A MIRROR FOR PRINCES

A MIRROR FOR PRINCES

TOM DE HAAN

19 88

ALFRED A. KNOPF   NEW YORK

THIS IS A BORZOI BOOK
PUBLISHED BY ALFRED A. KNOPF, INC.

Library of Congress
Cataloging-in-Publication Data

De Haan, Tom.
 A mirror for princes.

 I. Title.
PR6054.EI335M5   1988   823'.914   87-45241
ISBN 0-394-56359-X

Manufactured in the United States of America

FIRST AMERICAN EDITION

A MIRROR FOR PRINCES

I

And sithen in the eyre an hiegh: An angel of heuene
Lowed to speke in latyn: for lewed men ne coude
Iangle ne iugge: that iustifie hem shulde,
But suffren & seruen – : for-thi seyde the angel,
   'Sum Rex, sum Princeps: neutrum fortasse deinceps.'

Then in the air on high: An angel of heaven
Came low to speak in Latin: for common men ne'er could
Argue like advocates: for acquittal of their sins,
But must suffer and serve – : for thus spake the angel,
   ' "I am a King, I am a Prince," you say,
   But you will perhaps be neither, one day.'

Langland, THE VISION OF PIERS PLOWMAN

What was that cold rush of air, frightening the papers on my table so that they rustled and fluttered? Serena has just come in. She smells of autumn, letting in the chill as she opened the door; she disturbs the quiet warmth of the room. I think she's brought some food with her. She's not a bad girl, Serena.

She hasn't seen me busy writing, like this, for a long time. Work is in short supply, as it is nearly winter. No one wants letters written in the winter. No business is transacted. But this is for no one. At least, I can't envisage anybody reading it. No one in the village can read – except, I think, for Serena's father, but his reading matter is limited to inventories. When I'm gone – dead or departed – Serena will keep this for as long as she can, and look at it sometimes, probably upside-down for all she knows; but when she's gone, someone will put it to a good use and light fires with it, or wrap fish.

I remember when I was in my early twenties and Lord Olivah, that fat middle-aged man whose greatest achievement in life had been to hold a second lieutenantship under my father's command – and if you, paper or person, want more information, you shall have it all in good time – well, I remember when Olivah, considering he had lived as interesting a life as any man of his close acquaintance (that's probably true), an-nounced the completion of his memoirs. Hearing this news, I thought: 'What a ridiculous waste of time! How can he imagine that any of us' – this was when everyone who counted was young – 'would be in the slightest bit interested in whatever incidents from his dull life he's scraped from that sieve he calls memory?' Fragments of too thick and heavy a nature to slip through the little holes.

That's nothing to do with this, really; except that Olivah wrote his memoirs, and that, I suppose, is what I'm about to do. I'm not interested in setting the record straight, or clarifying my place in history, or cleansing my reputation: these memoirs have only one purpose, which is to pass the time. At first I thought I'd write a diary, but that wouldn't keep me busy. I need to have something to occupy the winter days that are coming on – days, so I'm told, when one rarely stirs out of doors, and snow wraps up our little village. With what proud proprietorial stirrings I wrote that! 'Our little village.' My little hut. My roots of my roofing tree. My plain Serena, thank you. I'd been chewing at my pen for two hours before you came in. I've never written memoirs before, if that is indeed what this will turn out to be. Should it have a plan? A thematic, schematic framework? On the other hand, should I tear this page up, throw it in the fire, and forget all about it?

Look at her. You call her plain, as if you were fit to judge with your old man's eyes. For you are an old old man when women look plain to you. Watch her bending over the fire. She is outlined by the flames, the flickering shadows falling on my face, re-enactment of a thousand memories that have nothing to do with her. Sometimes I wonder how much she notices of me when I think she is not aware – if she senses me watching her. She is lighting a long and slender slice of wood: how the little flame bursts and hisses at the end. One by one she moves from candle to lamp and lights them. I'm sorry I forgot to shut the window. Now look at her, profile set square in the window-frame, sunset dying. The last rays are lending her hair a sort of pale halo, diffused through the tangle of its strands, but it cannot last, she is shuttering the window to with a click. Just then, in that moment, she was beautiful – what woman is not, with her head crowned by passing sunlight, the glow of fire warming her cheeks, shadowing her hollows, all her outline of thigh and shoulder blurred and the curve of her throat sharp against the evening sky? If nature can perform these miracles, so quickly passed, so quickly regretted and forgotten, when light and heat can raise a beauty even in Serena's face, can I still not bring myself to feel any desire for her, even for so short a time as in that second when she was lovely?

Serena's unexpected moment of beauty has come and gone. What's passed is past. I see that I have discovered my theme, which is useful so early on. My name used to be Reyhnard Rorhah, Prince of Brychmachrye. King Reyhnard Rorhah Tsyraec, Lord of the Fahls, Son of Gods, God of Gods, Son of Kings, God of Brychmachrye . . .

Which all depends on your point of view, really. Some things, however, are incapable of change. I will always be Reyhnard, third of the four sons of King Basal the Great and his wife Ursula Andaranah. I will always be the brother of Hans, and Alexi, and Peter whom I love. My wife's name is Beulah. I, Reyhnard Rorhah, brother of my sister Madeleine who was, in everything aside, perhaps, from the date of her birth, which we never knew, truly my twin.

She was beautiful. She needed no deceptive sunset to set her aflame, for me; nor anything as coarse as a fire, with its spitting sap and its black smoke, to make her warm for me. Now all I am left with is the sun and the wood, in my sky and on my hearth, and warming my hands – fascinating hands, mine, when you look at them. I never thought they would turn out so well. Blue-veined and thin, though the prominent bony knuckles can be a pain when I jar them inadvertently against a low-hanging root. These days my skin is always white beneath the fingernails. It's the cold. I stand in front of the fire trying to get warm, turning my hands palm to back to palm, roasting first one side and then the other – by which time the skin on the back is crawling with cold again. It only goes to show the staying power of external heat.

Thinking about cold has made me feel cold. I forget that night falls a little earlier every day, and I'm always surprised to see it grow dark before supper. I need a new coat. A blanket would do; I could use it as a cover on my bed at night, and to wrap around me when I'm working. I never used to feel the cold; or maybe my memory is playing me false, and I did, but I bore it better. That means I'm getting old. What a surprise. Putting my fingers inside my shirt, they're either chilly or my skin is warm, or both, more likely. My shoulders are as bony as they ever were. My ribs have never not stuck out, not even when I ate well. We were not a fat family. Last week's bruise is still aching. It gives me a pleasant pain to worry at it, down on my knee, and it has taken on a lovely mauve-yellow colour. My nose is cold, my ears are cold, my hair is still black, my eyes are still green, all is as it was yesterday. Two yesterdays. Here-yesterday, when I sat and stared at the sky all morning, watching the clouds float by, and walked down to the bonfire in the potato field to get a light for the hearth, which I had let go out. Breakfast of bread, lunch of bread and soup, dinner of soup, here-yesterday all one time . . . and real yesterday.

Real yesterday unfurled between the turrets of Tsvingtori, the pillars of Ksaned Kaled, and Madeleine: my three palaces. Then I was something, when I was all those things. Things worth remembering; remembering worth more than most things. For they were the sum of what I was, and what have I left to do but remember? Remember what I can, and set down what I recall.

1

I may as well begin in the time-honoured fashion, with my birth. It occurred in the sixteenth year of my father's reign. I was born on a day like this, a chilly day at the fag-end of autumn, when the year is winding down towards its end. It was a short and easy labour, so I'm told. I slipped into the world with little effort, arousing no excitement, and so there were three of us brothers.

At the time of my birth my eldest brother, Hans, was nine years old, and my other brother, Alexander, whom we always called Alexi, was eighteen months younger. The years before Hans had been full of miscarriages and false hopes. It is easy to understand why my father loved Hans right from the start, and of course he had no reason to rejoice over a third son as he had for the first. I was no real extra security for our family's hold on the throne – at least, that's how my father would have seen it. At that time it was forbidden by law to mention my uncles, and of course he never did, but he could not have forgotten that my mother had once had seven brothers, and that he had stolen the crown from them all.

My nanny told me about them. Her name was Bronwen. She must have been over sixty when I was born, though to a child anyone who is not a child looks the same age: old. I used to scare myself by imagining she was a thousand years old. She looked it. She had been Hans's and Alexi's nanny before me; in fact, she had once been the nanny of my dead Andaranah uncles, but this was supposed to be a secret. My mother had tracked her down and, keeping her past quiet, had reinstated her in her old post at court.

Bronwen used to come and wake me up in the middle of the night, bringing sweets and fruit as a bribe for my attention. While I ate she would sit at the foot of my bed and tell me the tales of my uncles. 'The Andaranah princes were great men . . . ' Her stories always began like this, and they always ended with the same moral: no matter what I did, I could never hope to be half the man that any one of my red-haired uncles had been. They were true royalty.

If anyone had found out she was telling me these things, she would probably have been executed, but since I know now that she was a lunatic I cannot give her credit for true courage. She had plainly worshipped her Andaranah children; their extermination was most likely what drove her mad. I was not fooled by her attentions into thinking that she was fond of me, or even liked me – how could she? I was my father's child, with his features and his colouring: a misbegotten half-breed foisted on a ravaged Andaranah princess. Still, Bronwen had to pour her memories on to someone, and with a crazy shrewdness she chose me. I was a child, I was in her charge, and she knew I never talked to my father.

My mother and her seven brothers were the children of King Michael Andaranah, who was descended in direct male line from Michah the Conqueror. My many-times-great-grandfather Rori was Michah's second in command, and sailed with him in the flagship from Andariah. After the conquest of Brychmachrye, Michah created Rori one of the fifteen Fahlraecs of his new administrative system and the province took its name, Rorhah, from him. Rori was also given Michah's daughter Berengaria; and this distaff descent was all the claim my father had on the throne when he, the elder son, came down from the mountains of Rorhah to the court at Tsvingtori.

I can't begin to assess how much right my father had on his side. His emotions and his morality are his private business; his actions speak for themselves. He wanted to be King. He made himself King, and he was very good at it. The motives of his supporters are much simpler to understand. My mother's father was not only incompetent but actively bad. He was a weak-willed, dissipated spendthrift – debauchery being not, as we know, a bad thing if you can manage it without injury to yourself. My father could: he had enough energy to spare for excesses. Michael's debauchery was a symptom of personal weakness. He never listened to his council; instead, he made merchants and bankers his private advisors, and in giving them his ear he was trying to repay the debt his borrowings had incurred. My father never had recourse to the bourgeois financiers. At court such measures are rightly regarded as shameful. And despite these dealings Michael's treasury was always empty. He raised the taxes to unprecedented levels, as well as inventing new ones. His sons, although brave enough in war (according to Bronwen), were grasping and arrogant – this, at least, is one charge no one could lay against the sons of my father. Michael's last act of misgovernment was to depose the Fahlraecs of Peat and Gurnah in order to provide two of his younger sons with lands and titles. No one knew who would be the next to suffer, and they didn't want to wait to find out.

My father gathered the disaffected around him. One night, during dinner, he murdered King Michael, stabbing him over a plate of soup. Then he rushed out, jumped on to his horse and galloped east to where his army had assembled. This was how the civil war started. If one believes in the Gods and in the divinity of the King, the Tsyraec God-on-Earth, then what my father did was a crime and an act of sacrilege. The only thing I can say is that it seems to me no one gets far in life without being a criminal: anyone who is successful is guilty of something. My father's right, if it is worth talking in such terms, derived from his genius as a general. At seventeen he was a Captain in the Guards; at nineteen he was commanding the war; at twenty-two, he was King. The Andaranahs were dead.

They all died before they reached maturity, and all but the two youngest died in battle. At the end of the war, when my mother had fled to Mindared and my father, pursuing her, had begun his siege of the city, the eleven-year-old Prince Henry killed himself by jumping off those once famous walls. In his pocket was a letter, intended to make my father think that my mother had escaped to another place. His army had acknowledged his kingship early on in the war, but until he was actually married to my mother his claim was no better than that of a dozen other noblemen. He was not deceived by the letter; later, when his troops stormed Mindared, my mother cut her brother Asah's throat with her own hands, to spare him a worse butchery. He was eight years old. Bronwen told me all this.

The capture of Mindared brought the civil war to an end. My mother's fourteenth birthday was her wedding day.

To me, my Andaranah uncles were on a par with the little shepherds' tales our governess would read to us when we were good. I loved the colourful, larger-than-life characters, but I never took them quite seriously. They were less real to me than the Gods. When I was five I believed with all my heart that the Gods were alive, but I had only Bronwen's word for it that my uncles ever existed. They were ghosts – or, rather, ghost stories – and didn't frighten me. I had a closer, more palpable myth to fear.

In the nursery we could hear his approach from far away, the unmistakable rumble of thirty or forty pairs of feet coming down the corridor heralding the deity, his train and his Guards. Usually they would go right past the nursery, but sometimes, at a whim, he would decide to come in and take a look at me. One of the Guards would precede him, announcing: 'His Grace the Tsyraec.'

This gave the governess and the other children time to prostrate themselves comfortably, flat on their faces with their hands behind their heads.

Alone among them I remained on my feet, to look upon my father's face.

He too was always old, though not as Bronwen was old. His was a monumental agelessness, like the statues of the Gods in the Temple. He was of average height, with a square build that would have been slender if his muscles had not been so well developed. His long Rorhah nose was flattened and twisted, the left side of his face and much of his body a mess of old, silvery scars, and his hair, once black, was grey now and still thick. His beard remained black, jutting forward from his chin like a spade. Two fingers were missing on his left hand.

The fable of the Great God Adonac tells how he raised humanity up in rebellion against the Gods, urging them to seize the mastery from their creators. This mythological revolt was put down, just as all the real ones are, and his fellow Gods tore Adonac to pieces for his punishment. Only the person, a human woman named Asdura, pleaded for him, and yet the Gods were so moved by her tears that they immediately reassembled Adonac, excepting his ears and his genitals, which they never could find. He was given a pair of golden ears, and his grandmother Vuna's bull was gelded to repair the rest of the damage. Then the Gods elevated Adonac to the Kingship of the Lands West, Hulsitoq, where the Sun sleeps. They set him above themselves and made him Supreme God, and while they were about it they apotheosised Asdura, whom Adonac gratefully married and made his Queen. When I was five I thought this was true history, and marvellous too.

I thought that my father, so scarred and broken, must have undergone an ordeal worse than Adonac's, and so must be commensurately greater than Adonac. My father was so far above all men he must be superior to any God. When I was not in his presence, I adored him with as much passion and more fear than I gave to the Gods, but when he appeared in front of me – when I had to stand on my feet and look into his unsmiling face, backed up by row upon row of unsmiling adult faces behind him – then I would feel nothing but awe in his paternity, and terror of his deformity.

After a minute or so he would turn to my brother Hans, smile at him, make a joke. All the adults would laugh, and laughing they walked out. From the rear of the train Alexi would throw me a look and a grin, but he and his friendliness seemed worthless to me.

Their noise died away down the corridor. The children and our governess got back on their feet. They began to play again, snatching the toys from my hands.

I had one living uncle. When he was born his name was Henry Rorhah, and he was my father's younger brother. He never came to court, so I have no idea what he was like; but he sent his son Nikolas. When my father became King, his brother, who took over the inheritance of the Fahl, was forced to relinquish the family name, and so the Fahlraecs of the province I now live in are no longer Rorhahs, but Rayallahs. My cousin became Fahlraec after his father's death –

When I came face to face with Nikolas, about six weeks ago, I was afraid he might recognise me. In this I did Beulah, my wife, a gross injustice. I should have realised she would make such a convincing job of my funeral that Nikolas, and everyone, believes I've sailed west to Hulsitoq. It would never occur to him that I am who I am, and therefore not dead, when there's a far more plausible explanation for my face: if Nikolas were to think about me at all, he would assume I was his brother. Quite a number of the peasants in this region have the Rorhah features, so I'm not out of place, and though I washed up here by accident I couldn't have chosen better if I tried. Round here the by-blows of Nikolas's family are to be met with every few miles. In fact, Serena tells me that her little niece is Nikolas's daughter – this must make us relatives.

Our little house is snug. My sister Madeleine – who came from the mountains herself, who took such pleasure playing with the cottage our father built for our mother on Ksaned Kaled – she would have loved this place, this tiny mouse house, this glorified hole in the ground. The main room, in which I am now sitting, is approximately six paces by six. The ceiling is so low I must stoop whenever I stand up, and when I look out of the single small window my eyes are not far above the level of the grass. The two bedrooms, Serena's and mine, each about an arm's-breadth wide, lie one to either side of this room. They are windowless, hollowed out beneath the roots of two pine trees which hold up the earth of the roof. I could never sleep in mine in the summer, but now, with its rugs, it is warm. Before I came Serena lived here alone, except for her goats, which she keeps in a lean-to behind the pine trees.

She loved listening to my stories about Tsvingtori. When I arrived in this village I could lie to the natives about my origins, but Nikolas knows the Tsvingtori manners and the court accent. He quizzed me. And I thought I'd made a fine job of disguising my voice! So I told him I'd been a clerk at the Palace.

I liked that – and it was, in a way, an honest answer.

Serena, how could I explain a city like Tsvingtori to you? You would see the cliff it is built on as just another mountain, its broad cobbled streets as goat paths. North of it the river Wastryl falls in a thundering cascade down to the sweet waters of the bay, more magnificent than you can imagine compared to the thin, transient waterfalls that tumble over these rocks during the spring thaw. Serena, the truth is I can't describe it. I've been down to the city docks a mere dozen times in my life. I've never been into a city shop. I could count on one hand the merchants' wives I have seen, and I have spoken to none. Tsvingtori's back lanes, tall, cramped houses, small gardens, schools and university, busy marketplaces, dealhalls rowdy with all the languages of the world, its courthouses and its temples, are nothing to me but a memory of red tiles seen from above.

The Palace has no other name, but when we, my brothers and sister, my family, my court, when we said Tsvingtori, it was the Palace that we meant. From the heart of the Palace – from, say, the fish-pond – it is a good twenty minutes' walk before you reach the closest part of the encircling wall. Five men can stand side by side on top of the Palace walls; if you do stand on it, and if you are very tall, you can catch a glimpse of chimney-pots and roof-spines through the thinning branches of the horsechestnut treetops. The Palace is a hotch-potch of architectural styles, part of it going back to before the Conquest, the rest added over the years, a bit here, a bit there, with no real eye to the overall design. It's a rambling complex of kitchens, staterooms, halls, salons, dormitories and apartments, barracks, mews, stables, kennels . . . I have no idea how many rooms there are, but they run into many hundreds. There is another place on the wall from which, at this time of year, when the trees are bare, I could see the windows of the room where I was born. I could now, if I were there.

This village has one building which, for lack of anything better to fix on, reminds me of Tsvingtori. That is the Temple. I suppose there is some sort of moral to be found in the fact that it is built of sandstone, with no resistance to the elements, for it is dedicated to me.

If I had Alexi's sense of humour I would go in and pray. As it is, I never go in, and the villagers quite rightly consider me to be without religion. They know King Reyhnard is dead, but they haven't replaced the lintel with one dedicated to the new King, Beulah's son Basal. Perhaps, being conservative, as the native people are, they prefer a dead god they know to a live one they do not.

Brychmachrye is thick with temples, but they are not real temples. We all know that, it being an article of faith. There is only one true temple: the Temple of Tsvingtori, my Tsvingtori. It is one of the buildings put up by my father at the beginning of his reign, replacing the old temple with one made of granite and faced with marble. Brychmachrye prays to the King, and the King, the Tsyraec, stands in the Temple of Tsvingtori to converse with the Gods his equals.

I don't want to talk about Tsvingtori with Serena. I could never explain it in a way she would understand, and whatever she can understand is really not important. Tsvingtori was my home. Tsvingtori and Ksaned Kaled: two separate and very different places, one home. Home contained within a place and a time. This is a familiar concept, but I don't think Serena could grasp it.

In some ways I am like a tortoise.

As if, when I stand with the sun behind me, I can see the shadows of great beloved towers stretching away over this mountain snow; but I know it isn't really on my back. It can't keep the wind out any more.

In Hulsitoq – and I used to believe this – there is said to be a better home, another kingdom, a warmer Tsvingtori, a Ksaned Kaled where it never rains, where the roses are always in season. Where we, having died, will live for ever. But I do not believe this any more.

I was a God, and I should know.

2

Serena's niece is a pretty little thing, all yellow curls and blue eyes, fat-cheeked, well-fed, native to the tip of her snub nose – and so I doubt she can be Nikolas's daughter, because the Rorhah blood is strong and always shows. Be that as it may, they've named the child Niccola, probably hoping to ensure her some future advantage. Nikolas has so many bastards he'd never bother to deny this little girl.

Serena's family is suspicious of me, as is the rest of the village. I'm a stranger, and living with Serena – what man, I imagine them asking, would live with Serena? I don't much care for children, on the whole, not in the consuming way some people do, but to fill my time I've made the little girl a wooden doll with joints that move. Alexi once made a horse for Peter, and he showed me how. Now that I've finished it, Serena's family can't decide whether to take it, which is a pity after all my time and effort – and children with new toys are always a delight to watch.

What I'm doing is drifting back towards the subject of my childhood. Before I start again, I will lay down a rule. When I write, I must write of what I felt at the time, and hope that I am recalling it faithfully. I will not say of people what I know them to be *now* – yes, good, Reyhnard, you were very restrained about Nikolas. I'll write of them as they seemed to be then. They will change, because they did. Even I, who seemed static, changed.

I've already jumped around, getting muddled. Obviously it will be easiest if I do this chronologically. How old am I? Just gone five years old. I spent the first five years of my life in one room. Of course I know I didn't really – I learnt to ride, for one thing. I remember feeling slightly afraid, grabbing at the horse's mane because the ground looked such a long way away; and I remember learning that when you fall the ground is not as far away as you think. One moment you're in the saddle, the next, winded and aching.

But in my mind those five years assemble within one room. It was a large room with a smoky fire, giving me a continual cough from November to April. The inhabitants of those five years were my nanny Bronwen, my governess, whose name I can't remember, and fifteen or twenty children my own age. 'Your friends', the governess called them, but they weren't.

They were the sons and nephews of the Fahlraecs, brought to court at my father's request to spend their days with me. His aim in this was not to provide me with company but, as I have understood for some time, to have me thoroughly squashed. Teach that boy humility, were his instructions concerning me. I would grow up to be no threat to my elder brothers.

We were told that we were supposed to learn the manners of society together; without example, how could we learn? I was small for my age, and they were many against one. I was shy and arrogant by turns. Shy by nature I suppose, since it must come from somewhere, and arrogant because when my father came into the nursery I was the only one who remained standing.

Nikolas was the governess's favourite. Although only a few months older than me, he was taller and stronger. He was the leader. Everyone wanted to be his friend, to sit next to him during prayers, to play with him.

Our toys were mostly those Hans and Alexi had grown out of. Nikolas claimed all the new ones. When I grabbed them as my royal prerogative, the governess would take them from my hands; or else, pretending not to see, she would allow the others to fight with me and pin me down. This was to teach me that I wasn't really special, and it did work: by the time I was five I had more or less come to understand that the reason I was allowed to stand in the presence of the King was not because I was in any way personally outstanding, but only because I had been lucky enough to be born his son. I had nothing to be proud of, except, of course, him. Because he was my father, I was something more than those other boys were; yet except during those few minutes when my father was in the room, I was something less. When we were given a box of toy swords the governess would not let me touch them.

'They're going to be lords and generals one day,' she said, referring to the other boys. 'They must learn to handle arms. But it's not suitable for a priest.'

Which was what I learnt my father had decided I should be. I had only a vague idea what it meant, but I knew it was something inferior.

Daughters can be farmed out almost from the moment they are born, and later married right out of the country; sons are a permanent problem.

Of course it's always useful to have one or two spare – you never know when they might come in handy – but if they all live, they all have to be provided with some sort of livelihood. My father had three sons, more than enough.

I once asked Serena which of the Gods she makes her devotions to – or, rather, I guessed and told her, but it was an easy guess. Mathred, the mother of Adonac, who holds all birds and animals under her protection. It is hardly surprising that Serena, who is little more than an animal herself – a gentle, soft-spoken, hare-brained animal – should love her. When I was five I loved the Goddess Asdura. I thought she was my mother.

In the nursery we made our prayers to Asdura morning and evening, as all children do. Bride of Adonac, Queen of Hulsitoq – I haven't forgotten my catechism. She was so beautiful on the icon, smiling, yellow-haired, open-armed, robed in the silver wool of the stars. I didn't know that the icon was the product of an artist's imagination. I thought it was a portrait. I thought she was real.

I had never seen my mother, or at least not that I remembered. I know very little of her even now; I know that she was excessively religious, probably because she was unhappy. It often takes women that way. I don't know what she was like in the first years of her marriage, or whether she ever took an active part in court life; by the time I was born too many pregnancies, too many fasts, and too much fervent prayer kneeling in damp cold chapels had broken her health down completely. She hardly ever left her apartments or got out of bed. I suppose she never asked to see me, and it never occurred to anyone else that I ought to be taken to see her.

All I knew, when I was five, was that my mother was the bride of Basal, Queen of Brychmachrye, and that she lived in the Palace. With this information, my faith, and a child's logic, I constructed for myself a family whose members were neither contemptible nor awesome, but loving and beloved. To me the Gods had a bright, solid, sunshine and rainbow reality that could pierce through stone, and that was as different from the grey solemnity of Tsvingtori as my fantasies about myself were from the truth. Why shouldn't the Gods be my family? My father was a god. If he lived in the Palace, Asdura must live there too: the Palace was where gods lived. My father was the greatest being in the whole world. He was really Adonac, or Adonac was really him – at any rate they were identical. Therefore Adonac's wife was my father's wife, and the Queen of Hulsitoq was the Queen of Brychmachrye. Obviously Asdura was my mother. Who else could be?

I never spoke about this. It went without saying. I thought it was one of those things grown-ups knew so well they took it for granted. My father was never mentioned by name, or so addressed – except once I did hear his Chancellor, Edvard filcLaurentin, call him 'Basal' when he thought no one else was listening – and it was the same with my mother. For years I didn't know that her name was Ursula; in my presence she was always referred to as 'Her Grace your mother' or 'The Queen', and so I could never overhear or be a party to any conversation which would have disabused me.

Perhaps I also got Hulsitoq and Brychmachrye confused, and thought that Hulsitoq was simply another name for this country. At five years old I hadn't quite grasped what death means, or fully understood the doctrine that only dead people live in Hulsitoq.

I did not merely believe in the Gods. You cannot *believe* in the sky, or a tree, or the durability of a rock: these are things you *know* exist. When faith is as convinced and as happy as mine was, you can only call it knowledge. And when knowledge is proved false there is no way you can argue for it, as you can with belief. Belief, needing no proof, resisting every assault of reason, cannot be disproved as knowledge can. Just look at these peasants. Every day I see them going into that temple, and who are they praying to? To me. To the God, the Tsyraec, divine-born King. I'm supposed to be in blessed Hulsitoq, whispering into the golden ears of Adonac, making their crops grow and curing their boils. It's pathetic. The only thing I can take seriously is their credulity.

However, when I was five I thought Asdura was my mother. Nikolas might be my cousin, but for all his swaggering and popularity he was no relation of the Gods, so one day, when I lay on the floor with my arms pinned beneath his knees, I told him as much, adding that one day soon Asdura would come to hug me and kiss me as I had seen his mother kissing him.

The governess pulled us apart. Nikolas immediately sneaked on me. She held me at arm's length, slapping my ears hard as she said, '*That's* for your rudeness and *that's* for your pride . . . '

I was crying, more from the frustration of being misunderstood than from the sting of her slaps, and I blurted out angrily that it was no more than I ought to expect from Asdura, because she was my mother.

The governess looked very startled then – for which I don't blame her; I was her responsibility – and asked sharply, 'Where did you get that idea?' I kept my mouth stubbornly shut. She grabbed me by the neck and stood me in the corner, where I spent the rest of the day.

The next morning Alexi came to the nursery. He must have been about twelve, and already close on six feet tall. The governess was obviously expecting him because she let him come in. He had a bag of sugared cakes, which he handed out, but I stood aloof and refused mine, looking away sullenly when he smiled at me. All I knew was that when Hans walked at my father's side, with my father's arm around his shoulder, Alexi walked behind like a thing forgotten. I wanted nothing to do with him.

Presumably our father had sent him to do this little errand. He gave me one of his hands, and with the other took hold of Nikolas. I don't know why Nikolas was brought along. At the time I thought Alexi must suppose he was my special friend because he was my cousin. Nikolas jumped up and down, chanting, 'Where are we going, where are we going?' I remained mute.

Alexi gave my hand a friendly squeeze and said, 'We're going to see the Queen.'

At that I perked up, though 'perked up' would be the wrong expression. A deep, joyful sense of spiritual adventure buoyed my spirits, making me feel as if I were walking on a carpet of incense as Alexi led us through more corridors than I had ever seen before, mazy and bewildering. The panelling was scrolled like folds of linen, or carved with animals, flowers and strange geometric shapes. My child's eye was especially drawn to the brightly coloured tapestries, their shiny cloth sewn into pictures: tales of the Gods, my family. There was Mathred, with her brown hair and brown eyes, hands scooping brown earth. Another was horrible, all red like blood: Adonac dismembered. Nikolas tugged boldly at my brother's hand, reaching out to touch the hangings, then breaking free to chase a mouse that ran from the wainscotting. Alexi laughed good-naturedly. I was too moved to be naughty, for now I saw the unmistakable portrait of golden-haired, blue-eyed Asdura crying for her murdered lover, and her tears were stitched-on pearls.

At last we stopped outside a door. Alexi told the Guard to announce us. He went in, coming out again after a moment and holding the door open for us to pass through.

I remember wanting to cry with disappointment, because She wasn't there after all. It was a large room but very crowded, full of religious paraphernalia, portable altars, statues, incense burners, wreath brackets and candlesticks, all of which was still there, gathering dust, when I moved into those rooms years later. It smelt sour, and the whole of it was dominated by an enormous bed covered in red satin, more than big enough for all us children.

A woman spoke; I realised then that I had missed seeing her because she was dressed in red, and she was lying on the bed. The pillows which propped her up were almost the exact same shade of red as her hair.

I stood on my toes for a better view. This woman looked older than

Bronwen – and since Bronwen had been my mother's nanny, this woman couldn't possibly be Asdura. She was too old, and too ugly, and all wrong. Obviously Alexi had made some mistake – well, what else could you expect from him . . .

She said, 'Come over to me, my son,' looking at Nikolas. I knew she was not Nikolas's mother.

Nikolas started to giggle.

I wanted to ask Alexi to take me away.

Of course I know now that she must have been only thirty-six, but she looked so hideously, terrifyingly old. She was fat. Everywhere the flesh sagged from her bones, as if it was too tired to bother any more. Her face was like a mask: matt white, with dark holes for her eyes, nose and mouth.

She glanced from Nikolas to Alexi, and frowned. The flesh between her brows puckered thickly. She turned her eyes on me.

I can pity her now as one pities a chance-met stranger; at that moment I had to stifle a scream.

She said, 'Alexander, bring Reyhnard over here.'

I struggled desperately when he picked me up, fighting against being brought any closer to that bed. I hid my face in his shoulder rather than look at her.

'Aren't you going to say hullo to your mother?' she asked.

I remember now that she had a nice voice, hardly more than a whisper. She probably wasn't as hideous as she seemed to me then; it was as much my disappointed expectations which made me flinch from her.

'You're lying,' I said. 'Put me down, Alexi, she's lying, she's lying.'

I had often been beaten before, but never with a stick. This time I was. She sent Nikolas away first, and then called for a servant to beat me. I didn't cry. Alexi did, though I saw him trying to hide it behind his sleeve.

We were dismissed from her presence. Nikolas had disappeared, but Alexi would not let me go. When we were alone in the corridor, he crouched down until our eyes were level and ran his big hand up my forelock. I jerked my head away.

'I'm sorry,' he said. 'I'm sorry. I didn't think she'd hit you.'

'I hate her.'

'You mustn't. Try not to.'

'I hate her and I hate you too. And I hate Nikolas.'

And the Gods, I could have said I hated the Gods too. But only a child hates the stone he's stubbed his toe on.

The snow is falling again. Serena has a rabbit, poor child, that got caught in her snare. I hope it was dead when she found it. When she has to kill a thing it makes her cry for hours. But she is not crying, and I see she has been given some onions. So there it is, we will have rabbit stew tonight, and rabbit soup tomorrow. You treat me like a king, I tease her, and she blushes.

Poor simpleton, she thinks the animals have souls. She thinks every rabbit she knocks on the head will hop away to the clover fields of Hulsitoq, and when she gets there they will all stand on their hind legs to greet her. Serena, there are no gods. A rabbit once dead is dead for ever. What we are eating is all of him that there will ever be. But I cannot tell her this.

3

Paper is a luxury in these parts. When I last went to Rayalled, which was about six weeks ago, I took the precaution of buying as much paper as I could carry, and even so I may end up having to write between the lines of pages I've already used. To save space I'm forcing myself to write in a tiny crabbed hand; if my tutor Aneurin could see it, he'd have one of his quiet fits – he worked so hard to teach me the exquisite penmanship of the court clerks. In Tsvingtori there was an abundance of paper but, as with all things, its value increases with its scarcity. When I look at this rough grey-tinted stuff I'm using, which cost me so much and which I hoard with such passion, I begin to realise how I took paper for granted, and I remember the day I first discovered it for the precious thing it is.

In the nursery we had no paper. Our alphabets were painted on cloth and bound with wood, and we practised our letters on wax tablets. The sharp points of the styluses were more often used in pricking each other, though not mine. I don't say it smugly. I would have, and tried to, but the others were quicker at getting their jabs in first, and I remember there was some sort of rule about 'no returns'.

I can't remember a time when I didn't know how to read and write. Alexi told me everybody says this; but I do remember that when I was five I knew, and Nikolas and the others didn't. Too busy digging their pens into each other, probably. Day after day the governess took us over the same ground, and I was bored while they struggled.

One day I escaped, I'm not sure how. It was a few days after I had seen my mother, and I was still in disgrace: no one was allowed to speak to me because I had been wicked. So, while they played with their wooden swords and the governess hung over them, gazing devotedly at Nikolas, I must have slipped out. Retracing the route by which Alexi had taken me, I was soon back in the wood-carved corridors. The tapestries no longer interested me. I chose a door at random. Hanging on the handle, I threw all my weight against the heavy wood and managed to push it open.

It's mid-afternoon now, an early winter afternoon which means only another two or three hours of sunlight. If I were in Tsvingtori now – I don't need to be in Tsvingtori to know how the library will look at this hour. I don't need to shut my eyes to see it.

The light will be coming from the west, a silvery, wintry light. Those windows must still be there: large, rose-shaped, five panes and a circular pane in the centre. Their glass is cut like diamonds, magicking prisms through the air. In those bands of blue, and red, and yellow, the dust is slow-dancing; and the smell of that dust, and of leather and ink, is the smell of my boyhood.

Five years old, I stood in the doorway and was entranced. It was the most wonderful room I had ever seen, a sculptured cavern of wood and leather and light. Shelves rose up into heaven and beyond to touch the ceiling; they were built of stained oak, roused in the sunlight to a rosy black glow. Ranks of books stood to attention, too many to count, turning their spines towards me: dull maroon, dull gold, dull green, rich old colours. A fantastic carpet covered the floor. It was black and white, patterned in senseless swirls and dots, and so soft that for the first time I could hear my footsteps making no sound as I walked into a room.

The silence, the colours, the smell, all were so different from everything I was used to – the nursery and my bedroom, stone walls and bare floors – that I started to panic, imagining I had entered another world through that door and would never be able to get back to Tsvingtori. Perhaps no one would ever come to look for me.

I tore back across the carpet, my fear doubling because I still made no sound. The silence was like something dead. I wrenched open the door – there was the corridor, there were the tapestries.

One of the library windows had been left open, and through it came the sound of women laughing. This reassured me. I decided to stay. Someone was coming up the corridor, so I shut the door and ran behind a bookcase. I didn't know how long I would be able to hide, but having made my escape I was going to stay free as long as I could. The footsteps passed by.

After a while I plucked up the curiosity to come out and clambered on to one of the benches to reach for a book. It was far too heavy for me to hold; I dropped it, and it fell fluttering, landing with a soft thud on the carpet. I held my breath, expecting the noise to have attracted someone's attention; but no one came, so I climbed down to the floor and turned over the pages of the book. Its script was impossible to make out. I tugged forth another, smaller, book, and another, but they were all the same and I soon got bored. I jumped back on to the carpet, tracing its pattern with my feet in sweeping circles, until I got dizzy and fell over. It didn't hurt at all, falling on that carpet.

My eye was lured by something bright.

A desk was built up on a dais, under one of the windows, and on this desk were pots of ink. The sunlight was caught in them, firing the colours into liquid gems, rubies and emeralds and sapphires. They looked good enough to eat. I scrambled to my feet and rushed over, kneeling on a stool to investigate the desktop. Lying flat upon it was a sheaf of paper.

No cheap, provincial paper this; it was royal paper, thick as a fingernail, tinted a rich pale yellow. When I crumpled a piece in my fist it made a sharp crackling sound. I lifted it to my nose for a sniff: it smelt faintly, not unpleasantly, of urine. Holding it up to the light, I could just make out the shadowed silhouette of my fingers wriggling behind it.

I tore it in half. This time it made a sighing sound – as if it had sensations. Along the line of the tear it was jagged and frayed, showing layers of pulp pressed together. Turning it over in my hands I felt a twinge of pain, as if I had cut myself on a blade of grass. A thin line of blood was welling at the base of my thumb. I screwed that sheet into a ball and threw it away, licking at my cut.

After I had knelt for a while gazing at the inky jewels, I was inspired to pick up a brush, and on the next sheet of paper I drew a large, lopsided R in red ink. Then I took another brush and filled in the space at the top of the R with green ink. The colours danced together, glistening like the waters in the fish-pond.

With two more brushes I painted large circles around the R in blue and yellow. This done, I held the masterpiece up, the better to admire it in the light, and all the wet ink dripped together, turning dirty brown.

I threw that page to the floor and took another. This time I chose black ink, and wrote:

I am Reyhnard Rorhah. My father is the Tsyraec. My father is the King.

I filled up the page writing this, but immediately threw it away because I felt it was. all wrong. I had something else I wanted to put down.

This ink and paper seemed marvellous stuff to me, sturdy and adult. No palette knife could smooth away what I had written. It would never be erased to make way for tedious repetitions of the alphabet. What I had written would last for ever. If they tore it up it would still remain, in separate pieces, like a puzzle. Even if they burnt it, it would not be destroyed. The dead are burned but they are not destroyed: they live for ever in Hulsitoq.

This last thought did not ring true. I stared glumly at the paper for a moment, wondering what I was in search of. At that age, I suppose, I didn't really connect my new doubt in the Gods with the episode in my mother's room, but all the same I suddenly knew what I wanted to write. So I cheered up, dipped the brush in ink and began on a new page:

I don't believe in Gods.

After a moment's thought, I added beneath it:

Nikolas is a dogs dirt.

This was the worst insult I knew, the one we muttered under our breath in the middle of our battles.

Spoken insults drift away into the air and are forgotten. This one was written down. It had all the power of a prayer, and the eternity of a mountain.

By this time I was utterly enthralled. My letters slanted and dribbled awkwardly, refusing to keep in their lines, so I threw that sheet down and tried for better shapes on another.

Ink spattered over the desk as I worked away. I used up nearly all the paper, piling stained and tattered discards around my feet. My attention was so concentrated that I never heard the library door open. The carpet must have absorbed the sound of their footfalls as it had mine, for when I suddenly heard heavy breathing behind me it seemed to have come from nowhere.

I jumped with fright, and my elbow knocked against the red and yellow inkpots, which overturned, washing across the desk and spilling to the floor to drench the carpet in bright orange.

Next thing, I was lying in the pool of ink, my ear throbbing. He had knocked me off the stool.

'You dirty bastard,' he shouted. 'What do you think you're doing? Look at the mess you've made in here, you brat.'

And he kicked me.

I ought to say that I don't, of course, remember the exact words everyone spoke, but I do remember their general drift, of which this is a fair approximation.

'How did you get in here?' he shouted. 'God, you're filthy – Aneurin, look at what he's done, ink everywhere, and the books – '

He was about to hurl the empty red inkpot at me, when another man came up behind him and grabbed his arm. I heard new footsteps arriving, and from my vantage point on the floor I realised three Guards were standing in the doorway. They had come to investigate the commotion.

The two men hadn't noticed them. The first was still red-faced and fuming, but the second, Aneurin, was white. He gripped the other man's wrist and said, 'Geraint – this is one of the princes . . . '

Geraint's hand went slack, and the inkpot dropped, luckily missing me by several inches. Lucky, that is, for me: I already had a thick ear and bruised ribs. As far as Geraint was concerned it would have made no difference whether the inkpot hit me or not.

He fell on his knees – I suppose he collapsed – gasping for breath as if he had been throttled. Aneurin held out his hands to help me up. They were shaking violently. He seated me back on the stool, and then he also got down on his hands and knees, crawling around under the desk to collect the soiled papers.

Now it was my turn to start feeling scared, because I knew what I had written.

The Guards came in. Geraint heard them and looked round; seeing them, he buried his face between his knees and began to moan. Aneurin heard them too, and bumped his head under the desk when he tried to stand up.

The Guards said to Geraint, 'On your feet.'

He hauled himself up, never once looking at me. Nothing he could say to me would help him. It was not my place to accept his excuses. I was nothing in all of this. On my father's orders the lowest of the under-kitchenmaids could knock me about until I was dead, but if the most powerful Fahlraec in the country so much as pinched me without my father's command, then he was a dead man. It was not to me that Geraint's apologies were due. In kicking me without permission he had insulted my father, and he knew this.

The Guards said to him, 'You'd better come with us.'

'Oh God,' he said. 'Oh God.'

This was the first time I had ever heard fear of death, pure fear like perfect pitch. I believe it will be the last sound I make. Poor Geraint. You were right, I had made a mess. The boy deserved a beating, but not from you. What a thing to die for.

'I didn't know,' he said.

I wonder how Aneurin knew. I never asked him. We never talked about it.

Aneurin, who I suppose found it as terrible as I did to look at Geraint's face – though I could not look away – Aneurin, for something else to look at, was staring at my papers; then he said, in a strained voice, 'Look at this,' and held out the sheets to Geraint.

Geraint grabbed at them. I wanted to tell him to be careful, or he would cut his hands. Gradually, as he ruffled through them, his colour returned to something like normal.

He glanced at me. 'I see you're a philosopher, sir,' he said unpleasantly.

I felt Aneurin's hand resting on my hair. 'Too much so,' he replied.

Geraint was becoming very excited. 'I'll take these, I'll show them to His Grace . . . '

My stomach turned over with a fear to match his fear.

'You'll only get the Prince in trouble,' said Aneurin. 'And it won't help you.'

'It might, it might. Look at what the Prince wrote. "I don't believe in Gods." Any man might lose his temper seeing something like that. It's treason. It might help me. The King might pardon me. It might help.'

It did not. Geraint was buried alive. His treason was worse than my treason. The great King my father was a practical god: a soldier, a builder, a politician. He rarely punished words as harshly as he punished actions. I was merely beaten until the skin came off my shoulders and sent to spend a week in the Temple, after being curtly reminded that the Temple would be my home when I was twenty-one.

Thus the affair was officially treated, and my father was officially angry, and the court officially shocked. But Alexi, who came down to the Temple to visit me with his pockets full of marzipan, grinned and said I was a 'bagful of surprises'. Perhaps my father was pleased. I wouldn't be surprised. It was the first conscious naughtiness I had ever committed, and maybe he imagined it showed a spirit of independence, and of courage, which for a while might have led him to hope I would turn out like Hans. I don't know. He smiled at me before he sent me away. In that week, I suspect, he liked me more than ever before, or since.

I hated that week in the Temple. I was miserable, bored, lonely and frightened, and I could have spun round with relief when the last day came and a man arrived to take me back to the Palace. Actually it was Aneurin. I recognised him right away. He held out his hand, and never then nor ever again did he speak one reference to our first meeting. As we walked back together he told me he was going to be my tutor.

Aneurin was unmarried, and up to this time he had held a post as a clerk in the royal archives, where he had worked consistently but without distinction. He was now thirty-one, and in line for a small promotion.

He came from a native family which, before the Conquest, had owned estates in the south-west marshes. Most of the ruling families had been wiped out; Aneurin's survived by surrendering with a firm sense of self-preservation to the inevitable. They gave up their lands without a struggle, and turned to make their living as court clerks. The experience of generations had taught Aneurin's family that pride was no substitute for bread, or for their heads – Aneurin got more pleasure out of telling me that his grandfather had translated the entire corpus of the acts of King Conradin into the native than he ever did in recalling the once-glorious deeds of more distant forebears. Survival and humility were in his blood, and thus my father saw in him the right man to teach humility to a third prince.

Aneurin had the best handwriting in the court, and no ambitions to be a philosopher, either political or metaphysical. He was something of a linguist, though a competent rather than an inspired one; grammar and the study thereof was his great delight. He was my tutor for eleven years, and in all that time we did not have one lesson, or even one discussion, on theology. My father might have told him to steer clear of the subject, but after eleven years of studying Aneurin I am pretty sure that he had that easy-going sort of faith which belongs to people who accept what they are told in childhood and never think much about it afterwards, except to hope that it is true.

His sister, by the way, ran a brothel down by the city wharves, or so Alexi told me when I was old enough to understand. I never mentioned it to Aneurin. By then I knew him well enough to realise he would be ashamed of it.

Everything I've so far said about him I came to know over the years. When I was five all I saw was a pleasant, smiling young man with thin hair and inky fingers, who told me I would never need to go back to the nursery. He spent his time in the library with books and paper, and was going to teach me to do the same. I liked the prospect. I liked him.

I have since seen many fathers with their children, playing with them, teaching them, scolding them when they are wilful or foolish, but always loving them. Perhaps this is what all fathers should be like. It's hard for me to say. No one alive now had my father for a father. When I was five I never expected such things from him. If he appeared in front of me now, I still couldn't. He was my Tsyraec, my King, my father. Aneurin was never my father in my heart, that bloody smashed thing – but in fact, day to day fact, he was all the father I ever had, such as he was. Which is to say he was the man who primarily brought me up.

I have tried to write about Aneurin clearly and prosaically, because I want to make some memorial to him: this little cairn of words. I think he would like it. He hated exaggeration. He knew what he was, and what he wasn't, as well as I do. I did love him once, and for years I never knew his faults, because he never had cause to show them. He's the only one left now who would care about what's become of me. Poor Aneurin, I've just realised – he thinks I'm dead too.

This is all I have to say about my first eight years. Aside from those two or three very strong memories, on which I have already used up far too much paper, the rest was an unvaried but to me interesting round of growing up and learning. Getting taller, mastering arithmetic, learning the native, understanding poetry, all the milestones of a boy's education – they are well known and need not be described. Aneurin's company cured my loneliness. I was no longer bored, except during geography. The companionship of those sons of the Fahlraecs, boys my own age, was never regretted, because they had never been companions.

I still had all the faculties I was born with. Love, for my father and for Hans, and more mundanely for my tutor; faith, transferred from the Gods to my studies, and towards the distant, ill-defined goal of manhood; joy and excitement in learning. I was rarely unhappy and never for long, and sometimes I was so happy I thought I was the luckiest person who ever lived. Alexi said most children feel the same at some point. He said a lot of things.

I once read somewhere that an inability to remember events from one's early years is the mark of a happy childhood. So let's leave it at that. I have now reached the point at which my real life begins.

Peter.

4

Soon after I became King I moved into my mother's old rooms, and one day I was poking about in the attic above them, checking for anything that might appeal to me before the servants cleared the lot away, when I found a painting. It had been taken out of its frame, rolled up, wrapped in rags and pushed out of sight behind a trunk. I pulled it from the cobwebs and, blowing off the dust in clouds, held it up to what little light there was. At first I thought it was a portrait of Peter; then I realised that the eyes were brown, not blue, and that the face belonged to someone older, close to manhood. Presumably it was one of my mother's brothers. The painting was Chatiennese and so rather idealised, but within the iron limits of their set proportions it was a good portrait, and you could see the man behind the graph paper.

When I try, like a painter, to describe Peter's face, it sounds ordinary, which it wasn't at all. How can I show him as he was? He had red hair, the colour of beech leaves in autumn, brown sometimes in the shadows, and copper in summer. His blue eyes were always blue, not that indecisive grey-to-blue-to-green that some people have. Blue eyes neither large nor small, set in a face that was round when he was a child, and later thinned out to squareness. A strong short nose with wide nostrils. This is hopeless. No one going by this description could ever pick Peter out at some court function.

I think what I've just given is no more than, as the artist might say, the canvas of his face. His character is not found in the angle of his cheekbones or the width of his brow; it is Peter behind those things – Peter in the flash of his eyes, Peter in the crackling of his hair, Peter in the lift of his shoulder, Peter in his quick smile – and if I try to draw him, all I will produce is the Peter-of-my-words. Only what I make of him, and not himself at all.

Peter was so full of energy, so abundantly vivid with life. I do believe that, if he had been given the chance, he would have become the perfect man. He had so much hope and intelligence and talent, so many plans. Nobody is perfect, but he came close, or at least his promise did.

I have taken on something beyond my ability. I can't make anything of Peter, for the truth, the great and sole truth of my life, is that he and Madeleine made me between them. I can't begin to explain him. I love him. He was my brother. I can't explain because I do not understand. Peter, to begin with you is never to end.

This is a picture of the day my brother Peter was born.

High summer. Big white sun in a hot white sky. Haze confusing the horizons, steaming over the downs; salt water running down our faces and itching beneath our clothes. Cold water in a mug gratefully taken and gulped. Round the window the vine leaves had been crisped by the heat-wave, their tips burnt brown. The buzzing of flies, and other insects, and a crowd of people chattering in the courtyard down below. We – Alexi, Hans, and I – were alone together, locked away in a room upstairs, in obedience to a custom as old as, perhaps older than, our possession of Brychmachrye.

A bee was trapped in our room, throwing itself against the window-pane, wings raging, so maddened by the smell of flowers and the damp heat that it could not find its way to where the window was open.

Cutting through this picture – this sleepy, sweaty, bright, buttery sort of picture – was a scream like the sound of a fingernail on slate. It scraped down the corridors and burst through the windows, silencing everything to a hum. Renewing itself, it crescendoed, growing louder than a human voice should be; then it peaked, and died away on a gasp of sudden quiet. We breathed. It came again.

We were just finishing lunch in the early afternoon, and this screaming had been going on since daybreak.

It is not a sound one can ever become accustomed to. It was like blows thudding again and again on a bruise: after a while the pain radiates out and takes over your whole body. You want to vomit.

Alexi pushed his plate away. He hadn't touched his food. The screaming swelled, and he clapped his hands over his ears.

I had tried to eat, but could not. Only Hans had wolfed his lunch with an unaffected appetite. The screams were screams of agony, and he was hearing them as we were; he knew what was happening, he knew his mother was in labour, but it meant nothing to him. We were listening to the sound made by pain which can be neither escaped nor endured. At eight, I had no experience of it, but I could imagine it. Hans could not.

'I wish she'd get on with it,' he said, tilting back his chair to plant the broad soles of his feet on the wall. His boots were tossed in a corner; he'd been about to go riding when the summons came. 'The groom told me he found the spoor of a wildcat in the north woods,' he was telling Alexi. 'I wanted to stake it out today.'

Alexi was roaming restlessly back and forth, not really listening. At that moment he paused by the window and looked down. 'Bloody crows,' he said.

'Why crows?' asked Hans, picking at some dirt under his fingernails.

The whole court had assembled in the cobbled yard beneath our window. Against the greys and browns of the Palace walls the figures stood out brilliantly in an abstract of silken colours, scarlet, azure, saffron, green and gold. It was custom which forced them to stand there and wait, just as custom confined us to wait in that room.

Alexi turned around and shrugged. He hunted the depths of his pockets for chocolates and offered us each one, but Hans shook his head, so I did too. I would not take what Hans had refused.

Hans said to Alexi, 'Listen, if she gets it over with before dinner, we can have a ride round the woods. You'll come?'

'Of course,' said my other brother.

I was eight and a half years old, Alexi fifteen, and Hans, my big brother, seventeen. Our imprisonment dragged interminably on. It was dull being locked up on such a beautiful day, and the day itself was made ugly by the screaming, but all the same I treasured this opportunity to be close to Hans. Now and then he would throw me a word to complete my happiness. It was like being locked in a cage with a glorious lion whose mane you have always longed to stroke. Next to him Alexi appeared, in my eyes, to be Hans's shadow, a long, insubstantial, cast-behind thing.

My father loved Hans with a pure affection I never saw him show for anyone else. He asked nothing of Hans except that this son indulge himself from morning to noon to night with whatever took his fancy. Of all of us, Hans was the one physically most like our father, giving an impression of strength rather than height, with large long muscles that would have turned ropy with age, had Hans lived so long. He had a longish square face with a broad forehead, and flat square hands.

As far as his character went, Hans had less of our father in him than any of the rest of us, even Peter. Our father had a rapid, sometimes vicious sense of humour, like Alexi, and a wholly practical brand of wisdom. Hans's intelligence was the instinct of the woodsman. Our father was widely read; Hans was barely literate. He was not a fool – he could read a spoor better than any of the court huntsmen, and could out-think even a fox. His mind was fitted to the trees and the stars, to the hunt and the smell of blood. He was immensely strong. By the age of ten he could lift a Guard's broadsword, and I once saw him strangle a lionhound to death in a fit of temper. He grew out of these rages as he got older.

As a soldier, Hans was more of a hero than a strategist, better suited to standing at the head of a death or glory charge, laying about him with his sword killing four at a stroke, than to the command of an army. Our father was a military genius. Other kings sometimes used to send ambassadors to request his advice, if a war was going badly for them. I may add that he charged them pretty heavily for this service. Nothing if not astute, my father.

Hans could smell rain a day before it came; he could see colours by moonlight; he could hear a rabbit break a twig from over a hundred paces away. He understood animals. He knew where the boar would feed, and where the wolf would break cover. He knew the exact moment when the stag would lose hope in running and turn to fight for its life.

On the other hand, he found people incomprehensible. Hans was not cruel. When hunting, he killed quickly and neatly. He was not even uncaring. It was simply that for him pain, and fear, and jealousy, and shame, and sympathy did not exist. He took no notice of them in others, and made no excuses for them.

He was loved. Our father loved him. I loved him, everybody did. Hans attracted so much love, and yet most of the time one felt he hardly noticed it or knew what it was.

No, I'm wrong, I know that. I know he loved Alexi. Or rather, I know Alexi loved him. I'm getting on unsure ground here. I don't know if Hans loved Alexi, not with what I would call love.

Those two were inseparable. I must be careful here, because while I know what went on in Alexi's mind, I have to guess at Hans's. They were so completely different that I doubt there were more than two or three pastimes they wholeheartedly shared. Hans's life revolved around hunting and riding, and the only food he appreciated was hard bread and red meat. Alexi preferred chasing the maids, and food was one of his greatest pleasures: I always remember him with sweets either in his mouth or in his pockets. He also loved mental challenges like chess and cards.

Physically they were often apart, but emotionally, or spiritually, or wherever it comes from, Alexi always put Hans first. He would have done anything for Hans. He spent long hours in the saddle with him, and in his turn Hans played long games of chess with Alexi. Often Alexi let Hans win, though Hans never guessed. Knowing Alexi was good at chess, Hans assumed he was too, and he could never understand why other people beat him so easily.

If Alexi had put Hans to the test, I don't think there was anything Hans would not have forgiven him. But he never did put him to the test.

If those screams had been Alexi's, Hans could not have sat there frowning, full of his own impatience.

At seventeen he was fully grown, as much in the spirit as in the flesh. As we get older we think and wonder about the stars, about life and religion, about love and what we're doing here, or whether there's a reason at all. We draw conclusions and we change them. I'm older now than Hans will ever be, and I'm still doing it. Hans never did. He had no sense of wonder. Life, for him, held no mysteries. It was wind and earth, speed and blood, and for him those things never altered or lost their power.

Everyone, without exception as far as I know, loved Hans. Theirs was the love for the unique. There never was, and I doubt ever will be, anyone like him. Even I, whom he rarely noticed, who did not even want to grow up to be like him, adored him. I knew how much he loved Alexi, and I was jealous.

Alexi was pacing up and down, occupied with a thousand different thoughts. He'd be thinking about our mother, and the pain she was suffering; about the court gathered beneath our window, and what each individual might be thinking; about Hans, and me, and our father, and whether the new baby would be a boy or a girl. Hans sat on his chair, watching Alexi pace, waiting to be set free. I sat on my stool and looked at Hans. Alexi settled for a moment beside me. 'Well, Reyhnard,' he said, 'how would you like to have another brother?'

I ignored him and gazed at Hans. 'I have brothers,' I replied, determined to imitate Hans's lofty unconcern with all this pain and anguish.

'How about a little sister?' Alexi suggested. Just then another scream wrenched, and he shivered.

I thought: He's weak. Weak and useless. No one cares about him, except Hans. Why does Hans like him so much? Our father doesn't, I've never even seen him smile at Alexi. I don't want to be friends with him.

Of course I know why I hated him. He was too close to what I was, and treated in much the same way by most people. An unnecessary prince, but a potential threat which had to be kept firmly in its place. I wanted to be associated with Hans's glory, not Alexi's ordinariness.

'I don't think she's going to live through this one,' he said.

Hans uttered a brief noise of contempt, adding, 'Bitches never make so much fuss.'

'She's a woman, Hans, not a dog.'

'Is she going to die?' I asked with interest. I slipped into their way of referring to our mother as 'she'; for Ursula had always been a name to us, a title, never really a mother, and the impersonal 'she' was the best reference we knew.

'I hope not,' said Alexi.

'She's making enough noise about it,' said Hans.

'Presumably it does hurt, rather.'

I asked, 'If it hurts, why does she do it?'

'I'm afraid she hasn't got much choice,' said Alexi.

'Well if I was a woman, I wouldn't.'

Alexi's burst of laughter annoyed me, because I couldn't see that I'd said anything funny.

'If she didn't, you wouldn't be here,' he informed me.

This struck me as peculiar reasoning. It had never crossed my mind that my birth had hurt my mother. Why would she have gone to so much trouble for someone she took no interest in?

'Does it always hurt?' I asked disbelievingly.

'Well, Lady Gurnah had her son last month, and she said she didn't see what all the fuss was about.' Then he added, 'But on the whole, I think it does.'

I turned this over in my mind for a bit, and came to a decision. 'When I'm married,' I announced, 'my wife won't have children.'

This set Alexi's laughter off again, louder this time. 'Stop it!' I cried. 'I mean it. I won't let her.'

'I can see your marriage is going to be a bag of fun.'

'Shut up.'

'Don't you know what married people do, Reyhnard?'

Hans interrupted. 'Leave him alone, Alexi.'

'He's eight years old! Someone ought to tell him, and from what I've seen of that tutor of his, he doesn't know any more about it than our little brother here. God, Hans, I can't remember a time when I didn't know.'

'You think you're such a know-all,' I said.

Alexi went to the cupboard and found a pack of cards. 'Come on, Reyhnard, let's have a game.'

'No thank you.'

Hans yawned. 'Leave him alone.'

'Has it ever crossed your mind he might be upset at what's going on?'

'Reyhnard,' Hans turned to me. 'Do these screams upset you?'

'No,' I lied.

'There you are,' said Hans.

Alexi dropped the cards and wandered back to the window. He hung out of it, tilting further and further forward until his feet were off the floor and he was balanced on the sill.

'Hey, Hans,' he said, 'come and have a look at this.'

Hans's chair toppled backwards when he stood up. He walked, cat-footed, to Alexi's side and put an arm around him. 'What?'

'Look down there, by the pump – that maid in the white dress, see? She's new.'

Hans scratched his leg, and said, 'Not my type.'

'Have you got a type? What is your type? Rohaise?'

'Too fat.'

'Genevieve?'

'Which one?'

'You know, Michael filcGaston's daughter.'

'No, too skinny.'

Alexi was chuckling again. 'Your problem is you're too picky. You may not know it, Reyhnard, but those two girls I've just mentioned are famous for being the most gorgeous girls at court. And this great hairy lump says "too fat, too skinny". Father's not so fussy about his mistresses.' Alexi started to sing:

The prettiest girl you've ever seen
Keeps her geese on Temple Green.
Meghan her name is,
And widely her fame is spread . . .

Hans hummed along. He could never remember the words of Alexi's silly songs. We were treated to several verses of Meghan's adventures sung in Alexi's rich tenor, and then he broke off to wave to someone.

'You really interested in them?' Hans asked Alexi.

'Who?'

'Those two girls of his – '

Alexi grinned. 'Good God, no. I wouldn't dare even if they weren't – He'd kill me if I got one of the court girls in trouble – '

I asked, 'What's a mistress?'

Alexi turned around and smiled at me, and said, but gently, 'Someone you have sex with without being married to.'

I must have looked blank, because I remember him asking me in a very surprised voice, 'You do know what sex is, don't you?'

I stuck my tongue in my cheek, and said, after a moment, 'Maybe.'

'Well, do you or don't you?'

So I said decidedly, 'Yes.'

'Tell me, then.'

'Come on,' said Hans, 'this is boring.'

I wasn't going to tell Alexi I didn't know; but he was twice my age and he could see. He came over, sat beside me and said, 'Well, I'll tell you.' And he did.

So long ago, I can look back and smile at that boy named with my name, who listened to his brother's matter-of-fact descriptions with amazement and a giggling, disbelieving disgust. Alexi could easily be lying to me, I thought. He would, too.

I couldn't hold out for long, though. Maybe we are born with the knowledge of it; maybe the understanding of sex is an instinct in itself. At any rate, I had to admit that it sounded somehow right. And Alexi was very good at breaking things gently to people. He tried to persuade me that it was fun, better fun than anything I could imagine, and he racked his brain trying to remember childhood pleasures of his own to hold up for comparison. I was well on my way to being convinced, when Hans spoilt it all in trying to help by adding, 'Haven't you ever seen the dogs?'

I had. The bitch running away, dragging her backside in the dirt, snapping at the dog who grabbed her neck between his teeth and jumped on top of her with an ugly, stupid expression, tongue hanging, eyes rolling; that quick jerking of his hindquarters, lasting only a few seconds before the bitch managed to throw him off. I had seen it, but never watched for long. It made me feel uncomfortable, as if all my insides were changing places, so I always hurried away from the scene.

She's a woman, not a dog.

I didn't want to believe them. People couldn't act like that, not like animals. It was so demeaning, so wrong. My father was the King, he was a man, he could never, never have acted like a dog. Alexi, yes, maybe

– anything was possible with him; but not proper people, not my father. It was awful: I couldn't stop imagining my father's face wearing that dog's expression.

It took years to rid my mind of this picture.

Alexi saw that they had said something wrong, so he patted my shoulder – 'Don't worry about it' – and changed the subject. Daylight stretched into night when I should have been in bed, but no one came to fetch me. The servants were bringing the court their dinner on platters, although it was still almost too hot to eat outside. Indoors it was cooler, and as the hours passed and I pushed to the back of my mind the lies my brothers had told me, I grew hungry. At last a maid came in with food. The sun was a vast yellow ball now, dipping towards the west. The birds were singing, but the Palace was silent. We had heard no screaming for some while. The courtiers, bored, tired and stiff, could find no more to chatter about beneath our windows.

'It must be over now,' said Alexi.

Hans yawned. A wasted day.

As long as the screaming was going on time had been full of purpose, an agonising push towards an end. Now, with the silence, we were suspended in aimlessness. Was it born? Was it over? Was it dead? Was she dead? Nothing was happening.

I think this was the first time I took refuge in a book from thoughts I did not want to think. I lit a candle and opened a book of poems I had brought with me, mouthing the metre soundlessly.

Alexi sat down on the floor with another candle, and a book he had found in the cupboard. His voice was like a lullaby, though the stories he was reading were bloodthirsty adventures. Hans never got tired of hearing the same story. Like a child with a favourite shepherd's tale, he preferred a plot he was acquainted with, and a foregone conclusion: the fall of a savage soldier, the death of a mighty beast. Soon he was asleep, snoring loudly.

Aneurin started off my poetic education with Isumbard Shoemaker, whose solid, balanced metre and inevitably upright morals used to make Peter writhe with boredom. Serena, however, loves it when I recite them for her, nodding her head in agreement with each well-worn analogy of virtue. Unambitious as poems, they may be dull, but they are faultless – suitable plain bread to breed minds on. I ignored the morals. I loved the rhythm. Poetry was like song, without music. Rhyme, cadence, the expressive flow of the whole, these were the things I was exploring. I had noticed how the melody of a tune can change ordinary words into sad or joyful ones; so, I had begun to feel, it was with poetry. Poetry makes words work hard under the yoke of the metre, drawing their deeper meanings through strict arrangements. All the little catchphrases we prattled out in daily speech without a second thought were, in poetry, stripped, their meanings refreshed, forced to pull their weight.

Even in Isumbard's dreary little verses I could sense the beauty of this discipline. I was beginning to realise that language was not just for communication – not just for 'Hullo, how are you?' and 'Pass me the salt', not just for learning geography and mathematics – but for expression, something I could use to talk with myself. I could reach inside for all those nameless things that were agitating in me, pull them out, dissect them on paper, and I would know what they were.

I could not, of course, have expressed it like that when I was eight. Then I could only have said, 'Poetry is interesting, I like it.' Maybe, if pushed, I could have told Aneurin – but no one else – that I thought I could do something with poetry that would make me stronger.

Alexi had put his book aside and was deep in thought. I tapped out the metre with my foot. Hans would have snarled at me to stop, but Alexi didn't mind. Hans twitched in his sleep, and muttered. We had all almost forgotten why we were there.

The candles were flickering on their stubs when someone knocked. 'Wake up, Hans,' said Alexi as the door opened. Two footmen came in, followed, unexpectedly, by Chancellor Edvard filcLaurentin. I shut my book and we all stood up.

He said we could go to our father now. Before any of us moved he started speaking again, unevenly, telling us that our mother was dead. I don't know what sort of reaction he expected from us. He looked more upset than Hans or Alexi, much more upset than I could feel. Chancellor Edvard was a very good and kind person; he was, as far as I know, the only man whose opinion my father ever respected. My father might have asked him to break this news to us, but I think it's more likely that Edvard took the duty upon himself.

Then Hans, leaving his boots behind, stalked out of the door and down the corridor. Alexi held out his hand to me, but I hugged my book to my chest and hurried off in front of him.

We didn't have far to walk, and the corridors were deserted. Nearly everyone who could fit had squeezed into my mother's rooms. The crowd parted to make way for Hans, who went straight to our father.

Our father put his arm around Hans's shoulder, draping a sleeve across his back. 'Another son,' he said.

The crowd gave no response to this. They seemed subdued, as if they were waiting for someone to indicate what the proper emotion should be.

Alexi braced his back against the wall, next to me, out of our father's field of vision.

My father, of course, could do anything he liked with this newest son. He might not want it. He might decide to expose it. He might have wanted a girl. There was no way of telling whether he was happy, or angry, or sad; and the face of every other person in the room was just as inscrutable.

Finally a woman spoke, high-pitched and nervous. 'Sir – what is the Prince's name?'

My father blinked, looking slightly irritated. 'Peter,' he said. Then, linking his arm through Hans's, he walked with him towards the door. Hans was telling him about the wildcat. 'Tomorrow,' said my father. 'We'll go and have a look tomorrow, together, how about that, hmmm?'

Soon there were only four people left in the room: myself, Alexi and two women. One was the woman who had spoken. I could see from her dress that she was a lady, not very rich, but young and clean-skinned. The other was my old nanny Bronwen. I waited for Bronwen to say something, wondering if she would show signs of being glad to see me after all these years; but she was hanging over the cradle, muttering to herself, and never looked at me.

The lady, who was to be Peter's wet-nurse, started enthusing: 'Her Grace was so brave . . . ' and I saw she was moving closer to Alexi – perhaps not consciously, but quite obviously – finding in him whatever it was that women saw to like and seek out.

'Oh sir,' she said, 'it was terrible. When I had my own baby, that was only three weeks ago – I didn't know it could ever get so bad. The child was lying feet first, wrong way round you know, sir, and you can see for yourself how big he is. In the end the doctor had to use his hands and I reckon that's what did her, Prince. She was so brave, she really was, and you could see, in her eyes, she knew it was all over. And then something gave in her, further up, you know, not in the place where the baby was, if you'll pardon me – all that straining, and then she started bleeding from her mouth too, and then she was gone, like that.' The woman wiped her eyes and said, 'I thought you'd want to know, sir, how brave Her Grace your mother was.'

Bronwen broke in, 'She died like a princess.'

An old phrase kept going round in my head: she died like a dog.

That thought was worse than the gory tale the wet-nurse took such delight in. Since the details all came to me second-hand, and since I had never seen anything bloodier than a cut knee, the picture she painted couldn't really upset me.

Alexi's height and build, and his striking handsomeness, made him seem older than he was, and the wet-nurse was lulled by his open, friendly manner into prattling on. 'His Grace is such a – such a *firm* man, sir. Most fathers I know of cry, or faint, or have to leave but – but then, His Grace isn't just any father, of course. He never turned a hair: In fact if I may say so, Prince . . . ' Here she stopped, some sense of discretion getting the better of Alexi's charm and her own garrulousness.

'Unsympathetic?' said Alexi. 'His Grace thinks he knows everything there is to know about pain – '

I squirmed and pleaded – 'Alexi' – shamed to hear him talking like this about our father in front of someone who was only a step above a servant.

He bent down to me. 'Did you know, Reyhnard, Father once had a septic arrow taken out of his back, at Mindared. He never said a word the whole time they were digging it out, and as soon as it was over he got on his horse, stormed the city, and – rescued – our mother.' His voice teetered close to sarcasm at the end. Bronwen snorted contemptuously.

The wet-nurse's eyes were wide. 'Is that so, sir? But women are weaker creatures, you know – '

Alexi raised his eyebrows. She reddened, and looked away. I hated watching all this. Then Alexi put his hands on my shoulders and said, 'Let's see this little brother.'

Bronwen moved away and busied herself at the other end of the table.

We looked into the cradle.

He was so tiny, surely too small to be alive. Could this red and naked animal, his wrinkled, waxy face screwed up like an old man's, be a human being? His eyes were wide open – blue eyes, and what is this? Red hair? Slit of a mouth closed in a narrow line, he regarded us solemnly. Beneath the mottled skin of his chest I could see his heart beating with rapid strokes, like a bird. He seemed so brave in his fragility, red-raw and defiantly alive, with his large awkward head, bloated belly, stick limbs.

'Isn't he a funny little thing?' said Alexi.

My brother Peter, a red dollop of life born from a dead woman.

Alexi said, 'Watch this.' He put his hand – spider-fingered, pad-palmed, bigger than Peter's head – into the cradle, and brushed his index finger against Peter's fist, which immediately unfurled, each finger smaller than a thumb-joint, to close round Alexi's finger with a firm grip. I was amazed.

Those blue eyes stared up at us with grim intensity.

'Why doesn't he smile?' I asked.

'He can't yet. Go on, you try what I did.'

I stood on my toes to give Peter my hand, and he took it.

At that touch he curled into my heart, and I fell in love. 'He's mine,' I said.

'So babies aren't so bad after all?' Alexi laughed, seeing the transformation in my face. 'All right – that's only fair. I've got Hans, and you've got this sweet little Pea-eater. You'd better take care of him, though.'

'I will.'

I will. I remember so clearly. It was a promise. I never forgot, Peter. Like all the other promises I made to you, all kept in the end, as if keeping them could actually do some good. To the best of my ability. That's what hurts most, the proof that my best ability was so very little. No it isn't. Anyway, it wasn't.

I went out for a long walk after I wrote all of the above. I think I must always do this in future, when I feel the temptation to rave. Raving will achieve nothing but a waste of paper. Good resolution. When one has inadvertently wasted as much as I have, every small conservation counts. I still have space left here to finish this off.

Alexi lifted Peter from his cradle, wrapped him up in a blanket, and said, 'Looks like I'll have to be the one to do this.' I followed him to the window. In the courtyard the crowd was still waiting. Alexi held Peter up, turning him so that he was in full moonlight, and announced: 'Peter Rorhah, Prince of Brychmachrye.'

There was a moment's dull hush, then a desultory cheer, and the crowd dispersed.

5

I can't say that the court quickly recovered from my mother's death, for it, like her children, had little loss to recover from. We all enjoyed the funeral. Down in the lower levels of the Palace, among the footmen and carpenters and cooks, were many who still retained a certain loyalty to my mother's family, and since the donkey-work fell to their lot they prepared for the last of the Andaranahs a farewell worthy of a goddess.

Her death ship was anchored in the bay. Every man and woman in Tsvingtori, and from as far around the environs as could be reached in a week, brought their tribute piece of silver or gold. With these the mast was gilded, the deck tiled, and the rail plated with electrum; from bow to stern the ship was wreathed with yellow roses and blue delphiniums. I could just catch a glimpse of it from the top of the west tower, rocking gently on the sunny waters.

My father had recently acquired some new toys from the land south of the sea. These were made of grey powder, smelt of sulphur, and each had a wick. When a flame was put to the wick they shot into the air and exploded fiery colours. A page-boy stole one of these fireworks to play with and had his hand blown off.

As they cut the ship's moorings and put it to the torch, they lit those fireworks. I'll never forget the sight. I have seen more majestic funerals – my father's, for instance, his was a flotilla – and I've seen more glorious fireworks, but when I was eight I'd never seen either before. I was young enough to be stirred by the spectacle, while forgetting what had made it necessary. The ship became a floating fireball of orange, its sail dissolving under the flames, throwing rippling sheets across the still waters. Above it the fireworks screamed like hawks on their prey. They dripped golden rain, whirred in sparky green wheels. The night was every colour but black, the court awed into silence between outcries of amazement at each new burst of rainbow stars above us. Last of all came a rocket of blue and gold, diving towards the horizon, where the ship, now a faint glow, was dipping beneath the sea.

It was so stately, so bright, on such an immense scale – so compulsive – that for an hour or so my firm belief that the Gods were a lie and Hulsitoq an invention was shaken.

I thought the funeral was lovely. Like the child I was, I hoped we'd have another soon. I couldn't cry over a woman I had met only once, especially not when her death had given me Peter.

Four sons watched her go away, four brothers ranging in age from eighteen to the newborn boy I carried in my arms. Peter grizzled all through the ceremony, hating the noise and the brilliance of the fireworks.

My mother's daughter was not present. None of us was aware of this omission; none of us knew she existed. My father liked to keep up the traditions of the Andaranahs wherever possible, as long as they did not interfere with his plans for the government, and consequently our sister had been sent away soon after she was born to be raised with a family on the north marches. I don't think my father intentionally kept her a secret. If he never mentioned her it was because he had no reason to. No one did, not even Alexi. They had all, I think, forgotten her, as the court tends to forget anything they have no immediate interest in or use for.

To be honest, I suppose it isn't such a bad tradition. Madeleine had her regrets, but she would be the first to agree that anywhere is preferable to the court for bringing up a girl. When I compare them, the court girls born and bred, with Madeleine's simplicity, modesty and lack of affectation, I have to say that our father did the right thing.

While I was grappling with education in the library, Madeleine was growing up on a mountainside, running wild, learning to swim and ride and shoot with a bow, growing straight as an arrow herself. It's easy to picture her looking just as I did at that age, for they never cut her hair. At court, of course, little girls keep their hair short until puberty, just as little boys never cut theirs until they are thirteen. I don't know the reason for this custom either, but I do know that we brought it with us from Andariah. When I was eight, my own hair looked as Madeleine's did when I first met her, eleven years later: thick, straight, black, done in a tight plait so the ends wouldn't trail in the wet ink.

Four sons. Here we are, Father. Tell me, Father, weren't you a satisfied and secure king? True, you proved there was no safety in numbers against a military genius, but then again, how many outstanding generals can one age produce? And you were the one. You had Hans to follow in your footsteps; daily, with great love and painstaking care, you were teaching him the complicated craft of kingship. How do I know it's so complicated? Funnily enough, I do.

So tell me, Father, what would you have done if all those years ago soothsayers had come to you and said it was not Hans but I who ought to be taking those lessons?

You'd have had them buried alive, probably. After laughing in their faces.

I'm afraid I would have laughed along with you, the moment you gave me my cue. I believed that everything you said would come to pass. You knew everything. I believed there was nothing you did not have.

It was true. You had a dozen palaces, only two of which we ever lived in. You had a hundred castles. You had armies and ranks of Guards. You had any woman you wanted: in forty years, did you ever once hear the word No? You had the Treasury of the realm, packs of hunting dogs, stables full of horses, fleets of ships, more servants than you could name. You had cities and towns, villages, farms, woods, rivers, mountains. You had a country. You had Brychmachrye and all the people in it. You had four sons and a daughter. We all belonged to you.

Listen, Father, I've had all these things too. I know what they are worth – which is precisely nothing, if their possessor lacks a man's qualities. Me, Reyhnard, your son, your 'teach-that-child-humility' son – or, if you prefer, 'that boy' – I know you. I was what you were, and that either makes you grind your teeth, or bust a gut laughing. What a turn-up! What a joke! Did you always suspect I would come to a bad end, or did you arrange it?

You were very gifted, Father. I'll admit it. What do you think, that you've raised a son who won't give his own father credit? You probably do. Actually, Father, I'm not lacking in perception. You were gifted beyond any other man of your generation, both physically and intellectually. You turned Brychmachrye on its head and then set it back on its feet. You made yourself king and then proved to be a great king. Whether you were a good man or a bad man is not in this question.

When I was young your spade beard and scarred face terrified me, but even so I was sick with pride to be able to stand up and look you in the eyes when the other boys were prostrate on the floor. I feared and adored you. I could see nothing you ought to have done and had not. That mighty trinity of king and god and father could do no wrong. You were my own, blind, personal religion. You loved Hans: I loved Hans. You gave me a tutor and I worked my guts out for him, to please you. You took no notice of Alexi, and so I tried not to. It was the hardest thing I ever did, and I did it for you.

You were the hub of my universe, the root of the world and its farthest stars. You embodied justice. Week after week you dealt with the petitions, stamping them granted or not granted, and from you there was no appeal. In the Justice Hall you occupied that throne suspended from the ceiling, never touching the ground, for how could the purity of divine judgment be sullied by contact where the human things walked? You made the crops grow and cured boils, didn't you? We know – you, and I, and the crumbling stonemasonry Gods.

Did you ever believe in the Gods, Father? Did you really believe that what you were doing was sacred?

One can't be much of a king without wisdom, courage, authority, the ability to command respect, and since it is now as much my right as yours to dispense justice, I'll give you some. You did have all those qualities: in human portion, not divine.

When did I finally know this? That's an interesting question, Father. When I became what you were, though I'd had my suspicions. You were never a God, not even when I believed you were. There are no excuses for you, no special allowances because you were exceptional. You were no more of a man than I am. And as Madeleine said, you weren't much of a father either; so all that's left is your kingship, at which, admittedly, you were outstanding. Yet even in that you made some mistakes. Believe me, I'm more sorry to have to say this than you are to hear it.

Too late now to reach out to me and tell me that these things I say are true. I know they are. You're dead, King. Dead as my brother, dead as my beloved, dead as a rabbit, and it's a long time since I cared to make you proud of me.

I wish I could have told him all this while he was still alive.

———

When I was ten we went to war with Ruffashpah. I ought perhaps to call it Ryffachpye, which is the native name for that land to the north of us, the unconquered part of Brychmachrye. The Ruffash, who should by rights be subjects of our crown, call their land 'Brychmachrye', and they call our country 'the enslaved place'. As I said, the natives have long memories. The border was established during the Conquest, but not fixed, and as the Ruffash don't recognise it in any case they are for ever spilling over and making trouble in the north marches, which is why we have to go to war with Ruffashpah from time to time. Hostilities last for three or four months, and little by little we eat away at the 'unenslaved' territory – though quite honestly, who'd want to conquer it? There's nothing up there but mountains, snow, wolves and wild men. In this particular war Hans distinguished himself by slaughtering thirty-six of the Ruffash in one afternoon.

Peter was just old enough to listen with rapt attention to these tales of our brother's heroics. His blue eyes were huge in his round face, but he could never listen silently; he was always breaking in, asking questions, screwing up his face to think hard when something didn't make sense.

It amazed me how fast Peter grew. Seeing him new-born I had thought, Surely I could never have been so small? Alexi used to say, 'Oh look, I think Pea-eater's going to turn into a human being . . . ' but he had always been that to me. His proud, brave, stubborn individuality was stamped on him at birth.

When he learnt to walk, he was determined to get up and have another try every time his legs let him down. When he had a new word, he would repeat it over and over again until everyone but me got sick of hearing it. I've stored up every inch he grew and every minute of his years. Perhaps it is because those years turned out to be so short that I remember them as fuller than most people's – yet I'm sure that's not true, because I remember how at the time they seemed so long, packed with milestones. I remember going in to look at him on the evening of his first birthday. He had fallen asleep, with his mouth open, and he had such long eyelashes that fluttered in time with his breathing. I could look at Peter for hours and feel no time had passed. I thought then, How can so much have happened in twelve months? The sun never slowed down. It was Peter who made those months longer, taking charge of them with a time that was all his own.

Each day was like my birthday, or like his, with some new surprise to look forward to. At times I felt as if I could look down into his blue eyes right through to his core, and see the rapid, incessant learning going on in there; other times he would smile mysteriously and I would wonder what he was thinking about. Really I believe he was remarkable, because I've never met any child who was as endlessly fascinating as Peter. I carried him about when he couldn't walk, and held his hand when he could, scaling down my steps to his and wishing, in a way, that he still needed to be carried. I can't remember ever having as many questions in my head as he asked me between the ages of three and seven. 'Why, why, why?' It was his favourite word. I did my best. I spent hours looking things up for him, and trying to teach him to read. I hated having to tell him that I didn't know the answers; and sometimes, because he made me think about something, I would mentally work my way through to a solution I had never considered before.

He taught me things too, such as how it feels to be truly afraid.

This was when he learnt to ride. I had been taught badly, but Peter had a born skill, and he rode as well at seven as I did at fifteen. We would go out together, I on a sedate mare, Peter on a savage, shaggy pony that he adored. He was fearless, jumping over hedges and streams, turning acrobatics in the saddle, while I with my love in my throat twisted the reins and knotted my toes, on guard for the terrible moment when he might need me, ready to jump out and put myself between him and any danger. Children don't know their own frailty, but the ones who love them do; and it is as hard to forbid them to risk something as it is to watch them do it. I was always poised to catch him, hold him, keep him from being hurt.

I was so afraid that in some moment of my absence he might discover a new word, or invent a new game, and I would miss it. The first word I ever heard him speak was 'No'. Remembering it now, I don't know whether to laugh or cry. He was always fond of those two words, 'Why' and 'No'. The second word he spoke was my name, or as much of it as he could manage. This happened one evening when we were playing together. Bronwen came in and tried to take him away for his bath, but he shrieked, 'Reyn, Reyn! No!' I was so happy it hurt, in that strange way, in my heart and up my throat. I made her leave Peter with me.

Bronwen didn't like me. She never had liked me much, nor either of my elder brothers as far as I can gather; it was my ear she had needed. Now she had Peter's. And now – well, for the last twenty years I've wished I'd told someone, even Alexi, or Aneurin, about the things she used to say to me.

I didn't like her either. I suppose I resented her as much as she resented me, and for the same reason. If she could have objected to my coming in and taking charge of Peter, she would have; as it was, she handed him over sullenly, because she could not refuse. In my turn I hated her for being with him when I couldn't be, which was most of every day. He was fond of her. Peter was naturally full of affection, and so I tried not to forget that I had once been fond of her too, in a shallow way.

However, I did say to Aneurin that I thought Peter should have a new nanny. In answer, Aneurin simply gave that tic of his head which meant he wasn't going to think about things outside the small scope of his influence.

'She did well enough by you,' was all he said.

One afternoon in autumn, when Peter was seven, we dressed ourselves up in fur and leather and went out for a canter. The sky was that stark blue you get only on cold, dry October days; if you could have reached up to tap it, it would have rung like crystal. Our breath trailed behind us in clouds of steam as we raced through the woods, dodging amongst the trees, throwing each other challenges. When I had started to feel a bit tired – I was always worn out long before Peter – we came to a hillock and dismounted. Peter scrambled to the top and collapsed in a heap, his face flushed. I laboured up after him. An old beech tree flourished on the crown of the hill, littering the ground at its roots with papery copper leaves and the spiky shells of beech-nuts. I sat down with my back propped against the rough trunk, taking Peter between my knees to ruffle his hair. He loved that. We both smelt of warm sweat, kennels and tack.

After chattering about all sorts of things, Peter suddenly asked me, 'Reyhnard, can someone be born without a father?'

At first I thought nothing of this. He was always asking questions, and this one was less strange than some he had come out with. I replied, 'No, of course not.'

He thought this over silently. 'Are you sure?'

'Positive. Are you thinking of anyone in particular?'

'No.'

He said this in that shy, drawn-out way which with children means Yes. He must have spent the next few moments picking and choosing his words, which was unusual for him, as he generally blurted out whatever he had to say without stopping to think. When he next spoke, he sounded wary. 'So, Reyhnard – is the King really my father?'

'Of course he is. You're my brother, stupid. And Hans's, and Alexi's – '

'But – '

'What?'

'People can be brothers because they have the same mother.'

'That's true. They can also be brothers if they have the same father. In our case, it is because we have the same mother *and* the same father.'

'But Reyhnard' – he was squirming uncomfortably – 'Bron says I don't.'

'What?' I leaned forward, sure I couldn't have heard right.

'Bron says I didn't have a father.'

I pulled at his hair, not roughly, just to draw back his head so that I could see his face. He was biting the inside of his cheek. I could find no trace of laughter in his eyes. Straight up from his heart, he meant every word, and he meant me to take it seriously too.

'Are you angry with me?' he asked.

'Not with you. What else does Bronwen say?'

'She told me Mother's in Hulsitoq with our uncles and when Father dies Adonac won't let him in and she said he's not really my father and not – ' He stopped to take a breath, and looked reluctant to continue.

'Peter, what? Not what?'

'Not really the King,' he whispered.

Oh no, I thought, wondering why I didn't feel surprised she could say such things.

'Do you believe her?'

He turned his face away from me.

'Peter,' I shook his arm. 'Peter, who does she say *is* the King?' Though I could make a guess.

He said, as I was afraid he would, 'Me.'

It was only then, during the course of that conversation with Peter, that I realised Bronwen was insane. Previously I had considered her a garrulous old woman with some funny ideas, someone to dislike but not to be afraid of. When I called her a lunatic before, it was only because I know now that she was one. It takes a madwoman to torture a child with such lies.

'Peter, you trust me, don't you?'

He nodded.

'If I told you something, and then Bronwen said it wasn't true, who would you believe, her or me?'

'You,' he answered unhesitatingly.

'Good. Now listen to me. I'll tell you how it really is, and I promise you this is the truth . . . '

I told him all the facts I knew about the civil war: our grandfather King Michael's delinquencies, Brychmachrye's need for a good and able king like our father – everything that I had managed to extract from Bronwen's highly coloured tales. I glossed over the manner in which our father had married our mother, though I've no doubt Bronwen filled Peter with horror stories about that as well. I highlighted all our father's achievements, his genius, his power; I said what I truly believed, which was that he was the only man in the world fit to wear the crown of Brychmachrye. As I saw him then, so I painted him: the most wonderful, gifted, awesome being in the whole of creation. If there were gods, he would be one. In a way he was one, being so far above the common run of mortal men. If we were allowed to choose our fathers, who would want to be anyone's son but his?

When I had finished I asked my brother, 'So if someone came up to you and asked you "Who is the King?" what would you say? Honestly, from your heart?'

'The King,' said Peter.

Thank God, I thought. 'Peter, you know Bronwen's very old. She's a bit funny in the head. You shouldn't pay any attention to her, she doesn't really know what she's saying. What she told you is rubbish, you see that now, don't you? You can't be born if you don't have a father – '

'But Reyhnard, listen, you know when Vuna made the world she wasn't married, she had Vishnac on her own, by herself, and then she married him. Vishnac didn't have a father.'

'That's a story.'

'No it's not, it's true. That's how I was born too. I didn't have a father. Mother made me on her own.'

'Did Bronwen tell you that?'

He looked at me as a scholar looks at a simpleton. 'Some, but I worked it out. I'm not stupid. I know how people get babies – '

'Well, then – '

'But that's why it *must* be true.' He jumped round on his knees, waving his fists excitedly. 'Because Bron says I don't have any of the King in me and you do, and Hans and Alexi, and that's why she tried to make me believe I'm the proper King because she says I'm an Andaranah prince and not a Rorhah prince, but I don't believe *that* . . . '

'Why not that, if you believe the rest?'

'Because he's *always* been the King.'

'Well, that's a small mercy. Peter, how long has Bronwen been telling you these things?'

'Ages.'

I remembered then that a year or so previously there had been talk of a woman in the provinces who had given birth to twins, although she was a virgin.

Of course there was never any doubt that Peter was our father's son – no doubt, that is, in anyone's mind except Bronwen's crazed one. Peter took after our father in many ways, if not physically, but Bronwen would not want to look any deeper than the surface. The mad are lucky in this:

their dreams come true, at least in their mind's eye. Bronwen could never look at me, with my black hair and green eyes, and pretend that I was not my father's son, but Peter, I am sure, looked exactly as our Andaranah uncles did when they were his age. Like the youngest, Asah, who died when he was eight. One of her lost children had returned to her, reborn out of the womb of her dead Princess, and it was not only easy but necessary for her to believe that Peter was the product of parthenogenesis. For her he had to be pure Andaranah without one stain or blot.

Even lunatics have their brand of logic; but if she had twisted Peter into madness too, then nothing could excuse her.

I said, 'Tell me honestly, do you really believe all this?'

'Honestly, Reyhnard, I don't know.'

I hugged him close and laid my cheek against his. 'Peter, please listen to me. Bronwen's lying. She's mad, so she doesn't understand that what she says is untrue, but it is. It's not true what she told you, you know it's not. Everybody has a father and the King is yours.'

'Vuna – '

'Vuna was a goddess. Our mother wasn't, she was a human being.'

'She's in Hulsitoq and Vuna's in Hulsitoq.'

'Well – maybe. But she wasn't in Hulsitoq when she had you. She lived in the Palace, like we do. You were born in the Palace. I was there, Peter, and so was Alexi. Ask him, he'll tell you. And she could not have had you without a father. You ought to be proud. She was only a queen, but father's the Tsyraec – Peter? What's the matter?'

His face had closed up. I had never seen this expression before, this smoothing out of his features while he retreated inwards, but I was to see it again many times. It meant he was thinking something he didn't want to tell me. Always, when I saw it, I felt like shaking him hard, knocking him open so I could read his mind.

He only said, 'It was nicer before.'

'Why? This is the way it happens with everyone, me too, and Father. Everybody's got a father.'

'But Reyhnard,' he whispered, 'I don't like him.'

'I see.' I was getting angry, because I was frightened for him, and furious with Bronwen, and unable to find something to say which would settle this matter for good.

'Now look here,' I said sternly. 'You had better not go around spouting all this nonsense Bronwen makes up, because people will just laugh at you. They know he's your father. And what's more, you'll be in big trouble. And so will Bronwen, and she ought to be. He's your father whether you like it or not, and you ought to love him.'

He suddenly looked very frightened. 'I do!' he shouted, grabbing my arms.

'Peter – '

'Reyhnard, Reyhnard, shut up.'

'What's wrong with you?'

'It's the King,' said Peter. 'He can hear us.'

I glanced around, feeling as scared as Peter looked, expecting to see my father come striding through the trees with his courtiers straggling behind him. But all I heard was a blackbird, and all I saw was the deserted forest.

Peter took hold of my hands and urged me up. 'Come on,' he said, feet fidgeting in the dead leaves. 'Let's go home.'

We rode back mostly in silence, except for those sudden spurts when Peter would let out a howl and send his pony vaulting over some obstacle. He didn't look particularly happy, which I supposed I could understand. I hoped he was thinking over what I had said, and was accepting it.

When we were nearly home, he asked me, 'Do *you* love him?'

'Of course I do.'

Peter didn't mention this subject again, but I could not forget it and I was sure he hadn't, either. He was still in Bronwen's care, under her influence, still in danger no matter what I said to him. I felt there must be more I could do: something that would solve it once and for all.

Out of the question to go to my father. I never even considered it. Briefly, it occurred to me to confide in Aneurin, for Peter was his pupil too now, having come to join me in the library when he was five.

It was then I realised, I think for the first time, that whatever little Aneurin might be able to do he would not have the courage to undertake. If I did tell him, and he did nothing – which was likely, in view of his disinclination to do anything all the other times when I'd said Bronwen ought to be removed – then I would risk his life in making him an accessory in knowledge to her treason.

I never felt so helpless as I did then, when I understood that I could not turn for help to the only person I had. Probably I should have gone to Alexi; I didn't, for obvious reasons. Since I couldn't think what to do, I did nothing at all except worry myself sleepless, and hope that Peter had taken my words to heart.

Peter was so fierce, so strong-willed. He hated to be thwarted. I was watching him one day as he took his pony over jumps. They looked far too big to me, and I wanted to cry out, 'Don't try them!' Instead I tried to keep quiet, knowing he needed me as an audience to admire his skill.

He galloped at a rail taller than I was. The pony refused. Peter jerked its head down, kicked it, and came at the rail again, cursing and drumming his heels. The pony would have none of it.

I had to say, 'It's no good, the rail's too high.'

He threw me a stubborn look as he wheeled his pony round, cantered to the end of the paddock, and charged. At the last moment the pony dug in its hooves – and between one breath and another Peter was lying in the dirt and I had jumped the rails to come running. He sat up, but he was crying.

'Are you hurt, Peter, are you all right?'

He pushed his fist across his eyes, smearing his nose with dirt, and scowled at me. 'I'm not crying 'cause it hurts,' he stated, sniffing. 'I'm crying 'cause I'm angry.'

Best and most delightful of all surprises was finding that Peter loved to draw. He had a real talent for it. When Aneurin left him alone to practise his handwriting, Peter would sketch instead. He was marvellously competent: I thought so then and still do. He made drawings of the parade ground and the hunt, mostly horses, dogs, swords and soldiers. If Aneurin ticked him off, Peter would stick his tongue out; but Aneurin rarely chided. Having himself no talent, he was not disposed to criticise it in others, and that, I suppose, was his best virtue.

In the summer evenings we would go for long walks or rides, and in the winter play cards and other games. Peter was a terrible loser, putting his whole passionate heart into the desire to win. Sometimes, when he could see I had the advantage, he would throw a fit and hurl the board across the room; but he was always sorry afterwards, picking the pieces up. He was quick to lose his temper, and quick to apologise.

I don't know whether this is helping or hurting. The best thing is to keep on. Peter had other friends, a little gang of ruffians his own age. They prowled through the Palace, stealing things, teasing the kitchen cats – once there was a great furor when they were caught playing hide-and-seek up on the battlements of the roof. These were games I was too old for. But when he fell and gashed his knee open I was the one he came crying to, the one to kiss it better. I bear every one of his childhood scars inside me.

Peter was such a proud child, a child anyone would be proud of – but our father never came to see him as he had come to see me. When our father saw Peter running around in the gardens, shrieking with laughter, then our father would stare at him as if trying to remember who he was. I was destined for the Temple, Alexi for the Council and Hans for the throne; there were no plans for Peter.

Alexi often came to see us. He was so tall he had to crouch on his haunches to look Peter in the face. He was as much older than I as I was older than Peter; between Peter and me, eight years was nothing, but perhaps fifteen years is too great a gap to conquer. Or maybe it was Peter's looks, or his character, or the lies Bronwen told him, I don't know – they all added together and I knew Peter felt like a stranger in our family. It seemed everybody but me viewed him in the same way.

One afternoon Peter and Aneurin and myself were in the library. I was translating a piece of Duccarnese poetry, very badly, mixing up the gender endings, while Aneurin was doing his best to force the rudiments of metre into Peter's unattending head. I knew this game of Peter's, who always wanted to see how far he could push someone's patience. My own, as he knew perfectly well, could be pushed to the ends of the earth.

For the third time Aneurin began at the beginning, carefully simplifying his subject. Peter was supposed to be taking notes. When Aneurin finished, he bent down to have a look at them. All the time he had been speaking, Peter had been busy drawing a dog with large teeth and a feathery tail. It looked hungry.

Aneurin astonished me by losing his temper. He took the sketch and ripped it into little fragments, exclaiming, 'Can't you ever pay attention for five minutes, you stupid, stupid child?'

'Give it back!' Peter screamed, punching his desk. 'Leave it alone. It was bloody good.'

'Don't you swear at me.'

'I will if I want to, you horrible dirty old man. I hate your horrible stinking poetry and I hate your bloody lessons.'

'Peter!' I reproached him.

'Well I do, I do hate them.'

Aneurin was dropping the pieces of sketch into the fireplace. 'Let me tell you,' he said, 'it's no pleasure for me to have to teach a blockhead like you, but since we both have to endure it you'd be better off making an effort and not wasting my time with silly, badly drawn doodles.'

'It was a good drawing, and *you're* a blockhead.'

'Peter!'

Aneurin shouldn't have spoken like that. I could see he was already sorry he'd lost his temper. He tried to remain stern, but now approached the situation rationally. 'Oh, do try to attend, Peter. You know it's the wish of His Grace your father that you apply yourself and acquire an education befitting a prince and a gentleman, and I am doing my best to please the King. Do you want to disappoint your father?'

This tactic had always worked with me, on those rare occasions when I proclaimed I'd have no more doings with geography and arithmetic. I looked at Peter's face, expecting signs of repentance; his complexion had gone an ugly red, which meant that in a moment he would start saying things he had no control over. I got out of my chair, but before I could reach him Peter had blurted out, 'The King's not my father, he's not, I don't have – '

I grabbed Peter by the throat. Aneurin had gone rigid with shock. I tried to clamp my hand over Peter's mouth, and he bit me. He sometimes had these fits. His teeth drew blood, and I had to let him go.

He ran out of my reach and hurried on talking: 'Reyhnard says it's a lie but I know it's true because Bronwen told me, I asked her, and she said it was true and she knows, Reyhnard – ' He threw me a look, begging me to understand. 'She's old, she knows all about Mother what no one else knows and she said I was an Andaranah re-re-renesk – '

'Renascent?' asked Aneurin incredulously.

'Yes, that's it. How come you know?'

One must give credit for virtues that are struggled for. Aneurin fought for bravery, and found a good imitation. He said to me, 'What does the Prince mean?'

Peter opened his mouth again, eager to explain to someone who looked willing to believe. I forestalled him. 'It's that old woman Bronwen, his nanny, who used to be mine. Didn't you know she used to be our mother's nanny?'

Aneurin's lower jaw hung wide.

'And our uncles',' Peter interrupted.

'Be quiet, Peter.' I went on to Aneurin, 'She's old, and rather touched in the head, and she – well, she's got this mad fixation that Peter's a sort of – virgin birth, like that woman from the provinces everyone was talking about. You remember?' I was as red as Peter's hair. Aneurin would have joined me if he hadn't already been white.

He looked scared to death, wringing his hands. 'I never wanted to tell you this,' I said, which was a mistake, as he looked more frightened than ever.

Aneurin knew the difference between omission and commission. He knew that, with the King, there was no difference at all. I guessed whom he was thinking of: Geraint, who had kicked me all those years ago. Dead bone now.

'Oh dear Vuna, help me,' he whispered. 'What am I going to do?'

'Don't say anything,' I suggested.

He looked at me with horror.

As it turned out, he neither said nor did anything. He merely walked around more hunched and self-effacing than before. When he looked at Peter, I saw in his eyes the expression I had always imagined condemned men would have when they stand on the edge of the freshly dug pit.

6

I was nearly sixteen, and what have I said about the court? I can't say much, except things I know now which I did not know then. In those days I lived – as we all did to some extent – in the court, but not as part of it; rather like small pebbles dropped into a great mill-wheel, too tiny to clog up the works. Aneurin, of course, would remind me that writing is worthless taken outside its proper context. In my defence I'd reply that the court is no more my proper context than this village is. I existed above it as I now live outside. I would add that these are memoirs, not proper history; the men who stride across history barely stepped into my life then. I did not, and do not, live in history. In my world Peter was the centre, Aneurin loomed large, and my father was the distant sun which kept us all alive.

The court was his court, and it is for this reason that I should write a little about it, for it reflects something of him. I suppose history will confirm what everyone always said, that it was a great court. A great court for a great king. My father had that gift of great men for gathering other great men about him – Bernard Derondah, for instance, who was a master of diplomacy. Officially he was of peasant birth, and my father forced Lord Derondah to adopt him; everyone believed he was my father's bastard brother, for he had the Rorhah features and the extraordinary talents of that generation. Then there was Gilles Mehah, uncle of Valentine and Lord Mehah, who gave up his Fahl to his cousin in order to qualify for a seat on the Council. He ran the Treasury and made two fortunes, one for my father and one for himself. A flair for finance seems to run in the Mehah family. I've already mentioned Edvard filcLaurentin. My father made him Chancellor at the age of twenty-five: he held that post for thirty years and in all that time I don't think one person ever levelled a word of criticism at him.

The great assistance these men had given to my great father in his great work was over before I was born. By the time I knew them, they had outlived their usefulness, holding on to posts that had titles but no real functions. Even so, I remember them as outstanding amongst the collection of idlers and self-seekers who mostly made up the court.

On the whole, courtiers' lives consist of nothing but pastimes. My mother's death gave them something new to play with: a game of speculation. When would the King marry again, and whom?

Rohaise and Genevieve, those two girls my brothers had studied and spurned, were the front-runners. I came to know Genevieve later; I once asked a favour of her and she granted it. Her beauty was the sort which becomes more elegant as its wearer grows older, brown-haired and olive-skinned with fine big bones. She married the second son of Lord Vacled and had six splendid daughters, of whom four lived to adulthood. From the thin gossip which trickles up here I understand these girls are much in demand on the marriage market. Genevieve was an 'ornament of the court', as they say in those little history books written for women and nitwits – in her case she really was. She was a well-bred and gracious woman, a Lady in a place crammed with ladies.

Rohaise, in my admittedly biased opinion, was less fortunate in her looks. She rejoiced in that sort of pink-and-blonde dimpled charm which is so popular but wears so badly. She was more to my father's taste than Genevieve; neither was sufficiently to his taste for him to marry them, and in time it became clear that he had no intention of marrying anyone. So Rohaise sailed off to Andariah with her brother, where she crowned her career, so to speak, by becoming King Francis's official mistress. The Queen of Andariah had no children, but Rohaise has produced two daughters, one of which should be married to Beulah's son and heir by now. It's a small world, as Alexi would say, given the slightest chance; but not so small that a king can't lose himself and all he loved within it.

My father found a new mistress. She had a native name, Caryad. I think there might have been a little native blood in her. She came from a very minor family – Alexi told me she had been on the point of making an unexpected and advantageous marriage into the family of one of the Fahlraecs, when my father crooked his little finger and she dropped it all to come running to him. She loved him. She showed how much in giving up everything.

Caryad was small and delicate. I loved to watch her hands, which were very expressive, because her pink fingernails were the exact shape of almonds. She wasn't really beautiful, but unless she was tired or ill you never noticed this. Her hair drew all attention. It framed, crowned and burdened her; when it was loose it fanned out in a mass of crinkly strands that gave off visible sparks on dry nights. The individual hairs were coarse; the effect of the whole was amazing, with the colour and sheen of honey. She asked for nothing from my father except to be allowed to love him. She never intrigued for marriage. She was quiet and self-composed, and never threw her small weight around, which nonplussed the great ladies. I liked her. She was kind; she used to give me presents, and when she saw me she never forgot to ask after Peter.

Quite a contrast indeed.

Alexi had got another one of the kitchen girls pregnant. She had to go, as my father would not tolerate little half-royal bastards littering the underbelly of the Palace. The general opinion was that it was the girl's look-out. Alexi wheedled me into going down with him to say goodbye, and I must have been at a very loose end, because I said 'All right.'

I remember nothing about her except her pretty eyes, which were big and golden and damp, full of sadness. She was alone in the room she shared with the other maids. They were all at work. Stupid girl, I thought, why did she do it? She knew what it would lead to. Is Alexi's charm so overpowering? No shortage of girls keen to work at the Palace: they come, they get pregnant, they disappear.

He had a fat wallet, which he gave to her. She opened it up. Her eyes widened at the amount, but the sadness never left them.

He said, 'You can rent a room until you've had the baby, then we'll see. I'll come down . . . '

She was no older than me, but she was wiser. I thought he meant this and would do it. She knew he meant it, but would not.

I stood to one side and viewed the scene with contempt. I wasn't revolted by the fact that he'd slept with this servant, since he'd been doing that for as long as I could remember. Neither was I ashamed for what he had done to her, and for what she would now have to endure alone. I was humiliated by his attitude.

He allowed that girl to stand on her feet, to talk to him, look at him, touch him, as if they were common lovers. This is his fault, I thought, she knows better. When she saw me she had done the proper thing, and then Alexi had helped her up.

'I must go, sir,' she said soon.

Alexi said, 'When you've found a place, send me a letter. Send it through the footman, the one I know is a friend of yours. He'll see that I get it. I'll make sure you're all right.'

When she had gone, Alexi sat down on her bed. He seemed subdued, though not particularly unhappy. In no time at all he would find another – if, indeed, he did not have two or three others already.

'Let's go,' I said.

'What did you think of her?'

'Alexi – aren't you ever ashamed?'

He looked up sharply, startling me with such an odd look in his eyes, slightly cold, half-way between anger and sadness.

'What do you mean?' he said, and I was sorry I had mentioned it.

'Well?' he prompted.

'Of having them treat you with such disrespect. It's bad for them and worse for you.'

'Oh,' he laughed. 'Oh yes, I should have guessed. Oh Reyhnard, you must have some funny ideas about sex if you think that I order them around and they call me sir while we're – '

'I know what I see. It's not good for the servants to have us mingling so familiarly with them.'

'What a sweet little prig you are,' he said, not unkindly. 'Can't you ever unwind? I brought you down here to do you a favour. You might be married one day, who knows? And how will you feel if you haven't got a clue what you're supposed to do? Not to mention the poor benighted woman who has to marry you. It's there to use, you know. It won't drop off.'

'Yours ought to, the way you use it.'

Alexi roared with laughter, rocking back and forth and making the mattress squeak.

'Look, are you coming?' I asked impatiently. 'Because I'm going.'

He sat up, and suddenly shot out an arm to make the elbow-joint crack like a whip. This always got on my nerves. 'Come on then,' he said. 'Hans is busy with Father. Let's go and see Peter.'

In those days there were times when Alexi almost succeeded in making me like him. No matter how much I disliked his attitude – and there were times, like that day, when I loathed him so much I'm ashamed to remember it – there was something about him which made his company stimulating, perhaps because it was so frustrating. I could never find the angle from which he was looking at the world. At the time I thought he did it to irritate me. To some extent he probably did.

Alexi seemed to see the world in different colours from everyone else. I thought he was morally colour-blind. I thought I couldn't talk to him, and I thought that was why. To my own disgust I realised I envied some things about him. Other times I considered him beneath contempt.

I thought all sorts of things about him, none of which he deserved. I have known this for many years.

7

Though dead, to live: that is the ambition of poets. When their throats are dust and ashes they will continue to speak, their words for ever fresh. I am thinking of Caryllac.

I met him between the pages of a book which should not have existed, let alone have been read by me. From the power of his words I formed an image of Caryllac: tall, golden, muscular. I found strength in the poems and so pictured strength in the man. Other boys make heroes out of athletes and soldiers, taking their ideals from great feats of valour and physical prowess. I made mine out of a voice.

He was under the same ban as my Andaranah uncles. Aside from his name I knew little about Caryllac, though I know more now. His mother was a fish-gutter. He was born in Sylaeg, on the south-west coast, a town buffeted by sea tides and winds seven months of the year. The great shoals of cod lying a few miles off the coast have helped establish the town's prosperity; all the same, a fish-gutter in Sylaeg is a synonym for down-trodden poverty. Caryllac's mother was a great beauty in the native way, or so the legend goes. She was caught sheltering Andaranah partisans during the civil war, and was put to death. I understand that Caryllac's father, who was a son of the Fahlraec of Floriah, also died in the war. Caryllac was taken in by the Floriahs and brought up to be a servant in their household. When he was sixteen, he ran away and came to Tsvingtori.

He wrote poems and plays, and for a while he was very much in vogue at court, charming them with his elegant comedies and shepherd's tales. Yet if you read his later poems, and especially those that he wrote in the native, it soon becomes clear that he no more believed in the Gods than I do.

Uncomfortable attitudes crept into his verses. The Gods became quarrelsome and petty. His lords and ladies walked in less than divine gardens; his rosebushes sprang thorns. He opened his heart to his hand and began writing about the things he really cared for: tramps and servants, pimps, prostitutes, thieves, beggars – and, above all, fish-gutters. I recall one poem so clearly, describing a row of fish-gutters crouched along a dock, piles of gleaming fish in baskets at their feet. Suddenly a mackerel flaps, once, and lies still again. How beautiful those women are! The rhythm of their arms is like music – until you see their eyes, dead as the eyes of the fish they are cleaning.

Caryllac's crimes, if crimes they were, snowballed from such small beginnings. His poems gave the people of the city heroes and heroines from their own ranks to admire. He exalted what had always been contemptible; he portrayed more courage in one impoverished widow's struggle to keep her children fed than was shown by both sides during all the long years of the Conquest, that favourite theme of his predecessors. He put peasant ecstasies and gutter sorrows on the same level as the acts of gods and the feelings of kings.

The Official Publishers refused to take any more of his manuscripts. His books were removed from the Palace library. He and his friends, for ever anonymous, laboured by hand to produce a series of three poems.

These poems are almost artless, written in a doggerel which Caryllac could never have intended to be read; rather, they are for reciting in the open air, memorised by the hearts of an illiterate crowd.

The first poem recounts a meeting in the street between a lady and a prostitute. The lady lifts her nose; the prostitute steps to one side; each goes her separate way. Back home the lady nags her husband, beats a servant, criticises her children and then sits herself down in front of a mirror, eating chocolates and trying on for size the new necklace her lover has sent her. The prostitute also goes home. She cooks supper for her children, cleans the house and is visited by a client. Caryllac cleverly does not tell us directly who this man is. He is too tired for lovemaking, and wants only a sympathetic listener; in the course of their conversation we discover that he is the lady's husband.

The second poem is in the same vein, dealing with a rich merchant and a galley oarsman.

The third is very different.

A young girl barely into her teens comes to work as a maid at the Palace. She hopes to fall in love with and marry some handsome young groom or gardener, who will tend her and cherish her as she deserves. Unfortunately a powerful lord conceives a passion for her and rapes her; she becomes pregnant, and is packed off to seek refuge in a brothel. This poem was terrible partly because it was too true – and even more because any man or woman of ordinary intelligence could have read the symbolism between the lines. The great lord's name was Basal filcMichah. The girl's rape was a metaphor both for the civil war and for the subjection of the native population by Michah and his followers; and Caryllac goes out of his way to drive this home.

He never made any attempt to hide. When the Guards came for him, they found him sitting on the little stool where he always wrote, and in the middle of composition. Caryllac wasn't afraid. He had teased death and dared it to try him – but he wasn't executed. Geraint, that cringing clerk, had been put to death for as petty a crime as kicking me. Caryllac, thumbing his nose in my father's face, was exiled.

My father had the measure of Caryllac. He chose the most appropriate punishment possible. Apparently he said to Caryllac, 'You've gone too far, but nowhere like as far as I can send you.' He had Caryllac escorted to a warship, allowed him every freedom aboard ship, and transported him to the south. This was the place he had chosen for Caryllac's exile, the land on the other side of the water, beyond the straits of Duccarn, where spices and fireworks come from. In the south there is nothing but sand and rocks, dry heat, white sky, no springtime, no winter, no rain.

Since Caryllac had no religion he was not afraid of death: he knew that in the nothingness of death one cannot be aware of what one has lost. But living, in exile, he would not forget the cornflowers blooming in fields of green wheat, the mossy banks of summer streams, snow, hollyberries, the autumn clouds and the song of the birds in the morning. He would remember these beloved marvels every day of his life, contrasting them with the desert he now inhabited. He would wake every morning to the memory of Brychmachrye and the knowledge that he would never see her again. This is what my father did to Caryllac.

All his books were burnt, just as their creator was daily being burnt under the desert sun. I don't know how the copy I had survived. Nor do I remember how I found it, but I had it in my hands and I kept it safe.

I memorised all his poems. At night, between whispered recitals, I would talk to Caryllac, knowing he couldn't hear but wondering if he could sense me. I believed he must: I felt my own admiration for him so strongly. He had allowed no fear to stand between him and his voice. He had looked my father in the eye and never regretted a single line. I thought he must be happy, and not with a common, everyday sort of happiness, but with the happiness of a god who has created things he knows will never tarnish or die.

I made a promise to Caryllac. When Hans was King, I said, I would persuade my brother to bring him home and give him all the honours he deserved. I never worked through how I would do this, but I thought that if I took Caryllac's poetry and courage as a model, I would grow up enough of a man to achieve anything.

Peter must have said something, or unknowingly let it slip, because Bronwen was arrested. In order to get her from her room to the prison they had to pass the library, and despite her age she found the strength to break free from the Guards and run down the corridor, bursting in on our quiet studies.

She tumbled through the door screaming Peter's name. Peter ran over and tried to drag her in, shouting 'Shut the door, Reyhnard! Shut the door!' with desperate insistence; I could not move, and Aneurin stood wringing his hands, drawing back a pace for every inch Peter dragged Bronwen towards us. She was fat and old, and Peter's face flushed pink with the effort. He was panting. All this took no more than a few seconds before the Guards came in. They were breathing heavily, creaking leather and clanking superfluous swords, shamefaced that so much manpower had failed to subdue one crazy old woman. Seeing them, Peter threw himself over Bronwen, and the Guards just stood there helplessly. They were not permitted to use force on him.

'For God's sake, sir, take the Prince away,' the Captain said to me.

Aneurin had the right to use whatever methods he thought necessary in order to control recalcitrant schoolboys, and in the end he was the one who peeled Peter off the old woman. Peter stood like a wooden doll with no joints while Aneurin held him by the arms. The only signs of life he gave were the tears running down his nose.

Bronwen was still shouting mad things. The Captain hit her on the mouth, and she fainted. He was wearing leather gauntlets which must have broken her teeth. I saw a red stain spread over her chin. They lifted her by the arms and legs, shapeless as a dead mare, and carried her away.

The Captain remembered to shut the door behind him.

Immediately, Peter turned on Aneurin. 'It's your fault, you filthy dirty liar, I hate you . . . ' beating weakly on Aneurin's chest with his fists. Aneurin made no attempt to catch Peter's wrists or defend himself in any way, but he looked at me with a sort of mute resignation. I knew he was not guilty.

I took Peter by the shoulders and led him away. He was choking on his sobs. We made it as far as his rooms before he threw up.

The issue was clear. Bronwen was the guilty party. Guilty of stuffing him with fantasies and lies until it made him sick. She had allowed him to see that scene in the library. She wanted him to see it. She had betrayed her guardianship. She was guilty of hurting Peter, and I was glad they had taken her.

I tried to talk sense to him.

'Peter, don't cry. She told you lies, and that was wrong, you see that now. Father punishes people who tell lies.'

He said between gulps, 'Do you love me?'

'You know I do. I love you much more than she did. I've never lied to you.'

'Do you love me more than him?'

'Who?'

'The King.'

I did not need to stop and think, because the answer came right up from my heart. 'Yes, much more, more than anyone.'

Twisting my shirt in his fist he cried. 'I'm scared, Reyhnard. He knew. I don't know how he knew. He knows everything. He can see inside our heads. He is the King, I know, I know now – he can hear everything, he can even hear what people *think*. He's going to kill her, isn't he?'

I stroked his hair and said nothing. The answer was probably yes.

'Maybe he'll kill us too.'

'Oh Peter, what a thing to think! Father's not going to hurt us – '

'Not *you*, because you never thought anything bad about him, but I did and he knows – '

'Peter, Peter, shhh, he's not going to kill you.'

Peter snuffled thickly. 'Would it hurt?'

'Stop thinking about it.'

'I cut my leg on Hans's sword once, really deep, and it bleeded but it didn't hurt, not for ages. It hurt later, but not then. So if they took a sword, you know, and stuck it in your heart, you'd be dead right away, wouldn't you, and it wouldn't hurt, would it?'

'No, I expect it wouldn't hurt. You must stop thinking about things like that, Peter. No one's going to kill you.'

'What's it like to die?'

'You're so silly. How could I know?'

'Are you scared?'

'Everybody's scared of what they don't know.'

Peter rolled on to his back and thought about this for a while, beating a tattoo on his bare stomach. I saw a new idea come into his eyes. 'Reyhnard, what if they made a mistake, and they thought you were dead but you weren't, and they put you on the ship and you woke up and you were bur-bur-burning?'

'I don't think that's ever happened.'

'But Reyhnard, but what if it did?'

'Well then, you'd be dead after all, wouldn't you? Or you could always jump overboard and swim to shore. That would surprise them.'

He started to laugh, in that high frantic way which soon disintegrates into tears. I held him tight and let him soak my shirt. His crying was so painful he whimpered, clutching at his chest.

I think in a way, though he probably wasn't aware of it, he was relieved things had come to a head. I can't deny he was fond of Bronwen, but she had put him through a nightmare and I think he was guiltily glad it was over.

His eyes were shut and he was breathing heavily. I thought he had fallen asleep, but he suddenly said, 'When I'm King I'll kill Aneurin.'

'Oh Peter, why?'

'He told on Bron.'

'He didn't. I told him not to tell.'

Peter drew back, just a little, and raised his eyes to me. I saw his love there, and a different devotion, the childish one, both more passionate and more fickle. Trust too, child to father and man to man. And one more thing which united us: the knowledge that what we said and did had no influence over anyone else. He did not need to say this; instead he pointed out, 'Aneurin's scared. He's scared of everything. Haven't you seen the way he jumps every time someone knocks on the door? Aneurin's scared he's going to die.'

I thought I should get his mind off this subject, so I said, 'You know better than that, Peter. You know you won't be King. Hans will be King after Father.'

He asked me very seriously, 'Won't you ever be King, Reyhnard?'

And I said No.

'I don't think that's fair,' he said.

Alexi came in without knocking. He climbed up beside us, rumpled Peter's hair and stretched out his long legs so that the feet were dangling off the end of the bed. His next move would be to reach into his pocket for some sweets – chocolate, or marzipan, or toffee – and so he did, offering us each a bull's-eye. I gave Peter mine.

'I hear you're in a scrape,' Alexi said to Peter, whose cheeks were bulging like a greedy squirrel's.

'How do you know?' I asked.

'I keep my little ear to the ground. I came to see if there was anything you wanted.'

Through his mouthful Peter asked, 'Where've they taken her?'

'Prison, I'm afraid.'

'Can I see her?'

'I don't think so.'

'Alexi' – Peter swallowed one of the sweets – 'why don't I look like you and Reyhnard and Hans?'

'Oh Peter!' I exclaimed. 'Does it matter?'

Alexi touched my arm, almost imperceptibly, and said, 'That's one of the great mysteries of the world, Pea, which means I don't know. You take after our mother and Reyhnard and I take after Father, and that's how it is.'

'But why am I the only one?'

Alexi folded his arms, looked Peter straight in the eye, and said, 'You know, you're not. Ages before you were born, before Reyhnard was born, when I was very small, Mother had another baby and it looked just like you, only it was born before it was ready to live.'

I wished I'd thought of that.

'Oh,' said Peter, crunching up the other bull's-eye with his strong teeth. 'Bron never told me that.'

'I guess she doesn't know everything, hmmm?'

'Alexi, why was it born if it wasn't ready to live?'

Alexi threw me a harried look. 'I don't know. It happens.' He leaned back, studying Peter from under his eyelids, and asked him, 'How old are you now, Pea-eater?'

'Seven and seven months and two weeks and three days.'

'Good God, that old? I see you're doing all right in arithmetic. How are you getting on in your lessons?'

'I hate them and I hate Aneurin.'

I wanted to tell Alexi to stop egging Peter on, but at the same time I wondered what this was leading up to.

He said, 'That's a bit strong. Why do you feel like that?'

'I just do. Anyway he doesn't like me either.'

'That's not true,' I protested. 'He just wants you to do well.'

Alexi grinned, tapping his nose. 'So that's it. Bet you don't like lessons because you're backward – bet you can't even read and write – '

'I can too!' Peter leapt up. 'I don't like my lessons 'cause they're boring!'

'All boys have to be educated.'

'No they don't,' said Peter decidedly. 'All my friends don't, not like with Aneurin. They're learning fencing and riding and things . . . '

'Is that what you'd like to do?' asked Alexi. 'Leave the library for good, and join your friends' lessons?'

Peter's face lit up; and then he glanced at me, and wavered. 'Reyhnard can come too.'

'Ah, I'm afraid he can't.'

'But what will he do, all alone?'

A good question, I thought. Peter flickers in the library like a living fire, illuminating all my hours. I need him there.

Alexi saw my expression, and kept back whatever else he was going to say. Stretching himself, he rose, gave Peter another bull's-eye, and told me to come and see him when I could; he wanted to talk to me. Later, when Peter had fallen asleep with his head in my lap – he was so worn out, I knew nothing would wake him for hours – I quietly disentangled myself and went to Alexi's room, impatient to hear the half that he had left unsaid.

'Want a drink?' he offered.

'No, I'm not thirsty. What is it you have to say, Alexi? I don't want to leave him on his own for long.'

'No, I know you don't, but it's about him.'

'About that rubbish of him giving up his lessons?'

'I don't think it is rubbish. Now calm down, Reyhnard, listen. You don't have to tell me, but I wish you would . . . about what's been going on.'

'You said you knew.'

'I lied, sort of – '

'You lied about that baby too, didn't you?'

'Not really. She did have a miscarriage, though I've no idea what it looked like. Awful, I should think, it was only four months – '

'*Alexi!*'

He inclined his head in apology. 'I forgot how squeamish you are – no, please listen. I do know a bit about what's happened to Peter. I know old Bronwen's done something pretty terrible and involved him – and that's about as much as anyone knows for certain. Of course they're speculating like mad. I've heard some pretty wild stories this afternoon, but I'd like to know the truth. I just didn't want to talk about it in front of Peter.'

I gave him credit for this, grudgingly.

'What did she say to him?' Alexi asked.

'Filthy, stupid lies. Not worth repeating.'

'You can trust me, you know.'

'I hate her,' I said.

Alexi sighed heavily.

And I hate you, I thought. I hate your grinning handsome face and your big tall body. I hate those girls you let touch you with such freedom. I hate the food you eat. I hate the fact that I can't understand why Hans loves you.

All the same, I told him. I had to tell someone.

Alexi took a seat and listened without interrupting while I told him everything I knew. Furrows appeared between his black brows, and he chewed his knuckles. When I finished, I had to ask him – hating the necessity, hating knowing he would have an answer, hating knowing that I had no one else to ask – 'What's going to happen now?'

He took his hand out of his mouth and said, 'Bronwen's done for, of course. It seems so sad – you can't blame someone for being crazy . . . '

'Who else is to blame? I told you what she did. I hope he buries her alive – '

'He probably will.'

'I don't care, I want to know what's going to happen to Peter.'

'Reyhnard, I don't know what he'll do to Peter.'

I tried to stand up then, dizzily clinging to the back of the chair, my knees like water, at the same time trying to say something that I couldn't get out because my throat was blocked with a great lump of irrational dread and panic. Alexi took hold of my arm, unbalancing me; I half tumbled and was half pushed into the chair. 'Sit down,' he said. 'Don't – here, take this, drink it . . . '

It was as strong as acid. I spluttered.

From a long way away I could hear him asking me a question. I shook my head, and it began to clear. I heard him say, 'You'll break it,' and felt him gently remove the glass from my grip.

'What is it?' I coughed.

'Potato spirits.'

'It's horrible.' But it helped, putting a foreign warmth into the pit of my stomach, fuming up to melt away the blockage in my throat. 'It's not his fault,' I said. 'No one could blame him. He's only seven.'

'I know. I'm sorry, what I said was stupid. I didn't realise you'd – I didn't mean he'd be executed or anything like that, Reyhnard, come on – '

'What then?'

'I said I don't know.'

'But it's bad?'

'Peter's been going around telling people the King isn't his father, and that's a lot worse than saying the Queen isn't your mother, and you know what they did to you.'

'He's only seven,' I repeated.

'You were only five.'

I exclaimed, 'I have to do something!'

'What?'

There was nothing we could do. I stared at the glass in his hand, not seeing it, wild pointless pictures filling my mind of the Palace torn down, everybody dead, Peter and I standing safe in the midst of the smoking rubble.

Alexi broke in on my thoughts with, 'Does Peter really hate his lessons that much, or was he just saying it?'

'I don't know. I never thought about it. I thought he had to do them . . . '

'Well, think about it now.'

I wedged my hands in my armpits, remembering Peter's restlessness, how he was for ever staring out of the window or drawing when Aneurin's back was turned, taking three days to learn what had taken me one – and not because he lacked ability. He was simply bored stiff, as I ought to have noticed long ago.

'I suppose he doesn't like them very much.'

'If that's so, then it's hardly surprising Bronwen's notions got such a hold on him. All that time he's spent mooning over something he doesn't want to do – and probably doesn't do, does he? It's given him time to brood. It's not good for a child his age. He ought to be out with the other boys, in the fresh air, learning fencing, fieldcraft, drill, all that sort of thing. It's obvious he's never going to be a scholar – even I can see that, and I don't see as much of him as you do. He doesn't want to be a scholar. So he ought to be a soldier if he's going to be anything. Look,

Reyhnard, I know Aneurin suits you but he doesn't suit Peter – don't interrupt. The other thing is this. He shouldn't go back to Aneurin, not after what you've told me happened today. He doesn't like Aneurin, and what's more he doesn't trust him – and I'd guess Aneurin would rather not have him back, though he can't say anything. Am I right?'

I have to admit that I had never thought any of this out as clearly as Alexi obviously had. My objectivity was always weakened when it came to Peter. All the same, what he said sounded fairly accurate, so since I could not deny it, I said nothing.

Alexi waited until it became clear I would make no comment, and then he went on.

'There is something someone else could do. I'm afraid Father's going to come down pretty hard on the little bugger, so listen, Reyhnard – I don't know if this will work, but I'm going to ask Hans . . . Actually, on second thoughts, Hans wouldn't do. I'll go and see Heloise, you know, Edvard filcLaurentin's wife. Maybe she can get Edvard to talk to Father, try to persuade him that Peter should be taken out of the library and sent to join the other boys. Father might listen to Edvard. And if he can be convinced that that would sort Peter out, he might not be so hard on him.'

I believe that, as I listened to this scheme of minor intrigue, my face became cynical and suspicious, because Alexi flashed a smile and added, 'It's the best way. The only way really. I would ask Hans, and I know he'd want to help if he knew. It's just that somewhere between me and Father, Hans would forget; and I couldn't stand there prompting, that would only make it worse.'

'How can you talk that way about Hans?' I protested angrily.

'I'm not blind to his shortcomings. He is human, you know, he doesn't have to be perfect. Now, what do you think, can you come up with a better plan? If not, then I'll go ahead with this one, because it's the best I can think of.'

I sat up straight, put my chin in the air, and replied – I'm ashamed to remember with what an unpleasant, sarcastic tone – 'It's terribly good of you to go to so much trouble, especially as you don't really care one way or the other. Do you?'

Alexi crossed his legs, giving in return for my cold stare his frank equanimity. 'Do you really think I'd bother if I didn't?'

'You care as much about Bronwen as you do about Peter. I don't call that really caring. You know what she did. You're doing it because you love interfering – '

'I know why she did it, too,' he interrupted, getting to his feet and gesturing. 'Come over here.'

'Oh, what for?'

Three of his long strides bridged the space between us. He took hold of my arm and hauled me up; Alexi was much stronger than one would guess from his indolence.

'I want to show you something,' he said, dragging me across the floor to stand in front of the window. 'What do you see?'

'Nothing.'

'Now don't sulk. You must see something.'

'The grounds.'

'What else?'

'The sky, trees, some birds – what am I supposed to see?'

'Don't look at the scenery, nitwit, look down there, at the people – '

'They're always there.'

'Indeed they are.' He prodded me in the neck and pointed. 'Look at that man, see him? The fat one, going bald. Maybe he owes a fortune in gambling debts, and he's going out of his mind wondering how to raise the money. He can't think of anything else. And see that woman in the yellow dress, the pregnant woman? She's got a husband and a lover and she's been found out, and she doesn't know which is the father – and if it's blond like her and her husband she'll be allowed to keep it, but if it's dark like her lover they'll put it out, so she's trying not to love her baby because she doesn't know if she'll ever be allowed to hold it. That gardener, the one with the limp, pushing the wheelbarrow. He's got a wooden leg. He was going to be an athlete, a runner, but a dog bit his leg and it had to be amputated. He's not much older than you. And there – '

'Alexi! Stop! Do you know all this or are you making it up?'

'I know it and I'm making it up.' He ran his hands through his hair. 'If what I've said about them isn't true, then something else is.'

'So?'

'Doesn't that mean anything to you?'

'Should it? Alexi, what are you trying to do?'

'I'm trying to talk to you.' He was becoming agitated, which I found more disturbing than anything else, for I had never seen him in such a state before. 'Every one of those people has their own problems, as if being alive wasn't enough – they're *alive*, Reyhnard, just like you. They're each the centre of their own world and in that world you, and I, and Peter, and even the King, Reyhnard, even the King, we all count for very little.'

I was honestly puzzled; and because I thought he was wasting my time for no better reason than to confuse me, my temper rose.

'What's that got to do with Peter?'

He thrust his hands into his pockets. 'I don't know.' The fit seemed to be over. He sloped away from the window to sit in my chair, throwing his legs over the arm so that his feet touched the floor. 'If I ever work it out, you'll be the first to know.'

Then he waved a finger at me and started again. 'I'll tell you something else about them – they all sleep and eat and fart and fuck and the gardener with the gammy leg takes real pleasure in growing beautiful – '

'Oh shut up. I don't want to hear about them. I'm not interested in them. I want to know what's going to happen to Peter.'

'We shall try to get him out of that library.'

'You are such a bloody fraud, Alexi. You haven't bothered to think about my feelings.'

'I thought you'd want what's best for him. You keep saying how much you care about him – '

'I *do*. You don't, that's what you've been saying. Nothing's important to you. You don't care about him any more than you care about all those people out there, those strangers – '

'Strangers?' he said quizzically, as if the word were foreign to him. He began to grin, slowly, tigerishly, all his white teeth, teasing. 'You know, if you looked at yourself through someone else's eyes, you'd see a stranger too.'

This idiocy was enough to snap the last of my patience. I was fed up with his silly games, his empathy with trivial misfortunes, his lack of self. He had no shame, no pride, no honour; he was a prince, he was the son of a god, such as gods are, he was my brother – and he made servants his equals. Some vital part must be missing in his brain, I thought. Rather no help than his.

I left him, and went wandering aimlessly about, resisting the urge to go back to Peter and tell him things he would not understand. In my room I took my copy of Caryllac out of its hiding place, stuffed it under my shirt, and made my way to a deserted corner of the gardens, near the woods, where it was damp and few people came.

8

Bronwen did die, retaining her defiance to the last. She killed herself, more by the strength of her will than anything else, and in a strange way. She jammed earth from the floor up her nostrils, and ripped up her clothes to stuff the strips down her throat, thus suffocating herself. She must have had a monolithic hatred. I always imagine her dying with silent laughter in her blocked throat, thinking in her madness of how she had cheated my father of the kill.

In fact he could not have cared less. He had bigger potatoes to dig, as the saying goes. Some people are sympathetic to lunatics, and my father didn't believe in making martyrs, so if this had all happened in a quiet year he might have done nothing more than retire her to a far-flung corner of the country. But unrest had been brewing for some time around Mindared, always a centre for Andaranah disaffection, and in that year it blew up. A week or so before Bronwen's arrest, the Fahlraec of Mindarah and several lesser lords of that region withdrew from court and began to muster their followers. What they hoped to achieve is anybody's guess, since from the start they had no chance. My father had done such a good job of putting right the misrule of the Andaranahs and controlling the local lords, and the country was so prosperous, and my father so popular, that even in the west only a small proportion of the population could be roused to rebellion pitch. Hans, who was under strict orders from my father to restrain himself, took out several battalions to deal with the problem. He bloodied the rebels up a bit, captured their ringleaders, and brought them back to Tsvingtori. The rank and file were pardoned and sent off with an injunction to concern themselves with crops, not politics. The lords and their lieutenants were executed in a common grave where Bronwen's body had already been laid – a suitable degradation. The families of the condemned were allowed to keep their lands and titles; they fully appreciated this generous gesture. He would never – said my father – visit the sins of the husbands on their wives and children.

I was old enough to understand the wisdom in this, and to appreciate what a useful tool for a king mercy could be.

As it happened, Peter was taken out of the library and sent to join the other boys, after being so thoroughly whacked he couldn't sit down for two days. His delight at being free from his lessons enabled him to take this beating with admirable fortitude. Everything seemed on the point of working out well for him, when some idiotic young woman told her son the details of Bronwen's death, and he gleefully passed them on to Peter.

My brother had terrible nightmares, from which he would wake sweating and screaming, crying out both for her and for me. I took to sleeping with him. I didn't mind, I liked it. If I couldn't spend my days with him I would spend my nights, lying awake to watch him sleep, telling him stories to take his mind off things, often playing games into the small hours until he dropped off from exhaustion. For a long time Peter was afraid to go to sleep because it opened the door for his nightmares. Seven or eight weeks later he caught measles. He probably caught it from one of the other boys, and since I had never had it I caught it from Peter. Neither of us was very seriously ill. I still carry a souvenir of it: a rather large pockmark on the inside of my right elbow. Peter took a long time to shake off the illness, but as the measles cleared his nightmares started to fade too.

The library was gloomy. Aneurin was a bundle of shuffling nerves, always glancing over his shoulder. I told myself I should not blame him, but I did.

Reading all this over, I suppose I've made our lives out to have been concerned solely with blood, death and terror, wave upon wave of strong emotion. Far from it: it is because these events were, so to speak, like pockmarks on the smooth complexion of Palace life that they are so memorable. Serena tells me her first memory is of seeing a rabid dog shot to death with arrows. The archers, she says, were so frightened of being bitten that they stood too far away, and their aim was bad, and the dog a long time dying. Yet who could have had a more tranquil life than Serena?

Now, Reyhnard, you really must make up your mind who you are writing this for, or to, because so far it's a bit of a mess. It's too disjointed and awkward. Too level in some places, too lumpy in others, and personally I think the punctuation is rather poor. How will that do for criticism, Aneurin? He'd disapprove of both the style and the structure. Aneurin, I'm grown-up now, I'm the King, I can do what I want.

I don't care, damn it, let me rid myself of some useless baggage. If I'm not free at last, up here, when will I be? I write what I want, as I feel, what I am – and you know, I suspect the real aim of it is to empty myself. Ink like blood, you see:

When I am drained
I won't be pained.

I wrote poetry, of course. Anyone might have guessed. I was just the type. Boys who have soldiers for heroes swing swords and go hunting. A boy with Aneurin for a mentor and Caryllac for a hero would write poetry. I don't much, any more.

Time to time, it comes; I've never known from where. I will be walking in the snow, or sitting here writing, or eating, or watching Serena sew, when it materialises. Suddenly I'm filled with it, milling in my brain, so that my fingers itch for a pen to put it down before it dribbles away.

Aneurin had one teaching talent: he knew how to turn his pupil's interest to advantage. When he discovered I wrote poetry – and it was quite by accident: I left a piece lying around and he recognised the handwriting – he decided to encourage me, and he used to set me subjects:

The Growing Tree – twenty lines, hexameters
The Siege of Mindared – thirty lines, heroic
The Good Deed of a Noble Friend – sonnet

Cheerfully I churned out undistinguished work. It was not all bad; in fact, none of it was actively bad, and there were some lines that were positively good, and encouraged me in my hope of being an heir to Caryllac.

Long beneath the leafy larch I lay . . .

I was immensely proud of that line, which began my poem to the growing tree, until Aneurin asked me whether I didn't think the alliteration a little over-done.

We would sit nose to nose across the table, Aneurin peering at the sheet I had scribbled over – he was becoming very short-sighted – and underlining the good lines with blue ink, the bad with red. Then he would send me away to re-write it. I don't suppose he ever thought he was forging a great artist. His major family trait, after all, was realism.

Bad or good, it doesn't really matter. What mattered was that I wrote them. I was now sure of what I had long ago guessed at in the poems of Isumbard Shoemaker: poetry is where you can put your heart. I laboured away at those set pieces, but what I enjoyed most were the poems I wrote for myself, about myself: about my love for Peter, my adoration of my father and Hans; about my contempt for and growing confusion with Alexi; about my ignorance of women which, in my ignorance, I thought was from choice; about my high disregard for the petty concerns of court life. Of course I never showed these to anyone; and of course I modelled myself on Caryllac. My best pieces have a strong smell of plagiarism about them.

I am reminded of a little poem which Alexi was fond of quoting to me in those days – for he had, somehow, found out my ambition:

I tried to write of love
When I did not know it.

'Twas mere imagination;
All my works show it.

And now that I love you,
I am confusèd quite,
For I have used up all the words;
There is no more to write.

Poetry is a second-hand joy:
My heart knows this is true.
I have no need to write of love
When I can be with you.

Alexi hardly ever managed to get to the end of this ditty, he was laughing so hard. However – note the little accent on 'confusèd', an artificiality to adapt a word to a metre in a poem which doesn't scan anyway. I used to be terribly keen on such conventions. I suppose that's just one small symptom of the whole necessity, for me, of writing poems. When one is at the age that I was then, one's mind and emotions, and one's whole being, are so unstable and confused – though of course at the time one does not feel unstable and confused at all, but rather as if one is coming across every day a hundred truths which the old fools have never known or have forgotten, and which you yourself forget by the next day – anyway one does, or I did, seize upon poetry because, as I've said, the discipline of the metre forces you to reflect upon jumbled thinking and half-formed ideas, and whips them into shape. It is also, when it works, immensely satisfying, at a time when there is very little satisfaction to be found anywhere else. These days I prefer prose. I don't have to squeeze and twist my thoughts into tight spondees, as if they were a middle-aged woman struggling into a corset. This mountain village confines me enough.

When I was sixteen poetry was my heart and soul, literally. All there was of me I put out, open to the fresh air and the wet ink. It's so hard to remember now, that I gave all the enthusiasm of youth to that one thing. Since then I have known greater joys than poetry.

One poem in particular pleased Aneurin no end. I remember nothing of it now. It was very undistinguished, except, perhaps, in its sincerity. It was about my father. I believed it said I loved him as a God, feared him as a King, and was proud of him as a father, and that my life could have no thrill in it equal to having been born his son. Or words to that effect. I can be cynical about it now, but it was not put so bluntly: it was a very flowery tribute to him. It was not one of my set pieces, but I had not intended it as a completely private one either, and it was not totally by accident that Aneurin found it. I had left it lying in a very obvious place. Aneurin did what I hoped he would: by some hook or crook he managed to place it before my father's eyes, and word filtered back that he had been very pleased by it, very pleased.

Aneurin wrung his hands with joy, then wiped them over and over his thinning pate, overcome with pride and the flush of success. Very pleased, His Grace was very pleased, oh well done Aneurin, what you have achieved.

I'm sure my father clearly saw the demerits of that poem. He was not averse to a little tease; I think it was because he had not been brought up to be King that he had a sense of humour about the situation. He, after all, had never toed his King's line. If his courtiers had not given him the obeisance he demanded, they would have been dead quicker than he could blink, but all the same I think he despised them a little for it. One day he and his train came upon me in the garden. I was in that out-of-the-way spot I usually preferred, and I think my father knew this, and came that way on purpose.

I was deep in Caryllac, mouthing the words into my brain so that I would never forget them, and in the hope that some of his creative power would rub off on me. I didn't hear my father approaching until a cold shadow fell over my book, and I glanced up, frowning, intending to motion whoever it was out of the light. Seeing him, I jumped up, twitching and fumbling, trying to hide the book and knowing it was too late.

He was in a good mood.

'Ah, Reyhnard. Studying, I see.'

'Yes, Sir.'

'Splendid to see such application in the young. Hansli, you see what trouble your brother goes to to improve himself? I think we can forgive such a scholar for not noticing us – bigger things filling up your mind, eh, son?'

'You took me by surprise, Sir; people rarely come this way. I wasn't expecting . . . '

He hadn't heard me, was not interested. He inclined his head to address the court.

'Ladies, gentlemen, did you know that as well as having a scholar in our family, we have a poet?'

Polite murmurs of interest. I felt sick, with a mingling of pride, apprehension and fear. Most of all, I squirmed with a racking shyness which I had never, until that moment, known I possessed in such abundance –

for never before had the attention of three score men and women been focused on me. I marshalled my nerves and stood stiffly. If I didn't move, I wouldn't embarrass myself with some awkward stumble. Looking past Hans, who was watching a hawk circle overhead, and past Alexi, who was winking at me, I saw Caryad, slender quiet thing with her mass of hair fluffed out round her head. She clasped her hands, smiling at me with her soft mouth and dove-grey eyes. She knew my father better than any of us.

'Yes, a poet,' my father repeated. 'A very gifted young artist. Our own son the Prince Reyhnard. We must say it fills us with pride to have such talented children.'

One eager-beaver sycophant at the back cried, 'Perhaps the Prince would be so generous as to recite us one of his verses, Sir.'

My father's eyes locked on him, making sure of the face. Then he smiled, saying, 'I daresay he might, with a little persuasion. Young poets are always shy of their work' – swinging round – 'aren't they, Reyhnard?'

'I would be happy to recite a poem for you, Sir, if you wish it.'

'One of your own,' said my father.

I found enough courage to glance past him at Caryad. She nodded once, with a smile of encouragement.

I did not need to ask him which poem he would prefer. He knew only one, which had, so to speak, tickled his fancy. And the joke would not have been complete had the subject matter of the poem been anything other than him.

Attentive silence – coughings – Alexi winking, Caryad smiling, my father not smiling, not exactly, but with the pleased expression of a man who has set a booby-trap over the door and is about to see someone open it. Who was the booby? That was the question. No help for it now. I began.

It was a short poem, thirty lines or so having used up my fund of superlatives. It was replete with alliteration, which I thought gave it a grand and stately sound, plus a few onomatopoeic battle noises. Now – with this listening audience, with my father in the front row – I became fully aware of each lame phrase, all the worn conventions helping the metre along. Every fault glared. My voice grew louder, as if I could drown out those faults. My father's face, twisted and amused, never altered its expression; I stumbled at length to the end.

'Ve-ry good,' he said, stretching the syllables. Wild applause broke out.

'Excellent, Your Grace, and so well recited, very acute analogy I thought . . . ' They fell over themselves to congratulate him on himself, and his son, and the poem – splendid poem, not of course that it did justice to its subject, young author, but delightful . . . They tangled and tripped in their flattery, torn between the need to praise the King's son, the obligation to exclaim that mere words could not describe His Grace's magnificence, and the assurance that his son's poem came as near as possible to doing so.

My father took all this with a bland satisfaction, as if he had been given the very present he had asked for. When they had finally worn themselves out and were beginning to repeat their protestations, he turned back to me and said, with a little glitter, a gem, really, of irony, 'Thank you, Reyhnard, for that excellent entertainment. Now I think we've kept you from your studies long enough. May I see your book?'

I had hoped he would forget. But he never forgot. He noticed everything, and made it his business to inquire after everything, however seemingly irrelevant. If I had wanted to keep out of trouble I should never have opened that book. As it was, he had put me through so much in such a short space of time that I handed it over without a pause, with a sort of resigned despair.

His reaction surprised me; that is, because he seemed to have none. Keeping my place with his thumb, he ran the two fingers of his left hand down the spine. Caryllac's name was inlaid there in red letters, but my father gave no sign of recognition. He opened the book, flicked over one or two pages, and handed it back to me without a word. Lifting that deformed hand he stroked his beard thoughtfully, then said again, 'Thank you, Reyhnard.'

He took Hans's arm and they walked on down the path, talking of horses.

Caryad and Alexi waited at the back of the train. When the court had all passed along a little way, they came up to me.

'I enjoyed that very much, Prince,' Caryad smiled. She smiled so sweetly. She seemed to be always smiling, even on those rare occasions when she frowned. 'I suspect you've quite a talent,' she went on. 'Though it's still a little raw yet, as I'm sure you know. I'd be so pleased if you allowed me to listen to some more of your poems. You know,' she put her head to one side and smiled more deeply, an unaffected gesture, 'I've always been fond of good poetry.'

She reached out to offer me her hand. I looked with delight on her slim fingers and almond nails. Caryad gave my hand a squeeze – I raised my eyes to her face. Her red lips were painted, blue shadow on her lids, pink powder on her cheeks. The skin of her palm was soft, warm and dry. I pulled my hand away and glanced involuntarily after my father, now a tiny head bobbing in the distance.

Caryad misread my thoughts. Giving me a maternal pat on the arm, she said, 'I must go now,' picked up her skirts – she really was very small, with bird-thin wrists and ankles – and hurried after the court.

In that second I had felt a link with my father. I had seen what he saw in her. She had no real beauty, only skin and perfect fingernails and extraordinary hair, but she glowed from inside like Asdura.

Alexi hadn't mistaken my look. 'She's only a woman,' he grinned. 'And not so young and not so pretty.'

It was true. She had that puckering of the skin round her eyes and the corners of her lips; but since her beauty was not skin deep, it didn't matter.

My thought, which she had misread, was that she was the first woman who had held my hand as a woman touches a young man, rather than a naughty child or a little boy. It was only for a moment, and she had changed it to a mother's touch, believing I thought she should not lag behind my father; but Alexi understood.

'Showing an interest at last, are you?' he said. 'She's far too old for you, and not for sale to boot, but if you like her looks there's a kennel-maid – '

'Not that,' I said, meaning a thousand things.

'Waiting to fall in love, are you?'

Why should I confide in him? I waited for him to go away.

'Suppose you must be, being a poet, because they're so ro-man-tic.' He rolled his eyes. 'Crappy poem, by the way. You can do better than that creepy bullshit.' He didn't say this unkindly. Alexi said nothing unkind, ever. He had a sort of friendly but forceless bullying.

'Alexi, how old were you when you first got someone pregnant?'

'Not sure. Fourteen – thirteen, I think.'

'Do you have any idea how many bastards you have?'

He shrugged. 'A dozen, at a round guess. Maybe more, if they all lived. Probably more.'

'Alexi, don't you care? I mean, don't you care about your children at all? Don't you ever want to see them – '

'Of course I care.' He rubbed his hand across his mouth. Because he was so tall, Alexi was very good at hiding his expression from people: all he had to do was look over their heads. He was doing this now. 'But I can't change the way things are. I do try to look after them, you know. I find out where they've gone. I send them money. I do go to see them if I can – but you know it's not easy to get out of here, and then they move away and I lose track of them. And some of them do get married. What's that book you've got?'

'Haven't you ever loved any of them?'

'Ah, no.' He was laughing at me. 'I'm a heartless beast deep down. Come on, what've you got your nose in, let me see.'

'No need, I'll tell you. It's Caryllac.'

His hand was waiting for the book, so I gave it to him. He flipped it open.

'It's very good,' I said. 'You ought to read it. It might improve your mind.'

He shut it with a snap and sat down, jackknifing his knees. 'I don't know whether to laugh or cry. Sometimes, Reyhnard, for all your studying, you can be incredibly stupid.'

'Give me my book back.'

'Oh well, read it while you can.'

'Father didn't say anything.'

'He wouldn't.'

'It was all a long time ago, the trouble with Caryllac.'

Alexi crossed his legs. 'Did you know he's still alive?'

'Of course he is.'

'Of course he is,' Alexi mimicked.

'Please don't do that.'

'Terribly sorry – I just forgot about the immortality of poets for a moment. Anyway, he is still alive, you know. Still away in the south somewhere. Didn't you know that every ship coming in from there brings Father a poem? Caryllac's nothing if not defiant. Still, if you must be a poet I suppose you could have a worse model. Want some toffee?'

I'm tired now. My memories need a rest. I'll take an easy subject: Serena, beginning with the particulars.

Her hair is coarse, brown, thick and straight. Her eyes are brown – or, let me be exact: they are the colour of damp mud, slightly green, not unattractive. In fact, the prettiest thing about her. She has the native face, flat-cheeked and low-browed, but flatter and lower on her than on most. Her complexion is reddish-fair and rough, like the rest of these mountain peasants. Her fingers are flat-tipped, square-nailed, not nimble. She is fairly short, neither thin nor fat, with strong arms and legs, wide hips and a flattish chest. That seems an adequate portrait.

Serena's eyes are simple things. I can look right through them, and read in them an unwavering belief that all of life is as straightforward as herself. Lies are beyond her. Deception and dissimulation she does not understand. She has the eyes of a dog, adoring and accepting. The physical and mental cruelty her family has meted out to her, the mockery of the village, are to Serena in the same category as the wind and the snow: harsh, but inevitable. She can conceive of no world in which things might be different. It has never occurred to her to question religion. She has faith in the same way that she has hunger and thirst, and in her there is no dividing line between the life of the body and the life of the spirit. Belief is too positive a word to describe Serena's faith, for that implies decision, where Serena only accepts. Hulsitoq is as real to her as Tsvingtori, and she has seen neither of these places. It is more real, perhaps. She has no hope of ever seeing Tsvingtori, but she has every expectation of going to Hulsitoq one day. Even in Hulsitoq, though, she can imagine no other life than one shared with the goats and chickens, the dogs and cats. I think – though she hasn't said it in so many words – she has some idea that in Hulsitoq she and the animals will have a garden to themselves, and the people will be somewhere else. After all, Hulsitoq is purported to be a place of perfect bliss, and that is Serena's ideal of bliss. It will be on a mountain, of course, and there will be seasons, but the winters will not be so cold, nor the summers so hot, and she will not have to kill to eat.

Serena is a half-wit. I think I've said that already. You can see it in her eyes, in her lack of co-ordination, in the hang of her jaw. Yet sometimes I do wonder how half-witted it is to take life as it comes, ask no questions, and greet each morning as if it heralded the best day ever. Her silent, patient, natural optimism may be a symptom of idiocy – or it may be what helps her to survive. Serena is perfectly suited to her life. The other young people in this village chafe with boredom, sometimes run riot, yearn for the town and dream of Tsvingtori. They are restless and rude. Their elders are disappointed versions of the youths they were. Even if they are content to be farmers and goatherds and cheesemakers, which on the whole they are, they all seem to be tarred with dissatisfaction. But Serena, who has grown up to expect nothing, takes everything, even the sunrise, as a gift.

I may as well write a little bit about this village. There are about a dozen huts like this one, half a dozen proper houses, a granary, barns and pens, the mill, the hall – all built of wood or wattle and mud. There's also the Temple, which I've mentioned. I suppose it's quite a big village, compared to some I've seen. The town of Rayalled is ten or eleven miles south-westish, and Nikolas has his castle there. Rayalled used to be Rorhed, but that was before my father became King and appropriated the family name to his exclusive use. Then Nikolas's father had to find a new name for his family, his town and his Fahl, and he took it from the river Ryal which, as a matter of fact, runs past this village. I'm getting mixed into history here. Back to the village.

I remember Aneurin's geography lessons. The main source of revenue for the village is wool. This is sold to factors in Rayalled, and various luxuries which the villagers cannot produce for themselves, such as wine, are purchased in the village. There are quite a few acres of level ground around the village, stony-soiled, producing a small rye crop of poor quality. Many of the huts have little gardens where they grow cabbages, turnips, onions and carrots. The village has an orchard of stunted apple trees, and a communal potato field. And that's about all there is to it. The diet of the village is black bread, potatoes, the odd onion, and mutton mutton mutton cheese cheese cheese.

In the winter the sheep are penned in their folds, the goats in their byres, and we might starve to keep these precious animals alive on root vegetables and barley stalks.

Serena's father is one of the richest men in the village, though once upon a time he was among the poorest. Serena was born in this very hole-hut. Her father stinted his family until he had saved enough to buy a prime ram at the sales in Rayalled. The investment paid off: his flocks prospered, and now produce some of the finest wool in the region. His ram lambs are sought after for thirty miles around. Out of his profits he built himself a large wooden house next to the Temple. He has a finger in every pie going.

Serena is one of the seven children that lived. She comes somewhere in the middle, but isn't sure of her age. She was born at a bad time for her family and the village, when foot-and-mouth was decimating the flocks. Wool prices had risen, only the village wool was of such poor quality that it went for very little. Her mother was starving when she was pregnant with Serena. It may have been this deprivation which stunted the girl. Apparently she was a tiny baby, born with a cowl, which to these superstitious villagers is the worst of bad omens. For some weeks they thought – hoped – she would not live, and it is only for this reason that she was allowed to survive at all: when it became clear she was not going to die of her own accord the time for deciding whether they were going to put her out or keep her had long passed.

I don't think Serena knows any of this. At least, I hope she doesn't. She's never mentioned it. Perhaps she wouldn't understand what it meant, that the only reason her parents didn't expose her is because they thought she was going to die. I heard it from other mouths than hers, malicious gossips who thrive here just as well as they ever did at court. The only reason I risk writing it is because I know Serena can't read, and at any rate she only speaks the native. On the other hand, perhaps it would have no power to hurt her after all this time. Serena has no talent for introspection.

Two of her brothers are in the army. Another works in Nikolas's stables, and a sister in Nikolas's kitchens. I understand her eldest sister married out of the village. It is her youngest sister, aged fifteen or sixteen, who claims to be the mother of Nikolas's bastard. This daughter lives in the big house, and her parents burst with pride in her, for she is a real beauty. Serena envies her. Not for her beauty, not for her so-called lover, and not for the devotion their parents lavish on her, but for her little girl.

I have lived here for years and years, so it seems.

A day passes in a flash when one is busy. Yet it seems to drag on for ever when there is nothing to do. I've been thinking about this, and I have come to the conclusion that time is motion. A man whose life has been crammed with activity has lived much longer than a man who sits and thinks and broods, and yet the busy man, when death comes, says: Was that all? So little time . . .

The days when I had and was so much, how can they be over so soon? Now I sit and think and brood. Time is like a pool to me now, a puddle, thick, stagnant, sluggish. Time is these mountains. Time is this sky. They are not timeless – that must have been said by a man who had something to do and somewhere to go. No, I am time-full, and they are time. Time cannot move forward from here. It will not go back. I can no more wind time to my will than I can shift the mountains or pull down the sky.

I came here at the end of summer. I was dirty, starving, covered in sores. Serena found me and took me to her home, this hole of a hut where we live under a tree. Maybe I did think it was strange – but what is strange? Do you think I would do time the favour of finding anything strange?

Serena fed me, looked after me, nursed me back to health. Having nowhere else to go, nowhere I want to go except places that no longer exist, I've stayed. Why not? It is simple, like life with Serena. I've found some work as what might be called a day-labourer clerk, especially useful for letter-writing, and the finest hand in the village – actually, the only one. I've starved before, so I know we're not starving. It could be worse. I could be dead. I suppose I might well have died if Serena hadn't found me. So I stay. It makes Serena happy. What more can I do?

Well, the truth is that she loves me. Not much achievement: a battered dog loves any gentle hand. She was the butt of this village, their official idiot; now I am her protector. Since my arrival they've stopped playing tricks on her. They haven't sent her on wild-goose chases, or teased her for a kiss, or buried dead mice in her house, or done any of the other hundred things that amuse them. To them I'm a middle-aged vagrant, but I'm also Serena's man.

Her family is agape, amazed. They're also suspicious. What man would consort with Serena? A very strange sort of stranger. In their prosperity they are ashamed of their goat-girl daughter. They threw her from their house (this was long before I came here), they – disowned is a melodramatic word – but then her whole story is too melodramatic for what she is, which is not a heroine. As a dog cast out from the hearth goes to the kennels, so Serena moved to this hut. She never complains, never utters one word of criticism. Her mother may pass her in the street without acknowledging her, and Serena will not mind.

What more can I do? We live here on the edge of the village, one idiot and one foreigner, together in our little menage. But we are far more at home than any of those who were born here and who belong. It is Serena's natural habitat; and I am at home in its desolation.

As if I didn't know what more I could do. I can look at her right now. She has a cast-off shirt of her father's which she is taking in for me. There are onions and carrots in the larder, stale bread that she has begged. She's going to make me onion soup for dinner. She loves me. I'm all she's got, the only human being who talks *with* her. We live together like a married couple of many years' standing. I have my routine, my little habits, and she caters to them all. That stitching is so difficult for her. She keeps losing the needle. She frowns, holds it up to her eyes, squinting. She is clumsy. Now she is looking at me, lifting her head from the work. Her cheeks are flushed.

Does it matter that she is plain? If she were loved, she would be beautiful to the man who loved her. She loves me, but she remains flat-faced and dull-haired, and I must work hard to find a prettiness anywhere in her.

I know she would like to marry me, but she doesn't talk about it. I don't think she really hopes for it. She would be happy with my child, a child; after all she is a woman. I can see her very eyes ache when she looks at her little niece.

I can't marry you, Serena. I am married already.

I don't need to marry her, or love her, or think her beautiful – but I can't even bring myself to want her. Night and day we are together, rarely more than an arm's breadth apart in this tiny room. If I wanted to, I could reach out and take that trusting girl. I wouldn't have to say a word. Serena would not refuse me.

I could take her. I could make a sort of home with her. I could give her what she wants. She has given me everything, and I have given her nothing but an avuncular protection and the appearance of living with a man. I've been in her house for six months and I have not touched her once, except accidentally.

I don't want to. I don't want to want her. What is more, I cannot want to.

I had buried my head in my hands. Serena rose silently, crossed a few feet between us and put her arms around my shoulders. She sensed something, as dogs do, when they come to lay their head in your lap because you are troubled. She touched me only for a moment, accustomed to my moods; now she has returned to her sewing.

Her touch is so sexless. Is she neuter, arousing no lust, sparking no interest, because she lacks even an animal urge to mate? Or is it me? She has everything a woman needs to make her desirable to a desperate man, and I am desperate. But not for her. The only ache her touch can arouse in me is the ache of loss.

Serena, you don't know, you can't imagine what love, what knowing you are loved by the one you love, is like. I don't think you could begin to dream about what making love to your beloved feels like. It is a thousand miles removed from what you have seen the dogs do. I am desperate for it. But not with you. I am unable to love you, or want you, or anyone. I am unable even to use you.

I am a walking illustration that part of you dies with the one you love. That part of me which was given life by Madeleine – my manhood, my selfhood if you like, my joy in participating with the rest of creation – is the deadest part of me now. Sometimes I see a woman with her hair, or her smile, or her way of walking, but I am not deceived. She is my compulsion to chastity. I have no choice in this. And if I did, I would choose no other way.

The houses of this village dot the valley, the valley curves up into the mountains, the mountains rush towards the sky and the sky arches over the world: all this space is filled with Madeleine. The dawn is a reflection of her beauty – to me it is. I can see it. To me she was as clear as a looking-glass, the mirror of the world. All beauty, all love, all desire, all good things were wrapped up in her, and the dawn is precious to me because anything beautiful reminds me of what I loved in her.

Sometimes I think I can hear her speaking in the cold winds that rise from the glaciers, and I must remind myself that I cannot, she is not, she is gone. If I try to deny that, I will go crazy, and then what is left of this half of us will go too. Madeleine, everywhere I look in a window or a pond or a polished spoon, I see my face, your face. We were as good as twins, having one heart between us. It cannot cease to be yours simply because you are no longer here to bear your share of the double burden. I have to hold on to it. It is all that sustains me. Without you I am a cracked mirror, useless and distorted. I am bits of your brother held together only through love of you: the hollowed-out shell of a person you made whole. Madeleine, I think our love is more resilient than I am. It has all the strength of will. I think it is too strong ever to die. When I die, it will keep on beating and roaming the world.

Serena, listen, you must find some other man to be your husband and give you babies, because these jumbled fragments of a man that you have taken in, that you love, they are no good to you. Without his glue of faithfulness he might as well be dead.

Serena, don't you ever ask yourself *why* this vagrant was running? I suppose she doesn't. After all, rain falls from the sky without offering an explanation. Who knows what makes the weather? The peasants think the King does. I stopped wondering years ago.

9

Several days after that little scene in the garden, Hans broke his leg while out hunting with Alexi. He tried to force his horse to jump a hedge too high for it; the horse shied, and Hans, for once caught out of synchronisation with his mount, was thrown.

As a result of his accident he was confined to his bed with a plank of wood strapped on his leg from hip to ankle. I should mention now that despite this his leg did not set straight, probably because he would not stay still. For ever after it bowed slightly inwards, almost two inches shorter than the other one. This impaired the grip of his seat, but it did nothing to alter the recklessness with which he rode.

Alexi took me along to Hans's rooms. I expected no cheerful welcome, and got none. Trapped in bed, Hans was peevish, and Alexi had invented a game to keep him amused. It was, as it had to be, a simple game. With calculated appeal Alexi called it 'Hare and Hounds', and it was a variation of chequers, with one marker, the hare, chased around the board by five hounds. The object was no more than seeing how long the hare could avoid death. Peter would have tired of it in ten minutes, but Hans loved it. Alexi patiently manoeuvred the hare while Hans, grunting and chuckling, pursued it with his hounds, stopping every so often to correct Alexi's moves, saying a real hare would not have done such and so.

I played a few games with him. Hans was curt, talking to Alexi, rarely noticing me, and when he did he addressed me as Hare. I didn't mind at all. It was a luxury just to be in his presence. I always felt safe when I was close to him. I had been put down and kept back, I had been beaten, I had seen a man and a woman hauled off to their deaths, and my Peter crying with fear. Hans had known none of these terrors. He was the eye of the hurricane, and when I was with him I no longer felt as if I was perched on the fringe.

The game approached a crucial point. Hans's hounds closed on my poor inept hare, which made little effort to escape. Hans leaned over the board, his long Rorhah nose wrinkling as if, among these gold and silver pieces, he could smell damp earth, fur and blood. His heavy eyelids awakened: the room had dissolved and he was in the woods, pounding over black mulch, chasing the bay of his hounds.

Alexi was leaning out of the window, watching people passing and things happening. Hans's bedroom was a good vantage point for this, with its broad view sweeping over the gardens and the treetops, away across the rolling meadows and the distant forest until sky met earth at the horizon's inclination.

He turned around, glanced over us, and said, 'Reyhnard, you must move your hare, or he'll corner you. To the left.'

'Rubbish,' said Hans. 'Hares freeze.' I left my hare where it was, trusting to the dice, but Hans threw a double and the hounds were upon me: teeth gnashing, barking, splash of red.

'Another game?' I offered.

Now Alexi was trying to stand on his head, waving his long legs in the air to attract our attention. I concentrated on setting the board up again, but Hans, always amused by the slightest idiocy, started laughing loudly. Alexi jumped to his feet, grinned and began to play a different game. He hollowed his shoulders up and round, clasped his hands behind his back, and stalked around the room with a worried look on his face.

'So who am I?' he invited us to guess.

Lowering his voice, he began to speak in a voice of vibrant intensity, nothing like his own: 'So you see, Sir, the facts of the matter are these, but we must further take into account numerous other regional factors and if I may mention my wife in this context, since she happens to come from the Fahl under discussion – '

It was so accurate I had to laugh. 'That's easy,' I said. 'Chancellor Edvard.'

'All right, you've guessed so now you do one.'

At that moment a maid slipped through the door with her arms full of bed-linen. Alexi caught sight of her, puffed out his chest, rolled his eyes and galloped towards her, bellowing, 'A doe, a doe!' and shaking his fist in the air as if about to transfix her on the point of his spear. Like a doe, she froze, glass-eyed; then she dropped the sheets and bolted.

Alexi somersaulted to the floor and lay there, laughing. 'Sorry I took your turn, but that was too good to miss. Come on, Hans, who was I?'

'Can't guess,' said Hans.

'Good God, it was you, you great oaf.'

I thought Hans would be hurt by this, as I would have been. I took up his cause and said to Alexi, 'You're an idiot.'

He jammed his tongue under his bottom lip, bulging out his eyes and cheeks with air. 'If the wind changes, you'll stick like that,' I warned him.

'Do you think so? And if I did, the question is, would anybody notice? What do you think, Hans?'

'More than you do,' I replied for him; Hans had lost interest in our argument and was rolling the dice.

'I don't think, I am,' said Alexi.

'To think is to be,' I pontificated.

'Oh, really? And where did you pick that up, Aneurin's arithmetic class? Life is just a happy little equation, sitting on your arse all day putting two and two together and adding up the meaning of it all.'

'I don't – '

'I thought that's what poets did.'

'It was mathematicians a minute ago.'

'Come on, Nardo, don't pretend you're stupid.'

I winced. 'Don't call me Nardo.'

'Hare, it's your move,' said Hans.

I turned back to the game, rolled the dice and played my move. We had a few moments of peace, and then Alexi went on, 'Anyway, if to think is to be, then to be is to think. So I do think, because I am. And worms exist, so they must think too. And rocks are rational beings. So stuff that for algebra. Poor Nardo, thinking so hard so young. You'll use up all your brains by the time you're twenty.'

'Don't call me Nardo.'

'It's your new nickname.'

'I never had an old one.'

Hans interrupted suddenly. 'He's trying to get your goat.'

'You haven't got a goat to get,' Alexi answered back.

They were smiling at each other. Alexi never smiled at anyone else like that, wholeheartedly, all his sharp edges sheathed. It was a smile that said: I want nothing from you but to have you the way you are.

Alexi, why did you love Hans so much? He was fierce and honest, a plain true heart. Was he all the best parts of you, as Madeleine was for me? The one without whom you were no longer sure who you were? I knew them both so well, but when I think about them together they sometimes seem like strangers.

He asked Hans, 'If you could go anywhere in the world, where would you choose?'

This was a variation on another of his parlour games, entitled 'If You Could . . . ' for example, be someone else for a day, or be an animal, or live in a particular period of history, who or what or when would you choose?

Hans said, 'The moors, north of Mindared. I went there once after the rebellion. It was beautiful. Grouse and wild deer. Lots of heather. Where would you choose?'

'Don't know. Anywhere – or everywhere. Everywhere, if I could.'

'What, in a ship?'

'No.' Alexi had his teasing grin. 'I think I'd like to fly, like a bird. It would speed things up, anyway. Something with great big wings – an albatross. I think I'd make a wonderful albatross.'

'Hah!' Hans snorted. 'More like a cock, you mean!' He laughed with delight at his own joke, his body shaking so hard that the chequer-board tumbled off the bed, and his leg, with its plank, tangled up in the sheets. Alexi started mimicking the cry of a cockerel with great precision.

In the middle of this uproar we heard someone knocking at the door. My throat constricted out of habit; Hans lay back, still chuckling, unperturbed.

'Come in,' said Alexi.

A page came in. I recognised him; he had been in Peter's gang until he was elevated to his present high position. When he lifted his face I saw it was flushed, and guessed this was due to the excitement of being in my brother's rooms. Hans's stature as a hero had assumed legendary proportions among these small boys. The page's eyes darted round, storing up details for a later retelling; then he remembered his duty and said with keen officiousness: 'His Grace requests the Prince Reyhnard to wait on him in the library in fifteen minutes – '

I started to stand up, but the floor was moving under my feet as if I were on board a ship.

Alexi said, 'Tell His Grace the Prince is coming. You can go now.'

The door closed. I held on to the bed rail, trying to find my balance. Alexi touched my arm. 'I'd better take him,' he said to Hans.

'Oh rubbish, you know Father hates that. Anyway Reyhnard should learn not to be so wet.'

Suddenly I found my legs again.

'No.' I brushed Alexi off. 'I'd better go by myself.'

My fear was evaporating in the dry challenge of Hans's comment. At sixteen I ought to be able to face my father without leaning on someone's shoulder, least of all Alexi's. The page was still lurking outside the door but ran away when I opened it, and I walked on my own along the corridors to the library.

My father's Guards were posted outside the library, and one of them opened the door for me. A group of young men were standing in the middle of the floor. Seeing them, I stopped, brought up sharp by disappointment. I had hoped my father would be alone.

My friends, they had been called, though everyone knew they were not my friends. I had scarcely seen or spoken to them since those cloudy nursery days. Nikolas still stood out. He remained the leader, at ease in his prominence, having fulfilled every promise of his childhood. His friends – his band, his followers – grouped themselves around him. They were muscled from their exercises and tanned by the sun. My contemporaries. My age, and men.

They had invaded my territory. I knew their preserves: I hunched when crossing the parade ground or visiting the gymnasium. This library was mine, my school, my sanctuary. They stared at me as if I were a stranger in my own home.

Nikolas didn't smile. He didn't need to. I saw it in the poise of his head. His body laughed.

Aneurin was also present, standing to one side, diminished by these vibrant young men. He was trying to fade away and almost succeeding, shrinking into himself, seeking a hedgehog's escape. His face, always pale, was white. His hands, always nervous, were a messy knot of fingers. He stared at me with weak eyes, as if I had betrayed him.

My father's chair was set under a slab of light. The left side of his face was in shadow. As I felt I was expected, or ought, to do, I went across to him. I stood in front of him, looking into his face.

He said nothing.

I wondered what was going on. I didn't feel afraid – or rather, no more than I always felt when he was near; it was less fear than a sort of awe that made me particularly conscious of my shortcomings.

When he decided the silence had gone on long enough, he said: 'Reyhnard.'

I couldn't pull my eyes away from his face. I understand now that most people felt like this when he looked at them in that way – but at the time I believed it was unique to me because he was my father, and because there was nothing else worth looking at while he was in a room, nothing else as important. I still think this is true, in a way. He was the Pole Star around whom all things circle and return: the axle of the wheel of existence. No rut was too shallow for his attention, no pebble so small but he bent down to move it aside. No harm he did but it cleared the way for a greater good. No thing he destroyed but it was replaced by something better. He was a God, he was the King, he was my father. No one else in that room was his son. I started to feel a little braver.

'Yes, Sir,' I said.

'I have a book here. Does it belong to you?'

My copy of Caryllac was lying in his lap. I knew at once that the servants must have raided my rooms for it.

'Yes, Sir,' I said.

Oh brave Prince Reyhnard, remember how frightened you were and how determined not to be? And how you remembered then that you were a prince only because he was your father? I remembered. I wasn't going to debase his paternity with cowardice.

The presence of Aneurin, and Nikolas and the other young men, should have been enough to warn me; but Hans's taunt was still smarting. Hans was my brother, not Nikolas or any of these others. I trusted my father. I would be his son. I would be like Hans. I was afraid of my father, but because I was afraid of him I was afraid to be afraid. Paradoxical, isn't it? And I was so convinced of his justice.

He said, 'Will you tell me how you came by it? Did someone give it to you?'

Aneurin's teeth were chattering audibly.

'No, Sir, I found it in a cupboard, I can't remember where.'

'You must do better than that. This book was someone's responsibility.'

'I have had it for several years, Sir.'

'Are you aware that all copies of this book should have been destroyed?'

'Yes, Sir.'

'And yet you still read it, and kept it hidden?'

'You must know that I did, Sir.'

I scored a point with this. A spark of amusement flickered in his face. Hand to beard, a softening of his tone, inquiring, 'Is it Caryllac who has influenced you to write poetry?'

'Not completely, Sir. But it is in Caryllac that I have seen what can be achieved with poetry.'

'You admire him?'

'I must do, Sir.'

My father leaned back, looking very comfortable with one elbow resting on the arm of his chair. He ran two fingers thoughtfully over the book's cover, as if about to open it and read us a poem.

Sometimes I think most of my life has consisted in learning that people are capable of things worse than I ever imagined, and in being forced to think badly of people I would rather think the best of. When my father caressed that book, hope, which was always at the ready, leapt up in me.

I realised – or thought I did – that those young men had been assembled for a lesson in the twin tinctures of justice and mercy. They would see fairness done to a man, Caryllac, who was as great in his way as my father, and whose virtues outweighed his faults. It seemed my father thought the same.

He said, 'I'm told Caryllac is considered an excellent poet, in fact one of the finest living. I've heard people say that time will probably place him among the classics. Of course, this was some years ago.'

Encouraged by his gentleness, I warmed to my subject. 'Sir, Caryllac is – one of the best poets I've ever read, really *the* best, and as you yourself said, Sir, a – credit to our country . . . '

'Go on, Reyhnard.'

'Sir, I – I know that I was wrong to read it, but now that I have read it, I can't be sorry.'

Again I hesitated. There was much more in me struggling to get said, and with my father in this mood I might have said it, had we been alone.

He saw this, and urged me on. 'Don't be afraid, son. Tell me what it is you're thinking.'

I struck about for a place to begin, but nothing seemed opportune, so I plunged right in with, 'I want to know, Sir, if you'll ever allow Caryllac to come home.'

Before I'd finished blurting this out I was amazed at my own daring. My father smiled. 'You think I should?' he asked, making it sound like a real question.

You want to know what I think, Father? I doubt you do but I'll tell you anyway. I'm thinking how surprising it is that Nikolas and his cronies, all these interlopers, haven't vanished right away, considering how hard I've been wishing they would. When I'm with you, Father, I don't think. I wish. I wish I could be alone with you. I wish you would put your arm around me. I wish you would make one fatherly gesture and lift that awe you put on me. I wish I could talk to you. I want to talk to you and have you listen with all your attention, without distractions. I think we should go outside together, alone, just you and me, and walk there in the wide fields under the sky. Because maybe, out there, I could tell you that I love you, and maybe in all that space you could find the time and the room to say it back to me.

That's what I used to think. That's what I used to wish. Where my father is concerned there is no end to wishing. But of course we are talking of Caryllac.

I took a deep breath. 'Father – ' and it gushed out. 'Caryllac's a great man, Father, you should bring him back. Surely he's suffered enough for what he did – he ought to come home, he belongs here. If you read his poems, you'd see. There's no malice in them, only such – beauty, they're perfect – you couldn't be so unjust as to keep a man like Caryllac in exile for ever. He's not a traitor. He only writes about things that matter to him, and he can take the ugliest subjects and transform them – look, I'll show you.'

I stepped forward to take the book from his hand. In retrospect the only surprising thing is that he permitted me to babble on for so long. He said: 'Reyhnard,' very softly, and I was caught off balance; I would have toppled over if I hadn't reeled awkwardly on one foot. No one else moved.

My father repeated my words, drawing out the syllables in his usual tactic of reducing the meaning to idiocy: 'He – can – take – the – ug-li-est – sub-jects and transform them. Don't you find something contradictory in this? A rebellion against order, a confusion of what things really are?'

Stunned by my abrupt fall into the trap, I was unable to make the reply that there was a beauty in everything, and the gift of a poet was to seek it out.

He said, 'I'm not going to play at sophistries with you, Reyhnard. But the truth remains that there is an order which must be preserved, and an armed uprising is only one, and in many ways the least threatening, form of treason. So much for Caryllac.

'There is still the fact that you deliberately obtained, read and kept a book which is proscribed.'

He held out his hand. Nikolas put a whip in it. This was not a birch, like the ones that had reddened my childhood, but a leather cat-o'-nine-tails.

'Aneurin,' said my father, 'you have failed to discharge your responsibilities.' And my father beat him.

The first thing I lost was any vestige of respect or admiration I had ever childishly held for my tutor. He was so lacking in courage he didn't even attempt to protect his head with his hands. The sounds he made were like a kitten crying. There was blood on the leather tips.

Perhaps I remember it as having gone on much longer than it really did. In the back of my mind I thought my father might kill him. And Aneurin was spread out on the floor, unresisting, as if to say: You can kill me if you want, you're entitled to.

Now Aneurin had never known that I read Caryllac. I had kept it secret from him for precisely this reason. To beat him for my crime was the rankest injustice. For a few seconds I was truly angry. I wanted to cry out, like a schoolboy, 'It's not fair! Stop! Stop!' as if I were the one being wounded, and not on my skin but inside, because every quality I had endowed my father with – justice, mercy, wisdom – was being, quite literally, whipped away.

It took me those few seconds to understand the look on my father's face. Then I realised that he knew Aneurin was innocent. Immediately I was as sure of this as I had been sure, five minutes before, that he would pardon Caryllac and bring him home. Aneurin was being punished for a fault all his own: incompetence. He *should* have known that I read Caryllac. It was his job to find out what his charge was up to. I had liked to pretend that I was protecting Aneurin by not telling him, but of course the only person I was protecting was myself: I knew Aneurin had no right to keep my secrets. He owed his loyalty to my father.

At last I understood why those young men were here.

Aneurin stood up, with his shoulders curved in and his neck drooping, his face that of a chastened ass.

'Take this,' said my father, 'and give that boy a real lesson.'

Aneurin was too badly injured to beat me with any force. My father snatched back the whip and, grabbing my shirt, ripped it open from my shoulders to my waist. I wondered if he would beat me himself – but 'that boy' was not to be so honoured. My father gave the whip to Nikolas.

Nikolas set about his task with great vigour, as I knew he would. He has no shame, my cousin, never has had; but the real lesson of that afternoon had not passed him by.

Objectively, this essay in humiliation was a thing of great beauty, worthy of a great man. The trusting victim so well drawn in, persuaded to betray himself. A work of art. He had seen my faith in him, he had promised me a fair hearing and led me on, and then he had levelled my illusions as flat as the walls of Mindared.

His eyes were placid. I don't think he really saw me. I knew he could not have punished Hans with such detachment. I knew also that in his opinion I had no one to blame but myself. I had broken the law. Why should I expect special treatment? He had never asked me to love him, never done anything deliberately to win my trust and admiration. If I gave it unrequested, what did he care? This kinship of father and son was the result of one brief thrust with my mother. What meant everything to me was as nothing to him. But he knew: my poem would have told him everything I felt for him, if he hadn't known already. He knew, and he did not care.

No one can imagine what it feels like to be thrown away and trodden on like this, by your own father, by a triple weight of disregard. He made an object of me, knowing how easy it would be. The whole charade he played out in that half-hour was for the benefit of those young men. I was the example given, the blackboard, and blackboards have no feelings. Whip your son in front of them, those hot-bloods, those young nobles so like what you once were, and scald away subversion, because if you do this to your own child what won't you do to them?

I tried to focus on his face but it kept slipping away, a stranger's face. The foundation of my identity had been ripped from me as if I had no right to it. Nikolas hit me and I hardly felt the pain. I was burning with shame. I was ashamed to be my father's son.

I wanted to curl up and mourn, for it was as though, in whipping me, my father had killed himself. Instead, I gritted my teeth and made as little noise as possible. Sad, really the saddest thing of all, that I could be braver when I was ashamed of him than I had ever been when I was proud. I didn't want him to think I was crying about the pain.

I had nothing left to believe in but Caryllac, who had been betrayed as I was by a justice in which he put too much faith.

'That's enough,' said my father, taking back the whip. 'Stand up, Reyhnard.'

I was not so fatuous now as to expect some homily from him. He was already walking towards the door, followed by the young men who, their school-room exercise over, would remember me as just another instance of one who had overstepped the mark. Oh, I had been very handy. I had finally made my birth worth while. I had come in useful for something.

I shouted after him: 'I still respect Caryllac!'

Petty defiance, to which my father gave no answer. He walked on as if he had not heard. Perhaps he hadn't.

10

I waited until I could no longer hear their footsteps, and then I left the library in the opposite direction to that which my father and the young men had taken. As I walked, I pulled my shirt off. This pinched me with pain, because the cuts were clotting together and frayed cloth had stuck to the dried blood. It was a hot summer's day, hot even in the corridors, but I was shivering. I heard voices coming my way and slunk into an alcove to wait for them to pass. From the clink of their armour and the slap of their boots I knew they were Guards; and they were laughing.

Now I know that they could not have been laughing at me, but then it seemed they were. What little blood I had was all in my head, drumming round my ears. The Guards walked on, the shade of their laughter leaving silence, and that silence seemed to me, as I crept along, full of more, distant, louder laughter. The whole court was laughing, chuckling, giggling, having a wonderful time, and the notes of their merriment jangled discordantly in my head. I understood what was meant by salt in one's wounds.

Go on, laugh at that boy, who was so foolish. How could that boy have believed anything he did, or said, or was, could be important? That cry of defiance which no one heard was just so much hot air, Reyhnard, and the only person it stung was you. Whom can you hurt in return? Whom can you blame?

I was in search of a door, any door, and finding one ran outside. I avoided the crowded gardens, the smiles in the roses, and even my damp corner, which was a pillaged place. I ran into the woods, and took a path which led to the river. Soon I was standing on the bank. It was mossy and green: flowers, trees, young birds, high summer and everything flourishing. Even the water washing over the rocks was clear, cold – and laughing.

I sat on the bank and hung my feet in the water.

I believe I had some notion of drowning myself. For nearly half a minute, I remember, my resolve was fixed.

He'll be sorry when I'm dead, I thought. He treated me like a dirty rag, once used then useless. He'll be sorry when he finds out what he made me do.

I stared into the water, carried away by a vision of how it would be. My face white and cold, my hair wet, wearing the beatific smile of one who has been released from his sufferings. Gentle hands carrying my body to my rooms, the news flooding the palace, my father rushing to my bedside, his heart clutched, fearing it was true but hoping it was not. Caryad at my side, one of her beautiful hands resting on my lifeless arm, raising her eyes to his face with maternal reproach, saying, 'He died so young, so full of promise. What a tragic waste.' And then my father snatching my limp hand up in his broken one, crying, 'It can't be true. Reyhnard, my son, open your eyes.' The realisation would break on him that he had done this to me. 'My fault!' he would exclaim. 'It is all my fault!' And he would regret those years of neglect, regret all those times he could have had me at his side, getting to know this son whom he had thrown away. He would stroke the damp hair back from my marble brow, and put that heavy head on my chest, and say, 'I love you.' And he would weep, because he would know it was too late for me to hear him.

I indulged in this little fantasy for a while, until the numbness of my feet, trailing in the chilly water, woke me up.

The question was – honestly, now – would he really be sorry?

The cuts on my back itched and throbbed. I could no longer delude myself. Peter would be heartbroken. Caryad might grieve a little. But the King would not care.

'What a histrionic gesture,' he would say. 'Exactly what I would have expected from him. I always knew that boy was unstable.' And he would say, 'What else did that boy think he was *for*?'

If I held my breath and dived into the water, I'd no doubt just float to the top. That was the sort of useless thing Prince Reyhnard was. And even if I did manage to die, what would my death achieve? I was never going to get the words I wanted from him, not now, and certainly not when I was dead.

When I was dead I wouldn't be able to hear him. When I was dead, what would it be like? Like being asleep for ever? No pain, no thought, no sense of time, no memories. No future, no tomorrow, no Hulsitoq, no Gods – no sunshine, no Peter, not ever again. Everything lost, everything over with, the good equally with the bad, as if the one were worth no more than the other. No possibility of any sort of 'again', nor a mind called Reyhnard with the ability to hold such concepts.

And what about the act of dying itself? The water closing over my head, congesting my lungs, the sinking, down and down. What would it matter then if the whole world was sorry I was dead? I wouldn't know about it. Their sorrow would occupy only a small part of their lives, but my death would be the end of the whole of mine. It would happen no matter what I did. Death was not a gesture I could gloat over. If I threw myself into that water I would gain nothing but the inevitable. Tomorrow, next week, fifty years from now, one day it had to end.

There was no way out. Not to be born was just as bad as being born to die: the same non-being. Out of non-existence we come, back into it we go, and in between a tiny space packed with terror of what we left and what we are compelled to return to. My mother had died, the King would die, my brothers and I would die – we were all either dead or dying, and the Gods are nothing but the invention of a desperate desire erupting from the middle of our great fear.

I am still afraid; nineteen years more afraid now than I was then. I am so afraid that it sometimes wakes me from the deepest sleep, and I lie there praying for it to be no more than a nightmare. If I had even less than I have now, I would clutch at it, I would defend it, the proverbial straw of a drowning man. That straw is the fact that he is still alive.

Bronwen's lunacy defies belief, for anyone who lets death in before its time can have no grip on reality. One more minute is as good as a lifetime. One more day is all I want, and then another one-more-day –

as many days as I can get, and more. No matter what sort of a life it is, it must be better than being dead. I don't care if they are all dead. If it had to be one or the other, then I'm glad it wasn't me, glad I'm not dead. I can't even care if that's a terrible thing to say. I can't even care that I can't care.

Fortunately these panics never last for long. After I finished, or rather burst out of, the last paragraph, I went out and walked in the snow for about half an hour, and that has cleared my head. I presume it is in the nature of life that fear of death can't always be so overwhelming; otherwise we'd kill ourselves to escape from it. I don't want to look at what I wrote above. When I get like that, it makes me say things I know I don't really mean. All the same, I'll leave it as it is. I can always come back to it when I begin to panic again, and maybe it will shock me out of it.

In the same way, all those years ago, my terror ebbed and I was rather surprised to find I had not died of fear. I was able to think, rather than panic, and I realised that I was no more capable of flinging myself into the river than I was of winning the King's admiration. This being the case, I must continue to live as I had always lived. However bad that was, it was better than being dead.

'Reyhnard?' came Peter's voice behind me.

His hair stood out brightly against the dark leaves. A dog crouched at his ankles, sniffing the earth. Peter tugged the lead, pulling harder than he needed, biting his upper lip and staring at my back. I turned round on my knees to face him.

'What are you doing here?' I asked. 'You know you shouldn't come into the woods alone.'

'You're here. I saw you come in. I followed you.'

'Did anyone see you?' I asked, thinking that if they had they might have seen me too.

He dropped the leash and fell on me, his thin arms around my neck, his hair tickling my nose and my bare chest – and he was crying. Peter, his hair the colour of a brother's blood, his blue veins clear and alive in his brown skin, his tears wetter than that river, and so much warmer that I was drowning after all, in love for this young, live, loving boy.

Even Peter will grow old one day, I thought. His joints will boll and lock, his chest will cave, his red hair become as grey as coal dust, all burnt out. Those big unblemished hands will be wrinkled and spotted, clutching at the blankets while his eyes roll up, blue eyes white in death. I shut my eyes against this picture and held him as tight as I could, as if that could protect him; I held him so close I couldn't tell whose heartbeat was whose.

'Who did it?' His voice was too deep for his years, his fingernails digging into my shoulders. 'It was Aneurin, wasn't it? I'll kill him – ' He made fists, small, hard, clean, punching my back for lack of some better target.

'No, it wasn't.'

'Then who – '

He stopped, because he understood. If it wasn't Aneurin, it could only be one other person. No one else had the right. I didn't tell him about Nikolas. Nikolas had done it on the King's orders; he had been an extension of the whip, a sort of extra hand. I didn't want to confuse the instrument with the author. That whipping would not be sufficient reason to hate Nikolas, but I have others. Perhaps I should have told Peter. I feel now that I ought. I didn't, because Nikolas was a hero to my brother and his friends. Not, in Peter's heart, on the same ground as Reyhnard, but only a little lower than Hans in the ranks of the admirables.

'I hate the King,' Peter whispered, sneaking a look beneath his lids as if the leaves were ears of the God. 'Don't you?'

I said nothing, from the empty space inside of me that had been my father.

Peter said, 'Why didn't you stop him? Why didn't you make him stop?'

'Oh Peter. How do you think I could have done that?'

Instead of answering, he said, 'It must have hurt awfully.'

'It doesn't matter now.'

With his arms around me, I thought: I am not the most awesome thing in Peter's world, or the most exciting, or the most admired, but I am the most important. When he clings to me like this I know that I am the only person he can rely on, the only one he can love as an equal. He makes much out of what I am. This filled me with joy, but also with a certain fear. Peter, my brother, more like a son to me than any real son could have been, our bones and blood spun out of the same material. No son could have struck at me as he did; no son could have clutched at me so insistently, nor wrapped around my heart with such tight need that I cannot, cannot tear him out. No son could have put so much weight of responsibility on me. I held his pride in my hands, like an egg.

Peter said, 'He'll be sorry one day.' It almost made me laugh.

It was then that I should have disabused Peter. I let him trust too much when nothing can be relied on – especially not a small boy's protestations. Peter's trust always had a quality of arrogance about it, as if people could become what he wanted them to be, and everything sort itself out to end happily ever after, no matter what messes he had carelessly strayed into. I had wallowed in the same mistakes, and it was then I should have warned him to put no faith in me.

My punishment was fair in a way, cruel certainly, and exactly what I should have expected from the King. And I should have told Peter this. I should have said, 'If you break the law, look what you get.' I should have given up the comfort of his arms and refused to let his love gloss over my stupidity. That was my chance, I know it now. Instead, though, I let him hug me as if I were some suffering innocent, some holy martyr, because it made me feel better.

Whatever else the day was, it was sunny and hot, and when we felt better we stripped off our clothes and went swimming. The cold water stung my wounds, but afterwards my muscles weren't so stiff. I think the dog swam with us too: three young animals climbing on to the bank, shaking their wet hair. Our skin stuck to the dry clothes when we dressed, Peter kicking and laughing as he tried to force his legs down his trousers. Then he took the leash, I took his hand, and we walked back to the Palace.

I thought I had lost my whole world that day, and had even been prepared to throw myself away with it. It's strange, but it is only when we lose the last of our innocence that we realise how much of it we still retained.

My life changed after this. I was removed from Aneurin's official tutelage, but this was more a gesture than anything. We were allowed to spend as much time together in the library as before, though things were never easy again between us. The only thing permanently lost was his title. In my new mood this seemed final proof of how little I counted for with the King. I would have been happier if I had been treated with less generosity.

Up to this time I had been living in the Palace, but not in the court. I now found I was required to take my place in court routine and functions. I had been kept in the schoolroom long past the age when Hans and Alexi came out, and this of course was because of the position for which I was destined. Probably the King decided, in his disinterested way, that if I had more 'real life' to fill my time with, I wouldn't cram my brain with poetry. It was not unlike the solution Alexi had intrigued for with Peter – but after all, if a thing works once, use it again! I was introduced to society: I ate my meals with the others in hall, I attended the salons, I joined the train for the garden walks, I went to balls and recitals, I hated every minute of it.

Whether they are really empty-headed sycophants, those men and women of the court, or whether they are first-class dissimulators, I don't know. They're all of a breed, and don't really interest me. Some had minds, I knew; I could tell this from the way they treated me. They had a sarcastic deference, such as is accorded those who demand it in theory but do not deserve it in practice. Some of them were skilful with a word. Their 'Prince' when they addressed me told me they thought less of me than of some old and valued retainer.

My moments of agony were endless. Merely to remember them is to feel the same embarrassment: the itching flush, which was bad enough in itself, and my clumsy hands spilling wine when a pair of blue eyes, painted and lined, were watching me. My voice stuttered and squeaked, taking any important chance to humiliate me, as if it were ashamed to be mine. Most of all the exclusion of laughter. Whether in the throes of embarrassment, anticipating it or remembering it, it goes on rankling until any laughter hurts.

There were pockets of kindness. Caryad would reach her beautiful hand out to mine, telling me to build up a wall of unconcern against those eyes and that laughter. Alexi took time away from his favourite pursuits to be with me and draw the teeth of the worst occasions. Sometimes, when I'm writing, I feel his big hand on my shoulder, his long frame between me and the light, shadowing the page with greyness. He is leaning over me, with a real interest in what I have to say. He reads it – I can hear him laugh, one good laugh among all the bitter ones. He sees what I have written, and doesn't take offence.

'Nardo, you prick,' he would say. 'Enough of the soul-searching. Put it down and come and have some fun. I've just met this girl . . . '

He would bend down and turn a page, his touch leaving the corners sticky.

But Alexi, even you are ink, now.

About girls – women: they are glass beauties, every one of them, so polished and brushed, neatened and powdered. They would look lovely scaled down and arranged on the mantelpiece. Their hems are heavy with dew as they walk through the gardens, stalking beneath the weight of their dresses. Women are survivors; they easily excel men in the art of life, or of keeping one's head above water. They know what their best bet is and they grab for it, with none of this dithering and staring at the stars. If their aim misses, they make the most of what they can get. Look at Beulah; look at Serena.

I remember quite well that when I was that age – sixteen, seventeen – the idea of putting my boneless bit of extraneous flesh into someone else's body was repugnant to me. I didn't have much to make me different from – superior to – the other young men, so I was rather proud of this feeling. Admittedly it seems unlikely that I really was never disturbed by the faintest twinges of desire, but if I did feel any lust I can't remember it now. No faces, no names come to mind. Probably the memory is too painful, like all the other humiliations.

I could relax only with Caryad, since the King's claim on her rendered her sexless. I decided I did not like women; certainly women didn't seem to like me.

Two years passed. There now, that was quick. Hurry some on, slow some down. I was eighteen. Nikolas got married. She was a pretty girl, just fifteen, and she adored him. She wasn't the only one who adored him, but she was the only one lucky enough to get him. The King's nephew is a pretty good catch; even so, had he been any Fahlraec's son Nikolas would still have been eagerly pursued for his prospects and his personal qualities. He was broad-chested and tall, with a cultivated moustache and an air of dignified modesty. He was admired by his contemporaries, approved of by his elders. The King enrolled him in the Guards and soon promoted him to Squadron Second. This was partly because he appeared to deserve the honour, but also because even if the King had appointed someone else, Nikolas's innate authority would still have taken the lead.

I ought to say more about Nikolas, illustrate his character, show what sort of man he was. I won't, because when we were young I didn't know him. He seemed not extraordinary, but rather superordinary – that is, containing in finest example all the qualities a young gentleman ought to have. Oh, Nikolas turned into a surprise for all of us, even for Beulah, which is the most surprising thing of all.

Peter was growing like a weed. Every week he looked taller. In those years I saw less of him than ever before, my time being taken up by the rigorous schedule of court activities in which he was mostly too young to participate. I absconded when I dared and went to him; he was rather like a friend still living in my old homeland, whom I would visit as often as I could in order to recapture a memory of what it had been like to live there. Whenever some special grief fell on him – when his pony died, or his best friend was taken away to the country – he would seek me out, holding back his tears like a man. I always knew when something was wrong, although it might be hours or several days before he would talk about it. I never pressed him; knowing he came to me for comfort was enough.

I held on to my love for Peter as the one good reason for bearing with everything else in my life. It was a tough and sturdy plant, that love. It makes me think of another weed, the dandelion, a plain, golden flower, called a weed although it is really very lovely, and abused thus only because you can never eradicate it. If you cut it back in one place, it returns two-fold somewhere more secret. I hoped that when we were older, when the difference in our ages no longer formed such a gulf between us, we could again be as close as in the years when we had spent all our days and half our nights together.

In my seventeenth year Peter won the boys' junior athletics competition, and the horseback hurdling race. The King shook his hand as one stranger to another; Hans did him the honour of praising his pony, which Peter had broken and trained himself; and Alexi got his friends in the kitchen to ice a cake with Peter's name on it, most of which Alexi later ate. But I was the one who felt as if Peter's victories belonged to me. I was responsible, not so much for Peter's particular talents as for Peter himself. I was proud enough for five.

One of the best memories I have from those years is my eighteenth birthday party. Caryad arranged it all as a surprise for me. There were no more than nine or ten people there: a few of Caryad's nicer friends, Peter and Alexi, and even Hans, though he didn't stay long. They gave me my presents, and we ate and watched a performance by some players Caryad had hired up from the city. I don't think I enjoyed the party particularly – I never felt easy as the centre of attention – but of course what mattered was that she had gone to so much trouble for me. I don't know if she asked the King's permission. He never mentioned it.

So there I was, half-way through my nineteenth year, but no older really than I had been at fifteen, or even ten. I was still a boy, in spite of, or because of, what I chose to view as my worldly-wise cynicism and aloofness. It is less painful than one might think to remember myself as I was, because what I was then, I am not now, and I can look back on that boy with mingled regret and pity for his naïvety.

To quote Serena: before the sun rises, the moon must set. I think she means by this that things have to get worse before they can get better.

11

A tiny trickle of a stream, too small to be dignified by the name of tributary, runs through a dingle behind the kitchen gardens. Between the kitchen gardens and the garden royal is a long, narrow patch of land run to weed and wild lawn, encircled by a privet hedge. I was sitting there, trying to read, on a very hot summer's day. The wasps and flies kept bothering me, and the sickly sweet smell of the privet was almost overpowering. But if it was hot, it was also peaceful, and I had chosen to sit there in order to get away from the footsteps and the laughter and the chattering that roared through the halls and reached at last in whispers even to the attics.

It was a breezeless day. The birds were silent, their feathers damp with humidity; plucked roses wilted like the ladies who had gathered in the cellars to drink chilled wines. Peter and his friends were a siesta-ing pack, tumbled limbs sweating in sleep. It was too hot to move a fan. No one was outside: all craved the vast shade of the Palace.

From the distance a premonition of lightning shivers across your skin. Your body waits for thunder and rain. Somewhere beyond the glassy horizon the relief of a climax is hidden. Despite their bleached loveliness, these are days of foreboding. We pant and twitch in their tight expectancy.

I never believed in natural portents, but maybe I do, now.

I heard a rustle in the undergrowth at the edge of the dingle. It might be a rabbit. What, I wonder, do rabbits look like out of the sight of man? When they are alone, or with other rabbits, are their noses calm, their flanks no longer vibrating tensely, their eyes relaxed?

It wasn't a rabbit. It was a girl.

She crawled out of the bushes without noticing me. Her hair was thick and yellow, curling perfectly: not too tight, not too straight, fat and rich as twists of butter. Twigs and dirt were tangled in it, and as she stood up she started to brush them out with her hands. She was wearing a white dress. The back of it, which was turned to me, was smeared with mud. Damp and stained, it stuck to her, rucking up around her thighs. How old could she be? She was like a child, with a child's smooth plumpness: firm round arms and small white hands, and a complexion of gold-dusted pallor. Her muscles rose and fell with a sliding grace.

Her hands roamed over her body, flicking at the dirt, tugging her skirt down. It was like watching an animal, and oddly disturbing, for every motion was done with a conscious elegance and an ease of long practice, as if she had spent years perfecting this imitation of a grooming cat. The pace was measured, allowing every now and then a slight gaucherie to suggest all the charm of young girlhood. She was giving an accomplished performance and, so far as she knew, for the benefit of none.

When she turned round, her head curved first, her spine following on, and her whole body seemed to ripple from her neck to her ankles like a snake. How could she, so small and round, express such sinuousness? A small red tongue licked across damp teeth.

She saw me, and stopped.

I'd already recognised her. I didn't know her name, as she had been at court for less than a week, but the freshness of her beauty had stood out from the moment she arrived, a peach among so many withered apples. Now, seeing her closely, I realised her eyes were not large and limpid, as the impression was, but small, hard and glittering. At my stare she dropped her lashes. When she raised them, I saw she could widen her eyes at will.

So glossy, sleek and juicy, cheeks flushed to a rosy gold; despite the dirt and dishevelment, she stood all in place, parted her teeth in a smile and started to walk towards me.

My stomach turned over, as if a toad were hopping towards me or a spider creeping on my flesh. Her eyes, her sixteen-year-old, deep brown eyes, were filled with such cold age they made my skin crawl.

Another rustle came from the dingle. The girl's wet lips parted, her laughter trilling like a flute played by a virtuoso. She winked at me, gathered her mud-hemmed skirts around dimpled knees and ran off in imitation of a fawn towards the Palace.

Alexi crashed out from the woods. There were grass-stains on his knees and his shirt was torn. His eyes scanned the garden, glittering with the same heat as had the girl's, but since all he saw was me they gradually cooled down to their usual lazy expression.

'Oh, hullo. Nardo,' he said. 'Hot enough for you?' He strolled over, digging into his pocket. 'Want a chocolate?'

They were melted. I made a face and said, 'How many times do I have to ask you not to call me Nardo?'

'It's a term of endearment.'

'Piss off.'

'Oh, bad word, how wicked of you.' He was rocking on the balls of his feet, and I knew he was not as contented as he made out. 'Where's she gone?' he asked.

'Don't know. Palace.'

Never one for the thrill of the chase, Alexi lay down on the grass beside me, his handsome face unruffled.

'She's your toy, is she?' I asked.

'Can you be showing some interest at last? How abnormal, my child.'

'Normally you confine your attentions to the servants.'

He put a blade of grass between his thumbs and tried to whistle.

'What's her name?' I asked. 'I've seen her around.'

'Beulah. She's Lady Uhlanah's protégée. Pretty little thing, isn't she? Interested?'

Interested? She was a snare of golden skin and hair, rich breasts, pale thighs. Beulah exudes sex as a marsh exudes the scent of rottenness.

'Because if you are,' he went on, 'I'll see what I can do. Never let it be said I was not prepared to make sacrifices for the sake of my brother's manhood.'

I ignored this old dig, and asked, 'How old is she?'

'You *are* interested. I'm not sure. Fifteen or sixteen – I gather she has a horde of brothers and sisters, dirt poor. She's the eldest.'

'Come to court to make her fortune?'

'Come to make anyone she can lay her hands on, so to speak,' said my brother crudely.

'Like you?'

He grinned. 'It's not hard to make me. Show me a sweet and I'm anybody's. What've you got there?'

I gave him my book. It was in Duccarnese. Their alphabet is so different not many people can read it, and I expected it would mean nothing to him; but he flicked it open with sticky fingers, his chocolate joining my sweat to mar the pages, and read me a poem, translating as he went.

'Pretty,' he said at the end. 'Wine and love and jollity. Better than that gutter stuff you used to read.' He snapped it shut. 'I've surprised you, haven't I?' he teased, waggling his eyebrows.

'I didn't know you could read Duccarnese.'

'Just goes to show you don't know everything, doesn't it?'

He lay flat on his back, folding his arms behind his head. With his eyes shut to the sun he said, dreamily, 'You think I'm a bit of a – bumpkin, I think, might be an apt word. Don't you? I give you credit for not thinking me a fool. Or maybe you do. In which case, I wonder which of us is right?'

'I think you spout a great deal of nonsense.'

He stretched a leg in the air, the sinews cracking, and asked me, 'What do you think your great virtue is? Or let's put it another way, your best point?'

I replied promptly. 'Realism.'

He started chuckling.

'Well, what's so funny about that?'

'Nothing, really, only I always thought that was *my* best point.'

'You?' I was astonished. 'You hide from reality with your – with all the things you spend your time doing, and – and you smother reality in a coat of pleasure. All your life is is fun, really.'

'Isn't that what most people want their lives to be?'

'Alexi, don't you ever want to do something more? To be something more?'

'That's an extremely interesting question, young man. I also appreciate that little phrase, "reality in a coat of pleasure", like a sugared pill . . . '

'I don't know why you bother to start serious conversations if you're just going to turn them into a joke.'

'But Reyhnard, that's all I can cope with.'

I tucked my book under my arm and stood up, saying, 'I know you're only pestering me because you're bored, and I don't feel much like being pestered – '

'Ah Reyhnard, don't go.' He pulled at my arm. 'Talk to me. Divert me. Tell me about yourself.'

'I thought you were the expert.'

If he had said something more, I probably would have walked away. Instead, he rolled on to his stomach, burying his face in the grass. I found this non-sequitur of a manoeuvre so confusing that I sat down again.

His voice came muffled through his hair. 'Have you ever noticed that words mean more than what they say?'

'Not with you, no. With you they usually mean less.'

He swung over to look at me with a mock-sincere face, and said, 'There's nothing more to me than what you see.'

Liar.

Alexi scratched his hair, already bored by this line of discussion. 'Do you think I'll get into trouble?' he asked me.

'What about?'

'That bit of fluff. That white velvet glove. That girl.'

'Shouldn't you be worrying about whether she gets into trouble?'

'Well now, if you ever want any advice on that subject, you come to me. But anyway, in her case, no.'

He took off his shirt. Alexi's back was broader than a man's forearm is long, and in those days it was still hard and ridged, with sun-black skin. On it I saw fresh scratch marks. He noticed me staring at them, and he grinned, and said a strange thing: 'They're all the battle-scars I'll ever have.'

We sat in silence, our ears strained in hope of thunder, a break in the weather, and the end of enforced inactivity.

After a while, he said, 'Caryllac is a gutter poet, you know.'

'He's one of the finest poets we have.'

'Did I say he wasn't? There's nothing wrong with gutter poetry, provided you can do it properly.'

He had to play out his little game to the end: he recited a poem I knew well, about the death of a prostitute from venereal disease.

'But Nardo,' he added when he had finished, getting to his feet and brushing himself down, 'he's not the best model for you. There's no dirt in your life. Just clean grit, and you can't stain pages with that.'

Off he went, humming to himself.

———

I saw her again at dinner. The weather still had not broken, and all the windows were thrown wide. Heat dripped in. We young men stood against the wall, watching the women at the table, waiting for them to finish with the dishes so that they could be handed on to us. It was almost too hot to be hungry.

I would have stayed away if I dared, but I was not so stupid as to think that the King, who never cared what I did when left to my own devices, would not notice my absence from things I ought to attend. The taste of luke-warm fish congealed in my mouth. I refused the rest, and watched Beulah.

She was sitting at the far end of the table, outstanding like a rare gem in her setting of second cousins and poor relations. The women fanned with one hand, sighing and phew-ing about the weather, picking thinly at the food on their plates. What bad manners to eat as if you were hungry – though everyone knew that everyone had fruit and cheese and biscuits lardered away in their rooms, to be fallen upon as soon as the meal was over.

Beulah had no such manners. She ate daintily but rapidly, her small teeth snapping on the meat like a half-grown cat. Her pointed tongue slithered out to lick the sauce from her lips. Once, when she thought no one was looking, I saw her steal a piece from her neighbour's plate.

The King was weighed down with his clothes and restless from the heat. Caryad sat beside him, head aching with hair, forehead plastered with small curls. She looked very drained, very plain. The King pushed his chair back and started to wander, exchanging words with the men, sitting now with one woman, now with another. Caryad's eyes were blank. If I had shut my own I could have followed the King's progress. A trail of animation attended him.

A plate of tomatoes, lettuce and cucumber, sprinkled with ice, came round. I took a tomato and a handful of ice, sucking at the cool acidity to rid my mouth of the taste of fish. Alexi squeezed the maid.

The King had roamed to the end of the table. From the way he sat down there, planting himself firmly, squeezing in next to her thigh, it was obvious that he had been heading for this particular seat all the time.

White porcelain bowls full of dark red cherries had been placed on the table. No one made a move towards them.

Until the King reached out and pulled a bowl over to him. He picked out a pair linked by their stems and, taking each between a thumb and a forefinger, held them apart without bruising them. He put one in his mouth, and as he crushed it with his tongue he raised the other to her lips; she curved forward to seize it between her teeth, biting it. Their faces were an inch apart, connected by those stems. Red juice ran down her chin.

The breathless air shifted like an exhaled gasp. Fans started moving again, bowls scraped across the table, laughter bubbled, and the King glanced at Alexi, who was fiddling with the maid's ear-lobe.

Beulah chose to look at me. First she lifted her head, then her eyelids, then her eyes, as if she were slowly and deliberately taking off all her clothes piece by piece. Her cheeks were flushed. She swallowed the cherry and smiled at me, dark little flecks of fruit-flesh on her white teeth. She smiled at me for less than a second before she returned her eyes to the King, but by then it was far too late.

That languid strip of a glance had carved me up from groin to brow and made me feel that I was naked.

Whatever it is that makes a man want a woman – one particular woman, so that no other will do – I felt it then for the first time in my life, and the force of its blow nearly made my knees cave in. I had met lovelier women, gracious adult women, kind women, charming women, slender, beautiful, witty women and not one of them had provoked this feeling in me, that if only I could have her, I would be her slave.

It's a disease, a sick rust of the soul. I didn't know why it had happened and didn't care. A man dying of starvation wastes no time on metaphysics when he finds bread. He just wants to eat. Beulah, like the miasma of plague, enveloped a man and made him know for the first time his unslakable hunger and thirst. The promise of gratification ran like sweat from the pores of her skin; but it was all salt, the salt water that sends desire for a cold spring spiralling up, when still there is nothing but salt, no water but her sweat, and a man could die trying to drain her.

I wish with all my heart what I couldn't wish then, because she with one glance had deprived me of all self-will. I wish I had been blessed with the omniscience that is said to come with the crown of Brych-machrye, for if I had, I would have killed her then.

Later, as I walked back to my rooms, shaken and dreaming, I passed Caryad. She was trying to hide behind a badly-drawn curtain, and she was crying. As the measure of what Beulah had done to me, I must write that I was unable to pity Caryad. I only envied the King.

Beulah dragged the dank stole of her sexuality after her, and Reyhnard the dog followed. I sniffed behind trees. I lurked in corners, scratching my itch. Wherever she walked and whatever she touched bore lingering traces of her smell. I lolled my tongue. Tail between legs, I cowed at a distance, but I trailed her.

I know now what a loveless person Beulah is. At the time, however, I viewed the world as neatly divided into black and white: masculine and feminine, her lovers and her haters. The senses can be misleading, and in my innocence – or ignorance – I mistook the sound and smell and sight of love for love itself. I believed I loved her. I wrote a lot of poems, squinting and scrawling by the light of the moon. Most of them were dreadful, but fortunately for my future reputation they have all been destroyed: as dawn broke I would ceremoniously burn them. My brain was a boiling pot of adjectives: magnificent, lovely, divine, exquisite . . . I might not feel sorry for Caryad, but I almost pitied Alexi for his loss. Most of the time I wore out my emotions in love for Beulah and pity for myself, who had nothing, while the King, once again, had everything.

I know perfectly well now that I was acting like an idiotic, lovesick boy. I don't enjoy remembering it. I am well aware that even the court was not totally populated by caricatures, and that there were men whom Beulah left cold, and wives who did not hate her. I write about it in this off-hand manner because that makes it easier, but there was certainly nothing off-hand about the state of my feelings. They were not in turmoil, but blindingly clear-cut. I loved her. I wanted her. More accurately, I wanted her and so I thought this must be love. The thing about Beulah is that she really is an extraordinary woman. This was clear from the start, when she achieved what no other woman had ever achieved, that breaking down of my combined defences of fear and disgust to make me feel desire. It's true that the other women had never tried very hard, but the point is that Beulah didn't either. She didn't have to try.

I should have told you all this, Madeleine. You understood everything, you would have understood this. I let you think that I had always hated her, because when you came it did seem as if I always had. I know now that even if she had been a completely different person I could never really have loved her, for I was bound to loving you. There's so much that you don't know. Although all this happened before I ever met you, it still seems like unfaithfulness.

I might as well confess, now that she can't hear me.

It was suddenly as if my world had opened up. Before Beulah, there had been only me, for myself, my place and my routine, and nothing else had anything to do with me. I was like one of those magnets we used to play with, the ones that repel anything that comes too close. The ones that will not stick. I read, wrote, slunk around the edges of society and waited to be sent to the Temple. I considered myself to be a complete person, with all my doors locked. Alexi tried to show me that I was a heartless house, crammed with antique furniture – but who listens to Alexi? And all my boyhood was in Peter.

Then Beulah woke up my senses: threw open my windows, so to speak. My ears were keen for every conversation, my nerves alive to every nuance of speech and manner, my eyes fascinated by her and by everyone else who seemed, then, to have no meaning except in relation to her.

It was a straightforward little play with a cast 'of hundreds, typecast adoring men and envious women, and here was a part ready-made for me: the forgotten prince, the sensitive young poet who nursed an un-requited love for the heroine, the leading lady, the King's mistress. I fell into my role as if I had been rehearsing for it.

The theme of this play, of which I suppose I was the author, was that Beulah was so pristine, so perfect, that she could rise above all the envy and hatred, as well as the admiration and desire, which surrounded her. Perhaps she really believed that article of religion which says all the King's possessions are sacred. She strode about the court as if nothing could harm her. She wore an invisible crown.

Now what is true about her is that she ate up strong emotion. Like the ghosts of the dead who have not been laid in water, she fed on souls. She liked to own people, to make their wills hers, or at the very least to make their reactions to her the most important thing in their lives. Love and hate were equally her way in to possession. Alexi's soul was still his own, because to him Beulah had been nothing more than another pair of legs between which to idle away an afternoon. He watched the interplay of King, girl, court and his ridiculous brother with wry amusement, at least at first.

But Reyhnard, at last, was interested.

Did I really call her the King's possession? I meant that she possessed the King. She was his last mistress, the one who supplanted Caryad, and she had no rivals and no successors. The King also followed her.

Late morning on a day in early September. It had rained the night before, washing the dust from the garden's colours, and the grass was wet and cool. Beulah was wearing a pink dress with a belt of beaten gold, her small feet with their rosy toes sinking into the silver-rimed grass. Her round white arms moved gracefully as she clipped red and white roses with a pair of golden scissors. Behind her the King was walking with his councillors. He nodded when they spoke, but his dreams were of Beulah, and he was so attuned to her that he leapt forward almost before she pricked her finger, to kiss the place where the thorn had drawn blood. Such precious blood, Beulah's, each drop a ruby – these were my thoughts as I hid in a hedge behind their backs, wondering how this scene could best be put into poetry.

Beulah craved security. She wanted a territory no one could take away from her. The post of mistress, impermanent and unofficial, held no joys for that ravening mind. The King was old – too old to live as long as she did and continue to ensure her pre-eminence. She says she was never afraid, but she never denied she was greedy.

I had to give up the track at last, because the King left his councillors in mid-mouthing, took Beulah's hand, and led her indoors.

12

I learnt her history. She enjoyed telling me, listing her lovers, if you can call them lovers. To call them lovers is to drag that beautiful word through a cesspit. She enjoyed telling me, and there was something sick in my nature which made me need to listen. Of this, as well as everything else that happened between us that year, I am ashamed.

Her family's estates aren't far south of Tsvingtori. They were small – of course, they're much bigger now. They are situated in the fruit-farming area, and Beulah – I can't resist this – was their prize-winning peach. Her family was poor. Not as this village is poor, with the poverty that can grind away almost any shame except mine, and that lifts food and warmth and shelter to the status of luxuries. Beulah's family was just poor enough to put real luxuries beyond their grasp. Such families, the petty nobility, are cheaper than potatoes, and the King knew their price. They are the mainstay of the government. Beulah, whether by birth or upbringing or instinct, also knows this. She gives them their due, and they adore her.

By her own account she was a beautiful baby and a lovely child. I have also heard other people, who knew her when she was young, if she ever was, say this. Apparently she was born with those yellow curls that were never enough of a crowning glory for her. I can imagine. Aunts cooing over the cradle, what a charming little poppet, nothing is too good for her. She took one look at the pinching and scraping that went on around her to enable her family to keep up their end in the world, and realised she could do better. On high days and social occasions she was taken to the castle of the Fahlraec, where she saw their clothes and their jewels, and, if all ambition springs from the same source, their power, from which the only appeal was to the King. She studied it carefully, decided she wanted it, and set out to get it, never once doubting that she would succeed.

I'm not guessing at these things, or the way her mind works. She told me, in little bits, though not in that year. Much later. I suppose it is an old story, this birth of boundless aspirations from mean beginnings. The King himself reached for the crown, and got it, but then his beginnings were not as mean as hers. Who could have followed through on that determination to better one's lot as well as Beulah has? There were setbacks, of course – me, for one – but she has always been a lucky woman.

Can such a faultless woman be flawed? Yes indeed. Her first lover was a farmhand. She was eleven. He raped her, she says. I can't see any reason for her to have lied about that. At any rate, it began as rape but ended with her coming back for more. According to Beulah, their copulation was so hectic and so frequent that she avoided getting pregnant only because she was too young.

She soon saw the error of such slumming and moved on to a cousin, then an uncle, then a friend's brother, and then the son of the Fahlraec. She learned fast. Mostly they gave her little trinkets that weren't worth much, but she hid these from her parents and stored them away. They were her professional trousseau. One day the son of the Fahlraec gave her a gold and sapphire bracelet, and then, as she said, 'My eyes were opened.' I don't doubt she thought: 'Maybe some day someone will give me a crown.'

Lord Uhlanah began to show an interest in her. So did Lady Uhlanah. A son's infatuation is one thing, a husband's quite another. This woman was obviously very astute. She didn't make a scene, but offered to bring Beulah to court, where the girl would soon lose interest in her minor conquests. Beulah sold the bracelet and bought herself a wardrobe.

Her flaw is her sensuality. She knows this. It also happens to be her greatest asset. She would never have got where she is without it. She has never been able to control it completely, but now, since there's nowhere higher for her to climb and no one to look down on her, her appetites are taken as much for granted as the King's were. At the time, though, it could have been her downfall. Oh Reyhnard, don't be stupid, you know nothing could have harmed her. I know that she had at least two other lovers during that time when she was supposed to belong exclusively to the King; she judged, correctly, that no one but Hans would have the courage to tell him straight out, to his face; and she knew that to Hans it would not seem worth the telling. Perhaps she had Hans, she always was coy about that – no, I'm wrong, she couldn't have. She wouldn't have been able to resist boasting about it.

People of Brychmachrye, your King is talking to you. Here she is, the woman of whom you speak with such pride in fields, on roads, behind tavern doors. I've heard you. This is she, the Queen you love. She always said she loved you too. I don't. Listen, peasants, not that you'd care so long as you get a big harvest in every autumn, I never really thought about you at all. Did you notice? So here she is, I've given you over to her divine protection. Don't bother to thank me. It was a pleasure.

I'm sure the King knew what she was, and what she did. But she held him in such thrall that he could refuse her nothing, and forgive her everything. She had every reason to think he'd give her anything she asked for.

I can come up with only one explanation for his refusal to marry her. It does you a sort of honour, King, that in the heat of your passion you kept an ounce of cool sense. There are some loves that grasping bitch could not foul, some things too pure for her to reach, preserved from her trampling climb to power. You knew that if you married her and gave her legitimate children, she would use every claw and every wile, and every part of her, to push Hans aside, and you knew that once her son – your son – was in your arms, you might not be able to stop her, or want to stop her. King, great King, there's your greatness, the greatest thing you ever did: you were a match for that woman, that vile, stone-hearted, poisonous fiend. You and Hans, I and Madeleine – we did our best, King, we kept them as safe as we could, we shielded their purity and stored them away in our hearts. But now you know, and I also have always known that we are not gods, only men. We could not protect them from Death, the one bitch stronger than Beulah.

So it was heard about court that you would not marry her. She cried and had hysterics. She always was good at that. She threw her other lovers in your teeth. She spread herself out and promised you new treasures in return for what she asked. Well done, King. Your finest battle.

I've forgotten to write about Caryad.

I had promised to take Peter drawing. He wanted to sketch down by the river, and he was not allowed to go there alone. He carried his paper and paints, I had a book; we walked through the woods together, and – how could I have done, but I did – I wished he was Beulah.

'Look,' he said, 'Hans and Alexi.'

They were away to our right, beside a rhododendron bush. Alexi was lying on his stomach with his face in Hans's lap, and Hans was stroking his back.

Peter said, 'Alexi's crying.'

So he was. I started to turn away, having no desire to intrude on my brothers' exclusive love for each other; but Peter ran over to them. Hans looked up and frowned.

'What's wrong?' said Peter.

Well, I couldn't stand there like a stranger, so I sauntered over to them, nonchalant, as if we four were together every day of our lives.

Alexi had sat up. His face was crumpled, but still handsome. I suddenly felt I was looking at the face of the boy he had always been too old for me to know. He smiled, rather sadly.

I said, 'What is it, Alexi?'

He rubbed his eyes and said, 'Caryad's dead.'

For nearly a month after her fall from favour, Caryad had remained at court. I know this because I remember the ripple of gossip when she left, and not because I remember seeing her during that month. I can't remember seeing anything except Beulah. Then, as I said, she disappeared at the end of August. No one knew where she had gone, and no one bothered to ask. Her clothes, which she left behind, were given to the maids. Beulah already had her jewels.

This was the first news I had heard of her. Peter said, 'Caryad? Lady Caryad?' and started to cry.

I hugged him, asking my brothers, 'How do you know?'

'Hans's groom comes from the same Fahl,' said Alexi. 'He went to visit his family last week. They told him. She went into the temple. She lay down in front of the statue, Nardo – she cut her throat.'

Caryad, your beautiful clothes abandoned, your beautiful hands holding a knife, your beautiful hair clotted with blood. Too violent an end to your gentleness.

I asked, 'Does the King know?'

'I told him,' said Hans.

So even Hans had cared for her.

'We only found out today,' said Alexi.

That very morning I had seen the King wandering hand in hand with a golden girl through a summer garden, as if he hadn't a care in the world.

It's his fault, I thought. Beulah can't help being loved. Is it his fault? No one can help loving Beulah. She is innocent and thus makes him innocent. So then I thought: Caryad was a fool to trade one inevitability for another.

Alexi said, 'She tried to be a – a sort of mother to us. As much as he would let her be.'

Peter was shivering under my hands.

Caryad, what did you hope to gain from a man who had already forgotten you? Was it courage or cowardice? Sometimes, on this mountain, I think that it must be the latter. Caryad, tell me your secret: the thing that makes death preferable to life. I loved, as you did, and I lost her, but in that grand gesture I cannot follow you. What you did has put you beyond me for ever.

Our mother is the sea, our mother is the earth – or so we are taught. Rocked in our mothers, in the womb of the earth, we sleep a real, dreamless sleep, and we never get any closer to her heartbeat than in that sleep. So what does she do? She throws us out, thrusts us into the world, and it's no wonder we squall and mew, for what is there to look forward to with our newly opened eyes but their final shutting, that terrible sleep, that nightmare death. Everything that lives comes out of the earth, and is cut off by the earth and allowed to die. It's not a mother. It's a monster. If this is the way of nature, then maternal love is the most unnatural thing in the world.

Throughout those months of summer and autumn my obsession, like bad fruit, ripened.

I can say now that I was the victim of my innocence. As Alexi repeatedly told me, if I had known more of sex I would never have mistaken lust for love. I hate her now; I hate seeing the image of her in my mind, hate knowing that I can't wipe it out of my unselective memory. I can't forget the impress of those days: her hair shining in the candlelight, beneath which she had positioned herself so carefully. Her breasts fuller than ever above a tight belt. Her thighs evident beneath her dress. Beulah is a sister of time, a thief who feeds on what she steals and gives back nothing. I hate her even more for those promises. It was a false front that she enjoyed tearing down, showing the ugliness underneath what I had chosen to make my goddess.

She knew I wanted her. How could she help but see it, when my hands shook as violently as my voice every time she came near? Most people could see it, and Beulah is a not unperspicacious woman. Later, she said it amused her. In October the King of Pravarre sent us a crate of pomegranates, and she, like the greedy thief she was, adored those fruits, pippy and bloody and sweet.

One day I found her without the King, sitting with, of all people, Hans. The King was absent because it was petition day. It was raining, and Hans was mending the string of a long-bow he had clamped between his knees. I had been wandering from room to room, hoping to find the one she was in, and I could have killed my brother for the sake of that proximity. She was right next to him, her rounded hip pushing against his thigh, her hand on his arm, using to the limit that force I have rarely seen fail. Hans seemed to take no notice.

Alexi was sitting in a corner, on the floor, grinning like a wolf.

'Prince Reyhnard,' she said, 'what a pleasure.'

A lie, like everything about her.

Her hand, white and heavy with rings, patted the cushion beside her. 'Come sit down, sir,' she said.

I nodded, unable to find words for the treasure she was offering. I sat an inch away from her skin. Her scent – it comes from a bottle – span my thoughts into giddy gibberish.

'Now you are quite a family,' she purred.

Alexi barked with laughter.

Her fair brows curved down. Mine, less fair, followed suit. She never liked Alexi. I hope she dies where no one can find her. I hope she rots alive.

She arched her back and swung round to Hans. 'Are you going to the hunt tomorrow, sir?'

'Uh,' he grunted, pulling at the bow.

She poised her fingertips upon his shoulder. 'Oh, this rain, this weather. It's so enervating. Don't you find it a little dull? I hope it clears by tomorrow. I'll come hunting with you, if you go, and perhaps His Grace will too.'

' 'Spect so,' said Hans.

She knew perfectly well that wherever she rode the King rode after.

Beulah yawned, showing a wet pink mouth. She stretched, each arm lifting like a dancer's, and the pit of her arm was in Hans's face.

I've heard people speculating about the jungle, that jungle further south than Caryllac's place of exile. Few people have seen it, fewer go there, and practically none return. But I have seen it. I have smelt it in the heart of green Brychmachrye, in stone-grey Tsvingtori. Sweat steams up from its armpits. Sap runs along the shining creepers, caught in the combs of her hair. Pithy trees thrust among the vines. Sucked down into the stinking roots men die of fever, sunk and lost in the depths of her flesh. Her presence is the hum of insects, the crawling fly upon my itching skin.

The next day Alexi tracked me down in the stables. Peter was showing me his new horse, a fine little bay mare, all eyes and legs and swishing tail. He was grooming her mane, taking burrs from the hair with small deft fingers, tongue clamped between his teeth. I was leaning on the stall door, happy to be the audience for the pride he took in his skill. I felt as contented as I could be with never a moment free from Beulah.

Alexi tapped me on the shoulder. 'I have to talk to you.'

I put my head in my palm and stared at him.

'It's important,' he said.

'Important to whom? I didn't think anything was important to you.'

He shook my arm impatiently. 'I mean it.'

'What is it?'

He jerked his head, meaning, I don't want to talk about it here.

We went outside and into a barn behind the stables where the hay was stacked. It smelt of fresh essential things: new-mown grass, molasses and sweat. In my sickness it reminded me of Beulah.

Alexi sat down on a bale of straw. 'What do you think she's up to?' he asked.

Who – Beulah? How could that guileless woman, that radiant enrapturing girl, that paragon of all virtues be 'up to' anything?

'You left in a rush, yesterday,' he said.

Of course. My rigid passion made it impossible for me to sit still so close to her whom I could not take in my arms, kiss, taste, unfold my servile heart to. And how can you ask a young man as much in infatuation as I was to sit calmly by while the object of his pure poetic fantasies flirts with his brother, squandering the delights of her voice on his dumb ears? I would have stopped my heart-beat, I would have forbidden any sound to interfere if she spoke to me as she had spoken to Hans, pouring the pearls of her tongue on to my lap.

'She wants Hans,' said Alexi.

'What?'

'Or, at a pinch, and it would have to be a pretty tight one, she might settle for me. But she definitely wants Hans.'

'What are you talking about?'

'What are you talking about, what are you talking about,' he mimicked. 'Who, or what, as you so accurately put it, I am talking about, is Beulah. That little piece of white thigh, that delightful morsel of snake who's got her coils so tight round Father he'd give her the moon if she asked for it. I think you know the one. She wants to marry Hans.'

'You're mad.'

Deep in her heart my sweet heroine, my innocent flower led astray by a corrupt and goatish old man, really wanted her prince, her faithful servant, her Reyhnard.

'I'm not. Snap out of it, Nardo, you're like a man in a dream. You saw the way she was yesterday. She is deadly serious. The King's no good to her. How long can he live? Another ten years, fifteen maybe. She'd only be thirty-two or -three, a young woman in some ways but too old to marry, if anyone would take her. She's nobody's fool, and if you were less besotted you'd see what it is she's after.'

'She's not like that, Alexi, she couldn't be. She's only a girl, she's younger than me – '

'She has the heart of a whore and the mind of a banker.'

I threw my fist at him, a wild and straying punch which he easily caught, keeping my hand imprisoned in his. I panted, sparks in my eyes, hating him, hating Hans, hating the King, hating everything and everybody who conspired to keep me apart from her.

'When are you going to wake up and see she's not worth it?' he exclaimed. 'She's caused nothing but misery since the day she got here. First the King, then Caryad, then you, and now maybe Hans.'

'You can't blame her for the way other people behave.'

'I don't "blame" her,' he said. 'There's no profit in blame. In a way you have to admire her. She knows exactly what she wants, and if she doesn't get it it won't be because she didn't try – it'll be because I'll kill her if he tries to make Hans marry her. Do you know how she screws around? Do you? And he lets her get away with it. She's tried it on with me, more than once, but I won't have any of it and that's why – well, partly why she doesn't like me, not that she really likes anybody – '

'Stop talking to me like this! You won't make me believe you.'

'You really are besotted, aren't you? Nardo, listen to me – Hans or Father, it doesn't matter to her which one she gets, but she wouldn't have you on a silver platter. And a good thing for you, too. The best thing you can do is go work it off on one of the maids – '

'You don't understand.'

'No. No, I suppose I don't understand. I don't understand what's going on in this place any more. I've never seen him make a fool of himself before. I didn't think he could. Thank God he's not going to marry her – '

'I don't believe you.'

'He won't marry her, Nardo – and she's tried hard enough. Don't you understand? She wants to be Queen. So if he won't marry her, Hans will do just as well – either way she'll get what she wants sooner or later. Couldn't you see what she was trying to do to him yesterday? If he was any other man she'd have won by now. Father would never be able to stand up against the two of them.'

'You're crazy. If the King won't marry her, he'd never give her to someone else.'

'Don't be so stupid.'

'He'd never allow it – '

'For God's sake, Nardo! Where do you live? Haven't you realised that what Father wants doesn't matter any more? It's what *she* wants.'

'You're making it up!' I shouted back. 'No one could be like that. You only have to look at her – '

His burst of laughter drowned my protests. He sat down heavily on a bale of hay, clutching his stomach and shaking his head. 'Nardo, I'm – lost for words.'

How sad to remember now that we could ever have fought about Beulah. Right as always, Alexi, and in your kindness you blocked up my bolt-hole. I can't say, 'Where were you when I needed you?' You were there, you knew I needed you, even when I didn't know myself. You tried to show me what was wrong with me, and you tried to help me out of it. I am laying bare scenes and emotions I would far rather forget, and I am doing it for your sake. Let no one say Alexi was less than the best of brothers and the best of men, for I cannot continue with this until I have made up in full, and more, all the justice I refused him then.

Of course I was fed up with his lecturing. I thought to myself: what a feeble thing this great, tall man is, to be so easily twisted by his failure to keep one precious girl; so I turned my back on him, and walked away.

What's that sound? It's like water dripping. I'm looking out from my seat by the window, and all I can see is nothing more or less than I expected: snow, the village huts, some villainous crows perching in the bare trees. I can't find the source of that sound, but it's somewhere close by. The icicles hanging over the window seem to have lost their crystal chill. They are melting.

I believe it is spring. Or at any rate, it must be a thaw. Life smacks my artistic pretensions right in the mouth. This has come at a very inappropriate place in the narrative.

Nature will have its joke, but I'm not going to join in. I won't palm off this part of my life so lightly. I owe it to Madeleine to scrub through right to the last stain; then I shall have something clean to give her.

It will undoubtedly be painful, but it will be worth it. And if I feel better when I've heaved up the last of it . . . well, as Alexi said, there's no profit in blame.

13

It was December before the King came to a decision.

Never before had I been in the throne room, never having a reason to go there. This time I was summoned. I had to go, most unwillingly, with the same old sickness of dread in my stomach. Whatever it was about, it had to be something more awful than I could imagine, if he was using the throne room.

Since I expected to see him, the first person I noticed was Beulah, sitting on a stool below the dais. Her appearance shocked me. Her shoulders were slumped in an attitude of defeat, and her hair was plaited away from her face, which was pallid with dried tears. Her expression was sullen and angry. The set of her body was unforgiving.

The King was on the throne. When I first sat there I noticed two deep, thin grooves pale in the dark wood, carved by two square nails on a damaged left hand. He marks everything his own.

Hans stood next to the King, scratching his thigh.

Above the King's head hung that famous canopy. It was – I presume still is, since she'd have no reason to move it – bolted to the ceiling above the throne, its length drawn back to be held in the angle of ceiling and wall by a gold-plated rod, from which it falls like a curtain to the floor, where its hem lies in bunches. This canopy is older than our possession of the country, and it is the banner of kingship. The native kings had no crown, the idea of which we brought with us from Andariah; all they had was this canopy. It is a piece of archaic symbolism: blue sky and stars for the section above the King's head, and the hem is brown earth and green water. Between them stands the God Adonac, robed in royalty. His right hand curves to the sword at his hip, while his left holds a sheaf of wheat. Madeleine told me it is a work of appliqué: Adonac's limbs, head and torso have been cut out of material and sewn on to the backdrop. I have no idea how much of it is original, but I should think very little. The moths are always getting at it, and I can't remember a time when some or other part of it wasn't being repaired. It's very heavy drapery. That two-dimensional Adonac can easily lose an arm or a leg, or half his face, if the cloth is hung badly. As I said, it is symbolic.

The walls of the throne room are faced with marble, their dado picked out in gold and cobalt. They opened out towards me where I stood at the far end, my back to the double brass doors. The floor is tiled in ceramic diagonals of blue and yellow, which are always crumbling and expensive to replace. My eyes tracked down their zig-zag, diminished with distance, angling in perspective, all pointing towards the King.

What new trick did he have up his sleeve? For what purpose had I suddenly come in useful?

The room was jammed with courtiers. You can never make them keep quiet. No matter how solemn the occasion, they whisper and gossip, flutter and flirt: the swish of the sea in a shell.

I approached the dais along the line of the tiles. Beulah's eyes were narrow. Her hands grappled in her lap, the knuckles whiter than bleach. I could see her rings would cut those soft hands; I wanted to take each finger and uncurl it, prevent her hurting herself.

She glared resentfully at me. Her lips were drawn tight over her teeth, and she looked impatient and humiliated. He's betrayed her, too, I thought – and this idea gave me a drunkard's courage.

I stood up so straight the bones in my spine grated together. From the dais the King gazed mildly at me. He asked, 'How old are you now, Reyhnard?'

'Nineteen, Sir. I was nineteen last month.'

His hand waved the irrelevance of the second statement away. 'Nineteen,' he mused, tapping his lower lip with a finger. 'Old enough to have sown your wild oats, hmmm? Old enough to stop chasing skirts and settle down.'

At the age of nineteen he had already murdered the King of Brychmachrye.

'Ah,' he said, 'the young generation.'

Tittering in the ranks.

He said, 'Old enough to marry, really. What do you think, hmm, Reyhnard?'

'As you say, Sir.'

'My father – your grandfather, Hans.' He had taken his son's arm and was shaking it softly, with affection. 'Your grandfather was married when he was fourteen. And now look, you brute, you bear' – pet names – 'you're twenty-seven. Three grown sons, and where are my grandchildren, eh, Hansli? Who'll guide the country when you are gone? You've no sense of duty.'

A blank lack of comprehension crossed Hans's face. He rolled his glance around the room, hunting for Alexi's nod or wink, but Alexi wasn't there. Hans wrinkled his nose and looked at me, smelling a friend.

'I didn't know you wanted me to get married,' he said.

The King gave his arm a loving tug. 'Time enough. No hurry. When you feel the need is soon enough.'

Hans said, 'I thought you wanted to tell Reyhnard – '

'Ah,' said the King, pointing up his two left fingers.

I heard a smothered imprecation from Beulah. She must have been glued to that stool, because nothing less would have kept her there.

The King said, 'It's time you were married, Reyhnard.'

'Yes, Sir.'

'Marriage is a sacred state. Not to be taken up lightly. Especially for a priest. Marriage and fatherhood, both created by the Gods – hmm, Reyhnard?'

'Yes, Sir.'

'Created by the Gods. Not only for pleasure and personal fulfilment but for – what shall I call it? Self-control. Self-discipline. I was married to your mother for twenty-four years. One cannot easily put aside such a length of time. Tragically, we lost her, but I have another marriage, one more sacred to me, much as I loved your mother and grieved for her. I am married to this country. I am responsible for her – to love her, cherish her, keep her and protect her. It is the will of the Gods that men's marriages should derive from and emulate this fundamental marriage between a King and his realm, and as it is the duty of a King to care for and protect his country, so it is the duty for a country to honour and obey her King. Do you understand what I'm saying, Hans?'

Hans had been wool-gathering, but the sound of his name prompted a reflex nod.

'I am speaking to you all now,' said the King, pitching his voice to carry past the heads of the courtiers. 'Whenever two young people embark, with love and hope, on the holy state of matrimony, then it is a time for us to reflect upon the nature of the world and its relationships, and to recognise the worth of the models which the Gods have given us as paradigms for our own lives . . . '

He went on and on in this vein. His mouth rolled out grandiose phrases and pious rhetoric, while his eyes remained acutely watchful, noting the reaction of every person in that room: the young man yawning at the back, the two girls giggling behind their fans. He knew everything about them, and this was the sort of method he used to obtain such knowledge.

Beulah was crying openly now, but he paid her no attention. It occurred to me that he might be trying to rub salt into some wound he had given her. She must have offended him deeply to earn such treatment.

If I had known her then as well as I do now, I would have realised that those tears were not the hot tears of remorse, but cold tears of fury and indignation. Her plump jaw was clenched so tightly it appeared angular.

'. . . and so,' said the King, 'it is not only with great pleasure, but with solemn reflections and sincere prayers for the future, that we announce the betrothal of our son Reyhnard to the Lady Beulah.'

Applause. Cheering – or was it jeering?

I think I've said enough about what I felt for her, that I can spare myself delving into the depths of the joy I felt when he said this. I was stunned, it's true, and I was also incredulous, but I was mostly overjoyed.

He came down off the dais, pausing to whisper in my ear, 'Shut your mouth.'

He held out his hand to Beulah. For a moment she looked ready to spit on it, but then she extended her arm – she wouldn't touch him, though – and gave the merest impression of holding his hand. He took mine and laid it on top of hers. Her fingers were like ice.

'Reyhnard and Beulah,' he proclaimed.

He leant over to her. I heard him clearly, he asked her, 'What's wrong with you? You've got what you wanted.'

I felt her hand tremble in mine. I thought she was going to smack him across the face, so I closed my fingers slightly on hers.

Her eyes deserted him and alighted on me. She began to smile, gracefully, beautifully, shyly, and if people can die of ecstasy I would have died then.

The rest of the props for the farce were laid out in one of the small dining rooms. No one knew what to say to me, and since they never had said much to me they couldn't make a start now, so they said nothing. I was perfectly happy to stand and look at Beulah, who was sitting down. She was smiling, smiling, smiling at me.

Apparently there is an animal which lives in the rivers of the jungle, a large variety of lizard called a crocodile, big enough to prey on men. They say that while it eats them, it smiles. A pretty obvious parallel.

Hans sought me out. 'Alexi told me to tell you he'd send his congratulations only he's saving them for when you wake up.' Hans shook his head. 'What d'you think he meant by that?'

'Tell him he can keep them, I don't need them.'

'Well, hope you're happy.' Then he had a thought. 'Tell you what, Nardo. My mare's going to foal in a couple of weeks. It's by Brindle. You can have it if you want.'

Then the King came and took him away.

Beulah knows every screw on the rack. She took what he had done to her . . . and I don't know what to call it. It wasn't really a punishment. A discipline, perhaps. Is there a word for it, this giving someone what they asked for in such a way as to turn it into something they would rather not have? At any rate, she paid him back in his own coin. She was the perfect betrothed. Her old lover seemed completely forgotten: she was deaf when he spoke to her and blind when he smiled at her. She treated him as if he were not only the King, but a stranger, with a distant, correct politeness. Me, she attached herself to with all her tentacles, behaving like someone devotedly in love, lavishing more endearments on me than I had received in the whole of my life. With her public kisses and embraces she reduced me to a state of inebriated hallucination, reeling with my own luck. She made him watch it all. He was suffering, but he was patient. This went on for ten days. We were married before the mare foaled.

We never learn, never. By this point I should have known that nothing coming from him could do me any good. I should have apprehended his purpose, recognised myself in the role of tool, his tool, her tool, their tool.

I didn't because I couldn't see straight. Or, to be precise, I was looking straight, but in only one direction: at Beulah. I focused on her with tunnel vision, let her fill my view, and was unable to perceive the true state of things in the round.

We were married. In my eyes the ceremony had stamped her legally, irrevocably, as belonging to me, and I to her. Not a single one of my thoughts or desires didn't centre on her. I wanted to glut myself on her body. I could not stop touching her. I was possessive of her beauty: this wasn't the same thing as lust, but more like a man closing his hands around a priceless piece of china which he alone owns.

How could I have comprehended my true situation? I couldn't think about myself. She took me over; she occupied me like an invading force. When she was lying beneath me, effortlessly voluptuous, my only thought was 'she's mine', the thought going round and round in my head until I lost the ability to think, and was too congested to see her yawning.

If she hadn't had an ulterior end to gain by fucking me, she would have thrown me off her just like the bitch with the dog; but of course I couldn't see this either.

Afterwards, the echo of my heart fading in my ears, I would remember who and where I was, and turn my head to look at her. She smiled passively, where a few moments before she had been violent; but whether violent or passive, her narrow eyes were unchanged by the act, and I knew that once again she had slipped through my fingers when I was too far gone to notice. We had lain inches from each other, and had never been one. Every night was like the first: the night in which I hoped, this time, she would give something of herself away. I didn't just want the use of her body. I could have got that from anyone. I wanted her, her self, her being. I wanted her to react like me, to abandon control of herself as I did. I wanted her to be like me: to be me. I never wasted a thought on any of the other men she had had, not even the King, because she was mine now, and I could think of nothing aside from having her.

I had imagined I would be happy when I had her. But I never had her. *She* had *me*.

It was the most elusive form of frustration. Intercourse with her left my body as empty as my hands, and I lacked the most fleeting impression of any real union. I threw the whole of my energies away on it, and she gave me back nothing. In the morning I felt as dried-out and brittle as a stale loaf.

I know, now, that what we did together was not making love, nor what I felt for her love. But for four weeks I thought it was.

When I look back on it, I have to say that those four weeks, those twenty-eight days, were the last days of my childhood. Right in the core of me there must have been some part retained since birth in its pristine state, with its natal energies of trust, hope and love not yet exploited. Unerringly, Beulah stuck her tongue right in that part and withered it dry.

They duped me so thoroughly that I can't even feel ashamed of it. They could do it only because I was innocent, and that is nothing to be ashamed of. I can even be proud that my innocence was so strong and resilient that it could see nothing wrong. I feel no embarrassment to write all this. I feel fury against the two who made it happen. Especially against her, that bitch of a whore, that despoiler. He threw me to her, but she was the one who consumed me. She ravaged me of the last of my virgin territory, which I had offered to her in all good faith.

And though he, the King, probably knew what would happen to me, as he undoubtedly knew what I felt for her – again it doesn't matter. If 'that boy' wasn't important, then neither are you, King. I make you peripheral. She was the criminal.

Alexi, you were too right. If I'd had other women before her, she could never have done this to me. Then, perhaps, what I did in innocence would not, under the hot sun of remembering, have rotted into obscenity.

14

Not all of those four weeks, or the twenty-eight nights, were passed together. After five or six consecutive nights with me, she might not appear. Or I would wake in the night and find her gone. She eluded: she said she would wait for me somewhere, and then wasn't there; she failed to show up when she had promised to come. Things like this happened:

The King put his arm around her and kissed her, and she didn't pull away or make any attempt to stop him.

Seeing this, Reyhnard thought, 'She's afraid to show her true feelings. She doesn't dare risk offending him.' None of us did.

'Of course the King still loves her,' thought Reyhnard. 'What man, who has had her, could stop wanting her? He has made a mistake, and it's too late now.' After everything he had said the day we were betrothed, I thought he respected marriage.

When I asked her what she had done or where she had gone, she simply giggled and kissed me.

She had a set of two rooms, which the King had given her when she was his mistress. After we were married she refused to give these up. She claimed she needed a place of her own, and wanted to feel free to sleep there when she chose, because to be too much together made her feel claustrophobic.

Reyhnard thought, 'These don't sound much like real reasons,' but all the same he accepted them. He was afraid to press for real reasons, because she would never give any. All she gave was empty answers that he couldn't latch an argument on to, which was just as well, because he didn't want to argue. Sometimes, in the middle of the night, I went looking for her in those rooms, but she was never there. When I asked her about this, she pleaded insomnia, saying she went for a walk or to read in the library. Throughout these conversations she chuckled happily, as if they were a private joke. She never allowed me to get serious.

She said, 'Really, darling, you're very funny.'

Did I suspect? No, Reyhnard clung to the last of his faith like a starving man with a hunk of rotten cheese.

This is, in essence, an old story: I did not know because I did not want to know.

Four weeks after our wedding I was sitting alone in my bedroom. A book of poetry was open on my lap, but I wasn't reading it. I was staring at the neatly-made bed I hadn't slept in, because I couldn't find her and so could not sleep at all. I don't recall thinking anything. Thinking leads to logic which leads, in the end, to unavoidable truths. I rejected clear thinking in favour of a numb faith.

Alexi knocked on the door and came in. 'I thought I'd find you here,' he said.

He glanced around the undisturbed tidiness of the room. There was no trace of her in it.

'It's cold in here,' he said. 'Why don't I get someone to stoke the fire? You must be freezing. What are you doing?'

'Reading,' I replied, failing to pretend I was really absorbed by my book.

Sentences started talking of their own will, rushing half-formed from my mouth: 'Have you come from the court? You haven't seen Beulah anywhere around, have you?'

'Actually,' he said, 'it's her I've come to talk to you about.'

He sat down on the bed, stooping forward to pin his hands between his knees. His posture was very strange. He sat stiffly. Stark. Most unlike him.

He said, 'I don't know how to tell you this.'

A childish instinct for protection told me to clap my hands over my ears. In childhood we learn to despise that lying phrase 'for your own good' and we never stop hating it. But there was an adult voice overruling my impulse to hide; it told me that Alexi was here for my sake, not his, and if he had to he would tear those boy's hands away and force me to listen like a man. So my hands lay futile in my lap.

He said, 'I can't let them make a fool of you any longer. I can't stand the way they laugh about it, as if they were so bloody superior. I'm sick of it. You have to know.'

I have to know. I must know. I did know, though I refused to admit it.

He said, 'She's still sleeping with the King.'

It was so obvious. My empty bed, her disappearances, their public embraces – all of which I had covered up with wishful excuses as if that could make it invisible.

The court had never been deceived. They had no intention of deceiving anyone. I had chosen to deceive myself, but now, with the truth straight out in front of me, I no longer had a choice.

Alexi said, 'I'm sorry. I'm really sorry.'

'No congratulations?'

'Oh Reyhnard – it's not your fault. You were like a sleepwalker, you couldn't see where they were leading you. It's better you know. Reyhnard – I really am sorry.'

I could have held out my hand and touched Alexi, and I know he would have taken it – but all this time, while I stared through him, he appeared to be moving further and further away, so that in reaching for his fingertips I would have to stretch across a chasm.

'Why me?' I said.

Why had they picked on me to be her security, and the name of her respectability? Was it because I had been a willing victim? I had made it so easy for them. It never crossed my mind to say no.

'What did I do?' I asked – not, to deserve this, but rather, to be so undeserving of any consideration?

'Reyhnard, Reyhnard.' His voice sounded faint, as if he were speaking from the far end of the room. 'It's not your fault. You didn't *do* anything. It always had to be you. Try to understand, think about it. I told you she wanted Hans, but he would never have given her to him.'

No, not Hans, whom the King loved better and more truly than he loved her He would never have given Hans a wife and then taken her back again.

'She doesn't know how to put a lid on her ambition,' said Alexi. 'She made no bones about wanting to be Queen – she asked him, more than once. But he wouldn't let her. I think he likes to know that he was able to refuse her something.'

'What about you?' I said. 'You said at a pinch she'd make do with you.'

'I'd have said no.'

'Would you?'

Alexi shrugged. 'Tried to. Of course he could have made me. But

Father has some funny ideas about me. I think he was afraid that if I had her, I might be able to keep her. Really, it's ludicrous – I had her before he did. Also I think he was afraid she might try to get rid of Hans and make me King when he's gone. Honestly, as if I could do that to Hans – or want to keep her. You know, Nardo, I think she's completely destroyed his sense of judgment . . . '

'Did she tell you all this? How do you know?'

'It's obvious,' he said.

And so obvious why it had to be me.

What was the point in knowing? Where was the good in being told? Nothing had changed, except I now had this stinging wound in me where an admission of the truth had been forced through.

He had come to help me, but he could see from my face that he hadn't achieved anything. 'Oh God,' he said, 'you can't – '

I said, 'You've always known that I don't – love her. It's not that – '

The door swung open and she swayed in, trailing her skirts and talking. 'Darling, you haven't seen my purple belt anywhere, have you? This moving . . . '

She realised Alexi was in the room, and stopped abruptly in mid-flow. Brown eyes flicked from his face to mine, then settled on a spot on the wall while she put a hand to her hair – either to stroke back a non-existent straying curl or to smooth her surprise, for she was so rarely taken by surprise.

She decided to smile, and let both hands fall in a clasp to her hips. 'Hullo, Alexi.'

He said, 'What a surprise to see you here.'

'I didn't think you'd come to call on me, darling,' she answered sweetly. 'Reyhnard, have you seen my purple belt? The one with the diamond buckle. I can't find it and I want to wear my lilac dress. All this moving about, it's so annoying, nothing is where I expect it to be. I don't know which room to call my own.'

'So we've noticed,' said Alexi.

I was surprised to see that his antagonism irritated her. I thought Alexi and I were so much in the same position that nothing we said had any effect on her, or was considered to be important. This shows how little I knew of her, then.

She was an army on patrol. She conquered with no weapons but her legs, her breasts and her scent. She carved a totalitarian kingdom, and was piqued at any show of self-will from the least of those she wanted for her subjects.

'Why don't you and your brother continue your little chat somewhere else?' she said. 'I'm very busy – I must have a bath.'

Alexi folded his arms, stretched out on the bed – her side of it – and gave her his tiger's smile. 'Go ahead, Beulah. Don't mind me. Unveil yourself. I'm sure I won't be struck blind.'

Considering what a physical woman she is, Beulah doesn't easily lose her temper, nor does she have any of the other weaknesses that usually go with such a nature. She replied, 'Very funny, Alexander, you're so droll. Now please do me a favour and run along.'

While she talked she had seated herself at the mirror, taken the pins from her hair and started to brush it. The brush was drenched in her favourite perfume. Its odour filled the room. I motioned Alexi up and pulled him to the door.

'Please go,' I said. 'I have to talk to her.'

'Don't. Don't give her the satisfaction. Anyway, believe me, you can't – '

'What are you two whispering about?' she called.

'Go,' I said.

'Come and see me later.'

'Maybe . . .'

I shut the door on him and leant against it. Beulah knew I was watching her. I saw her smile in the mirror.

I tried to see her as I knew I must if I was to get through this intact. But she, with that steady flow of arm against hair, was drawing me back into the tunnel. She was so sure. She had every reason to be confident.

She said, 'If you're just going to hang around doing nothing, why don't you do it somewhere else?'

'Am I in your way?'

'Darling – of course not.'

She began to hum, pulling open a drawer, lifting the lid of a jewellery box. The room was already beginning to look untidy.

'Damn,' she said. 'Where are they?'

'What are you looking for?'

'My diamond rose earrings, to go with the belt, if I ever find it.'

'You were wearing them last night.'

'Yes, I know.'

Before I could lose my nerve I forced myself to say, 'Maybe they're in the King's rooms.'

She stood up, unlacing her blouse. Beulah was very agile at shedding her clothes, though she liked having someone to dress her. 'They might be,' she said. 'Reyhnard, be a dear and see if my maid's outside, she can go and look.'

I suddenly felt the exhaustion of not having slept for a day and a half. 'Beulah, why didn't you tell me?'

She glanced up from her stocking. 'Tell you what?'

'What Alexi told me.'

She did look slightly taken aback – but whether honest or acting, who knows? She replied, 'We thought you knew.'

'You? Who? You and the King?'

She rolled down the other stocking without giving me an answer.

'But you must have been able to tell!' I exclaimed.

'I thought you were just being funny.'

With a twist the rest of her clothes were off, and she stood there in her vest. She didn't need to give me a performance, not now, but she couldn't help it. Crossing her arms, she took hold of the vest's hem and slowly pulled it inside-out over her head, wriggling her hips. Perfect grace, perfectly artificial, memories of the hot summer's day when I first saw her.

Naked now, she dropped her vest on the floor and went on with her business as if I wasn't there, thoughtfully tapping her foot, making up her mind, crossing the room in a wave of pink flesh to take a fur robe out of the closet. Every step sent her curls rippling across her back, wafting fresh pulses of scent through the room. She wrapped the robe around her shoulders.

'Beulah – '

'Oh, what is it? What do you want?'

I want what I have always wanted, that things should fall out the way I dreamed, and not as they really do.

I said, 'Do you know how much you're hurting me?'

She lifted her eyebrows in delight. 'Oh, really – '

'I don't think you do, or you wouldn't be doing this.'

'Doing what? I wish you'd stop being so melodramatic.'

How could she say this? When I felt as if I was lying in bloody gobbets on the floor, doing violence to myself and unable to resist the pain. At last I started to feel some proper anger. In order to ring the bell for her bath she had to pass close to me, and I snatched her bare arm. 'Let me go,' she said softly.

'You're married to me.'

'So? That's not my fault.' She tossed her head, swirling her hair around. I grabbed it, all that fat yellow hair, and jerked backwards as hard as I could. Perhaps I hoped to break her neck.

She slapped me on the ear.

I hit her.

Her knee came up and kicked me in the groin. I had to let go of her, pain racking me in spasms, staggering back to fall on the bed with my knees cramped to my stomach. She waited happily for me to be able to speak.

To think that I used to think she, and our marriage, were worth fighting for.

Finally I coughed, 'I'll kill you.'

She smiled sweetly. 'Poor jealous Nardo. Who would have thought it? Well, I did. Poor Nardo.' She came round to the other side of the bed, hitching up the fur to flash glistenings of dimpled whiteness.

'I hate you,' I said.

'Oh, you little liar.'

She crawled on all fours across the blankets, mouth parted, tongue to tooth-tip, until she was poised above me. Her hand stroked the thing that she had bruised, and it, helpless and repulsive slave, tried to struggle up, while Reyhnard, partly in pain and partly with desire, panted like the pet dog she had made of him.

She slid along my body to hold her mouth above mine. 'No more right now, puppy,' she said.

I grabbed her face. Lovers should not grab, but she had taught me all I knew about love and tenderness; and in any case we were hardly lovers. She has these games. She bites, hoping to be bitten.

Shifting her weight to balance on three limbs, with her left nails she carefully drew blood from my wrist to my elbow. 'I've left you the other one,' she said, sliding out of my hands, coiling back like a snake from the bed to the floor.

'Beulah, I *won't* let you do this.'

'Oh, my poor darling.' She laughed, and shrugged, one shoulder slipping out of the dark fur. Then she got up and went to ring the bell, saying, 'He told me you were a fool. Oh Nardo, I suppose I am sorry you deceived yourself, but honestly, why should I be? You got what you wanted.'

'That's what he said to you.'

I scored a tiny victory with that. She yanked at the bell and said testily, 'I'm not ashamed of being his mistress.'

As she was ashamed to be my wife.

You are not alone in this feeling, Beulah.

She could forgive him for making her marry me. She couldn't forgive me for being her husband. She looked at me contemptuously, her eyes those of a general surveying the slain bodies of men too weak to win.

I said, 'Beulah – '

And I begged. I begged like a trained dog, and the words stand like a monument between her and me, for which *I* can never forgive *her*. I said, 'Please – '

She rubbed her hands, a gesture I had come to recognise as one of pure delight. 'I must tell him! He said you wouldn't be jealous, wouldn't make a fuss. But I was right.'

She pulled the robe tighter and gave me a stern frown. 'Listen, Nardo, don't make a fuss. It's bad enough for me the way it is. Don't make them laugh at you.' She punctuated this with a little sigh: That I should have to *explain* this to him. Then she patted my feet as she walked past the bed. 'Roll over, darling, and play dead. I'm going to have my bath.'

I don't know what to call the emotion I felt for her. It wasn't love, and it wasn't hate, but it was as strong as either of those emotions. The one thing it definitely was not is indifference. It may be that I am the first person ever to have felt this emotion, and so it has no name because previously it did not exist to need one. I hope this is the case. I would not wish such a feeling upon my worst enemy.

It's essential to find the proper name for each thing, so as to know what precisely you must direct your energies against. You must be able to say: 'This is a stone, and this a root, and this a broken cobble', in order to identify the thing you have tripped over. Then you can concentrate on removing it. If you call everything 'thing', you can never point your finger at your enemy, and you exhaust your forces raging impotently at the entire world. And you keep on stumbling. I am sure it is because I could not define what Beulah made me feel that it took so long for me to conquer it. Since I must give it a name, I will call it compulsion, for lack of anything better. The difference between it and true compulsion is that it came from inside me, not outside; and it was she who burrowed into me to put it there.

She deprived me of my integrity. I could not resist her, every time she whispered in my ear or ran her hands through my hair. I felt such a desperate, shamed joy when, once or twice a week, she gave herself to me. That phrase, that common euphemism is so incorrect. She didn't *give* herself; she let me throw myself away in her. She fed me on looks and kisses and then took it all back again. She was curled up inside me like a tapeworm.

No, I know a better analogy. To be crudely accurate, she had castrated me in all but the most crassly physical sense. She had taken my balls into her possession. I loved her on those occasions when she condescended to lend them back to me; when she withheld them, I hated her.

I wanted to be able to refuse her, but I couldn't. She had castrated my will-power too, that soft, purring, golden, sixteen-year-old girl.

After a few days I found myself going to Alexi, trying to tell him the gist of what had happened between Beulah and me. I couldn't think of much to say.

'You were wrong,' I said at last. 'I was offered to her on a plate, and she took me.'

He said gently, 'Try to forget about it. You must try. Try to make it not matter.'

Impossible. I was absorbed in her and she was inside me: the reverse of a natural embrace. I wanted to tell him, 'I can't', but I didn't need to. He could see.

'You must find someone else,' he suggested again.

I shook my head. I would not find in any other woman what Beulah had taken from me.

I'm sure Alexi would have said, 'It doesn't make me think less of you. I always knew what she is.' He was very kind to me. I could see him being so understanding. And I thought: It would be nice if I could appreciate this. But I couldn't. Beulah had appropriated to herself all the power to rouse anything in me.

I don't know how else to put it. Except that even after having been told what she was, and having seen it for myself, I still could not stop wanting her. Having married her, and slept with her, and been teased and taunted by her – none of this made any difference. I was as sick and obsessed as I had been before our marriage. The only difference was that I now knew I did not love her. She possessed everything about me, not just my sexuality: she filled my thoughts, my spare time, my sleep, my nerves, my appetite, my breathing, all my emotions, the clean and the filthy, the good and the bad. She made it all a part of her, every bit of it coloured by the dingy light of my association with her.

The colt was born with three legs and had to be put down.

15

Beulah would not leave me alone.

I mined for poems in a dead seam. Sometimes I fell asleep at my table and she would wake me with a shake. She was dressed for the evening, the sky was black, the moon shining off the snow as brightly and as coldly as the sun.

'It's dinner,' she said. 'You must come down.'

I shook my head, my shoulders hot where her fingers touched.

'You must,' she insisted. 'I won't let you embarrass me. I refuse to have an empty space behind my chair.'

And I must, as I must do whatever she says.

That winter was very cold. Every night the wind jammed the snow up in drifts against the doors, and all day the servants fought a losing battle to keep the paths clear. At dawn I would see dead birds frozen on their perches. Other birds smothered in the chimneys, where they had flown to look for warmth. The wind knocked up and down the flues, and the trapped birds choked and scrabbled in the smoke.

Hans enjoyed that winter tremendously, for it brought him some good hunting. The wolves, who generally keep well outside the cultivated areas, were driven by hunger right down into the streets of Tsvingtori, taking old men and children. I remember Hans looking like a shapeless parcel of fur and leather, wearing a wool mask that showed only his eyes, climbing on to a shaggy horse with his bad leg dangling. The halls reeked of dead wolf; the Palace dogs went mad rubbing their noses in the new fur rugs.

Alexi usually accompanied Hans. One day they cornered a wolf, which bit Alexi's hand and tore it badly. We thought he might lose it, and the arm, but the cold saved them, and the wound healed into a patchy red scar. He complained more about his chilblains, and the aches in his joints. 'These old bones ain't what they used to be,' he grinned.

Hans got some liniment from the stables and rubbed him down, like a horse.

Fires were kept burning twenty-four hours a day in every room in the palace. The roar of their flames drowned out the wind, casting moving light as the bare trees cast their moving shadows. Carpets and tapestries had been unrolled, laid down and hung up: we were enveloped by material. On the whole it was quite warm in the palace, if you didn't stand too near a window or in a draught.

These ubiquitous fires did nothing to warm me up. I felt at one with nature: bleak.

All around me I saw the warmth of physical and emotional bonds, love or whatever. There was the King and Beulah, who were enough to steam ice; all husbands, wives, lovers, mistresses, brothers and sisters; Hans and Alexi, mothers and their children . . . all the infinite permutations of human affection. Like flint and steel, it required two to strike a light.

Genevieve's crop-haired little daughters tumbled round her skirts. Nikolas's wife sat with the women, her fingers busily wielding a needle through two pieces of linen, a shirt sewn with love.

Outwardly, I had no less than before, but what I did have had been sneered at and smeared, not worth the having. In fact I had more. I had that compulsion inside me.

Even when I was outdoors with Peter, making snowmen, having

snowball fights, watching him romp through the powdery snow and his hair standing out brightly against the whiteness – even then I stood far away from him, and his laughter echoed faintly to me across a bottomless divide.

I felt as if I had been excavated, diverted, drained into Beulah and made into an island.

In the earliest hours of the day, when a band of pearly grey horizon was broadening at the incurve of a black sky, I would sit at my window, my pen drying, my paper white as snow. I could sit like that for hours. A maid would come in and stir the fire. The fat cold sun, like a moon, would winch up, and the purple cast of buildings darken on the snow. Hans and Alexi would come out, the elder pushing the younger; Alexi yawned, and Hans threw a handful of snow in his face. When they passed on, they left wide rumpled prints where they'd had their mock-fights. A little later, Peter and some friends would emerge, their dogs bounding ahead of them through the drifts. They were going to hunt snow hares. There was a craze that winter among the boys for the scuts of white rabbits, and they used to play marbles for them. Peter gave me one. I kept it for years, but I don't have it any more.

Inevitably, Peter would turn around and look up at my window.

He was far too old now to be hugged, wriggling away when I held him in order to remind myself of affection. He was also outside my prison. When I was with him, I felt my unsteady grip on the edge of the chasm. Rumours and whispers had come down even to the children. They only half-grasped the facts, but they understood the shame. I could neither keep her nor keep away from her, nor free myself of her as she coiled, like death, inside me.

All the same, after he had disentangled himself from my hug he would smile into my face, touch my arm and suggest that we do something together, just him and me.

That's love, Beulah, but you wouldn't recognise it.

He looked up at my window, and I knew he was wondering what had happened to me. The dull daylight reflecting from my window-panes made me invisible.

Then a friend would pull his arm, and he would turn and walk on.

I did struggle against it. I was not yet resigned. I had flashes of resistance.

We had a quarrel, a real one. I went up to my rooms at lunchtime to find her asleep in my bed – still nominally our bed – and from the door I could smell a stench of gone-off anchovies. She didn't bother about baths when she came into my room.

For once I didn't feel a weak delight at seeing her in my bed. I wanted her out of the room. Peter was coming to show me some drawings, and I had promised to teach him a new game of cards. I didn't want her smell and her taint to permeate him.

I threw open the window. Wind blasted in, whipping her hair across her face. She woke up, bleary-eyed, and said drowsily, 'Shut the window, darling.'

'Get up,' I said. 'If you want to sleep in the middle of the day then go to your own rooms.'

'This *is* my room, darling, and my bed. It's so cold, please shut the window.'

'It stinks in here.'

'Oh, let me sleep. I'm so tired. I'm aching all over, all that dancing!' She stretched beneath the sheets. 'Oh, oh, I'm so sore.'

She leaned up on her elbow, letting one breast fall plump on to the pillow. I grabbed the covers and threw them back. 'Naughty,' she giggled. 'Why don't you get in?'

'You get out. Get out of here.'

She arched her body, as if she had no bones and all her joints were arbitrary, and pulled herself into a sitting position. Wrapping the eiderdown around her shoulders, she swung her legs over to dangle off the bed; she was bare below the waist.

'I mean it,' I said. 'I'm sick and tired of this.'

She gurgled deep down in her throat. Trailing the eiderdown behind her, she got up, eyes fixed on mine, and came over to me, laid a hand on my shoulder, circled it over my back while she curled forward to put her mouth against my ear. 'You really must learn not to tell lies,' she whispered. Her hand worked round and down my stomach, felt for it, had held it fast. My face was burning.

'Poor Nardo,' she said. 'You can't even make your own cock do what you want.'

I hit her, hard enough to knock her back on to the bed. She lay there for a moment, her eyes glittering with an odd sort of gratification. Then she tried to sit up, and winced, touching a hand to her arm. 'You've hurt me,' she said.

'I didn't think that was possible.'

'Listen, you ever hit me that hard again and you'll wish you hadn't.'

I knew that this was not an idle threat. She had already got rid of Edvard.

She went for him like a plumb-line, Edvard filcLaurentin, who had been Chancellor since before any of us were born. He and Hans were the only men – as Beulah was the only woman – who could have persuaded the King to do something he did not want to do. Both men fell short, because Hans never used his influence and Edvard over-estimated his. Only Beulah both knew her power and used it, treating it with love and care like a robust growing child.

Edvard was unshakably loyal to the King, but he was also, as I've said, an irreproachably virtuous man. He had never approved of any of the King's mistresses, not even gentle, harmless Caryad. Nevertheless he acknowledged that they were necessary, in fact inevitable, and he quietly tolerated them.

Edvard and I were probably the only people who expected the King's affair with Beulah to finish when she married me. Nor was Edvard prepared to keep his opinions to himself when he saw that it had not. The King had a Council – Edvard was on it – but for all the notice he took of them his councillors might as well have stood on their heads and recited nursery rhymes, except for Edvard. He took the King aside for some plain speaking; what he said calmly into one ear, Beulah countered, pouring herself insidiously into the other. Edvard spoke with loyalty and sense. Her tongue licked around the lobe and probed the tube. Once or twice the King wavered. I got to know these times: they were when I would find her in my bed three or four nights in a row – but Edvard shot his bolt when he set an ultimatum: either this ends, or I go.

He went. Once he had had friends. The day he and his wife stood in the snow, handing their trunks into the carriage, they stood alone. His friends were indoors, sitting around the fire, drinking tea with Beulah. I sat at my window and watched Edvard climb into the carriage. As it drove away he put his head out of the window, and looked back. I was sorry to see him go. He had never spoken to me about it, but along the corridors and through the walls and up between the floorboards the knowledge had reached me that he had been a sort of friend.

Beulah had a replacement all lined up. Gilles Mehah was made Chancellor, the Council was reshuffled, and the empty seat was filled by her protégé, Dominic filcRandal, who was a cousin of Nikolas's on their mother's side. He was twenty-five, undistinguished in any way, except perhaps by his cloyingly insincere politeness. Well, I could say all sorts of things about Dominic, but he was never really important, and he has paid for being stupid.

The harshness of the winter had meant that all transportation and communication virtually ceased. The bay was frozen over; the docks of Tsvingtori stood empty. By early March prices had escalated alarmingly. There was a great deal of privation in the city. Naturally we were not aware of this – I mean by 'we' people such as myself or Hans or the ordinary courtiers, not the King and Council, who obviously knew, or

Alexi, who presumably knew this as he knew everything. I'm sure Beulah knew: it was the sort of thing she makes her business.

Down in the city riots broke out, in the course of which some wealthy corn merchants were murdered and their grain stores looted. For the time being these incidents were allowed to go unpunished, the King recognising that the city populace needed an outlet for its hunger and frustration. Three or four days later a mob of stevedores broke into one of the marketplace temples and killed a priest. This sacrilegious act could not be ignored, so the King sent Lord Peat's brother Michael, accompanied by a bodyguard, down to the city to calm the rioters with pious exhortations. The mob tore the deputation to pieces and tried to storm the Palace. The Guards went out in force to drive them back.

From the window of Alexi's room I could just make out the square figure of Hans hacking men in two, and wiping his sword on what was left of the slushy, bloodied snow.

Beulah was so upset by this incident that the King had to make her a present of a new pink dress and matching ruby jewellery. She threw a fit one evening: a plate of rare steak and creamed potatoes had been set in front of her, at which she began to utter small choked coughs, trying to push it away. It knocked against her neighbour's arm and spilled into Beulah's lap. The gravy trickled down her skirt and she started to scream. Anything like this, but especially meat and swords, could set her off. However, as I said, after she got her new things she forgot all about it.

Several days later a fleet of corn ships arrived from Pravarre. A detachment of Guards was sent down to the docks to supervise the unloading. It all went off calmly, and was distributed to the population, so everything settled down.

I can be cool about it now, for I have seen many worse things since then, but at the time it did disturb me. We weren't in any danger, and Peter got quite over-excited, rushing through the corridors waving his toy sword and shouting battle-cries, until he had to be forcibly restrained from running out to join Hans.

What disturbed me most of all was the quality of Beulah's hysterics. They were like her gracefulness: perfect, but unreal. Of course when she had them the young men came swarming round, and the older men too, slapping her wrists and fanning her cheeks, and crying, 'Give her more room', and pressing brandy and sweets on her, while pages and footmen lurked in the background and hoped they would be called upon to do something. Alexi stood to one side, arms folded, wearing an expression of undisguised cynicism, and said to me: 'She's so sensitive, your poor wife.'

When she fainted, I noticed she locked her knees and swayed in such a way as to roll carefully on to the floor, never bruising herself. After-wards, when she was seated on a sofa recovering, her small feet up on a cushion, I saw that her eyes were dry, her complexion rosy, and not one curl was out of place – and yet she could make you doubt your own eyes, disbelieve your own doubt. The King would come running from wherever he was, even from the other side of the Palace – his face was worried and white. She would extend an arm so precisely, neither too fast nor too slow, from elbow to wrist, the fingers at last uncurling for him to take her proffered hand and kiss it. Every time she did this I was reminded of the day I first saw her come climbing out of the bushes, when she ought to have been dirty and dishevelled and taken by surprise and yet, even though I could *see* she was all those things, the only impres-sion I retained was of her complete self-possessedness. All in place.

Her self-control was a cunning old soldier, and it unnerved me. I knew I had nothing to match it.

In all things regarding her character I was becoming gradually clear-headed. I knew she did not think about me any more than was necessary, in the same way, I believe, as the captain of a ship must keep any number of variables – the winds, the tides, the shifting sand-banks in the river mouths, the stars, the tempers of his crew and the state of the rations – clearly in his mind in order to steer a safe and steady course. To continue the analogy, my ship was being tossed about in stormy waves, breaking up, taking on water, while its captain – myself – was sitting on the poop with his hands tied behind his back, brooding about the weather.

I understood all this, but it was no good. What I knew about her could not mitigate or remove that compulsion. I would have been better off *not* knowing. I would have felt less demeaned by my servitude.

She was rather like a dog who keeps running back to some deserted corner, to make sure the bone she's buried is still lying quietly. She knew all my hiding places. Fast as I found new ones, she dug them out, and she and her followers would descend on me to play for the hundredth time that scene the King had first written by a shadowed bench at the edge of the gardens, long before any of us ever dreamed Beulah existed.

If I refused, she would dig her nails into the soft flesh at the base of my neck, saying, 'But *why* don't you write them any more? It's such a waste, darling – oh, what a disappointment . . . '

She never let a chance slip by. She might ignore me all one evening, flirting with numerous other men, and then, when she had demonstrated that I could do nothing about it, come up, slip her arm through mine and whisper secretive giggles in my ear while the King watched her with the indulgent smile of a father.

You see, King, how much like father like son? You, too, were happier believing.

When I say that Beulah's behaviour was artificial, I don't mean that it was glaringly so. Beulah wasn't just a slut, not even then. She has always been an extremely clever woman, one of the cleverest people I know. Her artifice was like a spice: there was just a hint of it, a sort of make-up on her character, and it fascinated one to find out what this intriguing girl was *really* like. Alexi, of course, had seen through it at once. I took much longer to understand exactly what she was.

Summer came, and Peter turned eleven. His arms and legs were growing faster than he could keep pace with, a gangling boy tripping on the step up from childhood. He fussed with his hair in hot weather, saying, 'Can't wait till I'm thirteen!' He always had something to look forward to.

He had taken up with a new set several years his senior. They, the gang, would lounge about in the shade of the porches, sniggering and staring at the women. Whenever a lady, amused by their fumbling interest, turned to smile at them, they would redden and fall silent, dropping their eyes; but once she had walked away they collapsed into giggles.

He would stand in front of a mirror, pulling faces and straining his eyes from side to side in hopes of seeing the first traces of a beard that was nowhere near ready to start growing. I hated it. I hated watching him trying to be what he was not, when it was years yet before he needed to grow up.

If it had been possible, I would have grappled with Peter and held him back physically. I wanted to prevent this one thing from changing, this friendship and love which we shared and which had nothing to do with anyone or anything else. Nothing should be allowed to affect it: not the King, not the court, not women, not time.

I was afraid for him; even more, I feared that world ahead of him which I knew, and he didn't. It held infinite dangers, and might change him from the child I loved to a being who, perhaps, was harder to love and who loved me less. I know it was silly, but I used to want to say, 'Peter, stop growing up. Stop being so impatient. It isn't worth it. I know it looks bright and exciting but it isn't, and worst of all it is inevitable. Once you've grown up, Peter, it's too late to wish you hadn't.' I thought there was so much time for him. More fool I. I wanted to tell him to wait; but now, he can wait for ever to be twenty.

The court was in the gardens. I wanted to be alone, so I went to one of the smaller salons. As I paused in the act of turning the handle I heard two children giggling inside the room. I thought up something stern to boot them out with as I opened the door.

Framed by a sunlit window, Peter and Beulah were sitting on a table. He was wearing shorts; she had her skirts hitched up to her thighs. Her knees were dimpled and pink, his brown and scabby, and they were barefooted, swinging their legs in rhythm, eating sherbet out of a bowl with two spoons.

She must have just finished telling him a joke, for he threw back his head and laughed, and with a cry of 'Hah!' Beulah thrust a spoonful of sherbet into his open mouth. Peter sputtered, bit the spoon, and swallowed the ice.

She slid the spoon out.

'Pig!' he gasped, laughing.

She inclined towards him, laying a hand on his brown leg. 'You're the pig,' she smiled. 'You've eaten nearly all of it, and it was mine.'

Even with him, Peter, a child, she could not stop performing. She arched and curled, she smoothed her hair, widened her eyes, smiled and dimpled. He was innocence enthralled.

I thought I would be sick.

That look in his eyes was so familiar. I had seen it in the King, and in many other men, and in my own mirror: oblivious of everything except Beulah. Thank God he had no name yet for the sort of delight there was in being with her.

He didn't know I was standing in the doorway, but she, probably, was aware of my presence. She put a finger to his lips and said, 'The rest is for me, piglet.'

Piglet, puppy. No more now, puppy. I had to stop this.

'Beulah – '

Oh yes, she knew I was there. Her neck bowed, sweeping her chin round and up in a circle to turn wide conker-coloured eyes on me.

Peter jumped off the table, landing awkwardly on those big feet he hadn't yet grown into. His face was red, even those pure boy's ears. 'Oh, Nardo, hullo,' he muttered.

I longed to shake him, hard. He looked guilty; he felt guilty. He felt the guilt before he knew the reason for it. 'That's her!' I wanted to shout. 'That's what she does. You think she's going to give you something worth having, but she never lets go of it, and all you end up with is a sour taste on the back of your tongue.'

Instead, I said a lie. 'Peter, your friends are looking for you. You'd better go and find them.'

He tried to slink past me, heading for the door, but I had to catch his eye. What have I done? he asked me silently. He bit his lip and blinked, I'm sorry.

Of course he wasn't to blame, he was only a child. He couldn't even understand why he felt guilty. I ruffled his hair, which was a way of saying, 'I'm not angry with you.'

He smiled in relief, shedding his guilt like a coat too big for him, and sprinted off.

Beulah had come down from the table to recline on a sofa, holding the bowl in one hand and mopping up the rest of the sherbet. She waved the spoon at me. 'You're in a bad mood. What's eating you?'

'Beulah, this has got to stop. This is where it stops.'

Her mouth was full. 'What are you on about now?'

'I can endure most things. I can bear the King. I can just about bear the others, because I have to. But I won't put up with this.'

She scraped the spoon round the bottom of the bowl. 'Oh, not again, it's so boring.'

I grabbed that bowl and threw it across the room, smashing it against the wall. This so startled her that she sat up and regarded me with real attention.

'I've had enough,' I said. 'Isn't it enough that you've made me a laughing-stock? Isn't it enough that you've got the King wrapped round your little finger and half the other lunatics all panting after you – '

'Not to mention you,' she said.

'Not to mention me. Let's not mention me. Just leave my brother alone.'

She put her hands to her throat and said in an injured tone, 'Why, what on earth were we doing?'

'You know! Sitting there with your skirt up round your armpits, fluttering your eyelashes and putting your hands all over him – '

'You are so ridiculous. He's a child.'

'I know he's a child!'

She rubbed her hands together. 'Then why are you so jealous?'

'I'm not jealous!'

'Well, you could have fooled me.'

'I don't care what you think, just leave Peter alone – '

'Keep your voice down,' she said. 'Everyone can hear.'

'So what? They all know everything already – '

'Reyhnard, I've asked you not to shout at me. Really, how can you accuse me of making a fool of you? You do a fine job all on your own.'

'Just tell me what you want!' I shouted. 'I try and I try but I just can't see it. Tell me what you want and I'll give it to you if you'll leave him alone. Do you want to get me on my knees, is that it? Do you want me to tell you you're like a knife in me? I will, you are. How much more of me is left to give you?' I had her by the shoulders and was pushing her back and forth, bumping her head around. 'How many more do you have to have?' I cried.

She grabbed my hair and tugged it back – not hard enough to hurt, just a sharp tweak that made me realise what I was doing, and try to pull myself together. She stroked my cheek. I caught her wrist, pressing her palm against my skin.

'How do you think it feels to be punished when the person hurting you doesn't even notice?' I asked her. 'I need to know what I have to do to make you stop it.'

Her hand relaxed in my grip. 'I notice,' she said huskily, pulling herself up to kiss me. When she drew back, still clinging to my shoulders, I saw her mouth had softened and was trembling.

'Oh – ' She was crying. 'Oh Nardo, I didn't think I was doing anything wrong. It's not my fault I wasn't brought up here and I know I don't always do things properly, but I didn't think this was wrong. I only asked for some sherbet, and while I was waiting I saw Peter and I asked him if he wanted some and he said yes, so we came in here, because I wanted to talk to him, because he is my brother too, now. I don't understand why you're so angry. He's only eleven. We were only telling jokes and things. Please don't be angry. I'm sorry, I'm sorry I said those things, but you're always saying that everything I do is wrong and I don't know what to do – '

'I don't, you don't do everything wrong – '

'I do,' she cried. 'You do, you do . . . ' She was crying and stroking my chest. How could I have stopped holding her, or kissing her hair, or telling her not to cry?

She had done this to me many times, and this time, like all the others, I was pliant. Her tears and distress unmanned me. I was deeply moved by what seemed to be a sudden expression of need, for me, for my gentleness and forgiveness, and it reminded me how young she was, not much more than a child herself and far away from her own family. In short, I was duped, lulled and out-manoeuvred. 'Please don't cry,' I said, 'I can't bear it.'

'I can't help it, I feel so awful . . . '

I found a handkerchief and pressed it into her hands. The business of sniffing and wiping her eyes took a minute or so, during which I watched her anxiously, feeling a brute for having made her cry. She laid her hands on her forehead, smoothed them back over her hair and raised her eyes.

'You're not angry any more, are you, darling?'

Conker-hard confident eyes, the lashes slightly damp – but there was no redness, none of the ugliness of real crying. I had been manipulated yet again, and again I had let her do it. I knew this, but at the same time I tried to tell myself that no one could fabricate such sincerity from nothing; maybe she meant it despite herself, for it had to come from some honest part of her which even she, perhaps, didn't know she possessed. 'She will grow up,' I told myself. 'She could change.' But less and less was I able to believe this.

'No,' I said.

'Honestly?'

'No, I'm not angry.'

'Oh good.' She smiled, and started to kiss me, tentatively at first, then more wildly as I responded. I was overjoyed to find she had forgiven me. In the honest back of *my* mind I knew it was an act, that all my emotions were as artificial as the means she had used to stir them. I knew this even while she made me fuck her on the sofa with the windows open. Fuck is a perfect word: it is precisely, exactly, what we did together. At the risk of being repetitive I must say again that while I knew all my feelings, such as joy, guilt and so on, existed only in so far as she made me feel them, my real reactions had been pushed so far to the back of my mind – by her – that they could not be associated with the world at large, or even with my own thoughts. I do sometimes wonder why she bothered to fuck me at all. I know now that she got no proper pleasure out of it, at least not from me. I expect it was for the pleasure of controlling me. I was, after all, her husband, and as she said, 'Anything can turn out to be useful.'

Commotion in the Palace.

Caryllac is coming home.

I found out only half an hour before his arrival. Obviously something was up: the servants were bustling and the court was a-twitter with excitement. Aneurin – I hadn't given a thought to Aneurin for months – was looking quite smart in his old-fashioned clerk's finery, making himself visible where usually he effaced. The King strolled about with a genial smile.

I went to find Alexi, who always knew what was happening.

He was in the foundry with Hans. The Palace has only a small foundry, a plaything; the Guards' armour and weapons are made in factories in Tsvingtori. Hans preferred to make his own. He said this was to get the weight right, but we also knew, though he did not say, that he derived great physical pleasure from the labour of smithying.

My brothers had taken their shirts off. Hans had bull shoulders and a bull's neck. Hard tight muscles balled under his skin, sweat rilling down the valleys between each strong tendon. Alexi worked the bellows. His flesh was a little looser, the muscles slipping and sliding where Hans's knotted.

I stood at the door, hot dryness belching out at me as from an oven. The heat and the noise were intense. I wiped the sweat from my eyes, watching Hans's thick arm rise and fall like a chant: raise hold down strike, raise hold down strike – the ring of the anvil like the clangour of battle. I knew I ought to find this all very beautiful, but at the moment I couldn't feel it mattered.

When Hans stepped back for a breather, I broke into the sudden silence, 'Alexi – '

The bellows wheezed as he let go, turning round to grin at me. 'Nardo! Hullo, what are you doing here – I mean, why aren't you busy jumping over the moon?'

'What's going on?' I asked him.

Hans wiped his hands on his trousers. 'I'm thirsty,' he said. 'Let's get something to drink.'

We went outside together. The summer day was cool after the smithy, and Hans blinked in the sunlight. We walked over to a rain-barrel standing in a patch of shade.

'Alexi, tell me – what's going on?'

'You really don't know? I'd have thought – still, everyone must have thought someone else must have told you. Pretty close to your heart, this.'

'Well, go on.'

'Oh well, it's not so much really, just that Caryllac's exile has been rescinded – hey, Hans, look, I think I've killed Nardo.'

'You're joking,' I said.

He decided not to tease me. 'Cross my heart, I swear it's true. He's coming home today – just in time for tea.'

'Here?' I asked.

'Of course here. What do you think Father's looking so pleased about?'

Hans dunked his head in the rain-barrel, threw it up and shook out a spray of drops. 'Don't know what all the fuss is, about one old man,' he said.

'He is not old, Hans,' I said. 'He's younger than the King.'

Alexi added, 'Yes, but all that time in the south would probably age a man pretty quickly, so – don't expect too much. Remember he's been away a long time. It'll probably be a shock for him.'

Nonsense, rubbish, what did Alexi know of the bond between Caryllac and myself? I had whispered my invocations to him in the dark night, and he, caught between white sun and white sand, must have taken them on the wind.

Heroes have no age. However he walked, I would see Caryllac walking like a hero, plumed poetry. In my mind's eye I had always envisaged him as a tall, slender man, purple eye-hollows in a burnt face, his bleached hair shorn ragged. He would stride like a king, the cloak of his defiance thrown about his broad shoulders.

He would stride in and see me immediately. He would look at me and he would know that he was my ambition: that I had tried to be better than I was through being as much like him as possible. He, my first obsession, would lend me a new strength to fight the second obsession, the base one. He would give my poetry back to me, Caryllac in the flesh.

Heavens moving, clouds parting, Caryllac coming home. I was too preoccupied with my own joy to think of asking why.

'I must change,' I said, because I was wearing some old trousers and a brown shirt, frayed at the elbows, quite unsuitable. Back in my rooms I threw the contents of my wardrobe across the floor. Not white, too southern. Not blue and yellow either. I needed something appropriate, like the right word in the right place. Jammed at the back I found a pair of moss-green trousers and a jacket which I hadn't worn for several years, but I knew they were the ones. Green, the green of Brychmachrye, grass green, Caryllac's colour and his essence.

Beulah wandered in, looking sulky. She saw what I was doing and showed her teeth.

'You must be simply thrilled,' she said.

I saw it annoyed her that I had some joys which didn't depend on her. I almost did not mind – Caryllac was helping me already. However, she might tell me what I couldn't wait to know, so I asked her, 'How is the King?'

'Oh, pleased as punch, stupid old fogey. I'll say one thing, men certainly know how to carry a grudge. You'd think it was the long-lost love. You can tell him I'm not coming. I'm not interested in any fusty old word-merchant. The whole thing's ridiculous.'

I was glad she wasn't coming. I could bear with no distractions. Nothing should come between Caryllac and me. Leaving Beulah to her pique, I hurried downstairs.

The royal salon, with its mosaic of blue and gold tiles and its silk-papered walls, had been chosen as the setting for this historic occasion. It was packed with a noisy crowd waiting to welcome Caryllac home. I pushed through the knots of courtiers, thinking: This isn't good enough. He should have used the Justice Hall. He should have had some poetry . . .

Caryllac, burnt and burnished to absolutes, walking in to face the King; the King descending from that suspended throne, approaching Caryllac, standing on the same ground as Caryllac, sealing this reconciliation . . .

That would have been poetry.

The room was stuffy with all those people, and the heavy scent of lilies in blue vases. The King, resting one knee on a chair, was talking to Gilles and Lord Mehah. Chilled wine circulated. Men and women moved around, talking and gesticulating, filling the room with themselves and their cacophonous bustle.

I wanted to exclaim that this was all wrong. They ought to do Caryllac the homage of waiting in silence. They were treating it like a party, when it ought to be a triumph.

A large, thin book was being passed from hand to hand. They opened it, showed it to each other, read bits out and enthused over them. I couldn't hear the words of what they were quoting, but obviously it was something they liked.

'Oh!' said a woman. 'This turn of phrase! Don't you think it's absolutely . . . How right His Grace is to bring that poor man home.'

The King's eye caught mine. 'Ah, Reyhnard, come over here. I'm glad at least one of my children has seen fit to welcome the most noble of the sons of Brychmachrye . . . though of course' – he chucked me under the chin – 'I should have remembered I could count on you. Where's the Lady Beulah?'

'In – her room, Sir.'

'Sir?' said a footman.

The King smiled at me, and took his time bringing his gaze round to where the footman indicated, to the spot and the man I was already staring at. My first thought was: how did that old farmer get in here?

He must once have been of average height and weight, but age had shrunken him into deformity. His skin was too baggy for his frame, and his head was too big for his body. The effort of carrying it had hunched his spine. All his features were small and regular, except his nose, which was swollen with fluid. His skin was chalky grey, like cold ashes.

He needed a cane. One of his legs bowed inwards, double-jointed. He must have broken it badly many years ago. Someone had given him clean clothes and his hair had been recently shaved, close to his scalp, but he still looked verminous. The women nearest to him had drawn back their skirts.

The King smiled at this man and nodded, giving him permission to approach. He took one step, listed sideways, and buckled his bad knee. Then he fell down on both. He clasped his hands behind his head in a gesture he had not forgotten, and lay with his face flat on the cold tiles, prostrate before the God-King of Brychmachrye.

The King sat down in his chair. And he smiled and smiled and said, 'Get up, Caryllac.'

Caryllac tried to stand, getting no further than a sort of crouch when his joints locked.

'Go and help him, Reyhnard,' said the King.

Caryllac's skin was dry and scaly. It took some seconds to get him into an upright position, and I tried to avoid looking at his profile; but in the end I had to. His face was seamed, puckered, wrinkled: the erosion of the desert.

He grabbed my arm very hard for support, and we went up to the King. Caryllac would have fallen on his knees again, but the King put out a hand to indicate that this was not necessary. 'Bring a chair,' he said.

Caryllac snatched his hand, put it to his lips and kissed the signet ring. 'This seal', he said, 'has brought me home.'

This was in fact not true. The royal seal is a large heavy thing like a stamp, and is. kept in a safe in the Council offices.

Caryllac's lips were the colour and consistency of putty. His voice was cracked, as if there was no moisture in his lungs.

Twenty-six years. All those years in the south. I thought: This isn't a man. This is a carcase.

What were my nine months of marriage to his twenty-six years of exile?

'Your Grace, please, forgive me,' said Caryllac. 'I am overcome. I cannot find words enough to thank you for your generosity.'

The King patted me on the arm which was not being used by Caryllac. 'This is my son, Reyhnard. He's a great admirer of yours – I think I'd be right in saying that, wouldn't I, Reyhnard? I should think he remembers any number of your poems that you've forgotten.'

Now, surely, Caryllac would look at me, and see in my face the original of a prayer that had reached him across the desert. He would know me and remember me. We had met so many times in my imagination, though never like this, and I had never imagined he would be so old and decrepit – but there was still the possibility that none of this mattered. I could examine the windows of his house, and perhaps it would make no difference that his façade was battered. Inside that sloughed insect-case of a body I might yet find my hero.

He turned his eyes to me. They must have been blue, once. They were rheumy. The irises were a bluish-white and the pupils dark grey. All I could see on those eyes was a dullness like the reflection of the sun; blank, and white, and tired.

Caryllac said, 'I don't suppose many young people read my books these days. We must have a talk some time, young man.'

The King said, 'Sit down, Caryllac. Have some wine.'

Later, when Caryllac had been helped away to his room, the King picked up the volume the courtiers had been leafing through and handed it to me.

'His latest work,' said the King. 'I'm afraid his handwriting's a bit crabbed, but I'm sure you'll be able to make it out.

'You know, Reyhnard, I think you were right about Caryllac. This court has been sadly lacking in culture recently. I'm considering making him poet stipendiary – anyway, have a thumb through that and tell me what you make of it.'

This was the last refuge of hope. I put the book carefully under my arm and went outside, walking through the gardens and over to the other side of the woods, where I could climb up on to the wall, although strictly I wasn't supposed to. From there the towers of the Palace were hidden by the trees. I could see distant hamlets, dusty roads, the river, the downs, the meadows and copses, and all the greenness of Brychmachrye.

I opened that book and read it from end to end.

Long before I finished, I knew why the King had let Caryllac come home.

The title of the work was 'Constantin and Larissa'. Having poked my head into several schools in various towns across the country, I understand that this long poem is becoming a sort of compulsory text, as Isumbard used to be, so anyone who comes across these writings will probably know it well. It was written in epic allegory. I say allegory because the hero, Constantin, was clearly none other than the King, and the heroine, Larissa, was my mother Ursula. The plot is a simple shepherd's-tale.

Constantin comes down to the court from the northern mountains and falls in love with the beautiful Princess Larissa. Her father, the King, an evil tyrant, has already arranged a marriage for her with an elderly and debauched King from the south. Larissa is easily wooed and won by her dashing suitor, but her father locks her up in a brass tower in the western marshes. Constantin then embarks on a long career of chivalry and derring-do. He raises an army against the King and his seven sons, who are a bad lot, and slaughters them all very gallantly. He then has to undergo numerous trials by magic before finally releasing his Princess from her tower. They marry, and everyone lives happily ever after, while peace and prosperity reign.

Of its genre it was a pretty piece, and executed with great craft. But Caryllac's genius with the language, which had pressed mud from the gutter into jewels, illuminating his lyric and epigrammatic works – it might as well have never been. This poem was hack work. It was the work of a man who writes not for the sake of the thing, but for the price of it. It was such a blatant mockery of history, such a turncoating of his own attitudes, that Caryllac could have written it with only one aim in view.

One small section did move me, though not with its beautiful writing, because it had none. By what it said, rather than how it said it, this passage alone managed to do what Caryllac's poems had always done to me: reach inside and make contact with what I felt. It is the speech the commander of the Andaranah forces makes to his aide-de-camp, Thierry, when he, the commander, is dying on the battlefield:

> *'Has Constantin won the field?'*
>> *'He has, sir.'*
> *'How many dead men grace this field of his?'*
>> *'On their side, many; on ours, many more.'*
> *'Thierry, their cause has become my cause.*
> *We have fought and we have lost the great war.*
> *What now is left but uniforms on corpses*
> *To tell the victors from the vanquished?*
> *And what have I won with this death of mine?*
> *Only what no man need struggle for:*
> *Bought my father's inalienable bequest,*
> *The one thing every mother gives her son,*
> *A heritage of death down generations.*
> *I am beyond being helped by your tears,*
> *And ever was since I entered the world.*
> *Keep them, for if I had lived, Constantin*
> *Would yet have killed me with slow banishment.*
> *Since death must come, this swift end is best.*
> *I would not want to die in exile . . . '*

Intimations of mortality. Even for Caryllac.

16

A regiment of soldiers has been billeted on us.

I ought to have expected it. The last time we went to war against Ruffashpah must be – what? Eight years ago now. It seems like yesterday.

For the last month or so the first of the summer's crop of vagrants have been passing through the village – unlike me, they don't stay – and one of them had spent the winter in Amanah-in-Peat. He said the Ruffash tribes had been making border raids again. That place has always been a literal pain in the arse.

The scout came up here only a week ago, and since then Serena has been in a state of bubbling excitement. They had soldiers in the village last time, eight years ago. Her eldest sister married one. Serena was too young to be of interest to them, but she retains an impression of to-ings and fro-ings: life on a wider scale. Yesterday afternoon I was sitting in a patch of spring sun outside our door when she came galloping up, chirping, 'They're here, they're here,' and dragged me off by the hand to come and see. They were marching up from Rayalled. The sun glinted on their swords and pikes and armour, making them visible from several miles away, a glittering column weaving between the hills like a thick thread of metal.

The villagers made the most of their small stock of treasures. Carpets were hanging from the windows as if this were any ordinary cleaning day – but these carpets had already been beaten, and were the best each household owned. One woman sat on her doorstep, polishing the family pewter. All the women had taken their bright summer dresses out of the chests, shaking free the dust and moths, and were strolling back and forth as if they always sang when they went about their daily chores. Two young girls, dressed in red, sat on the roof of the miller's house and plaited head-dresses of flowers.

The Commander, his Aide-de-Camp and the Captain rode at the head of the column. I had a shock, because the first thing I recognised was the Commander's horse, a flashy chestnut called Brack that used to belong to me. I can't remember the Commander's name, but I recognised him too, a heavy-set man with a collection of sparkling teeth above a curly beard. He came to court just before I left, and made his way into the outer edges of Beulah's coterie – presumably he has been promoted.

I found a place where I could be inconspicuous and watch the parade. Serena, entranced by the show, didn't notice how uneasy I was. The soldiers filed past, jaws set, shoulders swinging; the villagers find this uniformed mass a pretty impressive sight. The girls waved and whistled, but the soldiers marched straight on, eyes front – all except for one wag who turned and winked, and stuck out his tongue at the two girls in red. The village boys scrambled in the wake of the column, running to keep up and puffing out their chests.

Last of all came a little brown and black dog. It followed them through the village, over the bridge, and into the camp on the other side of the river, where the pitched tents blended in with the muddy greens and browns of the spring countryside.

Serena kept up a constant stream of meaningless chatter all afternoon, but what she said went in one ear and out the other.

The Commander returned to Rayalled the same night, without ever noticing me. Caution was replaced by curiosity, so this evening I went over to the house which has been converted by its owner into a temporary tavern (in order to part the soldiers from some of their wages), and there I ran into the Captain.

He was trying to order some wine, but the landlord found his lame native incomprehensible. I went up and spoke to him in court-speech. 'Tell me what you want,' I said. 'I'll order it.'

The Captain was, at first, understandably startled to hear the accents of Tsvingtori in this village. Once we had our wine and were seated he relaxed, expressing his relief at being, as he put it, 'finally able to have a decent conversation.'

He was an inoffensive young man, with tousled brown hair and earnest eyes. From the speed with which he got drunk it was obvious that the responsibility of keeping so many soldiers under control was beginning to daunt him. He told me it was his first posting on active service.

'I'm from Tsvingtori,' he said, in a tone which made it evident he thought this village a pretty poor place by comparison. 'My father's a merchant – family's been in it for generations, but I couldn't settle in the business. Itchy feet, you know? So when the recruiter came round I joined up. See foreign places. Meet new people. Officer school was good fun.'

He told me proudly, 'I was a member of Lord Thomas filcValentin's entourage when the embassy went to Andariah to arrange King Basal's marriage.'

I made suitably impressed noises. 'Did you see the Princess?'

'I did. Pretty little girl, and only ten, poor thing. She cried all the way home. I think it's a shame to send them away from home so young.'

'So the King and the Princess are married?' I asked.

'Yes, just before the solstice. Good lord, this is a backwater! You didn't know?'

'Most news takes a long time getting here.'

'I've noticed. They've still got the Temple dedicated to King Reyhnard.' He tossed down the wine, and grimaced. 'Foul stuff – still, it gets one drunk, which is the main point.'

'I thought you were in charge.'

'They can look after themselves for one night, the buggers. They know if there's any trouble I'll hang a few. They're like animals, the only thing that keeps them under control is fear of the whip. I suppose one has to expect to get sent up here sooner or later – '

'An occupational hazard?' I suggested.

'You could say that. It makes one think. What did I give up, you know? It's not a bad life, can be exciting, and on the whole one has no regrets, but at times like these one does rather wonder if one hasn't made a cock-up. We deal in wine, you know, back home. I got a letter from my father saying they've just had a shipment of Duccarnese Cadini white in.' He stared gloomily at his glass, and sighed. 'I could do with some of that right now.'

Then he shook his hair from his eyes, as if to clear his head of preoccupation, and asked me, 'So tell me, what's a chap like you doing in this hole?'

'I live here.'

He wagged a finger. 'Now you can't fool me. You never learned to talk like that in this dump. You're a Tsvingtori man, I'll bet. Educated too, I can tell – like me.'

I said, 'My family comes from these parts,' which was true enough. I added, 'I used to be a clerk at court.'

'Well there you are, I knew it. You've obviously got a bit of culture about you, not like these louts. Do you want to know what I've spent the day doing? Interviewing prospective soldiers, hulking great ox-heads who think all soldiery consists of is sticking swords into people. I mean, they'd be a liability. We haven't got time to train them, and anyway one doesn't exactly need an army to deal with these Ruffash. If you know what I mean. I mean, we've got an army, but we've got enough. Could you get another round in? I'll pay . . . '

His news came right from the heart of the country, and it was fresh. He gossiped on endlessly about who was in favour, who was out, what marriages had been made, political ups and downs.

I asked, 'Is Lord Thomas filcValentin married yet?'

'Don't think so. Tell me, what department were you in? Foreign, domestic or judicial?'

'Well, I moved around a bit.'

'My cousin is in the Foreign, that's how I got on the embassy staff. Maybe you know him?'

'It's been years since I was at court . . . ' I didn't want to talk about myself, I wanted to hear all his news from home, and I steered him back to it. He took special pride in describing the splendours of the Palace to me. Several times, when he mentioned a particular room or person, I nodded or said, 'Yes, I know it,' but of course he assumed I would.

He held up his cup – his seventh – and toasted loudly: 'The Queen, to the Queen – though one should say, the Queen Mother. Fine woman, damn wonderful.' He leaned across the table and hissed conspiratorially, 'You know what? They say she really ran the country, you know, I mean, the old King – King Reyhnard, may he be blessed by the Gods – they say he wasn't up to much. I'm not saying I know, but I can believe it of the Queen. You know, we only met twice and the second time she remembered my name, even though I'm regular army, not a Guard or anything. One wouldn't expect her to remember, I wouldn't have been offended, but she did and that means a lot, you can see that. I reckon she'd be equal to anything. She's a real man's woman, and that's saying something, not many of them around. You know what else?' He was right in my ear now. 'They say all the Guards are her lovers, you know? And she arranges their duty rosters to suit her. Well, I've heard some people criticise her, but what I think, what I think is, she's the Queen, damn it – and what's more, they say she's nothing compared to Basal the Great in his prime. Three girls in a night, I've heard, now that is what I call living. There was a king for you!'

I'm afraid my laughter only bemused him.

After a dozen cups, he staggered to his feet. He was extremely drunk and a great deal happier than he had been at the start of the evening.

'Tell you what, old man,' he said. 'Tell you what. When you get sick of this place, you come down to Tsvingtori and look me up. You do that. We'll have some of that Cadini white, and look round the old haunts. Look up my cousin. You'll do that, promise? Excuse me, I think something's wrong. I don't seem to be able to walk. Could you give us a hand, old chap?'

He leaned heavily on my shoulder.

'The nag's just outside the door, bloody beast, here it is. Hssst, horse, come here – take her head, if you'd be so kind. Could you just hold this stirrup for me? You're a friend, you know. Really.'

He clambered up, falling into the saddle more by luck than good judgment. The horse pricked up her ears, and I saw an almost human expression come into her eyes: Here we go again.

I laughed and waved him away. The horse trotted down the road, bouncing the Captain's body from side to side. I put my hands in my pockets and strolled thoughtfully home.

I wasn't unhappy – this might have been the wine – but I did feel curiously divided. My feet were taking the familiar route along the village street, seeing by moonlight those wattle-and-timber houses, chipped doorsteps, smoke grey against the night, and the huge faint shapes of the mountains beyond . . . while my head was back in that vivid, sunlit, multi-coloured world made up of people I knew and places I loved. Either

I or my body must be walking through a dream, for only one of these two places can be real.

Anaesthetised by wine, this splitting has so far caused me no pain, but I know that tomorrow I will be in agony worse than any hangover, and the reason will be my self-indulgence.

In Tsvingtori the salons are still rippling with the highpitched tittle-tattle of the courtiers; the servants still move like shadows, never thought about until you have them no longer and wonder what else is missing; Beulah still sweeps along the corridors, dragging her skirts behind her, choosing her Guards with a nod and a smile. The children I knew are growing up and getting married, men I never met are being promoted, and neither I nor any of us are there to see it as we ought to be. In Tsvingtori and Ksaned Kaled life runs blithely on without me, without Madeleine, without Peter or Alexi or Hans, and it seems – oh, it seems a fraud and an illusion, our lives have been taken over and we pushed aside to make room, make room.

None of it is mine any more. I knew this when I left, I knew I wasn't needed – but still, I feel like a ghost, who creeps back at night to eavesdrop on the people he knew, while they recline in comfort beside the fire, eating, drinking, enjoying what is forbidden to him.

As I reached the hut I had another thought. Why, I wonder, did that sodden Captain not include in his list of fascinating royal debaucheries Madeleine and her brother Reyhnard? Has Beulah really succeeded in preventing it from spreading beyond the court?

As the Captain so neatly put it: I reckon she'd be equal to anything.

It was dark when I came in. The fire had gone out, and the lamp wasn't lit. I stood here shivering in the chill and the damp, feeling rather angry, because Serena appears to have gone out. I lit the fire myself. After all this time one would think I'd have got used to the smell of earth. I sat down to write this and wait for her, but now I'm not angry so much as worried. Serena never goes out at night. She always waits up for me. Where would she go, and why for so long as to let the fire go out? I know some of the village girls go across to the camp to flirt with the soldiers, and for whatever that may lead to. Serena wouldn't. It's not like her. She might have gone to check her goats – or anything, really. Hopeless to try to guess. You never know what ideas she'll get into her head. I think I'd better go and look for her. She might have fallen down and hurt herself. That's not very likely though, she's goat

It's morning now. I'll just finish off that last sentence, where I meant to say she's goat-footed herself. I can hear her goats bleating. They want to be milked. Serena is asleep. I can't go out, because I should be here when she wakes up. I doubt I could milk the goats anyway. I've never tried.

She came back as I was in the process of writing the last paragraph but one. I heard her coming towards the hut, and I went to the door, to open it. I was about to give her some lecture on going out without telling me, but I never got the chance. She stumbled in with her face averted, and tottered across to her bedroom as if both her legs were broken. She shut the door. Through it I could hear her crying.

I picked up a candle and went to her door, intending to go in and find out what was wrong. But she cried, 'Go away.'

I knew then that something was very wrong, not one of her strange little griefs, such as finding a baby bird dead in the grass. Serena never tells me to go away. She always comes to me when something's troubling her, looking sad-eyed like a dog.

'Serena, is there something wrong?'

'No.'

I knew she was lying. This behaviour was even more unlike her than flirting with the soldiers would have been – and *that* I know the poor girl isn't guilty of. I told her I was going to come in, and did so.

Her room is tiny and windowless, nothing more than a bed really. On that bed was a huddled creature catching the candleflame in rabbit-brown eyes. She stopped crying when I came in, and when I got closer she tried to turn her face into the pillow, but even that small movement was too painful for her. I knelt down beside the bed, holding up the candle to see what had happened to her. Her eyes were all red and bulged with crying. Her cheeks had been beaten black and blue, her mouth was bloody, and some of her teeth, and her jaw, were broken.

I asked her who did it, because – I don't know why – I thought it might have been her father.

She opened her mouth to speak. I heard the broken bones grate to-gether. She was in so much pain, and she couldn't scream because scream-ing made it hurt more. She started crying again, coughing blood from her mouth. 'It hurts, it hurts, it hurts . . . '

Nardo, where were you? It hurts.

I didn't know what to do to make it better. I tried to stroke her hair, but even that had been ripped out in handfuls.

Finally, over the course of several hours, I found out everything. Her favourite goat, the little white one, Snowbell, didn't come home with the rest of the flock, so she went to look for it. Under the bridge is a thick growth of dock, and she went down there, calling for her goat, thinking it might have strayed along the river. She was jumped by three or four soldiers; and when she, my uncomprehending little animal, resisted, they beat her into this state and then did it anyway.

When she had told me everything she could grasp of what had happened to her, she asked me, 'Why?'

It's strange how her simple mind brings everything down to its simplest form, and in doing so too often makes it unanswerable. I don't know why. I wish I did. People call this sort of behaviour 'animal', but if I said to her, 'They were animals', it would only add to her bewilderment. The animals have always been her friends. I stroked what was left of her hair. She was shivering like a trapped hare, her broken teeth chattering. I know she still does not understand what they did to her and why they did it, only that it hurt her, and that out of the gentle night and her beloved fields, where she has always been so safe, has come an unimaginable brutality that cannot be, cannot be allowed to be, a part of nature.

In pain, and terrified as she was, she still managed to push her head against my hand and look at me with trust. I held her hand until she fell asleep. I'm going to sit beside her until she wakes up, so she will see me and know that I am here.

After she has woken, and I've made sure she's all right, I am going to go across to the camp and hang them with my own hands, and first of all the Captain, who was busy pouring his fuddled gossip into my ear when he should have been sober, drinking and whining when he should have been protecting Serena, preventing this obscene ravishment of trust.

17

After Caryllac's return, I gave up.

It was as if at some point during that day I had died without feeling it, and now was isolated inside a large glass bottle. Aside from me it was empty, but it seemed full of smoke because everything I saw looked grey. I could see green leaves, red poppies, yellow butterflies, but I was unable to make a connection between these colours and the colours I used to know. I felt as if I was living in some fifth season that shared not one attribute with any of the others, yet had none of its own either. It was never going to move on to any other season. Everything sounded and smelt and tasted grey, and had a dull chill. I found eating a struggle. I often felt that it would take more effort than it was worth to do something imperative: when I needed to relieve myself, or when I was hungry, I would sit and sit, motionless, until I knew I ought to be in pain; but I could not feel it.

Sometimes, if I compared this numbness to the acuity of sensation I had felt a year before, when every one of my nerves had been sharpened to unbearable pain, I would feel a black rage. My anger never lasted long. It was stifled by four words which went round and round in my head: nothing is worth it. This phrase droned in circles until it drowned out every other thought. It seemed impossible that anything should ever change, either to improve enough for me to feel happy, or else to get so bad that I would feel intense suffering.

I had no energy for arguing with her. It wasn't worth it. One day, just after I had woken up from a nightmare, she came striding in with her skirts billowing round her and flung her gloves down carelessly on the table.

'You lazybones, do you know what time it is? It's nearly lunch, I'm starving – look at you, lounging around in bed. I don't think you've any idea of time any more. When did you go to sleep?'

It sounded as if she was talking inside my head. Her words re-echoed round my skull.

'Are you all right, Nardo?' she asked.

'Yes.'

'You're not ill, are you?'

'No.'

'You don't look well. You know, Nardo, you shouldn't sit up half the night reading, then you wouldn't feel so tired during the day.'

'Whatever you say.'

This took her aback, though it hadn't been intended to and in any case I was in no fit state to appreciate my small success. She looked at me as if she had pulled back the bedclothes in expectation of a living body, and had found a heap of pillows instead.

She prodded me harder. 'Reyhnard, at your age this is appalling. You should have half my energy – or your father's. We've been up since six, riding since eight, not to mention the fact that I only got three hours' sleep last night.'

Leave me alone, I thought. It did not seem worth saying out loud: she never listened to me or did anything I asked.

I stared up at the ceiling.

'Oh, get out of that bed,' she said. 'You're irritating me. If you did what we do and fed yourself properly and got some decent sleep you'd soon put on some weight and feel much better.'

'Would you love me then, Beulah?'

'Oh, not again – '

'Let's suppose I was all the things I should be. Suppose I was tall and good-looking and charming like Alexi – '

'Nardo – '

'All right, suppose I rode around all day on a sweating great horse and had muscles like iron and, in general, suppose I was like Hans? Or what if I was old and covered in scars and had a broken nose and no fingers, suppose I was the King – '

'Reyhnard,' she interrupted crossly, 'what is wrong with you?'

'Nothing.' It was so apt I smiled. What's wrong with me is that I feel nothing. How can I know I'm hurt when I can't feel pain? I cannot remember what I used to feel like, what things I used to enjoy, or dislike, or find annoying. Nothing seems pleasurable any more. Nothing seems worth the bother of avoiding. I wanted to scream at her, 'What have you done with me?' Instead, I smiled. I suppose she could not see the truth in that grimace, because she rolled her eyes and said, 'You're so strange, Nardo.'

She watched me for a moment, licked her lip, and went on, 'You *are* strange. You don't have the least idea about anything, do you? You certainly don't know anything about love.'

'I loved you.'

'You don't *love* me.' She stressed the tense sweetly; I knew she neither meant this nor believed it. 'Or, if you do, you have a funny way of showing it. If you loved me, you wouldn't always be thinking about yourself. You'd think about me, about what makes me happy. And you wouldn't keep trying to hit me the way you sometimes do. If you loved me.'

This was a common ploy of hers. My proper response would have been, 'So, you're just using those other men to spur me into loving you more, is that it?' She would then reply, 'You don't understand me at all . . . ' and in the end I would fall to my knees with protestations. This time, though, I could not give her what she wanted. I had nothing left to give.

It turned out that this conversation was leading up to her asking me a favour. While they were out riding that morning, the King had said he was going to give her some new rooms, bigger ones. I'd like them, she said. The problem was, she had grown so awfully fond of my rooms. 'These have such a splendid view,' she said. 'I really would miss it – and you know there aren't any other apartments as nice on this side of the Palace, except Hans's – '

Ah, I thought, she doesn't understand. She's talking about rooms when I'm talking about my being. First she occupied me, now she wants my rooms.

I started to laugh, soundlessly.

'What's so funny?' she said. 'Stop it.'

I could not control myself. At last she went out in a huff, leaving me laughing helplessly.

I didn't see her for twenty-four hours. I spent the next morning in the library, not reading, but because it made a change from sitting in my rooms. As I was returning along the corridor, I looked out of a window. On the edge of the woods I saw the King, and Beulah, and the court, riding towards the Palace. She was indefatigable.

I pressed my head against the window-frame. She would get my rooms, of course. My permission was not necessary. She could take whatever she wanted. She has me surrounded, I thought. Every possible future I could imagine, every road my life might take, she blocked. There was no way around her, never would be; it was pointless to resist. My hope was exhausted. I had no plans, no poems unwritten, no energy left. She had engulfed them all. Peter, my brothers, the King, my writing, all my emotions and my will-power, the whole tapestry of my being consumed by subtle degrees, and none of it, nothing, was worth fighting for any longer.

I felt weightless. I could feel neither the wooden window-frame nor the bone of my brow pressing against it. 'This hurts,' said my skin. After a while I heard it and stepped back.

I sat down and looked through the window, watching Beulah ride up to the Palace, that great concentration of power trailing behind her. The sight overwhelmed me with an extraordinary, tender awe, stronger even than anything I had felt for the King as a child. 'Isn't she wonderful?' I thought. 'She has everything.'

I am trying to be honest, and therefore I have to say that in those moments, and at no other time in my life, I really loved Beulah; or I was on the point of loving her. I loved her power, her absoluteness, her contentment, her total absorption of myself. It was with Beulah, in those few minutes, that I began to know what true love was. I wanted to be her, knowing no other way to regain control of my life.

Madeleine, I wish with all I am that I had told you about this. You would have understood; you understood everything. In recompense, I am writing all my shame out now. I have out-faced it. Madeleine, it wasn't the Beulah we knew, that fat, blonde, flat-footed, plucked and painted woman. I never loved her. I loved that all-powerful everything because I wanted it to give me back myself, still unaware that such a gift was beyond her power.

I'm not sure how long I sat there. Twenty minutes, probably, or half an hour, giving Beulah enough time to come indoors. I saw her climbing the stairs, heading for my room, and at the same time as she approached me a flurry of movement in the courtyard attracted my attention. I looked down; Beulah was beside me.

If Madeleine looked up, what did she see? A monster with two heads. One round, pink-and-white face with bright lips and small brown eyes; a second face, thin and long-nosed, stubbled and grey beneath green eyes, untidy black hair. Two faces as one . . .

Beulah turned to me, looking very put out, and said, 'Oh, it's your sister. I didn't think she'd be here until tomorrow.'

. . . those two faces separating, reclaiming individuality, one woman and one man.

Madeleine might have thought: That woman's beautiful, but why is she frowning? She doesn't look very friendly.

And that man – he looks as if he's seen a miracle.

Almost a miracle, Madeleine. A proof.

All my life I'd had this sense of something lacking, someone missing, a person I had once known very well who had inexplicably disappeared. It was like having a name always on the tip of your tongue, or thinking you'd seen someone you knew in a crowd. I felt that if only I waited, we would be together again as we ought to be. Now, how could I have explained this feeling to Alexi? He laughed at me enough as it was. And, to tell the truth, I did my best to shake it off. I thought: Most likely it is all in my mind. And then, after Beulah, I lost faith in the feeling altogether.

I should have known better. My only mistake was believing that, in Beulah, I had found her.

Madeleine looked up at me and I saw my own face redeemed, stripped of its past, made good as new so that I could start again and do it right this time. She erased all my mistakes and fumbles and despairs as if they had never been. She came to me so quietly, along the one path Beulah could not have foreseen or guarded, and she bore my future in her face – such an unexpected future and yet, for that reason, the only one I could ever have or want to have, because it was the only one nobody could predict, nobody could thwart.

Madeleine, did you have a score of Guards, or ten-score? Plumed prancing horses, and fluttering standards of blue and gold? A hundred porters, two hundred maids? Young girls with baskets who ran before you to lay a carpet of flowers at your feet – the choir of the Gods, and all the birds and beasts, kings and lords of the whole earth bowing, fireworks, canopies of silk, drum rolls, ranking soldiers to line your path, the sun and the moon crowding the sky together, the flames of every temple's porches flaring up to make the day brighter for you?

Well, no, of course there were none of these things. We didn't need such fanfare. The King hadn't bothered, though he had summoned you. There were some strolling nobles staring, several ladies intrigued, a gaggle of lurking pages and one scratching chicken. Alexi came out of the kitchen door. I think he told me you were coming, but it hadn't registered. I know you won't be offended by my telling you this. You rode in on your bay pony, straight-backed you were as always, accompanied by one maid, a pack-horse, two sagging Guards. You slid from your saddle – no hands to help you – and planted your feet firmly on the cobbles, smiled shyly at Alexi when he introduced himself. You lifted your face to ask him a question.

I saw your face. Did you see mine? Did you wonder: Who's that? Is it my own face reflected in the sunlight on the glass? Is it me? It is you, Madeleine. My face raised up to me. You are all my mirrors, my thousand reflections in my two green eyes.

I turned from the window and made for the stairs. Beulah followed me, but I left her behind and ran down, three steps at a time, out into the courtyard to greet my sister.

II

Suppose next that we added one to one; you would avoid saying that the cause of our getting two is the addition, or in the case of a divided unit, the division. You would loudly proclaim that you know of no other way in which any object can come into being except by participation in the reality peculiar to its appropriate universal; and that in the case which I have mentioned you recognise no other cause for the coming into being of two than participation in duality; and that whatever is to become two must participate in this, and whatever is to become one must participate in unity.

Plato, PHAEDO

18

Alexi waved me over.

'Nardo, shut your mouth and open your eyes and you will get a big surprise! This is Madeleine – our sister, will wonders never cease? We've just been introducing ourselves – though I knew you weren't a stranger the moment I saw your face,' he told her. 'Madeleine, this is our brother Nardo.'

'Reyhnard,' I said firmly.

Her eyes ran back and forth like the darting of birds, coming at last to perch on me with a bob and a shy smile. She pulled off her hood, shaking her head, and I saw that hair, my boy's hair, her hair, tangled entrancing blue-black ropes of hair falling straight to her hips. She held out her hands, my hands, to me, smiling the smile I still see in a mirror. Smiling, I see her face, my face, ageing for her who can never now age.

How did I manage to hold up my head? How could I possibly explain my surprise? I could not say, No one told me you were coming, that your name is Madeleine, that I even have a sister. Alexi had told me *a* sister was coming, not this particular sister, this girl, this image of myself planted in front of me like a tree sprung in its full leaf.

With her eyes level before mine, she stretched into me and back over all my memories, so that I could in truth have said that I had always known she was there, and I had always known she was coming, and I had always known she was mine.

I held her hands and felt her wrists. Her pulse was racing. She was nervous, trying hard to be brave. I wanted to hold her as close as I could, yet I was afraid to touch her in case this miracle should vanish as suddenly as it had come.

She glanced quickly from one to the other of us, and asked, 'Am I expected?'

Alexi laughed. 'That's a moot point. I know Father sent for you, but we expected a sister, not another Nardo.' To me he said, 'Have you noticed how alike you two look? You could be twins.'

Shyly, she threw her head forward, her hair unfurling about her.

'Alexi,' I said, 'remember we used to have hair like this when we were children?' I took a length of black softness in my hand, telling her, 'But never this long.'

'It's never been cut,' she said. She looked straight out at me from under her brows; then she coloured and twisted away, hair dripping like water from my open hand.

Alexi had been calling for a servant to come and unload the pack-horse. The soldiers had sloped away. He cupped Madeleine's elbow, and put his other arm through mine.

'So – sister – there's a new word for us to get used to – anyway, Madeleine, you've rendered me quite inarticulate.'

'Which is some achievement,' I said.

He said to me, 'I don't think Beulah will be as pleased as we are.'

Madeleine's eyes met mine again across the breadth of our brother.

'Well,' said Alexi. 'Well.'

He couldn't stop grinning, that delightful ear to ear grin which made one forget so many things about him. It drew a response from Madeleine, little creases appearing in the smooth skin on either side of her mouth. Alexi grinned wider. Abruptly he swooped down and kissed her cheek; when he lifted his head I saw she was blushing again.

'Couldn't resist it, sister,' he teased. 'Now, where to start? I don't want to confuse you. Let's begin at the beginning – do you know how many brothers you've got, sister?' Madeleine shook her head. 'Well, good lord, there's hundreds of us. Four, anyway – God, four, it suddenly sounds like an enormous number. Hans is the oldest, of course, I'm sure you know that – then me, then Reyhnard here, and little Peter, though you wouldn't guess it to look at him. I'm tempted to give you some potted characters, but you'd never remember them now.'

'Give her a chance to catch her breath,' I said.

He said, 'Why don't we find somewhere to sit down? We don't have to go up right away. They're in lunch, and I happen to know you weren't expected until later.'

I said, 'Are you hungry, Madeleine? Are you thirsty?'

'Tell you what,' said Alexi. 'Let's go into the kitchens, there'll be nobody about but the servants. You can have lunch with us. We'll help you find your feet, tell you what's what and so on.'

He paused. 'If it all gets a bit too much for you, say so. I'm sure you'll find it a bit overwhelming at first.'

'Yes, perhaps, a little,' she said. 'I've been on my own a great deal.'

Madeleine, your voice. As clear as glass. I must catch you, wrap your shadowy hair around me and keep fast this little sister who looks ready to fly away back to the mountains she came from.

Alexi led the way to the kitchens. On the doorstep Madeleine hesitated, and looked back to me. She too could hardly believe it, finding herself in this self, my self in her. I ran my hand down her hair from the crown to the nape, ruffling it as I did with Peter. 'Come on in,' I said.

A bug-eyed maid by the fire stared.

'What would you like?' Alexi asked Madeleine.

'Oh, anything. Whatever there is.'

He chuckled. I could see this laughter confused her: she was too new here to allow herself to be either amused or offended. I glared at Alexi, who then pointed out kindly, 'Just about anything you can think of is in these kitchens, Madeleine. So tell me what you fancy, and I guarantee you can have it.'

'I'll have what you're having,' she said.

'It's venison pie for lunch upstairs. Would you like that? And some salad? And fruit cake for afters?'

'You'd better say yes to the fruit cake,' I advised her. 'Alexi's got the sweetest tooth in the country.'

She smiled at that, her first true smile in a flash of happiness. 'I must confess I like sweets myself, so I will say yes, thank you.'

'I can see you're a sister after my own heart,' said Alexi. He sent the maid away to bring the food, and sat our sister at the table. 'Now, how about some wine, or cider?'

'Just water, please.'

'You're sure?'

'Yes, please.'

'Well, think about the wine. I don't want to alarm you, but you never know, you might need it.'

'Don't pay him any attention,' I said. 'Alexi loves to exaggerate.'

'You slanderer!' He cuffed me.

I sat across from her, unable to feign interest in my food. Her movements fascinated me: the way her arm arrowed out as she lifted the glass, the rotation of her shoulder-joint, her tight grip on the knife; the clench and release of the muscles working in her jaw, the flare of her nostrils, the quiet little gulp when she swallowed –

This was how I looked, when I ate.

She was so intense, clean, bold: the blackness of her hair around her fair skin, her deep green eyes, and her face that could not keep still. There was nothing blurred about Madeleine.

Alexi asked her, 'Have you ever met the King?'

She finished her mouthful and, still gripping the knife, answered, 'I'm told I have, but I was too little to remember. It must have been at least sixteen years ago, when we were fighting the Ruffash. He came north and stayed with Lord Randal – he was the father of the family I live with. They told me' – she was reddening again – 'that when I saw him, I screamed, so it's probably just as well I don't remember.'

This I found impossible to believe. Of course she might well have screamed – I remembered my own sick dread of his broken face and spade beard – but I could not, cannot believe that she existed before I saw her, that she had any memories or any life which were not also mine.

She was saying, 'I've been told he's rather scarred and grizzled, but I really can't imagine what he looks like.'

She had simply dropped from the sky, newly created, half an hour old and as old as I was, as if the Gods had suddenly decided to prove their existence by answering my prayers in the most fundamental way, by giving me Madeleine. It was the name on the tip of my tongue . . .

'Nardo, what are you muttering?' asked Alexi.

I said to my sister, 'You've got a very pretty name.'

'Thank you,' she replied, bobbing her head to hide her blush.

'Don't embarrass her,' said Alexi. He smiled at our sister. 'Had enough, Madeleine?'

'Yes, thank you.'

'Well then, just sit here and relax. I'll go up and see what's happening. I'll leave you Nardo for company. I'm afraid he can be a bit grumpy at times, but you can always pretend you're talking to your own reflection.' He chuckled, stuffed some cake into his pocket, and went off.

Madeleine sat straight up in her chair, elbows tucked in, looking any-where but at this man who stared at her.

Now that we were alone, I couldn't think of anything to say. The idea of making forced conversation with her, small talk, was ridiculous. I just wanted to go on looking at her, for reassurance, and to touch her, to make sure that she was real, warm, living flesh, not a wish or a dream.

Madeleine broke the silence. 'Who's Beulah?' she asked.

'She's – I'm married to her.'

'Oh. And he – Alexi – he said you're the youngest?'

'No, no, Peter's the youngest, he's only eleven. Alexi's in the middle, and Hans is about a year and a half older than him.'

'You're the only one that's married, though?'

'Yes.'

I looked up at her. Madeleine's eyes were fixed on her plate. Her hands lay folded in her lap. From a distance we heard the clattering of pans and the crackle of a fire.

'Do you have any children?' she asked.

'No, no, I don't.'

'How long have you been married?'

'Less than a year.'

'She – your wife – she's not foreign, is she? Not with a name like Beulah.'

'No, no, she comes from Uhlanah.'

I couldn't understand why this made Madeleine sigh. 'Oh, that's nice,' she said sadly, glancing down when I looked at her. 'Nice for her, I mean. To be so close to home.'

I couldn't help laughing at that; Beulah had gone to such lengths to shake off her origins. Madeleine retreated into silence. The far-away kitchen noises didn't intrude through the quiet that surrounded us, two people, one man, one woman, one person.

'You don't mind me asking all these questions, do you?' she said.

'No, go ahead, I'm happy to tell you whatever you want to know.'

She fiddled with her knife; then suddenly, before I had time to think, she threw up her head to meet my eyes and demanded, 'Do you think we could be twins?'

'Well – it's possible . . . Has anyone ever said anything to you?'

She shook her head. I think she expected me to know. I couldn't think what to say, how to explain to her the way things were here. 'Well,' I said at last. 'Just because no one's talked about it doesn't mean it can't be true.'

'How old are you?'

'Nearly twenty. How old are you?'

'I don't know. When I was old enough to ask, no one could remember exactly.'

'You're obviously not forty-five.'

I said this to make her laugh, because she was beginning to look very serious. I was rewarded with a half-hearted smile before she went on, 'I suppose the King – I mean, Father – would know. I might be twenty-one. That's the age girls usually come home, if they're not married already. Do you think I look older than you?'

I think that we are the same in every way, that I was born with you and you with me, and that we will die together, Madeleine, night-haired and star-eyed, my perfect polished mirror of a sister.

'I don't know,' I said. 'It's hard to tell.'

She asked me, 'Do you know why I've been sent for?'

As it happened, she thought she had the answer to this question, but was hoping I would come up with a better one. I didn't know this. I only wanted to say: Why doesn't matter. You are here and you came for me.

'Does there have to be a reason?' I replied.

Madeleine was playing with her hair, winding and unwinding it around her fingers. 'Lady Catherine – Lord Randal's wife, you remember, the lady I live with – she said that the King, Father, was arranging a marriage for me with a Prince of Pravarre. I was wondering if you knew anything about it.'

'No,' I said, meaning, No I don't know anything about it, and also, No of course it's not true, life would not be so perverse as to give you to me only to take you away.

She pushed at her hair, wiped it back untidily from her face. Her eyes, my eyes, were close to tears, and her mouth, my mouth, was trembling, and Madeleine, my brave Madeleine who had so much courage, needed mine. 'I'm so scared,' she said, hiding her face behind slender, bony, familiar hands.

I shoved my chair back with a clatter and went round to her, taking her hands to chafe those cold fingers between mine. 'Don't be,' I said, tucking her hair behind her ear. 'Don't be scared.'

I knew, of course, that it was highly unlikely that the King, who had ignored her for nearly twenty years, should now bring her home for no reason at all. I ought to have been as frightened as she was; instead I felt happy, kneeling beside her, holding her hand. I was quite sure then that she would never marry this man. I seemed to know that, just as I had always sensed she was there, so she would never leave.

Alexi came back in.

'It's all set,' he said. 'He'll be waiting for you in the Dove Salon in about an hour, which just about gives you time to change – Nardo! You've made her cry.'

'No,' she said. 'No, he didn't.'

Madeleine, I will never make you cry.

'Well,' said Alexi. 'Perhaps you'd like that wine now?'

I promised Madeleine I'd wait while she changed. She came down in a russet dress, and I took her to the salon.

The air was noticeably hotter when we reached the threshold, gusting out from that noisy room crowded with people. The door gaped. Madeleine stopped. Wide-eyed and shy, poised like a doe at bay, wanting to flee but ready to make a stand – she put a hand on my arm.

Don't you know yet that I would tear my insides out for you if that could make this easier? I would lay myself down like a carpet to carry you through this. They will swoop and point and chatter, they will catch at your arms, your legs, your hair, anything they can get their hands on. They will try to pin you against the flat boards of this court like some alien butterfly. But they can't hurt you if you don't let them. I'll show you. I'm here, and whatever I can do for you, I will.

As I thought all this, she listened to it gravely; then she nodded, lifted her hem, and plunged in.

Soon the worst was over. Madeleine held her chin up and met her ordeal. the King kissed her, presented her to the court, called her his beloved daughter, and set her free in the room; she didn't scream once, and the King made no mention of the rumoured marriage. Her shoulders tensed up as she moved about, enduring the introductions. She walked so carefully, like a wild bird put into an aviary, afraid to take wing because the nets might be anywhere. Madeleine has a grace which is as far removed from Beulah's as a waterfall is from a fountain, and her natural modesty took refuge behind her courtesy. It wasn't long before she made her way back to my side. Her breath was coming short and quick, little beads of sweat clinging to the short hairs at her temples.

'I'm sorry it was so awful,' I said, low enough for only Madeleine to hear. 'It's over now. Are you all right?'

Her eyes were unlike any I have ever seen. They were like Peter's, when he was new-born. Like mine must have been on the first day I opened them.

She breathed deep, and said, 'It wasn't as bad as I thought it would be. That's the best way, I suppose, to think something's going to be worse than it turns out to be. Anyway, I'm silly really to be scared of meeting big crowds of people. If I – '

But she broke off there, her attention drawn away to the crowds that were parting as Beulah came through.

Madeleine must have caught some of my tension, for I felt her stiffen too, though her eyes remained frank, friendly, honest.

'Darling, I'm so sorry I'm late.' Beulah manufactured a smile at once contrite and delighted. 'Are you going to introduce us?'

So I had to go through the motions: 'Madeleine, this is the Lady Beulah; Beulah, this is the Princess Madeleine, my sister.'

'Darling, one can see *that* without being told. Now I would have said one of you was as much as anyone could hope for, but then that's just my opinion.'

'Beulah – '

'Oh – ' Her nails bit into my wrist. She had come closer to me than

Madeleine was, and pressed herself against my arm, speaking to my sister across me. 'You mustn't take offence, Madeleine – my husband's always telling me I'm a terrible tease. Seeing you standing together here gave me such a funny feeling of seeing double.'

Madeleine extended a hand and said, 'It's lovely to find one sister among four brothers.'

'These northern manners are so pretty, aren't they, Nardo.'

Innocent Madeleine, innocent of the snub. Beulah, though maintaining a gracious smile, failed to take my sister's hand. She did this in such a way that one might believe she hadn't seen it.

She said, 'That's a lovely dress. Where did you get it?'

'Thank you. I made it.'

'No! Really? How competent you are. It seems to run in the family, doesn't it, Nardo?' Beulah paused, as if considering a notion; then she continued in generous tones, 'Would you be offended at a word of advice, Madeleine?'

'Oh no, please.'

'Well, dear, the thing is, at court we don't make our own dresses. It's rather a pity really, you're obviously a wonderful seamstress. Of course we embroider and sew shirts for our men – ' This was beyond a joke: I've never seen Beulah embroider, and I doubt she can. 'Now I hope you're not angry with me. I do think it's a splendid dress, but I thought I ought to warn you straight away, before somebody said something.'

It was a perfect dress, velvety and straight, as much a foil to my sister's beauty as Beulah's pink-and-silver ruffles were a frill around hers.

Madeleine ran a hand down her hip, suddenly aware of some unexplained feminine gaucherie – and to you, Beulah, must go the magnificent credit of being the first one to humiliate her.

My sister said simply, 'Thank you. I hadn't realised.'

Beulah waved a hand gaily, 'Well, there's no reason why you should.'

'At home – up north – all the girls make their own dresses. We're all expected to be able to do that.'

'And a very useful thing too, but remember, you're in Tsvingtori now' – and I am Queen here, so watch your step, interloper – 'Ah!' Beulah cried. 'I see a beckoning finger. I must away. I'll come and find you soon and we can have a proper chat.'

I watched her walk through the crowds, feeling the same incredulous astonishment as, perhaps, a man might feel to wake and find his amputated limbs have been restored to him.

This could not be the same woman who, less than three hours before, I had watched riding at the head of the court. That woman had been a conquering deity with the gift of all things in her hand, before whom I had been ready utterly to abase myself. In her place stood this girl-sized imitation: a Beulah who was short, plump, chubby-cheeked, with a flat-footed walk and an insinuating nastiness. This was the girl Alexi had always seen.

I watched her trip through the parting courtiers, and for the first time I realised her plumpness made her slightly knock-kneed. She gave her hand to the King, who stooped to kiss the top of her head. She was a round young girl. And he was a burly, middle-aged man, thickening at the midriff.

'She seems very popular,' said Madeleine. 'Is Father very fond of her?'

'You could say that.'

Contempt, amusement, relief, plain happiness – it all came out in my voice. Madeleine, listening, furrowed her black brows and said thoughtfully, 'You don't like her, do you?'

'I loathe her.'

'But – but you're married to her.'

'That's not my fault.'

Madeleine began to tug at the short hairs behind her ear, craning her head round to study Beulah. 'I should think a lot of men would envy you,' she said. 'I envy her. I always wanted to look like that – small and blonde and beautiful.'

'You're better the way you are.'

'Skinny and sallow.' Madeleine laughed. 'That's what Lady Catherine used to say. She said I was lucky to be a King's daughter, because she couldn't imagine who would look at me twice otherwise.'

'She sounds to me like a very stupid woman.'

Madeleine opened her mouth to protest, green eyes wide. Oh, I wanted to laugh and hug her, kiss her, pick her up and dance her around the room to thank her. More than limbs restored, I had been given a new pair of eyes to see Beulah with.

Those eyes were watching the crowd again. While Madeleine was thus occupied, her thumb came up to her mouth and she began to chew it, making clicking noises, seeming to be unaware of what she was doing. I saw that the poor thumb, precious as even the smallest part of her is infinitely dear, was red and sore.

'Your poor thumb,' I said.

She snatched it down and folded it under her fingers, looking guilty, 'I'm sorry, it's a bad habit – I know it's annoying. Lady Catherine used to put garlic on it and tie my hand behind my back. I was cured, but it's come back.'

'Pity to ruin such a pretty hand.'

'Oh – ' The thumb was fighting to reach her mouth, but Madeleine fisted it down. 'Please, I'm sorry – you make me feel uneasy when you flatter me – '

'It's not flattery.'

'You're only saying that because I look like you.' She tried to change the subject, asking, 'Does everyone call you Nardo?'

'Yes, unfortunately. Well, not the King. It was Alexi's nickname for me, and it stuck, but I hate it.'

'Then I promise not to use it. Where is he?' She stood on tip-toe, scanning the crowd. 'I haven't seen him.'

'He isn't here, neither is Hans, or Peter. I'll take you to see them later.'

'Why didn't they come?'

'As you can see, it's not much fun. None of us comes if we can avoid it. And Peter's too young.'

'Look, that young man over there, the one talking to your – Beulah. I think I met him, but it was all so fast. He's not one of our brothers, is he?'

'No, that's Nikolas Rayallah. His father is Lord Rayallah, the King's brother. He's our cousin. He's supposed to be one of the best-looking men at court.'

'Is he?'

'Don't you think so?'

Madeleine seemed fascinated by the two of them. 'I think *she's* a flirt,' she said, watching Beulah's movements.

'Why does she interest you so much?'

'She's in my family. My family interests me. I've never had one before.'

Her expression grew puzzled as she watched Beulah kiss the cheeks of first one man, then another. I realised I had to warn my sister, now; to leave it a day might be to leave it too late.

'Madeleine, I have to tell you something . . . '

Irises green Brychmachrye, mirror-black pupils holding two Reyhnards intently returning my gaze.

I said, 'I hope you can understand this, but if you can't it just shows you're a better person than she is. Since I'm the only one that's married, Beulah is – she takes precedence over all the other women. She opens the dances, sits at the head of the table, receives the ambassadors, that sort of thing. The thing is, it means a great deal to her. More than anything else, really. And now you're here so you – you're going to take over from her. Supplant her, I suppose, is how she would see it.'

Madeleine was very quiet, taking this in. When I had finished she said, 'I wondered why she didn't like me.'

'Believe me, "didn't like" is far too mild a phrase for her. And "hate" isn't subtle enough.'

'But I don't want to take any of those things away from her. I don't want to do any of them. I'd hate it.'

'That's the way things are.'

Madeleine bit her thumb hard, saying round it, 'I don't think that's a very good reason for anything.'

I drew her hand away from her mouth, closing mine around her thumb to protect it. 'It's the only one there is,' I said.

She disengaged her hand, took a step back and looked all around her, seeing the way things were: ceilings and walls closing in on her, the locks on the window shutters, a roomful of nameless strangers distinguished only by the varying smartness of their clothes, talking together so loudly that it was impossible to hear what anyone was saying. The mountains and the sky were out of reach.

She hugged herself in her thin arms. I would hold her, if only she would ask me. In this place you have no one to rely on except the ones whose blood you share. I don't know if that's how it is in the rest of the world, but that's how it is here, and this is where I live.

Madeleine said, 'Would it be very rude of me to ask you why you don't like her? You can tell me not to be so nosy, if you don't want to talk about it.'

'I don't.'

'I'm sorry, I shouldn't have asked.'

'It's all right. I don't mind. I will tell you one day. But I don't want to talk about it now.'

I intended to hold on to the integrity I had rediscovered in my sister, who takes me at my own worth, who, more than that, gives it back to me. Soon enough someone would tell her, and enjoy it. Before that happened I would have put such palisades around my sister that they could never reach in to cripple her straight-backed judgment, or drag her down the dirty alleyways of court intrigue and gossip, smearing their greasy fingers across her flawlessness.

Madeleine, I am a strong-box. I have you locked in my head for safe-keeping. Every word, every gesture, every smile is remembered. And now here I am putting you down on paper, Madeleine, giving my treasure away.

I need her now as much as I ever did. I needed her when I didn't even know her name or who she was. I was like a puzzle to myself, knowing I had a piece missing and wondering what it was. I cannot forget what my life was like before she came; and now it is the same again, the same gradual destitution of my soul. These scribblings make being alive so much harder to bear when I get up from the table, from the paper, leaving her behind.

19

I was happy to let Madeleine drag me all over the Palace and its grounds. She was as bursting with energy and curiosity as Peter had been when he was three years old. 'What's this?' she asked. 'What's that? Who lives here, what's this for, isn't this lovely, isn't this strange?' It was so long since I had spared a thought for such things that our discoveries fascinated me as much as her. All too often I didn't know the answer – 'And you've lived here your whole life!' she would chide. She taught me anew what I had first learnt with Peter: how much can pass you by when you start to take things for granted. I never wondered, for example, whether the little purple and blue flowers that grow in damp earth had a name. Madeleine knew it: soldiers and sailors. 'Look at this panelling, can't you see the little faces? I think it was carved like that on purpose.' 'Look, look at this sunset, we never have sunsets like this in the mountains.' 'Look at this step, it's worn away. How many people have walked over it, do you think?' Indoors she was always on guard, thinking twice before she spoke or took a step, but once under the open sky she would hoist up her skirts and run, dashing from a flower to a statue to a snail's shell, or to whatever her insatiable interest might alight on next.

She liked to feed the fishes in the pond. We sat on the marble rim, looking into the water, watching the carp swim in and out between the lily-pads, fat brown wedges with golden eyes. In the early evening the water rippled with a warm bronze light, breaking into circles of silver where the fish rose to the surface. Madeleine was throwing them breadcrumbs from a pile in her lap. 'Oh look!' she said. 'That one's so greedy.'

'Are you settling in?' I asked her.

'I like my rooms. My bedroom's bigger than the one I had at home, so I felt a bit lost in it at first. But I can just see a bit of the city from my window. What's Tsvingtori like?'

'I don't know. I've never been down there.'

'What, never?'

'Not into the city. None of us do – well, we're not supposed to. Alexi goes down sometimes, I think, but he shouldn't really. Hans goes down once in a while, to keep Alexi company.'

'I wish I could.'

'Why?'

'I've never seen a city. I think it would be exciting, all those people. But there's lots of people here, too – I suppose I should get used to this place first. Haven't you ever wanted to go down?'

'Not really. If you're not supposed to do something, it's a waste of time thinking about it.'

Madeleine laughed. 'I'm afraid I do, all the time. But you're probably right, it's better not to.' She scattered crumbs across the pond, and when her hand was empty she let it fall, splashing into the water. 'It's warm,' she remarked, and looked up at the setting sun. 'The light's different here, too. I think it's because at home it shines off the mountains morning and evening. It gets cold very quickly when the sun goes down. Have you ever been to the mountains?'

'I haven't been anywhere but here.'

'Don't you ever feel – well, don't you ever want to get out?'

Her brows were lifted, her lips slightly parted, her head bent a little forward and to one side, all seriousness. Perhaps I looked like this when I was asking something important. This idea so intrigued me that I said automatically, 'I am out.'

'I mean outside the Palace grounds.'

'As I said, if you can't, you don't think about it. Hans has been all over the place, though. Alexi has this game, when he asks you where you'd choose if you could go anywhere in the world. Do you really want to go back to the mountains?'

'I didn't want to leave. Now I'm here, I don't know any more. I didn't have lots of friends at home or anything like that, and I'm not missing Lady Catherine and everyone as much as I thought I would. He seems very fond of you.'

'Who?'

'Alexi.'

'He's . . . ' But suddenly I no longer knew what I wanted to say. Even the gist of my thoughts had become elusive, so instead I said lamely, 'He seems to be a lot of things.'

'Of course Hans is his great friend. Like you and Peter. I feel a little sorry for Peter.'

'Why?'

'I don't know, because he's still a boy and you're all grown up.'

'Alexi is as much older than I as I'm older than Peter.'

'I know. He's lucky to have someone who loves him as much as you do. I like him. I wish . . . '

'What, Madeleine?'

She was holding her breath, eyes shut, wishing hard. Then she breathed out and said, 'Millions of things. You know, at home Lady Catherine had two daughters, but they were both so much older than me, they got married years ago. I am glad I came here. I hope . . . I'm not boring you, am I?'

'Far from it, I'm fascinated. Go on.'

She reached for my hand and turned it over in hers. First she looked at my palm, then at my face, and leaned forward to kiss my cheek. 'When I was growing up,' she said, 'I knew about you, I mean about all you brothers, but you didn't seem real. I never thought I'd meet you, any more than I'd meet Michah the Conqueror. And now all of a sudden you're all real. I don't want to sound silly, but it does feel strange. In a nice way.' She curled her hand round mine. 'Something nice to get used to. I like all of you, but I like you most. I suppose that's not the sort of thing people say here.'

'If they don't, they ought to.'

'Maybe they can't. I think a lot of them don't know what they feel, but I'm probably wrong. Here,' she filled my hand with crumbs. 'You feed them.'

Writing this out has jogged my memory, and I've thought of something else she asked me. I'd forgotten it because of what she said immediately afterwards, which stuck in my mind and overshadowed the first thing. She asked me, 'Do you like it here?' Also, I think I forgot it because at the time it was a meaningless question. I had nothing to compare it to. Do I like living in this village? Not much, but then I have no reason either to stay or to leave.

'Do you like it here?' she asked.

'It's my home.'

She got up, shaking out her skirts, and said quietly, 'I hope he lets me stay.'

About three weeks after my sister's arrival, we were informed that the court was to move to Ksaned Kaled.

I had never seen it, that green house on a gold island which the King had built in the first years of his reign. Hans and Alexi were both born there, but the court hadn't gone back since Alexi was five. Hans became more than usually taciturn when he heard this news – there's practically nothing to hunt on Ksaned Kaled. Alexi, however, was in high spirits. Madeleine and I asked him what it was like.

'It's not like anywhere. It's the most beautiful place in the world.'

Later, when we happened to be alone together, he said to me, 'I'm pleased, of course I'm pleased. I've been dying to go back. But I wish I knew why we're going *now* . . . '

'Maybe he just wants to.'

'Come on, you know him, he's always got a reason. Have you asked Beulah?'

'I never see her if I can help it.'

He slapped me on the back. 'I must say I've noticed the improvement. Congratulations. Oh, by the way, you don't think it could be what Maddy said, do you?'

'What?'

'That he's fixed a marriage for her with whatshisname, Prince Julius of Pravarre. It's the only explanation I can think of. You see, the way it sometimes works is, the prospective groom comes over at the end of the summer, spends the winter with the bride's family, and then they get married in the spring and go home. Gives them a chance to make sure they're not completely incompatible.'

'Oh no,' I said, 'surely not. He could do that just as well here as on Ksaned Kaled.'

'But Ksaned Kaled's so much more impressive, and a better place to spend the winter in, especially for a man from Pravarre. Nardo, don't look so worried – they won't be sending her away just yet.'

'She's only just got here.'

'I know, but that's how it works. Anyway, you know Father wouldn't have brought her here for no reason. What's wrong? You've gone quite white – you have got attached to her quickly, haven't you? I've noticed you're becoming very close. I suppose it was bound to happen. You know, I think Peter's getting a little jealous. Not to mention Beulah.'

'I wouldn't care if I never saw Beulah again, and neither would she.'

'But she'd be over the moon if she never saw Maddy again. You saw her face last night, when Madeleine opened the dance with Father. Poor thing, a blind man could have seen she hated doing it, but that doesn't cut any ice with Beulah. You mark my words, little Maddy's going to be posted off to pastures new faster than Beulah can bat her eyelids.'

'Alexi,' I said, 'please, do me a favour. Please don't mention any of this to Madeleine. You know how frightened she is. Just let her – let her think it's nothing out of the ordinary.'

He rubbed his finger across his upper lip, and went on doing this for some time, saying nothing; though his eyes were half-shut I knew he was examining me closely. Finally he said, 'You know, whatever people say, she's not really all that much like you, although physically you could be twins.'

'What do you mean?'

'If it's true, I think she'd want to be told. She's a grown woman, and she has grown up knowing what's in store for her. Don't you think she has a right to know?'

'She has a right to be happy for as long as she can. Anyway, you're not sure about this, it's just speculation.'

We travelled by ship, which is the right and proper way to approach the island. This is how myths are born, and one can uncover their origins by looking at our own lives: for the man who dreamed up Hulsitoq must have been thinking of Ksaned Kaled. It was night when we arrived, weighing anchor off the beach, and so my first sight of the island was in early morning. I rose before the others and went out on deck, leaning on the rail.

Watercolour blue waves rocked our ship, rippling on past to brush up the pebbly white sand. Beyond the beach was a thick wood of cedars and umbrella pines, and between the two was a narrow patch of yellow earth and scrub grass, dotted with poppies. Turnstones and sandpipers bobbed through the shallows. The seagulls were on the wing, hovering above our ships, their coarse screams urging us to hurry up with breakfast.

In the damp breeze, slightly salt, very fresh, I caught a hint of the fragrance of flowers.

Lilies-of-the-valley, violets, carnations, lavender, freesias . . . Madeleine could name them all, but I cannot. I know the scent of roses, though, field upon field of roses that shame the meagre bushes of Tsvingtori to call themselves a garden. These flowers take up almost the whole of the island, and are harvested to become the most famous perfumes in the world.

The factories, where the flower essence is distilled, used to be on the island, but they were moved to the mainland when the King built the Palace, and a town has grown up around them. The villages on the island come back to life during the summer, when their erstwhile inhabitants are allowed back to care for the crop. It must be a life spent breathing flowers that makes the natives of Ksaned Kaled such sunny, blooming people. When we are in residence on the island, most of the servants, except for favourites we bring from Tsvingtori, are recruited from the local population, and they make part of the pleasure of living there. One has the sense of being buoyed up and supported by a sweet, living carpet of contented humanity.

I understand there are all sorts of reasons why Ksaned Kaled is so suited to the cultivation of flowers. The woods which fringe its coast act as a break to the mild wind, so that the centre of the island is sheltered, warm and calm. The climate is very temperate; on the east coast palm trees grow, the only ones in Brychmachrye. But these scientific explanations don't interest me. Ksaned Kaled is a place of magical beauty, a wonderful abundance of scent and colour, an island so awash with flowers that to live on it is to lie like a honeybee in the heart of the flower itself.

Standing there, gazing across the sea and the land, I saw a doe. Trumpet ears and liquid eye stepping out from the woods, dab of brown against green poised to regard our fleet. Suddenly she shied and bolted through the trees. I turned to see what the doe had seen, and found my sister.

Weight thrown on one hip, elbows on the rail, resting beside me. 'Good morning,' she said.

I kissed her cheek.

'It's so lovely here,' she exclaimed. 'I can smell the flowers.'

'I saw a doe.'

'Where?'

'Just down there – she's run away.'

'Don't tell Hans.' Madeleine smiled. 'Oh, I wish we could go over there now and have an exploration, before anyone else is up.' She turned to me eagerly. 'Why don't we?'

'How could we get there?'

'We could take down one of the little landing boats. Or, no, that would make too much noise. We could swim.'

'Not in your dress.'

'I can take it off. Oh, come on, let's.'

'They might think we'd drowned.' I picked up a knot of glossy black from her shoulder. 'You haven't even brushed your hair yet.'

'I hate brushing it. Lady Catherine made me brush it a hundred times every morning and every evening. It's so tiring, and I hate having the maid do it, she never knows when it hurts. I wish I could have it cut short, like yours.'

'Oh no – don't cut it, it's beautiful.'

'Lady Catherine said it was my only beauty. That's why she'd never cut it. She said, "I don't care what they do at court, I won't have her shorn." '

'Honestly, Madeleine, you think far too much about that woman and her pearls of wisdom. You're with your family now.'

Her fingers reached down and gripped the rail as she swung back, balancing on her heels, the tangled hair unravelling off her shoulders. 'Are you happy?' she asked me.

'What does that mean?'

I was treated to a very long-suffering look. 'You pretend to be such a cynic sometimes,' she said. 'But I know you're not really. I feel I could be happy, here – I don't know, it just seems as if one piece is missing.'

'So what's the piece?'

'I don't know. The not knowing, I suppose.'

'About what?'

'Why we're here.'

'Madeleine, if the King was planning a marriage for you, he'd tell you.'

'Would he?'

I cannot lie to Madeleine's eyes. 'No. Probably not,' I admitted.

Madeleine retrieved a length of hair and began to plait the tangles. Her thumb crept up to her mouth, but she saw my frown, put the thumb away, and said, 'Can I tell you something?'

'Anything you like.'

'It's about being happy. I thought, maybe you're right, it doesn't mean anything. But then I thought it *must* do. At least, one knows what it means to *want* to be happy, just like you know what it means to be tired or hungry, so – '

'Nardo! Nardo!'

My little red-headed soldier, not so little any more, but still small enough to give his brother a hug in the morning. His cheeks were crumpled from sleep, bearing the crease-patterns of the pillow; his shirt-tail hanging out, eyes sparkling with the dawn sea air.

'Say good morning to your sister,' I ordered.

'Good morning, Madeleine.' Then quickly back to me, 'Nardo, what a super place. I bet there's lots of rabbits. Can we come here tomorrow and look for some burrows?'

'If you want. Madeleine can come too.'

'Nardo – ' Peter leant up to my ear. 'I want just us to go.'

Madeleine overheard, but her good nature never faltered. 'That's all right, Peter. I'll have far too much to do tomorrow.'

'Do come if you want,' I said.

'Everybody's getting up,' Peter informed her.

Madeleine glanced behind her, and said, 'Then I'd better go and brush my hair.' She walked away across the deck. The outer strands of her hair were lifted by the breeze, as was her skirt, folding and refolding like living sculpture around her legs.

When she was gone, I said to Peter, 'You were very rude.'

'No I wasn't.'

'She is your sister, you know, and she's a stranger here.'

'She's just a girl.'

'I thought you were getting rather keen on girls.'

Peter reddened, rubbed his nose, but managed to hold up his end. 'Not on sisters,' he said firmly. 'Anyway, she isn't even pretty.'

'Yes she is, she's very pretty.'

'Not as pretty as Beulah.'

I don't know what to say about that. It's so easy now to recognise all the chances I let slip. I should have said something then. Really what I should have done was kill her. I could have done it so easily, that morning, gone to her cabin and wrapped one of her stockings around her sleeping throat. Instead, all I did was laugh, tug Peter's belt and say, 'Let's go and find our breakfast.'

We disembarked several hours later. The King rode in the carriage ahead of us, sitting next to Hans. Peter had climbed into a carriage further back, where he was wreaking havoc with his friends. Alexi, Madeleine, Beulah and I were together. Beulah was wearing a wide-brimmed hat which shaded her face. She was sitting beside me, her thigh bumping against mine until I shifted away from her. She looked up from under her hat, showing big brown eyes and biting her lower lip. That old trick. I was more interested in the scenery.

Madeleine's face was slightly sunburnt, making her green eyes greener, and she twisted about in her seat as Alexi pointed out this and that to her. 'That clump of trees,' he said. 'Hans and I used to have a sort of fort there. Wonder if it's still standing.'

'I can see it!' Madeleine announced. 'Did you build it?'

Our procession moved slowly up a poplar-lined avenue running per-spective-straight across the undulation of colours which is the landscape of Ksaned Kaled. Fields of yellow roses, red roses, white lilies, pale blue lavender, squared into blocks by box-hedges.

Madeleine cried, 'Oh!'

At the end of the avenue a green and white palace lifted its proud roofs into the air. The entablature was of abalone marble, the fluted pillars of serpentine, the frieze banded by a narrow circlet of flame, sunlight on gold. From this distance it looked oddly one-dimensional, like a book illumination, against its pastel-brushed background of smooth blue sky and silk-cocoon clouds. Perhaps it was the dew steaming up in the hot sun which made it shimmer, but I prefer to think that this delicate, stately house had so absorbed the essence of the island that it really did float amongst its palette of flower-fields. The solid draperies of stone were hazy, as if they were melting.

'It's like a sugar house!' said Madeleine.

More than a work of architecture, a work of art, monument to a great King: the palace of Ksaned Kaled rich in the sun. So fragile and acute was its perfection, it seemed a sacrilege to walk in it.

Beulah said, 'I hope they've aired it properly.'

'Don't worry,' said Alexi. 'I'm sure they've heard you're coming.'

We drew up in front of it, and saw that it was after all set firm in its foundations. The footman helped Beulah out, her skirts tucked up to show an ankle, and she set her small foot down on the marble step. When she lifted it, she left a print in the dust.

She took off her hat, threw it to a maid, and walked up to where the King was waiting for her.

Madeleine watched them, and saw the King's fingers run down Beulah's neck. I heard my sister make a little noise, the sort of noise Peter used to make when he was five years old, when he was playing with a join-the-dot puzzle and had finally seen the shape.

I was standing out of the carriage, waiting to help her down. She held my hand tight, and even when she was on the ground she would not let it go.

'I see,' she said.

'Were you told?' I asked her. 'Or did you guess?'

'Neither, I just saw. Reyhnard, I must either be very naïve or very stupid. It is obvious, isn't it?'

'You're simply innocent. You should be proud of it. They don't try to hide it. They've got no reason to. Everyone knows, everyone accepts it. He's always had mistresses. It's a standing thing.'

'It must be awful for you. I can see now why you hate her.'

'Yes – no – it's not just that. She was his mistress before he made me marry her.'

'He *made* you?'

She was staring at her toes in embarrassment, which left me free to say, 'Yes, he made me.'

And so Madeleine never knew.

After a while, she asked, 'Why didn't he marry her himself?'

'She'd like to know that as much as anyone. At the time he made some long speech about having loved Mother too much – '

'Did he?'

'Who knows?'

'Did Mother love him?'

'I don't know. I mean, their marriage didn't have anything to do with love, did it? Most marriages don't. I don't know, Madeleine, I don't know what goes on in his head. No one does. I can't tell you why he hasn't married again, but I'm sure it isn't because he's sacred to the memory of our mother. Alexi thinks it's because he likes to know there was something he could say "No" to Beulah about. And of course he loves Hans.'

'Yes, I see. I think. Oh, it's so confusing.'

'He's not the only one.'

'Who? What?'

'Not her only lover. Any place, any time, any one – that's her motto. She's a hateful person.'

'I am sorry.'

'Don't be. It would be far worse if I' – and Madeleine was still not looking at me – 'loved her.'

'Yes, I see. Oh, what a mess – still, people make their own messes, they've got no one to blame but themselves. Except you, but you're blameless really. I remember you saying it wasn't your fault you're married to her. I thought that was funny, but I see what you meant. I'm afraid – I'm afraid I don't think much of him.'

'He's a great king.'

'He's not much of a father, though, is he?'

'He loves Hans.'

'Yes, you said. But there are three others of you.' She paused. 'Lord Randal was a good father.'

'I don't think I've ever heard you mention him.'

'I loved him. Perhaps one doesn't talk much about people one loved. He died several years ago. He used to think up the most marvellous games.'

Listening to her, it made me wonder whether sending Madeleine away to be brought up in a strange family, that custom which other kingdoms think is so cruel, was not in fact the kindest thing he ever did for any of us.

'You must be very sorry to have left them.'

She brushed my hair from my forehead, and put her thin strong arms around my shoulders. 'It was my home, you know,' she said. 'But not any more. Reyhnard? I'm glad you're not hurt.'

I laid my hand on top of hers, holding it against my neck. Beneath her wrist I could feel the little bones, and the blood beating. I encircled it with my fingers, that narrow wrist, and brought it down to kiss as one should kiss a sister's hand. 'Come on, mountain-goat,' I said. 'Let's pick some flowers for your hair.'

20

In that first year on Ksaned Kaled I had rooms at the back of the Palace. My windows opened on to the kitchen courtyard, where the maids sang early in the morning; if I leaned out I could see, right against the wall, beds of wallflowers arranged in patches of bright colour like the paints in Peter's box. Bay trees stood in tubs on the cobbles, and on the far side of the courtyard was planted an efficient-looking herb garden sending up aromas of thyme, sage, rosemary, mint, fennel . . . Beyond this was a landscaped wood, with a little stream that ran by the toy-house the King had built for my mother. On the horizon ran a feathery line of cedar-tops, their green so dark it was almost black against the blue-white sky.

A secondary staircase ran down from my bedroom to the kitchen passage on the ground floor. This passage forks off about ten yards left from the staircase: one arm leads to the dining hall, and the other, curiously, follows the outer perimeter of the Palace walls until it reaches a set of steps leading up to the library. Ksaned Kaled's library is very different from the one at Tsvingtori: it is cool and airy, marbled and tiled, full of clear light.

The morning after we arrived on the island, I was dawdling along this passage and enjoying the view through the windows when the library door opened and Beulah came down the steps.

'There you are,' she said. 'I want to have a word with you.'

'I don't,' I said, pushing past her.

'It's about your sister.'

This stopped me. I turned around. Beulah was looking very put out about something. 'Well, what is it?'

'Nardo, you ought to remind her that she's a princess, not a goat-girl. She was wearing a wreath of flowers when she came into dinner last night.'

'I know. I thought they looked very pretty.'

'I might have known. *You* may choose to behave like a lout but that's no reason for her to look like a peasant. Didn't you see people staring? The King was very embarrassed.'

'Why doesn't he tell her, then?'

'I'm telling you.'

'Beulah – I'd be extremely surprised if the King ever noticed anything anyone did or said or wore, except for you. I really don't care what the court thinks, and I think those flowers looked lovely on Madeleine, so I'll tell you what, if you didn't like them, you go and tell her. Go on, have a treat, go and snub her. Except you don't need my permission for that, do you?'

'Oh, Reyhnard – ' She put a hand to my cheek. 'What's got into you lately?'

'Nothing.' I pulled away from her touch. 'Who's got into you?'

'As if you'd care.'

'Quite true, I don't – oh, stop that.' She was making her upper lip tremble, her eyelashes tremble, her eyes glisten. She said tremblingly, 'I don't believe you care at all for me, any more.'

'It's a bit late to tell me that that matters.'

'Oh Reyhnard, how can you talk like that?'

I had to bend down steeply to bring my eyes level with hers – and I am not particularly tall – and I said, 'I know you too well for this. You can't get round me any more. If I ever find you in my rooms again I will go out and sleep on the floor in my brothers' rooms. It's over, and I don't think you can actually pretend it matters to you, not with a straight face.'

'Who is it?' she demanded.

'Who is what?'

'Who are you in love with?'

I straightened up. Did she really think I needed another woman to make me lose interest in her? Did she honestly believe I was in love with someone else? She sounded as if she meant it, but that never counts for anything with Beulah. I was on the point of reassuring her, when I decided not to give her the satisfaction.

'If I was in love with someone,' I said, 'do you think I'd tell you?'

'I'll find out.'

'What makes you so positive I am?'

'Oh, but Nardo, why have you changed towards me?'

I could have laughed at this unexpected streak of naïvety, only I didn't believe in it. 'Because I'm better off the way I am now, obviously.'

She sidled up to me and replaced her hand on my face, rubbing it silkily up and down. 'Don't you miss me at all?' she asked, giving a splendid impersonation of wistfulness.

'Of course. Like you miss a rotten egg when someone's cleaned out the cupboard.'

I felt a sharp pain in my cheek. Beulah stepped back, showing her teeth in what can't be called a smile. I touched my face, and when I looked at my hand I saw a bright dab of blood from where her ring had cut me. I wiped my hand on my trousers, and walked on.

In the afternoon I went to look for Madeleine, who had promised to meet me but hadn't turned up. On the way I met Hans and Alexi. I asked them if they had seen her.

'She's in her rooms, I think,' said Alexi.

Hans added, 'You'd better go and see her.'

This was enough to make me run.

Dim twilight filtered through the closed shutters of her windows. At first I couldn't see her. Narrow slats of light lay across the carpet, rising to curve round the solid of a human form. She was sitting at the end of her bed, wearing a white shift. A yellow dress, one of her new ones, was crumpled on the floor.

'Madeleine, why are you sitting in the dark?'

'I had a headache. I went to bed.'

'Can I open the window?'

'If you like.'

I pushed the shutters wide, sunlight pouring in to harshen her outlines.

'Do you feel any better?' I asked.

She grabbed her hair in two swathes and flung it over her shoulders, bringing her head up to give me a dull stare.

'Madeleine, what's wrong?'

'It's true. It's true, it's true, it's true.'

I sat down on the bed beside her, but she immediately got up, hurrying over to the window and leaning out, taking deep breaths. 'It's so beautiful here,' she said.

'What's true?'

'It's nothing. I know I'm being silly. It's all this hair makes my head ache.'

'What's true? Madeleine?'

'I always knew I'd be married one day.'

'Who says?'

'Beulah told me. And she must know, if anyone does.'

I felt chilled, as if my hands were full of time. Time is like snow: the tighter you close your hands to keep it in, the faster it melts.

'When?' I said.

'In the spring. He's coming here next month, or the month after,' she said. 'To spend the winter here.'

'Who?'

'Oh, I was right about that.'

She turned around and sat on the window ledge, sweeping the floor with her long bare toes. 'What's Pravarre like?' she asked conversationally.

'I don't know. It's south, a long way, south of Chatienne. Hot, I suppose. Not as hot as Duccarn. I don't know.'

'You don't know much, do you?'

She let go of the window and sank to the floor, hands on her knees, hair unravelling everywhere. 'I'm sorry,' she cried, 'I'm sorry, I'm sorry, I didn't mean it.'

I knelt down beside her. I should have put my arms around her, said something to comfort her as any friend might, but I couldn't. It would have sounded too fatuous. I was excluded; I suppose that is why she hit

out at me. I couldn't say, 'I'd feel the same if it were me', because it
could never be me. Her tears were shed around the limits of a friendship
I had stupidly supposed had no limits; I felt our friendship being broken
apart while she cried about something I could never suffer with her. I sat
there dumbly, listening to her sob and choke, and I felt so lonely I thought
I might just as well go away and be all by myself.

'I don't want to go!' she cried, and turned to me, grabbed my shoulders
as Peter used to do and pressed her head against my heart.

I looped back her hair. 'There, don't cry, lie down.' I drew her head
to my knees, stroking the soft skin behind her ear, telling her, 'I used to
do this for Peter when he was little.'

She almost laughed. 'But I'm not little, that's the problem.'

'We'll run away,' I said.

'Where?'

There was only one place. 'The mountains.'

'Oh, yes.'

'You can leave your husband behind and I'll leave my wife. We could
leave them to each other.'

'Where will we live?'

'In a little wooden house.'

'What will we eat?'

'Well, what can you cook?'

'All sorts of things. Lady Catherine thought all girls ought to know
how to cook. I suppose Beulah wouldn't approve of that either. We could
live on goat's cheese, like those little mice – do you know that song?'

I hummed:

A little brown mouse and a little white mouse,
Both lived together in a little mouse house.
And all they ate was cheese and bread,
And they lived together till they was dead . . .

Madeleine sighed, 'That's nice. Lord Randal used to sing that. But I
always cried at the end, poor little dead mice.' She rolled over on to her
back and looked up at me, her eyes stinging red but dry now. 'Reyhnard,
what happened to your cheek?'

'The barber cut it, he's not very good. Madeleine, when did Beulah
tell you all this?'

'Right after lunch.' She gnawed at her thumb. 'You don't think it
might not be true, do you?'

'I don't know much, and I don't know about that. Do you want me
to ask?'

She shut her eyes. 'No. I've found out wondering is better than know-ing, after all. I don't know what to choose – it's terrible to think anyone could hate me enough to lie about it.'

'You're wrong,' I said. 'Beulah doesn't hate anybody. Hate is too simple for her.'

'But you hate her.'

'Yes.'

For the next quarter of an hour or so Madeleine said nothing. Her head grew heavy and I thought she had fallen asleep; then she moved her hand, smiling, saying drowsily, 'Can we go some day?'

'Where?'

'To the mountains. I could show you where I used to live.'

'You do miss it, don't you?'

'Yes, maybe. I don't know. I miss the mountains. Will you come?'

'If I can.'

'No excuses allowed for a brother. Promise.'

'All right, I promise.'

This promise also has been kept. Here I am, Madeleine, but where are you?

I did run away. I ran away here, holed up in this little mouse-house of a peasant's hut. Madeleine, I see your mountains, but they are a desolate place.

21

It was the middle of September. The roses were full-blown. When their petals began to fall, at the end of October, Prince Julius of Pravarre would be arriving on Ksaned Kaled.

With a lifetime to fit into those six long weeks, the end of October seemed a lifetime away.

The routine of the court became fraught with the threat of lost op-portunities. Our evenings were eaten up by plays, dinners, concerts, dances; but we didn't have time to waste on resentment. When these things were over we would walk out into the cool night, and with our backs to the shuttered, sleeping Palace we would sit amid the scent of flowers, listen to the crickets, and talk. I had never dreamt I could find so much to say to another person.

Peter's jealousy calmed down a bit, I suppose because he knew she would soon be going. In those days it was not difficult to tear him away from his friends. He came looking for me, insisting on his fair share of my time. The best days of all were those golden, half-summer, half-autumn ones when we – Peter, Madeleine, Hans, Alexi and I – would walk the three miles to a broken jetty where we could have a picnic, and fish, and talk together like the family we seemed at last to be.

Alexi had an inkling of what I felt. He said, 'Odd how there seems to have been this place vacant for her. I can't think why, since we managed to get on fine without her – but it's a definite improvement, don't you think, Nardo? Maybe it was just the feminine element missing. It's strange I can't remember her being born. Hans wouldn't, but I should – I feel, in the back of my mind, as if I did sort of remember . . . '

This feeling that Madeleine had always belonged to us, had always been there – I couldn't have expressed it any better than Alexi did. I'm not superstitious, never have been, but I don't think I could have put my own emotions into words, and at the time it seemed as if I ought not to try.

Certainly it was enough for us to be brother and sister. I wanted nothing more than her company, her friendship, her conversation; to indulge in the fascination of watching her hand, the same shape as my hand, same crooked little finger, run down a white pillar or dip into a blossom to come out dusky with pollen. Madeleine's curiosity was inexhaustible, and her observations about people and things were straightforward, un-blurred by ifs or buts. It was knowledge I had forgotten, or had had cheated from me, but which I found safe preserved in her. Madeleine, you are my reassurance and my truth. You returned self-trust to me: what I saw, and what I believed in, were not flaws in my perception, but also what you saw and what you believed in.

Twin moons to twin suns we were, reflections of clarity.

We did not speak about what was waiting for us at the end of our six weeks, but it was never out of our thoughts, spurring us to almost frantic activity. We busied ourselves exploring the uncharted beauties and secrets of Ksaned Kaled, trying without words to reassure each other that these shared discoveries could somehow bind us together for ever, no matter how far apart we were sundered. In those days it felt as if Ksaned Kaled too was running out of time, for that man, when he arrived, would by his presence kill what my sister and I had made out of the island.

We spent a good deal of time in that little toy-house I've already mentioned. Its façade was a scaled-down replica of the palace, with three rooms inside perfectly proportioned. To enter it we had to stoop through the door, and the windows were no bigger than my head. We went there in twos or threes or fours, with books and paints, wine and cake, and we locked out the world. Time was barred entrance. We were all brothers there.

Madeleine would be deftly sewing tapestry work while Hans and Alexi played chess. I lay on my stomach, raising my head from my book now and then to see how the game was getting on. Outside Peter was climbing trees, but from time to time he ran in to show me some treasure, a brilliant feather, or a robin's eggshell as blue as turquoise. There were many days like this, days which seemed as if they could not end if we did not let them.

Those days were painted round my sister, in her clear colours: dancing with her, talking to her, picking flowers and watching rabbits, becoming accustomed to the duality of seeing myself asleep when I found her curled up in the sun. She has disarmed time, I thought, with this breaking of rules, this two in one, confounding the laws of nature. Time could not really be rushing forward to that day when she would be taken away from me. She had become a part of me so quickly I could barely remember when she was not. It wasn't like what I felt for Peter. There was such urgency about it: so little I could do and so much that would be missed.

I don't know when it changed for her, if it ever did, or if she always felt the same – nor if it really ever changed for me. We never asked, never needed to ask. That time runs so smoothly into all time that to look back is to see it coming. But in those weeks it never crossed my mind. It was, at least for me, desperately unobvious. I knew it would be impossible for me to be ripped in half and remain alive, and so I knew it would be impossible for Madeleine to go away and marry someone else. Maybe I made myself blind, because I had to in order to get through those six weeks, because losing a sister was bad enough – and then the scales were so firmly stuck it was an agony to pull them off. I don't know. I'm not making much sense.

Maybe I always knew. I knew then that I loved her. But I loved my brothers too.

Then, one day, it arrived. It had been sent for from Tsvingtori. I went up to her rooms to fetch her for an expedition, unaware of what a leap time had taken. I went right in. A maid was holding a long mirror, three other maids standing by with their arms full of lace while ladies crowded round to give advice. Beulah, Madeleine's only female relative, was smiling prettily and rubbing her hands. Madeleine caught my eye in the mirror, and shut her own – she couldn't bear to see the look on my face any more than I could endure seeing what they had done to her. Her hair was plaited and coiled around her head, stuck with pearls. They had made up her eyes and her mouth. She was wearing her dress, a blue and gold dress, royal colours for a queen, and stood straight-backed beneath the weight and the layers and layers of her wedding dress.

It was like watching a robbery in the heart of one's home.

'Doesn't she look lovely, Nardo?' said Beulah.

I turned around and went out.

Later, in the evening, not having seen her at dinner, I went down to find her in the toy-house.

'Madeleine, what will we do with that dress when we run away?'

'When are we going to run away?'

'Tomorrow.'

'Do you promise? No, you can't promise. He'll be here next week, Reyhnard, we must stop pretending.'

'I mean it. I will run away with you, anywhere.'

'We can't. Not even Alexi, and he's trying so hard.'

'Alexi?'

'Don't you realise? He can run while he's standing still. He's so clever and so – well, what has he done with it? He stuffs himself with sweets and sings silly songs and chases the maids, he just fills in his time because he's got nothing to do and never will have. He pretends he's busy so that he'll never have to think about what a waste his life is . . . Reyhnard, help me. Will you help me? I should have asked you before but I was so childish, I thought if I didn't talk about it it would just – go away. Will you teach me some of their language? I know you know it. I want to be able to talk to him at least.'

'Let's go outside. Come outside and walk with me.'

She gave me her hand and we went out, strolling up and down the bank of the stream. The evening was very mild. Far away stars dazzled in the sky, the full moon shedding a pale yellow light. A sea breeze ran across our faces and stirred our hair. The sounds of Palace life were fainter than the stars; close by we heard a nightingale in the willows, the frogs hidden among the reeds, the swish of a fish's tail. Beside me Madeleine lost her form in the moonlight, like my shadow.

We walked for an hour, but at last we had to return to the Palace. She went up the stairs in front of me. Halfway to the top she hesitated, and turned around to look at me where I was standing, looking up at her – she reminding herself, as I was reminding myself, that we were indeed two separate people, that it should be no surprise to look into the face of the other.

She hugged her body with her arms. Watching this gesture, I had the most sudden, vivid picture in my eyes: Madeleine on her wedding night, married to a *him* without a face or any character, a husband who could be anyone holding her in his arms, doing with her what I had done with my wife – a Madeleine who was less like me than like Beulah. It was such a shock I stepped back, and stumbled. I remember Madeleine stretching out her hand to me, to help me. I didn't take it. I was afraid to touch her, and I couldn't understand why.

This can't be absolutely true, though it is what I remember. I must have known by then. I knew and I did not know; or I felt the new constraint without realising what had happened – it's so tangled. But I believe Madeleine always knew, with that confidence of hers which never looked back, admitting no doubt, allowing no denial. She was never afraid to acknowledge anything.

'Pull yourself together,' said Alexi.

'I can't.'

'You'd better bloody try. Can't you see how much harder you're making it for her? After all it's her and not you who has to marry this man. Anyone would think you were being exiled. I thought you were so fond of her, but you're making that poor girl carry a double burden.'

'She's my sister.'

'She's my sister too, since we're being so possessive. And Hans's. And Peter's. You really can't do this to her, Nardo. You're acting as if it's some great tragedy, the like of which the world has never seen, when really getting married is the most normal thing in a girl's life. She's got twice as much guts as you.'

'So?'

'Try, Nardo, you must try, and not only for Maddy's sake but for yours too. You've always been far too emotional about the smallest things – '

'Try, try, try, that's all you ever say to me. When have you ever tried with anything? What have you ever really cared about?'

'Remember what I told you about Beulah? I told you that if you tried you'd get over it, and you did.'

'It's hardly the same thing.'

'No!' He laughed sharply. 'Admittedly. Not the same thing at all. But the principle is the same – '

'Since when have you been such an expert on principles? Shall I tell you something? Shall I tell you what she said? She said you squandered your time on pointless things so that you wouldn't have to think about how trivial you are.'

'Obviously perceptiveness runs in the family.'

'Your lecturing makes me puke.'

'Oh Nardo, would it really make you feel better if you could make me angry? I'm afraid I know you a bit too well for that.'

At the end of October one ship did arrive, and a party disembarked, and came to the Palace, and they told us that the King of Pravarre had died, and the day after his death the Prince Julius, now King Julius, had taken his mistress up to the temple and married her there. So Pravarre had a new queen, and no longer needed my sister.

Madeleine stowed the blue and gold dress at the bottom of a trunk. Then she and I, and our brothers, went out for a gallop across frost-etched fields of flowers.

22

The new King of Pravarre, by way I suppose of compensation, sent us a boatload of presents: satins and brocades, wine, jewels, fruit, statues, paintings, gold-plated tableware, and also some showpieces of armour which could not possibly have been fought in, and at which Hans sniffed disdainfully. Beulah managed to appropriate most of these presents – but we were happy to let her have them; she was the only one who needed compensation for ruined hopes. I did filch from her one beautiful piece of blue-white satin the colour and sheen of water, which I knew Madeleine would like.

Some of these gifts were living ones. Hans was very taken with a small, barrel-stomached pony, striped black and white with a tail like a cow's. Peter too was fascinated, and spent hours sketching it. Caryllac said he had seen large herds of these ponies roaming the vast meadows south of the desert where he had lived. It was not broken; Hans tried to ride it, but couldn't, and very soon it died, probably because it wasn't used to the feed we give our horses. There was also a dancing monkey dressed in a red velvet jacket and trousers. I didn't care for it, with its sad half-human face, but Madeleine became very attached to it. They shared the same habit of chewing their thumbs. The greatest success was the parrot, blue and green and yellow, with angry unblinking eyes. It hated the monkey, who would sneak up behind it and pull its tailfeathers with a lugubrious smile. Beulah took this bird and chained it to a perch in her sitting room, rewarding it with chocolates every time it said 'Your Majesty', which is the title used by the kings of Pravarre. I doubt parrots are as intelligent as some people think, for this one used that form of address indiscriminately for anybody, maid or Fahlraec, who entered Beulah's room.

So the court wiled away its time with these new toys and pets, and by imperceptible stages the season moved on into the mild winter of Ksaned Kaled.

I was twenty. I was living in repose on a sort of plateau: no more mountains to climb, and I'll gladly forgo any further heights if only I can stay here for ever – that was my attitude, for a while. It was an easy attitude to cultivate. I didn't suppose I was giving up much, for what could be better than what I now had? The people I loved were close to me, I had comfort, beautiful surroundings, leisure and interests. Viewed objectively, there was no scope for improvement.

And yet, as I lay on that plateau I spent a good deal of time trying to work out why I wasn't as happy as I had every reason to be. I had no reason to be unhappy – at least, none that I could identify – and most of the time I was happy, in a quiet way. It was just that I was not always at ease with my happiness. It did not feel secure; I felt I had to be vigilant or someone would damage it.

I know *now* what the reason was. It was like a shadow of what I feel all the time, now, waking and sleeping, felt then with only a fraction of its present force. Then, it was a gentle hum. This is a scream. At that time I didn't know what was missing from my life. Now I do.

I could see nothing wrong with the present, so I thought it must be misgivings about the future which made me unable to relax. For lack of a better or more obvious explanation, I settled for the knowledge that I would not be allowed to stay on my plateau for ever. This time next year I would move to the Temple in Tsvingtori to begin my training, and this life, though it would not be ended, would be altered.

The coming year was the one in which I should have been preparing for my career, but no one mentioned it and I wasn't going to. I shut my eyes on my little plateau, and made no effort to raise the subject.

Then, in an unexpected manner, it brought itself up.

Late one morning I was alone in the library, reading in front of the fire, when Beulah came in to inform me that she was pregnant.

'It was bound to happen sooner or later, wasn't it?' I said. 'What are you telling me for? It can't be mine.'

'It might be.'

'Come off it. We haven't slept together for the last four months.'

'That was your choice, darling, not mine.'

'I shouldn't think you even know who the father is.'

'It could easily be yours,' she said calmly. 'I thought I was pregnant at the end of August, and I've been sure for several months now.'

'Then why didn't you mention it before? You're lying, Beulah – and even if you're not, even if you have been pregnant since the end of August, that doesn't mean it's mine, so don't think I'm going to go around pretending it is. Have you told the King?'

'No . . . '

'Why not? I would have thought that by the law of averages he was the favourite for fatherdom.'

'Oh Nardo.' She laid a hand on my sleeve. 'You're right. I know I deserve this. I'm not going to try to convince you that you're the father, even though you probably are – but you're still my husband, and legally you're his father. You'll give him your name. He'll be part of your family.'

'We've had bastards in the family before. Usually we boot them down to the city.'

'Stop it.' She folded her hands in her lap, looking at me as if I was some unpleasantly wilful child. 'I didn't come here to ask you for anything. I only came to tell you. I thought you should be the first to know. I never dreamt you would be so nasty about it. I didn't know you could be so – so cruel. I wish I'd never told you now. And as soon as my back's turned you'll be running off to tell everyone my baby's a bastard – '

'It *is* a bastard. Why should I bother to say anything? Everyone knows. I'd simply look an idiot if I claimed the responsibility. The whole subject bores me, Beulah. In fact, the thought that there might be a part of me growing inside that stomach of yours makes me feel sick. I don't even want to think about it – '

I broke off, because I did feel suddenly nauseous. I put my hand over my mouth, hoping she would leave. She sat on, saying nothing. I could feel her smile.

I said through my fingers, 'What does it matter, anyway?'

'It matters to me.'

Then I realised I had been holding my breath, and my lungs were aching. I exhaled, and said to her, 'Well, if you're so concerned about the tender sensibilities of your little bastard, why don't you try to behave a bit more like a respectable woman? Otherwise that poor thing in there is going to grow up knowing his father could as easily be a footman as the King – '

Her hand was on my arm again. 'Do you really want me back, darling?'

I blinked. 'Don't you listen to me? I don't want anything from you except to be left alone. In fact, with you it's not a question of *wanting* anything, I simply don't care what you do or who you do it with.'

Perhaps she thought I was protesting too loudly. Her hand slid up my arm. 'I want to move back to your rooms,' she said.

'No.' Then, 'What for?'

'Well, you see, the reason I haven't told the King – is – well – ' She twisted the material of her skirt between her fingers. Her eyes, raised to my face, were wide under their brows, dark brown and a little tearful – but I felt nothing, nothing, nothing, nothing, nothing but a distant contempt. She went on, 'Well, the reason really is – is that he once said he found pregnant women repulsive.'

'I see. Back to your husband, the last resort.'

'You said I should be respectable.'

'Nothing between us was ever respectable. Go and sleep on your own, try something new. Anyway, you do surprise me. How could you allow the King to find you anything other than ravishing? You must be slipping. Just tell him it's his, he'll be delighted. Or if not, try any of the other two or three dozen. I'm sure one of them will be happy to shoulder the blame.'

'What's happened to you, Nardo? You used to be sweet and giving, and now you're so hard.'

As if she needed to ask. The last thing I wanted was to be wheedled into another one of those 'How I expect too much from people' and 'Why can't I understand that she has her own life to live' discussions she used to drag me through, so I shrugged and opened my book; then I thought I ought to remind her.

'Have you given any thought to the fact that soon after it's born we'll be moving to the Temple in Tsvingtori? It'll be all right for you if the court's there, but what if he decides to stay here?'

I think I was hoping she would say, 'I'll stay with him, of course', but instead she told me, 'Don't worry about that, it's fixed.'

'Fixed? What do you mean?'

'He's putting it off.'

'You asked him?'

'Of course I did.'

'You had no right to do that!'

I shouted so loudly I ruffled the curls on her forehead. She remained placid. 'Darling, you can't mean you *wanted* to go. You don't even believe in religion. I can't understand why you're so angry.'

'Can't you?'

'He could have sent you without me, you know. I do this for you and what thanks do I get?'

'That's crap and you know it.'

'All right.' She stood up, her fingers easing a curl back into place. 'But I don't want to go and we're not going, and that's that.'

She walked out as collectedly as she had come in.

I stared at my book, torn between relief and anger. It was true, I hadn't wanted to go to the Temple. I didn't believe in the Gods I would be trained to serve. Nevertheless, it had been my future. Mine, belonging to me. I hadn't liked the thought of it much, but my duty and my education had been directed towards it. She had taken it, even the choice of it, out of my hands.

I had no feelings left for her, except dislike. She had lost all the power she once wielded inside me. But the power she had over me was undiminished. It was the same in quantity and quality as the power she held over the footmen and the maids: come, go, stay, as she tells the King we shall.

While I'm on the subject of babies, it's quite certain now that Serena is going to have one.

I'm a busy man these days, doing my inept best to cook and clean and look after her animals. The goats kick me, hard, when I milk them – it's a punishment for my cackhandedness. Serena does nothing but sit in the sunshine all day long, a blanket around her shoulders.

In her beaten eyes is the same expression of slow thoughtfulness I have seen on the faces of pregnant ewes. Her situation intrigues me. I have little inkling of what goes on in her mind, but this I do know: she does not seem to have made a logical connection between her rape and the child now in her womb. Given her character this is not surprising. Her pregnancy is gradual and natural, like the ripening of the year we take for granted. The act of violence which precipitated it was abrupt and terrifying, a freak. It is not grief, her silence, and even less is it self-pity, of which she has none. It is more like winter than anything else, when the earth seems dead but beneath the snow the bulbs are already sprouting. Perhaps she is making a choice. It's hard to tell. The working of her mind is a lengthy process. If she is, I think it will be a choice between surrendering to the shock of that irruptive violation of her natural order – in which case I am afraid she may go mad – or forgetting it and accepting that she is filled with new life, like the fields and the animals she knows. She will either come back into harmony with them, or she will cut herself off from everything.

As I say, I can't be sure. Maybe nothing is going on inside her head. She may simply be dulled with pain and horror. But for the moment, while I wait to see what happens, it is too early to feel sorry for her. If nature does win, she will be left with the child she has always wanted.

I did go to see the Captain. He was hung-over, and I was furious.

'So what are you going to do?' I shouted at him.

'My dear chap, I am sorry but you must admit the girl was a dunce to go walking in that area at that time of night. There have been billets here before, she ought to know the risks, and quite frankly it's more than one's job is worth to take exception over such a minor matter.'

'They beat her up and broke her jaw.'

'So you've said. Perhaps I could come and take a look at her?'

'You're not coming anywhere near her. I want to see the men responsible for this.'

'I expect they wouldn't remember.'

'They raped her!'

'Well, we've only got her word for that.'

'And mine. She's a mess; they nearly killed her.'

'Now look here. I'm not having you coming in here telling me what to do. It's hard enough trying to keep that lot in a straight line on parade, and you're asking me to risk a riot for the sake of some peasant girl. You come from these parts, you know what these girls are like, they're used to it. I don't want any trouble.'

'Your soldiers caused the trouble.'

'That's your claim.' Then a crafty, hopeful expression crossed his face. He said, 'Now it may be the case that your girlfriend's a little roughed-up, and it may be the case that beating up one's woman gets one a bad name around here, but you haven't got any proof, you haven't got any witnesses to point the finger at my men, have you?'

'What are you saying?'

'You're the one who lives with the girl, aren't you? It certainly seems to me that a man who comes home to find his woman playing around with another man might lose his temper, especially if he's had a bit too much to drink, and might knock her around a bit and then, when he's sobered up in the morning, try to pretend it was all someone else's fault.'

'You bastard. You were so drunk last night you could hardly sit on your horse and now you think you can accuse me of practically killing a girl?'

'I'm not the one making accusations.' He picked up some papers and started to shuffle them into a neat pile. 'I've got a lot to do this morning, and you really are wasting my time, so I suggest you go home quietly before I arrest you for slander and disturbing the peace. Now get out of here.'

Hearing our raised voices, the Guards outside the tent had come in.

They clutched their pikes and stared at me. I glared back, wondering whether it might have been one, or two, or any of them – but they could have run me through in a second, so I had to give up. I made my way back across the fields and the bridge and the goat-path, back to the hut, where Serena had woken up.

My anger has faded, though Serena's jaw will never be straight again, and her face will always be a little scarred.

Already the whole village knows she is pregnant. These old women can tell the very day it happens. They all assume that I'm responsible, both for her damaged face and for the child. Probably I've risen in their estimation – 'At last!' I imagine them saying. 'He must be more of a man than we thought.' But since I can't think less of them than I already do, it doesn't matter.

23

I am back, back at my table, back with my writing, back in Ksaned Kaled.

My trouble – the source of my restlessness – was like distant music. You catch a strain of it coming from another room, but someone speaks and drowns it. You hush them, hold your breath, and turn your ear towards it. The tune sounds familiar. When did you first hear it? Long ago, when you were a boy, and you have almost, but not quite, forgotten it. Now you realise there is something wrong with this rendition: a note out of place, or a chord missing. You remember, or you sense, that this music ought to make your skin prickle with its perfection. It ought to fulfil you, but it is not complete. You need something more.

I think of music. Alexi is singing. He has our sister by the hand, twirling her round the room, her hair swinging to follow her like a descant. He lets her go, and it is my turn to catch her. We spin in a circle, trip over each other's feet, and collapse in a dizzy, laughing heap on the sofa.

'Isn't it funny,' said Madeleine. 'All that agonising, and in the end I needn't have worried at all. It only goes to show – '

'Not to count your chickens before they're hatched?' Alexi suggested.

'Not at all. Perhaps "tomorrow never comes" – now there's one I've never heard you use.'

'Can I help it if I like truisms? They're so apt, they spring so readily to the tongue – you don't have to think about what you're saying. Anyway, they only sound trite because they've been used so often, and they wouldn't be worn to death if they weren't true – '

'Hence the name,' I said.

'Imagine if you were the man who first thought them up,' said Alexi. 'You'd feel quite a bright spark.'

Madeleine said, 'I wonder if I'll ever get married.'

'I thought you didn't want to.'

'I didn't want to leave all of you. It wouldn't be so bad to marry someone from the court. I'd love to have children.'

Hans was at the door. Alexi got up.

She asked, 'What about you, Alexi?'

He started to laugh, and went out with Hans.

Madeleine asked me, 'Is it true you're having a baby? I mean, that Beulah is?'

'Can't you tell?'

'I thought – no, it does show. Reyhnard – '

'It's not mine.'

'Oh. She says it is.'

'You mustn't ever believe anything she says. Anyway it's quite impossible.'

Stupidly, I expected her to blush at this, or look away. I should have known better. She looked me straight in the eye. I was the coward, the one who looked away.

Scarcely a change in the weather: light chill, a morning frost, no snow to mark the march of winter. Beulah swelled. I thought, maybe it is true, and if the baby is born in April I will never be sure.

My little plateau was growing less and less comfortable. Sometimes it closed in on me until I could hardly breathe. I told myself it was the weather making me feel like this. The question of the Temple had been resolved – or rather, brushed aside – but the uneasiness persisted, forcing me to admit that it never had been anything to do with the Temple, or the future. It was here with me, in the present, every day. So what was it? Winter had not quite ended, spring was about to begin – that's it, I thought, that's what's making me jumpy and irritable. I'm not used to these mild Ksaned Kaled seasons. Spring fever, it's a natural thing. I looked for an answer in any old excuse: dinner disagreeing with me, rainy days, being woken up by barking dogs in the middle of the night.

I had trouble falling asleep. Some nights I couldn't sleep at all. When this had happened in the old days with Beulah I had known what I was waiting for; now I felt I was impatient for something unexplained and unguessable. I lay awake and stared at thoughts that had no meaning. They were coloured inks spilled at random across a page. Flat on my back in the dead of night, head buzzing, heart pounding for no good reason, I could have screamed at the unfairness of it. I had finished with Beulah: why hadn't I regained control of myself? I was still tossing and turning around my hollow core.

When it was at its worst I sought out Madeleine as I used to seek out Peter. I really worried that I might be physically ill, but she was calm and gentle, never remarking on my state, and so I reckoned there couldn't be much wrong with me if she hadn't noticed anything. Yet even when I was with her – so much of every day – my discomfort was not alleviated. It changed, from agitation into something too quiet for excitement, yet not unlike it.

I tried to write a poem about it, but was brought up sharp before I had finished a line. The pen dripped and the ink clotted while I dug, and dug, and finally had to admit defeat. I didn't know where to begin. Language, like everything else, was inadequate.

Alexi said, 'You're like a dog that's lost its lead.'

One day Peter looked at me with a frightened face and said, 'Nardo, you're not sick, are you?'

Actually, Peter, I think I am and I can't sleep for worry. What if I never get better?

Regret became desperate when I looked back to months only just passed, to a time when all I wanted was for Madeleine not to go away. I had that now, but it was not enough. Being indifferent to Beulah was not enough. Knowing I had escaped the Temple was not enough. In my heart and my mind I was no better off than I had been a year ago, when I was still trying to be married to Beulah.

One day the servants left my bedroom door open and a cat got in. I returned to find she had given birth to four tortoiseshell kittens in my bed. She hissed when I came in, baring small, sharp teeth. Why my bed? I asked her. The sheet was wet and bloody, but I didn't mind. Even as she hissed, she purred, and the four tiny bodies with their flat ears and glued-up eyes tugged at her teats, patting their paws against her clean, furry belly. There was nothing in this scene to disgust. In fact, I found it soothing. I held out my hand for the cat to sniff and lick.

Suddenly I thought I would like to bring Madeleine up to see the kittens, so I went to find her.

'In the stables, I think.'

At Ksaned Kaled the stables are half a mile away from the main palace. I set off down the road, and after several minutes I saw two horsemen riding towards me. Soon they came close enough for me to realise that one was a young man-about-court, and the other was my sister.

'Reyhnard,' she called. 'Thomas and I are just going for a ride.'

'So I see.'

'Oh, why don't you come? We'll ride back with you, we can wait for you.'

I could see from the young man's face that riding with the brother had never been part of his plan.

I wanted to push him off his horse, jump into the saddle and ride away with her.

I said, 'You go. You go on.'

'Did you want me?'

'No. It's not important.'

'You're sure?'

'Yes, go on, go on, and have fun.'

'I'll see you later.'

She dug her heels into the horse's flanks and raced off, pursued by the young man. Her unbound hair was like a banner, whirling and whipping – the last thing I could make out as they grew smaller in the distance.

Much later, after she had returned red-cheeked and wind-swept and we had eaten dinner, I asked her if she would like to see the kittens.

'Oh, yes please.'

Scarcely eight hours old, the little balls of fur were fast asleep. The mother cat lifted her head as we came in, but Madeleine, who knows her way with animals, kept back, and was content to admire them from the end of the bed.

'Shouldn't they be moved?' she asked.

'I wouldn't like to be the one to try.'

'She's purring.'

'She knows me now.'

'Do you think she'd let me hold one?'

'Ask her.'

Madeleine carefully approached and made herself known. She rubbed a hand over the hard, silky cat's head, and very slowly slipped her fingers under a kitten. The cat was watchful, but calm. Madeleine raised her hand; the kitten woke up and stretched, mewing blindly. The cat widened her eyes – I laughed at that, for it reminded me of Beulah.

Madeleine whispered, 'They're so little. I can feel its heart beating. They won't be drowned, will they?'

'I suppose she's my cat now. They can stay here, I'll get them a box. Madeleine – '

'Yes?'

'What's he like – that young man?'

'Thomas filcValentin? Oh, quite nice, I think. I was at a loose end and he asked me to go for a ride with him. Why do you ask?'

'He's a friend of Nikolas's.'

'I thought so.'

'He used to share a nursery with me when I was so high.'

'Were you friends?'

'No, not really, not that I remember. He rides well. Did you have a good time?'

'Quite-ish. We didn't talk much.'

'Madeleine – '

'Yes?' She was watching me from under her lids, with a hint of a smile, a sort of tender, amused patience.

'So,' I said. 'What do you think of him? Will he do?'

'What for?'

'For your husband.'

'What? Oh!' She threw back her head, all the white length of her throat vibrating with laughter. 'I'm not on the shelf yet, am I? I don't need to start looking just yet.'

'I just thought – I just wondered – whether you might be in love with him?'

'Oh, silly, I hardly know him.'

'He's very good-looking.'

'Honestly, Reyhnard, you must have such low standards – you think everyone's good-looking. Maybe he is, but looks aren't everything and I'll tell you one thing, he hasn't got much of a sense of humour.'

'You found that out?'

'We did talk a bit, you know.'

'Madeleine – Madeleine, you would tell me, wouldn't you? I'd like to think you felt you were able to tell me. If you were in love with someone.'

She put the kitten in her lap and said, 'Reyhnard, you don't have to worry, not about me – you can if you like, it's nice when you're protective, but the thing is there's no need. I mean, I've never been one of those stupid girls who are always getting crushes on people.'

'Have you ever been in love?'

She picked up the kitten and kissed it. 'Never. Have you?'

'No.'

'No, I remember you saying. I think it must be something in the family. As far as I can gather none of us has ever – been in love. But . . . Can I tell you something?'

'Go on.'

'I've seen the way all the women here have one affair after another, one man after another. I don't want to judge them, but I do think that apart from anything else it must be a very unsatisfactory way to live. I can't see why they do it. I could never be like that. When I fall in love, I will always love that person, for ever, I know I will.'

'Don't you listen to Alexi's songs? Everybody thinks that.'

'But I mean it. There are some things you always know about yourself, and I know that's how I am. I don't think anything less is worth it. I mean, you might as well not start at all if you're going to stop, don't you think, Reyhnard? If you assume it has some sort of time limit, like a race – if you can see the end at the beginning, there's no point. I couldn't love anyone like that, just for a while. And I think that's how we all are, you and me, and Alexi, and Hans, and probably Peter too when he grows up – that we haven't fallen in love, yet, because we haven't found the person who is – who is the one . . . '

She had forgotten the kitten, was looking at me.

I heard someone, myself, replying, 'Do you spend much time dwelling on this subject?'

Madeleine, sometimes you must have despaired of me.

The kitten was once more the sole recipient of her attention. She nuzzled its softness, saying, 'It's hard not to, in this place. Oh look, they've woken up, they're nursing. I'd better put this one back.'

Madeleine, I am coming to suspect there is a secret in you. Everything about you is without deceit. Every colour is pure: green eyes, black hair, white skin, your straight, uncluttered form. I am looking in my mirror, turning left profile, then right. I study my eyelids. I see they have thick blue veins, drawn in with a soft pencil. There is a scar on my cheek where Beulah cut me. My thick hair stands up when I draw my hands backwards through it.

I was sitting on my own, half-asleep, when suddenly, without warning, my whole being took fright.

My heart-rate shot up, pounding, rapid, arrhythmic; the blood in my arms and legs bubbled; my skin crawled; my breath was caught in my throat like a stone, as if I had been kicked in the stomach – the same symptoms, but much worse than before. Sweat itched on my nose, down my back, in my armpits. A spasm of muscles heaved my body to its feet. My legs wanted to move, so I obeyed, hoping that if I let my body have its own way I could out-run whatever this was. I went outside and walked around the fields for hours, the clammy earth sticking to my shoes. My lungs were crying out for fresh air.

This is it, I thought, I'm dying.

Another time Alexi said to me, 'You're looking awfully strained these days, Nardo. Are you sure there's nothing bothering you?'

I'm dying, Alexi, can't you see?

Hans added, 'You've got very thin.'

Oh God, I thought, even he's noticed it. Still Madeleine said nothing.

I honestly did not know what it was. After Beulah I imagined myself immune to that sort of thing, and, knowing no other woman, I knew no better than to assume it would be the same with anyone: painful, ugly, degrading, and quite unmistakable. And I really believed that it would kill the possibility of feeling any true love – I mean, the sort of love I have for Peter and Madeleine – for the object of one's desires. There is a difference between wanting the woman because you want sex, and wanting to make love because you love the woman, but I didn't know that then. I didn't think you could feel both needs for one person. I didn't know, though perhaps I should have suspected, that Beulah perverted sex just like everything else: she couldn't touch something or give it without spoiling it first.

Also, I could say that I failed to see the truth because she was my sister. As I said to her, 'If you know you're not supposed to do something, you don't think about it.' She was my sister and I loved her: thus to me it seemed doubly wrong to think of her in that way, so wrong in fact that the thought couldn't force its way across my mind. I had to suffer while my misconceptions were turned on their heads, until I finally understood that I felt this way precisely *because* of who she was, and not in spite of it.

It was neither ugly nor degrading. It was painful, but it was a good, true pain, like passing one's hand through fire and water to purify it.

We were treated to a play. Caryllac had written it. It was very dull. Peter sat next to me, whispering in my ear all the way through. In front of me was Madeleine, wearing her blue dress. She had pinned up her hair. Wisps of black curled at her nape, like smoke. When she moved her head, the small bones of her neck rippled beneath the skin. She appeared, suddenly, as easily breakable as a glass vase. All those little points of bone: her wrists, her collarbones, her shoulders, the join of her jaw and throat, they made my heart ache.

Afterwards we danced. 'Look,' she said, holding up her hand. 'Put yours against mine. We used to do this at – when I lived with Lady Catherine.'

'What does it mean?'

'Oh, nothing, it's just to compare. Your hand is bigger than mine, but my fingers are longer than yours. They're the same shape, though . . . Do you think we'll ever get used to it?'

No, Madeleine, your hands, your arms, your hair, the whole of you is mine. Madeleine, it's spring, spring on Ksaned Kaled and already the roses in the shelter of the Palace are bringing forth buds, as they were then. Don't you remember remarking how early the flowers blossomed on Ksaned Kaled? Listen to me. I thought I was dying. You know how afraid I am of dying. I thought you didn't notice when I was crying out for help. Madeleine, you had to help me up, make me as straight as your straight back. You had to show me what we always knew, because I didn't know it, I couldn't see it, all I knew was that there was something killing me. You stood there waiting, running out of patience, while I was dying of my inability to see.

24

It was a cold day in the middle of April. Purple and yellow crocuses were growing outside the windows of the library passage. I was looking out at them. Presumably they're still there, or their descendants, unless someone has dug them up. It was several hours after lunch. I had eaten a fair amount, and was feeling quite well. Every time this happened I thought my illness had gone for good. I was in the passage looking through the windows at the crocuses. My arms were full of books. The windows of that passage are high and wide, rising from knee-height to touch the vaulted ceiling with pointed arches. Panes of leaded glass are set in square pillars: it's a sort of glassed-in cloister. In the afternoon sunlight falls directly through those windows, casting bright squares of white light and sharp lines on to the flagstones. The light plays tricks at the end of the passage, where the steps descend from the library door. Those steps are cut at so acute an angle that even on the sunniest days they are obscure in darkness. Walking down them, you are suddenly blinded, stranded in the windowlight until you blink.

It was a cold day, but fine and clear. Blackbirds were singing in the kitchen garden, their song faintly audible through the glass. I was on my way to return the books to their shelves and choose some more, humming one of Alexi's songs, surprised to find myself feeling more or less content. The passage was so pretty, its solitude so calm.

Then, while I stood admiring the crocuses, I heard a noise coming from the library, and tensed. Someone was opening the door. I was the only person who ever came this way – except Beulah, when she was looking for me. Afraid that it might be her, I half-pivoted, ready to retreat. But it was Madeleine who stepped into the light.

She put her sole down on the smooth-worn paving, one foot resting on the step behind her, the other tip-toe, poised on a creaking sandal. Its strap had come loose.

Because of the light, Madeleine didn't see me. She stooped to tie up her sandal, her hair fluent in waves down her arched back, sunlight dazzling in her eyes, running in and out amongst her hair, gleaming blue and black and gold like water.

It was as if I had never seen this woman before. The sight of her caught me unawares, as it had the day she tried on her wedding dress. This time I could not walk away. I could not move.

I said, 'Madeleine' – or maybe I didn't say it, maybe I only thought it.

She heard it, or some sound escaping from me. Hands arrested on her hips. Surprised in the motion of smoothing her white dress, the sun bright on her back, Madeleine looked up at me.

Myself in her green eyes, she in mine, my sister, my mirror, myself. We had no chance to conceal what was plain on both our faces.

I heard her catch her breath, her impatient eyes asking me, telling me: You understand now?

I am the son of a king, and she is his daughter. She is my peer, the only woman in the world who can match me blood for blood. We stir the myths in each other's veins. I always thought there was nothing in those old fables of our divinity – but I am more than a god when Madeleine touches me, better than a god, for when my sister looks at me all that was divine in me she makes into a man.

I must give her all of me, love all of her. She will not let me get away with less. I cannot say, 'I'll have this of you, and not that . . . ' for we are entirely interchangeable. The differences in our bodies, judged by appearances so alien to one another, are only skin-deep; we must strive to incorporate them in order to be together. We want, in each other, the same thing – not to take a private pleasure while the other pursues his, her separate ends, perhaps achieving them and perhaps not, but to reach each other through it, and use it to shatter the false limits imposed by having to call this my flesh, and that her flesh.

Nature had wronged us when it tore us in two, giving us each a body, mine a man's and hers a woman's, as if we had always been two individuals – as if we would not know the moment we saw each other that there had been a mistake. Madeleine knew, right from the start. It took so long for me to see, and hurt so much – and in the end it was so easy. I saw her standing half in shadow, half in light, my sister, myself. All the time I had imagined I was dying, this was closer to me than any other woman could be, closer than a wife, or a mother, or a daughter could be; as close as the one who is as much my blood and my bone, my heart, my past, my future, as I am.

She ran down the passage, window to window through light and shade, the tails of her hair in pursuit. She ran to me, holding out her hands.

She refused me any more time to think. Reason is an overrated faculty: given enough time and enough bloody-mindedness we can persuade ourselves into any folly. If she had done this sooner, held me and kissed me without saying anything, we wouldn't have wasted so much time – nine months of my ignorance and her patience. Now she would allow me no more chances to make the wrong decision.

She kissed the voice out of me, speech, thought, doubts, drained me of inconsequentialities and filled me with knowledge of herself. No inch of her was a surprise. Her skin smelt of musk and summer rain, tasted of milk and salt. The vital, superficial distinctions that made her the sister to my brother, she gave me those, she said: These also belong to you, are you. My sister is my sixth sense. What she feels, I feel; whatever pleasure and pain I give her she not only gives back, but I feel it through her.

When we were together all things took their substance from us. Looking at the world, its rounded self-sufficiency, I see us. That evening was beautiful. It might have been beautiful on its own, but I in looking at it made it beautiful. Does that make sense? It does to me, but then I know what I'm trying to say.

The afternoon set in a flush, arrayed itself with a sky-wide rainbow of colours. Long sweeps of cloud were illuminated from behind, ribbons of smoke and fire striping the sky down to the horizon, where the sun sank hot and huge and yellow. Already the moon had risen, transparent as a disc of water. Then the voice of the watchman broke into my dream, calling the twelfth hour, and I knew I must wake Madeleine, or we would be missed at dinner.

She was curled in the bed, a nest of sheets rucked around her, arcs of rib curving from her stippled back. Her shoulder blades were folded like wings. Black hair fanned across the warm pillows, her sleeping face turned to the fire. As the sun set, the shadows of daylight that had sculptured angles on her body gave way to the glow of the flames, and she looked dusky, malleable. Sparks exploding from the fire burst reflections like stars in her hair. Her breathing was deep and even, her limbs boneless, quiet, resting.

Coming away from the window, I began to feel the cold and wrapped one of the cast-off blankets around me as I picked up my clothes. Then I sneezed, which woke her. She sighed in her throat, rolled on her back and flung a long arm across the pillows.

I pulled on my trousers and came to sit beside her. She sat up, throwing back her hair, her hair all tangled and tumbling down her skin, black ropes against ivory. I watched the way her neck moved on her abrupt shoulders, each tendon in high relief as she stretched back her head and yawned. Then she dipped forward to rest her brow on my arm. I wanted to kiss her collarbones, her smoky nape, her blue-veined wrists, take her and snatch back the afternoon. But time is always our enemy.

She rasped her knuckles across the stubble on my chin. Her breasts and cheeks had pink sore places where my beard had scratched. I touched them. They felt hot, slightly feverish. She kissed me between my throat and my jaw, and got out of bed.

She sat in a chair while I combed her hair for her. I undid each knot with my fingers, laying the lock flat in my hand, and combed it until it fell about her in a smooth polished sheet. I span out the task purely for the pleasure of brushing her hair's abundance.

After this we had to hurry. I put on my shirt; she put on her stockings, her petticoat, her vest, her blouse, her collar, all that superfluity of clothes girls wear, and her crumpled white dress. I think I felt the most joy in that moment when I watched her bend down to pick up her dress from my floor. She shook the creases from her skirts, and I did up the laces. Then it was time for dinner.

25

In late April Beulah had her baby. I was told afterwards by the midwife that it had been a fairly easy birth, compared to most first deliveries, and I suppose I'll have to take her word for it. I had to attend and watch the whole thing, and that was unpleasant enough. Perhaps I would have been moved by it, as I've been told men are, if it had been my child, or if I had loved her, or even merely liked her. As it was, I couldn't feel any sympathy. Such suffering was nowhere near enough punishment for what Beulah had put me through.

As Alexi remarked some twelve years earlier, it's hard to accept that we came into the world in no other manner than this. So much ugliness and noise and pain. No wonder we are what we are.

So, as Beulah predicted, the child was born in April. And so, if it – the child, the boy – had served its nine months' term, then it had been conceived in August. I have my doubts. It was very small, unusually small – the midwife pointed this out, but I'd already noticed for myself. I do know that there are ways of inducing a birth before its time, and certainly that child had an almost monstrously unformed look. I wouldn't put it past Beulah. She took a pretty dangerous risk, but it was alive, born with some strands of black hair which later grew quite thick, and gummy pale blue eyes that soon turned green, and its nose promised prominence, so it probably was the King's.

At any rate it doesn't matter, as it died before it was three. But I'm getting ahead of myself.

I did for it what Alexi had done for Peter: carried it to the window and showed it to the assembled court. They cheered my son who wasn't really my son, and the King's grandson who was probably his son; then I handed it back to Beulah, who gave it a fat teat and told me to make myself scarce.

Her energy and powers of recuperation are daunting.

It was Hans all over again. The King was besotted. He carried it everywhere. He rocked it and sang to it, calling the whole court to come and look whenever it grabbed his finger or raised its head or, later, smiled. Beulah insisted on nursing it herself. This was partly because she was producing more milk than a cow, and also because it acts as a sort of contraception. Since the King couldn't bear to be parted from it, he made her sit down and suckle it right in the middle of wherever he happened to be.

One day he was at the far end of the salon and Beulah was up at the other end, surrounded by admirers who treated this like some exquisite new variety of entertainment specially invented for them. Alexi said to her, just loud enough for those near-by to hear, 'Does this satisfy your craving for exhibitionism?'

In reply, Beulah gave him her new smile, the bare savage smile of a lioness.

It was not that the King loved Hans less. I am wrong, it was not Hans all over again, only a fraction. Somewhere in the back of his mind the King must have been glad, now, that he hadn't married her. Bowled over as he was by this new child, what might not have happened to his first real love, his true love Hans, if the child had been legitimately the King's? By law it was mine, so if he wanted to do anything to favour that child, he'd have to favour me first – but he would never be able to push Hans aside for me. And this is as far as I care to speculate into the King's mind.

Beulah, waiting and stalking, caught me on my own. She told me the new plan.

'He's not so concerned now about whether Hans ever marries or not,' she said airily, adding, 'Alexi does seem to have this distressing ability to reproduce himself, but I don't think he'd ever marry unless Hans did.'

'Do you really want to rely on that?'

'Hans won't marry unless the King pushes him into it. You know what he's like. Fortunately we don't have to worry about Peter.'

I saw. Simple. Hans would become King, outlive us all, and die without issue; Alexi would have no legitimate children. This would leave Beulah's child, who was, as far as the legal niceties of succession were concerned, the King's eldest grandson. He would take precedence over Peter and step on to the throne when Hans died. Brilliant. What a perfect arrangement, and so well designed to suit the King's desires. Oh King, your great schemes: such scope, such forethought, taking such pains to implement your every ambition. What happened to them all? They would have suited me.

It's hardly worth looking back on these empty intrigues, these true castles in the air. However I did point out: 'Beulah, I know you're not stupid. You must realise that when Hans becomes King, Alexi will do everything he can to make sure Hans marries and has children.'

I saw she did realise this. She had no answer, but wouldn't admit it. Thoughtfully she showed her teeth and went off to see her child. I soon forgot all about this conversation.

In those lengthening days of summer such things seemed as far away as puffy little clouds in my sunny sky. Beulah and her scheming, the King, the court – all clouds so insubstantial that Madeleine, in the breeze she made tossing her hair or waving her hand, could drive them right over the horizon.

Escaping from the Palace we would lie together in the hot grass, tickled by ants, eating green grapes, and spend drowsy hours watching the butterflies. I didn't pick up a book all that summer. Time itself felt as tranquil and fragrant as the air of Ksaned Kaled. We took long rambles along the flower fields, through vineyards and pine woods, coming at last to a meadow where we could look down on the pebbly beaches rattling under the waves, rolling in the warm pleasure of the sun. Our feet were always dirty from going barefoot, the nails broken and the soles rough. One behind the other we walked through the wet sand, delighting to leave one set of footprints where two people had walked. We carved our names in the sand and waited for the sea to rush up and erase them. A tangle of brambles sweeping the ground made a shady cave, where we hid amongst the thorns. In the very early morning, at midnight, or during the heat of siesta time, my sister and I would meet down at the toy-house and make love in its cool, abandoned interior.

We found a hundred hiding places. In company we were so correct, so properly siblings – we were ready for any risk except the one that someone might find out and take us from each other. This was no hardship: secrets are fun, and in that first year we were both a little childish. But it was not a game or a child's love. It was our essence, the acid test in which we assayed the other things in our life and found them dross, frivolous, transitory.

I love her. I so much more than merely love her, more than the sun merely shines, or a hurricane merely blows. I need her more than fire to keep me warm and water to drink, more than the earth I walk on and the air I breathe. Not much variety in those eternally hot, eternally blue months – but what perfection craves variety?

Now also there is no variety. But this is nothing, and that was everything. There's no other way to put it. Existence is meaningless without her and Reyhnard could be anyone. I would give up the endless months of drab survival I endure in this nameless village if I could have just one of those summer days – it doesn't matter which, they were all perfect – to end my life in.

Of course you would, Reyhnard. But you can't. Time will not drive bargains. What king would stoop to haggling with his subjects? What can I offer time? All time gives me in its lack of charity are these cold coals and scrap ends of memory it expects me to fill my time with; and ultimately, maliciously, time will make even these more violent and bitter than I can bear.

I'm old. I'm an old man, old before my time. Time has made me old. It will let me do nothing but sit and write and remember, recalling that time when I was too young, too innocent, too happy to pay attention to time. Time has exacted the price of my disregard.

Just one day, time, it's not so much to ask. One day from that limitless supply you guard so jealously. Just one, and not even a new day, I don't ask for that. All I want is a day I've already used. One of those days in the last summer before everything started to fall apart.

You know, what gets me most is the fact that the King thought the crown was the best present he could give to anyone, and that the lucky recipient ought to consider himself highly favoured.

One day Madeleine was busy being fitted for winter dresses, and I was at a loose end, when Alexi found me.

'What're you doing, Nardo?'

'Nothing much.'

'As usual. Me neither. I don't seem to be seeing much of you these days. How are things? Did you have a good time the other day?'

'What do you mean?'

'Fishing with Peter. He said he was going to ask you. Did you catch anything?'

'He never did. We didn't go fishing.'

'That's odd. He was very keen on it.'

'When did he say this?'

'About four days ago. I haven't seen him since.'

'Well, I haven't seen him for a few days either.'

'Really, Nardo, you have been neglecting him recently, poor sprat. Come on, let's go and find him. We could go fishing now, down behind the weir.'

'Where's Hans?'

'Busy with Father. Come on.'

First we looked for him among his friends, but they had last seen him three or four days previously. Neither the kennel master, nor the fencing master, nor any of the grooms knew where he was. I sent servants to ask those ladies with whom Peter was a favourite, but it was always, 'Haven't seen the Prince for three or four days.'

When we asked the servants who did his rooms, they said that Peter had not slept in his bed for the last three nights.

'Well,' said Alexi, 'we'd better find him.'

With a posse of servants we searched the kennels, the barns, the attics and the cellars, calling his name, only to be answered by echoes. He had vanished. It seemed futile, so we sent the servants away, warning them not to say anything.

'Where can he have gone?' I asked Alexi.

'The jetty?'

We galloped down to the sea, but there was no Peter, not even a footprint in the sand to show any human being had ever passed that way.

For the first time I realised just how large an island Ksaned Kaled was.

Impossible to search it – it was full of a thousand places where a not-so-small boy could hide himself if he was really determined. There were no wolves or boars on Ksaned Kaled, nothing that could do him harm so long as he did none to himself. But what if he had somehow managed to leave the island?

'How could they let this happen?' I cried angrily. That army of servants and retainers who should have kept an eye on him, grooms, dog-handlers, Guards, maids, footmen . . . How could he manage to evade them all? 'Why didn't they notice? Why didn't they say something?'

'Why didn't you notice?' Alexi countered gently. I couldn't answer. He was right. If Peter was anyone's responsibility, he was mine.

'He's obviously not here,' said Alexi. 'Where next?'

'It's pointless, we'll never find him – '

'We must. You must. Why do you think – Nardo, listen, I have an idea Peter's hiding somewhere where he can easily be found. He wants us to find him. Or I should say, he wants you to find him – '

'I'm trying to find him!'

'That's not the impression you've been giving him over the last few months.'

'What are you saying, that he's done this to frighten me?'

'Nardo!' Alexi punched his saddle, and the horse shied. 'Nardo, you're so dense! He's jealous, plain bloody jealous – '

'I thought he'd got over that.'

'He tried. But recently you've been giving him about as much attention as a toy you've grown out of. You used to treat him as though he was the only person in the world who mattered. I can appreciate how you feel about Madeleine – '

I couldn't help tensing, wanting to look away from Alexi's face; but bravado and stifled panic combined to keep my eyes on him. '– She came into your life when you were going through a bad time and it was her friendship that helped to pull you out of it. It's understandable you've become close, she's more your age, you've got things in common. I can understand that, but then I'm not twelve years old, and also, Nardo, I've never looked up to you the way Peter does. Don't you ever consider his feelings?'

'I thought – '

'What? What? Did you think at all?'

'He's got so many friends – he's always busy with them – '

'You thought you didn't mean this much to him? How could you be so stupid? Well, now you know. Come on, we'd better go and find him. I think I know where he might be.'

'Where?'

'That old fort Hans and I used to play in. I took him there once. It's only a shed, about four miles west of here – '

I dug my heels into my horse and raced over the fields ahead of him.

Even before I dismounted I could see Alexi was right. The little shed-fort was camouflaged among the trees, but there was a small smoking fire outside, and the whole place had an air of habitation about it. I pulled up my horse, jumped off, and ran to the door.

'Peter! Peter, are you there?'

No reply. He would make me work for my forgiveness.

I got down on hands and knees to crawl inside. A murky light filtered through the oiled parchment covering the solitary window. I couldn't see anything. He's not here, I thought. If he was here, he's gone.

'Peter?'

I squinted, and as my eyes got used to the light I saw a figure crouched in the corner. Red hair, wet red hands: Peter was skinning a rabbit.

'Peter, I can see you.'

There was no room to stand. I crawled over to him.

'Well,' I said. 'You gave us a good scare.'

'Have you been looking for me?'

'Of course I bloody well have. What on earth possessed you to do this? I've been sick with worry.'

'Don't know. I've been here for three days.'

'I know how long you've been missing. It's a big island, Peter, we've been looking everywhere. Are you all right? Have you been sleeping on this dirt? What have you been eating?'

'Rabbit,' he said, holding up the glistening stripped carcase.

'Well, at least you're intrepid, but that doesn't excuse you. What a stupid stunt to pull. You might have got really sick, living like this. You might have caught pneumonia.'

'So why are you angry? What would you care?'

'Don't be stupid. Why do you think I've been riding around like a maniac looking for you? Put that thing down, Peter. Let's get out of here. Let's go home.'

'Who's outside?'

'Alexi – he came with me.'

'Just Alexi?'

'Yes. Come on, let's get you home and into a bath.'

'Nardo?'

'Yes?'

'I knew you'd find me.'

He crawled out and stood up in the sunlight, blinking. He was filthy. Dirt matted his hair, mud and blood and fur caked under his nails. His face was black. He wasn't much shorter than I was, now, but all the same I grabbed his arms and gave him a good shake.

'Are you really angry?' he asked.

'Yes – no – I was angry because I was frightened. But you're all right, that's the main thing.'

'Did you think I was dead?'

I shook him again, harder, until I found my voice. 'Never, never say that, not even as a joke.'

He rubbed his hand under his nose, leaving a smeared trail. 'I'm sorry.'

Alexi called to us from the edge of the coppice. 'Hurry up, you two, it's tea-time and I'm starving. You're certainly a sight for sore eyes, Pea – though not for sore noses, pooh! Don't come any closer. You stink. You certainly put the wind up Nardo.'

Peter climbed into the saddle behind me. When we returned to the stables, he slipped off first and held the stirrup as I dismounted. 'Nardo,' he began, handing the reins to a groom, 'are you doing anything to-morrow?'

'Nothing special.'

'Would you like to go fishing?'

'Can we go on our own?'

'If you want.'

'Just you and me, then. Yes, I would.'

'All's well that ends well,' said Alexi.

Several weeks later we were told that the court was to return to Tsving-tori. Trouble was brewing in the west marches again, this time led by a young priest of Adonac. I think it was something to do with guild privileges. Also there was news of a present just arrived in the capital from the King of Andariah. Regretfully we packed our trunks and boxes, said goodbye to Ksaned Kaled, and set sail.

'We'll come back,' said Madeleine. A squall had blown up in the east, the wind whipping her hair across her face. We stood gazing back as the island slipped below the horizon.

I pulled a strand from her mouth. 'It will be harder', I said, 'in Tsvingtori.'

'But not impossible.'

We did not admit the proposition of change. There would always be another night for us. Tomorrow would always be like yesterday.

26

Grey and rambling, the Palace had a silver patina in the early autumn sunlight, and the rose gardens, though bearing no comparison with the fields of Ksaned Kaled, were still in flower. Peter's puppy was now a grown dog, but it hadn't forgotten him; he was reunited with all those friends of his who hadn't come to the island because their parents didn't go, or could not afford to send their sons – though ambitious parents try to do this. Hans was so plainly delighted to be back, and Alexi happy when Hans was happy, that despite all we had left behind it was not a sad homecoming. Ksaned Kaled was soon a hazy memory; Tsvingtori reclaimed the solid dimensions of reality.

I could say of every single line I have written that if we had not done this or that, then such and so would never have happened, but the fact, the fact, is that we did them. They happened. If we could have known what the outcome would be, we would never have done them; but we could not know until they were done. I have had a long time to think this all out clearly. Once we had done those things, we saw the results, but we might as well have never known for all the difference it makes. I should have written this right at the beginning, and called my whole life just chapters upon chapters of accidents.

The present from the King of Andariah was half a dozen horses of the breed for which that country is famous: four mares and two stallions. They were all handsome animals, but one of the stallions was a master-piece of a horse, a dappled-grey giant standing eighteen and a half hands high, with a black mane and tail, a large dished face, and eyes as big as apples. It was young and recently broken, very temperamental. The King gave it to Hans, for if Hans could not handle it, who could?

The first snows fell in early November, just before my birthday. We heard that a lion had come down from the hills north of Tsvingtori, probably driven south by the weather. It had been seen taking sheep and young cattle from the penfolds; then one day a shepherd disappeared. The trouble in the marshes had been settled, so the King decided to take some recreation and go lion-hunting. This was a great treat for Hans, because lions can usually be hunted only in the north and east.

We set out early in the morning, trampling the thick snow in the courtyard. Peter was in a temper because he was too young to come, and refused to see us off; all the rest of us were going, except for Beulah, who was still nursing.

Bells jingling, leather creaking, billows of breath from men and horses white in the frosty air. The squeal of cartwheels and the shouts of the bearers; Alexi singing; the lion dogs, with their wrinkled backs and pug noses, snuffling round our horses' hooves. Hans's horse reared and pranced, putting its ears back, aiming a kick at any dog that came too close. Despite his bad leg Hans sat his horse better than I did with my two good ones. His left side had no need of saddle or stirrup. The thigh gripped and his seat never lost contact; but his bent right leg pressed the arch of its foot into the stirrup iron. It seemed, in its weakness, not to belong to him. We were all muffled in furs and leather, wool scarves twined around our ears; and so we set off, with Hans in the lead, Alexi beside him, and Madeleine and I close behind. The King was further back, surrounded by courtiers: two hundred men and women, a bright and noisy train. We were to travel twenty miles to a small fort in the country where we would spend the night, and tomorrow we would hunt the lion.

Four miles out of Tsvingtori the dogs set up a tremendous baying. Hans pricked his ears forward at the same moment as his horse, both of them lifting their heads to sniff the air for the scent of prey. Madeleine and I exchanged a smile. Hans urged his horse into a canter to chase after the dogs, fast followed by Alexi; Madeleine and I pressed forward to keep up with our brothers. We sped down the snowy road with the wind in our ears, and were soon so far ahead of the court that we could no longer hear them.

The road narrowed, leading into a forest of pine trees. The woods on either side of us were impenetrably thick, tree-tops closing over our heads to leave us in a dim half-light. The ground was icy, the horses slithered, and we slowed to a trot.

Abruptly, Hans pulled up his horse. He sat at attention for a moment, rather like a retriever, and then turned round to shout back at us, 'I can hear something!'

'What?' called Alexi. 'How can you hear anything over these damn dogs?'

Just then the dogs fell silent, and stood stiff-tailed. My horse was shivering.

A jackdaw broke cawing from a tree, frightening Hans's horse. It shied, his leg bouncing against its flank. He put a hand on its neck to steady it, and quietly went on searching the woods with his eyes.

'There,' he said.

His horse's skin was twitching. It pawed the ground.

Between the trees was a grey shadow, a pair of yellow eyes. Hans sat very still. They stared at each other.

'It's a wolf,' said Alexi.

The shadow turned, limping, and melted into the darkness.

'It's wounded!' Hans cried. 'It must have caught its leg in a trap.'

'Leave it, Hans!' Alexi shouted, rising in his stirrups.

Mayhem broke loose: dogs barking and milling back and forth, Hans's horse bucking, Madeleine's horse dancing sideways, ready to bolt, and my own snorting, champing the bit. I tried to spur forwards to catch Madeleine's bridle, but as I did so her head, her eyes jerked away, and I looked where she looked, seeing Hans give his horse a hard kick – the horse leapt forward at the same moment as a dog came running between its legs, snapping and snarling, and the horse lashed out, threw its head back, missed its footing, and was slipping on the icy ground.

Madeleine was screaming.

Hans – *Hans* – was falling, falling from his horse, and the horse was falling too. Hans's leg could not keep a grip or control the horse and urge it upright. It was his leg that failed him.

He fell out of the saddle, a look of utter disbelief at his own helplessness on his face; he fell on to the frozen earth, and his horse fell on top of him.

All around the ignorant dogs were running and barking and waving their tails.

How could we not move? But we could not. We sat frozen in our saddles and stared at Hans. At what we could see of him under that thrashing horse.

Only Alexi – God, let me please forget his face – he moved. He jumped down, staggering for an instant when he landed, and stumbled over to his brother, saying nothing. I never dared to ask him if he hoped. But the horse was still alive. Its leg was broken. Alexi grabbed its mane and tried to drag it off Hans's body. He pushed, pulled, kicked.

'Help me,' he said.

Climbing off our horses, we ran over. We tugged and swore at Hans's horse but it was useless.

'Stop it,' said Madeleine. 'It's no good.'

Hans's eyes were half-open, sightless, showing their whites. Blood ran out of his mouth to stain and melt the snow. Madeleine knelt down, put an ear to his mouth, touched the vein in his neck gently.

'Alexi,' she said, 'he's alive.'

Alexi had been standing with his arms hanging like butcher's meat, but when Madeleine said this he started tearing at his clothes, stuffing his jacket under Hans's head, ripping his shirt into strips for bandages; he went on shredding the cloth when there was no blood left, until Madeleine caught his hands in hers and said, 'Sit down.' And then, 'Reyhnard, get the blankets off the horses.'

I ran over and pulled them from under the saddles.

Hans's horse had been lying motionless on top of him, panting, but as I turned round I saw it suddenly kick out with its back leg. This rolled it further up Hans's body; we heard the noise of something splintering, and black blood gushed out of his nose. Alexi threw Madeleine's hands off, and pulling out his sword drove it into the horse's flank, and yanked it out and pushed it in, again, stabbing it over and over while the horse screamed, going on long after it was dead and the snow a carnage; while I stood speechless with the blankets in my arms, Madeleine open-mouthed, both of us staring at Alexi and unable to believe that it was our brother tearing this animal to pieces.

He stopped. The sword fell with a clatter.

He sat down in the red snow next to Hans's head. His hands were dark with blood. He did not touch Hans, or say anything. He didn't look at us. He could have been alone in the middle of that forest, kneeling next to Hans, staring at him, as if by the strength of his will he could keep Hans alive.

Up along the road we could hear the court approaching, sounds of hooves and bells and laughter. The King came into sight, courtiers bunched around him and straggling behind. He stopped when he saw us. The others pulled up in disarray.

He must have thought Hans was dead already. He climbed out of his saddle and came over to us without another word, walking past me, past Madeleine, who was crying, until he stood in the bloodied snow and looked down on Hans and Alexi. Alexi did not raise his head or move. He gave no sign of having heard the King approach.

Madeleine, crying, trying to speak: 'Sir, Sir, he's alive, he's not dead, Sir – we must move the horse, we must get some bearers, we must take him home . . . '

I saw a man grow old in a moment.

He began to shake, his head, his hands, his voice. He cried, 'Alexander! Alexander! Why wasn't it you?'

Alexi said, 'I wish it had been.'

27

It took four men to move the dead horse. Hans was put on a stretcher and carried home. Few of his bones were broken, and he had only small cuts and scratches, but inside his injuries were too terrible to let him live. I don't think he felt any pain; he was unconscious all the rest of that day and into the next. We waited in the corridor outside his door,

Alexi and the King having locked themselves in with him. He died about noontime without, I think, ever knowing exactly what had happened to him.

On the evening of Hans's death I went down to one of the salons. Everyone was listless. Women, and some men, were crying. No one talked, or if now and then someone might make the effort to pass a remark, no one replied. I kept thinking of him as I had seen him the morning before, galloping like wildfire through the snow. The dogs whined and roamed restlessly, laying their heads on this knee or that, complaining as we could not complain. We knew what had happened. The dogs could only sense what we felt.

No one spoke to me when I left. I looked in on Peter. He and his pet dog were curled up together in bed, fast asleep. I went to find Madeleine. She was sleeping too. Her pillow was wet. I lay down beside her and put my arms round her, but she did not wake. Finally I also fell asleep.

By morning the servants had hung black felt over all the windows, and nailed the yew branches to the doors. All public holidays were cancelled. Up from the city we could hear the faint, measured rumble of temple bells tolling without cease.

It was as if, while walking in the gardens at noon on a beautiful summer's day, the sun had suddenly dropped from the sky, leaving us in darkness. Alexi cried, 'How can he be dead?' Hans, wind and light and speed, how could he be dead? How could he, so strong and well-beloved, have been crushed to death like an ant? He had seemed untouchable. If Hans is dead, then who is safe? Death was stronger than Hans, stronger than the King, stronger than all of us banded together. Black like the ploughing down of youth, the obliteration of power, the onset of old age.

The body was laid out in state in the chapel of Adonac. The King's bed was set up next to Hans's bier. He had his meals sent to him there, spent all his days and nights there, mourning his dead son with every eccentricity of grief.

We went down because it was our duty. Around his body they had lit a hundred candles, and in their yellow light the face seemed made of wax, with a pinched nose, glass eyes and brittle hair. A dead someone, or something, not Hans. Peter began to scream; Madeleine and I led him outside. It was a relief to get out, but it granted no lessening of our sadness.

All I could think was that those candles, that fire, that superfluity of fire could not bring one snap of flame back into that dead flesh.

Alexi would not come down to the Temple. He did not want to look at a dead stranger's face; still less did he need to. The King was mourning a dead son. Alexi had lost his living brother. That man-made temple with its man-made candles and its man-made incense was no place to grieve for Hans, who had always belonged in the greenwood, beneath the open sky.

Death had killed twice. It had taken Hans utterly away, and with Hans it had taken our Alexi. He had no laughter, no songs and jokes, no teasing. We sat with and talked to a man we did not know, a mountain of a man whose handsomeness seemed painted on to hide the face beneath. Peter, crying openly, wandered about with a lost and frightened expression, not knowing what to make of this top-turned world. Alexi looked neither lost nor frightened, but hard: grim determination.

We tried to be with him all the time, at least one of us. We sat with him and talked to him, having this hope if no other: that somewhere underneath it all he was still alive. Madeleine and I kept a close watch on him, afraid that he would succeed in the sort of thing he did in fact attempt.

She explained to me afterwards that she had simply felt a strange uneasiness, quite suddenly. She had been talking with him only half-an-hour before, but she went up to find him. He had said he was going to lie down, and he was lying down, on his bed, blood seeping from the cut vein in his left wrist. A sword lay on the floor. When she came in, he gave the first smile we had seen in a week.

'Ah, Madeleine – I don't seem to be able to do the other one.'

He had lost a fair amount of blood, but he'd made a bad job of the wrist and wasn't badly hurt. Madeleine tied it up and said to him, 'Hans wouldn't want you to do this.'

'He's dead. He can't want anything any more. I want, I choose, not to live like this.'

'It's not right, and not fair, Alexi. We love you too. Now that we've lost him we need you more than ever.'

'I've botched it up, haven't I. How embarrassing.'

'I promise not to tell anyone if you promise not to try this again.'

'I don't mind if you tell Nardo.'

'You must promise me.'

'I don't need to promise. You're right, but not for the reason you think. I should have done it six days ago. Since I didn't – didn't think of it, didn't do it then – it's too late for me to die with dignity. So I have no right. But I don't know how I shall live without him.'

'We all have to try.'

Telling me about this later, she said that when he looked at her then she felt guilty for saying this.

The King tried to prevent him coming to the funeral. Perhaps he had heard about Alexi's attempt, perhaps some servant told him about the blood on the bedclothes – at any rate, he said Alexi was forbidden to attend.

Alexi said, 'I don't think I heard you.'

'I don't want anyone making stupid exhibitions of themselves,' said the King.

'What are you saying? Do you think I don't know how to behave? How dare you suggest I'd degrade him in any way?'

'Don't you talk to me like that, young man.'

'Then I suggest, Sir, that you don't try to stop me going.'

They set the ship on fire and cut its moorings. We took off our hats. I saw Alexi's scalp. It was tenderly blue-shadowed, shaven down to the skin.

In the end it was the King who made an exhibition of himself. He broke down and cried, leaning on Alexi's arm.

Alexi, you crafty old bastard, there is nothing about you that is not ambiguous, except your love for Hans. I saw you standing there with a back like steel while the King cried on your shoulder. I saw you staring out at a past that was over and a future you wanted nothing to do with. I saw your shaven head, and in the middle of my own grief, God help me, I felt pity for you.

28

Time passed, as it really has no option but to do, and I, like most people, assumed it was in the nature of things that they would heal over, like a scar, and that it was as much an inevitability as a duty that we would regain our enthusiasm for living. Spring came round again, as it always does despite the death of winter. I thought this was reassuring.

In a room, Madeleine, Alexi and I. She pulled back the curtains and smiled, saying, 'Look, Alexi, what a lovely day.'

'Is it? Yes, isn't it. Funny how the sun keeps on rising and setting.'

But it did, and it was the question of the future that gradually revived the court.

It may well have been the first time that many of them took a good look at Alexi. They saw a tall young man, healthy, very handsome, quick-witted and intelligent. A few of the younger set began trying to curry favour with him, expecting at least an acknowledgment, which was more than they had ever got from Hans. Most of them, however, waited for some sign from the King.

They waited for the King to take Alexi into his confidence. They didn't expect him to give Alexi the degree of loving favouritism which had been Hans's due. Hans had been adored, prized, cherished; Alexi was a makeshift. Nevertheless, they did expect the King to make some attempt at grooming his successor: for example, to take Alexi to Council meetings as he had taken Hans, introduce him to the ambassadors, walk with him and discuss affairs of state. To spend a little time with him. Throughout that black winter and subdued spring the court waited.

But, quite simply, the King had lost interest. Never in his life had he been forced to make do with second best. He could not begin now.

His obsession with Beulah's child evaporated. She brought it to see him as often as ever, and he still dandled it on his knee, but with an air of aloof preoccupation. Strategically, she weaned it, and continued to sleep with the King; but I often saw him look at her as if she was far away. They walked and sat together a great deal, usually in silence.

Once, in the middle of a dance held for the reception of an embassy, he suddenly reached out for her hand and said loudly, 'Ah, my dear, you are a great comfort to an old man in his grief.'

Beulah, uncharacteristically, blushed and looked uncomfortable.

So Alexi's circle of courtiers never developed. They saw the King's apathy and, fearing to offend or make a wrong move, they gave up trying to cultivate my brother.

Alexi walked alone, and would not let anyone near.

Peter had retreated from the court. He spent all his days out of doors, down at the stables or the athletics track, coming back to the Palace only to sleep, and sometimes not then. Early in the morning he would wake me up and try to persuade me to go with him. Often I did. He hated being alone.

We stood watching Nikolas showing off his fencing to a gaggle of young ladies.

I said, 'It's as if you live down here, you know. In fact you more or less do.'

'I wish I did. It's deadly in the Palace. Nothing but long faces. I hate it, it's horrible. The King's hair is white now, have you noticed?'

'Yes.'

'Everything's so quiet. It's like a house full of old people, tiptoeing around.'

'Nothing's been the same since Hans died.'

'It's been six months. I miss Hans too you know – but if he could see the way things are now, he'd be glad he died. Oh, well done, Nikolas!'

'Don't applaud him. He's just performing.'

'He's good, though. He comes down here a lot these days. He can't stick the court either.'

'Have you become very chummy with him?'

'Not really. I talk to him sometimes. I like him, he's got a lot of – what's the word?'

'Self-confidence?'

'No – well, in a way. At least he doesn't sit around brooding. Alexi is like a different person. He always acts like he wishes I was somewhere else. We used to be friends.'

'It's harder for him, Peter.'

'Yes,' said Peter, 'I know.'

I asked him, 'Have you done any painting lately?'

'No, not really. Look, Nardo, I'm not all that good, really, I can see that.'

'You used to enjoy it so much.'

'I used to like playing with toy soldiers too. One gets older, one gets realistic.'

Coming from a twelve-year-old boy, this was so pompous I laughed. 'You sound like a middle-aged man!'

'Good score, Nikolas!'

'Pay attention.'

He turned back to me. 'Nardo, sometimes I . . . Painting!' he exclaimed contemptuously. 'What's it good for? I don't want just to have a hobby, I want – well, one of us ought to be a soldier, and the only one left now is me, so that's what I'm going to concentrate on.'

He shifted his weight to the other foot, shouted congratulations at Nikolas, and returned to me. 'Do you remember when I was little, and I used to say, "When *I'm* King I'll do something or other", and you always said that neither of us was going to be King, because Hans was – '

'Yes, what about it?'

'Funny it should turn out to be Alexi.' He squinted at the duellists for a moment, and added thoughtfully, 'Nikolas says he'll make a good King.'

'Nikolas is obviously an expert.'

'Don't be so sarky. If you knew him better you'd like him more.'

'I knew him well enough in the nursery, thanks.'

The match was at an end. We both turned to watch Nikolas. He flourished his sword, saluting first his opponent, then us; then he slid his sword into its scabbard and walked over to where his wife was sitting.

He, my contemporary, was at this time twenty-one, but even as I looked rather younger than my age, so he had the bearing of a man several years older. I seem to be leading into a description of him, and this is as good a place as any to give it.

Nikolas cultivated a rough, solid, no-nonsense image, and in those days seemed to be a rough, solid, reliable man, a soldier to the core. Our nurse had singled him out as exceptional before we were five years old, and so it remained. He was marked for a shining future: a general undoubtedly, an ambassador probably, and if he gave up his Fahl to his younger brother (who, like their father, never came to court, and was as far as I can gather a bit of a nonentity) he would have a seat on the Council as well.

Despite all this Nikolas retained a certain diffidence. Everything he did he did well, yet rather than come forward for praise he retreated from it, and it followed him.

He had many friends, but was not seen to have intimates. If he had a circle, it wasn't easy to distinguish. He seemed devoted to his wife, and I never heard of him having mistresses while she was alive. Over the last few years he had always been correct to me; though he knew as well as I did that there was no point in even beginning an attempt to make friends.

He seemed, he seemed – my cousin Nikolas seemed the very model of a good man.

He came riding through the village just the other day, with the Commander. He was wearing general's insignia, so presumably he is in charge of this war with Ruffashpah, which he could win with one hand tied behind his back. Never let it be said that I denied anyone their due. They took me by surprise as I was walking along the street. I had no time to get out of their field of vision, and so Nikolas greeted me. When I say me, I mean the clerk he thinks he remembers from that time last autumn when I took the inventories to Rayalled. I've often been told that he has this gift of never forgetting a name or a face, and as I said, his confidence never looks further than the obvious explanation.

I don't envy him. It goes too deep for that. I'm a good man too, as the poets say. I can't say 'the best'. Who is? I have my flaws and I made my mistakes because I am a man. I am not 'the best', but I did my best, and with fewer privileges than he had. I am not the traitor. So tell me, Temple Gods, with your weather-worn faces that look leprous but aren't even that because you have no flesh, you tell me: Why are the innocent punished while women trail their hair in their tears for the guilty, who end up with more honours than they had before? What about the men who followed where Adonac led? Did Asdura, sweet and gentle mother, cry for them?

I remember lying on a hillside, surrounded by the scent of crushed grass, warm earth, Madeleine – her hair twined round me, my head in the hollow of her shoulder, my nose burrowing drowsily beneath her ear, happy and half-asleep on a May afternoon.

'That's a horse,' she said, pointing at the clouds.

I got up on one elbow to join her game. It had rained the night before, cleaning out the clouds to leave them weightless and bleached. Madeleine's horse thrust its head and one hoof westward, rose up in a formless mass, and became . . . 'A castle,' I said.

'Wouldn't it be nice if we could go and live there?'

Change and no change. In the world at large everything changed when Hans died; between my sister and myself nothing had changed. We merely sought the outdoors more than ever, forsaking the Palace for a distant hill or hollow where we could be alone, happier on our own than we were with other people.

'I love you,' I said.

'I love you too.'

'But I love you more.'

'No, I love you more.'

'I love you even more than that.'

'How much, then?'

'About a million times as much as the sky is wide.'

'That's only about half as much as I love you. Oh look – look!' she cried. 'Look at that ship! Look at those sails puffing out! It's squelching right into your castle.'

I could write for all my life about every word Madeleine said to me. I remember everything, in the way they say drowning men do: all at once and as if it were of the moment. Pictures and words. The subterfuge, the risks that were fun and almost part of the delight. Shared daring. I remember we danced together so carefully and properly, hand in hand; and she would rub her thumb against my palm in circles, testing my endurance. Once she went too far and I cried out, softly. People around us heard me and I had to pretend I had twisted my ankle. I got my own back at dinner, making her drop her spoon by running my foot up and down her leg, under the table. She was angry then, but never for long.

One great day I finally took my courage in both hands and did what she had begged me to do: I showed her my poems. She sat down attentively and read each one through, while I hovered over her, saying, 'That one's no good' – 'I never liked that one' – 'How could I ever have written that?' – trying to labour their flaws when she picked out their best bits, and even snatched one from her hands. Patiently she asked for it back. She read them all, and said, 'I know I'm biased, but I do think they're good.'

And I said, 'But you haven't had a real education, not a literary education, you're no judge.'

She understood that I said this out of nerves, not unkindness.

I remember this conversation, which took place on the night following our day out on the hill.

I came to her room in the middle of the night, not to make love but for love. All alone in my room, in the dark, I had been panicking about death again. I could not get the image of Hans's dead stranger's face out of my mind, nor those thoughts which superimposed me, dead, in his place. Madeleine was awake, knowing I was coming, perhaps, waiting for me. My teeth were chattering. I climbed in beside her. She was so warm.

'You're freezing,' she said. 'What's wrong, are you ill?' She pulled the blankets up and held me tight.

'I can't sleep,' I said.

'Why not?'

'I'm afraid.'

'Of what? What's happened?'

'Of death,' I said; and this was the first time I had ever talked about it to anyone, this horrible, pervasive dread that over the years had become as integral to me as my organs. Just being with her, mentioning it, bringing it into the open, helped me to calm down. She put my hands on her breast so I could feel her heartbeat. 'You're all right,' she said. 'I'm here.'

'I wish I could sleep with you like this all the time. I hate sleeping on my own.'

'Reyhnard, I've never seen you in such a state before. Do you often get like this?'

'At night. It's worst at night. Not often during the day, it's not so bad in the light. You can see everyone just – just being alive, and you can say it won't happen for a long time, and when it does it won't be so bad. But you can't see anything at all at night, and it's so quiet, and I can't stop thinking – '

'Shhh,' she said. 'It's all right. You're here now.'

'Do you want to hear a paradox? When I'm this frightened I wish I was dead so I wouldn't have to feel afraid any more. But I don't wish I was dead. It's Hans, more than anything. I thought I'd got over it, but no. Hans. He's dead, he's dead, we'll never see him again, he'll never go hunting again. He's dead. He's gone. There's nothing left of him at all, not even ashes . . . '

'He's in Hulsitoq.'

'There's no Hulsitoq, don't give me shepherds' tales. I don't believe in it. It can't make me feel better. It makes me feel worse. I wish there was a Hulsitoq, then I wouldn't be so frightened.'

'How do you know there isn't a Hulsitoq?'

'Don't, Madeleine, don't. I'm not in the mood for arguments.'

'I'm asking you a question.'

'I know because I know. Don't tell me you believe in it.'

'I see no harm in believing,' she said gently.

'You can't choose. Either you believe a thing or you don't. You can't *decide* to, just because it sounds like a nice idea.'

'Whether there is or there isn't, there's still death. You can't go through life being afraid of it.'

'I know that. I *know* – I know better than most people because it looks like I'll have to – '

'Reyhnard,' she hushed me. 'Keep your voice down. Lady Vivienne and her husband sleep next door, their bed's right against the wall.'

I shut my mouth and pushed my face against her shoulder. She began to speak, softly, reasonably. 'I know that you're afraid. I know why. I am too, everybody is. Being afraid is as much a part of life as – as death is. Death is the price we have to pay for the privilege of being alive.'

'I didn't ask to be born!'

'Would you rather never have been alive at all?'

In her bed, in her arms, if I had said 'yes' it would have been through fear, not honesty. 'You know I wouldn't.'

'Well then,' she went on, 'if you're glad you're alive, and since you can't do anything about death, you must resign yourself, and not let it spoil life. You know, Reyhnard, they say that as one gets older one fears it less.'

'I don't believe that.'

'But you don't know, so you ought to believe it. Death is natural. It can't be such a terrible thing. Everything dies. It's part of the world.'

'It's easy for you, you're a woman.'

'Then maybe I know better than you.'

'You don't know, you just believe all that rubbish they teach us. You don't know what it's like to be as afraid as I am – '

She took my face in her hands, speaking my name over and over. I felt my panic ebbing out of me. It's going through her fingers, I thought, and she will put it away where it cannot hurt me. It wasn't what she said that I found reassuring, for I've heard many men say it, and it has never helped. It was her hands, her skin, herself. We lay down again.

'I have thought about it,' she said. 'It seems to me that it's only death that gives any point to life. Who would ever do anything, if they had endless time? If you lived every day as if you were going to die at the end of it, you wouldn't miss a thing. You'd get the whole of the day.'

'That's no argument.'

'There's no point in being afraid of the inevitable, it will poison your life.'

I was kissing her; then I remembered something, and pointed out, 'Madeleine, when you thought your marriage to Julius of Pravarre was inevitable, you were frightened.'

'Yes I was,' she agreed, stroking my hair. 'But I'd have faced it as bravely as I could.'

'So I'm a coward, is that it?'

She laughed and kissed me back. 'Of course not. You've got too much imagination, that's all. It's easy for people with no imagination to be brave.'

'You're imaginative, you're as much of a dreamer as I am.'

'Reyhnard, you can't compare a marriage with death.'

'A fate worse than death?'

Instead of laughing, Madeleine slid down under the covers to level her eyes with mine, and said seriously, 'Yes. I think there are fates worse than death. If I'd had to marry him and go away from you, that would have been.'

We made love stealthily, covering each other's mouths with our hands. In the candlelight her wide eyes were greeny-gold, glazed like the dazzle of sunlight on the sea, shining with my own joy in being alive, with her, loving her. I loved making love to her as she loved making love to me. Maybe the whole world does make love in the same way and use those words, but to tell the truth I don't believe it. It seemed entirely a part of us, our invention, our taste, our delight, our answer to the question Why? Why are we born, why do we eat and sleep and dream and work and love? For this, that's why. I would love never to stop, to go on through all the hours of the day, dawn to dusk and noon to midnight, for when we make love we alone are in motion: the world stands still and we are the spinning of it. If we could make love for ever, without pause or rest or weakening, we would never die. While we make love we are living in eternity.

We touch godhood, I thought, relaxing in that soft sleepy trough after the madness. A phrase of Caryllac's passed through my mind: 'brief ecstasies of timelessness', and in its wake the wretched sadness came creeping over me. I thought of Madeleine saying, 'It's the price you have to pay.' You always have to pay, I thought, paying with this grief for that little death. I've seen immortality and can't have it: I am right to be afraid. I know what I am denied.

I clutched at her. 'Madeleine, this will end one day – '

'Don't, please don't, don't say things like that.'

'It's true, it's true, I can't run away from it or make myself believe it isn't true. Whatever you say doesn't alter the fact that we'll both die one day, and this – '

Having no other way to shut me up, she kissed me until I forgot what I meant to say. Or, as the saying is, perhaps the kisses spoke for themselves – at any rate kissing in circles is better than talking in circles. 'Are you feeling better now?' she asked. I nodded against her hair. 'There, then, go to sleep.'

'I can't,' I said. 'I must go.'

'Did anyone see you come in?' I shook my head. 'Then be quiet, go to sleep. I'll wake you before the servants come.'

Madeleine, I remember sleeping in your arms, where nothing could ever hurt me. Sleeping in peace and waking in trust, jumping eagerly out of bed to greet the sun. I remember when I looked forward to each new day.

I remember something else she said to me that night. 'We have all our lives ahead of us.' I used to say that to Peter: 'Why are you in such a hurry? You've got your whole life ahead of you.'

I wonder if there's anyone alive or dead who hasn't said that at least once, or thought it. Perhaps Hans didn't: those were not the sort of terms he thought in. I never heard Alexi use it, though, which is strange. Or not. I suppose he would say it wasn't a truism.

It's not true. From the moment we are born we have a bit of our lives behind us, and more and more of our lives behind us until it is all behind us and we are dead. I see I have found a new way of expressing my present existence, this being both alive and dead: all of my life is behind me, and yet I am not dead. Oh Reyhnard, you are such a liar, no not a liar but such a neat little constructor of aphorisms, or whatever you call them. You have one thing left in life, and that is love for the people who loved you. That is what hurts you and that is what reminds you that you are still alive.

But then, when I had my whole life ahead of me, when we were grieving for Hans, and worried about Alexi, and wondering about the future, when I still had Peter and Madeleine, when I was happy, we thought things had changed at court.

What had happened, what we thought almost beyond endurance – it *was* terrible, it *was* almost beyond endurance. It was the first crack before the dam collapses, letting the flood in, and everything falls to pieces. And we didn't know. Like that joke which used to make Peter laugh so much when he was four.

Three wicked men, who didn't believe in the Gods and so lied and cheated and sinned their way through life, died and sailed to Hulsitoq. This surprised them, because they hadn't believed it existed. They were even more surprised to find that Adonac was real, too. Because they were so unregenerate, they were punished by being buried underneath the earth for ever.

'Oh Adonac, great Adonac,' came their muffled voices (I had to put my hand over my mouth and muffle my own, or Peter would make me start again). 'Oh Adonac, we didn't know, we didn't know.'

And the great God of Mercy replied, 'Well, you know now.'

29

At the beginning of summer we had some very hot weather. One day the King was out in the gardens, playing with Beulah and her child, when he suffered a seizure. He was carried into the Palace unconscious. The doctors said that: due to extremity of the weather, that is, the heat; and due to his debilitated condition, that is, he was worn out with grief, some blood had burst in his brain. It might have killed a lesser man, but it seemed nothing could kill him: he woke after a few hours and soon recovered, or almost. Externally his only symptom was a slight looseness down his left side; his face sloped, his left hand shook, and he talked out of the right corner of his mouth. Inside, though, it had affected his mind.

He became forgetful. I saw him put a thing down and then hunt for it, unable to remember where it was. Often, in the middle of a speech, he would suddenly stop as if he had dropped all his words; then he would repeat everything he had said. At times he was as sharp as ever. You could see it return. His brain would uncloud and the old look return to his eyes, and then all the courtiers around him would pull up their backs and look smart.

He knew what had happened to him – once or twice I caught a glimpse of his face when he didn't realise anyone was looking, and there I saw an expression of grieving desperation. And then I would think, 'That man is my father.' But it was too late. I didn't know how to pity him;

and sometimes, when he looked at me or Alexi, he did not bother to put that expression away, so I realised it was just as well I had no pity for him, since neither of us would have known what to do with it.

He might still have been capable of affairs of state, but he had no inclination for them, and no interest. He shook his head when they were mentioned, and then forgot them. It was when we saw this that we knew the King had gone.

The first instinct of everyone – court, Council and ambassadors – was to turn to Alexi. Obviously it would not be long before he was King. But Alexi turned his back on them. He showed them clearly that he didn't want to, and would not, become involved.

Meanwhile Beulah gathered control. I learnt of this in reverse, so to speak – by which I mean I realised she had accumulated power only after it had grown to a large extent, and working from that I went back to find out how it had happened.

It dropped into her lap.

Chatienne was preparing to go to war against a small country off its west coast. This country is composed of innumerable small islands, and as its real name is something impossible to transliterate, we call it Sogorah. It's part of Chatienne now, or so I will assume until news of something different filters up here; but in those days we did a good trade with Sogorah, mostly in spices and silks. The Chatiennese ambassador came to Tsvingtori in order to arrange a treaty of non-intervention. We would refrain from entering the war on the side of Sogorah, and in return our trade privileges would be confirmed; or rather, this is what they hoped we would agree to.

The ambassador put in at the residence in Tsvingtori and sent his proposals to the King. Sometimes the King glanced at these paper deputations; more often he rolled them up and put them to one side; the end was always that he forgot about them – if they had ever managed to penetrate his mind in the first place. Now, for an ambassador the one thing worse than coming home with a 'No' is coming home to admit he couldn't gain an audience or any answer at all. The poor man sat in his residence sweating with fear of death, until, desperate, he thought up a desperate plan, and sent his suit to Beulah. Perhaps a friend of his in the Palace, or some merchant seeking interest with Chatienne, had hinted to him how things stood at court.

Beulah – I discovered this many years later, and was furious with myself for not having seen it before – invited the man up, had a private talk with him and set a date; as promised, on that date and at that time, the King was ready to receive him. He had been briefed by Beulah, who stood next to him throughout the interview. Everything was settled to

Chatienne's advantage. Soon after this I saw her wearing a magnificent set of Chatiennese opals, but these were merely a courtesy gift. She was after something less tangible and much more valuable.

This is the first instance I know of Beulah taking a hand in affairs of state. Previously she had been a leader of court fashion, an organiser of society, stirring her finger in marriage contracts, fixing titles and property deeds so that they would go to her favourites. Of course there was her victory over Edvard filcLaurentin, but that was personal, not political.

So if, as I admit, I know less of government than a king ought, look no further for the reason than my wife.

This is rather dry, but then it is history, if hard to see as such. I find it all extremely boring, and always did. Government is boring, unless you have a taste for it. I don't. She did. She does. However –

An embassy from Andariah had also been cooling its heels in Tsving-tori, unable to reach the King. Good news travels fast in diplomatic quarters: they noted Chatienne's success, adopted the same method and were soon satisfied and speeding on their way. The next month a deputation came from the city of Amanah-in-Peat. This city had been troubled by border raids and was suing for a reduction in taxes. As if it was decreed, they sent in two petitions: one openly and with formality to the King, the other under cover of a letter to the Lady Beulah.

Everyone knows what happened after that. What, perhaps, they don't know is that it was Beulah who told the King to refuse the Amanaians, Beulah who selected the battalions sent up to deal with the ensuing trouble, and Beulah who appointed Nikolas as Commander, though his papers of commission bore the King's seal which at that time, as she told me one day when I came into the Council chambers and found her using it, she had had possession of for only a few weeks.

Well done, Reyhnard. A lovely dull catalogue. But then it was easy, really, for her to take control. Who else was there? Alexi didn't want to know, and nobody asked me – if they had, I wouldn't have been interested either. Alexi and I were both too engrossed in our own affairs to notice what alignments of authority were taking place. I dimly sensed, because Peter and Madeleine both pointed it out, that the aimless anxiety which had filled the court had been replaced by a sort of relaxation; as if a collective sigh of relief had been uttered at the sight of someone taking the helm. Those who saw what was happening did not question it. They were all too glad that things were sailing ahead once more; and if it had been, not Beulah, but even a clerk or a servant, I don't think anyone would have tried to stop them.

So, King Basal the Great, which seems to be the epithet posterity has decided to bestow on you, Great King – this was the sum of your years of rule which began with such glory and destruction: in the end, you let your mistress run the country for you. I know the moment when it all became pointless. That royal rug was pulled out from under your feet. Your broken hands, which had carved so many victories, grasped at air. Death respects no man's wishes. Why should it have honoured those of Basal the Great? Great King, I make you my model, that should please you. There are many ways of running away, and yours, Great King, is the easiest.

Piece by piece Alexi came back to us. First his smile, then his laughter, then his old lazy, provoking manner of speech. One day we heard him singing. Yet it was not the same, and we knew it never would be. It seemed enough to have back this much of him. Madeleine treated him with the same gentleness one gives to an invalid of war, who has seen too much and lost too much to take up his old life again – or to want to.

We let him come to us when he felt like it, and we were together more and more. I had never thought I would miss him so dreadfully. He became reflective, and his conversation was usually directed towards the past.

He and I were sitting in a salon. We had a walnut cake, and were each eating a piece. At the far end of the room two women were embroidering, their heads together, but we ignored them.

We talked about my childhood, nothing serious. With him it was always 'do you remember, do you remember?' As it is with me now. I understand how he felt. I know that he talked as men do who have nothing to look forward to but death, and no change that could be for the better. At the time, though, I thought talking helped him.

Reminiscing about my early days put me in mind of something I had always wanted to ask him, and now I felt an urgent need to seize this chance. 'Alexi,' I said, 'why have you always been so – I don't know how to put it. So nice to me? You know things about me that I can't remember. But I do remember when I was in the nursery, and the King came in, and everyone frowned but you always smiled at me, and you used to bring me things.'

'Who knows?' he said. 'Who knows? You were my brother and you were a baby. I've always liked babies. I even like Beulah's baby, though given its mother I dread to think how it'll turn out. I suppose you fascinated me – not you, not my old Nardo, because you weren't *you* then, just a baby. Do you remember when Peter was born, and I showed you how babies will grip your finger if you give it to them?'

'Yes.'

'It was your wet-nurse showed me that.'

'You must have bowled her over with your charm.'

'I was only eight. God, what a long time ago. Like another life. How old are you now? You're twenty-one, aren't you? You know, one gets quite attached to babies. And then you were growing up, and turning into this rather horrid little individual, and I saw that the same' – he broke off to put a piece of cake into his mouth, and went on talking while he chewed – 'I suppose I thought I could help you – make something of yourself. You were a little bastard when you were younger, you know. Sometimes you still are. Suppose we all are. The priggish things you used to say – '

'You pointed them out at the time, Alexi.'

'Ah well, I don't flatter myself my little lectures were ever taken to heart. It's Peter and Madeleine – '

The girls at the other end of the room were giggling loudly. I glanced round to see what they were laughing at – but it was us. I looked at Alexi, his mouth full, and down at the cake, and saw that he had eaten it all.

'I'm a glutton, aren't I?' he said. 'I didn't even notice.'

Beulah is a bitch with a cunning nose, coursing the main chance.

I had noticed that she was choosing her lovers with more discretion these days, and that there weren't so many of them. We assumed she still slept with the King. Any information to the contrary would have come down faster than bricks dropping. Of course she still slept with the King. She had her footholds and she took good care of them, but she knew better than anyone else what his death would mean to her. Alexi would have her out on her ear the moment he became King. I thought, and hoped, that he might even let me divorce her, though I never mentioned it to him: there seemed time enough and I was happy with Madeleine. I hardly ever saw Beulah – she was scarcely a part of my world. And there were two subjects we did not dare raise with Alexi: the Kingship, and Hans.

Beulah swept back into that familiar game which was no game, which she had played and I had watched her play three years before with my dead brother. She knew she was fighting a hard battle, though I doubt she could accept it was as doomed to failure as her assault on Hans had been. She was for ever ordering new dresses and jewellery, trying out perfumes, hiring and firing hairdressers and maids. Her prize was Alexi, and perhaps she thought, 'I had him once, I can get him back.'

I don't think she ever quite understood us, dog-nosed keen as she was – though in the end it didn't matter. We were all a disappointment to her. But she fought a good fight and I salute her, fit Queen for the men who serve her.

The salon was crowded. The King was not there. Peter had inveigled me into a game of cards, threatening to escape if I didn't play. Madeleine stood by my shoulder, both of us keeping an ear on the court: the atmosphere was strained, over-excited, as an audience is before the play begins. Alexi sat on a sofa close to us, reading. Beulah, whether in a corner or in the middle of a room, was always the centre of it, looking more beautiful than she ever had since the day she had borne her child – and I may say this, because she was beautiful. I ought to know, I was nearly smothered by her beauty. She was beautiful, and so are all sorts of foul poisonous things: the bright red berries children reach for instinctively, until we teach them that those berries are deadly.

Beulah came down the room, her perfume higher and stronger than any other woman's, her hems kissing whispers along the floor as she walked. She paused, fanned, exchanged words, took a hand and held it, slipped her arm through another's – she knew how to seem to be everywhere at once.

'That's a new collar she's got on,' Madeleine remarked to me. 'I like the lace, but it would be better with less.'

'We'll see a dozen of them before the week is out.'

Peter was also watching her. I told myself I ought to do something, or see what Alexi could do. Peter might welcome his advice. I didn't think he had slept with anyone yet, though Alexi reminded me that thirteen was more than old enough, and pointed out that Peter was not the type to hang back for long. If he had, I said, he would tell me – which he did. All stare and no action, said Alexi. Still, better the servants than the ladies, who cannot be sent off to the city if they get pregnant.

I watched him following Beulah's movements, and made up my mind to have a talk with him soon.

Finally she reached our little island. I felt Madeleine step back as Beulah came up behind me. She kissed the top of my head and kneaded my neck with her hands. I tried to shrug her off, but she dug in.

'I've got such exciting news, darling,' she said. 'Little Basal talked today, talked for the very first time.'

'Oh really? What did it say?'

No one saw her nails cut into my skin. 'He said Mama, and then' – she lied shamelessly – 'he said Dada. Isn't that thrilling, darling?'

'Wildly.'

'You must come and see him very soon, maybe he'll talk for you.'

From the sofa Alexi drawled, 'Is that performing parrot of yours still alive, Beulah?'

Sweetly she answered, 'We were talking about little Basal. Do pay attention, if you must butt in.'

The laughter, behind-hand for Alexi, was open now.

Her hand trailed down my sleeve as she walked round me, heading for Peter. She stood behind his back, put her hands on his shoulders, and bent forward to study his cards. 'You should keep that,' she said. 'Play that, or my husband will trump you.'

Peter tried to laugh – 'Whose side are you on?' – but it ended on a squeak.

'I shan't take sides between brothers.' Now that she had his attention, she took a step back and flicked the hem of her skirt. 'Tell me, Peter, what do you think of this dress?'

He stuttered, 'It's – it's very nice.'

'I'm glad you think so. I thought this embroidery down the bodice might be a bit too fussy – ' She fingered it, and shot him a look from under her lids. 'As long as you're not simply flattering me?'

Alexi said, 'Oh, Peter always says what he thinks, don't you, Peter?'

Red now to the tips of his ears, Peter glanced from her to him and back to her and tried to say something, and suddenly dropped all his cards.

'Don't move!' Beulah cried. 'I'll get them!'

She bent down, her tight belt pinching her waist, her breasts falling forward against the lace, her flesh bursting out of her clothes like a peach so ripe it was ready to split its skin. Then I felt Madeleine slip her cool hand into mine. She pressed it against her leg, hiding our clasp in the folds of her skirt. My irritation died away. I saw that when Beulah stood up she was curved to face not Peter, but Alexi. Well, I thought, he can look after himself.

When she gave the cards to Peter and her fingers touched his palm, his blush was shining red. She patted his hair and moved away. I watched her hover, chatting with two women, and then, at last, she sat down next to Alexi.

'It's your lead,' I said to Peter.

His head was stooped over the table, and I couldn't see his eyes; his fingers, which I could see, were shaking. We played out the hand and I won easily. Then he excused himself. I thought it better to let him go. Madeleine sat down in his empty chair, but didn't pick up the cards.

Suddenly I was surprised to hear Nikolas beside me, offering, 'I'd like to play a game with you, Prince, if you would be so kind. I've heard you're very good.'

No alternative but to nod. Madeleine half-raised herself to give him the chair; then we heard: 'Will you get away from me!'

Every startled head in the room turned as one to stare at the sofa. It was Alexi who had spoken. Beulah was sitting rigidly upright. Alexi folded his hands on his book and said, 'I do wish you'd stop rubbing yourself against me, Beulah. I must say you give me about as much urge as a dead donkey's armpit.'

I thought I had seen her angry before, but I never had, not like this, with the uncontrollable rage that lesser people suffer from. This was the first and last time I saw her hit someone – well, someone other than me – on the face, hard enough to leave a mark; then she leapt back as if she was the one who had been struck, and she shrieked with the voice she must have had before she came to court. 'You prick! You think a damn sight too much of yourself if you think I'm interested in *you*, you fat pig. You're just a fat pig stuffing yourself from morning to night, you don't know when to stop eating and it bloody well shows.'

'In that dress, at any rate, I think it's a case of the sow calling the boar fat, don't you?'

In the time it took her to think up an answer to that one, Beulah regained her temper, remembered where she was and saw that the situation was running away with her. What they said to each other – well, as I write it down, it's ludicrous. But no one was laughing. The words didn't matter. When dogs bare their teeth and growl at each other, no man knows what they are saying, but he knows what it means and he keeps out of their way.

Beulah stood up straight and folded her hands. She waited a long time, hoping he would make the mistake of speaking first. He simply looked at her. The moment was dying. So she put a forgiving expression on her face and said, 'Prince, I shall not ask for an apology. Your behaviour would be inexcusable in a servant, and still more so in a man of your position. However, I shall overlook it, for we all understand that you haven't been quite in your right mind since the tragedy of Prince Hans's death. So, sir, this is the end of it, and I shan't mention it again.'

Alexi shrugged, and returned to his book.

The moment was hers, for she had cared enough to seize it. When I was King she always made fine speeches. I suppose she still does.

She turned around with a grand sweep and joined back into the court. Soon she was laughing and joking and playing with her fan as if it had never happened. But once in a while I saw people sneaking a look at Alexi.

And once I saw him lift his head and stare at her. She had her back to him. He stared for a long time with eyes full of grief and hatred, and did not care who saw it.

Much later that day Madeleine said to me, 'She was right about one thing. He's getting terribly fat. I can't think how we didn't notice.'

'He's put on a bit of weight.'

'A bit? He's put on three stone at least.'

'He can't have, not in eight months.'

'He has, though. I'm worried. He does eat like a pig. He eats anything and everything, he's always eating.'

'He's always had a big appetite.'

'Not like this, Reyhnard. I know he can carry it, almost – but if he goes on like this he'll become immense. And he's lost all his muscles. Surely you'll admit?'

'He is a bit out of condition. Of course he and Hans used to go riding every day, and now he doesn't.'

'You must ask him to go with you.'

'Madeleine, I have. He won't.'

'He doesn't take any exercise at all. He just sits around and eats. You must say something to him.'

I tried, but he didn't seem to hear me. When I urged him to eat less and take more exercise, he went on devouring biscuits as if no one was talking to him.

High summer. The grass was burnt at the edges, the sky shivered. The roses paled in the hot brilliance of the sun. We had more than the usual number of thunderstorms that year. Gilles Mehah announced that he was resigning the Chancellorship and retiring from the Council. He wanted to go to his nephew's Fahl, where the weather is a little more temperate; the south-west coast of Mehah curves to embrace Ksaned Kaled. Who could blame him? We would all have liked to go.

I forced myself to take an interest in this, in order to force Alexi. I dragged him out for a walk. It was I who said, 'We have to talk about this.'

'You must go to the King,' I said. 'You must make him share the selection with you. I know you, you've always kept your eyes open. You must have a man in mind.'

Alexi said, 'Gilles is a loss, it's true. Not that any of them has much work to do these days.'

'They're all over fifty, except for Dominic filcRandal and Valentine Mehah – and he's pushing it. The Council needs some new blood.'

'Why are you so interested in it all of a sudden?'

'It's not *my* responsibility to be interested in it – '

'Oh Nardo, you are a bore.'

'You can't shut me up like that. Admittedly I "know little and care less", but if you don't make an effort Beulah will stock the whole Council with her own toadies, and you'll either have to work with them, which would be impossible, or get rid of them all and build one up from scratch.'

'Look, just drop it.'

'It's your responsibility.'

'Can we sit down here, please?'

We had climbed to the crest of a knoll. On one side we could look down across the gardens and the Palace, while on the other woods and meadows rolled away from us, rising into downland. Little grey curls of smoke floated up from the pleats of the landscape, showing us hamlets and houses. Alexi sat down with his back to the Palace, staring out to where the river Wastryl snaked under the sun, black and shiny like old silver.

His face, forehead and neck were dripping sweat, black curls sticking to his skin. I saw the beat of the vein in his throat. He was breathing heavily.

I looked at his neck. Once the sinews had shown through the skin, and the flesh curved in at either side towards his spine; now, beneath his short hair, there were three plump rolls of fat. His wrists were beginning to look like a baby's, podgy and wrinkled – a grotesque parody on a man who had once been so handsome. He sat awkwardly, unable to bring his cross-legged thighs flat against the ground. His body, once so deceptively powerful, was now flaccid.

How could eight months – half a year – have caused all this wreckage?

The only part of him that had not put on weight was his face. It was gaunt. His green eyes were huge under hoods of bone, and his Rorhah nose beaky. His lips were faintly blue.

Seeing the mess he had allowed himself to become, I got angry. 'A year ago you could have run up this hill and laughed all the way,' I said.

'Shut up.'

'Alexi, don't you ever look at yourself? You're fat! Fat! It's appalling! You can't even climb a tiny little hill before you have to sit down. How did you let this happen? I can see it in front of me and I still can't believe it.'

'I wouldn't have come if I thought you were going to nag me to death.'

I took a seat on the dry grass next to him. 'Can't we talk about the new councillor? Haven't you got anyone in mind?'

He named a man.

'I don't know him,' I said, 'but I've heard the name.'

Alexi was tearing at the grass. 'Well, that's about all you'll ever hear of him. You always were a long time taking in news. Beulah's already got her man in.'

'Who?'

'Basal Kyrah, but everyone calls him Kerry because there are so many Basals.'

'Basal Kyrah? But he's my age. He used to be in the nursery with me. He was friends with Nikolas.'

'Suppose he still is.'

'Well, Alexi – *Alexi*, what are you going to do?'

'Nothing, I should think.'

'But you must do something.'

'Why? Tell me why. Why should I do anything?'

'Because – because when the King dies, you'll have to pull her off the throne like a winkle.'

'Maybe I never will be King. Maybe Father will fulfil everyone's prayers and live for ever.'

He took out a bag of toffees and began to eat them, very rapidly.

'Put them away!' I shouted.

He went on crunching them up at exactly the same speed.

I tried to think of something that would stop him. 'Alexi! What would Hans say if he could see you now?'

I was glad I'd said it, because Alexi immediately stood up, and I saw he could still be light on his feet when he chose. He grabbed me by the front of my shirt and hauled me up; but he had lost some of his strength. Once, he could have lifted me off the ground.

'Do you think I eat for fun?' he shouted, shaking me by the collar. 'I have to eat, I can't help it, there's this bloody great big fat hole inside me where he used to be. But you can't even understand – ' He let me go. 'You've got no idea what it feels like, so shut up!'

'You're killing yourself.'

'I hope so!'

'You've got no right.'

'Listen Nardo, I know you do not give a shit. All you're worried about is that I might die and then *you'll* be the one.'

'How can you say that?'

'Because it's true. Because I know. Because I hate it all so much, you must feel the same. I don't blame you, I know how you feel – I *am* how you feel, I *am* what you're afraid of, can't you *see*? I hate it, I hate eating like this, I hate being a gross pile of flesh, I hate being alive. I hate missing him. I hate everything, nothing's the way it was supposed to be. He was going to be King. Everything's gone wrong. I hate it all.'

'Do you hate me, and Peter, and Madeleine?'

'Yes, oh God, yes, sometimes, yes, because it wasn't you. But myself most of all, because it wasn't me.'

'Alexi, he couldn't have lived without you.'

'Oh, you never knew him. He could. He didn't need anyone.'

'He needed you. He loved you, Alexi, you were the only person he loved.'

'I wouldn't call it love.'

'That's what it looked like to us.'

'Love is what's between men and women. This was different.'

'No it isn't. I love Peter.'

'Yes, you do, don't you?' Abruptly, he was not angry any more. 'Funny little Peter,' he smiled. 'Not so little any more. He's as tall as you now, isn't he? He'll be taller than I was, one day. You do love him. I loved Hans. I still do. I guess I've never loved a woman, but I've always loved him. He was always there, from the day I was born, how can he not be here now?'

'Alexi, people never die completely if you remember them – '

Alexi wrapped his arms around his head, saying quietly, 'Don't.'

'Hans is still here, because you love him, because he's a part of you – '

'God, where did you pick up that crap? You can't really believe it. I just hope you never have to find out what a lie it is.'

He turned round swiftly and walked away. I thought he was going to walk off somewhere on his own, but I felt I had to let him go.

After three or four yards he came to a standstill on the crest of the slope, and stood there with his hands clasped behind his neck, elbows jutting out, craning his head back.

'You probably don't remember,' he said over his shoulder. 'You once called me a very trivial person. I bet you didn't know that I really took it to heart. Sometimes I used to think it was true. I used to worry about it. I used to ask myself, "God, what am I going to do with my life?" I thought I was unhappy about it. But I wasn't, I know that now. Never, not once, was I really, honestly unhappy. I can tell now, because now I am unhappy all the time. And then after it happened, after he died, I thought, I can't go on feeling like this for ever. I've got to get over it some time. People do. And every day I wake up and I just hope that this day it's going to get better. But it never does. I don't think it ever will.'

He fell silent, folding his arms across his chest, standing there with his back to me while he gazed across the countryside.

Five or six minutes passed. At last it occurred to me that he might want to be left alone, so I was about to disappear quietly down the hill, when he startled me by flinging his arms into the air and shouting, 'Take a look at that! All this will be yours one day, my son!'

He spun around, walked briskly back to me and took my arm. 'Come on,' he said. 'Let's sit down. I'm still out of breath.'

'Alexi, you must lose some weight.'

'Yes, it's nothing but musts now, isn't it? You must stop eating so much, you must take an interest, you must be King . . . '

'Alexi – '

'I'm afraid I don't want to be King. I don't particularly want to do anything.'

'Peter told me Nikolas said you'd make a good King. For what it's worth.'

'Did he now? What a comfort. Well, I suppose I probably would, at one time. But it's no good, you know. They can't bring us up to do nothing, expecting never to have to do anything, and then shove this at us. All I want to say is, "Look, I'm not interested, leave me alone. Find someone else." Of course they can't. I *have* to do it. One has *responsibilities.* You are scared, aren't you? So am I. I've never had any responsibilities before. It's frightening.' Then a glimmer of his old self, saying, 'Not to mention boring.'

'Alexi, what you said, it isn't true.'

'What?'

'That I don't care about you.'

'I know. I'm sorry. I shouldn't have said that. We've had a lot of fights, you and me, so that must mean something.'

'It does.'

For a while we contemplated the view in friendly silence. Then after what was, for him, a long time, he took out his bag of sweets and started to open them.

I said, 'Alexi, give those to me.'

'Do my ears deceive me? Are you giving me a lecture?'

'No, just hand them over.'

'Ah me, the world's changing faster than I can keep up with it.'

All the same, he gave the sweets to me.

Serena is recovering. There was no flash of decision, no moment when she saw, or heard, or touched something that sparked an inner revelation and made up her mind to go on with life. That's art, that's Caryllac's style. Art is quick, but life is long and gradual. Every day Serena does a little more and broods a little less. She has fewer moments when she stops, stares, and pulls back inside herself like a wounded tortoise. It may be that she is recovering because the thing which hurt her gave her more than it took away. Apparently some mothers come to hate the child that is raped into them, because whenever they look at its foreign face they are reminded of its father; but I think Serena will forget, as animals do.

Since writing the above, I've been for a walk. I wasn't really in the mood for writing, and Serena came in saying something about how she wished there was some honey or a piece of fruit. She gets these terrible cravings for sweet things. Beulah used to devour quantities of raw beef, which I suppose wasn't really out of character. I took a walk over to the beekeeper's house, but as it happened he wasn't in – 'Gone to Rayalled,' said his wife before she shut the door in my face. I'm used to this reaction now. I was feeling in quite a good mood, so I decided to walk the long way back to the hut. I crossed the fields with my head in the clouds, not realising Serena's father was approaching until we were almost face to face. He had a spotless lamb hung over his shoulders. Presumably he was taking it for sacrifice. Spotless lambs are rare, and one either sacrifices them or keeps them for breeding – this I learnt from Serena, to whom animal sacrifice is as abhorrent as human.

'Well then, young man,' he said. 'How you keeping?'

Odd to be addressed as young man – though I suppose I am, compared to him. Or am I? He looks sixty, but he might be only a little over forty. Odder still to be greeted in such a comradely way by one who has been known to cross the street rather than my path.

I said, 'Very well, thank you.'

'How's that girl of mine? Keeping her nose clean?'

I was so startled to hear him mention Serena, whom he never talks about, that I couldn't think of anything to say.

He went on, 'So, young man, we hear you're going to be a father.'

I didn't think. I blurted, 'It's not mine.'

'Come on now, whose is it then? Not the Holy Tsyraec's, that's for sure.'

That certainly is for sure. I stopped and did think. I don't know what the village may have heard about Serena. I haven't mentioned what happened to anyone; the Captain, as far as I know, has said nothing, and the soldiers were probably too drunk to remember anything, let alone her face. I have no idea what the village may know or what they would think about it if they did; but in Tsvingtori rape is shame, so I shut my mouth and let him think what he liked.

I saw so many things in his eyes, but the most complex was this: that there are few men who would not boast of fathering a child, and few women a man would deny fathering one on; but of those few he could believe I was the man and Serena the woman. He spat. It lay there thick and coated with dust. My stomach churned.

He hitched the lamb up on his back. It bleated, which seemed to give him a thought. 'Now then, my son, tell you what. We'll be doing some slaughtering next week. You send the girl along and we'll give her some stuff. And tell her to ask her mother for some of them eggs the yellow hen's laid. She knows how to rear them. You do that. A woman with a baby coming needs a bit of meat. I've always took care of what's mine, you know that. I gave her that house you're living in.'

'I know, she told me.'

'Did she? Well, she's not a bad girl, if she is a bit dim. Still, a baby and all will set them straight, that's what I always say. Be seeing you.'

He strode away down the track, whistling.

Well may he whistle. His life is going well, and even that thorn in his flesh, his spotless lamb, has found herself a man and is going to have a baby.

I walked on into the village. The Captain came riding past with an escort of soldiers. He sat high on his horse, looking over my head, though the soldiers stared at me. I had other thoughts on my mind.

On the roof of the miller's house some women were threshing. Their flails hissed and the corn leapt up, like a swarm of golden bees in the air, and the wind blew the chaff away. Up down, up down, to the beat of the singing flails – at first it reminded me of a dance, then of Hans and Alexi forging a sword. Round about the miller's house the ground is powdery with white flour. Indoors, the donkey on the treadmill turns the grindstone. I could hear the scream of stone against stone, hooves plodding in a circle. Two chickens ran across my path, chased by a kitten, best of a bad litter of which the rest were drowned. I know this because Serena happened to walk past while it was happening, though too late to rescue any of them and bring them home. And they say peasants have no sentimental attitude to animals. I suppose she is the exception that proves the rule. The donkey in the mill-house brayed. Down the street a woman had hung her rugs on a rope and was beating them, sending up clouds of dust that made her sneeze. Three very small boys with snotty noses were throwing stones at a mangy dog, but their arms were weak and their aim was bad, and the dog could not be bothered to move. Old Raspberry was playing with his granddaughter on their front step. He's been given this nickname because he has some disease of the nose which has made it as red and pimply as a raspberry, though much larger. In the shade of a tree a boy and a girl were kissing.

When one of the villagers dies, or even if one of them is feeling low, they have a song they sometimes sing. It's not a hymn, just an old folk-song:

In strong bands with bloody hands they came;
From the sea they came like mist upon the foam,
And they brought chains,

And so they came
Like the clouds from the mountains,
Like the leaves from the tree,
Like the breakers from the sea they came.
We never heard their silent coming
Until they beat upon our doors like thunder;
And like the storm they came.
And so they came
Like the hailstones from the sky,
Like the swarming hordes of bee,
Like the children of the sea they came.

Once I asked one of them what exactly this song referred to, and he replied that he didn't know. But I know. It is about the conquest of Brychmachrye by my ancestors King Michah Andaranah and Lord Rori. Presumably this song was banned, which would explain why any direct reference has been removed, and why the villagers have so conveniently forgotten the sort of thing they usually never forget. How else could a song about the sea have come here? Not one of them has ever seen the sea.

Serena asked me, 'Have you seen the sea?'

'Yes, many times.'

'What's it like?'

I searched for an explanation she could understand. 'Like the mountains,' I said. 'But flatter, and made of water.'

'And it's blue, like the sky.'

'No, not like the sky at all. And not always blue. Water has no colour, you know that. The sea reflects the colour of the sky. Sometimes it's grey, and sometimes green.'

'The sky isn't ever green.'

'Yes I know, but sometimes the sea is. And when there's a storm, it's black.'

Who knows why they sing this dismal old song? What have they got to wail about? The Conquest passed them by. Nothing has changed in this village since time began. The mothers and fathers of their mothers and fathers were living here, in houses just like these and probably in the same places, when the old native Kings of Brychmachrye sat beneath the canopy of Adonac. They've worn the same clothes, used the same pots, named their children with the same names and ground their bread in the same fashion generation after generation.

In the winter their poverty is harder to endure, but hidden indoors or beneath snow. In the spring it emerges, and the bright sun points out its edges. This village is a mean and shabby place. It is so poor and cracked that even time recoils from touching it. The old people have the grime worked into the leathery creases of their faces, and they seem to wait for ever before they die. Why do they do it? They are so busy keeping alive that they have no time to be alive. Why do they go on and on and on? Grinding their bread, shearing their sheep, ploughing and sowing and reaping and rutting in the barns like the goats they share their lives with. Year after year after year. And then they die. Like everyone else. Like everything else.

These are the people of whom it was said to me: Afraid you'll have to be their King now, Nardo. Their God. They need one, and you're all we've got.

I spit on you, Isumbard, with your ridiculous name and your edifying verses about the rustic virtues of a bucolic life. I spit on you with the same spit Serena's father uses to water his stony fields. They're peasants, they're beasts, they've forgotten the meaning of that interrogative Why? And in forgetting that, they are no longer men. And they've never heard of your poetry. Or Caryllac's. Or mine.

30

After that conversation Alexi appeared to improve. He did eat less. He took more exercise. And, as if in proof that no Rorhah was ever meant to be so fat, the weight dropped off him. He tried –

Alexi, I know you tried. You old bastard, you old fox, you can't fool me.

He came to see me more often, not merely to play 'let's remember', but for a game of cards or chess, or to talk about poetry and even, sometimes, politics. Madeleine promised him that if he was down to his old weight by solstice-time she would make him a shirt for a present. 'Only *if*,' she stressed, 'because I don't want to have to make it too big.'

Still he refused to go riding. Peter saw to it that the grooms clipped his horses' hooves, for otherwise the animals would have been crippled through lack of exercise. Alexi fell into the habit of walking the court dogs, taking them for long strolls through the Palace grounds and beyond.

On the anniversary of Hans's death we went into deep mourning for a day. This is the custom at court, to mark the end of the funeral year. Alexi stayed in his rooms. The next day was a festival. The morning was given over to poetry, music and games, with a feast all afternoon, sacrifices in the evening and a dance late at night. Among the sacrifices were Alexi's three horses, so he must have asked that this be done; we didn't see him that day, or the next, or the next, and could not bring ourselves to enter his rooms.

On the fifth day he came out of his own accord. His beard, which he had let grow quite long, had been shaved.

'Madeleine,' he said, 'let me borrow your horse. I want to go riding with Nardo.'

'Yes, of course,' she said.

The snow was so clean, the sky pearly-blue. Alexi said, 'I feel I could touch it, if I reached up. Come on, let's race.'

I felt as light as my horse's hooves skimming over the snow, showering it up like white dust. Cold air in my lungs, slapping my brain, tingling, as I thought, 'We have him back.'

He reined in beneath a cedar tree. His cheeks were red and his horse's flanks were heaving, but he wasn't out of breath. He was a better horseman than I, though neither of us would ever be as good as Hans had been: still, we were good enough to be brothers.

'That was great,' he exclaimed. 'This air really burns down your throat, but it's refreshing. You were right, you and Madeleine. I couldn't have done this three months ago. I don't think her horse could have carried me.'

'Easy on, easy off.'

'I bet you learnt that little saying from Beulah – oops, sorry, I won't spoil the day by mentioning that name. What a splendid day! Hope the whole winter's like this.'

He stood up in his stirrups, unaware that the branch above his head was weighed down by a thick pillow of snow. It was one of those moments when you know what's going to happen next. He yawned, throwing his arms up; his arm jostled the branch and the snow thumped down on to his head. I nearly fell off my horse laughing.

Alexi growled and leapt at me, pulling me head over heels into a drift. We came up gasping with cold, our mouths full of snow, and wrestled, trying to shout and laugh at the same time. Once I would never have been a match for him, but now I made him work hard to win.

It seemed to me that it was almost the same as before. I also thought that perhaps, with time, he would let me be a substitute. Never a replacement – no one could replace Hans – but someone to make his loss easier to bear.

Alexi, I think that on that day I loved you no less than I love Peter and Madeleine. But you were right again, right as always. We learn a lot of tripe and present it with pride as if it was our own invention, when all it really is is something someone told us. You were right. Time heals nothing. What hurts now hurts as it has always hurt, and always will.

Peter had discovered a place on the far side of the woods where the wall had crumbled. Full of excitement, he insisted we go exploring – Alexi, Madeleine, Peter and I. There was a wide empty meadow on the other side of the wall, with a coppice in the middle. We built two snow forts and had a battle, Alexi and Peter against Madeleine and me. The snowballs we hurled disintegrated in mid-air, while the dogs barked and rushed to snap at them, snarling in surprise when their prey melted coldly on their tongues. We rolled in the snow and made people-prints, always trying and always failing not to disturb the perfect silhouette when we stood up.

'Come on,' said Peter, 'let's make a snowman.'

I argued, 'The snow's too powdery.'

'Oh no it's not. We can try.'

'I'll help you,' said Madeleine.

Taking the saddles off our horses, Alexi and I sat down at the edge of the coppice.

He said, 'That boy has endless energy.'

Peter was kneeling in the snow, a dark shape with a bright head, newly shorn red hair that I hadn't yet quite grown used to.

'Wish I was thirteen again,' said Alexi.

'Come on,' I laughed, 'you're only twenty-nine. That's supposed to be the prime of life.'

He was doodling in the snow with his forefinger. Then he said, 'The King looks very ill. I don't think he'll last much longer.'

With an abrupt, savage movement he grabbed a handful of snow and fisted it into a ball of ice which he flung across the meadow. It fell and exploded; Alexi turned to me.

'All right,' he said. 'I've been doing some thinking, serious thinking, about the government, which as you know is not something I normally do. I've been thinking over a lot of things and I want you – I want to talk them over with you.' He grinned. 'You never know, you might learn something.'

I quoted Isumbard:

Apply yourself to what is right,
And never go to sleep at night,
Unless you know that you can say:
'I have learnt something new today.'

'That you can *unlearn*. Get the lumber out of your brain, my child. Now look, I want to be serious. Much as I dislike it, I know I've got these responsibilities you keep insisting on. And I suppose it is better to have some idea of what you intend to do, instead of sitting with a glazed face wishing it would all go away – Pete, Pete!' he shouted. 'It's going to fall over. Prop it up, Maddy.'

He asked me, 'Do you think he's happy?'

'Who, Peter? As much as any of us are, I suppose.'

'I don't know. I know he's happy when he's with you. But I've been on my own with him, and sometimes I get the impression he feels – lost? No, maybe not. I think he feels as if he doesn't belong to us. To you, yes, but not to us. Maybe it's because he's so young. Or maybe it's because of all that crazy stuff old Bronwen used to tell him. She's been dead a long time, hasn't she.'

'I never talk about it with him. I think it's better not to.'

'You're probably right. Let sleeping dogs and all that. He's very prickly, little Pea, he's got a great deal of pride. I'm afraid I foresee trouble.'

'In what way?'

He spoke with strange earnestness – strange from him, to whom true sincerity was as foreign as true cruelty. In fact, I remember thinking that this whole long conversation was strange. But at the same time I thought, 'If he needs to talk, I am glad to listen.' I thought – I thought almost anything except the thing I should have realised.

Alexi said earnestly, 'You matter more to him than anyone else. I told you when he was born he would be your responsibility, remember? His mind works in a funny way. I don't know if you realise it. You've always been too close to be objective.'

'How is it funny?'

'Well, I don't know. He's very extreme. He pushes himself – he gives a lot and expects a lot. And he doesn't always think about the consequences of his actions – suppose that's to be expected, he's only thirteen.' I was well aware of all this, but Alexi went on. 'Nardo, I don't know what Peter might be capable of doing if he thought – if he thought you'd let him down.'

'I never will.'

'I hope not.'

I said, 'You've obviously been doing a lot of thinking about Peter.'

'A lot of thinking about a lot of things. I'm exhausted. Anyway, the first thing we must do is get him a wife as soon as we can.'

'Alexi! Don't be ridiculous, he's far too young.'

'No, I mean it. It should be soon, in the next few years. Preferably a princess – that's why I said we should start thinking about it soon, because these arrangements take time. He may be thirteen but he's not a child any more, you know.'

'I do know.' I was finding it hard to follow him.

'So – we'll find him a wife soon, someone he can be proud of. I think – I think we'll put him in the Guards, as soon as he's old enough. Give him a Captaincy.'

'He'll love that.'

'I thought so.'

The snowman had a large pot-belly and a sloping head. Madeleine was rounding it off, patting snow into the cheeks, and Peter had made an arm. He wedged it in.

'Look!' he shouted proudly.

The shoulder slipped and the arm fell off.

Alexi laughed and, still laughing, said to me, 'Now, what about your wife? The beautiful bitch. I'm afraid she's going to have to go.'

'You mean it?'

'Not just for your sake, though of course, Nardo, that is a consideration. I loathe the bitch, but it isn't really personal. It would simply be impossible to govern while she's around. She has got a tight hold. And she's very popular, have you noticed? Not just with the court, but with the people.'

'How on earth do you know?'

'I told you, I keep my ear to the ground. You ought to take a lesson. Now don't distract me, I know what I wanted to say. About Beulah. She's going to have to go a long way away, overseas. It's a pity . . . '

'What do you mean?'

'Oh, not a pity that she has to go. The bitch could carve a new empire for herself wherever she went. It's a pity, in a way, that she is what she is. She knows a lot about running the show, much more than you or I do. She would have come in useful, if only she weren't so determined to do it herself. But she's got to go. And Dominic. He's her creature. He's a bad influence in the Council and he's got no common sense at all. I'll try to get Edvard back. It was a shame he ever left. And that was her fault too.'

'I know.'

Alexi leant back against a tree-trunk, shutting his eyes. He was thinking hard. I can find no other way to put it. Hard thought reflected in his speech. He was afraid of leaving something out.

Alexi, Alexi, was this really the best you could do for me? I hope you were prompted by guilt. I hope you still feel guilt. I hope you can see me and I hope you feel so guilty it hurts worse than anything.

He said, 'Well, the first thing to do is get you divorced. I can't reshuffle the Council all at once, people might make trouble and things could get sticky. We'll have to take our time. Give them a couple of years, make them see that if they don't pull their weight, they're out. Then we might find out what they're really capable of. The thing is not to rush anything.'

'I can't imagine you rushing anything.'

He raised his eyebrows. 'You never know.' Then he said, 'This snow does make me feel sleepy.'

His eyes were shut again. I leant against the same tree and watched Peter and Madeleine. The snowman had completely collapsed, and the two of them were dancing madly in the debris.

'Thomas filcValentin is a good man.'

Alexi was looking at me again. I said, 'Is he?'

'As they come, he's not bad. He hasn't got much initiative but I think it's his nature to be loyal. He'd shape up well as a Secretary. Oh, and the Mehahs. Got to tread warily there, Nardo, especially now Valentine's so hand in glove with Beulah. I'd like to take the Fahl away from Lord Mehah and give it back to their uncle, but I suppose I can't really – on second thoughts, it wouldn't make much difference. Gilles was a brilliant councillor but his nepotism knows no bounds. Putting the minor families into the Council is the best answer, so long as they're talented. Second cousins and distant relations, not brothers and nephews.' He sighed. 'The Council's in bad shape, Nardo.'

'Alexi, could you possibly make one more good resolution?'

'Depends. Well, out with it.'

'Do you think you could stop calling me Nardo?'

He began to grin, slowly, broadly, spreading from ear to ear. 'Aren't you used to it yet, after all this time?' He cuffed the back of my head. 'You'll have to get a bit tougher, Nardo. Nardo, I'm afraid you're stuck with it. Peter's forgotten you've got another name.'

His hand opened behind my neck, and he pulled me to him and hugged me. Hugged me only for a moment. But fiercely.

'Hey!' Peter ran over, with Madeleine walking behind him. 'What are you two talking about?'

'About the multitude and magnitude of your faults, Pea,' said Alexi. 'What happened to your snowman?'

'We killed him.'

'You killed him,' said Madeleine. 'I thought he was rather handsome.'

'Oh, he wasn't much. Anyway, his head kept falling off.'

Peter flopped down between us, and Madeleine knelt behind me with her arms over my shoulders, resting her weight on my back. I began to forget all the things Alexi had said to me.

He took a parcel out of his pocket. 'What is that?' asked Madeleine sternly.

'Just a piece of cake, a little little piece.'

'Throw it away,' she ordered.

'But I'm starving!'

'Good. Throw it away.'

He made a face, but did throw it away. It landed three or four yards from us, and immediately a blackbird swooped down from the tree to pounce on it, bobbing its head and tail.

'Look at that bird eat!' said Alexi. 'I know how it feels.' He started to sing:

I saw a blackbird on the wing,
I heard the little blackbird sing;
I saw the blackbird in a tree,
The little blackbird sang for me.

Blackbird, blackbird, why are you singing
So sad and so sharp a song?
'A cat has killed my children –
I sing because I cannot cry, because I cannot cry . . . '

Madeleine said, 'Oh don't sing that, it's so sad.'

And Peter said, 'Anyway, the blackbird's song isn't sad at all.'

31

At the end of January we had a freak heatwave. The flowers began to bud, tentatively, as if convinced something was amiss. Fires were kept burning daily, in case we were surprised by a sudden freeze. The heat in the Palace became oppressive. The servants were caught on the hop. Most of the meat, which is kept indoors in winter but in ice-houses in the summer, spoiled. In Tsvingtori prices went up. This did not directly affect us, but I was told of it by Alexi, who had regained his old consuming interest in everything that went on around him.

Madeleine and I were in the kitchens. I feel there is a reason why we were there. I can't remember it, though I've tried hard to. If there wasn't a reason, then nothing makes any sense. We weren't often in the kitchens, but that day, that morning, we were. Perhaps it was cooler there. If we had been anywhere else, in the library, or the salons or the stables, or even in my room making love when he walked in to look for me, that would have been better, but we were in the kitchens and as far as I can remember we were doing nothing at all. Our being in the kitchens was one of those pointless things with no memorable cause which emerge abruptly as a pivot around which life changes course. Perhaps, as Madeleine said, if it had not been that, it would have been something else. But because it was that, it is that to which one looks back and says: If only I had known.

Nardo, Nardo, sometimes I think you don't think at all.

I do, Alexi, I do. Alexi, I have to know. Tell me the truth.

Truth? You're asking *me* for the truth?

Would it have made a difference?

Yes, no, I don't know – Alexi, why do we only see the result? Why can't we see the cause before it's caused it?

Well Nardo, that's just the way things are.

'Oh good, Nardo, here you are. I've been looking everywhere for you. I've just met the most fascinating man. Hullo, Madeleine. So listen – I was walking along outside when I saw Aneurin – you haven't forgotten Aneurin, have you? Did he tell you, Maddy, Aneurin used to be his tutor. Anyway, I saw Aneurin with this ancient old man, he had the biggest mop of white hair you'll ever see, bigger than Father's and much whiter. God, I'm hungry. Is there anything to eat? Damn this weather, they've thrown out all the meat.'

'There's some salt beef.'

'Ugh, not even for me, thanks.'

Madeleine said, 'There's some apple pie, and some fruit cake, and – '

'No, I don't want anything sweet. And don't look at me like that, dear sister. I'm a reformed character. I crave something savoury.'

'There's masses of fruit and vegetables. And I think they're making some kind of fish thing for lunch – '

'No, I don't want that.'

'Madeleine,' I said, 'we are deceived. This isn't Alexi, this is an impostor.'

'You can laugh. I'm training myself to listen to my taste-buds. I had the bad luck to see old Lord Olivah – you know the one, he's just published his life story or something equally unbelievable, the one who's too fat to sit on his horse. I had the misfortune to see him with no clothes on, can't remember how. Gave me a good kick up the backside, that did.'

'Then don't have anything,' said Madeleine. 'Get on with the story, we're agog.'

'Oh, be fair, be merciful. I'm starving. I haven't had anything to eat today but some toast and an apple. No, don't call the servants, I'll look myself. I like hunting.'

He shooed the maids out of the larder, and rummaged around in there, talking all the while.

'Anyway,' he called out to us, 'Aneurin asked me where the engineer's room is. I was surprised. He's lived here for what? Thirty years? More, probably. He's blind as a bat, you know, can't see further than the end of a margin. Ah, victory!'

He came out carrying a lump of pâté on a plate.

Madeleine wrinkled her nose as he passed her. 'That smells terrible. I'm sure you shouldn't eat it.'

'Don't worry. I like things a little gamy – and if I haven't got an iron stomach yet, I should have.' One of the maids brought him a knife and some fresh bread. 'Where was I? Yes – so I asked them what they wanted with it – the engineer's room. And it turns out the old man is a friend of Caryllac's. I mean, he must have been at least ninety. So I said, I doubted they'd find Caryllac in the engineer's room, and I asked the old man if he was a poet, because we had one in the family. It was really rather amusing, because Aneurin's so short-sighted he didn't recognise me, and the old man didn't know who I was. So he said No, he was a mathematician and an astronomer. So I asked him why he'd come to court. And then' – Alexi swallowed the mouthful he was talking through – 'then Aneurin blinked, and then he squinted, just like a mole when it comes out of its hole, and he said, "Is that you, Prince Reyhnard, sir?" I said no, and he seemed rather disappointed. You really ought to go and see him some time.'

'Yes, I know, I will, go on.'

'So then the old man said Caryllac had invited him to court to see the telescope.'

'That's not in the engineer's room, it's up in the South Tower.'

'We know that. But that's the joke. The old man's an astronomer, but all he's ever done is stand on the ground and stare at the stars. He didn't even know what a telescope was, all he knew was that you looked through it. And Aneurin! – well, the two old boys put their heads together and decided that since a telescope was some sort of mechanical instrument, it must be in the engineer's room. Neither of them knew where it was, but did that stop them?'

'Alexi,' said Madeleine, frowning and smiling together, 'you really shouldn't laugh at them.'

'I'm not, I admire them for forging out bravely into the unknown – anyway, I didn't laugh *then*, I promise you. I was very solemn – at least, I took them up to the tower. It seemed the least I could do. I tried to explain a bit about how it works, not that I know much about it. Anyway, the old man and I had a long talk, and he knows a great deal, really, considering all he's ever had to study with is the naked eye. I was gripped. He says there's going to be a lunar eclipse next month. I said I'd go up there with him tomorrow evening and have a proper star-gazing session. Do come, I know you're interested in that sort of thing.'

'Not all that much,' I said.

'If you listen to him you will be.'

Madeleine said, 'I want to come too.'

'Of course you can. But we'd better not let him find out who we are. He's just an old country boy, liable to get flustered. That was good, that pâté.'

'Alexi, you are naughty,' Madeleine chided him. 'It's nearly time for lunch.'

'Not for me. I'm not hungry any more. How about that, looks like my stomach's shrunk. I'm going to find Peter and see if he wants to take the dogs for a walk.'

We didn't see him at lunch, or at dinner either, but we thought nothing of it. In those days Alexi was a law unto himself. He followed no regular hours and observed court routine only when he chose.

Between dinner and the dancing I went up to my rooms. I had just got changed when Madeleine burst in.

'Reyhnard, Reyhnard, come quickly, it's Alexi, he's ill – '

She grabbed my hand and pulled me after her. We ran down the corridors, Madeleine stuttering, 'I just went in to see him, to ask him if he was going to come down – He's so ill, he was throwing up. He was covered in sweat but when I touched his forehead it was cold . . . He asked me to get you. He seems to have trouble talking. It's the pâté, I know it is, I told him not to eat it . . . '

In her haste Madeleine had left his door ajar. We stopped for a moment outside, in the corridor. Through the open door we could hear him retching. Madeleine covered her mouth with her hands, gnawing at the thumbs. I caught them and put them down. The vomiting stopped. I went in, and Madeleine followed me.

Alexi was lying flat on his back. His breathing sounded slightly strained, and his hands, which were stretched palm-upwards at his sides, were twitching spasmodically. He turned his head very slowly, until his full face was in candlelight, and smiled. This looked as if it hurt him.

'Thanks for bringing him,' he said. 'You're a lovely girl. Now go away, I have to talk to Nardo alone.'

She said, 'I'll fetch a doctor.'

'Not yet, sweetheart, please don't. I'm all right, don't worry. You just go outside, all right?'

She bit her thumb. I heard the nail split. Then she nodded. 'All right.'

It took Alexi some time to move his eyes from the door, which she had shut behind her, to where I was standing at the foot of his bed.

'Don't worry,' he said. 'It's not catching.'

He spoke fluently, but his words were slurred, as if his mouth was very cold or he'd had too much to drink. 'Come over here,' he said. 'Get on to the bed. It isn't so easy for me to talk.'

'What have you been drinking?' I asked him.

'Is that what it sounds like? Nardo, you know me better than that. A boozer is about the one thing I'm not.'

I climbed up beside him, taking his wrist to feel his slow, shallow pulse. His hands were like melting ice, chill and damp.

It looked like 'flu to me. Drunk and 'fluish, I thought, no wonder he's been throwing up.

'You're very sick,' I said. 'You ought to let me send for a doctor. They can give you something – '

'Stuff the doctors, I know what's wrong with me. It's ptomaine poisoning. I'm sure you've read about it somewhere. I don't need a doctor. They couldn't do anything, not that they ever can. I'm dying.'

'Don't be ridiculous.'

'Maddy was right, I shouldn't have eaten that pâté.'

'Well, if it is that which is making you ill – look how much of it you've thrown up.'

Deep in his throat Alexi was laughing. 'Doesn't matter. It's done its worst. I have to talk to you while I still can. I'm sorry about Beulah.'

'What about her?'

'Remarkable woman. The King's never really been able to control her, so don't lose sleep over it if you can't. You're going to need her.'

I thought I saw his game. Drunken and feverish with 'flu, he had decided to play some silly practical joke on us. I was in no mood to play along. Obviously he was ill, but he couldn't be dying. Not Alexi. Not my leg-puller of a brother, that great jumper-out from behind doors.

'I'm so sorry,' he said. 'I know I promised I would get you divorced. Nardo, listen to me. Don't do it. It wouldn't be worth your while to get rid of her. She's very popular.'

'You've told me this before.'

'She can help you, Nardo. Promise me you'll try to learn to live with her.'

'All right,' I said. 'A joke is a joke and this one's in very bad taste. I don't think it's funny to frighten Madeleine the way you did. You're not dying, but you are ill, and I'm going to get her to send for a doctor – '

'No.'

He tried to grab my arm. The effort of lifting his hand sent rivers of sweat gushing down his face. His skin was chalk white. He levered his hand into the air but couldn't force his fingers open – seeing him struggling to make them move was what stopped me.

He let his arm fall and said, 'I don't want them coming in here.'

I was suddenly afraid, and my heart felt as cold as he looked.

'You bastard,' I said. 'You did this on purpose.'

'I'm not going to fight with you now.'

'You bastard, you bastard, you can't die, you can't, you can't do this to me, you can't die.'

'I'm terribly sorry but I am.'

His body jerked up like a puppet on a string, and he retched. Nothing came out. When the fit was over he fell back on the bed, heavy as a log of wood.

'You bastard,' I said again, unable to think of any other word.

Then I said, 'I'll never forgive you.'

'Quite frankly, Nardo, where I'm going it really won't matter to me whether you forgive me or not.'

'You shouldn't have done it. You're incredibly selfish.'

'It's done now.'

His brow, his ears, his lips were all ashy, blue veins thick and prominent on his fixed eyelids. I heard a faint thumping as if from far away, and wondered for a moment what it was – then I realised it was Alexi's heartbeat. I wanted to throw up myself, but he gave me something to do by asking, 'Can you get me some water?'

I fetched a cup. He tried to close his fingers round it, and failed, so I held it to his lips. The water dribbled down his chin.

'Are you in much pain?' I asked him.

'No. Hardly any. There's just this numbness. Take it from me, it's not such a bad way to go.'

'Alexi, *please* let me get a doctor.'

'Do me a favour. Look under the bed and give me what's there.'

I got down on my hands and knees and groped around in the dark until I touched something hard and cold. It had a sharp edge, which helped me guess what it was, and feeling my way carefully along it I found and grasped the hilt. I dragged it out. It was almost too heavy for me to lift. Using both hands I managed to haul it up beside him.

As soon as it was in the light, I recognised it. It was Hans's sword. The one he and Alexi had made together.

Alexi sucked in air. 'I should have handed this over for his funeral. But I couldn't. It was the only thing I had of his. I haven't got much to give away. Would you like it?'

'It's yours, you should . . . ' I couldn't say 'take it with you'. I couldn't bear to. I think it was then that I began to believe he was dying.

'It's not mine,' he said. 'It's Hans's. It's a sword for a king.'

'I can hardly lift it. And you know I'm no swordsman.'

'Neither am I. So do you want it or not?'

'Well, yes, but – '

'Good.'

He closed his hand around the blade. After a moment a trickle of blood seeped into the sheet. Apparently this didn't hurt him. He smiled. 'She should have let me do it. It would have been better. Did she ever tell you? I tried to kill myself.'

'Yes, I know.'

'With this sword. I could have done it, too, if I'd fallen on it. But I was such a coward. And now it's happened anyway.'

'Alexi – I have to know, did you do this on purpose?'

No answer. His eyes were shut.

'Please,' I begged. 'Tell me.'

'Hans should never have ridden that horse,' he said. 'Not with his leg. But I couldn't stop him. I didn't even try. And with me it's food. Listen, there's something you can do for me.'

'Whatever.'

'It's quite easy. There's this maid, her name's Brigid. She's got red hair. She's pregnant, it's mine. Could you see to that for me? Give her some money. There's some in the chest. Don't let her go to the Rope and Anchor, they're all diseased there. The Tar-Barrel is a good place. Tell her I said so. I'm cold. Would you mind getting into this bed with me?'

Under the sheets he was fully dressed. I hugged him tight round his stiffening shoulders, resting my chin on the top of his curly hair. He pushed his head against me and looked up. 'Nardo, I'm so worried you'll do something stupid. You will remember what I said about Beulah, won't you?'

'Yes.'

'You must promise.'

'I promise.'

'I swear I'm sorry, really sorry, that it has to be you. I know you don't want it any more than I did.'

'You did do this on purpose, didn't you? This is what that strange conversation was about, a few weeks ago. Isn't it?'

'It is, it isn't, it doesn't matter. Did I say some sensible things?'

'It doesn't matter because you're not dying, I won't let you.'

He made a horrible noise, throttled laughter. 'And you accused me of selfishness.'

Then, after a moment, he went on in a different voice, one much more like his healthy one. 'Madeleine's a sweet girl, isn't she?'

'She's lovely.'

'All in all, having a sister turned out quite well.'

Humour him, I thought. 'I'm sure she'll be glad to hear you say so.'

'Nardo,' he said. 'I know.'

The tone of his voice made it clear what he meant. His eyebrows quirked as he regarded me sternly; I must have looked ludicrous with my mouth flapping open. 'Don't say anything,' he went on. 'I'm not shocked. Never was. It was inevitable. She's happy and so are you. So don't pretend.'

He might not be shocked, but I was. 'Alexi – how long have you known? How did you find out? Who else knows . . .'

'No one. It's because I know you so well that I could guess. In fact I think I knew before you did, if that makes you feel any better. When we all thought she was going to get married. She was so damn brave, and you were so bloody distraught – it wasn't like brother and sister parting. It was like lovers. I saw it coming.'

'But Alexi, if you guessed – if you suspected, why didn't you try to stop it?'

'Why should I do that? You don't think it's wrong, do you?'

'No –'

'Neither do I. Well, to be honest with you, if someone had asked me, theoretically speaking, what I thought about it in principle, I suppose I would have said it was wrong. But it's not abstract. It's you and Maddy. I can't make myself believe it's wrong when I see you together. You both light up whenever you see the other. God, Nardo, you don't know what it's like when you're not around. It's always "Reyhnard says this" and "Reyhnard says that". She worships the ground you walk on. I don't know how you do it. There's the two of them, Peter and Madeleine, thinking the sun shines out of your arse. Of course we know better. Nardo – tell me, how much do you love her?'

'I couldn't begin to tell you.'

'Is there anything you wouldn't do for her?'

'Nothing. You old bastard, can't you see that? I thought you knew everything.'

He said, 'Let me tell you something. I'll tell you what I was going to do. When I was King. I was going to send all over the world, find the best prince I could – the handsomest, richest, most talented, most virtuous, most bloody nice of the whole lot. And marry her to him.'

'But you just said – '

'I know what I just said. I meant that and I mean this too. And if you really love her, you'll do the same. You can't offer her anything except a life behind the curtains. No children. She loves children. No family. No home. You can't say you love her and refuse her a chance of all those things.'

'She wouldn't go. She loves me.'

'I know how much she loves you. I asked you how much you love her.'

'Would you have done the same with Hans?' I demanded. 'Would you have sent him away "for his own good"?'

He said, 'It's not the same.'

'It is the same.'

This disease, this poisoning, begins at the feet. They grow cold, but before they get unbearably cold they go numb. Over a length of slow hours the paralysis inches its way up the body until it reaches the heart. For a man who is afraid, it is the worst of ways to die. Under my hands I could feel his temperature falling. It was bad enough to hold him and know he was dying.

Alexi licked his lips. At last he said, 'You know, I think you might finally be right about something. What is it with us? All of us – except Peter, a little. No wonder he feels left out. Listen, say – I don't know. Say something to him from me. Tell him I wish he had been older. Or me younger. I hope you tell him you love him. I think he needs to be told. He needs to know he's not left out. I never told Hans. I never did. I thought I didn't need to. And I didn't, really – he knew. But after he died I was so sorry I never did, it was almost the worst thing. Which is why – which is why – I wanted to tell you. That I do love you.'

'I love you too, Alexi.'

He nudged my chest with his head. 'I know what you tried to do for me. It was good to see it. It showed all those years I spent fighting with you, and arguing, and trying to kick some sense into you, weren't for nothing. So you know now why I did those things. But it wouldn't have worked. You're not him, no one is. Next to my love for him, my love for you doesn't add up to a great deal, but you know, it's more than I have for anyone else except him. The way I feel today is no different from the way I felt the day he died. Nardo, I tell you honestly that I do not know whether I did this on purpose or not. But I think you know that I didn't much want to live. So don't be sorry for me.'

'I'm sorry for myself.'

' 'Course you are, should have known that. This really isn't such a bad way to die. I recommend it. It doesn't hurt much and I can talk to you. When I tried to kill myself I think I said some shit to Madeleine about dying with dignity, which was ridiculous, because I never had much.'

'That's not true.'

'Nardo, Nardo, if you're going to cry you can leave the room.'

'I'm not crying.'

We lay together in silence. At first it was almost pleasant, our companionship in the warm room. Perhaps it was my holding him, the heat from my body, but I even thought he was growing a little less cold. Far away in the rooms beneath us we could hear the sound of music, footsteps of the dancers, high-pitched laughter. Where we were it was very quiet. I thought, I'm sure he'll get better.

Looking down at him I had a brief start of fright: his eyes were shut and I thought he was dead; but immediately I noticed the twitch of movement beneath the lids. He must be sleeping.

Suddenly he heaved against me and gasped in air.

'Alexi – are you all right?'

He opened his eyes to give me an amused look. That gleam of humour was still green. When he next spoke, his voice was hoarse. 'Yes. Still got some time to go,' he said with difficulty. 'Listen. I'm not even afraid. Particularly. What happens next? And all that.'

'Alexi, do you – really – believe in the Gods? Do you believe in an afterlife?'

'I think I'll reserve judgment.'

'Alexi – do you think Hans is waiting for you?'

He shut his eyes again. 'Yes,' he said. 'I like to think so.'

A deep breath rattled in his chest. 'Nardo, please keep this to yourself.

I don't want Father and Beulah and the court piling in here until I'm well and truly gone.'

His throat jerked and fought the words, but he made them come out. After he had spoken, he let his head fall back, and relaxed. He lay quiet for a long time; that is, he – Alexi – did not choose to move, but his body moved itself. His arms and legs flinched at each heartbeat. His face was busy with tics. His breathing was ragged and erratic, with a sharp gasp before each inhalation.

He stared up at the ceiling. His eyelids were paralysed, so he could not blink, and his eyeballs were watering. But in his eyes there was an irony, as if he had always expected his body to take on a mind of its own.

Again he tried to speak. His lips were so stiff that the words were barely intelligible. 'Ask Madeleine to come in, if she would.'

I remember those last three words especially. They were not necessary, not really. But to him they were.

Up until the last quarter of an hour he had been talking so fluently, and sounding so cheerful – so much himself, not at all like a dying man. Not how I would be if I were dying. Surely tomorrow we would get up to find him lounging about with those long legs sprawled in front of him, those crows-feet of laughter in the corners of his eyes as he teased us: 'Hah! Fooled you! Look who's back from the dead.'

Now it was coming on so fast I had to believe it. Vein by vein and nerve by nerve, that big body was shutting down, all that length of him extinguished. Soon, tomorrow, tonight, that jerking would stop. His lungs would give out. His heart would give in. There was nothing I could do to stop it; and even if I could, he would not have wanted me to.

I heard his teeth chatter. He was getting colder again.

He was sweating less, but I was sweating more. My heart was pounding insistently, so much louder than his pulse. My teeth chattered in sympathy; in fear.

Slipping quickly backwards I got out of his bed, saying, 'I'll go and get her.'

I saw a fraction of a movement as he nodded his chin. He could not talk.

Madeleine was standing in the corridors, hugging her arms and looking chilled. Her muscles were all knotted up, her face tense, and her fingers were raw and bleeding from white nails. I kissed her and kneaded her shoulder. 'Don't cry,' I said.

'How is he?'

'Go in, he wants you.'

Her eyes were red and rimmed with salt. 'Reyhnard – Reyhnard – I heard what he said, all of it. I didn't want to, but I couldn't help it. It was so quiet out here.'

'Don't worry, don't worry about anything. I won't do anything you don't want me to do. Go in, he wants you.'

'I'm afraid.'

'Don't be, he's not. He's not in any pain, but he can't talk.'

'What shall I do?'

'Hold his hand. Sing him some of his songs, he'd like that.'

'Aren't you coming in?'

'No – '

She started twisting her hair anxiously round her wrist. 'Please – '

'No, please don't ask me, Madeleine. I can't. I can't.'

So then she let go of her hair, reached out to touch my cheek, and said, 'It's all right.'

Left on my own, I sat down on the cold tiles. I pressed my head against the hard panelling, sitting and staring at the wall, at the hangings, those old tapestries of the Gods.

Madeleine had left the door open. There was a silence; then I listened to her singing.

I have loved you through night and day,
I have loved you with all my heart.
This is the gift I give to you:
   A promise and a red red rose.

A red red rose from the heart of the garden,
Red red as your lips when I see you smile.
A red red rose that I plucked in the morning –
   How roses fade and promises break.

I have loved you through night and day,
I have loved you through autumn and spring.
And this was all you gave to me:
   A faded promise and a broken rose.

That was one of his favourites, that old country song. It had a bouncy tune that didn't go with the words. He used to love it. He used to make up his own words: 'And this was all she gave to me, two black eyes and a broken nose . . . '

Madeleine sang him all the songs he had taught us, and when she came to the end she began again. He died at three o'clock in the morning.

———

We came to terms with the fact that Alexi would never sing again. But not quite. I hear the birds singing every morning. He was like a bird, flying from branch to branch, beating his great wings. He was always a tail-feather out of my reach.

I have no words to write of my grief at the death of my brother, Prince Alexander Rorhah.

Even his death was an ambiguity. He did not know, or he would not tell me. When I love him I do not hate him, but when I hate him I cannot love him. At least he did not lie to me. We've had a lot of fights, you and I, but you were always, always good to me. Ambiguity, Alexi, an ambiguous good. Crueller in the end than if you had given me no kindness at all, for when I turned to you, you were always there, and then, one day, you weren't. Alexi, where were you when I needed you?

Dead, Nardo, dead. But that's life for you.

It may be just as well that such a grief, even after thirteen years, cannot express itself. For those who have known it will not need my words, and those who have not known it cannot understand.

32

Forty-eight hours after his death the freezing weather came back. We could not break the ice on the bay to bring his ship in, and the overland route was impassable, so his body was packed in ice and put in the Temple, where it would await the proper spring thaw. He would have enjoyed it, our incompetence. He would have laughed, tigerishly.

We were well into March and still the weather had not broken; but the route from Oysterport was not as impassable as we thought, because someone did come up it, an Andarian in fact, no less a person than the King of Andariah's cousin.

It happened that his arrival coincided with the predicted eclipse of the moon. I remember this very well because the Lord Chief Priest became extremely agitated over the so-called omen and wanted the King to refuse to let the Andarian in. I thought, What superstitious claptrap; and of course we did open the gates, but maybe the Priest was right after all. The Andarian told us he had risked the winter crossing of the sea in his determination to escape from Andariah, and as we are, in a manner of speaking, relations of their royal house, he had come to Brychmachrye, hoping for a welcome but not much minding if we threw him in prison – all he wanted was to stay alive. He brought us a warning: Andariah was in the grip of a plague.

He told us to shut all our ports. This is the sort of thing which gives rise to that old proverb about shutting the stable door after the horse has bolted. He had brought it with him, and he was the first to die.

Madeleine was also among the first to be taken ill. I nursed her myself, not really worried, because she was young and healthy and I could see she would recover. This disease is like a skilled farmer, weeding out the old, and the weak, and the children. I've sometimes heard it called 'Gardener's Plague', though gardeners, who lead active outdoor lives, aren't particularly vulnerable to it.

Before Madeleine was quite well, I had to leave her in her bed and take to mine. Alexi's death had had a serious effect on me; I was debilitated, and the sickness took a strong hold. I was told, later, that for a while it was thought I would die.

I was too sick to know or care. I was always hungry but could keep nothing down. It took me by chills and sweats in turn, and I was always coughing. My eyes, my nose, my mouth ran phlegm, and if I thought at all, which I don't remember doing, it would have been that death was not such a bad alternative to this.

Time passed, but I had no sense of it. I knew I was recovering when I found myself sleeping nearly all the time. I would wake up, note whether my window was light or dark, and go back to sleep again. By this point I knew I had nothing to be afraid of, because if the plague doesn't kill you in the first forty-eight hours, it generally does not kill at all. Sometimes when I woke up Madeleine was there. She would put flannels on my forehead and stroke my hair, and I would sleep again.

It was from such a sleep that Beulah woke me. She was shaking me furiously, her voice at first a part of my dream:

'Wake up, Reyhnard, wake up, you must get up.'

'Go away, leave me alone.'

'You must get up, Nardo, he's dead.'

'I know, I know, Alexi, Hans – '

'Not them, you idiot.'

My mind unfogged and I sat up. 'Madeleine – '

'*She's* all right,' said Beulah impatiently. '*He's* dead, the King – your father – '

'When?'

'Just now.'

'Oh no,' I said inanely.

'Oh yes, and the joke is you're King now, so get up and get dressed.'

'How long have I been ill?'

'About ten days.'

'Where are my trousers?'

'You mean these?' She threw them over.

I crawled from under the sheets, clambering over the blankets and feeling with one foot for the floor. Making contact, I tried to haul myself up by the bedpost, but my legs refused to do their duty – they slid weakly apart and I fell back on to the bed.

'God,' said Beulah. 'You'll make a fine king, I can see.'

'I can't walk.'

'Well you'll just have to.'

'Let me go back to bed.'

'It's out of the question. If you don't come now, anything could happen. The Council's waiting for you, what there is of it, because half of them are dead and the others are too sick to stand. But they're there anyway. Everything's in a complete mess. The servants are running wild – those of them that haven't run away altogether – and somebody's broken into the Treasury and stolen half of it, and they're rioting down in the city.'

'Oh God.'

Beulah cocked her head to one side and gave a snort of laughter. 'Spare me your Oh Gods. You're the God now.'

The spinning in my head faded and I found that, with concentration, I could stand. I put on my shirt, but the balancing on one leg to pull up my trousers was more than I could cope with. I sat down again.

'Get on with it,' she said.

'You obviously haven't been ill.'

'No, I've been lucky.'

'Is Peter all right?'

'Yes, he hasn't been ill either. Here are your shoes.'

'Send a servant for him. I can't walk on my own.'

'Hah, you'll be lucky if you can find a servant.'

'Then go and get him.'

She hooted, short bursts of mirth a note away from hysterical. 'Who do you think you are? I'm not your servant. There, you're dressed now, I'll take you there myself.'

'Who's outside the door?' I asked, hearing a shuffling of feet.

'Nikolas. There's a detachment of Guards with him. Reyhnard, his father's dead too, he only heard yesterday.'

I focused my mind and picked my way across the floor. My fingers couldn't keep a grip on the handle, so I leant against the door to push it open. Six Guards and Nikolas were there, standing at attention in their leather Palace armour and horse-tail helmets.

'Rayallah – ' I said.

'Yes, Sir?' Nikolas saluted.

For a moment I couldn't remember what I wanted to say.

'Rayallah – go and find the Princess Madeleine and the Prince Peter, and bring them to the Council. Don't bring them in, but knock on the door when you get there.'

'Yes, Sir.' He saluted again. The troop about-faced and marched down the corridor. I remained leaning against the door-post, amazed at how easy it was.

Beulah came up beside me. 'We'd better go. Put your arm around my shoulder.'

I had no choice, but as we made our way along the deserted corridors I had to tell her, 'It disgusts me to have to lean on you like this.'

She laughed, and squared her shoulders. 'Don't be a fool – although I know it goes against your nature. Not being a fool, that is. We can't waste time over our petty grievances. And Nardo – listen to me – you could do worse than lean on me. I've profited far more from your father than you ever did.'

'Profited is about right,' I said. 'I know – I know – what you've been up to.'

'Put it out of your mind, all of it. We've got enough to worry about with the matter in hand. If we don't manage to get things under control down in the city we might all be dead tomorrow. We have to give them a new god before they know the old one's dead, or there'll be no holding them.'

Suddenly, quite unexpectedly, her lip quivered and a tear, an honest tear, slipped out of her eye and ran down her cheek. I thought she was crying for my father. Then she said, 'You ought to know, little Basal's dead.'

'When?'

'Three days ago, early in the morning.'

After a moment I said, 'I'm sorry.'

We had arrived at the Council chambers. The doors were huge, black, carved with ravens and fishes, studded with bosses. I knew those doors well, having often walked past them; I came to know the chambers, but that morning was the first time I had ever been in them.

Beulah opened the door and offered me her arm. 'Go in, Sir,' she said.

I could not move. She held me with her eyes. Her hard black pupils gave nothing away, but those brown irises were pleated with cynicism, showing flecks of gold.

———

It was a depleted gathering. Those present had brains too bleary with illness to do anything, except that some wept openly, and others looked blank and old. Beulah suggested that we send three-quarters of the Guards, under Nikolas, into the city to deal with the rioters. Dominic, who, being younger, was fitter than the other councillors, would accompany them, and also three or four priests from the Palace college. It was hoped that these priests would confer some measure of inviolability on the deputation – though none of us had forgotten that occasion a few years back when rioting stevedores had murdered a city priest. Once in the marketplace, it would be Dominic's job to persuade the people that the rumours of the King's death were unfounded, and to keep them persuaded until we had rushed through with the coronation.

They are terrified to live in a country that has no god, for what may not happen when his protection is lost?

The rest of the Guards, the most senior, level-headed ones, would remain in the Palace to try to beat some order into the servants and re-organise the court routine. When this was done, said Beulah, we could set about tracking down the Treasury thieves who, she said, were most probably some of the servants who had run away. In this she turned out to be right.

We did everything she suggested. They had no other ideas. Even I, with my watery, stunned mind, had to admit that her plans were sound.

If Beulah grieved for the King and for her child she never showed it, except for that one tear. So I can't say whether she did or she didn't, though I prefer to think she did. I prefer to think her less monstrous whenever I can, for I am aware of more than enough of her vices to make me sick with shame when I remember she was my wife.

The King died of the plague, of course, though it could as easily have been a cold. After Hans's death, and his seizure, he had no resistance left. But to this day I have never been able to shake off my childish sense of surprise that something finally conquered him. The King was, after all, just a mortal man – but I was too old for this concept to displace the one from my nursery days.

That plague was like fire. In three weeks it had run around the coast and up the Wastryl into Ruffashpah. At first we could not tell how badly we had been hit, for its victims were mostly the very young, the old and the weak, who do no work or very little, and whose loss does not show up on the harvest registers and tax rolls. More recently, walking through the countryside, I have seen the effects of it: abandoned temples with no congregations, fields fallen into disuse, beech groves and hazel coppices overgrown with wild wood, villages half-empty for lack of the young men and women who died when they were children. I have yet to hear of a family that did not lose at least one member. Even now it breaks out in isolated places – I was talking about it with Serena, and she said that just before I came here their nearest neighbouring village had eight cases, and all died. Among others who were taken in that first, terrible month, we soon learned we must include Gilles Mehah and Edvard filcLaurentin. At court, two of Lady Genevieve's little daughters died, and Caryllac, and Nikolas's wife, who was seven months pregnant; and too many more.

Between King Basal and King Reyhnard, it was death who reigned in the Palace. Death, terrible and only god, omnipresent, inexorable, invincible, irresistible, stalked the corridors and knocked on doors. Death roamed through the gardens, devouring the roses. Death waited behind every corner. You never knew where you would meet it next. The court crept through days in silence, trying not to draw attention to themselves. What could I do? What could the King do, against death? We were as helpless as the next man. No one escaped untouched. Everywhere I looked I saw eyes as good as dead, terrified eyes that could not believe they had been spared, or eyes of anguish who would rather have died too. Eyes that glazed over in trying to count the number gone. No singing in the kitchens. No singing anywhere. Alexi too is dead. No laughter, no fluttering fans, no gossip.

Madeleine and Peter and I clung together. Peter could not talk. He could not or would not talk. He never made a sound except, if he thought we were going to leave him on his own, he would whimper softly. He was like a baby. Madeleine had to dress him and feed him and put him to bed, but she was still weak from her illness and finally the servants had to do it. I didn't know how else to help him. I couldn't see how to help myself. Fortunately, after about a week he began to recover of his own accord.

I think I understand what happened to him. He could find no words to come to grips with his violently altered world, the upheavals all around us and even between us. In desperation, he chose to say nothing at all.

We had lost so much, we had lost even the capacity to grieve. Grief could not encompass it. Who looks back to Ksaned Kaled looks back across a river swollen with rain, and the bridges are torn down, gone.

Very few of those left alive were over sixty. Few at court could remember back to the last coronation, and of those only Lord Olivah had been there. My father's coronation had been a makeshift battlefield affair. The one thing we all knew was that the new king ought to be crowned before the old one had died, living godhead passed to the living, but death had made that impossible. We had no choice but to spread the lie through the city that the King was not dead.

Those Lords who could force a passage through the snow came into the Palace one by one through the back gate, without procession and without fanfare, in order to keep the pretence, at least, alive.

I cannot avoid the obvious fact that my reign thus began with a falsehood. Beulah may have been right: if we had not lied, my reign might not have begun at all. The people might have panicked and attacked us. Beulah worked out the order of coronation by referring to the old annals. She organised everything. Thus my reign also began with her in control. Having written this, I see that these two statements more or less sum up my reign: a neat historical epigram. I stared out of the windows and was glad to let her do it. I didn't care who did it, as long as it was not me.

Madeleine and her seamstresses worked flat out to take in and hem up the robes. Madeleine had to work from memory, because I could not put them on before the day, and there could be no rehearsal. They measured the crown and then they measured my head, but there was no time to alter the fit, so they lined the rim with silk and stuffed it with wool. I think this made it marginally more comfortable than it would otherwise have been.

The night before the ceremony I was being dressed in my rooms, preparing to go down to the Temple (the intention being that I should there commune with my ancestors until dawn), when Beulah announced herself. She dismissed my servants, and said, 'The sword. I nearly forgot the sword. No one can find it. Do you know where it is?'

'I've got a sword.'

'But you need the King's sword.'

'This one will do.'

'Whose is it? Let me see it.'

'You can wait until tomorrow.'

She shrugged – 'Please yourself' – and went away. She had her own crown and robes to see to.

I could waste valuable pages describing the details of my coronation and transfiguration, but all that really needs to be written is that it occurred. One thing I do remember, which I think worth recording, was my inability through most of those three days to shake off the feeling that we were involved in an elaborate game, not the real thing – as when little children play husbands-and-wives with an old chest for a house. The actual Temple ceremony took place on the third day. At the very end of it, when I finally stood under the statue of Adonac with the crown on my head, one of the priests stepped out into the sunlight on the Temple porch, and announced to the world: 'Reyhnard Tsyraec, Lord of the Fahls, heir to Michah and to Basal; King Reyhnard King of Brychmachrye, King of Earth, King of Air, King of Fire, King of Water; Reyhnard Tsyraec son of Adonac, son of Uryg, son of Vishnac, son of Vuna; son of the Great Gods, Father of Brychmachrye . . . '

The Guards lining the avenue raised a deafening cheer, whooped, flinging their shields into the air with a rattle like thunder. 'Long live the King!' they shouted, clapping their swords together, and the court arose and shouted it too, and the choir burst into song. Beulah had orchestrated it all very nicely.

That was the moment when I knew it wasn't a game. I understood then, really comprehended: they had made *me* King, and there was no going back to what I had been before.

King Nardo.

King Nardo King Nardo King Nardo.

I'm glad Serena can't read. If she looked over my shoulder and saw this, she would think I'd gone mad.

I'm not a king any more. I've put it off. If that ceremony had meant something, if it was worth taking seriously, then I could not have put my kingship aside. Perhaps there never was anything to put off. Nothing happened in there. All that happened were the accidents which put me on the throne.

It would never have happened if Hans hadn't ridden that horse. Or if he had not broken his leg, all those years ago, so that he could have controlled that horse. If Hans hadn't been such a reckless, fearless horseman he might never have broken his leg. If he hadn't been so impatient his leg might have set straight. But if Hans hadn't been so fearless and impatient he would not have been himself, and we, and especially our father, might not have loved him so much. He would have been a different person. And so, then, might everything else have been different.

I didn't want to be King, but I was forced to. They all ran away – even you, King Basal. You most of all, Alexi. It should have been you. Hans couldn't help dying but you could. You rammed the crown down on my head and you ran away. You ran away right from under my nose and you did it laughing. Did I surprise you? For a while, you know, I did try. You all banded together in death and forced me to be King or join you. So I tried. I tried, Alexi, even though it should have been you. You never tried. I did. The attempt was honest and the failure, too, was honest.

What's that, Alexi?

Enough of these childish tirades.

Can I ask you something? How come you talk in my head so often when it's Peter and Madeleine I want and cannot, cannot have?

Someone's got to keep an eye on you. I'm so afraid you'll do something stupid.

Then why didn't you stay with me?

He always goes away again. Serena stirs up the fire, runs her hand across her belly, and asks me if I want to eat yet. What have we got? A chicken, luxury. Go on then, you must be hungry, and I'll put this away for now.

33

My first act as King was to arrange the funerals of our dead. Nightly from the west windows we could see the waters of the bay afire; even the paupers and beggars of the city had found a raft, or a barrel, or some vessel in which to sail their dead away. I myself had three relatives to provide for, though only two had been killed by the plague.

We decided at last on four ships: one for the King, one for Alexi, one for Beulah's son and one for the Fahlraecs and their close families. The rest of the dead would have to make do with berths in those ships.

Beulah nagged at me to put Alexi in the King's ship. 'Have you any idea how much it's all going to cost? And with the Treasury having been robbed we're not far off being broke as it is.'

But in this matter, I am proud to say, I stood firm.

The servants who had broken into the Treasury were easily caught. They had run, with their loot, no further than the city, where they made themselves conspicuous by throwing their ill-gotten gains around. They were buried alive; but the men who had been swift to hand them in and claim the reward were not so hasty about returning the money which had tipped them off in the first place. This wealth amounted to something over a fifth of the Treasury funds, most of it in loose jewels and coins. We got only a little of it back.

In the end, the sons and wives of the Fahlraecs came to me and asked, as an honour to them, that I allow their dead to share the King's ship – so we used three after all. Behind my back Beulah made them all fork out for this privilege, but I found out about this only much later, when there was really no point in getting angry.

I went to Lady Genevieve, asking her if she would let her little daughters travel with Alexi. He had always liked children. She agreed. Those dark eyes of hers were ravaged, the bone transparent beneath the skin. We all had that look, in those days.

I gave Alexi his sword back. It had served a purpose, though not the one for which it was made, and I thought: if he does find Hans, Hans will want to have it.

After all this was over and things were beginning to settle down, Beulah told me she was pregnant again.

That's good, I thought. At least it will keep her occupied, stop her interfering with affairs of state.

I said, 'Fine. But there's no way this time that it could possibly be mine, so don't try to talk me round.'

'Darling. As if I would. This child is the King's.'

'You expect me to believe that?'

'I've given up expecting you to recognise a pin when you step on it, but this happens to be the truth.'

'How can you know? It could be anyone's – except mine, I'm glad to say. We'll see when it's born. Which reminds me. I don't enjoy raising this subject, but I must. I don't know if you can manage it, but I'd appreciate it if you could choose your lovers with a bit more discretion, now that by some fluke you're Queen. I'm resigned to having no children, and I'll put up with bastards as long as they're from the nobility. But I will not have a bunch of half-caste servants running around being called Princes.'

'You're so amusing when you try to act like a king. It's so sweet, a puppy trying to bark like a dog.'

'You would do better to take what I'm saying seriously.'

'Oh, you're so out of touch, darling. I've had no one but the King since little Basal was born, and now – though I don't see that it's any of your business – I've got no one at all. At the moment.'

We were alone in one of the offices. Beulah was standing a few feet away from me. She remained composed even as I began to lose my temper and my credulity; she undulated forward, closer to me, smiling.

As if words could ward her off, I said, 'Presumably that's through your own choice.'

'Of course. You don't need to remind me of my position. I know my duties. But you, my sweet, do seem to have forgotten yours.'

I've omitted to mention that I was sitting in a chair. Beulah crouched in front of me, resting her hands on my knees and looking earnestly into my face.

'Oh Nardo,' she said. 'Why don't you come back and live with me properly? I know we got off on the wrong foot, but I was a different person then. I was so young. I know that I wasn't always – that I did things that weren't very kind. But can't we put all that behind us and start again?' She stood and moved round behind me, touching my upper arms, my shoulders, my neck. 'You don't have to be resigned to having no children,' she said.

How could she flatter herself that I was still susceptible to her? 'I'd rather go without than have children with you,' I said. 'No, Beulah, I do not want you back.'

She was playing with my hair, and didn't seem to be listening. 'You disgust me,' I said as calmly as I could; to which she replied, 'You've always said a lot of things you don't mean, darling. I never used to "disgust" you.'

'That was a very long time ago.'

'Not so long ago . . .'

She was trailing her fingers up and down my neck – I felt the same mingled pleasure and horror as when a brightly coloured spider runs tickling up one's arm. I suppose I am enough at one with my skin to feel a certain sensuality even when a dog licks my hand, but I write this down to show that a man's body and the man himself are not identical. Flesh is a strange thing, with its inadequate vocabulary. My hairs stood on end just as they used to, for her, but once it had been because she attracted me. Now, it was because she repelled me.

She couldn't read my mind, only my skin, and she must have thought she was on the verge of another easy victory. She leaned down, breathed through my hair, whispered in my ear.

'Not so long ago, but long enough for me to have grown up and to have learned how I ought to treat my husband, with respect. You should at least give me a chance to prove I'm sincere. Darling, why not? Apart from anything else it is your responsibility – but it wasn't so disgusting, it was fun. Don't you remember?' I could feel her tongue, hot and wet, a hair's-breadth away from my ear.

All it could arouse in me was horror of an old slavery and a longing to get as far away from her as fast as I could. When a man has been pulled out of quicksand no power on earth can persuade him to jump back in of his own free will.

I sat very still, as one does if a wasp is near. I kept my eyes fixed straight ahead, working out exactly what I wanted to say. Then, refusing to hurry my words, I told her, 'You do disgust me. You've always disgusted me, only there was a time, that time you call "rather fun", when I also disgusted myself. I'm not going to go through that again. I've been through it all before and there isn't one trick you have that I don't see through. Everything about you is repulsive to me. Your conduct is an insult to the dignity you have been raised to purely through the accident of being married to me, and what's more you insult me if you think all you have to do is snap your fingers for me to come running. I wouldn't touch you if my life depended on it. Your whole morality revolts me.'

By this point she had straightened up and stepped back. This was not because she wanted to get away from me, but in order to give me a clear view of her face. She was only slightly angry, and also amused. She was not going to lose her temper. She had something much better to strike back with.

'Oh, does it really?' she said.

'I'm sure you can make do with the thought that there's not a lot I can do about it, so why don't we drop the whole subject?'

She folded her hands in front of her stomach and put her head to one side, like a schoolmistress. But her smile – that ominous rictus of red lips and white teeth – set my own teeth on edge. It was a warning. I knew it, and readied myself. I think she had been waiting more than two years to say what she now said to me.

'You amaze me, darling, you really amaze me. Are you simply stupid, or so wrapped up in yourself you're blind to everything else? Where do you get the nerve to criticise the way I live, when the whole court knows you're knocking your sister off?'

Remember how she said this, as if she was correcting a child, as if she was asking a question, as if she expected an answer, as if she was pointing out that the sky is blue, as if . . .

Her smile had prepared me. I managed to sit there without changing expression. I think I even produced a laugh, and said lightly, 'What are you talking about?'

'Oh, Great Gods, are you really going to try to pretend it isn't true? I know it's true, everyone knows, you idiot. You're knocking her off and you can't deny it.'

'You have a filthy mind, and you use filthy words.'

'Call a spade a spade, darling, if that's what it is. There are other words too, and one of them is – '

I can't remember getting out of my chair or crossing the floor, but I remember the feel of her throat in my hands, soft and hot. I threw her so hard the wall shook when she hit it. Immediately I let her go. She braced herself against the wall and stayed on her feet, regarding me with an unfathomable expression.

I was sorry to see I hadn't hurt her. Then I realised that, in the blank moment between getting out of the chair and grabbing her neck, I had really intended to kill her.

I was the King. I could do it any time I wanted.

'If you ever mention this again,' I said, 'if you say one word, I'll have you killed.'

'Sir! Sir! Why don't you try it and see what happens?'

I was too angry to answer, but not so angry I couldn't see that her threat was as good as mine.

The corners of her mouth started twitching. Then it occurred to me that she might only have been guessing, but that I had now given her proof.

The whole court knows.

I said, 'Peter – '

'Peter?' She frowned. 'Oh – no, you don't have to worry about Peter. He's a prince.' She paused, as if that explained everything. 'He won't know unless you tell him. It's always the same. No one ever told you anything, did they? Or Hans. You might never have found out about the King and me if Alexi hadn't told you – '

'His friends – '

'They won't tell him. Believe me, no one will tell him. This isn't the sort of thing people talk about. They simply know it.'

The whole court knows.

'I don't believe you,' I said. 'They can't know – '

'*I* know,' she said. 'But believe whatever makes you happy. No one's ever going to tell Peter. No one will ever let Madeleine know they know. And considering what your family's like, Peter and Madeleine will never realise. You're such a strange family. The King and Hans, Hans and Alexi, you and Madeleine, you and Peter – even between you and Alexi. This thing with your family has been going on for years, long before she came here. Everybody's used to it, they think it's natural. I saw it practically the day I arrived – '

'Shut up.'

'– but it took me a while to work out what it was.'

'Shut up.'

'No, I will not shut up. This is quite beyond ridiculous. It may not be beneath your dignity to scrap like a pair of schoolchildren but it's certainly beneath mine. And you ought to make it your business to find it undignified. But you can't. You can't even see it. And that's what it is – this thing with your family – '

'Why don't you stick your filth where it belongs?'

'You're the one who's sleeping with her, not me. Oh, don't you *see*, Nardo? You're the King now. You can do whatever you like. Do you think they're going to titter behind your back and cut you? People don't do that to kings. You are the King, you stupid, stupid man. How on earth did you imagine you could hide what's going on? Don't you know what this place is like? You don't, do you? Your whole family lives in its own little world, seeing what it wants to see and unable to see anything else. You've lived here all your life but you've never really lived *here*. You've got no friends, except your family. The only friend your father ever had was Edvard filcLaurentin. Hans and Alexi had no friends. Madeleine doesn't. Even Peter – '

'Peter does.'

'No he doesn't, but you don't even see that. He has no friends. He has a gang of playmates. He rides with them and trains with them, but they don't share anything. For that, he comes to you.'

'You don't know what you're talking about.'

'I do know, because I've made it my business to know. Whether you like it or not, if you've got any sense you'll see that what I'm saying is true. Reyhnard, I'm not trying to insult you or make you angry. I simply want you to admit the truth. You are the King. You have to understand what that means. Brychmachrye must have its King. It can't go on without its God, and that's you. You are the King. As such your private life isn't particularly important. It's your public life that people see. And you know absolutely nothing about the government.'

'That's hardly my fault.'

'I didn't say it was. It's no one's fault. It's a simple fact.'

She stopped talking and allowed a silence to fall between us.

I looked hard at her. Between my anger and my disgust the silence allowed a thought to wedge itself: she had not called me darling since I hit her. This seemed to mean something, though I could not work out what.

I sat back down and took a good look at her.

Too plump in that tight-waisted dress. Flat-footed, her weight thrown squarely on her soles. Perfectly made up, but if you brushed the powder away you would reveal the raw area above her eyes where she plucks her eyebrows. Red mouth, red cheeks, gold-dusted lids.

She stands firm on those flat feet. She retains the contrived grace, the preciousness, the artifice of her stays and frills and cosmetics. But I no longer mistook the design for the designer. She had not called me darling for over ten minutes. She was telling me something about herself that rang true.

I perceived her. Beneath the clothes, beneath the powder, beneath even her skin and flesh and bones, I comprehended her.

As when you meet for the first time a man you knew only by repute, and you discover that everything you heard about him, all the inferences you drew from those reports, are true.

She said, 'We have to come to some arrangement. I know you don't like me, and I don't think much of you, so let's put our private feelings on the subject to one side. I will say that despite everything I am still prepared to give you children, your own children, and I will come back to you for that only, and only when it's necessary, for the sake of the country.'

'For the sake of the country! Forget it.'

'Fine. I can't make you and I don't really want to. You have your private life, I'll have mine, and that's all we need to say about that.

'But Reyhnard, it is too late for you to go on with your little life as if nothing had happened. It has happened. You are the King. And you don't know the first thing about it.'

'You, naturally, do.'

'Yes, I do. I know a great deal about it. Not as much as your father did, but I learnt what I could from him.'

'Why?'

'Why? Why not? It interested me, and everything's useful. Anything can happen, including your becoming King. You're the King and you can't change that. And I'm your wife. You can't change that either. To get rid of me would be more trouble than it's worth.'

'That's what Alexi said.'

'I hope you listened to what he said. He was a bastard, but he wasn't an idiot. Really he'd have made quite a good king. Reyhnard, I don't know what you want out of life, I never did and I don't really care. But I have what I want. You can call it luck or you can call it planning, it doesn't make any difference. I made it my business to be prepared if it happened, and it did. I have what I want.'

'I know that.'

'No, you think that all I wanted was to be Queen. Now, Reyhnard, you may not believe what I'm going to tell you, but you'll have to act on it all the same. I love my country. I have been put in a position of duty towards it, and I feel it's my responsibility to discharge that duty to the best of my ability. I don't think you feel the same way. I don't think you can look further than your family's collective nose. But that doesn't mean we have to fight about it. I happen to know that I could rule this country adequately and administer it, perhaps not as well as your father did, but a great deal better than you can on your own.

'If I were a man I'd do what your father did, and take the crown away from you. I could probably do it now, even though I'm a woman – Reyhnard, I'm telling you this because I want you to understand that I have no intention of ever doing so. The country would still need a king, and you're as good as any other. Better, really, because you're already

married to me. Look at it this way: I need a king and you need someone
to tell you what to do. You need me and I need you and that's all there
is to it. We can't afford to squabble. We have to put our personal feelings
aside and work together. We have to trust each other. If we can't show
a united front the government's going to disintegrate and the country
will be back where it was before your father took over. We have a
responsibility. That word makes you cringe, doesn't it?'

'You even sound like him.'

'I take that as a compliment.'

'Beulah, tell me something. Did you ever really love him?'

She raised her eyebrows. 'Is that all you can think about?'

'Well, he was my father, you know.'

She smiled at me. 'I admired him,' she said. 'He's the only man I've
ever admired. I can't imagine feeling that way about anyone else.'

So I see there is one other thing a man gives to the quicksand, the
crocodile, the wasp. Hating them, revolted by them, keeping well out
of their way, he none the less gives them respect.

It's odd that as long as she remained in the room I was able to stay in
control of myself. Or not so odd. Her presence always made me feel
hemmed in. She went away almost immediately after this, and as soon
as she had gone the reaction set in. I felt nauseous – partly because of her
and partly because my heart was racing. My first instinct was to run to
Madeleine and cry, 'We are discovered!' or something equally dramatic
and unnecessary.

I had my hand on the latch before I remembered Madeleine would be
busy sewing a tapestry with some other women. I hit the door with my
fist, kicked it, bruising my toes and fuelling my temper. It felt as if I was
being thwarted at every turn. I couldn't run to Madeleine and pour it all
out in front of other people, because one must never cause a scandal –
and what would the court think, what would the court think?

It was some time before I at last remembered to ask myself, 'What
does it matter what the court thinks?' This calmed me down. Deprived
of the opportunity to do anything about it there and then, I sat down,
and tried to think logically about the things Beulah had said.

She had tried to make me ashamed of myself. I thought: I remember
shame as I remember I was once obsessed with Beulah, that is, as if it
had happened to someone I did not know very well, rather than to me.
She had chosen her words – she'd had more than two years in which to
choose the most offensive phrases – to act like hammer blows ramming
shame down my throat. She was the one who had taught me the meaning
of shame. No doubt she thought she could still take hold of it and use it
as another lever with which to manipulate me. Shame was what I had

felt every waking hour, and in most of my dreams, during the first year of our marriage. Humiliation, the longing to crawl under a rock and hide from the people who knew: these were things *she* had made me feel. They belonged to her. They could not touch me and Madeleine.

Beulah can twist things any way she likes, but she can never stop me knowing, in my heart, in my bones, the difference between right and wrong.

I doubted the court *did* know, just as I doubted every attempt by Beulah to influence me. She lies through her teeth like breathing.

Even if the court did know, what did it matter? By their own behaviour they have abrogated the right to make moral judgments on other human beings. Their morals and their values are as despicable as those of the Queen they adore. If the court can sit in their rooms and gossip about shame, it is because they know what shame is.

Here I am, wasting my time and paper trying to justify something which needs no justification. No reasons are needed for what transcends logic. No proofs are needed for the truth. The truth is that we love each other. Sometimes I felt as if I had to put my hands around it and guard it with all my strength, because everyone was trying to debase it, bring it down to their level. But it is not fragile. It is stronger than any of them. Stronger even than my sister or myself on our own. It is its own defence, and needs none. They are so far beneath contempt they can never reach up to touch it. My sister and I have nothing to be ashamed of – and nothing to be proud of, for we are as much above pride as shame.

I do not need courage to challenge the rest of the world to pull my truth down, because I know they cannot do it. They could not spatter on us the shame they carry in themselves, with their cash-obsessed marriage deals, and their off-hand fornicating, and their all-change-partners. They no more know what love is than Beulah does.

34

I suppose there are many men – and women too, if this world holds another woman like Beulah, though one hopes not – who, while lacking Basal the Great's genius, are moved by his spirit. Men who would be King. I have been across this country from the coasts to the mountains, and in taverns where I have slept on straw, or walking through the harvest fields on a September afternoon, I have heard them, with their sunburnt faces and calloused hands, chewing dry bread and onions, talking with their mouths full: 'If I was King, I'd . . . '

When I'm King, said Peter.

He can say this because he is a prince, because he tells people nothing and they say nothing to him.

They came at the summer solstice, when the earth is full of the power of the sun. They came from all over the country. Some must have been travelling for months, setting off as soon as the roads became passable, making slow journeys with their blind eyes, crippled bodies, broken legs, or no legs at all. They raised temporary shelters outside the Palace walls. The wealthy had tents, but most of them made do with twigs and bark, or a moth-eaten rug spread over a branch. The lepers had a field to themselves where they slept on the wet grass. I am told that lepers feel no pain, but those who say so speak of physical pain. The fact that their flesh is corruptible shows they are men, and so – they turn the King's stomach.

'Sir, Sir, Sir – touch me, Your Grace, touch *me*.'

I had to go out and walk among them. Beulah followed behind me, round with her pregnancy, smiling like a goddess. The Council had asked her to remain inside for the sake of her child, but Beulah would not hear of it, and the people of Tsvingtori, who had barred their doors to these sorry specimens of humanity, spread among themselves the tale of her goodness. Nardo, however, had no choice but to do it.

'King, Sir, I fought in the battle of Amanah!'

One arm, half a leg. I remember that battle. Hans was there too. Do you remember him, soldier? You are alive, but he is dead.

'King, King, I sold my prize bull to buy gold for your mother's ship!'

What else did you hope to buy with that?

Please leave me alone. Please go away. What do you think I'm going to do? My crown, which no doubt you are disappointed to see I am not wearing, doesn't fit, which is more or less the truth of the matter. So true it's funny. Let me tell you something, cripple. My name is Reyhnard, though my brothers always called me Nardo. I write poems. That's what I'm best at, though no one but Madeleine ever takes them seriously. My father never did. He was the King. I am myself.

So much horror, too much, too many sores and wounds and amputations. I used up my reserves of horror more quickly than I would have thought possible, and walked on dully, wearily, impatient for it to be over.

Did they go home happy, if not cured? Who knows? Who cares? Their folly is not my concern.

Evening drew on, and we came in. The servants took our clothes away to be burned. Madeleine talked to me while I had my bath, about a new poet she had heard of, and a book she had read, and had I read it, and what did I think? Down to dinner: Madeleine on my right hand, Beulah at the far end of the table. Peter stood behind her, his face tanned, his hair bleached copper by the sun, his blue eyes expressive as he retailed some adventure to his neighbour. I could have called him down to share my plate with me, but it made him feel uncomfortable to be singled out, and I remembered the feeling, so I merely caught his eye and smiled.

Well, I thought, even the worst days have their happinesses.

And there were wonderful days. The embassies arrived bringing coronation presents. Pravarre came in six ships but left in five; the last was the present, and its ballast was jewels. Chatienne, having won its war against Sogorah, sent sandalwood chests loaded with spice-scented cloth. In the dead of night Madeleine and I crept down to the Treasury and picked over the silks.

'Oh look!' she exclaimed. 'This colour, it's like cinnamon, but look, it goes two ways when you move it in the light. You should give it to Peter.'

'Put it over there.'

She had flung open all the lids. 'This one's beautiful. Feel it – it's as if there's nothing there. It would go with an underskirt made out of this blue. It's a lovely colour, like the inside of a shell.'

'No, not that one.'

'But I haven't got anything pink.'

'I'm glad. Beulah wears pink. It's not your colour. She can have it, I suppose, since we have to let her have something. Take this white. I like you in white.'

'Reyhnard – what if they notice what's missing?'

This gave us pause. We looked at each other guiltily.

Then I said, 'But after all, I suppose this is all mine.'

'So it is,' she laughed. 'I think Beulah had her eye on that cinnamon, you know.'

We lumbered up to Madeleine's rooms, loaded with stuff, and dumped everything on her bed, giggling.

From Andariah, more horses, and also some very fancy armour, gold-plated things I could not have stood up in. An arsenal of swords.

'They must think every country's in as much of a mess as theirs is,' I said.

'This is a good one,' said Peter, picking up a double-edged broadsword with a silver hilt. 'But these jewels at the bottom get in the way. Can I have the hilt changed, Nardo? It's too good a blade to let it lie around in the Treasury.'

What did I miss most? When did I feel it most? High days and public occasions, they were the worst. When I had to sit in that groove-armed chair, feeling out of place and ill at ease, and look down on Peter's bright crown of hair, his bent knee. When he called me 'Sir.' I hated it. I wanted to say, 'Peter, get up, come and sit beside me, tell me what you've been doing. I never get the time to talk to you any more.'

Madeleine in a crowded salon, never too far away from me but always too far when she was not in my arms – Madeleine calling me 'Sir' with a serious face.

In the end I told her, 'I'll give you a dispensation, or whatever. It's too bad, I can't bear it. You can call me "brother" if you think plain Reyhnard won't go down too well.'

'But, plain Reyhnard, what will they think?'

'Let them think what they like. I'll tell Peter to drop the "Sir" too. I don't know whether it makes me want to laugh or cry, but whatever, I don't like it.'

Peter, however, could not be persuaded. 'Everyone else calls you "Sir," ' he said. 'I just feel happier with it, in public anyway. Do you really mind?'

'No, as you prefer.'

He groaned and punched me roughly. 'Don't be so stuffy. Nardo, when can we go riding again, just the two of us?'

'After the Andarians go.'

'When are they going?'

'Day after tomorrow, if the weather holds. Then we'll go riding, I promise.'

'Can we really go alone? What about your Guards?'

'Well, I tell you what. We'll sneak out before dawn and have breakfast on the other side of the river. But you'll have to see to the food.'

'All right, great!'

Work, work, work, work.

This time last year I had a job with a corn factor's office in the Fahl of Buranah. They were short of clerks, or they would never have hired unshaven. dirty, dressed-in-rags me. Where did you work before? they asked. And I said, In Tsvingtori. After a few days they noticed I was getting on quite well, which surprised them, as I'd said I hadn't done that sort of work before. Well, I said, looking up from the accounts ledger, I realise now that what I did was not so different.

When I was King I seemed to be required to memorise every inch of the map of Brychmachrye: the name of every·castle, every city, every port, the crops of every Quarter.

The Council said: 'Here are the returns from Mehah, read this, sign here, and here are the accounts from Gurnah, and Peat, and Rayallah, and here are the poll-tax rolls from Vacled and Fahl Tsyraec, and can we have a decision on this, and what do you think of that, and what should we do, Sir? and here are the guild levies, and the army requisitions, and the kitchen bill, and the bill for the new bed the Queen ordered . . . '

Until my head swam and I asked them, 'Who dealt with this before?'

'The King, Sir.'

No time for poetry now.

I came to the Council offices one morning before dawn, in order to do some work – or rather, to catch up on it, work I should have finished the night before. Instead I had gone with Madeleine to admire the new clothes of Sogoran silk.

Peter was torn two ways when he received his suit. He didn't know whether to be pleased or disdainful. He loved the colours and finery, but he remembered that such things had never mattered to Hans; and I could see that he was consciously, conscientiously, trying to model himself on Hans. Peter had said, We need one soldier in the family, and I'm the only one left. Peter, my beloved boy, my quick-tempered, demanding brother, you were fighting against your nature. We all tried so hard. I too.

Hans was Hans. Alexi was Alexi. We loved them; they died. We cannot bring them back. You cannot be a second Hans any more than I could – no more than I could reconcile Alexi to a world without Hans, or myself to a world without you and Madeleine. It is you I love and you I need.

Peter's curtness was half-hearted, and failed to conceal his real delight. He was always proud, which Hans had never been. Peter, our brother Hans was a pure heart, simple and savage and true.

Peter, doesn't Madeleine look beautiful in that green dress? Isn't her hair a wonderful thing? I wish you'd tell her so. She wants to be friends with you. I take nothing from you in what I give to her. She only gives me more to give to you. She makes me more myself. Why couldn't you understand that?

Madeleine put on my new clothes, and I put on her new dress. She pinned her hair up under one of my hats, and we stood in front of a mirror to see who was who.

'Maybe it's the hair – ' she said, 'because I can make mine look short, and you can't make yours look long – but I do look like you, and you just look like you in women's clothes.'

'They suit you better than me.'

'That's because they were made for me.'

'Here, take it off. They're far too tight, they must be dreadfully uncomfortable. Why do you wear these stays? You don't need them. Why don't you get rid of them, start a new fashion? You're slender enough.'

'Thinner than you, anyway, and you're not exactly fat. Turn around, I'll unlace it – no, not like that . . . '

The best thing about being King – and I hope someone reads *this*, because it would surprise them – the best thing of all was ordering that I should not be disturbed, and knowing my orders would be obeyed.

The next morning was petition day. I heaved myself out of a dead sleep long before the sun rose, because I still hadn't read some of them, and I thought I ought to go over them before breakfast. I knew, even as I decided this, that I couldn't possibly cover them all, for we received scores every week, and about such things! One in particular was more than usually trifling: a woman wanted the monopoly on selling ribbons in the neighbourhood of Mindared. It's remarkable that I can remember this one, or any of them, because I also remember thinking, as I walked along the empty corridors, how much labour for so little end result it was. After breakfast the petitioners would file in, but there were so many of them, and the number of their petitions was so immense, that I could never remember their names or what they were asking for. When I handed the paper back I had to glance at the seal to see whether it had been granted or not. Nevertheless the Council handed the petitions over to me every week, and I could never tell from their straight faces whether they were thinking what I was thinking: that we were trying to shift a mountain of trivia with a teaspoon.

I didn't ask, 'Who used to do this?' I had learnt my lesson over the Treasury accounts. The King, the King. Never let it be said that the King lacked conscientiousness. I rose before the birds to get my work done. People ought to know this, about my reign. I wasn't a great King, but I wasn't a bad one either. How much more can you ask from someone who never expected to be King?

Well, I suppose it doesn't really matter. Not to me. I know what I know.

I went into the Council offices and found Beulah sitting at the table, wearing the same dress she had had on the night before. A heavy pile of papers lay in front of her. The candles were lit; dawn was grey outside the windows. Her pregnant stomach nudged the table as she leaned forward to press the seal on to a piece of paper.

She heard me come in, but she finished what she was doing before she looked up and said, 'Good morning. You're up bright and early.'

Every time I found her doing something like this, I felt not just anger, though I felt that too, and not just 'What do you think you're doing?'

which I could see. Most of all I felt that I should have expected it, and was not really surprised. When you put something down, and later return to look for it but can't see it anywhere, you call to someone and ask, 'Can you see it?' And they reply, 'There it is, under your nose.' You've been staring at it all the time, too busy wondering where it was to see it. And what you feel is a fool. Every time.

Every time she made me feel a lap behind in the race, a move behind in the game. The pile of papers in front of her had all been stamped and sealed – some blue, for granted, and some black, for not granted. The one in her hand was the last.

'Have you been up all night?' I asked.

'Just about, yes.'

'Do you ever sleep?'

She laughed, and stretched, saying, 'That's the lot. I'll brief you on them if you like, but there's nothing you really need to know. You look terribly tired, darling. Why don't you go back to bed? I'll tell them you'll have breakfast there.'

I said, 'Is that my seal?'

'Yes and no. It's a copy.'

'I didn't know there was a copy.'

'It's mine. I had it made a few months before the King died. Before that, I used yours – his, I mean – but it was too much trouble to keep taking it out and putting it back.'

'Where did you get it made?'

'Ah, now that is my secret.'

'May I have a look at the petitions, or is that too much to ask?'

'Don't be sarcastic, darling. Look at all the trouble I've saved you. Open them if you must, but it's a time-consuming job sealing them up again.'

I sat down and pulled the pile towards me. I sorted it into two: granted and not granted. The No pile towered above the Yes.

I said, 'Does the Council know what you're doing?'

'I don't know. Does it matter? As long as the job gets done, what business is it of theirs?'

'It matters to me. All this time I've been handing things out with my seal on, and I've never even seen them. I don't know what they're about. I don't know what I'm supposed to have granted or refused.'

'It's not so terribly interesting, doing these petitions.'

'So why do you do them? Are you getting some sort of gratuity from these' – I indicated the Yes pile – 'for services rendered?'

'Don't be silly. They're poor, or peasants, most of them. The truth is, even if you did read them all you wouldn't know what to do about them, and you'd never remember what they were for. You have a mind like a sieve.'

'That's what I thought. I thought my memory was at fault, but all the time it's been because I haven't seen half of them. Beulah, how can you say you don't know whether the Council is aware of what you're doing? You must know.'

'I said it didn't matter.'

'It does matter. This is supposed to be my job.'

'Don't be so childish.'

'This is public business, Beulah. Either I'm the King or I'm not, and as you have so often said, I am. And what you're doing is treason.'

'That rather depends, doesn't it? I'd say it was criminal to put someone in charge of the petitions who knows nothing about them and cares less. Look, here's an example – ' She reached into the pile and pulled two out, slitting off the wax with a paper-knife.

'It's quite simple,' she said. 'Two of the petty nobility – let's call them Lord A and Lord B – are suing each other over the rights to a small deposit of gold. This little mine is in Lord A's estate – or it would be, if Lord A hadn't rented that section of his property to Lord B on a six-year lease that's still got three years left to run.

'Lord B discovered the gold, about four months ago, and he claims that it's his, since to all intents and purposes the land is his, at least for the next three years. But Lord A is also claiming it. He says he rented the land to Lord B for farming and not for mining, and no mention was made in the lease about the rights to anything *under* the ground. Also he says that Lord B knew at the time the lease was signed that there might be gold underground, and said nothing about it, and so obtained the lease under false pretences. They've both sent in petitions. So, what would you do?'

'This isn't a matter for the petitions,' I said. 'The provincial law-courts should deal with it.'

'They've been through the courts, and the courts can't reach a decision. If we – I mean you – can't solve this case through the petitions, then they'll have to come here in person for you to judge, which would be so much extra time and work wasted – mostly yours. So – I've opened the papers. Tell me what to do with them.'

She pushed the papers over to me. I unfolded them and began to read, but it soon became clear that the purple prose, pleadings and high invective would give me no further information to add to Beulah's. 'They'll have to come here,' I said. 'I can't decide from these. I don't know enough about the case.'

Beulah leaned back in her chair, tapping the paper-knife against her open palm. After a while, she said, 'As it happens, I know rather more about this case than you'd find in those petitions. What they don't say is that at the time the lease was signed, Lord A was living here, at court, leading the most extravagant life and running up all sorts of debts. He jumped at the first chance that came along to rent that land – even now he's still in bad financial straits, and he could do with that gold. He's the sort of man who'd rent his own wife out and then complain that the children weren't his – '

I interrupted abruptly. 'I don't think *you* are in a position to make that kind of comparison.'

'Do you want to learn something, or do you just want to be rude? I'm not telling you all this for my sake.'

'I doubt very much that you're doing it for my sake.'

'All right,' she said peaceably. 'Call it for the country's sake. We've been through this before. Now, as I said, Lord A is the sort of wild spendthrift who takes absolutely no interest in his estates, except for the money they make him. It also happens to be true that Lord B did suspect gold lay under the land, but it took him three years and a lot of hard work, and cost him a small fortune, to find it. Lord A would simply never have bothered. Nevertheless it's true that Lord B did, as Lord A claims, obtain the lease under false pretences.'

'I'd still say Lord B was entitled to it.'

'I'm sure you would, but you'd be wrong. There are other factors to think about. Lord A may be a wastrel but he's a glamorous one, very charming, and popular in his neighbourhood. The same can't be said of Lord B – he works hard and has doubled his inheritance, but he's also managed to set up the backs of everyone around him. His estates are very profitable, but that's because he has the highest tithes in the Fahl and will go to any lengths to make sure his peasants pay. In fact, if you were a peasant you'd much prefer to belong to Lord A – his adore him. He more or less lets them do what they like, and he's famous for the lavishness of his solstice festivals. So, if you give the judgment against him, you'll cause a lot of dissatisfaction in that part of the country.'

I asked her, 'What are the real names of these two characters?'

'Why don't you look at the signatures?'

I did, but the names meant nothing to me, called up no face or reputation. Beulah saw this.

'You ought to know these things,' she said.

Then I read the name of their Fahl. 'No wonder you know so much about it,' I said. 'That's where you come from.'

'I did know of them when I lived there, but I've never met Lord B – I mean, Maxim – and I only met Lord Lionel after I came to court. All this happened after I left my family. It's not just because I come from there that I know about it, it's because I – '

'Oh please, spare me. That phrase of yours gets on my nerves.'

'I wish it would get into your brain, darling.'

The servants were moving in the corridors, and the Palace beginning to stir awake.

'You might as well tell me,' I said. 'What decision have you come to about these two?'

'Well, I would suggest that you declare the gold your treasure trove, crown property. Appoint Lord B overseer and pay him a large salary, perhaps a third of the income from the mine, pay Lord A an equally large remuneration for the use of his property, and keep the rest.'

'That doesn't sound like any solution, they'll both be disgruntled.'

'We can give them some titles as well. Steward of the Royal Mine, or something like that. You don't know the petty nobility, that sort of thing means a lot to them. And we get some money, which we need. You could invite them up to court and give them a medal, or something.'

'I can't believe they'd accept such a decision.'

'They really have no option. Your father did this sort of thing all the time. That's where I learnt it. So there you are. Shall I seal them up again?'

'No, I'll do it.'

'You'll take my advice?'

Of course I would, of course I would, what choice did I have? She was right. I knew she was right. I hated her for being right. Is that so terrible a thing to admit? I am not ashamed of being human, no matter how hard she tried to make me feel so.

She said, 'I'll send for a clerk to draft your reply.' I nodded. She went out, shutting the door. I hate her, I thought.

She is strong. She's a tough one. She always was strong, I've always known that. I hate to say, 'She was strong, she was able, she was right,' because it sounds as if I'm praising her, when it is no more than the truth.

She has as many ways as there are thoughts in her mind of making me insufficient. Everything she did, everything she allowed to happen was by a conscious act, an effort of will. With her there were no accidents. In truth, as she said, no luck. Serendipity is a beautiful word. It is what she did not have.

At that time, in that first year when I was King, I had been studying some books on military tactics along with everything else. I thought: I hate her. Then I thought: a good commander never under-estimates the strength of his enemy. If the opposition has a siege train, then you build a better one.

I sent the clerk off to bring Madeleine to meet me in the library annexe, where the court rolls, censuses, genealogical tables, and Annals-of-the-King are kept. When she arrived, I said to her, 'This is what you have to do. I want you to take every name from the court rolls and cross-reference them everywhere they're mentioned in the accounts, the rolls, the censuses and all these other documents. I have to ask you to do this, because I haven't got the time.'

'How long have I got?'

'As long as it takes. If you like I can let you have some clerks, but I'd rather you did it on your own.'

'Then I will, of course.'

'Don't tell anyone what you're doing.'

'No, of course not.'

I hated asking Madeleine to do all this for me, but there was no one else. The only other person I could trust was Peter, and he was not old enough. I said, 'Anything else you happen to hear, about any of them – it doesn't matter how irrelevant it seems – write it down too.'

I would make it my business to know. I was determined that before the year was out, anything I did not know about the nobility would not be worth knowing. As the saying is.

I made a new arrangement about the petitions. Previously they had been kept in a large trunk in the Council offices. This was an old custom, and I had never realised before how insecure it was. I got a new trunk, a strong-box. As soon as I received them the petitions were locked in there, and taken to my rooms. I might not be able to get Beulah's seal away from her, and would not try, but I could restrict her access.

She said nothing about this, and I didn't discuss it with her. I made a note of which councillors protested. Dominic filcRandal was among them, but then I already knew whose side he was on. Few of the others surprised me.

35

Births and deaths: sometimes it seems that's all there is to life. A century or so ago there was a sort of intellectual craze for philosophers of the marketplace, the sort who hold forth on every topic under the sun, but write nothing down. This creed was adopted by their followers, so that nothing they said was ever written down, and now all we know of their philosophy is that they didn't believe in writing things down, which is rather amusing, when you think about it. They've been reduced to a paragraph in history, and they're that much only because a number of them were executed for treason – quite justly, I think, when I have my king-hat on. However, the reason I mention them is because, several years ago, I passed through a small town where someone (obviously a betrayer of the faith) had put up a plaque to the town's particular philosopher, recording his most famous saying: 'I was born, I am living, and I will die.'

If everything else they said was as obvious as this, you can understand why they wrote nothing down.

Beulah's baby was born in early October. This puts the date of conception in early February, so it is possible that what she told me was the truth. As it turned out, it didn't matter. It was a girl. Beulah named her Ursula and sent her to be boarded with a second cousin of Lord Mindarah; this was to reward him for the good work he had done supervising the local courts in the northwest quarter of that unreliable Fahl.

Solstice passed and we were in a new year. Peter was fourteen. Late one night I was sitting up, reading over the notes Madeleine had researched for me, when a knock on my door made me jump. I knew it couldn't be Madeleine; she had left less than an hour before. I called to the Guards outside to open the door. Peter came in, and shut it.

'Are you alone?' he asked.

'Of course I'm alone, it's the middle of the night. Come in. What are you doing up?'

'Couldn't sleep,' he said absently, scanning the room. I had moved into these rooms a few days earlier, and everything was still in disarray. He found some space on the sofa and sat down, cross-legged. Glancing from the piles of paper to the accounts ledgers, from the accounts ledgers to the books open on their spines, he started to laugh. 'God!' he said. 'God! It just goes to show – '

'What?'

'That things aren't really the way you imagine them. You've got more books in here now than you ever had.'

'What did you think it was, all embassies and killing people?'

He stretched out, sprouting legs that went on and on – and I was suddenly reminded of Alexi.

'You're awfully busy all the time,' he said.

'I'm sorry. I know. But it can't be helped.'

'I know. That's why I had to come and see you now – at night, I mean. I guess I could have sent a petition – '

'Don't be silly.'

'But I know what ages they take, and you're never alone, you're never free, so I just hoped you would be now.'

'It won't be like this for ever. I have so much to learn at the moment.'

'I know – I mean, I can imagine how it is. I wouldn't be bothering you if it wasn't important. I've been waiting to tell you for ages – '

'You should have come sooner.'

'I couldn't, I told you. But it's really important.'

He broke off there, and gave me an intent look which seemed to expect me to say something. 'Well?' I urged. 'What is it?'

He frowned. 'Are you going to make me tell you?'

I was completely at a loss to know what he meant by this resentful question, so after a moment's indecision I replied, 'You came here because you wanted to tell me something. If you've changed your mind I'm not going to force you. But why did you come and make this big thing about it being important, if you're not going to tell me?'

He bit his lip; then the shadow of something not quite like a smile flitted across his face.

'Peter,' I said. 'What is it?'

'You know.'

'Is this a game?'

'You're angry already – '

'I'm not angry. Peter, if you have something important to tell me, you should tell me. I am still your brother, you know. I won't be angry.'

'Promise?'

'Now you're making me suspicious. If it's so bad I have to promise, then I don't promise because I probably should be angry. But you know I can't stay angry with you for long.'

He turned his face from me, looked at the wall, then at the floor, then at the ceiling, looking all over the room in search of a way to begin. He seemed very uneasy, unhappy. I felt I had spoken too harshly. Sitting down next to his feet, I said, 'Please, tell me what's bothering you.'

'Nardo – there's this girl. I – I mean she – I mean, she's going to have a baby. Mine, I mean.'

I was so relieved I laughed. 'Is that all? What made you think I'd be angry about that? Do you want some money?'

'No – Nardo – '

'Alexi always gave them money. I think you should.' I waggled his foot and smiled at him, wishing he would cheer up.

He said, 'It – she – it – she's not a servant.'

I released his foot and sat calmly for a moment, confronting the obvious. I didn't want to shout at him, so I got up and walked around the room until I felt my temper was under control, when I could turn to ask him, 'Do you want to marry her?'

'What? Good God, no!' He laughed uncomfortably.

'I don't think this is anything to laugh about. You'd better tell me who she is.'

He set his jaw and for a moment looked so like a stubborn boy that I expected him to declare, 'I won't!'

'Isabel Mehah,' he said.

I knew her by sight, one of Beulah's ladies-in-waiting. A big girl – a woman, really. Rather raw-boned, and in the pink-and-blonde Beulah mould. I was glad now that I hadn't promised not to be angry. 'Peter! She's nineteen! And she's betrothed!'

'I know.'

'You knew and you still – '

'I knew you'd be angry.'

'Her uncle's on the Council!'

'I know.'

'You know an awful lot for someone who obviously didn't stop to think.'

'It's not my fault!'

'You're the one who got her pregnant – '

'That's what she says.'

I took a deep breath. 'Peter, that is not the way to deal with this, and it won't be solved so easily.'

'But you've got to do something, Nardo, she says she wants to marry me!'

'I bet she does. Well, you're too young, much too young, and they're the last family I'd have you marrying into. They're far too strong as it is. Oh Peter, what a mess, what a stupid thing to do. Do you realise what a stupid thing it was?'

'Nardo!' He threw up his hands. 'It only happened once!'

I remembered then that the Guards standing outside my door could easily hear every word we shouted at each other. 'All right, calm down,' I said, and took a seat on the far side of the room. 'You knew I'd be angry,' I said slowly. 'You know why I am. I am angry. But that's not going to help us. I'd just like to say that I hope you learn a lesson from this. Stick to the servants in future. Because if this happens again I will be furious. All right. Enough of that.'

I sat and thought, hand over mouth.

'I don't suppose', I said, 'that she could be persuaded to tell her betrothed it's his? I don't suppose there's any way it could be?'

'She says there isn't, and she won't.'

Of course she does.

'Well,' I said, 'the only thing to do is persuade her to leave court until she's had it. I don't know how her family are going to take this.'

'You're the King, make them.'

'The Mehahs are a very powerful family. I can't say "do this, do that, hop to it, jump", and expect them to jump.'

'Father did – '

'You don't know what he did. I didn't know what he did until I – well, I can tell you, Peter, Father would probably have made you marry her. I don't know what I'm going to do, especially if they refuse to send her away.'

'They can't.'

'They very well might.'

'They have to do what the King tells them.'

'Peter, if their daughter is pregnant and you're responsible then they have some say in the matter.'

'I think you're being a bit feeble – '

'Oh, you think it's so easy, do you?' I stood up angrily. 'You think you can just trot in here, sit down and say, "I've made this girl pregnant, she's a lady, send her away please," and snap, it's done? It doesn't work like that, Peter. I can't wave my hand and make everything all right, and sort out this mess you've landed yourself in – and me – through your sheer stupidity. If I can get you out of this and keep the whole thing quiet you can count yourself extremely lucky.'

He cried out, with a voice on the edge of tears, 'It's not my fault. She said it would be all right.'

Oh Peter, caught between boyhood and manhood with the oldest trick in the book. I shouldn't have stood there shouting at him. Time is too short for anger. When he is in trouble, where else should he come but to me? I sat down again beside him. 'I'm sorry,' I said. 'You're so tall, I forget how young you are.'

He said, 'Don't patronise me,' but without any real conviction.

'I'm not patronising you. You are young. It's not your fault. You weren't to know. She should have known better – and her parents and her young man ought to have kept an eye on her.' I put an arm round him. 'Don't worry. I'm glad you told me. I'll sort it out. One other thing though, Peter. Keep away from her from now on. No one else knows about this, do they?'

He shook his head.

'That makes it much easier. We don't want you to be associated with her in people's minds, so the less you're seen with her, the better. All right? They'll gossip anyway when she goes away.'

'You'll send her away?'

'Don't worry.'

Don't worry, Peter, because I was worried enough for both of us. He had only a vague idea of how serious a situation it was. I was under no illusions. Lord Mehah's brother Valentine was a member of Beulah's set, and Isabel's mother was one of her intimates – though I use the term loosely, because Beulah had no real intimates, any more than Nikolas had. But it would be to Beulah's advantage if Peter were, so to speak, married into her circle. I expected the Mehahs would use her influence to the full to push the marriage through.

If only he hadn't always been in such a hurry to grow up. At his age he should still have been playing with his dogs and ponies and toy swords, not with women. When I was fourteen the only women I had ever touched were my mother and my nurse.

I could see no way out of it. I couldn't find the nerve to speak to the Mehahs. As long as I didn't mention it, I wouldn't have to deal with a refusal.

Madeleine said, 'You're wearing yourself out. Send her away, it's the only answer.'

'You know I can't do that.'

'I'm sorry. I just can't think of anything else.'

I put it off and put it off. I did not want a test of strength with Beulah.

Then one day, about a fortnight later, she came to me. She talked of this and that, and then she remarked, 'By the way, Lady Mehah and her daughter are going into the country.'

'Oh,' I said. 'At this time of year?'

I was trying to work up the courage to seize this opportunity. But before I could say more, Beulah went on, 'They'll be gone for nine months or so. Apparently her grandmother's not very well. They don't think she'll see another summer.'

'Oh,' I said. 'Give them my condolences.'

She said, 'It would be a nice gesture if you gave them a present. A sympathy gift for their bereavement.'

'All right. You choose it. Take something from the Treasury.'

'Speaking of which,' she said, 'and of the Mehahs, I've been thinking – the post of Treasurer's vacant. Valentine might be a good man for the job.'

'I'll think about it.'

'Well, you know how these things are done.'

My relief was not real relief. I felt more like a patient after the crisis of his illness: less sick, but no less weak.

On top of everything else, I now had to be grateful to her, and I knew that this was why she had done it. See, Nardo, do you see what I can do for you? Things you could never do for yourself.

36

'There you are, off the hook,' I said to Peter.

'Thanks, Nardo, thank you. I can't tell you how grateful I am.'

He smiled, and his eyes said, 'I was never really worried.' Because Nardo always looks after Peter. Makes sure that Peter doesn't get hurt. Because he cannot bear to hear that small boy cry, 'Where were you?' Because he loves him, Peter.

I asked him, 'When's your next fencing match?'

'Day after tomorrow. Are you going to come?'

'I'll try to. Listen – Peter – I've decided that when you're eighteen I'll enrol you in the Guards, as a junior, and if you do well, and you like it, you'll be promoted. You might even take over from Nikolas one day. If you'd like that?'

'You know I would, I'd love it. Do you really mean it?'

'Of course I do. You're the soldier. But Peter, if you get into any more trouble I'll think again.'

'I won't, I promise I won't.'

We received an embassy from Duccarn.

I rather like the way this is shaping: embassies, petitions, Council meetings, births, death, embassies . . . I didn't do it on purpose, but I see now that it was inevitable. It was the rhythm of my life. Court music, the tempo of court life: a rhythm sometimes discordant, sometimes flowing smoothly, sometimes a pleasant harmony . . . an unending pattern-dance going on behind me.

I can't be bothered to remember what the embassy came from Duccarn about. It wasn't particularly important at the time. They brought more gifts. Our Treasury was filling up.

Beulah said, 'We're going to have to start sending some embassies of our own, soon.'

I said to Madeleine, 'I hope someone's made a list of what came from whom. I don't want to find myself giving people presents they gave to me first. I'd better see to it.'

When I went to do so, I discovered Beulah had already dealt with the matter.

I next discovered that she was still following her old policy of having a copy of all the diplomatic paperwork sent to her.

I could not trust myself to speak, and instead I did a ridiculous thing. I sat down and wrote her a memo in which I told her that this practice was to cease forthwith.

As soon as I had sent it I was sorry. I regretted having allowed myself to get so angry, and to no purpose, because my anger had no effect on her, and it seemed futile to work out how I could have let myself lose my temper so badly. She never replied to the memo.

Council business tails off in winter. One day we set aside more hours than we needed, and I was left with some unexpected free time on my hands. Madeleine was busy supervising a treat organised for some of the court children, Beulah had been invited to a betrothal party and Peter was down at the kennels, so I went back to my rooms to get on with my research.

There was Beulah, sitting on the floor. The petition strong-box was unlocked. All the petitions were scattered round her lap, except for the one in her hand. On my desk, neatly opened and obviously read, were the notes Madeleine had prepared for me.

This is the only time I have ever seen that woman look guilty. I found her expression so gratifying that I was able, instead of shouting, to say calmly, 'Get out.'

When she had gone, I put all the petitions back in the trunk and locked it. Silly really to bother, I thought, since she either knows how to pick it or she's got a key. I sat on the lid and said to myself: I can't take much more of this.

It was nearly spring again, and I had been King for a year.

Because Alexi shared his funeral with the others, we did not go into mourning on the day of his death; that is to say, not officially. It was the time of year when the days are growing longer, but they, for me, became grey with a twilight of might-have-beens. Especially the brightest days, when the sun glittered on the snow as it had the day he and I went riding together. On the anniversary of his death it rained. The sky was sludgy with clouds, pouring sleet. I felt strangely contented by this dismal weather: at one with it and more at peace with myself. Madeleine said she felt the same. We thought: this day last year . . .

If we had not been in the kitchens this day last year, if there had not been a thaw this day last year, if the food had not gone bad, then Alexi would now be King. I would be divorced from Beulah. We would never see her again. I would be living in my old rooms, carrying on with my old life and my old interests, happily ignorant of statecraft and politics, my free time abundant and devoted to Peter and Madeleine, with no one to ask where I was and say, 'There's something you have to do, sign, see, Sir.' My sister and I looked back across a year to the year before, when we had expected a future so different from the one we were given.

She started to cry and said, 'If we hadn't been in the kitchens, if there hadn't been a thaw – he would have found another way.'

On that day in March there was not one person at court who did not have a relative to mourn for.

We seemed never to have been out of mourning. We walked, dressed in black, from the Temple back to the Palace, and we looked at the budding crocuses with hatred for their insensitivity. The wood of the yew was dark brown, its needles dark green, its berries blood red – the eternal tree with the poisonous fruit. Everything seemed to have a meaning. The windows were curtained with black felt to shut out the sunlight, for the sun had no right to shine. I sat in the King's chair with the court all around. Many of them, men and women, were crying as they looked at me. What is this terrible joke? Where is the King? Where are their husbands, wives, parents, children?

Gloom commanded, brightness was banished. Black figures and more black in the shadows behind the candles. We shut out the day, illuminated ourselves with flames as if we were on our death ships. We mimicked death, played out a mock death, and the next day we could get up and say: We have put all that behind us. We have imitated death for our dead, now let us get on with living.

One day they would do this for me too, I thought. Dead king. The court puts on its black, grieves by ritual, takes off its black and goes on living. But not those for whom they grieve. Dead kings, dead gods. Ah, divine King, Sir, death rules a greater kingdom. Emperor death, from whom I hold my life in fiefdom.

I was not the only one oppressed by the atmosphere – that was the intention. We undergo this parody of death; we brave not death, but the watered-down aspects of it, the dark, the silence, the fire, so that when the real thing comes we can say, 'I've been through this before.' I don't know if this is the true intention or not. I often think it is. But it doesn't work.

In the hot silent darkness I could still hear my heart beat.

Beulah came up to me, touching my arm and speaking so quietly that only I could hear. As soon as possible after this, I left and went up to my rooms to be on my own. I sent my Guards as far away as I could, which meant round the corner down the corridor.

I ought to say a little bit about my rooms – not that I liked them very much. They were not the King's old rooms, Beulah had taken those, but I didn't mind. I would rather not have lived in them. Of course I couldn't go on living in my old rooms. They were far too small and undignified. I chose these particular rooms because no one was living in them. In fact they were my mother's old rooms, though all her stuff had been cleared out – except for the attic, which was crammed with junk. Behind the panelling in the bedroom was one of those secret doors with which the Palace of Tsvingtori is riddled. I don't think anyone knows how many there are. At one time or another all the larger suites in the Palace have been occupied by a king, and each had to have his own secret door; though not really so secret because they all link to each other in an intricate maze. I suppose they are a bad thing for security, but mine had an arsenal of locks on it, and only Madeleine had the keys. I used to imagine dozens of people sneaking off through those doors to various assignations, and all of them, to their intense surprise and embarrassment, bumping into each other along the way. But as far as I know it never happened.

Madeleine had a door in her room too. I had made sure of this, and not just because she was my sister; I would not have had any woman coming to me openly, because I like my privacy. I prefer not to let the whole world know what I'm doing. Now more than ever, since from getting up to going to bed I was, so to speak, public property, and I wanted to hang on to whatever privacy I had left.

I am meandering. Anyway, I was in my rooms, actually my bedroom, listening to the Guards shuffling their feet. I found it difficult to get used to this never being quite alone. It seemed excessive, and misplaced. Sometimes I thought that if I were to put the crown in the middle of the floor and then go out, the Guards would happily continue to stand and guard the thing that really mattered.

Outside the door one of them coughed. I listened to the noise first, and only afterwards said to myself, 'One of my Guards has coughed.' Then I realised I had been standing for any length of time thinking nothing at all. It seemed so absurd I sat down, on my bed, and laughed.

After I stopped laughing I asked myself: Why does this bother me so much more than the first two times?

Because this time there is not the remotest possibility that it could be the King's. I mean the old King's. The dead God's.

It's not as if I'm surprised. Beulah is the last person in the world I would expect to change her nature. New revelations, yes: like, just exactly like those layers of petticoats she has made the fashion, because she's putting on weight and doesn't want people to notice. Funny that she should be so vain. Vanity's always been called a weakness, but not in her, I suppose. Layer on layer of petticoats until you reach the woman beneath, the person who gives a shape to all those petticoats. To whom the petticoats offer a clue. I expected new revelations about her character. I was ready for anything, except a change in that character. I am not surprised she has not changed. So why does it bother me?

A voice I knew as well as my own was laughing beneath my windows.

I walked over and pulled the felt aside, blinking. Peter was playing with a court dog, two young ladies his own age having gathered as an audience. He was throwing a stick for the dog, in order to show how obediently it would fetch – but the dog scampered off with the stick between its teeth and refused to give it back. The three of them chased after it, shrieking and shouting.

He should have been inside, sitting quietly in the dark, thinking suitably solemn thoughts. I wasn't about to make him come in. I leant my forehead against the glass, reflecting that at least one of us was able to do what he wanted. What I would like to do is put the crown in the middle of the floor and leave the Guards to guard it while I go out and run around in the fresh air with my brother. I didn't in fact have the crown on – whatever the peasants may like to imagine: the King walking around all day with that big iron crown on his head (which incidentally we never got around to making smaller), sleeping in it even, or so they picture him – it was in the Treasury. I don't think I wore it more than twenty times in all.

Still carrying its stick like a trophy, the dog galloped into the hedge-walk, and Peter ran after it, with a girl hanging on to each hand.

Another nephew, or niece, for Peter. But not really a relation, not a member of our family at all. Me, Peter, Alexi, we all had children, but somehow none of us in the right way. I had no idea what the Mehahs intended to do with their daughter's child. Expose it, probably. It would be the best thing for all concerned.

Addressing the Council, in my imagination.

'Gentlemen, that woman whom the late King in his infinite lack of consideration made my wife is a whore. She is a prostitute of the worst kind, using her sex to manipulate men, paying them to sleep with her. She pays them with privilege, not that I'm naming any names. And when she becomes pregnant everyone calls the child mine, although everyone knows that it is not mine. And quite frankly I've had enough. I am sick of living one life in appearance and another in fact. That's what I'm sick of, that precisely. I'm sick of having to fight her every step of the way. I'm not prepared to put up with any more of her interfering uncontrollable behaviour, so I'm going to get rid of her, and what are you going to do about it?'

The Council, in my imagination, stand up as one man: at their head, Dominic filcRandal and Valentine Mehah. They exclaim: 'Sir! That wonderful woman, that credit to the court, mother of her country. Sir! Can you really intend to repay all her hard work, her care and devotion, with such ingratitude? Sir! Where would you be without her? Out on your ear, because that's where she'd throw you, Sir. Sir! And where do you get the nerve to criticise her morality, when we all know you're knocking your sister off?'

I let the curtain fall back, and turned to look at my bed. I realised there was nothing I wanted more than to get in it, and preferably never get out again.

So I did, thinking at the time that it was the second most sensible thing I had ever done.

I lay there for a while, chuckling to myself, 'Let's see her try to make me get up.' Then I curled into a ball and went to sleep.

I slept. And from time to time I woke up. Madeleine was always there, and Peter quite often. Sometimes I played a game of chess or cards with him, but mostly I slept.

My curtains were always drawn. The light shone through around the hems and I sensed the days were growing longer, brighter, stronger, warmer. My meals were brought to me and the Guards changed outside my door.

From time to time Beulah came in and asked, 'For God's sake when are you going to get up?'

To her I said nothing.

Every so often a councillor, or courtier, or Nikolas or some other official, would ask for admission, in order to request a command or a decision which supposedly only I could give. I knew they had been sent by Beulah, in an attempt to remind me of what can be called a sort of reality. And perhaps, to re-awaken my interest.

Madeleine told me that Beulah had informed the court I was suffering from 'nervous exhaustion'.

I simply saw no reason to get up.

Until one day, when Madeleine happened to be out of the room, I did feel like getting up, so I put on my dressing-gown, went over to the windows and drew back the curtains. I waited to see something more than a white glare, which after a few seconds I did. The first thing I noticed were the leaves. They had been pale sticky buds when I last saw them, and now they were unfurled, darkening. Like the colour of my eyes, my sister's eyes. Once we had all been green-eyed, the King and Hans and Alexi; now there was only my sister and myself.

She came in.

'Oh, you're up,' she said.

She was carrying an armful of butter-coloured daffodils.

I said, 'It's nearly summer, isn't it?'

'It's a lovely day.'

'Where's Peter?'

'I think he's down at the gymnasium.'

'He works so hard. Madeleine?'

'Yes?'

I put my arms around her and turned her face to mine, plumbed her green eyes. All I saw in their depths was two of me; I noticed my beard had grown rather long and straggly.

I asked her, 'What do you know that I don't know?'

'Nothing.'

I see that this is true. I see that if I could only get close enough I would find, in the eyes of my two selves reflected in her eyes, four reflections of Madeleine: into infinite refractions. So I closed her eyes with a kiss and let her go, and went to open the door.

The Guard's surprise nearly got the better of his training. He pulled himself from a slouch through a startle into a salute.

'Send for the barber,' I said.

'Yes, Sir.'

I went back to the window and sat on the sill, looking out at the bright, pretty greens and yellows and pinks of the late spring landscape. There were butterflies among the flowers. 'It will soon be summer,' I said to Madeleine. 'Do you know, it's nearly four years since we met?'

'Oh, I don't believe you, I feel as if I've always known you.'

'And always loved you.'

'And always will.'

'Yes,' I said. 'Madeleine, next month we'll move to Ksaned Kaled.'

My sister smiled and began to arrange her flowers.

37

Before the packing had begun, long before we set off for the island, I could sense a lift in the collective spirits.

Madeleine said, 'Everyone wants to get away. Too much has happened here too recently.'

The kitchens, the hills, the salons, the gardens, the woods, the grooved throne, the little smithy: all these things reminded me of death, and of the dead.

'They must all feel the same,' said my sister. 'There's hardly a room in the Palace that someone hasn't died in over the last two years. We must leave it behind us.'

We had no Hans now to be sorry we were going to a place where there was no hunting.

We still had a king. Men die; royal names change; families rise and fall; war, famine and pestilence scar her face; but as long as Brychmachrye holds her green head above the rivers and oceans she will have a man for her God, her Tsyraec, lord and lover and servant – I think this is something close to my father's understanding of the office. I occupied the great stateroom in the flagship. Obviously I did. If I were the King – I mean, if I were Basal the Great, my father – if he were penning his memoirs, he wouldn't have written that. It wouldn't have struck him as needing to be said.

It was night. Through the portholes I could see the navy-grey sky and the white sparks of stars, clustering in constellations. I could hear the blow and flutter of the wind in the sails, the creak of oak boards, the Captain calling to his helmsman, the slap and rustle of water. I could smell tar, brine, oil and my starched sheets, this last smell like the scent of land because everything else at sea is so different from land. I could feel the roll of the ship running before the wind. If I had shut my eyes and plugged my ears, that rocking feeling alone would have insisted we were at sea. I was happy to lie awake, enjoying the rise and fall of the ship across the swell, my mind full of those contented sorts of thoughts that do nothing but state facts: 'Here I am, lying in the great stateroom of the flagship, sailing to Ksaned Kaled because I said we should.'

I wished Madeleine was with me. She was in the second ship, with Peter, though Beulah was on board with me; perhaps it was just as well, because a ship is too small for secrecy, and better no opportunity than an impossible one. That's what she said, when I told her we would have to travel in separate ships. I liked it: I couldn't have put it half so well, but I knew exactly what she meant.

I remember lying there, travelling to Ksaned Kaled, missing Madeleine, knowing she was missing me, looking forward to seeing her again, feeling a little sleepy and good all over, and thinking, 'Well, just look at me lying in the King's bed.'

Abruptly I thought to ask myself, 'Why shouldn't I lie in the King's bed?'

I was wide awake, and for a moment I felt panicky, as if I was about to get caught red-handed doing something forbidden. I tried to laugh it off, but the other half of me argued, 'I *am* the King.'

Then I understood.

All of a sudden I knew what it was, the reason for the studying and the agonising and the renunciation of all the things I most enjoyed, and the sleepless nights and the work, work, work I had been driving myself through. The reason why I couldn't cope with Beulah. The reason why I felt pursued, cornered.

I had been waiting for a hand to tap me on the shoulder and say, 'Nardo, what are you playing at? Take off that crown, get off that throne. You shouldn't be there.'

Put like that, it sounded just as absurd as it really was.

The King was dead. I was the King. A chain of accidents, some contrived, others not; but I was the eldest surviving son, and who was the King if I was not?

I wasn't lying in that great stateroom through anyone's grace and favour. I didn't have to prove my right to it. I was the King. I had crowned myself and been transfigured – but what did that mean? Not much, apparently. I was precisely what I had been before and always would be. There was no reason why I should change, or try to.

I hadn't asked to be King. I hadn't wanted it. Since I had done nothing to bring about this state of affairs, I was under no obligation to do anything now. I owed it nothing.

I had no desire to wage unnecessary war, shed blood, dispossess the Fahlraecs, impose unreasonable taxes, or spend the crown into bankruptcy. I had no interest in doing any of the things which would foster discontent or throw the country into chaos. Hence, I could not possibly be a bad king.

The system of government which my father had established was so efficient it could be run with a half-wit or a madman as the figurehead. No doubt that's what many of the court thought they now had, I reflected. But it didn't matter, as long as the madman or idiot didn't try to tamper with the system. Which I had no desire to do. Some people might want to – there had been my father, and though his talents were unique his ambitions certainly were not. But why should I worry? I had Beulah to look after my interests, and she's a match for anyone.

Why have I been knocking myself out in competition with her? I don't want to run the country. I haven't been brought up to expect this would fall to my lot, and I have no more interest in governing than I have in sheep-shearing. And (being comfortably honest with myself) I haven't much more ability for governing than I would have for shearing sheep.

You can't force ability where there is no interest. Mugging up on accounts and geography bores me. Sitting up late into the night, sifting through piles of petitions, exhausts me and bores me. Diplomats set my teeth on edge. Two days after I've passed a decree I can't remember what it was about – that's how much it bores me.

It's not my fault. No one could begin to claim it was my fault. Such an argument would never stand up in court. No one could expect me to find it suddenly and compulsively riveting simply because my father and my elder brothers had died.

Alexi said, 'They can't bring us up to do nothing, expecting never to have to do anything, and then shove this at us.'

No, they can't. It's unjust and unfair.

When a merchant's heir, or even a peasant's son, runs wild, refuses to settle into the future they have arranged for him, and says 'I have other plans for my life' – a young man like the Captain, for instance, who can be held to blame for many things, but not for wanting to leave home, join the army and see the world – when a young man disrupts his parents' expectations, who is blamed? The father is blamed. It is certainly not the young man's fault.

God knows you only get one life, so it's folly to waste it trying to be and do what other people want. All I ever wanted was to be with my family, most of all with Madeleine and Peter; to love them, to share things together and to write poetry, which might be good and is mostly bad, but is at least what I enjoy. That is all I have ever cared for. I want nothing more to make my life worth living – and surely a man should be envied when he can say: I know what I want. These things, and nothing more, will make me happy.

It's not my fault that time and accidents conspired to throw the burden of government on to me. Alexi said, 'We've got *responsibilities.*' But the truth is, we have no responsibilities towards what we did not ask for. I have responsibilities towards Peter and Madeleine, because I love them. I love other things too: Ksaned Kaled, and the countryside of Brychmachrye, meadows of grass, great rivers, sweeping forests, the light of its sky, its colours, its rich variegated beauty. I love the earth of my country.

I don't love 'the country'. That's too vague for me. I certainly don't love 'the people', starting with Beulah and Valentine Mehah, and working my way down to the fish-gutters in Sylaeg. Why should I love them? What sort of a love would that be? So generalised, so diffuse – I cannot love in that wide, shallow way. Towards them I feel no responsibility and I'm not ashamed to admit it. To pretend otherwise would be hypocrisy.

It is my life and my country, and when they try to hold that whip of responsibility over my head they are as much trespassers as Nikolas and his cronies were in my library, all those years ago.

I'm not interested in running the country.

So, let Beulah do it.

Allow Beulah to do it. After all, why not? She is interested in it, she's competent, and she's created sufficient authority for herself. She's already got my seal.

Why am I competing with her for something I don't want? She's bound to win. She wants the thing we're fighting for, whereas all I want is to prevent her winning. But if I permit her to win, then she has no victory.

If I go on fighting with her over a worthless prize, then I am letting her and the things she has done to me – the reasons why I hate her – ruin the rest of my life. Let her have it. I don't want it. And the things I do want don't affect her. If I let her have what she wants, she may not try to spoil what I want.

I had come this far in understanding her: she was not vindictive when she was satisfied.

Beulah could not afford to be vindictive to me.

Then I realised what a position of strength she had put me in.

I don't like her and she doesn't like me, but we need each other, and no one else will do. In fact she needs me more than I need her. I could run the country myself; I don't want to, and so I need her to do it for me. But if I were not around – if she were not married to me – there would be no one who could allow her to do it. She was Queen only for as long as I was King.

I recollected what she had said about being able to raise a rebellion against me. But even if she did, she would still have to find another man to put in my place, and this new Tsyraec might have ideas of his own about the government. Any man who could be persuaded to take the lead in such a venture would undoubtedly have ambitions to be King in fact as well as in name. And of course he might not marry her, he might find a new queen. In trying for everything, she would run a great risk of losing what she had. She was better off with me.

My ace, my greatest strength, was her children. By law, if not in truth, they were my children and thus my heirs, and in dispossessing me, Beulah would dispossess her children.

What if she fell in love? Unlikely. Beulah does not fall in love. (I might as well say now that, as far as I know, she never did.) Love of human beings, for one particular person, was not in her nature. The only person she had ever loved was her son. There was only one thing she could want more than to be Queen, and that was to see a son of hers crowned King.

For that, all she had to do was wait. Of course there was a slight risk of some future attempt by her to depose me in favour of an as-yet-unborn son; but I think she knew I was prepared to deny her children were mine, if circumstances made this necessary. Her own behaviour would be evidence enough to give my assertions some chance of being believed, or at least sufficiently believed to give her a very rough ride. She would be wiser to wait.

I've written before that Beulah craved security. Not love, not the knowledge of being loved, she didn't need that. I have never met anyone as confident in this respect as she was. What she craves is security of position.

I am the King. She is married to the King. She loves that security, and needs it.

I folded my arms behind my head and gazed up at the ceiling, proud of my realism.

Clever Reyhnard. You see how simple life turns out to be if you work things through calmly and don't let your emotions run away with you?

Forget the past. Give her what she wants. You don't want it. Retire from the field, and this time you really will be free of her.

Free of her – this phrase conjured up such lovely pictures: Beulah sitting up all night labouring over the petitions, handing them to me in the morning so that I, refreshed from a long sleep, can distribute them. Myself day-dreaming in the Justice Hall while the protagonists plead their dreary cases, merely glancing down at my list when they finish to see what my judgment should be. Myself presenting the insignia of office to those men whom Beulah has patiently assessed and selected. Composing poetry during Council meetings, savouring the colour and finery of the embassies, the parties and plays and dances – because Beulah will send me a memo telling me what to do.

A happy life for a puppet king. A puppet king has no worries – least of all the worry that my puppeteer might cut my strings, because she knows and I know that she'll never find anyone as handy.

I was King and would be King until the day I died. Nothing less than death could de-apotheosise me, and while I was alive the godhood could not be bestowed on anyone else. Deposition would equal death; but Beulah would never let me be deposed. And my death was long long years away. I could fill those years with something more worth while than fighting with Beulah.

That night I saw those years of my future stretch away before me as full of beauty and happiness as the flower fields of Ksaned Kaled. I saw Madeleine and myself growing old together, tracing age in each other's face and feeling no fear. Peter growing up – he was already almost grown-up – to become a renowned and valiant general; marrying a proud and pretty princess, and giving Madeleine and me real nephews and nieces to love. I would carry on with my poetry. Time, and application, and happiness, would help it to improve. And perhaps I might write a monograph or two, on Caryllac, or Isumbard. And when I died I wouldn't be called Reyhnard the Great, but I might well be called Reyhnard the Scholar. I would have been content with such an epitaph.

I had worked it all out. We were going to live happily ever after.

I could not ask to have back what I had lost: childhood, religion, certain loves and passions, Hans and Alexi. But of the things I could have, it seemed to me that I could ask for no more than what I had already.

The next day, when we met on deck, I told Beulah the substance of my night thoughts, and promised her I wouldn't make any more attempts to block her essays in administration. She listened to me patiently, her smile pulled in at the dimples. When I had concluded, she said, 'But darling, that's what I've been saying all along.'

It seemed a vindication of my understanding of the world, my life and the future that this did not irritate me. I was free of her.

38

Ksaned Kaled, green house on a gold island, gem of houses, jewel of islands, wreathed with flowers, where the peacocks trail their tattered plumage in bright blues and greens along the flagstones. My sister walks through a garden of meadows, and when she returns to me her skin is dusted with pollen, her hair smells of roses. 'I love it here,' Peter said to me as we came up from the beach. His two pet dogs barked and rolled in the grass, relieved to feel the firm earth of Ksaned Kaled beneath their paws after four days at sea. He said, 'I wish we could stay here for ever.'

I too, Peter. Strangely, I find I have least to say about the times I best like to remember. They get elbowed aside by the clamorous memories of deceptions and accidents and mistakes demanding a hearing; it makes what I write misleading, for I have failed to emphasise the several long periods of tranquillity and contentment that I have enjoyed. These times ought really to be given the greater prominence, for they are what made my life worth living, as the saying goes. Our two and a bit years on Ksaned Kaled were such a time. I think I can allow myself to dwell here a little and redress the balance.

Among the few rules I had made was one putting the toy-house and its gardens out of bounds to everyone but my family, though Madeleine did often bring the children, sons and daughters of the courtiers, down to play. If I had a favourite place on the island, that would be it. We spent most of our time there in summer: it seemed always to be summer on Ksaned Kaled. Madeleine and I were sitting on a bench under a plane tree, roasting our bare toes in the sunlight, the rest of us cool in the shade of the leaves, going through the most recent batch of books – poetry, memoirs, history, various scholarly texts – to arrive from the Official Publishers.

Beulah called this job of mine 'encouraging the arts'. I need hardly say how much, or little, importance she attached to it, but I enjoyed it, and had taken it over from the Temple censors. Previously they had vetted the publications and sent me a selection of those books most approved of by themselves. My purpose was to decide which, if any, of the authors were sufficiently distinguished to merit the honour, if that is the right word, of an invitation to court, or perhaps the grant of a small stipend. I like to think that I carried out this job more fairly than the Temple had: I at least tried to find out which authors needed the money.

Aside from the singing and scrabbling of the birds in the leaves, it was very quiet. In the background, incessant and inescapable, droned the susurration of the court, but I was as used to this noise as a fisherman is to the ceaseless rush of the sea. It is only now, when I no longer have the murmuring all about me, that I – miss it is not the word. Think about it, perhaps.

Madeleine looked up, across the smooth lawn, the banks of hollyhocks and the box hedges, up the grassy incline to where the marble of the Palace took a matt sheen from the sunlight. 'It's so beautiful,' she hummed. 'Beautiful day, beautiful place. Everything in the garden's lovely – that's what Alexi would say, isn't it?'

'I wouldn't be surprised.'

'You still miss him, don't you.'

'Oh yes, in a way. As you said, wondering what he'd say about this and that. I'm sure we always will miss him. And Hans. It would be worse if we didn't.'

'I know what you mean. I miss him too, but not in a sad sort of way any more. Nothing's sad, here. You know what I think? I believe he's happy too, where he is.'

I smiled at her, not needing to say anything. She knew my convictions, and on a day like this I had no desire to dampen her cheerfulness.

I ought to say, although I have moved on several years beyond it, that Beulah's third child was born just before my twenty-fourth birthday. It was a boy, and she named it Basal. I thought to myself, 'If this one dies, she'll call the next one Basal, and the next, until she finally has another King Basal on the throne.'

It was a fair, fat, robust child, taking after its mother in every particular.

Impossible as ever to guess who might be the father – and I was tired of that game. To know that Beulah was its mother seemed the only fact of any importance. I never got acquainted with it. When we met on formal occasions we, that big, blond, arrogant child and the man who called himself its father, regarded each other as the strangers we were. It – he – Basal, is King now, but everybody knows this.

A pair of dogs came lolloping into the garden, sidled up to us, sniffed our hands and feet, and retired to pant in the shade. Peter followed them. 'Only you two', he said, 'could think of nothing better to do outdoors than read.'

He had just turned seventeen, my little brother, and was not far short now of his true height, almost a head taller than I was. His hair was clipped very close, so that in some lights its red had a pinkish tinge from the scalp beneath. His skin, though tanned, was naturally so fair that shaving was an ordeal for him, one he underwent with protests every six or seven days.

'I remember when you couldn't wait,' I used to tease him.

He would make a face and complain, 'Don't nag.'

'You'll have to keep it shaved when you're in the Guards, so you might as well start toughening up now.'

This always produced the desired effect.

The perpetual red-gold stubble against his brown skin and blue eyes gave him a striking appearance that some women found very attractive. I used to think it was a pity Alexi hadn't lived to watch Peter grow up. I think it would have amused him to see how much, in some ways, Peter was turning out to be like him.

'Have a look at this,' I said, throwing Peter a heavy volume. He caught it neatly in one big hand. 'What is it?' he asked.

'Olivah's latest masterpiece. An analysis of how history's great battles were lost, and whether the loser could have won them.'

Surprisingly enough, fat old Lord Olivah was still alive, the last surviving member of my father's inner circle. He had retired from court, half blind and completely deaf, to his Fahl, in order to work on the book Peter now held. It always seems to be the people like Olivah who go on living long after anyone who could possibly have cared for them has died.

Peter gave the book a brief inspection and said, 'It's rubbish.'

'Of course it's rubbish.'

He stretched out on the grass, knees up, arms folded behind his head. 'You must have something more important to do than wading through all this – stuff, Nardo.'

'This is important. Think of all the money the Treasury pours into the Official Publishers. If they can't find anything better to waste their paper on, I think I'll take away their subsidies and see how they like trying to survive on their profits.'

At that moment the dogs barked again, jumping up and pushing off through the undergrowth, tails feathering in pursuit of a captured scent.

Recently much of my spare time had been devoted to the question of finding a wife for Peter. I still thought he was too young, but I couldn't put it off much longer. His looks, as I have said, were striking in their colouring rather than handsome in their features – but I am being objective. When I allow myself to be biased, I say that he was extremely handsome. I suppose, also being objective, that he had less charm than Alexi, less power than Hans. Instead he had qualities of his own, hard to name exactly but making him the person he was. Why compare them? Peter was the one that I loved most.

Not long before this day in the garden I had been approached by a certain Fredric filcThomas, who was related by marriage to the Fahlraec of Peat. He wanted to register a complaint. His daughter, he said, was in his opinion receiving excessive attentions from my brother; he added, diplomatically, that he was sure the Prince's intentions were honourable but that this was beside the point, as his daughter was only thirteen. I could put no face to the girl's name, but after this I kept on the look-out for her. She was another one of those peachy blondes, and seemed to me a bit more advanced and mature than the sheltered young girl her father had described; after watching her for a while I was inclined to think the attentions had not been one-sided. However, now that he had complained about it I felt it my duty to say something, so, risking sulks, I mentioned it to Peter.

He took it in good part, though he did say, 'You really keep a sharp eye on me, don't you?'

'I'd prefer to think I didn't have to.'

He touched my arm with a meaningful look. 'Nardo, believe me, I wouldn't do anything to make you change your mind about the Guards. I want that more than anything. I've learnt my lesson. You can trust me.' He grinned. 'It was strictly flirtation, and anyway she's too young for me.'

But she was not the only young woman who chased after my brother. Seeing this, I realised it would be better to choose him a wife now, from among his equals, than to have some second aspiring Beulah forced on us. The episode with Isabel Mehah had left its mark on me; so now I began, quietly, to cast about for an appropriate princess.

Of course I could not keep it secret from Beulah. No transactions could be made without her finding out about them; no correspondence could come and go without passing through her hands. I went to her and told her of my intentions, feeling pleased with my own tact. Now that she had a living son safe in her arms, Beulah no more wanted Peter to marry a court girl, and thus promote that girl's family, than I did.

Politics. Dull, time-consuming, hateful. It was hateful to have to tie up my brother's happiness with politics. I would have liked to say to him, 'Go, choose anyone you want, choose the one you want.' But it was impossible.

And seventeen is too young to choose. Too young to marry. When I was eighteen I thought I was making a choice, when all I was really doing was committing an act of lunacy. I had been rescued from the consequences, and I wasn't going to let it happen to Peter. More than this, I wanted the best for him. This is the truth about my motivations. I suppose it was like showing him what he was worth to me. For Peter a proud and beautiful princess, nothing less.

I looked at him stretched out there in the sun, and I felt such a confusion of pride, and grief, and fear, and love, all mixed together. My sister and I often went to watch him training, long afternoons of hard work that he threw his heart into and his whole weight behind. He used both hands to pick up the broadsword, its steel as heavy as a man's body, as Peter's long arms and legs, his broad shoulders, though he was not a man yet. There comes an age in our lives when we settle down into the man we will always be. Part of me wanted to cry out for that time to hurry up, so that he would no longer alter daily in front of my eyes. I felt such pride in his height, and his strength, and in his skill at the things he valued.

I remember what it's like to be seventeen. It is an uncomfortable age to live through, but if it has its overwhelming despairs it also has its overwhelming joys. It is far harder to watch it happening to the child one loves. In Peter's blue eyes the five-year-old had never stopped being entranced by the rainbows a prism of light casts on a white wall. He still hated spinach, and still lost his temper when he lost at games, though he had learnt how to hide it. One day we were sent some paintings from Chatienne. Their subject matter was mostly dogs and horses, soldiers and battlefields, all his old favourites. I invited him to pick out those he wanted for his rooms, and he bounded ahead of me up the stairs to take a look at them. He walked studiously round the pictures, examining them all, a smile flashing when he found one he wanted. He showed me which ones were flawed, and why, and which were good, and why, and pointed out where the artist had used a trick of the brush to cover up a mistake. The interest remained, no matter how he might have tried to stifle it.

Sometimes I wanted to take that almost-man's body between my hands and tear it in two because I knew, I knew that the child I also loved was still somewhere inside it.

That time on Ksaned Kaled was the happiest of my whole life. Why couldn't it have gone as I'd planned, allowing us to grow older among the roses? I believe that on Ksaned Kaled one grows older more slowly than anywhere else. Why couldn't we have stayed there for ever? We were happy. How could we help but be happy, Peter and Madeleine and I, on Ksaned Kaled?

It is hard to write about happiness. There seems to be no need. You see, Madeleine, Peter – you see, the thing about Nardo's compulsive scribbling is that when you write it down you – I mean me, I – have distanced myself from it. It has been taken out of me. Not the happiness, but whatever it is I'm writing about. Do you remember what I said about being drained? I don't want to be drained of the happiness. We spent two years and five months on Ksaned Kaled and every one of those months was happy. I speak of what I know when I say happiness. Like – I'll go back to an old metaphor, and give this some sort of concentricity – like a starving man. Like a man dying of hunger in the middle of a wilderness, who knows he is going to die helplessly because there is no one left to come to his aid. That man knows better than anyone else in the world what bread means. And happiness.

39

When I look back on those days on Ksaned Kaled, I have to look at them through the recent past, which shadows that distant, happier past until sometimes I am pushed close to thinking that it was doomed by fate to end, that we were helpless – but I'm not superstitious and I don't really believe that. It's only for lack of any obvious, proper explanation that I sometimes entertain such thoughts, for one of the hardest things in the world is giving up one's faith in reasons. Better even a supernatural one than none at all: 'It's not my fault, the Gods cursed me . . . ' Who would not rather be the villain of a cosmic plan than the victim of random accident? But I still do believe there is a reason, or reasons, and I intend to find the explanation.

Autumn came round again on Ksaned Kaled, gilding the light with yellow mist. The chill in the air sent Peter into action. He spent whole days galloping round the island, in order, he said, to harden his muscles. A good deal of his leisure time was passed with men five or six years his elder, Guards of several years' standing, and he was often – too much I thought – in Nikolas's company. He was always making new friends.

They talked of arms and uniforms, of old campaigns and new tactics. He hinted to me that it was time he was measured for his armour.

For that, we would have to return to Tsvingtori. The island had no armoury, and there were no good ones in the nearby coastal towns. Other reasons also made it necessary to leave Ksaned Kaled, the most important being Peter's marriage arrangements. I put off our departure as long as I could, until any further delay would mean no time to pack before the sea voyage became dangerous. Most of all, I hated breaking the news to Madeleine.

'It's not that I want to go,' I said.

She pulled my head on to her shoulder, and her back was bronze in the firelight. 'We knew we couldn't stay here for ever,' she said. 'I don't really mind, except that you do. We came back once, we can come back again.'

'We will, next spring. Peter can sail from here as easily as from Tsvingtori.'

'Sail where? Have you found him someone?'

'I'm not quite sure. That's why we have to go back; I want to talk to the embassies.'

Madeleine said, 'I don't mind where we go, as long as you don't go somewhere without me.'

I don't seem to be able to keep to the narrative. And why should you? Because that's the point of this, if there is one. I never intended to ramble through my past and present thoughts, only through past events. Not that it really matters, since I can't see who would ever get their hands on this, but it matters to me. The thoughts hurt. I've done a lot of rambling, physical and mental: can't write while you walk, can't walk while you write. Action and dialogue, that's what we want, no more reflections. No attempt to understand, because to attempt the impossible is always to get hurt.

So make up your mind, Nardo.

I do try, but when I think, as I don't seem to be able to stop doing, another one of the things I think is this: How could I imagine I could ever put any distance between me and the past, or soften any pain? And why would I want to? As long as you're in physical pain, you know you're alive, and as long as you have the other sort of pain, you don't forget who you are. Trying to understand, to unravel, something like this is like trying to pull my veins out one by one through small slits. Look at that sentence. It *does* feel like that, but the paper isn't hurt by having that written on it. In one of the towns I passed through, a couple of years ago, I saw a man who earned his living as a street-scribe. He was very old and had rheumatism. The joints of his hands were swollen and red, the fingers stiff and puffy. When he wrote, he had to hold the pen between his knuckles. His script was the purest I have ever seen, but if you didn't see him in the physical act of writing you would never have guessed what pain he endured to keep it so beautiful.

We returned to Tsvingtori a week before my birthday. It was already very cold, the rose-hips nipped by frost, the palace stuffy with store-piles of green logs.

What's all that got to do with it? We know what the weather is like in November. We know when you returned to Tsvingtori. Either give up or go on. We know what you're trying to avoid.

As jewel-crowned time made its stately progress like the implacable emperor it is –

As time passed, I noticed a change in Peter's attitude towards Beulah.

And what was that?

He used to be alternately fascinated and flustered by her. She did it on purpose. She had always teased and flirted with him, ever since he was ten years old.

That troubled you?

It made me sick. It made me afraid. She makes me sick. I can't forget what she did to me. I was afraid for him, worried about him. I had noticed how much all his favourite women resembled her. He and I were not so dissimilar. I knew better than anyone else her power to attract him.

But on the whole, you weren't desperately concerned?

On the whole, no, of course not, because it could never go as far with him as it had with me. I simply worried that an infatuation might make him unhappy. She was a beautiful woman. She makes me sick but there's no point in saying she wasn't beautiful when she was. It was to be expected that Peter would find her attractive. She attracted most men, and he hadn't gone through what I had with her. He didn't deny he thought she was pretty, and so on, but that reassured me. It was too open to have intent. Also, he had done what I never did – found other women. He knew he couldn't have her, and that added to the attraction. Peter was a little thief when he was a boy, he and his friends. It was a boy's infatuation and, unlike mine, it would pass harmlessly.

And she had absolutely no serious inclinations towards him. She's always preferred men older than herself. She enjoyed leading him on, that was all, teasing him to make him blush. He knew this. He asked me once, when he was thirteen or fourteen, 'Why does she want to embarrass me so much?' I said it wasn't him in particular, she liked making everyone feel small. I told him the only thing to do was to pay her no attention. If she wasn't having any effect, she would stop.

Madeleine said it was his age. She said he would grow out of it. He started to when he was sixteen. I saw it fading on Ksaned Kaled. For a while he became indifferent to her.

Was this the change you spoke of?

No. After we returned to Tsvingtori they became hostile towards one another. It reminded me of Alexi, after Hans had died. Madeleine said so too. But it was less bitter, less full of hate. It looked like plain dislike.

She stopped flirting with him, sitting close to him, soliciting his views, all those things she did. She was busier too, getting busier all the time as I let her take more of the work off my back. So we all saw less of her. And when, rarely, she did throw a remark at him, he no longer stuttered and reddened, but answered back brusquely and returned to whatever he was doing. They didn't actually avoid each other, but there was no friendship between them. He found a new girl, a kennelmaid I think. I liked her looks; she was thin as a whippet with brown hair and eyes. I asked him once why he was no longer so . . . why he now disliked Beulah, and he said, 'You ought to know, you don't like her either.'

That satisfied you?

No, not completely. I didn't want to press him. He tells me what he wants to tell me, in his own time. Peter was always very proud, you know.

But all in all, you felt things were resolving themselves satisfactorily?

Serena's just made me some food. After I've eaten it, I think I'll go for a walk.

An hour's mobile reflection has helped me see what a silly way that was to carry on. The question and answer ruse didn't work. So now I'm going to try approaching what I want to say head on.

Peter had no need to tell me that he relied on me. I had always known he would, from the day he was born too young to be a brother to anyone but me; the day our father walked out of the room without stopping to look at his latest and last son, giving Peter the first name that came into his head because he simply could not be bothered. Out of all the crimes my father committed, this one remains the most unforgivable.

I knew he would rely on me. Alexi said so too. And I relied on Peter. That is a part of what love is. Often I believe it is the greater part of missing him.

I tried to be what he wanted, and needed, me to be. I tried to the best of my ability. I tried to live up to his expectations, because I believe, after giving this much thought, that I am to blame for those expectations. But 'blame' is the wrong word. I am responsible; and I always knew that.

The court is a cesspit and my life, where it touched the court, was also made filthy. This was through no fault of my own. I would have preferred to keep out of it, as I had always done before I became King. Once I was King I had no choice. I was not prepared to let the same thing happen to Peter. I never intended to keep him in ignorance, but only to preserve his innocence, for nothing else could have protected him from sinking down to their level. He was so easily influenced. I tried to keep him out of it, that mess of politicking and compromises and double-dealing, the crude and dirty soullessness of the court. I did all that I could do, and I admit it wasn't perfect, but it was for his sake. If he had been older, I think he would have realised this. If he had been older, he would have grown out of expecting me to be perfect.

It's easy now, looking back, to say I should have told him about what sort of King, or non-King, I was, and about having allowed Beulah to take over the administration, and about Madeleine and me. I distrust easy answers. It's easy to fantasise that telling him all this would have made a difference; but I do not, in fact, believe it.

Moreover, I'm still convinced I did the right thing in letting Beulah take control. As far as I can tell, the country enjoyed remarkable peace and prosperity during my reign, and if anyone is to take the credit for this achievement, it is Beulah. Also, as I've admitted, I had little choice but to let her do it. I knew when I was knocking my head against a brick wall. And I tried to tell Peter this, in a way that he could understand without losing faith in me, because I never, never abrogated my real responsibilities, the ones I owed to him. I believe I could have kept him safe, if he would have let me. And I believe he would have understood, if he had been older.

By the time I became King it was too late to start destroying everything he believed in. I had missed my chance years before, on that afternoon when my father had me whipped. I could have spoken to him honestly then, taught him what I had learnt: our father was far from perfect in many ways, and I was like him in that; I was mortal and terrified of it; I had no hope of ever being the sort of hero one finds in Caryllac. If I could have known, then, everything that was going to happen to us, I would have seized that chance. Afterwards it was too late. When I became King, Peter had reached the age where too many things are changing too fast; and not only that, but all our situations had altered out of recognition. I could not suddenly change as well.

Perhaps I should have told him about Madeleine and me. That's the easiest answer of all; but in fact I don't believe it would have made much difference. That was not the catalyst. He already knew I loved her, and this was what he resented.

How could I have told him? There is no right time for that sort of thing, not at his age. I was waiting for him to be old enough to understand – to have come to love someone himself, perhaps. And I do still believe that, not only was there no point in telling him things he did not need to know, but that to tell him such things would be harmful.

What is wrong about loving someone? I loved him. What is wrong about wanting the love and trust of someone I love and trust? What is wrong about doing my best for a child who relied totally on me, trying to keep him out of the filth when it would have been so much less effort to let him fall in? I could never have done anything other than these things. It is natural. It is human. If that is so, then I admit, without shame, without asking for pardon, that I am guilty of being human. And so is Peter.

Picking at all the faults in myself is another easy way out. I can deceive myself I'm getting somewhere, but in fact it only obscures the necessity of finding real, hard answers. If I had loved him less, I would not have cared so much about what was important to him. Perhaps that is the answer. That he died because I loved him too much.

40

It was spring, nearly time for us to return to Ksaned Kaled, before I could feel I had made any real headway with the question of Peter's wife. I had at last found what seemed to be the ideal young woman, or as near to that as possible. She was the niece of the King of Pravarre, that same erstwhile Prince Julius who had once been intended for my sister.

What swung me in her favour was the portrait the Pravarrian ambassadors delivered. It showed a girl with flaxen hair, hazel eyes and a heart-shaped face: a pretty model of her type, Peter's type. She was the daughter of the King's younger brother, and the only girl in their family. Julius had a number of children by his mistress, and these had been legitimised when he married her, but they were all sons. The Princess was only just fourteen – but then girls grow up quickly when they're surrounded by boys. I thought: she is young enough never to have been in love, so Peter will be her first.

I therefore planned that we should return to Ksaned Kaled where, on his eighteenth birthday, I would invest Peter in the Guards. After this I would tell him what I had arranged, and show him her portrait. He could sail to Pravarre in the early autumn, spend the winter there, and marry her next spring, when she would have turned fifteen. Madeleine would choose from the Treasury all the pretty things she would have adored when she was fifteen, and Peter could take these presents with him.

Before I embarked on serious negotiations with Pravarre, I was inevitably compelled to present my plans to Beulah. I could foresee no objections: that was the nature of our contract. I did not interfere with the administration, and she in turn refrained from meddling in my family's affairs.

As it happened, she supported my decision. She gave as her own all the reasons I've already mentioned, with a few political ones thrown in.

She said, 'The portrait was a good idea, don't you think? She's a very pretty girl. I'm sure he'll fall in love with that picture. I knew you'd want to see what sort of sister-in-law you were adding to your family.'

'It was your idea?' I asked, without surprise.

'Yes and no. I suggested it to all the ambassadors, but only Pravarre followed it up. The race belongs to those who care to win it, don't you think? You're right, she'll do very well. She's young enough to learn a new language without too much difficulty, and she's pretty enough to be popular.'

'Peter doesn't suspect, does he?' I asked her.

'Obviously I wouldn't tell him. As a matter of fact, I'm rather cross with my little brother at the moment. He used to be so sweet, and now I can hardly get a civil word out of him. I hope this trip abroad does him some good. He's become a bit too military of late.'

I could not help being mildly surprised that the court had caught no wind of my arrangements.

She said, 'If you ask me to keep a secret, I'll keep a secret.'

When it suits her.

Mistress of the back-door key, arch-dissembler, arch-bitch, I am so glad that you were born a woman when you said so often you'd have preferred to be a man. I don't care how much misery your womanhood has cost me. So you wanted to be a man – if I believed you, and I believe nothing you say – well, then at least there was one thing you wanted, however briefly, that you could not have.

Madeleine said to me, 'You ought to tell him soon. You ought to give him time to get used to it. You shouldn't spring it on him a week before he's due to leave.'

'I'm not going to,' I said. I thought it would be a wonderful surprise, a present.

The first of our ambassadors sailed off. His ship sank half-way up to its rails in the water, it was so loaded with presents. Down in the city the court-appointed craftsmen, goldsmiths and medallists and jewellers, were busy with my orders; and the court was preparing to return to Ksaned Kaled.

I don't know which of these I would choose as the truth: that I was unusually gullible, or that they were unusually crafty. They were remarkably careful, remarkably discreet. I don't think it was so much as whispered in the court. But I think of my brother Peter, and then I think of her, and I don't know what to think or what to choose.

It was not the worst day of my life. I wish it was. To know this is even worse than that day or remembering what I saw.

I went to his room early in the morning. I can't remember why. To talk, perhaps, a conscious effort because I was aware of how little we really talked those days. I opened the door and went in; came out and shut the door. I remember thinking stupidly, 'How silly of them, her room is safer.'

I walked back along all those miles of corridors. The sun was streaming through the windows. One seems to remember such tiny details. It was a lovely day. Guards were staring at me. People were getting out of my way with disconcerting haste. I went back to my room and was sick on the floor.

Someone must have sent the word around, because after a while I realised Madeleine had come in.

'You're ill,' she said, holding me up. 'You must get into bed. Come on, let me help you.'

'Go away.'

'Reyhnard – '

'Go away, please.'

'You're angry – '

'Not with you, not with you. But go away.'

She began biting her thumbs. 'All right,' she said, 'I'll be in my rooms if you need me.'

Finally, when I felt I could stand on my own, I went into the main room and opened the door. I wanted to call for the Guard, but I couldn't remember the name of the duty officer.

'Guard,' I said.

He came around the corner. I was glad to see it wasn't Nikolas.

'Yes, Sir?'

'Take an escort, and bring the Prince Peter here.'

'Yes, Sir.'

I stood and waited in the middle of the room, for about ten minutes. Beneath my feet I sensed the groundswell of rumour beginning to flood the Palace.

The sound of their return: five pairs of boots marching in time, and two bare feet. They knocked.

'Come in,' I said.

The duty officer opened the door. Peter walked in past him, and the four Guards followed.

I stared at Peter; Peter stared at me.

'You can go,' I said to the Guards. 'Down the corridor.'

They shut the door.

I stared at Peter; Peter stared at me.

He shouted, 'What do you think you're doing? How could you have me marched along like a common criminal? How could you humiliate me like this? How could you – '

'Sit down. And shut up. Until I'm ready to talk to you.'

'You can't do this to me!'

'You forget who you are.'

He shut up, and sat down.

I continued standing in the middle of the room. As far as I can remember, my mind was a blank.

Much later, he coughed, and I was finally able to speak.

'Where is she?' I asked.

'How should I know?'

'You mind what you say.'

He shut his mouth and tried to glare at me, but he couldn't meet my eyes. This weakened me more than defiance would have.

However, I said, 'I'm going. I don't know when I'll be back. You stay here. If I come back and find you gone, you'll be in even more trouble than you are already.'

I headed off down the corridors. Passing my Guards, I told them to remain where they were. It was still only the middle of the morning, and I guessed where Beulah would be. Where she usually was at this time of day: in the Council offices, seeing to the work she had made her own.

On the point of dismissing the clerks and servants, I remembered my manners and asked her to do it.

She spoke while she wrote, and continued writing after we were alone. There was no noise but the scratch of her pen. I should have known she wouldn't make it easy for me. She was no more perturbed than if I had caught her in the act of brushing her hair.

I didn't want to begin angrily. That would give her the advantage. I think she covered more than a page while I sat there, staring at her moving pen, trying to assemble some sentences before I attempted speech.

At last I surprised myself by saying, 'Could you stop that for a moment, please?'

She put the pen back in the inkwell, folded her hands and told me, 'You are such a fool sometimes. Why did you send the Guard for him? That was so silly.'

'How long has this been going on?'

'Oh, three or four months, on and off. It was pretty well drifting to its end. These things do, you know. They all have a limit.'

'Does the court know?'

'Does the court know!' she snorted. 'Darling, the times when you're most insulting are when you don't mean to be. Of course the court doesn't know. At least, up until today they didn't, but after the ludicrous way you've over-reacted I should think they're guessing wildly.'

It was intolerable to see her sitting there so calmly.

'You might at least have kept your hands off my brother!' I shouted.

'I would have had a job to keep his hands off me – or can't you bear to hear that?'

'What I saw – ' and the memory gagged me. I couldn't bear to hear or say any more, nor to keep my eyes open and look at her, nor to shut them and see it all again in my mind.

'Well – look,' she said. 'I am sorry about that. It was nobody's fault – or it was mine. I shouldn't have let him talk me into it. I thought it wasn't safe, but he said nobody ever came to his rooms. It was a piece of thoughtlessness on my part.'

'Thoughtlessness!'

'Throwing blame around isn't going to solve anything. It's a pity you came in, but what's done is done. It's over now. I told you it was coming to its natural end, and this has simply ended it a little faster. It never was anything serious, you must understand that.'

'Then why – '

I suppose she could not be bothered to listen to me.

'I'm surprised at you,' she said. 'You're the one that's so fond of him. You know, he can be terribly sweet when he wants to be, and he's rather attractive in that boyish way.'

'That's your excuse?'

'I see no need to excuse my behaviour. I'm telling you the facts. What would you prefer me to say? That I was in love with him?'

She punctuated this question with a little, deprecating laugh.

I said, 'Well, now you've got another skin to hang on your wall. You've had all of us, you must be pleased with yourself.'

'You really think your family is irresistible, don't you. I can see why; after all they are, to you.'

'Don't you dare bring that into this.'

She clasped her hands in front of her face, resting her brow on her knuckles for a moment. Then she looked at me thoughtfully.

'Very well,' she said. 'What are you going to do?'

'So I'm not making a fuss about nothing? You admit there's a problem?'

'There is now. You've made it.'

I had to ask her, 'What have you told him?' I hated asking her, but I had to know.

'About what?' she replied, though she knew what I meant.

'About me.'

'Oh, I thought you meant about his marriage. Don't worry, I haven't told him anything about anything. Why did you think I would? I told you, it wasn't serious, it was a bit of fun. I can assure you we didn't lie awake into the night sharing secrets across the pillow – '

'Beulah – '

'Nardo, believe me, he doesn't know anything about you and Madeleine. I said he never would find out. So rest easy. Now tell me – what are you going to do?'

I decided to test her. 'I'm going to send him abroad,' I said.

'When you intended, or sooner?'

'Sooner.'

She smiled, and cocked a finger at me. 'That's a very good idea.'

I said, 'I want to get him away from you.'

'Believe me, if I didn't want him to go, he wouldn't go. So send him away by all means, it's – ' and, abruptly, she used a very crude phrase which meant: It's no skin off my nose.

'So you see', she went on, 'you really have over-dramatised everything. You take things far too personally, dear. None of this was designed to hurt you. We didn't think about you at all, to be honest.'

'It's not *you* who's hurt me.'

She reached for her pen, saying, 'So I imagined.'

I went out quickly, leaving open the door through which the clerks hurried back in.

The corridors were deserted as I made my way back, except for the Guards, who were still at their posts. Everyone must have known I would come that way. I could sense the presence of the court, watching and listening, just out of sight.

If I was harder on Peter than he deserved, harder than I would have liked – lay the blame where all blame belongs, at her flat, fat, fast-rooted feet.

He was lying on his back in a windowseat, one arm propping up his head while he ate an apple. He jumped when I came in.

'Sit up,' I said.

He put his feet on the floor, holding the sticky core awkwardly in his big hands.

I knew why I had not felt this white fury with her. It was because I love him. The more you care about a person's safety, the angrier you feel when he does idiotic things. Peter sat perfectly still, staring at the apple core; the only sound was his breathing.

'I have to ask you something,' I began. 'When you answer, you must tell me the truth, yes or no, because I'll know if you're lying. Do you love her?'

'God, Nardo, what a question!'

'Yes or no.'

'No, no, no, of course I don't love her, no one could *love* her – '

'Then why did it happen?'

'I don't know.' He was blushing, stammering. 'It just did – '

'You'll have to do better than that. She's not one of your kitchenmaids, you know. She is the Queen. She's my wife – '

'Oh, come on! And *she* asked *me* – '

'She's a whore, Peter. She has a whore's nature. That's no excuse for her, but then I don't expect any better behaviour from her. It's certainly no excuse for you. You ought to have known better. Whether she initiated it or not is irrelevant. You should have refused.'

'It only happened once – '

'Peter!' I shouted; immediately I regretted it and tried to collect my temper, breathing deep. 'There's no point in lying to me. I've already talked to her.'

'Shit.' He threw the apple core across the room. 'She's a bitch,' he said.

'Yes, she is. It's your own fault you had to find out this way. I don't know which is worse, Peter – to have discovered your duplicity or to have been proved wrong when I thought you were the one person I could trust.'

'That's not true, Nardo, it's not. You're not being fair. You've never made a fuss about any of the other men she has. Of course I didn't think you'd mind if I did the same. I didn't think she mattered to you.'

'She doesn't!' I shouted. 'You do.'

'Then why are you treating me like this?'

'Peter, I know what she's like . . . '

He sat forward on the edge of his seat, and began to speak eagerly, rapidly. 'I know what she's like too, really, I do. You remember when you asked me why I didn't like her any more? And I said you ought to know, because you didn't like her either? You probably think now that

I was lying, but I wasn't. I didn't like her. I like her even less now. I know she's a bitch, she's always been a bitch to me, even when she was pretending to be nice. It's over now, today was going to be the last, really. I just had to . . . '

'Get her out of your system?'

Peter nodded, bright-eyed. 'You should understand. You think I'm too young to remember when she came to court, but I do. I can remember the crush you had on her. Even then I thought she was awfully pretty. I thought you were so lucky when you married her . . . But I mean, I know her better now. I understand everything much more clearly. I know you don't like her. I don't either, honestly – I think I loathe her really. But at the time it didn't seem to make any difference. I didn't even have to do anything, she chased me, honestly, she did – and when she offered, I just had to – or I would have always wondered, don't you see? I've got over it now. I mean, I don't even think she's attractive any more – '

I could do more than understand. I knew. That barbed mixture of subtlety and directness that was Beulah on the hunt, with us, seventeen or eighteen years old, innocent prey. No amount of experience was worth the treasure she made us pay for it.

'I don't want to hear all this,' I said. 'I'm afraid that right now I don't feel able to trust you, or anything you might say. You may say it's over. She says it's over. But I am going to make sure it's over.'

He leapt to his feet and came to me, his eyes as dark and active as stormy waters. 'Nardo – why don't you get rid of her?'

'Sit down.'

'Stop treating me like a child, will you? I'm not a child.'

'Some of your senses may act like a man's, but your sense of responsibility is certainly not one of them.'

'God, I hate it when you're sarcastic!'

'Peter!'

'Well I do. It's not fair. You ought to tell me, I have a right to know. I am your brother.'

'Now you remember that.'

'Why are you treating me like this? What have I done that's so terrible? Only what half the men in this court do, and they get away with it, and they're not your brothers. They're my inferiors, your inferiors. I'm seventeen years old, Nardo, and I don't forget that you're my brother – it's *you* who forgets, you shut me out of everything, you always have, ever since Madeleine came you've been shutting me out of your life.'

'That's not true.'

'It is true. Whenever I want to chat with you I practically have to make an appointment.'

'I came to talk to you this morning and look what I found!'

'Well, that's typical, isn't it. What do you expect? I never get to see you on my own, half the time I don't know where you are and the other half you're working, and when you do have some free time you're off somewhere with Madeleine. Whenever I come to see you she's always there. What makes her so special?'

'I give you as much of my time as I possibly can, Peter, you know that. I've always made time for you.'

'Made time! You make it sound like an effort. Maybe it is. You don't have to make time for her, do you.'

'Peter, please don't be so childish – '

'That's good, coming from you!' He laughed angrily. 'Nardo, when are you going to realise I'm not seven years old any more? I can't train twenty-four hours a day, I need other things to do, and I'm not stupid, I'm old enough to help you now, really help you with important things – *that's* the sort of responsibility that goes with my position. But you never give me a chance. You never even talk to me about your work. All you've ever done is hold the Guards over my head so I won't be "naughty", but how do I know what "naughty" is? When I do what I see other men doing you treat me like a criminal.'

'This is all very specious – '

'Look, I don't even know what specious means, all I know is that if you care so little about Beulah that you don't even care who she sleeps with, then you should get rid of her and get yourself a proper wife. Instead of spending all your time with Madeleine.'

'What do you mean?'

'Well, a sister isn't a woman, not really. You don't have any mistresses – at least I suppose you don't, though even if you did you probably wouldn't tell me. But I haven't heard any rumours. I'm worried about you, too, believe it or not. It's not good for you to live the way you do, it's not healthy. You need a proper woman, all men do. And all women aren't like Beulah, believe me – '

'Peter,' I said harshly, for I was badly shaken. 'When I need your advice about things like that, I'll ask for it – '

'You'll never ask me. That's why I have to ask you. Nardo – I really wish you'd tell me why you won't get rid of her.'

'Oh Peter, Peter, it's not important, it's too complicated . . . '

'It *is* important. It's to do with you and I want to understand, because I . . . '

Love you. I love you, Peter, and that is why I cannot tell you. I love you, and that is why I am angry with you. You do not need to know. I am allowed one unspoilt heart, that refuge of your not knowing.

I loved him, and so I remained angry with him and said, 'Sit down, sit down, it's none of your business.'

He was adamant. 'I want to know something else – are her children really yours?'

'Sit down!'

'Are they?'

'Yes!'

He said softly, 'Nardo – '

'Of course they're mine. I know my duty, I know the law.'

He returned to the windowseat, sitting with one leg folded against his chest. Wrapping his arms round it, he put his chin on his knee and just looked at me. With his heart in his eyes, as the saying is, though perhaps no one else could have seen his heart there. I could.

I have known that face for seventeen years. It has grown, hardened, matured. But it has not changed. The eyes will never change. They look at me as they always have, seven years old, five years old, one hour old. They say, You are the one who matters most to me – and they demand that mine say it back. But I cannot. There is Madeleine; she matters to me as much as you do, but Peter, please believe me, you do not matter less. What I find in her, what I give to her, could never have been found in or given to you. No one can take your place, Peter. No one else is you.

I did wish I was fifteen years old again, and he seven. If he was a little boy he could cry, he could put those bony thin arms around my neck, and I could forgive him his little crimes.

I sat down facing him. 'Peter,' I said, 'I suppose I should have told you this before, but it was going to be a surprise. I've made certain – arrangements, for your future. In fact they've been made for some time. What I found out today hasn't altered them or influenced them in any way; it's only – brought them forward.'

He dropped his other foot to the floor, leaning forward with a keen expression, looking so pleased that I guessed what he was thinking of. Better to disabuse him as quickly as possible.

'How would you like to be married?'

His answer came after a long, puzzled pause. 'Well, yes – I would. Of course I would, one day. But not yet. After I've got my Captaincy in the Guards.'

'No – before that.'

'How soon?'

'Next year.'

'If you say so.' This was grudging. He would rather have said No, but did not dare.

'Don't you want to know to whom?' I asked.

'Oh.' His tone was regaining its edge. 'So you've picked her out, have you?' he said carefully. After a moment he chuckled and added, almost cheerfully, 'Go on, tell, or am I allowed to guess?'

'It's Julius of Pravarre's niece.'

'Oh.' His eyes seemed to unfocus, and he scratched absently at his nose. Then he fixed his eyes on me again and asked, 'You've arranged it all?'

'More or less. It's all – wrapped up and waiting for the ribbon. To coin a phrase.'

'Nardo. Nardo. Why didn't you tell me?'

'It was supposed to be a surprise.'

'Some surprise. Not that I'm ungrateful,' he added hastily. 'What's she like?'

'Very young, she's only fourteen. Very pretty. Blonde, big eyes. Your type.'

'You chose her specially?'

'Of course I did. I am concerned for your happiness, you know I am. I didn't want you to end up with the first court girl who was cunning enough to trap you.'

'That doesn't say much for me, does it.'

'She's a princess, Peter. Peter, I wanted you to have the best.'

'I know. I know you do. I am grateful. Sorry I'm not more enthusiastic. I will be. I'm sure I will, when I get used to the idea. You've put a lot of thought into this, haven't you.'

'I wouldn't have done less, not for you.'

'I know. I'm sorry. I say stupid things sometimes. You're really much better to me than I deserve. I am sorry, Nardo.' He gave me a quick grin. 'I'm getting to quite like the idea already. Being married. So, when's she coming? I hope you give us some time to get to know each other before we do the deed.'

'Peter, she's not coming. You're going.'

'What?'

'To Pravarre. You would have gone at the end of the summer, to spend the winter there. It's the custom, you know it is. But after what I've learnt today, I've decided it would be better to send you as soon as possible.'

'But – ' He was resisting, wanting not to believe me. 'But when? What do you mean?'

'Next week, ten days. As soon as the ship can be fitted.'

'But how long for?'

'Until early next summer.'

'You want me to spend a *year* there?'

'She won't be fifteen until next spring. She's only just turned fourteen.'

'Oh, what's that got to do with it?' He bounded over to me, grabbing my arm to shake it, exclaiming, 'I'll be eighteen this summer. You promised me I could go into the Guards when I was eighteen. You've promised me for years!'

'Peter, what does it matter, this year or next? You can go into the Guards when you come back.'

'You promised me. I've been working for it for ages – you've seen me, you know how hard I've been working. Nardo, don't make me go – I don't want to get married, I want my post in the Guards, it's the only thing I've been looking forward to – '

'Don't exaggerate.'

'You promised! I've been looking forward to it since I was fourteen!'

'Well, when you come back and you're married, I'll put you in the Guards, I promise.'

'But you've just broken your promise.'

'You said you'd keep out of trouble and that's just about the one thing you haven't done, so I really am under no obligation to keep my promise. You're lucky I'm still prepared to consider you for the Guards when you come back.'

'Oh, I see,' he said slowly. 'This is my punishment.'

'Don't twist things. I've told you all this was arranged long before this morning.'

'Yes, but I wasn't going to go until the autumn and now I'm going practically tomorrow – '

'Peter.' I held him firmly by the shoulders and tried to speak rationally. 'You mustn't think of it as a punishment. It's not intended as one. I just want to get you away from her for a while.'

'I told you, you don't need to do that. I'm not interested in her, at all, any more. You don't need to send me away. Send her away.'

'I would have thought a man your age would jump at the chance to travel.'

'Well I'm not. I don't want to go. Can't it wait till next year?'

'Peter, please, trust me, I'm doing this for your own good.'

'That's shit!' He shouted this so loudly and so close up that my face was spattered with spittle; he wrenched out of my hands crying, 'I *know* you're doing this to punish me! Still treating me like a bloody child! You're always holding the Guards over my head. How do I know you'll ever put me in it? Today it's this, so you say "not this year", and next year it'll be something else.'

'That's not true. How can you say that?'

'Because it's what you do!'

'If I treat you like a child it's because you act like one.'

'Maybe I wouldn't have to act like one if you treated me like an adult!'

'I'm responsible for you, Peter – '

'You're not my father!'

'Peter!'

'You're full of shit, you always have been. You don't give a toss about me, I've thought so for years and now it's proved.'

'Look, Peter, don't try to blackmail me.'

'Why not? You've been blackmailing me for the last four years. I'm sick of it. I don't care if you never put me in the Guards, because you never will. I'm not going to go. You can write to Julius and tell him it's off.'

'You know I can't do that.'

'Well, I'm not going to go. I refuse to go. I don't want to go, Nardo, and you can't make me.'

He folded his arms and set his chin, looking exactly like the same stubborn boy who when he was five had refused to get off his pony.

But I said, 'Oh yes I can, Peter, and you're going.'

41

If I had made this decision only to punish him, I would have changed my mind long before he went away. Two weeks – which was the time between that day and his departure – two weeks of his sullen, sad face and mutinous silence were more than enough time for my anger to evaporate. But the imperative 'Go', to preserve him from himself and Beulah, remained.

No one at seventeen is wise enough to know their own best interests. I remembered how, at little more than his age, I used to argue so defiantly with Alexi over that worthless woman; I would without a qualm have murdered anyone who tried to send me away from her and from this country. A year later, though, I would have thanked them for it. I remembered all this, and I stuck to my decision.

Peter asked for no reprieve; I, loving him, hurt myself in giving him none.

A week before his departure we sent off a fast cutter to Pravarre, in order to advise the court there of his coming. He would travel in the slow state flagship. In his retinue we included Dominic filcRandal. This was partly because he could speak the language, but mostly because he was agitating for promotion in the Council and getting in Beulah's way. To compensate Peter for his presence, I let him have cousin Nikolas as well. Thomas filcValentin was also sent. I've never been able to like that man.

Sending Nikolas with Peter was a sacrifice for me. I knew that Nikolas already had a great deal of influence with my brother; I knew that if they spent a year together, especially in a foreign country, they could only become closer. I was afraid that whatever ground I lost in Peter's affections, Nikolas would gain. But I permitted it because I loved my brother. I don't think he ever realised that.

We assembled at the Palace gates to say our goodbyes. Nikolas and the detachment of Guards; servants; Thomas, Dominic and the rest of the retinue; Peter and myself; Madeleine and the rest of the court behind me. A sharp breeze was blowing from the west. I buttoned up his coat, when what I really wanted to do was ruffle his clipped hair and hug him. Perhaps it was because I couldn't do this, not with all those spectators, that I looked a little stern.

He said to me in an undertone, 'You're still angry, aren't you?'

I laid my hands on his collar. 'No,' I said. 'No, Peter, believe me, you're not going because I'm angry, but because it's for the best.'

He refused to meet my eyes. I gave his shoulders an encouraging squeeze. 'When you come back, you'll be in the Guards, I promise. The armourers have your measurements. When you come back it'll all be ready.'

He gripped my wrists, stared into my face and said, 'I hope you do get rid of her.'

Even then, at that last minute, if instead of holding my wrists he had flung his arms around me, told me he was sorry, that he loved me, asked to be allowed to stay – I couldn't have resisted. I would have brought him back inside, and his ship could have rocked on its moorings for ever for all I cared.

'It's hard for me, too,' I said. 'Harder for me.'

Abruptly, with heavy emphasis, he said, 'I'll be back in a *year*,' and pushed off my hands.

I thought, if he chooses to act like a man, then let him take it like a man.

He gave me a Guardsman's salute, and all his retinue behind him saluted me. 'Sir! Your good fortune and health until we return.' They about-faced and marched away towards the city, towards the docks where the ship was waiting. The wind was blowing in my direction, carrying Nikolas's voice. He said to Peter, 'Stormy weather, sir. I hope we don't have a rough passage.'

In my idle hours, which these days is most of the time, I often speculate that it would have been better for me if Peter's ship had been wrecked, struck a rock, gone down with all hands including my brother. But perhaps if that had happened, I would feel just as much the guilty party. I sent him away, and I was able to do so because I was the King, and I was the King because my elder brothers had died, and because Beulah was strong enough to keep me there. And I was the King because my father had murdered the previous King, and married his daughter, and made himself King, and because my father's father's and so on, and because Once upon a time the son of a god married a human girl and had seven sons to be kings, and so I am supposed to be descended from a god, and really you can go on for ever.

Have you ever heard the joke about the horse who broke one of the nails in its shoe, and the shoe fell off, and the horse stumbled, and the general riding it was thrown and killed, and the war was lost, and the country was conquered? Because of a broken nail.

You see, it's easy enough to blame the nail. But you have to ask, Why did the nail break? Because the horse stepped on a stone? Because the blacksmith fitted it badly? And what's to say the general would have won the war anyway? The broken nail might have had no real effect on the outcome.

I think about this in the same way that one picks at a scab.

If there is any magic in the world – which I doubt, since I don't believe in that magic which is part and parcel of religion, take it all or reject it all, the divine metamorphoses, the miracles, the oracular revelations, and that other sort of market-place, solstice-fair, he's-got-it-up-his-sleeve magic, which isn't magic at all: all magicians are charlatans and all priests are either dupes or hypocrites . . . However, if I believed in magic I would know where it lived. On Ksaned Kaled.

It's not magic, but medicine. I suppose medicine is a sort of magic. Take one sick body, one potion composed of various distillations, and lo and behold you have a third thing: health. Not always, but some medicines are infallible, and always produce their vaunted cure. Most, of course, are frauds. Alexi – where did Alexi get his mine of information from? – Alexi told me that sometimes a potion with no known medicinal qualities can effect a cure simply because the patient believes it will.

Soon after Peter had departed, we made our own short journey, to Ksaned Kaled. While on board ship, deprived of Madeleine's company, knowing that when we were reunited I would still miss Peter, I couldn't rouse any enthusiasm. What was Ksaned Kaled without both of them?

But once I was again among the familiar flowers, the faithful warmth and sunshine, Ksaned Kaled worked its medicine and soothed me until I could begin to look forward to my brother's letters.

Beulah and I did not talk to each other for two or three months. When she wanted me to do or sign something she sent me a note; when I had done it I would send her one back. Once I forgot to do something fairly unimportant, and she came to give me a lecture through my closed door. I didn't so much mind talking to her. It was looking at her that was hideous.

But after several months on Ksaned Kaled this emotion was also eased, though it never went away altogether.

For a long time we received no letters from Peter. At first I put this down to the delay inevitable with a long sea voyage, but time wore this excuse out and I had to admit that he was still hurt, still resentful. He wanted to hurt me in turn by refusing to write.

'He'll forgive you,' said Madeleine. 'Give him time.'

I said, 'It's not his place to forgive.'

But as I forgave him everything, I forgave him for not writing; and I forgave him completely when at last a letter arrived, towards the end of the summer.

The seal was broken. Beulah no longer bothered to keep up the pretence that she didn't read my correspondence. I didn't care; I was so pleased to hear from him that I had no time to be angry with her.

The letter contained little that could have given her food for thought. The Princess was mentioned, a brief physical description that told me nothing I didn't know already from the portrait. He added that he was given little opportunity to talk to her. Much more space was devoted to descriptions of the Pravarrian Army and Guards, the various hunting expeditions he and Nikolas had enjoyed, and the birthday celebrations they had arranged for him. This last made me think, as it was intended to – I know my brother – of the birthday present I had promised him, and the suit of armour still waiting in Tsvingtori. It also made me laugh. Peter doesn't give up, but I knew I had done the right thing. He sounded cheerful, as if he was having a good time, even if he couldn't bring himself to say so. It seemed I was missing him more than he missed me.

That letter, with its heavy underlining and poor spelling – he really hadn't paid any attention in Aneurin's lessons – could not, as the saying is, bring him back to me or make me feel he was present in the room. Rather, it reminded me where he was: in a foreign country, eight hundred miles away.

I guessed that someone, presumably Nikolas, had vetted the letter before it was sent, because all the 'Nardo's had been scratched out and

'Sir' or sometimes 'Brother' written above them. It had been read at least twice before it reached me, once by Beulah and once by whatever spy system the King of Pravarre operates, but that was to be expected. To have the letter was good enough. I couldn't have cared if the whole world had read it first, so long as it came at last to me.

This was the only letter I ever received from him. In fact, now that I think about it, it was the only letter I ever received from any of them. Beulah does not count, and neither do her millions and millions of memos.

I showed the letter to Madeleine. We spent the afternoon discussing his return – every day brought it closer – and the balls and plays and hunting parties we would throw for him and his new wife, and what rooms we would give them, and how she and Madeleine would become such good friends.

We – by which I mean the government, by which I mean Beulah – we as a matter of course received regular correspondence from our resident ambassador and the other executives of the deputation to Pravarre. I had insisted that Peter was not to be involved in the bargaining and negotiations, and Beulah agreed with me. When I told him that everything was wrapped up and waiting for the ribbon, I had rather anticipated events: we had only just opened serious discussions when I was forced to send him out there. Once they had my brother in their possession, Pravarre became much more demanding and our ambassador wrote endless letters of complaint; but I had guessed this might happen, and I wrote back telling him to agree to any terms. All I wanted now was for Peter to come home as soon as possible, and with a wife. I would rather have emptied my Treasury than have him think he had gone on a wasted journey. But whether my reply passed unaltered through Beulah's hands or not, I do not know. I imagine not.

Just before the onset of winter storms made sea travel impossible, one of our ships returned, bearing some of our ambassador's agents who carried by word of mouth news they did not trust to writing. King Julius, they said, was now prepared to consider the marriage only if I would undertake to depose one of the Fahlraecs and give that province to Peter. The ambassador's opinion seemed to be that I would not, because I could not, do this. A similar act had been the spark which set off the rebellion against my mother's father.

After we had received this news, Beulah cornered me in the offices to tell me what to do.

'Why don't we put it to the Council?' I suggested.

'Oh, don't make jokes, we can't possibly consider it. It's an absurd request, Julius must either be totally misinformed or an utter idiot. It would be better to marry Peter to a kitchenmaid than to try to depose one of the Fahlraecs. It would certainly cause less trouble. If those are the only terms he's prepared to consider then we'd better bring Peter home.'

'Just write and say no?'

'Well, really, I see no reason why anyone should be asked to risk sailing at this time of year. Let them wait. Peter can stay there until the spring. Let them cool their heels for a bit – your brother isn't a bad match at all for them. By the way, did you know the ambassador's been in that post for seventeen years? We should think about retiring him soon – he must be getting more Pravarrian than Brychmachrese.' She tutted. 'I wish we had a better diplomat out there. Thomas isn't bad, but Nikolas is hopeless, and as for Dominic! But we really can't send another or we'd have to send a reply with him. No, let them wait a few months. They may get tired of waiting. We'll see how they feel in the spring.'

Having sorted this out to her satisfaction, she crossed to the door, and was about to open it when she stopped and turned back to me, asking, 'I'm just a little curious. Tell me – would you have done it?'

I shrugged.

'If you had – just as a matter of interest – who would you have chosen?'

After a moment's thought, I said, 'Mehah.'

She rubbed her hand up and down her hip, smiling delightedly. 'I rather thought you might. Really Nardo, what you'd do if I wasn't here!' She went out, shutting the door on her laughter.

She was pregnant again. I knew it could not be Peter's. Aside from that I was not interested.

I resigned myself to receiving no more letters until the spring, and we settled down to enjoying the mild Ksaned Kaled winter. Peter always liked the colder weather, and would go rushing around in it on horseback or on foot – I wondered how he felt in that hot foreign country. In Pravarre they never see green holly with its hard red berries. They never know the pleasure of a roaring fire in a frosty room, roasted chestnuts, muffling up in furs and leather; they never understand that sense of glory and achievement in surviving the rigorous beauties of the white season. A solstice with no snow – unimaginable. I wondered how homesick he was.

I kept telling myself, He'll soon be home; and in a way that year of his absence was happy because I had something to look forward to. I could bear missing him, knowing it would end and knowing when. It was a delight, it was joy, it was a song and a dance, that missing him, compared to this. I wish he had stayed away for ever. Eight hundred miles seemed an insuperable distance, then, but it was near enough, compared to now. Now it is less impossible for me to touch the moon than it is for me to hold out my hand and have him take it with warm fingers.

I wish I had done it, no matter what she said. It might have made a difference, even if I didn't succeed but only tried to do it, for him. I should have deposed all the Fahlraecs, razed Tsvingtori to the ground, destroyed the law, slaughtered her and her children to save him. I was the King, or I was not. If I was, then what is a king? I couldn't keep them safe, not one of them. I couldn't even do that.

42

Last autumn, when I acquired my supply of paper and ink and pens, my original intention was to write a diary. As the whole point of this writing exercise is to provide occupation for my time and my mind, the diary scheme would have been a bit of a failure; I've written about everything that's gone on here which is worth recording, and I doubt I've covered more than thirty or forty pages – unless, of course, I in future reduce myself to writing: 'Today we got up, and had bread and milk for breakfast, and Serena did the washing, and I took an inventory for so-and-so . . . '

It's dull enough living it; I'm not going to re-live it by writing it down. All the same, it offers me an easy refuge when I can't go on with the other. Which I can't at the moment. Don't want to.

Serena must be almost five months pregnant now. It's beginning to show. Her ankles, wrists and face all swell up if she doesn't take enough rest, which, being her, she doesn't. The midwife comes round regularly to scold her. Apparently there is a chance the child will not carry full-term, and if it does the birth is going to be difficult. I'm surprised. I thought Serena would take to maternity like a bird to air, or, to be more exact, as easily as any cow, mare or ewe. I don't think she understands why she has to take such care of herself, so it's up to me to make sure she does as she's told – after all, this is the only child she is ever likely to have. She may yet find some reason to be thankful for her harsh upbringing, because the poor girl is going to need all the endurance she's got.

Thoughts of Serena are always prefixed in my mind by the adjective 'poor'. I don't know why I feel such pity for her. She has no self-pity. All she has is that strange sort of compassion one sees in dogs, when they lick another dog's wounds. I was so angry with the Captain and his soldiers, with everyone – but she's not angry. She has forgotten all about the crime and is looking forward to her baby. She never wanted much, and now she has everything she ever could want. Poor Serena – or lucky Serena? I don't know.

I want to write about an event which took place the day before yesterday. It was a particular piece of folly on my part; but then I knew it would be folly before it happened, which is not something one often knows. However, it was not in my power to refuse.

The day before yesterday I went to Rayalled. I gave Serena a lecture on staying in bed and not doing the cleaning, and then set out with the chief men of the village. We were going to present our – their – tax accounts, which I had drawn up, to the Fahlraec's agent. I think Serena's father, who was of the deputation, can read a little, but none of the others can, which is why they asked me along. Most of them rode on donkeys, but Serena's father owns a horse, a half-breed plough pony, all raw bones and shaggy fetlocks. He rode on this, looking very superior. He also owns a mule. This is a fine animal, which he must have bought for the prestige, since I can think of no other reason for his spending so much money on a sterile beast. The men consider it beneath their dignity to ride on a neuter, so he offered it to me. Probably he expected me to refuse – there's no way he could have known I can ride – but I was glad to accept. Rayalled is half a day's journey away and I didn't want to walk it. I had no saddle, but at home we were all taught to ride without one. It is supposed to improve your seat.

Peasants ride atrociously, slouching and bouncing, battering their heels against the calluses on their animals' flanks. Some of them even sat sideways, as if their donkeys were sofas. Their conversation was limited to the usual coarse jokes, crude talk, farming chat and repetitive village gossip, and gradually I fell to the rear, finding more to interest me in my own thoughts.

After a while I noticed they were getting quiet, so I looked up. They were staring at me. I wondered why, and then realised it was because of the way I was riding. I rode as it is my nature to ride, as I had been taught: straight back, heels down, knees gripping, no daylight between my seat and my horse.

I swear I could hear them thinking: Where did *he* learn to ride like that? and what do we really know about him, anyway? I tried to sag and slump as they did, riding on in great discomfort, but all the same I was rather pleased. I had always considered myself a middling horseman, but I was much better than they are.

Of course I am. I ought to be.

I heard my brothers laughing: Alexi, Hans, Peter.

'Nardo, come on, jump it! I did, it's easy.'

'Madeleine, let me borrow your horse. I want to go riding with Nardo.'

I would have liked to kick that mule into a gallop, flying from those men, disappearing in a cloud of dust to chase after my brothers.

Instead, I sat up straight and let the villagers think what they liked. We arrived in Rayalled just before noon, and went to have lunch at a place owned by one of the village emigrants, or escapees.

I wished I had not come. I hadn't wanted to, but they were paying me and there was no way I could refuse without engendering more ill will, and no plausible excuse I could think of. I hate going to Rayalled. Last year, when I was walking, I skirted round it. On the few occasions when I have been compelled to go there, I always feel morbid and listless for days afterwards.

I could not stop thinking about the King. I mean, my father. He was born there. I could not stop thinking that only a little over fifty years ago this town was called not Rayalled, but Rorhed. This Fahl was Rorhah. My name. The name of the Kings of Brychmachrye. If my father hadn't been born here – I mean, if he hadn't been born at all – the Kings of Brychmachrye would still be Andaranahs, and Nikolas would be Nikolas Rorhah, not Nikolas Rayallah, and I would . . . Well, if my father had been a different man, he would never have married my mother and I wouldn't have been born either. I don't want to start on all this again.

'Drink up,' said Serena's father, nudging me with his elbow. 'Get it down you, we're getting another round in.'

'All together, come what weather, that's the spirit,' said the landlord, who is, if I have assembled my information correctly, Serena's second cousin. He said, 'Here, d'you want to see what I've got round the back? You'll never believe it – come take a look . . . '

Dutifully we all rose and trooped round, and what we were supposed to be admiring was evidently a tree.

'Look at here,' said the landlord, pointing. 'Only found it in the spring, when I cut back a bunch of bramble. Mind the thorns. What d'you think of that, then? Draws the customers in, I can tell you.'

I in my turn found myself shoved up against the tree. A large irregular circle was carved on its trunk, the outline bolled and scarred with age. Inside it, awkward and angular but still legible, were the initials 'BR'.

'Basal Rorhah,' the landlord explained to the illiterates among us. 'The Tsyraec did that, Basal the Great, may he be blessed in Hulsitoq.'

It was only three feet up the trunk. He couldn't have been more than nine, or ten.

The landlord said, 'It's like a monument, isn't it? His own hand – '

'It's as good as a temple, what d'you reckon?' said Serena's father.

'They come from all over the town,' said the landlord, 'from all over the Fahl . . . '

'It makes you think,' said Serena's father. He took off his hat and the others did the same. 'It makes you that humble. To think he stood where we're standing now – hey, where you going? Where you going? That young man, he's so – '

By now I was out of earshot. I sat back at the table, picked up my glass, and drank. Then I drank his glass, and after that I drank three or four more glasses. And after all that I still felt stone cold sober, and still incapable of imagining my father as a child.

Had he been like Peter? Impossible. Like me? Even more impossible. I've never carved my initials on a tree.

There he was, in my mind's eye, a miniature version of the broken-nosed, grey-bearded King I knew, running around marking every tree his own. Did he even then, even when he was ten, nine, eight, plan to do what he did, and so predetermine my whole life before I was ever born or dreamt of?

'What's wrong with you?' asked Serena's father, peering into my eyes. 'You sick or something? You going to be sick?'

'Yes,' I said. 'No.'

'Not bloody surprised. You can pay for what you drunk, you daft – '

They slapped me round the face and put my head under the pump, though I tried to tell them I was sober. This treatment did do me some good. It reminded me what year I was in, and what my situation was, and why they could thus manhandle a son of my father.

The man-boy who had carved his initials on that tree killed a man for the crime of knocking me off my stool.

In the town square there is a statue of the present Fahlraec's grandfather, my father's father. I felt no emotion towards it. Dotted among the crowds were faces with black hair, long noses, green eyes, but they also failed to affect me. Not so the dirt under my feet. The King never came back to Rorhed-Rayalled after he left it at the age of seventeen, and I know that this statue was put up after Nikolas became Fahlraec. The dirt under my feet has always been there. My father probably, undoubtedly, walked along that street. When he was a boy. When he was seventeen he had his whole life ahead of him.

I've blotted up a whole page, covered it with scribbles and doodles, and now I've torn it to shreds and thrown it across the room. What's the point of writing about it? What end is there to gain in thinking about them, and remembering them, and writing about them? Trying to open up new pages when I know that the books of their lives are shut now, for ever.

As we climbed the steps to Nikolas's castle, I saw a small boy with curly black hair and bony limbs tickling a puppy's tummy. When he heard us, he looked up and smiled, showing very white little milk teeth. His nurse came round the corner, calling to him, 'Hans, Hans, come here,' in court speech. She picked him up. He wriggled, but she held him firm. 'Leave them alone,' she scolded him. 'They're only natives.'

Nikolas's son.

We were directed into a large hall, where we stood in a shuffling group. The men I was with cast xenophobic glances at the other shuffling, tight-knit groups. Those groups glared back.

I didn't expect to see Nikolas – Fahlraecs' agents usually deal with these things – so I was surprised when he came in. I suppose he has only just returned from the war (which we've won with our usual alacrity) and, since he was in town, considered it his responsibility to deal with us. Nikolas has always been a conscientious man, carrying out his duties with that extra touch of zeal which has earned him the name of virtuous.

The proverbial dark horse. I know too much about him to believe that it was only an aberration, though that was the plea which saved him, that and his lies or his flattery or his treason. Despite everything, Beulah must still trust him, and it would be a shock to my system to have to think her lacking in judgment.

He looked very well, sunburnt and healthy, with a new long scar, still a little raw, on his arm. His hair is white, but I know why. It is the sum of his punishment, the price of his life.

I've known him since I was three years old. I've never liked him and never trusted him. How could I have let that man, who whipped me just a tiny bit harder than he needed to, anywhere near my brother?

He opened his mouth to address us.

In justice, those teeth should be caked with earth. That mouth should be fleshless bone.

A man who, after everything he's done, still retains his reputation as a good man.

When I was a child I used to wonder, as children do when they enjoy scaring themselves, what it would feel like to be in a dream and unable to wake up. One of those bad dreams where everything is upside down: people walk on the ceiling, and familiar faces become strangers; you try to run, and feel as if you are fighting your way upstream.

I know now. I looked at Nikolas, and instead of the rage and hatred I ought to feel, which I can feel easily enough when I think about him, I merely felt uninterested and aloof. He is like a different man. I looked at him and saw the features of a cousin I have known all my life, but they stirred no response in me. He is like a dead man, a stranger dressed in Nikolas's skin. Perhaps this is because almost everyone else I have any feelings for, love and hate and all that comes between, is dead. Nikolas can't really be alive.

He thinks *I'm* dead. I shouldn't be frightened of death; I'm already dead. Beulah and I are the only people who know I'm alive, but she can't be sure any more. The villagers don't know who I am. Everything that I am is dead. Except it's alive, locked up here in my living skull. I'm a paradox, like a divine king. Because gods are immortal, but kings die.

The King is dead, but he is still alive, just as you always believed. I have become my own myth. How impressive. Fancy talk don't dig potatoes, as they say up here. The King is dead but I am still alive: now we have a definition.

Nothing untoward or eventful marked this my latest meeting with Nikolas. I presented the tax accounts to the Fahlraec, witnessed the village being ticked off on the agent's list, and then we remounted and came back up the mountainside. We arrived as dusk fell. I left the mule in Serena's father's yard and hurried back to the hut where, as I had suspected, Serena was up and about.

'Get back into bed, you stupid girl.'

'I'm just making your food.'

'I'll do it. Get back into bed.'

She touched my arm lightly, meekly, as a dog wags its tail when it has offended. 'Have you had a good day?' she asked.

'No, I haven't, and you're a bad girl to go running around as soon as my back is turned. Go to bed.'

She went, saying, 'There's soup in the pot.'

I sat stirring the soup, gazing into the fire, and after a while I started to laugh, thinking, perhaps it's self-preservation makes her get up when she shouldn't. Someone has to prepare the food, and I no more know how to cook than I knew how to be King. It all boils down – so to speak – to the same dregs: if I could have foreseen that I would one day need to cook, then I could have foreseen everything.

I took the food in to her, and sat on the end of her bed to tell her about Rayalled, and the Fahlraec's castle, and the people we had seen. She fell asleep, and I went to my own bed. Much later, as dawn was breaking, I slept too.

I had a dream.

I was sitting with Madeleine. We were holding hands. I did not know it was a dream.

Peter walked up to us. My sister and I jumped apart.

Peter opened his mouth to speak. A red thing came out. I thought it was his tongue, but it was a worm. His mouth was full of earth.

Then his hair was on fire and the flesh ran from his bones like water.

43

I could barely contain my impatience now that spring had come round again. He would be home in two or three months. March into April, the lilacs dripping their heavy scent like rain. April into May, horse-chestnuts flowering pink and white; it became very hot on Ksaned Kaled. But still no Peter and no letter, neither from him nor from our embassy. Despite Madeleine and her reassurances, I was worried. I thought, 'It's as if they are dead, they are so silent.' Though now I know that the dead are never silent, always whispering.

At last I had to go and see Beulah.

She was lying in bed, puffy with pregnancy. Her back and feet were propped up with pillows, but still her hair was smooth and fashionable, her face finely powdered. Over her knees stood a portable writing desk. Servants, clerks, officials and courtiers poured in an endless stream through her bedroom.

This gave me a simile: the court is like a river, like the torrent of the Wastryl, cold and frothing grey with water from the glaciers. Only hardened, cold-blooded creatures can swim in it and survive. But where Madeleine and I live it has tributaried to form a green pool, flowery with untroubled lilies, where goldfish flick and gleam –

Beulah put down her pen and said, 'Sir, come in . . . '

The servants and clerks and courtiers bowed with whatever degree of lowliness suited their rank, echoing, 'Sir, Sir, Sir.'

I collected my thoughts and said, 'Excuse us.'

When they had gone and the door was shut, Beulah said, 'Well, sit down, Nardo – or did you just come here to stand and dream?'

I took a seat, and felt I ought to ask, 'How are you feeling?'

'Since you ask, terrible.'

'You look all right.'

'Gracious, a compliment, how delightful. Would you like to tell me what it is you want?'

'Don't you think we ought to send some more people out to Pravarre? It's past time when we should have heard from them, but I haven't received anything – '

'Don't look at me; I'd tell you if I had.'

'I'd like to know if they're still alive, at least.'

She started chuckling. 'What a pessimist you are.' She pointed with her pen. 'If *that* had happened, we would certainly have heard. I expect they're on their way home right now. Haven't you ever heard the saying about no news being good news?'

'*Have* you heard anything?'

'I've told you I haven't. But think. They've been sent out with clear instructions, so if everything's proceeding smoothly there's no need for them to go to the trouble and expense of sending couriers home with news. We only heard last autumn because they'd had some unforeseen setbacks.'

'Maybe Julius is still waiting for our reply,' I suggested.

Beulah shrugged. 'Let him wait. She isn't the only princess in the world. He knows what our terms are. He must see that they're fair ones, unless he's a fool. And if he is a fool, we really don't want to be allied with him, do we? Not with something as binding as a marriage. There's no point in sending a reply when our answer is no.'

'So you're saying no?'

'No to his demands, and no to sending more men out there.' She tapped the pen on her desk, and smiled. 'Have you ever been in a marketplace?' she asked, wearing that schoolmistress look. 'No, of course you haven't. When I was a little girl, the servants used to take me to the market with them, when they wanted to buy some cheap jewellery or ribbons. I listened to them bartering. The trick is never to look too eager, otherwise the price goes up.'

'You really are a storehouse of useful information.'

'You can be as sarcastic as you like, it doesn't alter the fact that I'm right.'

'I want to know what's happening!'

'Trust me. Be patient. Give it until the end of June, after this baby's born. If they still aren't home by then, we'll have to send someone to find out what the delay is.'

I wasn't satisfied with this, but I had to make do. One more month – he might be back on Ksaned Kaled before the month was out. He might already be on his way home, as Beulah said.

Early in the morning at the very end of May, a letter arrived. It was brought to us by a clerk from the Palace in Tsvingtori, who said he had been given it by a wool-trader with connections at court, who in turn had received it from the pilot of a Pravarrian merchantman. Thomas filcValentin had written it. He told us the ambassador was dead, killed in a freak accident: a tile had fallen off the roof and broken his skull. Negotiations were at a standstill: could I please send instructions?

Beulah summoned me and wondered aloud, 'Why did he have to send it in such a roundabout way?'

I had little time to speculate on this, because late evening of the same day brought another letter. The messenger was a man I recognised as one of Thomas filcValentin's confidential servants. The letter was untouched by Beulah's hands, or anyone's, brought straight to me with its seal intact. No more than a note, I remember every word of it:

Sir,
We have just arrived in Tsvingtori. Please send word or come yourself if you are able.

In Tsvingtori? What's Peter doing in Tsvingtori? Doesn't he know we're at Ksaned Kaled? And what about the Princess? No mention of her. Trouble is what that note said. All its words meant one word: trouble.

Come yourself if you are able. Of course I'm able. Peter's home, what do I care about trouble? Peter's always getting into trouble. When he is in trouble he comes to me. He ought to come to me, he ought to know that I hold nothing against him. Peter out of trouble would be like Peter without red hair.

'Madeleine, get your maids to pack, we're going to Tsvingtori, Peter's home.'

'Oh, how wonderful – but what's he doing in Tsvingtori?'

'Who knows? Does it matter? We'll soon find out, we can be there in three days. We're leaving tomorrow morning.'

I immediately sent a messenger relaying overland to the capital. He would be there in forty-eight hours to tell Peter we were coming, and to wait for us, in case he had intended to come straight on to Ksaned Kaled.

Beulah was far too pregnant to travel. She knew she couldn't stop me going without her, and she did not try. She simply said, 'I'll arrange for the clerks to sort out the things that need your signature. You can do them while you're on board. And please promise me you won't try to reorganise things. I can't face the prospect of having a huge mess to sort out when I get to Tsvingtori.'

She did not ask me to write to her, to keep her informed on events or to ask her advice. She did not need to. She had an army of clerks and servants to do this for her. No doubt the waters between Tsvingtori and Ksaned Kaled would be choked with boats scurrying backwards and forwards with queries from the councillors and her replies. She could not stop me going, but she could have stopped the Council from coming with me. She chose not to. She has a thousand eyes for her surveillance, and the miles between the island and the capital are no distance at all to her long arm.

Only three ships were ready to be travelled in the next morning. Most of the court was left behind, to follow when they could. As I stood on the deck with my sister, I realised that since my marriage there had never been a time when I was out of Beulah's reach, not one day when I would not have had to see her if she wanted to see me. Now a whole month – perhaps more, if I was lucky – stretched in front of me. With Madeleine beside me, Peter waiting for me and Beulah left behind, what more was there to wish for?

She was not there to mar my reunion with my brother. That day, when I saw him again, and hugged him, kissed his cheeks, and couldn't stop laughing – no one has really lived unless they've experienced such happiness. The first minute that brought him in sight made up for a whole year spent without him.

'Peter, Peter, you're taller – I swear you're taller. You must have grown at least two inches.'

'You've just forgotten what I look like, Nardo. I haven't grown.'

'Of course you have, you must have. Madeleine, don't you think Peter's taller?'

'He's so tall already, what does another inch matter? You look very well, Peter.' She kissed him.

No princess, of course. I had guessed as much from reading between the lines of Thomas filcValentin's note. No wonder Peter thought he'd be in trouble. Everything seemed clear to me: whatever he had done, or failed to do, he had preferred to hide his head in Tsvingtori rather than face me at Ksaned Kaled; and for that I had only myself to blame. I could have cried with the pleasure of hearing his voice again, and with disappointment at his awkward, distant manner. Well, I acknowledged, it is up to me to mend the breach.

When he saw the chance he took me aside to ask, 'Where's the bitch?'

'Still on Ksaned Kaled. She couldn't come, she's expecting a baby in a couple of weeks.' His blue eyes counted silently; I couldn't help laughing. 'Oh Peter, you always were terrible at arithmetic. The only thing that matters about this baby is it means she couldn't come, thank God. So we're here and she's not, and that's that. Shall we go for a ride after lunch, the three of us?'

It was a beautiful, warm, early summer's day, when the leaves are at their peak of green youth. Briefly he tried to raise the subject of his trip, but I wouldn't let him. 'Tomorrow,' I said. I wanted to show him that explanations weren't important, not compared to having him back with me. I could tell he didn't really want to discuss it, because he dropped the subject and was at last his old self, laughing unrestrainedly, enjoying himself as much as Madeleine and I were. We raced our horses to the walls, went out for a row on the lake and later went to examine the new litters in the kennels. We all got a little drunk at dinner, being already half-tipsy with happiness. Once, without warning, Peter threw his arms around me, saying nothing, and hugged me until I was breathless. After dinner we ran about the empty Palace, startling the servants, teasing the court dogs, playing all sorts of marvellous, childish games.

I'm sure Beulah has this day locked in her files somewhere.

The next morning we settled down to get Pravarre out of the way.

Peter's story was almost identical to what Beulah had guessed. Julius had held out for confirmation that I would give my brother a Fahl – confirmation which, in the face of our silence, no one could provide. What we hadn't known about was the extra character who arrived on the scene to complicate matters: Prince Hans of Chatienne. He came to Pravarre after the ship which returned to us the previous autumn had set sail. He was also bidding for the Princess's hand, and Julius favoured his suit for various reasons, one of the more important being that Chatienne and Pravarre share a common border and too many common ancestors; but he could do nothing until he had received a definite refusal from Brychmachrye.

'I knew you'd say no,' said Peter. 'But the ambassador said we had to wait. I didn't see any point in hanging about. I knew it was a lost cause. Nikolas said so too. And Thomas. But the ambassador wouldn't let us go until he'd heard from you. Why didn't you send some word, Nardo?'

'Well, now you see how time-consuming these things are. I was about to, when I heard you were back. Tell me, how did Dominic acquit himself?'

'His pockets are practically dragging on the ground, he's made so much money out of this. Don't ask me how, can't think who would want to bribe him.'

Once the ambassador was killed there was no one in a position to countermand Peter's wishes, and no reason for them to stay on, so they packed up their ships and came home. Before they left, they attended the wedding of the Princess to her Chatiennese bridegroom.

'I felt rather sorry for her,' Peter told me. 'Did you know Hans Cha-tienyah's fifty-two years old? And has been through three wives already?' He made a face. 'I don't think his father's ever going to die. You should have seen her cry when we left. She'd have chosen me if it had been up to her. I had her eating out of my hand.'

'I don't doubt it.'

'She wasn't all that pretty, you know. That picture flattered her. She's got terrible teeth, and the most enormous hands, and bad skin too. If you ask me we're well out of a bad bargain – she definitely wasn't worth what they were asking.'

'Not worth writing home about, at any rate.'

'Don't nag. I'm back now. Anyway, you did old Julius a good turn. Our being there really pushed up the price he got from Chatienne.'

'Not broken-hearted?'

'Do me a favour,' he grimaced.

Aside from the bare facts, he had no information to offer me except his own opinions. When I questioned him, he would repeat that he didn't know this, he didn't know that . . . This pleased me rather than otherwise, for obviously my instructions had been followed far enough to keep Peter from being involved in the more venal aspects of a marriage transaction.

He remarked, 'You didn't have to come tearing over here, you know. We knew you were on Ksaned Kaled, we were going to go on there. I just wanted to pick up my armour.'

'I'm surprised it fits, considering how much you've grown.'

'Well it does fit, so obviously I haven't grown.'

Now, his eyes asked as he said this, now are you going to keep your promise?

'Since it fits,' I said, 'you'd better make use of it.'

'Really?'

'Of course really. You kept your promise, of course I'll keep mine.'

'You don't blame me?'

'What for?'

'Well, for – for failing to do what you wanted me to do.'

'Oh Peter. You can't really think that badly of me, can you?'

'No, not of you . . . ' he said slowly, scratching the back of his head, looking away from me. 'But I thought . . . ' His head darted up with keen eyes that searched my face, and he hurried on, 'I know what the court's like, I know how rumours get round . . . '

To set his mind at ease I said, 'Peter, whatever I hear against you, you must know that I would never pay it any attention. I never listen to slander. And I know that it's not your fault you haven't married that princess. The whole thing was out of your hands – if it's anyone's fault, it's mine, for refusing to give in to their ridiculous demands. So don't worry. Now, it's your birthday in six weeks, isn't it? Do you want to wait until then, or go into the Guards as soon as possible?' As if I did not know what his answer would be.

'Right away, as soon as possible.'

'All right, I'll tell Nikolas to start making arrangements.'

He frowned as I wrote this down. 'Do you have to make a note?'

'It's not for me, it's for the clerk. I'm not going to forget.'

Soon I noticed he was growing restless, though trying to hide it. 'What's wrong?' I asked him.

'Nothing, except I promised to meet Nikolas at eleven. We were going to course the puppies. And it must be gone eleven now.'

'You've just got back, why are you in such a hurry to rush away?'

'I'm not, don't say that. I wouldn't have fixed it, only I thought you'd be busy today. Do you mind if I go now? I could tell him it's off, and come back.'

He sounded as if he would prefer this, and so my stupid jealousy was mollified and I said, 'No, go on. You're right, I do have work to do and I should do it.'

'Why don't you come with us?' he asked eagerly.

'Don't tempt me. I must do my work. You go and tell Nikolas to make the arrangements for you, all right?'

He stood up, but now seemed as reluctant to leave as he had been to stay. Despite what I'd said about not blaming him, he still looked uneasy, almost indecisive. He was home, he ought to look happy. 'Go on,' I said, 'I don't mind.'

'Nardo, can I ask you something?'

'You don't need to ask if you can ask,' I laughed. 'Just ask.'

'Well – why hasn't Madeleine ever got married?'

I think I had been expecting this question, or one like it, for some time, because I found myself prepared. 'We just can't keep you off the subject of matrimony, can we,' I said lightly.

He was not to be diverted, and insisted seriously, 'There aren't all that many princesses in the world. I'm surprised no one's asked for her.'

'They have, don't you remember? Julius of Pravarre, before his father died. She was going to marry him.'

'Yes I know, but it never happened. Hasn't anyone asked for her since then?'

'Peter, what is this? Do you want her to leave us? I thought – '

'Please don't be angry. Of course I don't want her to leave. I like her. She's the only sister I've got. Things wouldn't be the same here without her. I'm only asking. If you think it's none of my business, then say so.'

In fact I had been about to say that very thing, but once he'd made that remark, I couldn't. I fought down my discomfort and told him the truth. 'As it happens, no one has asked for her. It may seem surprising, but they haven't.'

'No foreigners, you mean. But I know Thomas filcValentin – '

'I know him too,' I said, more harshly than I'd intended.

'You don't like him, do you. Neither do I.'

'Look, sit down.' I waved my hand. 'Since we've begun this, we might as well talk about it.'

'She's not interested in him at all,' said Peter, still standing. 'I don't think she even knows he's alive. That's why he's so miserable all the time.'

'I hadn't noticed he was, but that's got nothing to do with this. I would have thought you'd understand that Madeleine can no more marry someone from the court than you can – '

'You did.'

'And look how that turned out. I don't want to bring Beulah into this discussion, if you don't mind. Since she's not here, the best thing we can do is forget all about her. Please, sit down.'

'No, I'm going in a minute. Can I just ask you one more thing?'

'Ask.'

'Why haven't you ever looked for someone for Madeleine, like you did for me?'

'Because she's never expressed the slightest desire to get married. Because I know she doesn't want to leave us. Marriage is different for women, it can be dangerous. Why should she want to get married? And Peter, the truth is that I don't want her to go any more than I want you to go. I want you both here with me. If she got married, it would inevitably mean that she would have to go abroad, for ever, and I'll tell you, I would never have begun to arrange a marriage for you if it meant I would probably never see you again. And I would never, never try to force you into something permanent against your wishes.'

I thought this was a sufficiently comprehensive answer, but he would not let it alone. 'If she wanted to,' he demanded, 'if someone asked for her, and she wanted to marry him, you'd agree?'

'Well,' I said, 'of course. But I wouldn't like it, any more than I'd like it if you went out of my life for ever.'

He was watching me closely – and then, like, just like, the sun coming out from behind clouds, he smiled and his blue eyes danced. He said with a grin, 'Well, I'm home now, so don't ever try to send me away again.'

'I wouldn't dare. Peter, you'll be late if you don't hurry.'

'Yes. Nardo, don't you think it's strange that she's never been interested in anyone?'

'I haven't really thought about it.'

'Some people say it's a bit unnatural – '

'Then they're talking about things that are none of their business.

Madeleine doesn't pry into your affairs, Peter, and I really don't think we should talk about her like this when she's not here.'

He leaned his weight on the back of the chair, angling it towards him. 'You're right,' he said; and stood up straight, releasing the chair, which rocked forward and clattered on the floor. 'Well, I suppose I'll go.'

Even now he did not leave. He dawdled by the chair, and said, 'Nardo – I'm glad you told me.'

'All you have to do is ask. Now are you going or aren't you? Nikolas will get tired of waiting.'

'Yes, I'm going.'

At the door he hesitated. Slipping an arm up the post, he twisted round to look back at me.

'Nardo – ' he said.

'Yes?'

He didn't say anything, but he looked at me as if he had a question. I wanted to ask him what it was; I suppose I should have done, but if I had, I don't think he would have been able to say.

At last he said, 'See you at dinner,' and went out.

44

The court came back from Ksaned Kaled in dribs and drabs, but Beulah remained on the island. She had given birth to another son. As I've said, I never did see much of Basal, but occasionally I was in company with him, and I noticed he had a habit of holding his breath until he turned blue, or banging his head against the wall, if he was denied something he wanted. I hope this hasn't turned him into a mental deficient; not that it matters as long as she's around.

Before we heard this news of her new baby, Peter was enrolled in the Guards. I liked his armour. Some of the wealthier young men went in for highly decorated suits, gold curlicues, jewel-studded bosses, ribbons and fancy plumes. But Peter, who could have had whatever he wanted merely by asking me, chose a plain and serviceable suit of steel and leather – memories of Hans turning up his nose at the Pravarrian armour. Peter said he had taken Nikolas's advice, which damped my pleasure a little because it was always Nikolas this and Nikolas that in those days. But I reflected that I had only myself to blame. I consoled myself with the fact that his armour was one of the first things he had shown me when we were reunited, wanting my immediate approval. Remembering how jealous he had been of Madeleine, I swallowed my hurt. And I still, like an idiot or an honest man, thought that he could have made a worse friend than Nikolas.

When I remember Peter as a man, and not as a child, I like best to remember him as he looked that day. It was a late June afternoon of blue skies, green trees and golden sun. The swallows darted through the air, having returned from wherever it is they go – like Peter, safely home. He was as irresistible as a bolt of lightning, almost giving off sparks of happiness and pride, his armour, skin, red hair all burnished, smiling at me with such bright eyes that I couldn't mind when he smiled as he saluted Nikolas.

It's no good saying I ought to have realised, for what does that make Peter? Why should I, in the fact that he and Nikolas were together much of the time, that Nikolas looked boldly at me while Peter could not meet my eyes with any ease, in Peter's odd questions, have suspected anything? I thought that they spent time together because Peter was a new Guard and Nikolas was his Captain; that Peter was uneasy in my presence because he knew their friendship grated on me; that he asked questions because he wanted to know. Nikolas's new arrogance didn't surprise me.

When we came back to Tsvingtori and I saw him again, I noticed nothing changed about Peter. We were perfectly happy in each other's company. What else could I have thought? That he was such an expert in duplicity that it was all a pretence? I don't believe it now. I will not. He was as glad to see me as I was to see him.

Two weeks or so after his enrolment in the Guards, we were sitting alone together in the gardens. Peter was very conscientious about his duties, which meant we had less chance than ever to be alone with each other, and although he didn't say anything I knew he preferred not to be singled out from the others when he was on duty. But that afternoon he had come purposely in search of me, during his free time.

Having sat down next to me, he didn't seem inclined to talk. He took off his helmet and laid his sword across his knees; watching him, I wanted to laugh, so strongly did he remind me of the little boy who had gone hurtling up and down the corridors, waving his toy sword. Now he was nearly nineteen, playing with men's things. I must not laugh or I would hurt his feelings.

His eyes were fixed on his sword, but I could tell he wasn't really looking at it. The sun shone with a dull whiteness on his armour. He gave off such a powerful air of preoccupation that it affected me, too. I would have liked to touch him, stroke his hair. He looked sad, for no reason I could think of, and there had been a time, when he was a child, when a hug from me would have helped cure the sadness. Now I was not allowed to offer such babyish comforts. I folded my hands in my lap and made do with looking at him, thinking how good it was to see him once more on this bench, in this garden, in Tsvingtori, when he had been away so long.

He shot a quick, furtive glance at me and said, 'I wish you wouldn't stare.'

'Peter, what's wrong?'

'Nothing.' His shoulders were slumped forward. 'Nothing,' he repeated. 'What makes you think there is?'

'I wish you'd tell me.'

He ran a hand up and down the sharp blade. 'There's nothing wrong with me.'

'Then why do you always look so sad?'

'I don't.'

'You do right now.'

'Do I? Well, I'm not.' He forced a smile that came half-way up his face, realised it was a failure, and admitted, 'Well, maybe a little. I guess it's just a mood.'

'Guards not living up to your expectations?'

'No, it's great.' His hand kept stroking the flat of his sword. 'Maybe – I don't know – it's so nice without the bitch here. When's she coming back?'

'I don't know. In a couple of weeks, I suppose. Does the thought of her really bother you that much?'

'I hate knowing I'll have to see her again.'

'Believe me, I understand how you feel. I used to feel the same way. But you won't have to see much of her, you know, if you don't want to, and after a while it'll cease to matter. I think you'll be surprised how quickly it stops bothering you.'

Peter threw his head back, taking several deep breaths. Then he asked, 'Are you happy?'

'Why?'

'I just want to know, Nardo, all right?'

'All right. Sometimes I am, sometimes I'm not. On the whole I am. Much happier now you're back. Are you happy, Peter?'

'I'm asking about you. What – what things make you happy?'

I saw that this question, whatever it was really asking, meant a great deal to him, and so tried to give him an honest answer. 'Sometimes a lovely day, like today, can make me glad to be alive, but the thing is, when I'm sad a beautiful flower or a blue sky can't always cheer me up. The only important things that make me happy are you and Madeleine. Having you around, being with you, knowing you're happy. And my writing, poetry, reading, you know . . . I've always been happy with those things, and I couldn't be happy without them. Is that what you wanted to know?'

He nodded, deep in thought.

'Surely you already knew those things about me,' I added.

'Yes,' he said. 'I did. I don't think I was asking about that.'

'What do you want to know? I don't mind telling you.'

He twisted into an uncomfortable-looking position, with his elbows locked in front of his throat and his hands clasping his shoulders, legs wound together; he stuttered for a moment, then asked me straight, 'Do you like being King? Are you happy, being King?'

This took me aback. I had never expected such a question from anyone. Not even Madeleine had ever asked it – she knew what a meaningless question it would be. I thought Peter knew too, and so this, coming from him, was like being leapt on in the dark. For a blank moment I was unable to understand him.

'I'm happy with the way things are,' I said. 'I haven't got many complaints to make about my life.'

'That's not what I meant at all. Are you happy being King – happier than you were before? I mean, don't you feel – different?'

'What do you think "being King" means, Peter?' Before he could reply, I answered myself. 'I'm sure it means different things to the different men who are King. It must have meant a great deal to our father. He wanted to be King. I never did, you know that. And I never expected I would be. But it hasn't really changed my life. It's changed it much less than other things have. If you can call it change. The only things it changed were not – things I was, but only possibilities, things that might have been in the future but which, because I became King, never happened. Do you understand?'

'No, not really – well, maybe.' He scratched his stubbly chin.

I tried again. 'You remember, don't you, that years ago I was going to go into the Temple? I didn't want to but Father had decided for me, so I was resigned to it. Then it got put off, and Hans died, and Alexi – Alexi told me he would have done, oh, all sorts of things, but he died. And then the King died, so there I was. If you think about it, not about "the King's" life, but my life, about the things I've always done and enjoyed – well, the fact is that I can still do those things, and much more easily than if everything had gone to plan and I had become a priest. So in fact my being King has changed my life less than if all had gone as expected.'

I folded my arms, which I had been waving expressively in the air, and started laughing as I realised just how little I had said. Peter was frowning. 'But don't you think it ought?' he asked.

'Ought what?'

'Ought to have changed things?'

'It has, but less than other things would have.'

The beginnings of impatient little wrinkles were creasing between his brows. 'Anyway I wasn't asking about that. I meant being King – I suppose I mean the duties – '

'The work?'

'Well, the responsibilities . . . '

'The truth is, Peter, the work itself is pretty boring. Repetitive and tedious. There's always a new problem and none of them ever seems to get solved for good.'

He gave me such a complicated look; I could not fathom it then, but now, since I cannot forget his face, his eyes that day, and since I think about it so often, I decide that perhaps it was a sort of grief at finding what I said so easy to believe of me. As if part of him feared, or hoped, that 'being King' meant something special to me, and another part feared, or hoped, that it did not. As if he were both relieved and disappointed.

He said, 'You know, sometimes I feel I don't understand you at all, not like I used to.'

'But I've told you, I haven't changed. I'm still the same as I always was.'

Slowly, with his eyes half-shut, he measured out his thoughts. 'But you're – look, I don't know how to put this. But Nardo, you're supposed to be a – a god, now.'

I realised I would have to tread carefully here. 'Do you believe that?' I asked.

'I don't know.'

As if he wanted to, but could not, because it was Nardo who was King.

'Did you believe it about Father?'

'Maybe,' he said. Then his lids flew open like shutters thrown wide on a brilliant day and he asked breathlessly, 'Nardo, are you – '

His voice stumbled, his eyes fell, and he was abruptly silent again, withdrawing into himself.

'Is that what's bothering you?' I asked.

'No. I don't know. Nothing's bothering me.'

'I wish you'd tell me.'

'If you know so much then why don't you guess?' he shouted.

'Peter – '

'I can't tell you!'

I put out my hand to calm him. He shrank away from it, just a little, or at least I thought he did. At the time I thought it was my imagination, but now I believe he did recoil. I laid my hand on his arm and said, 'Why can't you tell me?'

He shivered. I patted his arm and removed my hand, believing he preferred me not to touch him. 'I don't mean to pry,' I said. 'But since you've come back you've – '

'Look, just leave it alone. I can't tell you because there's nothing to tell.' He sighed a deep, ragged breath. There was such profound unhappiness in him that I wanted to beg for his trust, insist that he tell me. But I did not dare.

'I'm sorry for shouting,' he said. 'Nardo, I – I don't feel too well. I'm so hot in this armour. I'm going on duty again in three hours. I think I'll go inside and lie down for a bit.'

I watched him stride away, feeling helpless. I could not force him to tell me. That would only make it worse. Obviously he was wretched about something, but what? If he could not tell me, I could not guess. I would have to be patient, and wait for him to open up to me in his own good time.

Thinking back to my own state of mind and heart when I was his age, not quite nineteen, I recalled, as one recalls a book read long ago, that I had been lovesick for Beulah. I had been wretched too, but in a delirious way. His wretchedness was melancholy. I had got over it, and he would get over this too. One day he would look at himself and wonder how anyone could have felt as he felt now, and whether he hadn't been a little mad. Patience.

Left on my own in the garden, I wanted more than anything else to know whether he confided in Nikolas what he would not tell me.

Later, I saw them standing together, arguing furiously.

I talked it over with Madeleine.

'So it isn't just me,' she said.

'What do you mean?'

'He looks at me sometimes as if – as if I'm somewhere I shouldn't be.'

'He hasn't been rude to you?'

'Oh no, he got over that years ago. We're friends now – or I thought we were. It's not that. It doesn't seem to have anything to do with whether he likes me or not. Sometimes I get the impression he feels – sorry for me. Maybe he thinks' – she laughed – 'poor old Madeleine, the old maid. But if we're together for any length of time, he soon starts acting like he used to. As if he's forgotten what's bothering him.'

'Something is, isn't it? I wish I knew what.'

'Perhaps he wants to deal with it himself. If he needs his privacy, you must let him have it.'

Someone sent me an anonymous note. I had from time to time received this sort of thing before; Beulah often had. Sometimes she showed hers to me. They came from self-appointed spies, warning me, or her, to be on our guard against such-and-so who was plotting this and planning that – which they generally weren't. These notes did not come from our 'friends', but from the enemies of those named in them, and thus Beulah could usually work out who the authors were. She paid no attention to them, unless they confirmed something she already suspected, because she always knew, before anyone else, what was happening.

I laughed at it. What it hinted was absurd. Then I did what I always did: tore it up, thinking as I did so that Nikolas probably had many enemies, but wondering who hated Peter.

I had promised him I would never listen to rumour.

One day, when I knew he was on guard-duty outside the offices, I had an idea: perhaps his failure to win the Pravarrian princess was rankling more than he would admit. I called him in and suggested that he think again about marrying, but this time choose for himself, because it would not be so impossible for him to have a court girl if his heart was set on one. He only said, 'Whatever you decide, Sir,' laughing rather sullenly to add, 'It doesn't really matter, does it?'

When I asked him what he meant, he asked if he could go.

Beulah did not return until mid-July. She stretched out a pleasant convalescence on Ksaned Kaled – and why not? There was no need for her to hurry back. A third of the court was keeping her company, and what little business I was transacting was relayed with efficient regularity to her. She sent me letters telling me what to do, but these I stuffed into a file, since there was nothing so urgent it could not wait for her, or so fascinating I burned to deal with it myself.

She and the remainder of the court returned in a flotilla of ships, a grand aquatic show. They paraded up from the docks with pomp and circumstance, and the people of the city celebrated an unofficial holiday, lining the streets to cheer, and clap, and throw flowers. They had done the same when Madeleine and I returned, but not with such enthusiasm.

Why don't you get rid of her? It's not that easy.

Beulah swept in, embracing and kissing first me, then Madeleine, then Peter. She smiled and ran her fingers down his armour, telling him how handsome he looked. We had lunch, and immediately afterwards she got down to work, briefing the Council, organising the petitions, the appointments and a ball.

When she walked away, and he thought no one was looking, I saw Peter spit on the dust where she had stood. And I saw Nikolas, watching him, nod slightly in approval.

What had she ever done to Nikolas, that he should hate her? I always thought they were two of a kind. Most of his honours and appointments had come from her.

She brought the new baby for me to see: another blond and brown-eyed lump. For something to say I asked, 'What's his name?'

'I haven't quite decided. I rather thought I'd call him Reyhnard.'

'Oh, come on, there's no need for that. Anyway I'd prefer it if you didn't.'

'What, then? He ought to have a family name.'

'Whose family?' I shrugged. 'If you're really asking me, call him after your father.'

'Oh, heavens, no, he was called Humphrey, that's a dreadful name. What about Alexander?'

'No.'

'Hans?'

'No.'

In the end she named him Rori. And that was the only discussion we ever had about him, or indeed about any of her children.

I don't know why I'm writing these irrelevancies. I am a coward, perhaps. I often think I am. Conversations about Beulah's children are not important, not worth remembering. Talking with Peter, though, I ought to write about that. And the note. And what Madeleine thought. They added up, but only afterwards.

And the good days, when the sun beamed and Beulah was busy some-where else, when Peter was at peace with himself and all was right with the world – I believed those days to be the pattern of the future. Like a necklace, snapped, spilling its beads so that later, in the grass, one finds a scattered jewel or two. If they are jewels, those days, and they are because their number is fixed, every day of his nineteen years, six thou-sand nine hundred and thirty days, each one of them more precious to me than – I don't know, than almost anything. As I see the end of the string coming, my counting becomes frantic and hopeful: perhaps I have miscounted, perhaps there is a day more. Those days, those memories, are brighter than pearls, harder to break than diamonds, and they should be described as jewels. Write about the good days and the times we spent together, for if they mattered then, they cannot be irrelevant now. All those days when I loved and trusted him.

Perhaps I should have seen it coming. Perhaps I would have done if I had trusted him less, loved him less; and then his salvation would have been in my lack of trust and love.

It was late one night, a week after Beulah's return, and Madeleine was with me. The door to my bedroom was shut. I heard the door in the further room open, feet enter and come shuffling across the floor. I thought it might be Beulah; the Guards would have refused entrance to anyone else. Telling Madeleine to stay quietly where she was, I put something on and slipped into the other room, shutting the bedroom door behind me.

'I can't sleep,' said Peter's voice, disembodied in the darkness. 'I have to talk to you.'

I lit a candle so that I could see him, but whether on purpose or by instinct he sat where his face was in shadow.

This time he did not hesitate. 'I've just been past the Council offices,' he said. 'It's midnight, you know, well past midnight. A light was on in there. Naturally I thought it was you, so I looked in to say hullo. But it was her. The bitch. Do you know what she's doing?' His voice rose, hoarse and high-pitched. 'She's got all sorts of official papers in there, I saw her, and she's working on them, she's got your seal! And she just smiled at me, as if . . . God! Nardo, did you know?'

'You're not supposed to go in there.'

'Well I did. And I saw. I want to know if you knew, and don't lie to me, and don't tell me it's none of my business.'

'Yes, I know.'

'You can't!' His fists flailed in the air; he was working himself up into one of those childhood fits of passion. 'I don't believe you!'

'I've just told you,' I said, thinking it best to keep calm. 'I know. Of course I know. Do you think she could do it without my knowledge?'

'That's as good as saying she's got your permission, Nardo – it's treason, what she's doing. How long has she been doing it?'

'Always – that is, since before the King died.'

'Does she really do all your work?'

I hesitated. 'Where did you hear that?'

'Does she?'

'Yes,' I said, and amended it to, 'Most of it.'

'I don't believe you!'

'You saw it.'

'How can you sit there and grin at me as if this was a joke? She shouldn't be in there, it's wrong, you're the King, it's your responsibility – '

'You've asked me and I've told you. I never wanted to tell you and I never wanted to be King, so just stop trying to tell me what I ought to do. You know nothing about it – '

'No, I don't, because you never tell me anything. I have to wait to find out by accident or from – God! God! I can't believe it. You know and you let her – '

'Of course I let her. She wants to do it and you know what she's like when she wants something. And quite honestly I have no desire to fight over it with her. It's not worth it – '

'No, it all suits you perfectly, you just said so. "It's so boring, I don't want the responsibility" – well, no wonder you won't get rid of her, you come as a bloody package. And all the crap you said about wishing you could get rid of her. You don't want to get rid of her at all, you might have to work then – '

'Peter,' I said. 'It's not like that. I never wanted you to know this – '

'I bet you didn't. How could you look me in the eye and preach all that shit about a sense of responsibility, and then send me halfway across the world for a whole year while you let her do your work and you spend your time – '

Whatever he had been about to say – and I can guess what it was – tailed off into silence, leaving his mouth open but speechless. He was no longer an angry man, but a frightened boy, afraid that his anger had gone too far. After our shouting, that silence too was like a shout, in which we heard the faint rasp of a door being opened, then shut, in my bedroom.

In the candlelight Peter's face was like a ghost's. He went on listening long after there was nothing to hear.

I waited for one of us to find the courage to speak first, hoping it would be me, but he suddenly whispered, 'That was Madeleine, wasn't it.'

I couldn't think of anything to say, no way to begin.

'Wasn't it.'

'Peter, listen, let me tell you – '

'I don't want to know, leave me alone!'

I could have grabbed him, held him, forced him to stay; I could have made him listen, made him tell me everything; but he ran away from me.

I could have run after him, chased him, caught him, made him listen.

I didn't. I didn't because I thought: What will the court think if they see the King, half-naked, running after his half-naked brother, both of them dishevelled, both of them screaming?

I thought he was bound to come back. I decided to wait for him. I sat up sleepless through the night, believing he would soon return.

At some point I fell asleep in a chair. I was woken by what sounded like a riot, shouting and confusion and dozens of feet racing up and down the corridors. I hardly had time to put my thoughts together and wake up properly before Madeleine came in, distraught, her hair unbrushed and her clothes thrown on anyhow. She grabbed my hands. Her thumbs were bleeding.

'What's happening?' I asked her.

'Oh, thank God you don't know. I hoped it wasn't true and you didn't know, didn't say – '

'What?'

'Peter's been arrested.'

'What?'

'Peter and Nikolas – and some others too, mostly Guards.'

'But Madeleine, no. Why?'

'I don't know.'

'Been arrested?' I was still half-asleep, and this seemed like some silly, bad dream.

'About half an hour ago,' she said.

It was too incredible to take in. I said, 'You must be mistaken, this can't be true.'

'No I'm not, I swear.'

'This is crazy,' I said. 'Someone's made a mistake. Let's find my shoes and I'll go and sort it out.'

Madeleine said, 'Listen.'

Boots were marching towards my door.

I have never felt so afraid as I did in those seconds. I hadn't ordered the arrests, so it must have been Beulah, and she never does anything without a good reason. Hearing those boots, I assumed she had taken Nikolas and Peter first in order to render me defenceless, and that now it was my turn.

She left the Guards outside and entered without knocking. Thomas filcValentin was with her. She and I had a short slanging match – pitiful, really, to remember – then she said to Thomas, 'Tell His Grace.'

He knelt on the floor and said:

That there had been a conspiracy.

That Peter and Nikolas had been planning to depose me, and put Peter in my place.

That it had begun in Pravarre.

That Nikolas had told Peter all the things I'd known he ought never to hear.

That they had tried to draw Thomas in, but he had refused from the start, and so he was never sure how far it had gone or how many men were involved. He had hoped it would never advance beyond bluster and half-baked schemes.

That when he wrote the note urging me to come to Tsvingtori, he had hoped my mere presence would put an end to it.

That he had also written the anonymous note, so that I could look into the affair without causing a stir.

That no one had done anything. That no one even seemed to suspect.

That last night, one of the Guards had come to him and said that the conspirators were ready for action, and that if someone did not take steps to prevent it the revolt would begin in two days.

That, after a night of agonising, he had gone to Beulah and told her everything he knew.

They had planned to kill us. All of us. Me. Madeleine. Beulah and her children. Anyone who stood by us.

Madeleine was crying so loudly I could hear nothing more that he said.

Loyal Thomas, afraid for his life. Why did he wait to tell me? Better to have kept his mouth shut, now that it was too late.

45

I said to Beulah, 'He must have a trial.'

'If you insist. If you really think you can go through with it. But he can't get off, none of them can. There's too much evidence. They didn't have a hope, they must be mad. Your family, Nardo, defies comprehension. You're all insane. How a man like your father managed to have such children I'll never, never know. I thought Peter worshipped you! What's wrong with him? And you were so unbelievably stupid not to see what was going on right under your nose. You're lucky I was here to put a stop to it. And Nikolas, I'm astonished at him, I always thought he was such a reliable, sensible sort. After all he is only your cousin, his mother's blood must have diluted your family's insanity – but obviously not enough. What a mess – and leaving personal sentiment aside, Nikolas is more of a problem than Peter. He's so popular and well respected, his condemnation will cause a lot of bad feeling, but we can't let them get away with it . . . '

She went on and on like this. To be fair, I suppose it was her way of dealing with shock. I was numb. I believed I wasn't really hearing her, but I remember it now.

I went to see him in the cells. Beulah did not want me to go, but she did not try to stop me.

His cell was as comfortable as a prison can be. I made sure he had everything: a good bed, sheets, cushions, proper food, books and candles. I was glad to see his dinner tray was empty – silly, I suppose.

In the back of my mind I knew it no longer mattered whether he ate or not.

I think he wasn't yet really afraid. This being in prison was his heaviest punishment so far, but all his punishments had come to an end. Though he had returned from Pravarre without the Princess, I had overwhelmed him with my joy at seeing him again, having forgiven him almost before he went away. He had been in trouble so many times. He was used to it. He thought prison was the greatest punishment there was. He thought it would be over quickly. Because Nardo always forgives him. Nardo knows Peter can't help being naughty, what with all those bad friends who lead him astray. Nardo always says, Come on then, come out of there. I don't think he truly realised the enormity of what he had done until the very end, and then only because of the enormity of the punishment.

Hearing my approach, he rose from his bed and moved as far from the door as he could, jamming himself into the corner of the cell. I stopped on the threshold. He stood with his back to me, pressing his face against the wall, torn between defiance and contrition.

'What do you want?'

'I have to talk to you,' I said.

'It's a bit late for that now.'

'It may not be.'

He waved a hand dismissively, as if his fate was a triviality that no longer concerned him.

'Peter, don't you realise what you've done? This isn't another one of your little scrapes. I can't treat it like a practical joke, though I hope it was, one that got out of hand. I am prepared to believe that you were led into this against your better judgment, by people who had more influence over you than they should have. I am willing to accept that you didn't know what you were getting into – '

'Nardo,' he interrupted, head bent as if reasoning with the wall, 'what makes you think I wasn't serious?'

'Peter – '

'You really think I'm ignorant, don't you. I'm not surprised, you did your best to keep me that way – '

'Peter, what have I done to make you hate me?'

He took a moment to answer this, and said slowly, 'If I hated you, you'd be dead already.'

The other prisoners were shuffling in their cells, rustling the straw, wooden bowls rattling against the grates. One of my Guards marched down and used his sword to rap the noisiest over the knuckles. The prisoner shrieked and dropped his bowl. 'Show some respect for the

King,' said the Guard, or words to that effect. Peter started laughing, a horrible sound like choking in his nose. Taking a deep breath he spoke in a monotone.

'When it started, in Pravarre, Nikolas just used to talk to me. He didn't tell me anything, I mean none of the things I know now. I suppose he was just testing the wind. He said he wanted to see if I knew already – he said he didn't believe anyone could be as ignorant as I was. Anyway, when he did start to – tell me things, I didn't believe him. I couldn't. I thought I knew you better than that. And when he started hinting, suggesting, that we do it . . . At first I thought I'd play along with him and tell you as soon as we got back. But by the time we came home he had me really convinced – and then I saw you again and I didn't – I didn't know what I felt. You didn't look any different. I was going to tell you, the day after you came back from Ksaned Kaled, remember? I don't know why I didn't. I suppose I was afraid. I think I knew all the time really that Nikolas was right and I didn't want him to be. But I liked him. I didn't think he was the sort of person who would lie. I never thought you would lie to me either.'

Without thinking, I said, 'I never lied to you.'

'Oh please. You did. When I asked you, you said, "Ask me anything and I'll tell you the truth," but you never did. You told me to ask you and then you lied. You lied to me about Beulah's children. And you lied to me about Madeleine.'

'I didn't lie to you, I – if I tried to keep certain facts about things from you it was for your sake, not mine.'

'You should have told me,' he said, but as if it didn't matter now. I would have preferred him to attack me physically or scream blame, rather than stay stiffly propped against the wall like some dead thing beyond pain or mercy.

'Suppose it had been me, instead of Nikolas, who told you. Would it have made a difference?'

He shrugged. 'Who knows?'

I ached to run over and touch him, hug him, bring him back to life. But I didn't. I was frozen to the spot, nailed there, fixed, afraid to touch him because I knew if I did I would start making all sorts of promises that Beulah and the law between them would not let me keep.

'Nardo, Nikolas said – Nikolas said that if it came down to choosing between me and her, you'd choose her – '

'That's not true, Peter, how can he – '

Peter wasn't listening. 'I always knew it,' he went on. 'Deep down. I think I've known for years that you – what you were doing. I mean it is obvious. I'm not as stupid as you think. It was never the same after she came and an idiot could have guessed why, but I – really I think I didn't want to know. I mean I always knew you loved her more, so much more that I didn't matter, compared, you know. But you should have told me *why*. The thing is, I'm not horrified or whatever you were afraid of. I was last night, but that was more because – more because I'd seen all the things Nikolas told me with my own eyes, coming one after another like that, seeing they were true and I didn't want them to be. It was that, more than because of – of just knowing about you and her. Do you understand?'

'I can't help the way I am,' I said, though I don't suppose now that this statement had much relevance to what he was telling me. 'If I love her it's because I love you – if I loved her less I'd love you less, can't you see that?'

'Look, it's not easy but I can accept – it. In a way it even makes it easier, funnily enough. Knowing that's the reason she means more to you, because she's a girl, and not because she's better than me or anything. But Nardo, you should have told me yourself. You shouldn't have left me to find it .out from other people, as if I was a stranger to you. And not just that. The other things, especially Beulah. I just can't understand why you didn't. Because you didn't trust me or . . . All those things you hid from me. That her children aren't really yours. Nardo, don't you know what the law is? If you have no children then *I'm* your heir, not her *bastards*!' At last there was life in his voice, a spark of anger. 'To know that you were prepared to cheat me out of my rights, Father's inheritance, because it was more convenient for you! That's the deal, isn't it? I mean, she's the King really, and that suits you just fine because it's so boring, it's so dull . . . And everyone knew but me. Everyone! When Nikolas told me, I said it couldn't be true and he laughed in my face, Nardo, he said it's been going on for *years*. Can you imagine how I felt? You should have told me, then maybe . . . ' He was making fists at the wall. 'If you'd told me right from the start, instead of letting me go on believing you were really – really . . . '

'What?'

'Perfect.'

'I never pretended I was perfect.'

'You ought to be, you're supposed to be.'

I felt hopeless, unable to approach him, denied the sight of his face. 'Peter, do you really believe that?'

That terrible laugh started up again, a nasal, childish giggling. From where I stood it looked as if he was crying. 'Do you want to know something?' he chuckled. 'I never knew Thomas had written to you when we came back from Pravarre. I thought you just knew we were back. I mean, the King is supposed to know everything. I think I sort of expected you'd know all about what Nikolas and I were up to, and stop it ages before anything happened. Father always did.'

'I'm not him.'

'No, I know that now.'

'I never wanted to be.'

'Remember when I was little, I used to be so scared he could read my mind? You never believed it, did you. Even before he died. God, you know, he must have been an amazing man, he made it look as though he really was omniscient, when he couldn't have been really.

'Nardo, why do they bring us up to believe something that isn't true? You're bound to find out sooner or later.' And then he added, 'I wish I did hate you.'

'Why?'

'I hated you last night. Now I just hate myself for having been so stupid – '

'Oh Peter, it's not your fault – '

'It *is* my fault!' he shouted. 'I know what I've done, I'm old enough to take the blame.'

Then, at last, after I had waited so long, he turned around and said, 'You're not fit to be King.'

'I know.'

He had that same look in his face as Alexi when Hans died, a brutal despair that would kill itself if nothing else came within reach to wound. He said, half to himself, 'I have nothing to believe in any more.'

I saw in his eyes that same death of faith I suffered when I was sixteen, in the library when my father had me whipped. *Do you understand now?* I wanted to shout. *I would have spared you this.*

I said, 'I can't stand seeing you locked in here.'

'Get me out.'

'I can't.'

'I didn't think so.' His expression never changed. I think he was beneath feeling disappointment. I know he was. I know how he felt. He added, 'She could. But you've never tried.'

'That's not true – '

'It is true.'

'Peter, do you know what the punishment is for treason?' I shouted; and he shouted back, 'You can't be a traitor unless there's a King, and Brychmachrye hasn't got one.'

'You might die, Peter – '

'So what? What would you care? I don't care. I don't care any more which one of us dies. I wish I had killed you. I wish I was dead!'

I could no longer resist. I ran to him, but he backed away. 'Please,' I said. 'Please don't say that. I'll see what I can do. I've always tried to do my best for you, or what I thought was for the best. All I wanted was for you to be happy. I didn't want things to go wrong for you the way they did for me.'

He took time to consider this, and replied, 'I know that.'

'Then tell me what it was that I did wrong.'

For a while it seemed he would not answer, lost in thoughts that left no trace on his face. I was about to repeat myself when, with a suddenness as if he had only just heard me, he said, 'I don't know. Maybe nothing. Maybe it was nothing to do with you. Maybe you did the best you could.'

It didn't sound like that, though. He said it to hurt. He knew it would hurt me. He didn't say anything else after that.

46

The trial was held two days later. Peter wanted to wear his Guards uniform.

'Certainly not,' said Beulah.

'Yes,' I said.

'If you let him, then you'll have to let all of them, those that are Guards. And you'll have to let Dominic wear his Councillor's robes.'

Dominic had also got mixed up in this. I suppose it was bound to happen. He always was an idiot. I had thought he was Beulah's, heart and soul, but I suppose even his idiocy could not prevent the realisation that he was wearing a little thin with her.

I said, 'Then let them.'

The trial lasted all day, dragged out by the repetitiveness of the evidence. Those who had been involved in the conspiracy, but who had not been rounded up in the first wave of arrests, lost no time in turning King's evidence.

What a phrase. The King didn't want their evidence. But they wanted their lives and so, in accordance with the law, they were given a free pardon in return for their evidence. There were nearly a hundred of them, all those little men – even some servants and a clerk or two. They would have cut the King's throat without a second thought if everything had gone according to plan; but since it had not, they turned around and with equal eagerness cut the throat of the King's brother. Beulah repeatedly expressed her astonishment at how widely the net of conspiracy had been thrown. I couldn't care about it one way or the other. Peter was involved, so it really made no difference how many others were implicated as well. Those witnesses for the Crown's prosecution were guiltier by far than any of the defendants. Whichever way they turned they were traitors, either to the King or to me. A hundred of them were not worth one of the red hairs on Peter's head; but four or five would have been enough to condemn him.

The trial was held in the Hall of Justice. The King sat in that throne suspended from the ceiling. Beulah had examined all the witnesses previously, but I had not. This was the first time I heard their sordid little stories of treason piled on treason. I grew more nauseous as the day wore on, partly because of what they were telling me, partly because of the way the throne slowly pivoted from side to side, and partly because it was all so dully, brutally monotonous.

The accused had no defence to offer.

Our defence against the world is a suspension of belief. I think Caryllac wrote that, in his youth. Or words to that effect.

It must have been someone with a morbid sense of humour who arranged to hang that throne from the ceiling.

Terrible how all these trivialities seem to fit together and compound into the appearance of meaning something, because they don't, not really; that they seem to, I think, is supposed to make us feel better. Secure, somehow. Justified.

The King swung back and forth in his throne.

I gave the impression of listening, but in fact I was off in the clouds. I soon realised they were all using different words to say the same thing, in different voices: different degrees of self-excusal.

All through that day I was obsessed by the idea that this wasn't really happening. I knew that it was, of course; but if I tried to focus my mind on it and treat it like reality, I couldn't. I would immediately think: This is too ridiculous. It's silly. Peter wouldn't want to kill me. What are they all playing at?

Beulah told me, several years later, that from time to time I smiled as I sat there.

The trial came to an end. People were looking expectantly at me. Beulah told me to make a sign, which I did, and the accused were led away in single file.

Beulah took me to the offices, locked me in, and talked to me.

It is not true that I took refuge behind the letter of the law. The law was the one place I could not hide either myself or him. It is not true that I could have saved him if I wanted to. I wanted to. My personal feelings were not at issue, and by that point I could not contemplate saving him. It is not true that I took this opportunity to assert my position as King. In fact that is the most absurd lie of all. Peter had accused me of being a failure as a King, and I have never denied it. I would with all my heart have continued to be one if that could have saved him. I have never had one-tenth the pride that he had, and I would never have sacrificed him in order to prove something that was not true. I could say that I was so shocked, stunned and bewildered by events and by the drawn-out trial, and because Beulah would not let me go to sleep, that she found it easy to make me do what she wanted. I was all these things, but even if I had not been it would have made no difference to the outcome. The law took this opportunity to exhibit its unbreakable authority over the King. It is only the law which maintains the King where he is, and the whole of society in ordered subservient rank beneath him. For him to treat it as if it does not exist is to invite his own destruction. The King is far more a prisoner of the law than any of his subjects. I cannot love the law, but I had no choice about respecting it. If I had ignored it, I would not have lived long. The King makes the precedent. The King is the law. Break the law, kill the King: every crime is regicide. Peter had brought himself within the jurisdiction of the law, and once he had done that it was too late to do anything to rescue him.

Beulah paced round and round the room, talking non-stop: 'They have to be executed. All of them. There's no way round it. It's the law.'

I said, 'Mercy can be a useful tool, for a King.'

'Not this time. They'll have to be executed. Letting them off with anything lighter is just throwing ourselves into danger. They are guilty. And it will discourage the others.'

'What others?'

'Whatever others there might be.'

Men like my father, women like Beulah.

'Peter most of all,' she continued. 'You have to show them, we have to show them that no one is above the law, not even the King's brother. He's the ringleader – '

'Nikolas – '

'Peter is the highest ranking, so inevitably he's the ringleader in people's eyes. He's the one they were going to make King.'

I hardly ever thought about that. It seemed so incidental, his wanting to be King, or so everyone said. If he really did. If he really had wanted it – if he had come to me and asked to have it, put his case, I think I would have given it to him if I could. I would have given him anything that was in my power to give. Except I believe that what he wanted was a figment of his imagination, and not the thing as it really is.

I said, 'Oh, he wouldn't have liked it so much.'

'Reyhnard! He wanted to kill you. And all of us. Kill you and all of us, kill you and all of us, kill you . . . '

I don't believe it. I can't. I don't know which is worse, to absolve him of any true intent and thus say that he died for no reason, or to believe that he really meant to kill me. I loved Peter, I brought him up. I spent my whole life with him. How can I believe that he wanted to kill me? Didn't he understand what it means, to be killed? Didn't he know me at all?

Beulah said, 'He wanted to murder you. And all of us. You can't possibly dream of giving him a pardon, Reyhnard, you'll never be safe again.'

A King may say to his servants: Go, and they go; Come, and they come; Do this, and they do it – after they've cleared it with Beulah. Or after I've made sure she won't oppose me. Or as long as it's not against the law. But I could not say: Come on then, come out of there – because I was not allowed. It is for this reason that I say: If I am a King, then what is a King? It is nothing the man isn't, nothing better, nothing more. Oh Peter, it is not worth having. Not at that price. Not for what you have made me pay for it.

The King cannot dream of pardoning traitors. But I have dreamt it, many times, and woken up believing it is true.

At last she let me go. I went to see him. He was curled like a puppy on his bed, knees drawn up to his chest. His face was buried in the pillow, but when he heard my footsteps he looked up. I almost turned and ran from the dread in his face.

'We never meant to hurt you,' he said. 'It's not true, what they said today. She probably paid them to lie. We wouldn't have killed you. Just her, the bitch. I would have got rid of her for you. You could have gone anywhere you liked, you and Madeleine, you'd have liked that better, wouldn't you, really? I never meant to hurt you, Nardo, I swear, I couldn't ever. I love you. Please believe me, believe that at least, it's true, I swear, please believe me, please don't go away.'

I could have cried but knew I mustn't. He was frightened enough already. I sat down next to him. Crawling up, he laid his heavy red head in my lap.

Perhaps I am entitled to no consolation, but I can't help looking for it. I wonder whether it is possible to punish someone for the crime they have committed, and even before you have punished them, during it, and for ever after, whether you can also be forgiving them.

'I'm so scared,' he said. 'I don't want to die, Nardo.'

'Neither do I.'

'But I told you, I was never going to hurt you, I told you. I swear. Please believe me, please – '

'I believe you.'

He stopped shivering, calmed down. His hair was cut very close to his head. It was stubbly, like a bristle brush. I ran my hand back and forth over its harshness.

After a while he said, almost cheerfully, 'Well, what are you going to do to me?'

We know what the law prescribes for traitors. Geraint, and the rebellious Fahlraecs, and the robbers of the Treasury, and Bronwen if she had not killed herself: they were all buried alive.

'I don't know,' I lied. There was no longer a reason not to. This was the full extent of his treason, this is what his actions had betrayed us into: honesty would have been cruelty, and lying was an act of love. I thought that if I could save him from nothing else, I would save him from fear, at least until the very end.

'Don't be afraid,' I said. 'Go to sleep.'

I know now that every crime, however small, whatever its motives, has its retribution just as much as the great crimes have. I should have told him. In some ways it is the thing I regret most of all, because it is the one thing I know I could have done for him. I should have offered him the chance that Bronwen, and Caryad, and perhaps Alexi took. I should have let him die with dignity, like a soldier; put his death into his own hands and allowed him a choice. It is so hard for me to remember what I felt then and what went on: I think, maybe, that I didn't tell him partly because I hardly believed myself that it would happen.

They were brought in one by one for me to pass sentence. Peter was brought in first. He smiled at me confidently. He trusted me, and I had told him not to be afraid. I realised I could not do it. What am I saying? I had known all along that I could not do it. I don't know what would have happened if Beulah hadn't been there. She was sitting below me, and when she saw my face she reached up to snatch the paper out of my hands. I jumped forward to grab it back, but not before she had read out his sentence.

Peter said 'No' – just that, so quietly. No. The Guards took hold of him by the arms and he started to struggle. Stupidly, I remember thinking, 'I could have told them he doesn't like to be touched.'

It all happened so quickly. He was calling my name. Beulah told them to take him away and do it. They were taking him out of the room; I was trying to say something, but I can't remember what, and I couldn't speak. I felt as if I didn't belong there, or wasn't there; as if I was watching it from a distance, and they were all people I had never seen before. Peter kept shouting at me to do something. I went on hearing his screams for hours after they took him away, as if he was still in the room.

What did you expect me to do, Peter? What do you think I am? I couldn't save you, I'm not a God. I thought you knew that. I thought that's why you did it, because you knew that I sat in that throne like a log: do nothing, say nothing, feel nothing.

III

. . . *my younger brother whom I loved, the end of mortality has overtaken him. I wept for him seven days and nights till the worm fastened on him. Because of my brother I am afraid of death; because of my brother I stray through the wilderness. His fate lies heavy upon me. How can I be silent, how can I rest? He is dust and I shall die also and be laid in the earth for ever.*

THE EPIC OF GILGAMESH

47

I woke up late this morning, frowsty-headed, and went outside for a breath of cold air. In the lee of the sunshine – though that is perhaps not the right phrase – on those parts of the grass that had not yet been liberated from shadow, a sharp glittering made it look as if it had been dusted with ground diamonds. Elsewhere the sun had melted this first, mild frost. I haven't been able to write for a while, because I have been harvesting. During the day I was too busy, during the night too exhausted; and when it was over my fingers had become so callused I couldn't hold the pen. I broke my back with the rest of them to get the harvest in, racing the inevitable frost.

A day in which we learn something new is a day well spent, according to that old tag of Isumbard Shoemaker's, but in my case it was three days before I learnt to handle the sickle any more profitably than a seven-year-old peasant child could have done. Most times I was detailed to pitchfork duty. Cackhanded as my efforts were, I have at least earned us our winter's share of bread. The camaraderie of an autumn field and aching muscles! What a fine and noble thing, and how good for the soul! Right up Caryllac's street.

Over the past few months I've been building up muscles that would not have shamed Alexi. I've been digging potatoes and turnips, patching barn walls, building stocks and pens. He'd grin at all the good clean dirt in my life and say: 'Well, that's not quite what I meant.'

It's meant to be so morally uplifting – I suppose because half the time you're labouring too earnestly to think of anything else, and the rest of the time you're too tired to do anything else. Anyway I couldn't refuse to participate when they asked, or rather told me to lend a hand. Even the women and children join in. And we have to stay alive.

I stood in that field, pitching the mown grain, stripped to the waist with the heat of hard work, although it was a chilly day. At first I often dropped a forkload or failed to aim it into the cart, but after a while I got better at it. Sometimes I took my turn with a sickle. I couldn't make sweeping arcs such as the peasants describe, but tentative nicks, bringing down perhaps a dozen stalks.

'What are you playing at?' Serena's father shouted across the golden-brown corn. 'Saw at it, don't hack. Anyone'd think you was eating your tea.'

'Now look at here,' he said, coming over to take the sickle from my hands. 'See them teeth? They'll do the job. You don't have to mangle it. Now you watch me – '

He swung from the waist, cutting a wide deep swathe, the corn falling like a retreating wave at the touch of the blade. Perfect as Hans on a horse. Perfect as Madeleine when she walked.

I went back to the pitchfork.

By the end of the first day my hands were red and swollen, painfully full of splinters. Serena picked them out with as much deftness as she is capable of, and smeared my hands with some sort of fat. Small pieces of straw, irritating and invisible, worked their way into my clothes and my hair, and even my skin. When I thought I had brushed them all out, I'd feel another one pricking insistently between my shoulder blades. I suppose I could have cried ineptitude and got out of the rest of it; but I don't think I could, not really. It was good to have no option. I never noticed the hours passing as I worked away in the fields. The sun, just like a sickle, arced from east to west, and I forgot how much it hurt.

And what would your father say, sir?

'I never knew that boy had it in him.'

Perhaps.

Would he be surprised, would he be proud to see his son joining in, hardening his palms with a man's labour, trying his best, wielding his sickle like a sword disguised?

A *man's* labour?

He'd say, 'I always knew that boy wasn't even fit to cut hay with the peasants.'

Probably.

On the last day they held a little competition, for which purpose half a field had been retained unharvested. It was a fine day, warmish and dry. Six of the best mowers in the village came with their prize sickles. They name their sickles, as we name our swords: Cutthroat, and Shearfast, and Eagle . . . Peter's sword, when he was in the Guards, was called Steelbite. Anyway, the object of the competition was to see which of the men could mow his strip of field the fastest. Great cheers and oaths and bets from the assembled villagers, and Serena got quite flushed with the excitement of the race, shouting and clapping her hands.

We were sitting a little way up a hillock, apart from the crowd, where Serena would have a good view and not be jostled. The duration of this competition was something over half an hour, and in the middle of it Serena's father wandered across to us. He seemed hardly to notice his daughter, but to me he said, 'Well then, young man, and I bet you wish you was out there with them.'

I am mildly curious to know why he is becoming increasingly friendly towards me; but only mildly. I assume it is because of Serena's pregnancy. Aside from that I have no idea. 'No, not really,' I said.

'Hands still giving you trouble, hmm?' He bent down and patted me heavily on the shoulder. 'You ought to be proud of them, shows you done real work. I'd of had to be blind to see you wasn't no farmer, but you've worked hard and that's something to respect.'

He straightened his back and put up his hand to shade his eyes, gazing at the competitors. 'That's the test of a man,' he said. 'To win that, that's something. When I was their age I won it, six times I won and five of them in a row. Wouldn't think it to look at me now, but on the Gods' honours. Six times. I was like the King.'

'How splendid,' I said, in answer to the tone of his voice. I had toyed with, and rejected, 'How nice'.

'Yes, it's something to remember. That I was the best.'

He doesn't expect me to be communicative; he does not need an interlocutor. So he went on, 'It's a record, five times in a row. Well, well, young man, you never know, maybe your son will take after his granddad. Maybe he'll win it, come seventeen, eighteen years from now. Old Serena's a tough thing, aren't you, girl?'

Serena nodded mutely.

'Hoping it's a grandson,' he said. 'I haven't got any of my grandchildren here, except the little girl. All my kids have gone off to Rayalled . . . '

The conquering hero was crowned with a wreath of the rye he had cut; the rest of his patch was gathered up, to be bound and presented on the Temple altar. The competitors, panting and glistening redly, wiped their brows with the back of their hands and gulped mugs of beer.

As soon as night fell it got very cold. The festivities went on, dance, drink and song to celebrate the store of food that will see them through the winter. The smoke from the Temple chimney smelled faintly of bread. Serena is too pregnant to join in with their wild whirling abandon, and it's hardly the sort of thing I would feel like taking part in, so we went back to the hut. I was about to write 'we went home' – words will get very slack if you don't keep an eye on them. Like ill-trained Guards. Let your attention wander for one minute and there they are, sloping and lounging all over the place, when they should be shaking their spears in defence of my meaning. My little army.

The ranks of my little army are full of gaps at the moment. Some have deserted, some are absent without leave, and some I have executed for dereliction of duty. However, like any commander worth his boots, I acknowledge that it may be partly my fault. Perhaps I do not marshal them correctly. Perhaps I play with them too much – this is bad for discipline. I had better abandon this little conceit and get on with what I was saying.

As we came through the door Serena uttered a weak cry, clutched her stomach, and staggered into a chair – my chair, in front of my table, where she has never sat before. She still has three months to go, so it was with some alarm that I groped for a candle, lit it and held the flame up to illuminate her face.

Instead of the look of stubborn pain which I expected to see, I saw a smile so much like joy that I was astonished. Self-joy, generated from within, a human delight I've never seen her exhibit before. She was pressing a hand on her stomach.

'What is it, Serena? Are you all right?'

She grabbed my wrist – I suppose she has seen other women, perhaps her mother, do this – and with more strength than I knew she had pulled me towards her, substituting my hand where hers had been. 'I can feel him,' she said. 'Feel!'

I didn't really want to, but before I could draw back I had felt him too, a definite motion underneath my hand, the kick or punch of a tiny hand or foot. He battered furiously as if in protest against his confinement – a person with a will of his own. I couldn't have been more amazed if I had suddenly heard him speak. Not once in all of Beulah's pregnancies did she grab my hand and make me acquainted with that second person tenanting her body. I've never really thought, before, that babies are alive before they're born.

'Does it hurt?' I asked Serena. 'Is it all right?'

'I think so. It doesn't hurt. Feels funny.'

I wanted so much to ask, What's it like? What is it like to feel that second heart beating beneath yours? For I have held both my little brother and my beautiful sister breast to breast against my skin, and felt each heart beating as if it were my own. Serena, tell me what it's like to know that the flesh and blood of your love is tucked away safe inside you, warm and protected, where you can stand between him and any danger. Once they're outside in the world, roaming all over the place faster than you can keep up with them, following their own inclinations, it's so hard to keep them from harm. They don't even want you to. Oh Serena, it's so impossible it will break your heart. Hans broke Alexi's heart; he cracked all our hearts a little, and he killed my father. It's difficult to believe that great man loved anyone, but he did, he loved his son Hans. After all this time I still cling to that fact, his one extenuating virtue.

Serena touched my arm to ask for attention. I looked at her, and for a moment, I suppose, a short moment, I did wish that it was mine, in a way. Something to leave behind that was half myself, that did not die either before me or with me, but somehow defied the laws of mortality to pass me on.

I know that's crazy, really. I more than most people should know what a pipe dream it is. It didn't work for my father. And if it works for anyone, it should have worked for him. He had five children. No matter how much I loved my brothers and sister, I can't stop them being dead. No matter how much their flesh and blood I am, no matter how faithfully and continually I remember them, their lives have ended. Children confer no immortality, not the sort I want. Not the sort that would stop me being afraid. Perhaps they are a consolation, I don't know, not having any. But they do not constitute a reprieve.

Serena's hand was insistent.

'What is it?' I asked her.

She said, 'What do you want to call him?'

I crouched down beside her, holding her stub fingers. 'Don't you think you should wait until it's born? It might be a girl.'

She looked at me with a grave sincerity, and said, 'What name do you like best?'

'Oh, you shouldn't ask me. You should choose it. You've done the work, it's your baby.'

'The father always names,' she informed me earnestly.

'But Serena – '

'Don't they do that where you come from?'

'No – but Serena – '

Fortunately I understood then what she was driving at. She thinks I am the father.

This realisation saved me from blurting out something I might regret, by rendering me speechless. Even now I can hardly find the words to deal with it. I don't know how she has managed to forget, but she has. And so do dogs, or any animal – if you take it and show it kindness, it forgets the kicks and cruelties it received from other men.

It's a waste of time protesting that she can't possibly have forgotten, because she has, and no amount of incredulity on my part is going to alter that fact. After thinking it over for a while, I now feel that it isn't as surprising as it first appeared. So, given that she has forgotten, or wiped it out, or lost her memory, or whatever – even given that, how did she manage to promote me to father? This is a far more fantastic feat of mental contortionism. I've never touched her. I've never kissed her, except on the forehead. I've done nothing to qualify for the role of progenitor. Yet it seems this does not matter to her.

It makes me think that perhaps she has an instinctive logic I've failed to give her credit for. How could something so good as a baby result from something so bad as a rape? In the simplest way possible in her simple mind, it did not add up, and so she substituted me. I am at a loss to know how she has done this. I don't know what kind of primitive feminine arithmetic she has used. All I know is that she believes it. The whole village thought it, and now she thinks so too.

What can I say to her? Serena, don't you remember when you went looking for your goat at night, and strange men jumped out at you from the dark, and pulled your hair and broke your jaw and hurt you, and you were so frightened and bewildered you didn't want to see me? Don't you remember that that's where your baby comes from?

I could also say: the facts of the matter make it quite impossible for me to be the father, and wishful thinking is not enough. Trust me in this. No one knows more about wishful thinking than I do. But it's a bit late for that argument. She has already made her wish come true.

I could say these things to her, of course I could. I could point out the facts of life of which she is astonishingly ignorant. And I am many things, but I am not cruel. So in fact, I cannot say these things to her. I cannot force her to remember. Alexi, you see, I'm not as selfish as you said. I know she has given me a great deal; in her terms, everything she has. She has asked for nothing from me, at least not in words. It's not much to give in return, that I keep my mouth shut and let her go on believing I'm the father. Considering the extraordinary way her mind works, she probably wouldn't believe the truth if I did tell her.

I've had so many fatherhoods foisted on to me, and once I didn't know if it was true or not. With Serena I know it's not true, but at least this time the girl believes it. It's not as if it would harm me in any way. The whole village already believes it, and it's probably due to this that they have accepted me to such an extent so quickly.

There is a great deal that I would like to ask Serena. I tried asking her things when I first came here, but I soon learnt her limits. Too often I threw her into confusion by asking questions beyond her understanding. Even what she does feel, she mostly cannot articulate. So instead of talking with her I have tried to read her face. Most things show up there. But what I will never know is when she forgot the rape, and made me the father.

I wonder what plans and dreams she has for this child. How does she picture him – or her – in her mind? What face does she give him? What character? Bold and reckless? Or shy and thoughtful? I wonder what sort of future she sees for him. A peasant like her father, the king of the reapers? Or something better, perhaps an education? Perhaps she expects that I'll teach him. Maybe she thinks I'll strike rich one day with my clerk's work, and we'll buy or build a house, a proper wooden one like her father's. Can she see herself cradling her son in her arms by the firelight, both listening wide-eyed to my stories about Tsvingtori? Or coming in with a frothy pail of milk, smiling to see her black-haired boy crawling in and out of his father's lap, learning to trace big letters in red and green ink? As a matter of fact, if he was my son he could just as easily have red hair as black, it runs in my family.

What am I saying? Come to that, what am I going to do? I never planned to stay in this village. I haven't thought about going anywhere else in particular; I've never looked beyond the present hour. If I considered the future at all it wasn't to see myself still here. And now I'm saddled with another bloody family that isn't even mine. The whole situation is nothing to do with me. I'm a bystander at the scene of the accident roped in against his will. I don't love her and I didn't make her love me and it's not my responsibility.

Everything was so straightforward until I found out what she thinks. Why does she think at all? She's too stupid to think. When she does think it all comes out wrong. This absurd encumbrance is the one thing above all others that I can do without. Even if I wanted to marry her, which I don't, I couldn't because Beulah, typically, is still alive.

Oh Nardo, I never thought you'd take any notice of silly little laws like that.

Dead or alive, there is Madeleine. Even if I could break my faith with her, which I won't, and even if I could forget her for as short a time as half an hour, which I cannot . . . Even if I had loved her with one-hundredth the love I do have for her, I would never betray her with Serena. That would be like spitting in Madeleine's face. It would be to cut off her hair, to close her green eyes. Serena, of all people. She's not mine. She's nothing to do with me. She's a native, a plain ignorant peasant, and I may owe her a debt of gratitude but that is all I owe her.

She can't make me stay, not if I don't want to. What am I worrying about? I detect in myself a note of concern as to what the village will think. Well, you can't sink much lower than that, though you made a good try, Reyhnard, that night when you didn't run after Peter because you were afraid of what the court might think. If I had run after him, tackled him, I could have made him listen, even though he was stronger than I. I could have persuaded him to talk. Only I didn't. And he didn't tell me. So after that, how can I care about what the peasants might think? How can I even think about what they might think about? They are as non-existent as the court. Even if they call me names and curse me, who cares? I won't care when I'm gone from here. I'll never see them again. One morning I'll pack up and go as suddenly as I came, and that will be the last they ever see of me. After all, Serena will have her baby, which is what she really wants.

Yes, I do think this is cruelty, a sort of cruelty, perhaps. But it is a necessary cruelty. I never told her I would stay. When I feel trapped, I have to run. I was cornered once before and I'm not going to let it happen again.

Time can take its course, for the moment. I'm here for the winter, come what may. Serena's baby should be born at the beginning of the new year, and she'll have recuperated long before spring. Peasants are tough. And her father does seem to be taking an interest, if not in her, at least in her baby. Maybe he'll let her move back in with them. He'll have his grandson – if it is a boy, which I hope it is, because that will make everything easier.

I've wasted far too much paper on this. There's no problem. It can be solved as easily as one footstep follows another. My decision is recorded, and the subject is now closed.

48

We had tethered our horses, my sister and I, and were walking along the patchy stretch of coarse grass and sandy earth that lies between the beach and the pine woods. It was autumn on Ksaned Kaled. The mist sat low, curling in and out among the tree trunks. It was morning. The sun was a pale effort behind low grey clouds. Pewtery waves rattled over the pebbles. In the distance was a cliff, a sort of bland dusty colour, dotted with black and white birds. A mile or so out to sea I could distinguish the faint shape of a ship with bright red sails.

'I wonder where it's going?' I said.

'Andariah, I suppose, by the direction it's sailing,' said Madeleine, who was walking behind me.

'That's probably the last we'll see this year.'

'Next year we'll see it coming back.' I heard her footsteps slow, and she exclaimed, 'Oh look!' as I turned around.

She stooped and picked something up to show me. It was a perfect pine cone, eight or nine inches long, frosted with dry gum at the tip of each woody scale. My sister was wearing a brown wool dress. A knot of material at each hip lifted the hem out of the dirt, revealing the scuffed toes of her boots. The long black tail of her plait dangled below the hem of a grey shawl she had wound around her head.

My eye fell on something that appealed to me: a thick straight branch, four feet long, lying in the grass. I took it up and started peeling the green bark away from the satiny wood beneath. I've always enjoyed doing that.

Madeleine lifted the cone to her nose and sniffed. 'I'm going to take it home,' she announced.

'You should give it to Thomas,' I said. 'The pine cone's his emblem, isn't it?'

'Is it? Anyway, I'm going to keep it.'

The bark came off in long, satisfyingly fat strips.

Madeleine pushed the shawl back and threw up her chin, taking deep breaths. 'I like it here, it's so quiet,' she said. 'So lovely. And everything smells so nice.'

'Well let's build a house here,' I said. 'Or why not a palace? Let's build another palace. Let's move the court down here.'

'That would spoil it.'

'Well then, let's build a lean-to. The court can stuff themselves.'

Going down a little hillock on to the beach, I started thrusting my peeled stick into the sand and pebbles, enjoying the force of pushing it, the rasping sound it made. I pulled it up, and it came out damp and muddy at the base.

Madeleine, pine cone in one hand, scrambled down beside me. 'Why are you so grumpy today?' she asked.

'I'm not grumpy.'

'Yes you are.'

'No I'm not, I've said I'm not grumpy. Just thoughtful. Grumpy is such a silly word.'

She thought about this for a moment, then walked away to sit on another clump of grass. 'I'm going to take my boots off and have a paddle.'

'It's too cold,' I said. 'You'll catch cold, probably.'

'Is it because Beulah's coming back tomorrow?'

'What?'

'That you're so thoughtful.'

'Oh. No, not at all. Madeleine, did I tell you she's having another baby?'

'Yes, you did. Last week.'

'I couldn't remember.'

'She'll have six children now.'

'When will she ever stop? She's very fecund.'

'Lady Peat is pregnant too,' Madeleine told me.

'Is she?' I was surprised. 'Surely she's too old.'

'She's only five years older than you, that's not too old.'

'You two seem to be great friends.'

'Oh no, not really. Lady Mindarah is her closest friend, they tell each other everything.'

'I tell you everything.'

'I don't like Lady Mindarah much,' said Madeleine, 'but I think Lady Peat's very nice.'

'Her husband's very good-looking,' I remarked.

'Lord Peat?'

'Of course, Peat.'

'Do you think so?'

'Don't you?'

Madeleine looked pensive, then said decisively, 'His eyes are too close together.'

'You don't have to go out of your way to find something flawed about him.'

'I'm not,' she protested. 'They are too close together, I've always thought so.'

'Did you know he's thinking of marrying his half-sister to Thomas filcValentin?'

'No, really?'

'It's a very good match for him,' I said. 'She's got a massive dowry, and he hasn't got much except his salary and a tiny estate in his cousin's Fahl.'

'She's not very pretty.'

'Well, one can't have everything. And Beulah approves. Thomas has got a great career ahead of him, he's top of her good books.'

Madeleine said, 'He is very devoted to you, you know.'

'Of course he is. He'd be devoted to a scarecrow if it had a crown on its head.'

She got up and came over to me, still clutching her pine cone, her skirts held up in her other hand. 'Reyhnard, why don't you like him?'

'You know why.'

'But he saved our lives, he – '

'I don't want to talk about it.'

'But Reyhnard, even before – that – you never liked him.'

'Why should I like him?'

'He's a good man, he really is.'

'That's no reason to like him. Has he been asking you to put in a good word for him?'

'Of course not. He hardly knows me well enough to ask that sort of thing, and anyway you know I never would, no matter who asked me – '

'It seems you like him enough for both of us.'

'Reyhnard!'

'But you always have.'

'If you don't want me to talk to him, why don't you say so?'

'Oh, I wouldn't want to be so ungrateful. Talk to him as much as you like, and while you're about it you might explain that there is no point in his trying to curry favour with me through you. It won't benefit him to rise in my opinion, because nothing's up to me. He'd be better off sucking up to Beulah. I mean, he's an idiot if he doesn't realise this, but I should think he does. I'm sure that man knows exactly what he's after. Heavens no, Madeleine, you see him just as much as you like. I wouldn't dream of spoiling your fun.'

I pushed the stick into the ground as hard as I could. It went in about two feet.

'What are you talking about?' she asked quietly.

I pulled the stick out again, grunting. 'I just don't think it's me he wants to like him.' I grabbed the stick with both hands and swung it round in the air. When I let go, it flew over the sand and crashed into the shallows. I stared at it floating on the water, and said, 'Haven't you told him yet how much you like him? I mean, he's the one you ought to tell, not me . . . '

My reserve of unfounded accusations ran out then, so I let it trail off into silence and stood there with my back to her. She made no sound. All I could hear, and see, were the waves and the birds and the wind coming in from the sea. I had an abrupt, terrifying sensation of being alone on that beach.

Needing desperately to look at her, I turned round. She was clutching her shawl, twisting the material at the base of her throat; against its grey her face was misery-white. The cloth was pulled over her brow like a hood, hiding her eyes, her head bent to gnaw her thumb. I was behaving appallingly, and I knew it. I knew it while I was doing it, but I couldn't help myself.

'Oh Madeleine – ' I rescued her hand from her mouth, and kissed that poor sad thumb. 'I'm sorry,' I apologised, kissing her hair through the shawl. 'Don't be angry with me.'

'I'm not, I'm not – '

'You would have every right to be.'

'I understand – '

'But you see, when I'm angry, when I'm upset, it's too easy for me to take it out on you. I don't mean to.'

'I understand, I don't mind – '

'You should mind, but even if you don't I have to say sorry anyway, because I am. Let's sit down.'

With my arm round her waist, I walked her back to the bank of grass. We sat together, her head on my shoulder, my hand soothing her back.

She said, 'I know I shouldn't mind when you're jealous, even when you say such strange things. I know that you know, deep down, that they're not true, those things you said.'

'I swear I don't say them to hurt you.'

'I know you don't. I do understand. But Reyhnard, you do know you haven't got any reason to be jealous, don't you?'

'It wasn't because I'm jealous – '

'Good, because you shouldn't be.'

'I got a letter from Beulah today,' I told her.

'Did you? How strange, she's coming back tomorrow.'

'Not so strange when you hear what's in it.'

'Bad news?'

It wasn't news at all, in fact. It was something years old, which I had never been told about.

'A shock,' I said.

'Not something that could hurt you?'

'I'm practically immune. No – she's freeing Nikolas.'

Madeleine frowned for a second, puzzled. 'Nikolas? But he's – '

'No,' I said. 'He's not.'

This is how it was done.

The Guards who were with him when he came in to receive his sentence had previously been given orders by Beulah, orders which the sentence did not supersede. When they took him from the hall, instead of turning right and proceeding outside, they turned left and took him back to his cell. No one saw them, because there was no one else in the corridor except three or four Guards: everyone was either in the hall or outdoors watching. Three days later, under cover of night, as the saying is, he was removed to the cells at the castle in Oysterport.

Most of the court knew, or guessed, what had happened to him, once they realised he had not been taken out for execution. I didn't know; of course I didn't know, who would tell me? Nikolas has always been well-liked and respected. Beulah gambled, rightly, that I could not bring myself to witness the actual executions, that I would be too lost in my mind to know what was going on.

The reasons she gave me for what she had done were these: that Nikolas was too popular and admired to execute; that up until the time of the conspiracy his record had been unblemished; and that she felt he should not have to pay the ultimate price for a youthful aberration. That is what she called it. Finally, she saved him because he has the rare true Rorhah gift for military matters, a talent she considered too valuable to lose. I make no comment on this. They are her reasons.

He had been in prison for four years, and his hair – she told me – had gone white.

What is four years compared to eternity? What is his white hair next to my punishment? Peter will never return, and this, Nikolas's return, was like dancing on my brother's grave and laughing in my face. How can she trust a man like that? He is a double traitor. He betrayed me, he betrayed Peter – he is a triple traitor, he betrayed me with my own brother. Nikolas used Peter like a sword or a noose, like something inanimate, when he was my beautiful, vibrant, fair-skinned child of a brother.

I know just how he used him – how he would have used Peter if everything had gone according to plan. I ought to say that I did not know this then, that day on the beach; Beulah told me about it much later, months later, when she no longer needed to keep it from me.

Nikolas had his own secret little scheme. After we were dead, Madeleine and I, he would have turned around and attacked Peter. The Guards were Nikolas's men, he was their Commander, he possessed their loyalty. He would have killed Peter, too. And then he would have married Beulah. And then he would have been King.

That is what she told me. She said he confessed all this to her in secret, the night before Peter died. And she believed him. Speaking of mercy, that's not mercy, that's her own vanity. But I don't know – I doubt she'd have spared Dominic just because he'd told her he wanted to marry her. Beulah has no mercy. She has no virtues at all. All she has is a dynamic pragmatism.

It's not simply because I hate him that Nikolas is completely beyond my ken. I used to think I understood him, until I found all this out. How can people want to be King? It's only because they don't know. It's as if I had some great diamond sewn up inside my body against my will: people would kill me for it, not really caring or even thinking about me, the hapless host – wanting only that diamond. It's as if I was one of those whales slaughtered for the sake of their ambergris. People wanting to do away with all of me in order to get one tiny thing that wasn't even a part of me.

I know it's true that I wasn't much of a King. I always knew that I would never be any good at it. I never pretended otherwise. But even if Peter had no faith in the King, he should have trusted me. If he had told me, if he had trusted me, he would not be dead. But since he treated me like a King, I was compelled to treat with him as a King. And since he did not tell me, since he did not trust me, if the King had not killed him, Nikolas would have. There was no escape for him except in trusting me.

Beulah wrote to me in the new language she was affecting in her letters, flowery and stilted:

He is penitent and ashamed, grievously and sincerely remorseful for the suffering he has caused, and humbly grateful for the mercy he has been shown . . .

She is so clever. Not once in that letter did she use an active verb with the pronoun 'you' or 'I'. It was all in the passive: 'He has been shown'; not 'You have shown', or 'I have shown', or even 'We have shown'.

He has exhibited every intention of deporting himself in future as a loyal and devoted subject and servant. He has been sufficiently chastised.

He is to be released from his present incarceration, and will be allowed to return to his castle in Rayalled, where he will remain under house arrest in exile from the court. He will not be permitted to travel a distance of more than three miles in radius from the walls of his castle, nor will he be allowed to receive any visitors whatsoever, excepting those members of his family in the first degree of relationship to him, and those who have been issued with a warrant . . .

He ought to be dead. He ought to be rotting away. He ought to be eyeless and noseless and stinking. Instead, he's walking around under the open sky. He can see the sun, and when spring comes he will smell it, and his blood will leap and sing with the joy of being alive. What do I care if his hair has gone white? It's still rooted in his scalp, it's still growing. He can scratch it and brush it and cut it, when he ought to have a skinless skull.

Madeleine said, 'He's never coming back to court, is he.'

'No.'

'I don't think I could bear ever to look at him again.'

When she said this, I thought for a moment that I could easily, with pleasure, have looked on him dead. To see that handsome, confident face mouldering and mottled with death's purple leprosy, those eye sockets empty, that grin which is due to a lack of lips, not amusement – but the truth is, I know I couldn't have borne it. To have seen him dead, or anyone dead, would be to know what Peter looks like now. To see him alive would be to remember what Peter no longer is. Either way, to look at Nikolas, or even to think about him, is a horror.

Why did Beulah write me this letter, when she could so easily have told me herself the next day? I don't know. It might have been so that, by the time she returned, I would have spent the first blast of my anger. Not that my temper ever bothered her, but with a day to think it over in I would have worked out some answers for myself, and so have fewer questions to pester her with.

In fact I wasn't angry; that is, anger wasn't my dominant reaction. It was all old feelings, like a scar that never stops aching, but aches worse in bad weather. The only way to cope with them is to ignore them.

Madeleine did not ask me, 'What will·you do?' and so I did not have to say, 'Nothing.'

49

After my brother's death, as soon as I was capable of planning something and seeing it through to the end – which was not for three or four months – I arranged for the court to remove to Ksaned Kaled. We lived there for the next four years, and I had every intention of continuing to live there until I died. This was made easier for me by Beulah, who commuted tirelessly between the island and the capital, spending one month in Tsvingtori for every three she spent on Ksaned Kaled. When she could she travelled by sea, and in the winter she went overland – it is to her, incidentally, that the excellent road which traverses the southeast of Brychmachrye is due.

On the other hand it made life more difficult for the court – not that this affected my decision. The most faithful and most ambitious among them trotted backwards and forwards with her, but it is an expensive business to maintain three establishments: one in Tsvingtori, one on Ksaned Kaled, and their own estates; and their incomes no longer stretched as far as they previously did, because Beulah had put up the taxes in order to finance her new system of administration. She did this as soon as I had made her understand that I would never return to the capital. There was less trouble over the new taxes than she expected: a few half-hearted moans and groans, and several deputations from the northern towns, but on the whole they acquiesced quietly. The memory of the executions was still fresh.

There are no marks on the shameful graves to show who lies there. Criminals are stripped of all lives, now and in the future. They are wiped out: we are not even to remember at what spot their bodies manure the earth. Graves are humiliations, signs of failure for the individual within them and the society he belonged to. Only traitors have graves. If the graves were left unhidden, they would stand as a memorial to the crimes that made them necessary. They are filled in, levelled down, ploughed over; they are planted with grass, or crops, or trees and flowers. Integrated into the landscape.

I never saw where they put him. All I know is that it is somewhere in the grounds. I never went outside. I didn't dare look out of the window. I was afraid of seeing bare black earth.

As time passed, I began to derive a distant pleasure from watching the court tossing and turning in indecision. Stay here with him? Travel with her? What will it cost? What are the benefits? Where's the best advantage? Where shall we go, what shall we do, can we afford it? It amused me. I had no part in it.

I cannot go back to Tsvingtori. I can never walk through those gardens, or ride in those fields and forests. He might be anywhere. I can never again eat the carrots and apples grown in the Palace grounds. I can't drink the milk from the cows that graze in its meadows.

Madeleine and I made our home on Ksaned Kaled.

Four years of trying to make myself understand again why people exclaim with delight at a lovely day. It was like learning to walk all over again, in a way. I would think I had mastered it, but then suddenly come up against a hard memory, and collapse. Trying to understand why one should stop and listen to a bird's song, why fresh bread smells delicious, why Ksaned Kaled is beautiful. Small things, but one must begin with them, make them matter again. I suppose, to put it this way, that each day was entire to itself, the one to concentrate on getting through with as little suffering as possible. Then night would come, and unconsciousness; after that, dawn, and it would begin again. Four years of trying, not to forget him, but to discover a way to remember him without pain.

Time passed and I came to be able to do this, more or less. Often more, but too often less. As time passed, a growing proportion of the court surrendered the frantic, costly to-ing and fro-ing and settled down on the island. Even if you do not have a good reason to stay, if you merely have no great reason to go, Ksaned Kaled works its medicine upon you, that tranquil singing isle. Even the least poetic and sensitive are gradually wooed by flowers between the sky and the sea, and find they cannot bear to leave.

At first it was their trips to Tsvingtori that dwindled, but in time their visits to their own estates became less and less frequent.

Beulah, surveying the somnolent court, said to me, 'Very impressive. Your father often said what a good idea it would be if he could lock them all up quietly, out of harm's way – and now you've stumbled upon it, quite by accident.'

She laughed, booming among the sleeping tiles.

In the summer before the autumn of which I am writing, an embassy came from Andariah bringing a tentative suit for my sister's hand. The ambassador, resplendent in his gaudy foreign clothes, presented the request in an almost offhand manner – as if he mentally shrugged a shoulder to say: Just doing what I'm told.

It wasn't King Francis who was asking for her. He, as I'm sure I've written, has a barren wife, and his mistress is that Rohaise who long years ago had been admired and rejected by my elder brothers. The King's younger brother, Prince Edvard, was – still is, I suppose – a homosexual, as the whole world knows perfectly well; nevertheless it was to this man, closer in age to sixty than fifty, that they had wanted to engage my sister.

It was so absurd I almost laughed in their faces. If I had, I think the ambassador would probably have laughed with me. Beulah chuckled to herself over the paperwork, beautifully phrased letters of refusal.

We could afford to laugh, especially Beulah. She had three sons and two daughters, with another on the way. Her progeny were all lined up to take my place. But for Andariah it was a serious problem. Francis and Edvard are the last surviving men in their direct family, but they have a horde of cousins, and various more distant relations, who will split the country in civil war if neither of them does their duty and provides an heir.

Beulah told me they had already tried for princesses from Chatienne and Duccarn, without luck. Our ambassador in Andariah had written to tell her this.

I said, 'Well, they can always have a go in Ruffashpah. As a last resort. Maybe I should suggest it.'

Beulah snorted, then added seriously, 'But try to be nice to them, if you can. What they're asking is ludicrous, of course, but it wouldn't do to offend them. I'm rather interested in one of their little girls.'

'Whatever for?'

'For Basal, who else?'

When I told my sister why the embassy had come, she almost went into shock, standing there wide-eyed and speechless.

'So you don't want to go, then?' I teased her.

'Good God, how can you – ' She saw my grin and started laughing. I took her hand to kiss all her fingers.

After a while, she remarked, 'All the same, it's nice to know someone wants me.'

'Don't sound so wistful. I want you, you silly girl.'

The ambassador took my refusal with another mental shrug, as no less than he'd expected. He was not put out – neither literally nor figuratively: he would not be put out, but settled in for a long stay, obviously in no hurry to get home. By the time the onset of bad weather made it imperative for him to begin his journey, he had wooed and won for himself a daughter of the Fahlraec of Kyrah.

'Looks like the end of his career,' was all Beulah said.

The Andarians departed, and the court went back to sleep.

Except for Beulah, who never slept.

Beulah, unlike me, needs no metaphors, no imagery, because she grew into her own imagery. The more she did and the more she amassed unto herself – work, authority, power, children – the larger, physically, she became.

It is because I cannot help it that I sometimes try to imagine how things would have been without her: how we would have lived and how some, perhaps, would not have died. But the reason I so often compare her in my mind to death is because she appears to be a thing of massive inevitability, too strong for me to shift or conquer. And so it seems that the life I had despite her was the only life I could ever have had.

50

I remember a beautiful scene.

The alabaster bowls are full of chrysanthemums, their papery globes the colour of bronze. The sun shines bright and dusty from the west, breaking the walls and floor into patches of tawny light and blue shade. Some of the rays are caught in a beaker of water that stands on the table; some of the rays halo my sister and stream around her, so that where they fall her black hair is gold, and where they retreat her skin is velvety purple. She curves among the sunbeams, sitting on her heels, her back uncurling upwards. Her hair catches in the rough weave of her dress, fanning and veiling her. A lock loops and purls down as she picks up a china doll; she twists from the waist to hand it to her companion, and the lights and shadows dance upon her. Between their smiles she hears my heart, throws back her neck, her head, rippling her hair, turning green eyes on me in the twilight.

She and half a dozen little girls were playing with a doll's-house. I watched them competing for her attention, pulling her sleeve, stroking her hair, crying, 'Look, oh look, please look at this!' the way she used to. Madeleine tried not to have favourites among these small friends, but I knew that the one receiving the doll held a particularly soft spot in my sister's affections. Madeleine had told me all about her. She had a lame leg, and her skirts hid a heavy iron calliper.

Madeleine was scratching fiercely at the back of her neck. 'I'm so thirsty,' she said. 'Brother, could you pass me that glass of water?'

Before I could move one of the girls said, 'I'll get it.'

I never liked watching Madeleine play with other people's children. I tried not to show it, but I am sure she could tell. It wasn't that I was jealous, nothing like that, and the last thing I wanted was for her to deny herself their company. It was the fact that they were other women's daughters. Seeing Madeleine with them made me painfully aware of how much she had sacrificed in order to be with me.

It may be because I believed for so long I could have no children that I thought I didn't care. What I can truly say about myself is that I have never felt any powerful and sustained desire to perpetuate myself, generate descendants, pass on my blood. I know I am unusual in this. If children have any appeal for me it is through kinship, not paternity – Peter's children would have made me as happy as sons of my own, if he had had any.

It was different for Madeleine, I knew that. I could not love her and fail to understand that in loving me she had agreed to the waste of a part of herself, the surrender of a dream. Childlessness was a hardship for her as it was not for me, and I didn't want it to be that way. I never wanted her to give things up for me, not unnecessarily. I did not selfishly, or wantonly, choose to deprive her of children – Alexi, I think, believed I was content to ignore Madeleine's desire for motherhood, or even deny its existence, because I had no corresponding urge to be a father. It wasn't like that. I always wanted her to have babies, but I couldn't see how. It was the one thing I would have changed between us.

I bled for Peter every waking hour. I didn't want to ruin Madeleine's pleasure in other people's sons and daughters, but neither could I share it. None of them was him. Since his death I felt her childlessness more than ever. She was all I had left, and it seemed so unfair that, for my sake, she should be without the thing she wanted most.

I say I bleed for Peter. I say this because it is the saying, and it is easier to parrot than to think. To be exact, it was not a wound. No blood, nothing, escaped from it. It never diminished. A closer approximation would be a bruise, large and new and raw, and every morning when I wake up it is beaten into me again. Only Madeleine prevented that bruise from taking me over entirely. She made it hurt so much less that sometimes it hardly hurt at all.

Believing I knew myself better than it turns out I did, I used to think: If I did not have Madeleine, I would do what Alexi did, because I cannot live without Peter and I have no one to take his place.

I said to the children, 'Go and play outside. I want to talk to my sister.'

They ran into the corridors, pushing and shoving noisily, with the lame one limping after them in a vain attempt to catch up. She was the daughter of a Guard. I don't think her parents had much time for her; the Guards are often more intolerant of physical weakness than other people.

'Poor little thing,' I said when she was out of sight. 'I sometimes wonder whether it isn't kinder to expose children like that as soon as they're born – '

'Reyhnard!' cried Madeleine. 'You can't!'

'Well, what sort of a life will she have?'

'Perhaps a wonderful one. Just because she has a bad leg doesn't mean no one will ever fall in love with her. Someone will, she's so sweet and she's got such a pretty face. I can't believe you said what you just did.'

'I'm sorry,' I said, because I was. Admittedly it was not a very kind thing to say; the fact remains that it is true. 'I can't help it if I sometimes think it.'

'And even if no one does, it's not the end of the world,' my sister rushed on. She was now, understandably, indignant, scratching at her arm in agitation. 'She's so bright – she's the cleverest of them all. I'm sure she'll never be sorry she was born, even with her leg. I mean, even if she never will be able to run for miles and dance all night at least she's alive – '

Poor Madeleine. I don't know what I looked like when she said that; bleak, I suppose. I felt bleak. I must have looked forbidding, because she crouched with her hand frozen half-way to her mouth, as if she would have fled from the room if only she could move. We had been through so many such moments, some caused by her, others by me, and far more by inanimate objects or any thing or word in the wrong place at the wrong time. You can get used to almost anything, and you come to realise it is a waste of time trying to put such moments to rights. You must simply hurry past them and forget they ever happened. I willed her to say something.

'Oh Reyhnard, I'm sorry, I'm sorry, I shouldn't have, I didn't think – '

In order to stop her I said, 'It's all right.'

I put it out of my mind – in those days I was learning how to, though latterly it has been growing harder and harder – and laid my head on my arms, mulling over the thing I had come on purpose to talk to her about.

Beulah once asked me whether, had I not had Madeleine, I would have divorced her and married a woman with whom I was prepared to have children. I told her she was being uncharacteristically speculative and left it at that. I am sure, now, that she asked me this during that same Andarian embassy, because it was then that I first started thinking about children, Madeleine's and mine, in a new light. At first it was a brief flash of an idea that disappeared before I could put a name to it; it returned, lasting longer and growing more imperative, until I was the one who was pushing it away, thinking it fanciful, impossible, not something to respect. It refused to be dismissed. It compelled me to take it seriously, to see it as more important than I had previously believed – as something essential – to peel away the difficulties one by one until I saw how it could be done. All that remained was to inform Madeleine.

I knew that what I had to say, while it would undoubtedly delight her, would also astonish her, and so I tried to lead up to it gently. I wanted her to understand I meant every word I said.

I began, 'I'm not sure how to put this. Madeleine, you know that while I have you I don't need anything else. It's not that I feel a desperate need for something more. I could live alone with you anywhere and be just as happy as I am now. The thing is, it is enough, but it doesn't have to be enough, if you see what I mean. We always thought it had to be, that we had to make do, but when you – when I really started to think about it, seriously, for the first time, I saw there isn't any real reason why we can't.'

'Can't what?'

'Can't . . . Madeleine, you know I hate seeing you playing aunt to those little girls. It's not good enough. I want you to have one of your own – '

'Oh. Oh.'

I saw that I really had taken her by surprise, and her reaction made me feel that I had perhaps rushed it: she was sitting very still, her face unexpectedly impassive. I was too far away from her up on my chair, so I came down to sit on the floor beside her. 'Don't you?' I asked.

Her hands remained calmly folded in her lap. She showed no excitement and offered no answer, only the patina of an old sadness.

'I know you do,' I replied for her. 'I know you've always wanted one.'

'It's impossible,' she said flatly.

Of course – that was it: she hadn't had months to work out the solution, as I had.

'It isn't,' I assured her. 'I've been thinking about it, it's not impossible at all, not if you really want one.' I was searching her face, sure that any moment now the spark of my enthusiasm would catch in her. 'It's not impossible. You could go away, I could find a place for you. Maybe the mountains – you'd like that. You could have him there, no one would know, and then – well, later you could come back to court, and after a while we could bring him here and pretend he was mine by somebody else.'

'Who?' she asked, raising her eyes to meet mine. She was smiling now. Her irises were a deep, sombre green, like fir trees in the winter. I took her hand. 'I don't know,' I said. 'We'd have to choose someone. You could choose her. I suppose we'd have to pay her to pretend. Maybe one of the servants – they're always getting pregnant, remember Alexi? I know it's a lot of subterfuge, I wish it didn't have to be, but it's the only way. I've been thinking about it for months. I've planned it all out and it would work, if you don't mind it being a bit underhand.'

'Do you want a child?' she said quietly.

'If you do. I will if you do. I'm willing.'

'For my sake?'

'If you want a baby, of course.'

She laughed, 'That's the nicest thing you've ever said to me' – then her neck seemed to snap, her straight back breaking down into my arms, and she was crying.

'Madeleine, Madeleine, why are you crying?'

'Because it's impossible. But because you said it, because you wanted to.'

'Don't cry. It's not impossible. Didn't you listen? I know you've always wanted children. I do too, Madeleine, it used to make me so unhappy when I thought we never could – '

'Oh yes, it's true, I used to think it would be lovely to have a baby, yours, ours – '

'Well then?'

'Oh Reyhnard, there's nothing wrong with your plan. It's me. It really is impossible. I can't have children.'

Still riding on the crest of my wonderful idea, I couldn't take this statement in, and asked stupidly, 'Why not?'

'I don't know why not, but I can't, I just can't. It must be something wrong with me.'

She crossed her legs, doubling over them as if she had a cramp, her hair sweeping the floor and hiding her face.

'Madeleine, you can't know – '

'Yes I do! It's been twelve years. If I could have babies I would have had one by now.'

'I thought you were doing something – '

'What?'

'I don't know.' I had never given it a thought. Because it was impossible, it wouldn't happen: that's how I had treated it. I was so taken aback I stammered whatever came into my head. 'I know there are ways – '

'At first I thought you were doing something – I assumed you were. It wasn't for quite a while, after Hans had died but before Alexi, and I think I'd begun to suspect you weren't, and I overheard two girls talking. They'd just got married and were – they were comparing notes. That's when I realised you weren't – '

'Didn't you do something?'

'I didn't know what to do. I didn't have anyone to ask. And I thought that if it did happen I wouldn't mind. But I knew deep down that if it hadn't happened by then it wasn't going to, and I just can't have babies. I just can't.'

'Why didn't you tell me?'

'I couldn't. I was so ashamed. And I didn't think you'd care.'

She wrapped her arms around herself and cried, 'It's a good thing I never did marry that prince, things would have been awful.' She wept on that cold floor as if she forbade me to touch her. But when I lay down beside her and eased her off the floor on to my lap, I knew, from the fingers that held on tight to my arms, that all she wanted was that – for me to touch her.

'It doesn't matter,' I said. 'It doesn't matter.'

'Yes it does. I love you so much. Most of the time I feel as if I'm nothing but love for you wrapped up in skin, and now you've asked me to do something that I can't do.'

'I don't care,' I said. 'It was for your sake. I only care that you're unhappy. You're right, I don't care about children. You never have children for very long anyway, they grow up, and even if they don't go away they're not children any more. I only want you. You're all I want. I wish I hadn't said it. Please don't cry.'

'Beulah can have children. Look at all the children she's got. It's so unfair, why can't I?'

She cried it all out, holding on to me like someone drowning, and for a long time afterwards we lay together quietly, peacefully, as tired as if we had made love, while the twilight turned into night. I could tell from her breathing that she was feeling better.

At last I sat up, saying, 'I'll light a candle.'

She pushed her hair out of her eyes and smiled. 'I'm so thirsty.'

'I'll get it.' I brought over the candle and handed her a glass of water. She gulped it gracelessly, panting for breath, and grinned in embarrassment. 'I've drunk so much water today, gallons of it. How can anyone drink so much and not blow up?'

'You've cried it all out. You'll feel better now.'

'I itch too, all over. I have for several days, but it's worse today.'

'It's the weather, it's been very dry.' I gave her my hand to help her up. She swayed as she got to her feet: I caught her and held her until it passed.

'I was dizzy for a moment,' she explained.

'You must be exhausted.'

'Yes, I am, a little.'

Strands of her hair were matted with salt. I tried to comb them clean with my fingers, and tucked them behind her ear. 'Madeleine, you should have told me all this a long time ago.'

'I know. I know now. I was silly, to think . . . '

'I'm glad you've told me now. You'll feel much better. I hate to think you had something on your mind you didn't tell me.'

'I'm so tired.'

'Of course you are, it's all the crying. You should go to bed.'

'Will you sit with me until I go to sleep?'

'I think I can do better than that.'

She laughed. It was wonderful to see her looking happy again. 'What about dinner?' she reminded me. 'It should have started ages ago.'

'Stop worrying. Come on, or I'll pick you up and carry you.'

'You couldn't!'

'It's a dare, is it?'

She was lighter than I expected. With her arms round my neck and her head on my shoulder, she was half-asleep by the time we reached her rooms.

An idea which grows gradually will not surrender its claim to attention without a struggle. After that evening the subject ought to have been closed. I knew Madeleine would prefer it to be. For her sake I tried to forget about it, but failed; it would not permit me to dismiss it as a thing of no importance. From the beginning I had considered it an inspiration of an idea, for her sake rather than mine, but after that evening it became, so to speak, as ugly as previously it had been beautiful, for since the sister could not welcome it, it began to savage the brother.

It was my turn to suffer in silence. I knew it upset her to talk about it, which is why, for some time, I did not. I hoped the doubt would either fade away, or else become so unbearable that I could be forgiven for mentioning it. Neither happened. What she had said to me was slowly eating away at my peace of mind, until I couldn't help but wonder whether my whole life had been built on an accident of nature.

I had to choose my moment carefully. I didn't want to distress her any more than was necessary. Her state of health was worrying me too. Up until that autumn I don't think she had a day's sickness in her life, aside from the plague. But in October she caught a chill and never really shook it off. My birthday passed and winter furled down, the Ksaned Kaled winter in shades of pastel. On the island autumn turns into spring with the briefest of nods at the harsh season, but this year Madeleine felt the cold weather. I saw her shiver in the warmest rooms.

One day she was well enough to come down and sit in one of the smaller salons. We were alone. Her chair was drawn so close to the fire, which she had asked to have heaped up, that I was afraid embers might fall on her. She looked unusually pale and fragile, but I set this down to the heavy black wool dress she was wearing. A thick blanket was tucked in round her knees. She was knitting, her fingers working the needles with sure dexterity, the click-clack rhythm never faltering.

Stop it, I wanted to say. Stop what you're doing and listen to me. Only I didn't really want to say it, or I would have. What I wanted was to forget all about it.

The longer I waited to ask her, the harder it would be: difficult for her to answer and painful for me to listen. I watched her knitting, and told myself I mustn't mention it now, not when she was feeling ill. But if I did not ask her – if I put it off and put it off through fear of what her answer would be – a time would come when I was no longer able to voice it. Since I could not forget it, it was better to hurt her by asking than insult her by being afraid to. Until I had asked her, I would not be at peace with either myself or her.

'Why are you so quiet?' she asked me.

'I'm thinking.'

I was standing by the window, studying the way the glow of firelight waxed and waned like a corona around her dark silhouette. 'How are you feeling today?'

'Much better, not nearly so tired.'

'I'll have you out galloping around the fields soon.'

'Won't it be lovely, when spring's here?'

'Not long now. Madeleine – there's something I have to ask you.'

She put down her knitting, prepared to give me all her attention, and all the patience I needed.

When she looked at me like that, with such tranquillity, the question felt its foolishness and began to slink away. Too late, though, for I had started and had to go on.

'When you told me, several months ago – when I asked you if you wanted to have children . . . '

She said nothing, and she maintained her calm expression; but her silent lack of encouragement said, Don't you know I don't want to talk about that?

'Madeleine – I wouldn't bring this up if I didn't have to. I have to ask this one thing quickly, and then I promise never to mention it again.'

'What is it you want to know?'

'I – Madeleine, would you have stayed with me, if you could have had children?'

'How could I have left you?'

'If you'd wanted to, if you'd asked, if you'd wanted someone else, I would have let you.'

'Would you?'

'Please, just answer me. I have to know.'

'You want the truth?'

No, I said. I said it in my heart, but to my sister I said, 'Yes.'

I had come down to sit at her feet, with my arms across her knees, but I was afraid to look at her. She is straight-backed, lathe-limbed, black and white and green: she is carved precisely. If I ask her for the truth, she will give it.

She said, 'The truth is yes, I would have stayed with you. And I hope you're ashamed of asking.'

Before I could reply, she went on, 'You're right, it doesn't make a difference. I loved you before I thought about children, and when I did it was only to know that I was happy to go without them, because I couldn't go without you. I was so frightened it might make a difference to you – but it hasn't, and that's all that matters to me. I couldn't have left you – that's what I meant, when I said "How could I?" Reyhnard, I remember when you were ready to run away with me rather than let me marry someone else. Would you really have let me go, if I'd asked you?'

'I'm afraid I lied.'

'You do love me, don't you?'

'Oh, I expect I probably do, yes.'

She started to laugh. 'I was going to say something else, but I'm not going to pander to your vanity.'

'Oh, go on, tell me.'

'Well, it's just that I'll never want to leave you, so even if you told me to go, I wouldn't.'

Of course I realise – I knew even as I spoke to her – that asking my sister this question was just about the most unnecessary thing I ever did. It's hard to explain why, although I knew what she would say, I had to ask her. It was something along the same lines as wondering whether, if you tried hard enough, you could make your heart stop beating. You know you can't really, and most of the time you're not conscious of that particular organ ticking away; once in a while, though, you can't help but wonder.

I'm glad now that I asked her. Nothing has been left unsaid. Her answer was less important to me than my doubts – no, not doubts, rather the fear that her answer might be something other than it was. She let me speak, understood me, and forgave me. I needed to hear it from her own mouth because – because it was good to hear. It was an added strength. One more statement of the truth to remember.

I am glad I asked her then, instead of relying on myself, because it means I never need wonder now. Half a love, like half a person, might have been too weak to withstand the tug of unanswered doubts. I am glad I did not keep secret from her a single suspicion which, if it had remained unspoken, might have warped the memory of the whole. Faithfully as I love, so do I remember.

51

By the beginning of February it was obvious that my sister was very ill.

The illness attacked her with a terrible discrimination, producing different symptoms in each separate part of her body. Her limbs, especially her fingers and toes, were often numb. She had difficulty breathing. When she could walk about her head span, but most of the time she couldn't walk or even get out of bed. No amount of sleep could overcome her exhaustion, and her muscles ached and burned as if she had been riding hard for days, although she had taken no exercise at all.

She didn't tell me these things; she never complained. I found them out from the physicians. She wouldn't have told them either, but I forced her, shouting, 'How can they help you if you won't tell them?' I wished it was me who was ill. She had an enemy to direct her pain and her courage against: her illness. I had nothing to fight but her gentle determination not to cause trouble.

She would get out of bed and stagger about, trying to carry on with her usual routine, when I could *see*, I could *feel* the effort it cost her. More than once she would have broken her neck if someone had not caught her when she stumbled on the stairs. My graceful sister, who used to flow when she walked as if on water, unable to climb up a flight of steps. Perhaps it would have been better for us both if no one had caught her.

Other things were happening to her which she could not hide. She vomited constantly. Her breath would come in shallow pants and she doubled over, fighting for it; then it would change to deep, heaving gasps.

And she was so thin. I watched, helpless, as she wasted away. Despite the nausea and the tiredness she was always hungry, always thirsty, so it was not a question of tempting her to eat things, which would at least have been something I could do. She ate ravenously. The more she ate the thinner she became, as if the process itself consumed more energy than she could spare. And the doctors didn't even know what was wrong with her.

There were days when she was so much better I could delude myself into thinking she would soon be well again. But the next day it would come back. When, looking for hope, I summed up the time she had been ill, I was forced to acknowledge that she was worse this week than she had been the week before.

I shouted at the doctors, 'Do something! Why can't you do something?'

I thought about all those times when I had never known what was happening until it was too late. Always, when it was too late, it had seemed to me that I could have done something to prevent it. Nothing is inevitable until it has happened. I could never work out what it was I might have been able to do, but this time, surely, there must be something.

So I did what I could. I shouted at the doctors. And at the beginning of spring they told me there was nothing they could do.

Beulah said to me, 'She is dying.'

'She's not, she's not. Don't even say that. She's not, she kept her breakfast down today, she walked around the room and sat up for half an hour, and she couldn't do that last week, she's getting better, the warm weather's coming and she'll get better.'

'She's dying, Reyhnard.'

'Reyhnard?'

I had been sitting by her window, looking out at the day. When I heard her speak my name, I came over to sit on the bed. Her hands were lying outside the covers. I took them into my own. The fingers were blue, cold, nothing but bone. I eased a strand of hair out of her mouth, saying, 'You're awake.'

'I'm glad you're here.'

'How do you feel? Sleep well?'

'Last time I woke up you weren't here.'

'I only went away for a little while. Look, I brought you some flowers.'

'They're beautiful.'

'They're the first. I know you can't go into the garden just now, so I picked the buds, and you can watch them open.'

She said, 'What's the time?'

'Middle of the afternoon.'

'Oh, I know, I can tell that from the sunlight on the wall. It's like a sundial. What's it like outside?'

'All right. Sunny. Quite warm. Not as warm as it is in here, though. I should think your flowers are happier in here.'

She had been smiling at me, but then her eyes unfocused a little and the lids started slipping down. I thought she was going back to sleep, but she forced them open and asked, 'May I have a glass of water?'

I brought it to her and watched her drink. She was so thin I could see the mass of fluid moving down her throat.

'How can I still be tired when I sleep so much?' she said with a smile.

'You should go back to sleep.'

'I don't want to sleep. I want to look at you.'

I kissed her cold hands. 'You'll see me again. Madeleine, if you feel you need to sleep, then you should sleep, otherwise you won't get better.'

Her eyes, which had always been bright and expressive rather than large, were huge now, sunk between her cheekbones and her brow. The muscles which had held them were wasting away. They were so pale, too – as if a vandal had gone over them with a brushful of grey water.

She said, 'Am I getting better?'

'Of course you'll get better, but you should sleep, you need it.'

'Will you stay here? I know it shouldn't really make a difference, when I'm asleep, but it's nice to know you're here. And I like to see you when I wake up.'

I kissed her, very gently; she looked so fragile a feather might have shattered her.

Heavy white lids crept round her eyes. 'Good night.'

'Good afternoon.'

A smile twitched on her face. 'So accurate.'

'Sweet dreams.'

I uncurled her fingers to kiss her palm. She was already fast asleep, having been only half-awake. I believed then, when I said it, that she would get better. I needed to. I chafed her fingers between my hands, then laid her hand in my lap and settled down to watch her sleep.

She seemed to me like a porcelain vase that someone had smashed and carelessly glued together. I could see every joint in her face. Her skin was very clear and dry, red and blue veins prominent beneath its transparency. She breathed with her mouth open, long dragging breaths that smelled sharp, and sweet, and a little acid. All the ridges of her windpipe stood out. I bent down to kiss her beneath her collarbone, laying my head very carefully on her breast, not wanting to bruise those carved ribs. Under my ear was her heart, pumping protestingly. It too was tired. It wanted to go to sleep.

I sat up.

She no longer looked like me. No one would mistake us for each other now, no matter what we wore.

Not my twin, not any longer. But still, even a stranger could have seen we were brother and sister.

I had never needed a mirror. If I wanted to know how I smiled or laughed, how I ate and drank, the transformation of my face when making love, or the agelessness sleep lent to me, I looked at her. She was me, my face, mine.

Her eyelids quivered for a second. I thought she was waking up, but it was not my sister. Death was stirring. Death was crawling in through her mouth and nose and ears, taking over all that belonged to me. Death in her skin had put itself between us. I couldn't see her, not when her eyes were shut and death sat on her eyelids.

In her dying face I saw my face dying. I couldn't see whether it was her or me or a mirror or death.

Madeleine and death becoming one on the other side of a sheet of glass, saying, We're not going to lie to you.

Death moving under her skin, beneath her eyelids, between each breath whispering:

– You're a lucky lucky man. Not many men have the chance to find out what they look like when they're dead. You've never seen anyone die. You've seen them dying and you've seen them dead, but you've always missed that moment when the one becomes the other. Wait, and you can watch yourself die, you lucky man –

After a time it becomes irrelevant whether you are walking away from something or towards something, because the motion is exactly the same for both. I did not run at first. I walked out of the Palace. I could see the clouds to the east were golden-pink around the edges; I could hear the birds singing, and the courtiers chatting, and the peacocks calling, and some dogs barking; I could smell the fresh air with its mixture of damp earth, new flowers and salt. I could taste the sweat on my lips. I could feel the sun in my hair. I would like to be able to say – though for whose sake I do not know – but I can't help feeling that I would like to be able to say that at that point I still intended to turn around after a while and come back. I did not make my mind up then: I did not have a mind about it to make up. Having begun to walk, it was easier to go on than to stop. I walked a little way down the road, and turned off it to cut through some flower fields. I went along five or six miles of them until I came to a little stream, which I jumped. When I landed, I was running. I ran through meadows and wild flowers, and came to the narrow wood of pine trees that fringed the beach. Running through that I churned up debris that smelt of evergreen and chypre, and as I ran on to the beach I noticed some stunted palm trees. I hopped on one leg, taking off my shoes, and ran barefoot along the sand. I liked that running. I liked the burning in my legs, the stitch in my side, the effort of breathing, the physical pain.

I stopped because I saw a boat. It had been pulled up on to the beach. Its prow was resting on the sand and its stern was in the water. A man was standing next to it, his arms full of logs.

I could see, across the channel, the low roofs of the town on the mainland.

The man had dropped his bundle of wood and was staring at me. 'What are you doing?' I asked him.

'Nothing, my lord, only getting firewood, only what's lying around. I picked it up. I ain't cut nothing, my lord.'

I asked him, 'Do you know who I am?' in order to make sure he didn't.

'No, my lord.' Then, ingratiatingly, 'But I can see you're from the Palace, my lord.'

'Do you live on this island?'

He hesitated. I said, 'Don't lie to me.'

'No, my lord. I live just over there –' He waved his arm in the direction of the town.

'Are you going back there now?'

'Yes, my lord, I was just about to go, just now, right away – '

'Take me.'

The peasants pretend to be slow-witted, but only because it's to their advantage. He was surprised for a moment, then stooped to retrieve his bundle of firewood and put it into the boat, no doubt thinking: What are the eccentricities of the court to me? When he stood up again he had a calculating look.

He began, 'Well, now . . . '

If I'd been Hans I would simply have got in that boat and said 'Row'. If I'd been Peter, I would have told him to do as I said or I'd cut his head off. As it was, I did what Alexi would have done. I took off a ring and said, 'You can have this, if you take me.'

He pocketed it. 'Get in, my lord, down astern. That's it. Makes the boat steady. Sorry it's kind of cramped.'

He pushed it off, jumped in with wet feet, grabbed the oars, heaved – and we were on the open water.

I thought about two things as I crossed the channel. The first was that I had no money with which to buy food or somewhere to sleep. The second was that I could not rely on this poacher keeping his unexpected passenger a secret. If he announced our encounter all round some tavern, any number of cut-throats might come after me to find out what profit they could make from my murder.

As we approached the coast I said to him, 'Put in at the beach there, below the town.'

'But my lord, I thought you was for the town?'

'Is it impossible to put in there?'

'Well, it ain't easy, and kind of out of my way, and me being expected half an hour ago already – '

I knew what he was after, which was my other ring. 'Do as I tell you,' I said. 'I have no money, but if you do as I ask you may have this.' I thought it would be better if I got rid of it, and remembered to add, 'I've nothing else.'

He took it, eyeing me doubtfully. I could only hope he would report my lack of wealth. The beach was shingle and spread with seaweed. He let the momentum of the boat run it on to the land, and waited while I got out. I picked my way between the seaweed. When I reached higher ground, I turned my head; he was still sitting there, watching me. I supposed he was wondering where I was going. If I hadn't run into him, I would simply have walked round and round the island. I had no destination in mind.

A grey evening was coming down, clouds borne low with rain. The walls of the town were far off to my right, and I kept my distance skirting them, walking across scrubby waste land until I came to a broad common full of cows. They were lying down in small groups beneath the trees, chewing their cud. They gazed at me thoughtfully. I walked past them and on through an orchard, the flowers of the fruit trees ghostly in the dusk. A fox with a rabbit in its mouth slunk across my path. It was night before I felt the packed earth of the Tsvingtori road beneath my feet.

I knew I was tired, but this feeling did not extend as far as my legs, which went on walking. There was no light. The new moon and the stars were blotted out by the clouds. I walked for two hours or so, and then it began to rain. I walked on through the rain, cold, hungry, wet and tired. After a while I caught sight of a dark shape at the edge of the road: a small building, a cow-byre. I went in. Inside it was warm and smelt of milk, manure and hay. I lay down in a large pile of straw in the corner. A rat scrabbled somewhere. I listened to the sound of the rain, and before I shut my eyes I wondered if I would be woken in the morning by bovine teeth chewing at my hair.

But when I shut my eyes, I saw her. I could not keep my eyes shut, or myself still. I had to walk. I was not tired any more. There was still the road ahead of me: if I stayed on it, I would not wander into some bog or moor, or a field with a bull. I went back out into the rain and continued walking west.

I think one is supposed to lose all sense of time when one walks like this. Later, months later, when I was walking absorbed in my own thoughts, I sometimes did – though even when I paid no attention to the sun, my stomach would remind me how many hours it had been since I last ate. But when you want not to think, you fix your senses firmly on external things, and let them occupy you. I marked the duration of the rain by counting my footsteps, running into thousands before I lost track. I kept my eyes open and alert, trying to see the owl that had hooted, estimating how wide the road might be, staring up through the rain at the sky – sometimes the clouds gaped for a moment to reveal the moon. So I know it was several hours after midnight when I heard a horseman approaching from behind me, at a gallop.

I climbed off the road into a ditch.

The hoofbeats grew louder, sped by me in an instant and thundered on. Gradually the sound faded away.

I got out of the ditch and kept walking, my feet soaking wet.

Just before dawn, the rain stopped.

Something rose up in front of me, indeterminate in the dusk. At first I thought it was a peculiar little hill standing all alone, but as the light grew stronger I realised it was a castle. I should have remembered it was there. It was one of mine. A cock began to crow inside its walls. I had stayed there once, when we took the overland route to Ksaned Kaled. It was a small, utilitarian construction, a sort of staging post. It stood a quarter of a mile away, at the end of a drive that branched off from the main road. I went up and the gate was open. I went in.

A servant was drawing water from the well in the courtyard. I have a bad memory for faces, but she must have once worked at Tsvingtori or Ksaned Kaled, or else had a very good memory from that one time, because when she heard the dogs barking at me she turned around to see who I was. She stared for a moment. Then she said, 'Sir.' Then she fell on her knees.

I suppose I passed out.

I must have done, because the next thing I remember is being propped up in a chair, with a plate of bread and eggs in front of me, which I ate. Hunger had kept me awake; having eaten, I could have slept in that chair.

I have a dream-like memory of hands under my arms, lifting me, carrying me upstairs. I shook my head clear for a moment and thought I saw a Guard, which made me sure I was dreaming. After that, I was standing in a bedroom, and the servant was on the other side of the bed, turning down the covers. I thought the sheets would be very cold. I was cold. She looked warm. I said to her, 'Get in,' and I think she did, and then I did, and I was asleep before I lay down.

I woke up because I was hungry. I was alone. It was dark outside, but bright and warm where I was because candles and a fire had been lit. Food was laid out on the table. I was too hungry to think, so I ate until I didn't feel hungry, all the while drinking the wine and calling for more. I drank until I was asleep again. I drank so much, so quickly, that I passed from sobriety to unconsciousness without going through the stages of giddiness, introspection and despair.

52

In my sleep I heard knocking. It woke me up, and I realised someone really was knocking on my door, the noise muffled by the blankets wrapped round my head. I heard the door open. I uncurled from the blankets and opened my eyes. Beulah was just closing the door behind her.

I was barely awake, and seeing her I thought perhaps I had been dreaming, and never left Ksaned Kaled at all. But the room, the furniture, even the way the light fell through the window, was unfamiliar. I wondered what day it was.

She took off her hat and gloves and laid them on the table. Her actions reminded me of something. This time, though, she did not fling them down carelessly and laugh as she approached me. This time she set them down neatly, quietly, and remained close by the door. This time she was thirty, not seventeen.

I said, 'How did you know I was here?'

'I had you followed.'

She added, 'We've got that peasant in custody. You can have your ring back.'

'Let him keep it, he earned it.'

'Why don't you get up, and get dressed? We'll go outside.'

'I can't, I don't know what the servants have done with my clothes, and anyway they're ruined.'

'I've brought you some,' she said, pointing to the foot of the bed. I looked down, and saw a suit draped over the bed-rail.

'I don't want to go outside,' I said.

'You ought to, you need some fresh air. You look terrible.'

'I feel terrible.'

'It's a beautiful afternoon.'

I got up, and dressed. Someone had put flowers in my room, a sunburst of daffodils in a rosy clay pot.

When I was fully clothed, Beulah picked up my wrist and felt my pulse. Then she dropped it and put a hand to my forehead. She checked my brow and temples, saying as she removed her hand, 'At least you haven't caught pneumonia.'

We went out on to a lawn behind the castle. There was a cedar tree, with a circular bench built round its trunk. Here we sat down. I expected her to start talking again but she did not. We sat together for a long time in silence. She did not need to say anything. I had known all along what she had come to tell me.

53

I stayed at that castle for a week. Beulah stayed with me. I created a pattern for myself whereby I slept as much as I could, and when I was awake I rode round the fields until it grew dark; then I would drink myself to sleep. On the seventh day Beulah said to me, 'Please understand that I wouldn't ask this of you if I didn't have to. I know you're grieving. I know how you feel. I know it's hard, but you must remember you have duties. You're not a private person, you can't indulge yourself like a private person . . .'

She tried to touch my hand, and said, 'Reyhnard, I think it's time we went home.'

She might as well have said, It's time we went to see Peter and Madeleine, they're expecting us.

I passed through a door into the garden, and sat down on the steps. Ksaned Kaled, I said to myself, but there was no joy in the name, no yearning in my heart. It's nothing but a house now. Ksaned Kaled and Tsvingtori.

Wherever Madeleine and Peter are is where I ought to be. I am her family. I am their home. Now it doesn't matter where I go or what I do. What does Beulah expect? Does she think I'll go back and sit in those huge rooms, or wander purposelessly along the corridors, growing gradually madder until I believe that if only I run fast enough I can catch them before they disappear around the corner? No. I know that they are dead. My life, what is left of it, will be lived on my own because they will never come back. I can never go back.

I could write pages and pages about what I felt, but it would all be the same. My decision had made itself before I stepped off the island.

I had no responsibilities left. I was not needed at court, or anywhere else. They needed Beulah, but not me. Her son is an acceptable substitute. I would never be missed if I never returned.

Beulah had followed me out on to the steps. She also sat down, moving awkwardly because she was so pregnant, but not close to me.

'I won't force you,' she said. 'But you should think about going home. No one knows you're here, except for me and a couple of Guards. There's things to do, we can't stay away too long. And, Reyhnard, there is her funeral to see to.'

'I'm not going back.'

'But surely you'll want to go to her funeral.'

'No.'

'Reyhnard, you mustn't try to pretend to yourself it hasn't happened.'

'I know she's dead.'

I have seen too many funerals. I would not countenance this one. No homage this time, death, no acquiescence. She is dead. She has no green eyes to search for mine and see that I am absent.

'I'm not going back with you,' I said.

'If not now, then when?'

'Never.'

She said nothing for a moment, but when she next spoke she did not sound surprised. 'What are you going to do?' she asked. 'You can't stay here for ever.'

'I'm not going to.'

'Then what are you going to do?'

'I'm going to go somewhere.'

'Where?'

'I don't know.'

'Anywhere in particular?'

'I don't know.' The moon had come up, a silver sliver hooked on the horizon. I said, 'It's a big country. I could go all over the place.'

'Just walking around? Like those tramps one sees at fairs?'

'Does one, do they? I suppose so.'

'But what will you live on?'

'I don't know. Does it matter? I suppose those tramps must get some food from somewhere, or earn it.'

'But darling, you've never had to do any work in your life.'

I stood up.

She said, 'You always did live in a fantasy world.'

'Look, for once in your life stop making problems for me.'

'I'm not making problems for you. They're there already. I'm trying to help you. You've got no idea what it's like outside the Palace. You'd starve.'

'Whether I do or I don't isn't your concern any more, Beulah. Take your son and make him King, I don't care, just leave me alone and I'll leave you alone. If you know me as well as you think you do, you must realise that I mean this. I'm not going to come back to court. Ever. So stop worrying. I've told you what I'm going to do and you can't stop me.'

As I spoke she also rose, languorous, stretching herself. 'I could,' she said. 'But I'm not going to.'

She walked back into the room. The servants were lighting the candles. She still moved with the fluency of a sixteen-year-old, despite her weight. Her pregnancy was in its seventh month, but she seemed to thrive on pregnancy as she thrived on everything. Partly her weight was that of the unborn child, but mostly it was her very own, those adolescent curves matured into the bulk of her prime. She stood with her feet apart, back broad with flesh, four-square, monumental. Seeming larger, perhaps, than she was – seeming to take up a room, whatever its dimensions. The little gap I left in my going she would expand and fill, she and her children.

She tossed her head and arched her shoulders, running a hand down her dress in that old gesture. But this time, when she twisted to look over her shoulder at me, she was a woman and not a girl. Her coiled sinuosity had been swamped by fat. In order to face me she had to shift her whole body round on her feet, a ponderous movement. The servants had withdrawn.

'You know I'm going to have to tell them you're dead,' she said.

I shrugged. It would be best for her, easiest for me. How she would manage to convince them I didn't care to know. She was bound to find a way.

She looked at me inscrutably, sighed, shut her eyes and tutted. 'I could say all sorts of things to you. I could point out all the difficulties lying in wait for you, and the fact that you probably will be dead before the year's out – but you won't listen to me, will you? So I'm not going to bother. Anyway, you're grown-up now . . . As grown-up as you'll ever be. Remember how much you wanted to be grown-up when you were little?'

'You have no idea what I was like when I was a boy.'

'Oh, every child longs to be grown-up. And now you are. Old enough to make up your own mind. I've got no right to stop you.'

'That sounds very unlike you.'

'I'm not a child any more, either.' She sat down in an armchair, propping her feet on a stool and rubbing her back. Glancing at me, she started chuckling and said, 'After all, Nardo, you can do what you like. You're the King.'

'Not any more.'

Easily on, easily off. Just a coat and a hat.

She seemed to have nothing more to say, and I certainly didn't, so I walked past her, intending to go upstairs to bed.

'By the way,' she said, 'when are you going?'

'Tomorrow. Tomorrow morning, before it gets light.'

'Very sensible. I'll go back to Ksaned Kaled tomorrow, then.'

'Whatever you like.'

I went to sleep thinking without regret that this was the last I would ever see of her. But when I groped my way down the stairs before dawn, she was waiting at the bottom with a candle. Her hair was a little disarrayed and her dress, the same dress she had been wearing the night before, was crumpled. She had been up all night, thinking whatever it is she thinks.

'So you really are going?' she said.

'As you see.'

I was wearing my own boots, good ones, and a linen shirt I stole from the laundry. My trousers and jacket I had found in a gardener's shed.

Beulah smiled. 'Good disguise,' she said. 'I was going to suggest it, but I see you do have some forethought after all. Come into the kitchen for a moment.'

She led the way with the candle. On a table in the kitchen lay a satchel.

She picked it up and handed it to me. It was made of leather and felt heavy.

'Where did you find it?' I asked her.

'Oh, I thought you might need something like this, so I hunted around a bit and this is what I found. There's a loaf of bread in it, and some cheese, and some apples. Mind the left strap.'

I slung it on my back. She followed me through the kitchen door into the courtyard. It was the cold hour which is neither day nor night, but the sky was beginning to purple. The servants would not sleep much longer.

'I'd better go,' I said.

'Wait . . . You'll need these.' She put a dozen or so silver coins into my hand. 'One of those buys eight loaves of bread, remember. I think you'll find they come in useful . . . '

I put the coins in my pocket. Their weight felt strange, unnatural, pressing against my leg. Beulah released my hand, and so I started.

'Reyhnard – '

I stopped.

She said, 'Don't go.'

I had hardly crossed the first field before I heard the cocks crowing behind me. A flock of birds rose out of the winter corn, wheeling away in a black mass through the sky. That night I slept in a barn in a meadow. The next night I slept in some stables in a village. They let me sleep there for free. At the end of the month I came to a town where a guild of masons gave me a job moving wheelbarrows. That was three and a half years ago.

54

Serena is in labour. I am sure it is too soon. There was a deep fall of snow last night, and this morning I was lying in my bed, cocooned with blankets against the cold, when I imagined I heard her go out. I ought to have got up then, but I was so sleepy, and told myself the noise was probably a mouse or some snow falling. I didn't think she could be so foolish. Ten minutes or so later I heard a loud cry of pain, and I did jump out of bed then, pulled on my clothes, went outside – I found her doubled up in the goat shed. She wanted to milk them. I helped her back inside and put her to bed. I could see in her face when the pains came, but between them she was smiling and laughing, exclaiming, 'It's now, he's coming!' as if someone had surprised her with a present.

I hope it's going to be all right.

It's evening already, but I know first babies take their time about entering the world. I am not at our hut – I was squeezed out by a horde of women: her mother, her sister, village gossips, the midwife, several guests from another village who are visiting relatives and didn't want to miss the excitement, and even Serena's little niece dangling at the end of her mother's arm. Serena's father, who had looked through the door and seen me elbowed into a corner by that press of women jabbering advice and encouragement, tapped on the shutter and called for me to open it.

'You're nothing but in the way here,' he said. 'I know how it is. You come over to my place.'

This is where I am, his house. Before I left, I gathered up all my papers and brought them with me. I was worried that if I left them behind they might get knocked down, trodden on or used to stoke the fire. Serena is in no state to tell them to leave my things alone. I've never been in her father's house before. No, I came into the kitchen once, or nearly inside, on the doorstep, to collect some vegetables her mother didn't want and had promised to Serena. At the moment I'm sitting at a large table, slippery with beeswax (I see where Serena gets her passion for house-cleaning from), in a sort of salon. I suppose I glorify it by calling it a salon: it's more a sort of communal room. His house is like a palace, it's so big. Five rooms, a kitchen, a larder and a workroom – how does he fill it up? I'm alone – his wife and his daughter are still with Serena, and he's gone out to look at his sheep. He does this sort of thing, leaning on the fence and looking at them, sometimes for hours. Counting his money.

What with Serena's cries, and the women bustling about, the air outside is in an uproar. Our hut is at the other end of the village, and I can't hear them in this room, but if I went into the street I could. It reminds me – well, but the court always looked so apathetic, almost resentful, whereas here all the villagers, even the ones who rarely exchanged a word with her, are on tenterhooks.

The walls of this house are thick, the shutters closed against the cold. The fire is crackling, and to pass the time I am writing. It's very quiet.

More than a year ago, on a May morning in the mountains, I saw a fair field full of sheep.

I had spent the night sleeping under a tree. Leaving the town where I had stayed for some weeks, I had been heading up into the mountains when night fell upon me in the middle of a forest. I had lost my way and was casting about for a path, but in the dark it was a hopeless task; I was tired and the night was warm, so I lit a fire to keep away predators, and went to sleep. Next morning the sunlight woke me, filtering through the leaves and dancing in patterns across my eyelids. I stretched, packed my satchel, stamped out the remains of my fire, and set off again through thick forest, still as lost as I had been the night before. The sun shone through the dense foliage in various shades of green, and from the angle of the light I could make a rough guess which direction was east.

Quite soon I found my way becoming easier: I was no longer tripping over roots, or running my face into a spider's web. I realised I was on a well-marked path which, with any luck, would lead to a stream, for I was very thirsty and the day fast becoming extremely hot.

In front of me the forest was thinning into woods; beyond the last trunks I saw clear daylight.

As I reached the edge of the woods, I heard men's voices. They were angry, shouting at each other in the native. Then there was a scurry, feet shuffling, leather creaking, and horses' hooves setting off at a gallop. I waited until the noise had died away, and walked out into the sunlight.

I was standing on the top of a hill or incline. Between me and the crest of the hill was a road, wide enough for a carriage, with deep ruts in its cracked earth; beyond it the ground rose up to a long peak and then dipped down out of sight, hiding from view whatever might lie beneath the hill. The road ran away to my left, gradually rising for three or four miles until it made a wide curve north and disappeared between the forest and the mountainside. The verge of the road was thick with flowers, poppies and bluebells and foxgloves, their bright colours dusted with grey. The thick grass which grew on the top of the hill was silver and yellow in turns as the breeze rippled over it, waving it like the sea. Far away the moving clouds were making vast patterns of light and shade across the landscape. Up in the air a bird of prey was hovering on motionless wings. It was a very pretty, tranquil scene, and utterly silent save for the wash of the breeze. The sound of the horses had vanished.

No sign of a stream, but if I followed the road I must soon come to a village where I could get water. I had just shifted my satchel to a more comfortable position and was about to walk on, when the wind changed in my direction.

I heard the tinkling of a small bell.

The wind died, and I could hear nothing. I thought it must have been my imagination.

The breeze returned: this time I heard the bell clearly, and the baa of sheep, coming from below the hill.

There must be a flock down there, and the bell must belong to the ram. Where there were sheep there would be a shepherd, and where there was a man there would be water. I crossed the road.

The breeze swelled, and underneath the bell and the sheep I heard a dog, whining.

I shivered. It was an ugly sound. Despite the hot sun my skin crawled.

I seriously considered turning back and going in search of that village; but I had come to the hill's crest, and I could now hear the sound of water running over stones. A few more steps brought me within sight of the stream. Part of it, to my right, was hidden behind a smaller hillock; the water looked cold and fresh. On its banks the grass was thick, lush and very green, the sheep like living drifts of snow against it. Overcome by thirst, I scrambled down the hill, startling two ewes which loped away bleating. I ran to the stream and knelt in the grass, trailing my fingers through the cold water and splashing it noisily over my face.

Immediately I heard the dog growling, very close to me.

I glanced to my left, but instead of a dog I saw, on the bank of the stream where it curved behind the hillock, a pair of sandalled feet, lying as if they had been thrown down there and did not belong to anybody. The torso they must join to was out of sight. I looked at the water. In it was a thin trail of cloudy red, floating down-stream.

The dog started whining again. It was clearly in pain. It must be wounded, for otherwise it would have gone for me by now. Standing up, I slung off my satchel and let it fall to the grass.

I walked around the hillock and found the shepherd. His legs were sprawled across the far bank, and one arm lay in the mud on this side of the stream; the rest of him had fallen face down in the water. I could see the point of an arrow thrusting out between his shoulder blades. The steel had been washed clean. Around his head the water was opaque with blood.

The dog snarled. It was a typical shepherd's dog, black and white with a foxy, devoted face. It bared its teeth at me. I kept my distance. After a while, the growl changed back to a whine; it seemed to forget my presence and went on with what it had obviously been doing before I interrupted: pulling itself towards the shepherd. The dog's tail was limp, back legs dragging along the ground. I realised its back was broken.

I took a step forward. The dog halted, growled in its throat, and made up its mind to ignore me. I went down to the stream and touched the shepherd's hand. The skin was still warm. I took off my shoes and waded into the water, grasped his shoulders, and after several attempts – his clothes were slippery with being soaked – I heaved him over. The dog began to howl.

He had a nondescript face, a young face. His hair, when dry, would have been fair, and the one eye that was open looked blue; an ordinary native face. One of his cheeks had been smashed when he fell, but it was not such a terrible sight. As I held his head out of the water a fly settled on his brow, and I brushed it away.

Only the feathers of the arrow showed. It had gone right through his chest. He had been dead before he drowned.

I laid him back in the water and climbed the bank. An incongruous, bright bit of colour in the grass caught my eye, and I went to see what it was.

It was a large neckpurse, the sort of thing I have often seen shepherds keeping their bread and cheese in. Made of tattered red and blue embroidery, with sequins worked in – a cheap thing. I doubted he had had any money. Shepherds don't need money. The purse was damp, and the string that had held it around his neck was snapped.

The dog sighed. I turned round. It had achieved its objective, and lay with its muzzle pressed against the shepherd's bare calf. Its eyes were filming over white.

Lying close to the neckpurse was a thick branch, which I guessed they had used to break the dog's back. I picked it up. The dog would die soon anyway. It is easy to kill a dog. At least I could save the animal from drawing out its death in pain. I took the branch firmly in both hands and jumped the stream, approaching the dog, who raised its head to look at me silently – knowing, perhaps, what I was about to do. I brought the branch down as hard as I could and caved in the dog's skull.

Dead, it rolled slowly to one side and slid down the muddy bank into the water. The stream ran through its broken brain pan, carrying the mess away in a flurry of blood, until nothing was left except white bone and wet fur. I waded in to grab the shepherd's ankles and haul his legs around; as I did so, his hand fell with a plop into the water. I laid him down in mid-stream, resting his heels on the dog's body.

There remained the branch, and the neckpurse. I fetched the purse and tied it to the shepherd's arm, for a man about to embark on the great journey needs his worldly wealth. No ship and no fire – I retrieved the branch, and managed to wedge it next to his chest. An oar was better than nothing. Then I sat back on my heels and surveyed my poor attempt at a funeral rite.

I have seen a dog die.

I remember now that I used to think, when I was young, that life would have some sort of culmination. I thought it would reach its completion round about the age of sixty or seventy: an end before the real end. At that age, I thought, one could lie back and bask in one's last days, having accomplished everything one had struggled for. Contemplating one's life from each angle: warm slow days like lizards in the sun. Then one could say: 'It was well done. Now I may depart contented.' I don't know when I had that idea. When I was fifteen, perhaps. Or during that first year on Ksaned Kaled.

Blow by blow death has kicked those juvenile assumptions away. I don't have to look at my own life; I can look at my family's. Did Madeleine lie back and watch her death approaching with the satisfied smile of one who is ready to go? Did I pat her hand and say, 'Every life has a purpose, and you have fulfilled yours'? Did she die at some approved time, her life rounded and complete like a rosy clay pot, serviceable and beautiful?

The answer is no. She did not. I am her purpose and I am still here. I still love her and I still need her. Death did not finish her off like an artisan. It tore her to pieces, like a murderer, and me with her.

Others death takes in one swift grab, but it is dragging my destruction out through years. It has looted my life of all my treasures, despoiled my happiness, and will in the end claim back even my bare existence from me. It has declared war inside me, pitting love and hate and fear against each other, wearing them out in a battle that none of them, nor I, can ever hope to win. I don't know why death sees in me a prize worth such efforts. No one would think it to look at me now, sitting here quietly putting sentences together, but often I want to rip apart everything I can lay my hands on, for the sake of this smashing going on inside me. I don't, though, because to do so would only be aiding and abetting death's universal vandalism. I may be its slave, but I will not be its henchman.

I think I am beginning to understand why, as my sister said, people fear death less as they grow older. Only I don't believe they do fear it less. I believe their life merely becomes more hateful to them. Penned up between the unendurable and the unimaginable, with no hope of escape from one except in the other, the will to fight is battered out of them. Death is so possessive, so greedy and capricious, that I think this surrender pleases it as much as the actual execution.

More than anything, more even than death itself, I am afraid that if I continue through years and years with this pointless persistence in being alive, I will come to love death as I once came close to loving that bitch Beulah: because she had everything I wanted.

She is a person and I can hate her. Death isn't a person. I can't love it or hate it. Death is an action, an event. Death is the shutting up of the body's functions, closing the doors and stamping out the hearth. I do hate it. I don't care what sense it makes, I hate it. I hate it not just in me, my death, but everywhere, in the nature of the world.

I see now why there is no word to denote what is on the other side of death, no word for the state we are in after we have died. It is because there is nothing on the other side to name. There isn't even death on the far side of death: it's the threshold into nothingness. Nothingness, and all the other words we are driven to use are almost metaphors: void, sleep, night. They really mean something quite different, having nothing originally to do with death at all. We try to imagine, but we can't. Hulsitoq of course is too ridiculous to mention; it's nothing more than this world shifted by fantasy across to the other side. However, since people seem to feel a need to use these words, I am again forced to ask: Why do I keep trying to find a name for something I know does not exist?

I have it. There is a word for it. Decomposition.

The only thing that occurs on the other side of death. Quick or slow, burnt to ashes on the sea or rotting in the earth, it is all decomposition.

Composition and decomposition. You should know about it, Alexi would say, you're the poet. Write a word and cross it out. I have spent more than a year writing this, and what have I achieved? The accumulation of a heavy pile of papers which I will either have to leave behind or lug around with me. Why bother to take it with me, when I already carry it in my heart? Either way, as I said months ago, when I'm decomposing it won't outlive me for long. It will wrap fish or light fires.

Alexi, I know nothing, except that I wish you had not died. And also, that I once believed I loved Peter and Madeleine so greatly I could not live without them, yet now I do. And I know this: that my heart has never stopped breaking with the burden of carrying them, and I will never stop loving them, and I will never give that burden up.

I was sleeping with my head on the table. Serena's father hadn't come back, so I didn't want to use a bed without asking. He came in just now and woke me up. It's dawn. He stood beside me, holding my shoulder with his hand and looking into my face. I could tell from his expression that something bad had happened.

'Do you know then?' he asked me.

I shook my head, and he said, 'It's a girl.'

I could have laughed. That wasn't so bad – he of course was disappointed, but Serena would love it whatever it was. I smiled and asked if I could go to see them. He told me she's dead.

I think he tried to explain what had happened but I wasn't listening. I can't believe it. I know they said it would be difficult, but I assumed it would be easier in the end for her than for some. She seemed made for it.

They leave me alone in here. I suppose they think I'm grieving. I don't really know what I feel. I am upset. Not for me. For her. I wish they would come in, talk about her, take my mind off myself. I don't know, I suppose she would rather be dead and have her child alive than the other way round. Poor thing. It's not right. I really don't think it's her death I mind so much, it's that she's been cheated. After everything she went through. I'm so glad now that I never did tell her the truth about her baby. I suppose I'll have to go and look at it soon.

Serena's father came in just now, but he went straight out again. He took a bow and arrows from the chest. He told me there's a wolf in the sheep pens.

A NOTE ON THE TYPE

The text of this book was set in a digitized version of Bembo, a well-known Monotype face. Named for Pietro Bembo, the celebrated Renaissance writer and humanist scholar who was made a cardinal and served as secretary to Pope Leo X, the original cutting of Bembo was made by Francesco Griffo of Bologna only a few years after Columbus discovered America.

Sturdy, well balanced, and finely proportioned, Bembo is a face of rare beauty, extremely legible in all of its sizes.

Composed by Crane Typesetting Service, Inc., West Barnstable, Massachusetts

Printed and bound by R. R. Donnelley & Sons, Harrisonburg, Virginia

DESIGNED BY CLAIRE M. NAYLON